The Trumpets of JERICHO

MONOCHROME
BOOKS MB

The Trumpets of
JERICHO

a novel

J. MICHAEL DOLAN

MONOCHROME
BOOKS MB

The Trumpets of Jericho: A Novel
J. Michael Dolan
www.jmichaeldolan.net

Published 2017 by
Monochrome Books
1911 County Road 306
Lexington, Texas 78947

Second Edition
Paperback ISBN: 978-0-99870-080-9
eBook ISBN: 978-0-99870-081-6
Library of Congress Control Number: 2017909834

Because of the dynamic nature of the Internet, any web addresses or links contained in this book may have changed since publication and may no longer be valid. The views expressed in this work are solely those of the author and do not necessarily reflect the views of the publisher, and the publisher hereby disclaims any responsibility for them.

Cover design by Austin Texas Print, Inc.
Interior design by Lulu Publishing, Inc.
Certain stock imagery by © Thinkstock

Monochrome Books (rev.) publ. date: 8/8/2017

Printed in the United States of America

*To my mother Louise, who helped with the
typing of the book and read it twice—
To my son Patrick and his wife Lisa, who endured
uncounted hours listening to me ramble on about it—
To my grandchildren Sebastian, Jolie, Alyssa, and
Julian, who I ended up writing it for—
And finally to the heroic dead, who stood at my shoulder
throughout the process to make sure I got it right.*

Author's Note

I consider Trumpets to be a work of history as much as one of fiction and have striven whenever possible to ensure its content adheres to fact. Of the dozens of people, for instance, who inhabit its pages, only a very few are imagined, the most prominent of them the Poles Witek, Pippel, and Menachem, the Hungarians Bela Lazar and Svoboda, the Russian POW Ustinov, and the German generals Steiner and Ehler. All other named characters are real. Please note, too, that though my research wasn't confined to the eighteen works in the bibliography at the back of the book, these were the most thumbed.

That being said, I did find it necessary on occasion to diverge from the historical record, mainly but not restricted to the timing of certain details. I did this not only in the interest of plot but to address the contradictions and bridge the gaps that exist in that record. Seldom, however, did I feel called upon to improvise—you as the reader can rest assured that the adventure you are about to embark on is as truthful to events as the novelist's pen can set down and him remain a novelist.

Military Ranks

SS	U.S. Army Equivalent
Reichsführer	General of the Army
Oberstgruppenführer	General
Obergruppenführer	Lieutenant General
Gruppenführer	Major General
Brigadeführer	Brigadier General
Standartenführer	Colonel
Obersturmbannführer	Lieutenant Colonel
Sturmbannführer	Major
Hauptsturmführer	Captain
Obersturmführer	First Lieutenant
Untersturmführer	Second Lieutenant
Sturmscharführer	Sergeant Major
Hauptscharführer	Master Sergeant
Oberscharführer	Technical Sergeant
Scharführer	Staff Sergeant
Unterscharführer	Sergeant
Sturmmänn	Lance Corporal
Rottenführer	Corporal
Oberschütze	Private First Class
Schütze	Private

Someday I will understand Auschwitz. This was a brave statement but innocently absurd. No one will ever understand Auschwitz. What I might have set down with more accuracy would have been: *Someday I will write about Sophie's life and death, and thereby help demonstrate how absolute evil is never extinguished from the world.* Auschwitz itself remains inexplicable. The most profound statement yet made about Auschwitz was not a statement at all, but a response.

The query: "At Auschwitz, tell me, where was God?"

And the answer: "Where was man?"

Sophie's Choice, William Styron

Why then do you say now: Let us persecute him, and let us find occasion of word against him? Flee then from the face of the sword, for the sword is the revenger of iniquities: and know ye there is a judgment.

The Book of Job, 19:28-29

1942

Autumn

For the first time in his life, Noah Zabludowicz felt like a caged animal.

The train sped through the Polish night, its gentle rocking belying the fear and uncertainty that gripped its occupants. That the cage was a moving one did nothing to lessen his feeling of entrapment. On the contrary, the analogy was as inescapable as it was ominous: there was little difference between the cattle this car was intended for and the hundred-plus Jews from the town of Ciechanow herded into it yesterday.

That it had been used to transport livestock was evident from the dirty, gray straw that littered the floor. This had turned out to be the sole "amenity" provided them by the Germans, so that by this, their third night aboard, the people packed inside weren't faring well at all. Along with the discordant chorus of coughs, snores, sneezes, and less polite emanations one might expect in such close quarters, came the spasmodic, muted rippling of tears.

Noah looked down to where his parents knelt, or where he thought they were. Though a few candles flickered here and there, he could barely see his hand in front of his face.

"Papa?" he said softly, should his father have fallen asleep. "Papa, you awake?"

"Yes, son, right here." The weariness in the voice was palpable.

"How is Mendel doing, papa? Has he gotten any better?"

Little Mendel was only eight, the youngest of Noah's one sister and eight brothers. The next youngest was Hanan, who was twenty-one. Their parents had been more than a little embarrassed at such a late-in-life pregnancy, but the rest of the family had applauded the middle-aged couple's continuing passion. As the fruit of this passion, Mendel's siblings had doted on him. It was a wonder he wasn't spoiled rotten, but in fact he was a sweet child, well behaved, undemanding.

He'd fallen ill yesterday. Nothing serious, at least not in normal times: a fever, some nausea, an associated loss of appetite. In normal times, before the war, before the SS, before the ghetto, there would have been little cause for concern. A stomach virus perhaps, easily treatable with a few days rest and his mother's warm chicken broth.

That was then, though, this was now, and the family was worried. After almost three years in the ghetto, three years of meager food and a raft of other wants, everyone's resistance was low, none more than the children's. People had learned to their chagrin, to their horror, that a small infirmity often had a way of flaring into something lethal.

"He's sleeping now, finally," their father replied, "but he's still got that fever. You heard him begging for water. If only we had a little water…." The words trailed off tiredly.

The Nazis had issued their *diktat* the evening of November 1st: by early morning of the 4th, all residents of the ghetto must be ready to vacate it, bringing only what they could carry. They were being resettled, they were told, somewhere to the east.

The news couldn't have been worse. Everyone was in a daze. For ages they'd been living under the threat of deportation, but after so long most were confident it would never come. Now here it was upon them, and with little more than two days to prepare. As in anguish as people were, this left them no time to sit around indulging it. What perishable food they had, they cooked, essentials were packed, valuables taken from permanent hiding places and made fast in portable ones, but no one thought to bring water, assuming it an easy enough thing for their SS handlers to provide. They'd been given none at the station, however, nor did it appear they were going to get any. The train had stopped for water once, to fill the boiler, but their guards had been impervious to the pleas coming from the cars.

Noah reached out in the dark until he found his father's hand. "It's going to be all right, papa, you'll see. I have a feeling this is almost over. I bet that by tomorrow we'll be settled in our new home."

From out of the blackness came another voice, smirking, sarcastic. "Uh-huh, and where will that be, this new home of ours? At the bottom of a pit, covered over with dirt?"

"You be quiet, Pinchas!" Noah hissed, not wanting to wake Mendel. "This is no time for that. You may be my older brother, but I'm telling you, not now."

"Yes, I am your older—"

"Noah, Pinchas! Enough!" It was their mother, her voice an angry whisper. "Shut up, the both of you! Aren't things bad enough without us fighting among ourselves? Besides, if one of you should wake this little boy...."

She waited a moment before continuing, awkwardness replacing the agitation in her voice. "Noah, come help your mother up. I—I have to— Just help me, dear."

There was no need for her to spell it out. He'd had to accompany her to the latrine before, and it hadn't been pleasant. Not so much from the effort involved in getting her there, or even the squalidness of the facilities, but from the guilt he felt at having to be a party to her humiliation—both the guilt and the shame at being powerless to prevent this assault on his own mother's privacy, her dignity.

He found their candle, lit it, and with him in the lead, mother and son plunged into the wall of people. "I'm so sorry," she said, as uncomfortable with the situation as he. "I'd have asked your father again, but at night—"

"Mama," he interrupted, squeezing her hand, "please. Don't say another word. I'd carry you there if I had to. You're my mother, I love you."

Actually, he had had to carry Mendel, several times, and it had been no mean feat. Fifty people in a freight car, with luggage, would have been torment enough; a hundred and more was a hell hard to fathom. Even after arranging their possessions so as to stand on the stuff, the deportees were crushed together in a near-solid mass. There was no room to sit, much less lie down. People had to take turns getting off their feet, and even then the best one could do was kneel, or if one absolutely had to sit, curl into a tight, muscle-cramping ball.

Breathable air was in short supply, most of it having been exhaled many thousands of times already. Those with respiratory problems, and the elderly and very young, had the hardest time of it. People panted like dogs, passed out, panicked, fought. The most coveted spots were a tiny, barbed-wire window next to the ceiling, and the occasional place along the walls where the odd crack in the wood let in some air.

Those who'd lost the battles for these were in no mood to be accommodating, and the space that Noah and family occupied was the length of the car from the latrine. At best it was a long, slow slog, at worst a potentially dangerous one. It wasn't easy for even those standing to move out of the way, while all but impossible for him and his mother, in the dark, balancing on bundles, not to step on those trying to sleep. As they followed the puny light of their precarious candle, curses, even threats, rose up around them.

One look at Noah, however, and even the surliest backed down, and not because he had an especially pugnacious appearance. In fact, his were the gently masculine, come-hither features of the romantic matinee idol, classically handsome in a non-rugged sort of way. Drawing-room, tuxedo handsome. The nose was finely chiseled, the eyes dark and a touch lazy, his lips in their fullness as close to being feminine as they could get while remaining a man's lips. Six feet tall, he was well-muscled, but not so heavily that it showed beneath his clothing. His hair was a light, wavy brown and just starting to bald at the forehead. He'd never worn a beard. His hands and feet were on the small side. He had a weakness for sentimental love songs. He rarely raised his voice.

Yet there was something about Noah that made one not want to cross him, the serene self-assurance of a man who knew how to handle himself in a fight. The stub of a candle he was holding may not have been much, but it was bright enough to reveal his face, and on that face was written this: "I have to get through, I have no choice. Please let me by or I promise you'll be sorry." People grumbled and were slow to move, but without exception gave ground.

Despite having been born in Ciechanow and spending all of his twenty-six years there, he knew none of these individuals he was squeezing a path through. There were the Vlasics, of course, and the Tabakmans from Silewski Street, but both of these families were situated near his, a few feet from the back wall. Everyone else, from their dress, looked to be rural Jews, collected by the Nazis from the outlying *shtetls* and villages and relocated to the ghetto. Ciechanow was by far the biggest town for miles, a terminus for the entire region's Jews. The Jewish population before the war had been about six thousand—the few square blocks later allotted to the ghetto ended up at its peak housing double that amount.

Just because he didn't know these people, though, didn't make it less distasteful for Noah to have to shove his way through them, no matter that he was all apologies in the process. But as bad as he felt about adding to their already considerable discomfort, it couldn't be helped. No way could his mother have made it to the latrine alone.

At last their objective loomed in front of them, a couple of bed sheets stretched across one corner of the car. Since the Germans hadn't given them so much as a bucket for this purpose, the deportees had been forced to improvise. The call had gone out for linens, towels, and cooking pots, the bigger those the better.

The smell was intolerable. Powerful enough to fill the car, here near the sheets it made one gag. Noah could only imagine what it was like behind them; this afternoon, the last time he'd brought Mendel, two of the pots were already overflowing. He handed his mother the candle and watched her duck behind the curtain. Her exclamations of disgust made his ears burn.

Later, the Zabludowicz siblings stood huddled together, all but little Mendel, who continued, thank God, to sleep. Not counting him, there were only four of them. The two eldest brothers had emigrated to Palestine years before the war; the twins, Ezra and Ehud, were trapped in the Warsaw ghetto; and on his twenty-third birthday, Joseph and a few hundred others were plucked off the street by the Gestapo, put on a train, and never seen again. Their mother still had the scarf she'd knitted him as a present, still wrapped in gay paper.

It was the blackest part of the night. Dawn was close by. Having extinguished their candles, most people were trying to sleep as best they could. But for the snoring of the adults and the whimpering of a few thirsty children, the only sound was the clickety-clack of the wheels on the tracks. The cattle car was less like a prison than a tomb.

"Pinchas, I'm sorry about earlier," Noah whispered. "I didn't mean to disrespect you."

The older brother shrugged unseen in the dark. "Forget it, you were right. It was neither the time nor the place."

Their sister Deborah, meanwhile, older than both of them—in her thirties but already a widow, nor did she have any children to show for the marriage—was less interested in her brothers' rapprochement than in what might be waiting for them at journey's end.

"But this *is* the time," she said, her voice impatient, "and I happen to agree with Pinchas. I've always agreed with—"

"Oh, swell," Noah groaned. "Haven't we been through this enough? Do we really have to have this conversation again?"

She ignored him. "And I've always agreed with Pinchas. Resettlement in the east…. just what does that mean? Can anyone trust the SS? Is that still possible?"

Noah didn't trust the buggers, either. Only a chump or a simpleton could. He did, however, find it difficult to accept some of the more outlandish rumors that had been circulating of late, the slaughter of entire communities, deaths in the thousands.

"I'll say it again, Deborah," he sighed, "and you, too, Pinchas. It doesn't make sense for the Germans to want to kill us. Things aren't going well for them in Russia. The *Shomeir* have a radio. I heard the news myself; the Wehrmacht is bogged down in Russia, some place called Stalingrad."

"And your point?" Pinchas asked, as if he didn't know already.

"I think the Nazis are going to need us. Victory is looking more and more elusive for them. The war has become a longer and more difficult prospect—maybe, as it was in the last one, even a stalemate. Trust me, the Germans will be needing all the slave labor they can get. Hell, they said as much themselves. We're being sent to work in some factory somewhere, to assist in the war effort. That's what their officers told our Council anyway."

"And you believed them?" Deborah scoffed. His sister's eyes were arched with brows as thick and black as her hair; he could picture them now bunched together in exasperation. "The SS would say anything, are capable of anything. You haven't, brother Noah, figured that out yet?"

This was hard to argue. The Germans had behaved abominably since their defeat of the Polish people, their conduct in Ciechanow being but one example. Life had been cheap in the ghetto. Aside from the fatalities brought on by SS indifference—disease from too many people living in too small an area, lack of medicine, lack of food, the shortage of coal and other fuels—stepping foot outside its boundaries without a work pass had meant death. The same for any Jew found outdoors after six in the evening.

Nor was disease or the unauthorized leaving of it the only means by which the ghetto had killed. The Nazis had drawn up a hundred infractions that were punishable by death. Permanent gallows were erected in the plaza fronting the main synagogue, long since shut down, and hardly a week had gone by that hadn't seen its share of hangings. Murder had taken other forms, too, much of it random and without provocation, on the whim of the Gestapo or SS man in the street. Boredom, drunkenness, or both were often at the root of these tragedies. Add to this the periodic roundups of those like Noah's brother Joseph, and by November the ghetto's population had been reduced by almost half.

"Capable of *anything*?" he said. "Maybe so, but I don't buy it. Bad as the SS are, as everyone knows they are, do you really think them capable, these Germans of yours—as a government, a people, a civilized European nation—of mass extermination? The murder of children, of whole populations?"

"What of Pippel then?" Pinchas countered. "Explain Pippel to me."

Noah's laugh was dismissive. "Ah yes, the famous Pippel. Which Pippel," he said, "the mad? Or Pippel the fool. Or Pippel the hopeless sot, the butt of a thousand jokes since even before the war."

For as long as anyone could remember, Pippel (last name unknown) had been one of the more colorful members of the Jewish community in Ciechanow. Most thought him demented in a harmless way, and the opinion had weight. He was a beggar by trade and a drunkard by inclination, though with the establishment of the ghetto, wine had grown scarce. But even sober, Pippel continued to suffer the occasional lapse into daftness. These could last for days and consisted of such behavior as animated conversations with himself, deciding to walk backward wherever he went, mild disturbances of the peace, and so on. During the warmer months, he slept in alleyways or on the stoops of the sympathetic. In winter, no one was sure where he holed up, but he was always there on the streets bright and early to beg.

Then one day the Gestapo took him and put him on a train. People thought that was that, until surprisingly, a week later, he showed up back in town, with a bandage on his head and a wild story to tell.

According to him, half an hour after leaving the Ciechanow station, the small train on which he and two hundred others were confined turned off onto a spur, went a short distance more, then stopped at the edge of a forest where everyone was ordered out. Awaiting them was a platoon of SS and two trucks. From one of these, a quantity of shovels was passed out, and the people led at gunpoint to a clearing in the woods. Here they were told to dig, and when the ditch was wide and deep enough, lined up in groups of six at the rim of it and shot.

Pippel claimed to have been only grazed by a bullet and left for dead. When he regained consciousness, he said, he clawed his way out of what should have been his grave to find the Germans gone—and silence, a deathly silence that spoke volumes. A friendly farmer later tended to his head and gave him food, and traveling at night, well away from any roads, he made it to Ciechanow and slipped back into the ghetto.

That was his tale, though few gave it much credibility, bandaged head or no. If it had been anyone else, maybe, but Pippel the *meshugga*? That he was as persistent as he was impassioned about his alleged ordeal there was no denying, to the point of stopping people on the street and forcing them to listen to him. He pressured, cajoled, begged, not for alms anymore, but simply to have his story believed. He'd been saved, he said, to warn them, to let them know what lay in store for them. Maybe then a few might escape.

But people didn't want to be warned, certainly not by the likes of him. They didn't even want to hear it. The whole thing was preposterous. If what he said was true, then everyone taken from the ghetto so far—every man, woman, and child—was dead. That was inconceivable. That just couldn't be. Those were the delusional rantings of a lunatic.

Spurned, Pippel grew morose and started keeping to himself, shunning everybody, and in the year that followed, the episode was all but forgotten. But not by everyone. Some remained suspicious.

"Madman, perhaps," Pinchas conceded. "Fool, undoubtedly. Butt of countless jokes, yes, but what if this once what he was saying was true? I heard him myself, and I can promise he's never sounded as lucid. Or as deadly serious. So it was a crazy story—it's been a crazy three years. What could be crazier than hanging men and women in the very shadow of the synagogue?"

Noah threw up his hands, though in the dark no one noticed. "You go ahead then and believe the addle-brained old drunk. I personally think he made it up to try and get sympathy, and the handouts that go with it. Did anyone actually see him put on that train?"

"Oh, come on, Noah," Deborah said. "That's hardly fair. How are we supposed to answer that?"

"Not fair?" he said. "I'll tell you what's not fair: the fact that this argument is always two to one, you and Pinchas against me. Well, guess what, tonight is different. Tonight a fourth party is present, someone who used to leave the room whenever we started talking about this, but who can hardly leave now. Hanan, what about it? What do *you* think the Germans have planned for us?"

Their brother Hanan had always been a quiet child, studious and somewhat solitary, more apt to stay indoors and read than go outside to play. As a result he'd excelled in school. His parents, everyone, had had high hopes for him; when the Wehrmacht invaded in 1939, he was a week away from the University of Krakow. He wanted to study philosophy, then teach.

Hanan didn't talk a lot. Neither was he much for argument or confrontation, which explained his silence so far. It didn't mean that he hadn't been listening, however.

"I—I'm not sure," he began, adjusting his glasses in the dark. "I think—I mean, it seems—Well, to me it's like this."

As if someone had pressed a button, his tone shifted from nervous to authoritative, to that of the professor he hoped one day to be. "If there were thousands dying, even death camps as some say, how could the SS hope to keep *that* a secret? Escaped prisoners, nearby villages, the partisans in the area…. the world would have to know, which would mean we would, too."

His next sentence took all three of them aback.

"As for Pippel and his story, if anything I find it encouraging. If he was telling the truth, then our chances are good. He said that the death train stopped thirty minutes out of Ciechanow. But we've been going for over two days now, and who knows for how much longer? I'd say we were out of immediate danger anyway, and then I'd say this: why would the Nazis go to all the trouble to transport us this far only to kill us when we got off the train? I have to side with Noah. They must need us for something."

Again, invisibly, Hanan slid his glasses up. "And if Pippel was lying, well, that's even better. Not only would it support the case for the resettlement being genuine, but undermine the validity of all those other horrible rumors. Let's hope he was lying, but if not then so be it. Whatever the truth, I don't see any reason to panic.

"Anyway.... that's how I see it." Suddenly, as if another button had been pushed, the professor went away and back came their little brother. "Please don't be sore, Pinchas. Or you, Deborah, please. The last thing I want is to make you mad."

Neither said a word, but not because they were upset with him. In fact, in spite of themselves, both found his logic comforting. Not enough to dispel their fears altogether, but some. Going by what Pippel had said, they should already be dead. Could Noah be right after all? Even if everything the beggar had said was true, his allegation of murder had occurred more than a year ago, with the German Army riding high. It was a different war now. Perhaps the swine did need slaves.

And with that, the argument was over. Everyone was too tired, their mouths too dry from thirst, to talk anymore. Besides, it was a good time to stop, on a positive note. Even Noah, who'd been trying to convince himself as much as he was anyone of their safety, even he felt better after hearing Hanan speak.

He found him in the dark and embraced him. "Thanks for being so damn smart," he whispered into the boy's ear. "I know you're not much for bickering, but believe me when I say you'd make a hell of a lawyer."

He'd always admired his kid brother's erudition. Though far from unintelligent himself, he hadn't taken well to school. He wasn't the academic type, preferred working with his hands rather than his head. He did think highly, however, of those able to pull off the latter, envying their talent, as he saw it, for living by their wits.

Pinchas was bright, too, but lacked Hanan's education. An electrician by trade, he played a prodigious game of chess. Noah had left school as soon as he could to drive trucks, ended up working for the Silvers, who owned a fleet of them. The Silver and Zabludowicz families were close, had been for years, but it wasn't until he started driving for them that he got to know, really know the second-to-youngest of their children, Godel.

Though three years his junior, Godel Silver and he quickly became the best of friends. People puzzled at the attraction; the two didn't seem at all compatible. Always careful, having chosen the rough-at-the-edges, blue-collar life, to keep his softer side private, Noah was on his way by then to becoming a man's man, all action and physicality, hard-nosed practicality. Though by no means a ruffian, he'd found himself skilled with his fists, and when it was called for had no compunction against using them. Godel by contrast was a self-styled lover, not a fighter, a dreamer, not a doer, a skinny kid who wrote poetry to try to impress the girls and claimed he wanted to be a serious writer one day. He wasn't a pushover, but though he would if provoked, didn't much care for pushing, either. Yet he and Noah had hit it off. The friendship was a mystery to everyone.

Noah wondered at it, too, at first, though it didn't take him long to figure out the dynamic in play. It was as transparent as water: Godel reminded him of Hanan. The two were alike in so many ways. Both loved words and reading, relied on brains rather than brawn, were complaisant but not cowardly, had integrity to spare. To Noah, the esteem in which he held his friend was plainly but a reflection of the even greater one he felt for his brother.

But there was another reason, too, an admittedly darker one, and though he would never have confessed it to anyone, had trouble acknowledging it himself, he had to allow it was a factor. It had nothing to do with why he and Godel had originally become friends. That had happened six years ago, and this had only arisen in the past three. But he couldn't deny that during those three years, it hadn't made him seek out Godel's company more than he would have. This "it" had a name—

And that name was Roza.

With the morbid talk finally ceased and the Zabludowicz's little patch of the cattle car quiet again, Noah was free to let his thoughts drift toward something more pleasant, to the remarkable creature that was Roza Robota.

He'd watched her grow up without being much conscious of her. He might see her on the street every so often, or in her father's hardware store when he stopped by with a delivery, but five years her senior he hadn't paid her much mind. For a brief period, they'd been fellow scouts in the *H'Shomeir H'Tzair*. Roza had joined the Shomeir when she was twelve, the first year she was eligible, but by then, almost eighteen, he was on his way out. He never even knew they were members together.

The H'Shomeir H'Tzair, Hebrew for Young Guard, was a Zionist youth group that on the surface promoted camping, sports, and other activities, but in reality had a more serious agenda. Simply stated, the Zionists believed there was no future for the Jew in Europe. The attempt at assimilation had failed. It was time to get out, start over somewhere else. This had nothing to do with Hitler and the ascendance of Nazism; by the turn of the century, Zionism was going strong. Though traditionalist Jews rejected it, believing that suffering should be endured passively and in submission to God's will, the movement had flourished. After a thousand years and more of discrimination, persecution, and not a few bloody pogroms at the hands of the Germans, Russians, and Poles, the Zionists argued that to be truly secure, the Chosen People needed a country of their own. Several geographic areas were considered, but in the end none was found preferable to their ancestral homeland: Palestine as it was known to the rest of the world, Eretz Israel, the land of Israel, to those Jews longing to return.

Enter the Shomeir, whose real purpose was to encourage *aliyah bet*, emigration to the Holy Land. Like any scouting organization set up for children, its main inducement was fun. There were lots of crafts and competitions—track and field, soccer, swimming—overnight stays in the woods, horseback riding, sing alongs. Accompanying all this, however, were instructions in Hebrew, Jewish history, and the fundamentals of farming, construction, and such. On Lag B'Omer, the feast day commemorating the miracle of the manna from heaven, the troops of the Shomeir, flags flying and trumpets blaring, would march to the plaza next to the synagogue. Once assembled, they would cheer speeches extolling the virtues of Eretz Israel and the freedom and opportunity awaiting them there. A well-known rabbi might speak, or a former resident of Ciechanow who'd actually made *aliyah*, returned from Palestine with a firsthand account of life in the land of milk and honey. Afterward, there would be singing and dancing into the night.

Even after he left the Shomeir, Noah remained an ardent Zionist. For him emigration was the only acceptable course of action. The Poles of Ciechanow had never hid their dislike of their Jews, an animosity that became evident as soon as one ventured outside the Jewish Quarter of the city. The refusal of some restaurants and other businesses to serve them, the stony stares in the streets, the literal stones sometimes thrown at them should they happen to wander into the wrong neighborhood—the list was as long as it was insulting, and though he'd lived with it his whole life, as an adult Noah continued to rebel at the mistreatment. Outside the Jewish Quarter was where he'd learned how to fight, and over the years made many a *goy* regret his bad manners. He was all set to follow his oldest brothers to Palestine when the German Army intervened, and would have attempted the trip regardless if it hadn't meant deserting his family.

Then came the SS, and with them the ghetto, and neither he nor anyone was going anywhere. Not that he was the kind to roll over and play dead, not without a struggle. Word reached him that the leaders of the Shomeir and some of the older scouts were fighting back after a fashion, sneaking out of the ghetto at night to steal food and medicine from the Germans and sabotage what equipment they could. They even had a radio capable of picking up the BBC in England, and were putting the information acquired there into an underground newspaper and distributing it on the sly.

It was Godel Silver who told him this. He'd been helping to write the newspaper, even accompanying the Shomeir on some of their midnight forays. Though never a scout himself, he had a new girlfriend that was, and it was she who'd persuaded him to throw in with them.

Noah was impressed. He wanted to help, too. He asked to meet Godel's girl, and agreed to do so the next day over some ersatz coffee at the Yellow Rose Café.

The Yellow Rose had once been hopping, the preferred eatery of the town's Jews, but though it wasn't much of a restaurant anymore, it still offered some things. Simple baked goods for the most part, and meatless soups and stews. That was on a good day; usually there was nothing but matzos and ghetto tea. A whole corner of the ceiling had caved in from dampness, the tables and chairs grown wobbly, the cutlery sparse. But to the great satisfaction of its customers, who looked on it as a link to the past and counted its survival a moral victory, it managed to remain open.

On the day appointed for Godel and his girlfriend and him to meet, Noah was the first to arrive. He sat at a table facing the entrance, ordered some "coffee", and waited. When the couple showed up, she wasn't at all what he'd expected. The only females he'd ever seen Godel with had been on the petite side, and quiet if not plain shy. This one was almost as tall as her partner, by no means fat but not skinny, either. She didn't wait to be introduced. Noah shook the proffered hand.

"Hello, I'm Roza," she smiled. The voice was husky, deep for a woman, but the more alluring for it. There was a throatiness to it that spoke of vigorous passions. "I hope you weren't waiting long."

The name meant nothing to him, nor did he recognize the face, but this he sensed right off: there was an earnestness about this girl, an intensity, inconsistent with her age. As soon as she sat down, her eyes locked onto his.

"You don't remember me, do you?" she said. "You used to make deliveries to my father's store."

Noah looked puzzled. He couldn't for the life of him….

"Roza Robota," she said. "Isaiah Robota's daughter."

He smacked his forehead in astonishment, nor was the gesture an exaggeration. It was she all right, but not. The last time he'd seen her, or could remember seeing her, she'd been all knobby knees and dental braces, her body as angular and spare as a box. Now here she sat in a flower-splashed summer dress, buxom, curvaceous, thick black hair to her shoulders, not the most beautiful face in the world, or at least not as quintessentially feminine as the rest of her, but one was drawn to it nonetheless. Her nose was a little aggressive, the jaw a bit square, but the mouth was sumptuous and quick to smile, her eyes intelligent. Noah couldn't recall coming across eyes like those before. So brown they shone black, penetrating yet kind, they didn't stop at the exterior of you so much as peer inside you. But though he couldn't escape the impression they'd already sized him up, taken the measure of him as not only a man but a person, not for one second did he feel judged. His innards exposed maybe, the core of him examined, but with a forgiving lens. No, he'd never seen eyes quite like those. They helped make her the kind of woman who only grew more attractive the longer one looked at her.

In age, however, she was as much girl still as woman. He wasn't expecting a lot from an eighteen-year-old. Then she started talking, small talk at first, but after ordering some coffee came to the point of their rendezvous. The Germans were evil, she said, her eyes seeming to get blacker, and the evil was just beginning, there was worse yet to come. Their people were in danger as never before. It wasn't just that the SS were killing indiscriminately, women and children and the old, but the casual way they went about it, as if squashing insects. There was no anger to their savagery, little emotion at all, and that was what had not only her but others worried. If a catastrophe were to be prevented, the Jews would have to start resisting.

"We already have," she confided, leaning across the table toward Noah, "but we've got to do more. We need men like you to help us. You're a fighter, Godel tells me, the terror of the *goyim* street toughs. He said he's seen you take on two at a time and whip them."

"Three," Godel said. "You should see him, he's murder."

Roza leaned closer, a smile lighting her face. "Well, here's your shot then to go up against the biggest bully of all. How would you feel about mixing it up with the son-of-a-bitching Nazis?"

Before he could answer, she beat him to it. "I can see that you're interested. It's written all over you. Tell me I'm not mistaken, my love, that your friend is just itching in his pants to join us."

"Far be it from me," Godel said, "to disagree with so convincing, and I might add, beautiful a girl. Noah?"

"Uh…. I don't see as I have a choice," he grinned in mock resignation.

"Good, it's settled then," Roza said, rocking back in her chair. "Now I get to shut up for a while, about business anyway, and drink, or try to drink, this ditch water they call coffee."

That was the way she talked, with a confidence beyond her years, a sassy exuberance that won one over instantly. Noah was interested all right, and in more than just her offer. After listening to her for only a few minutes, this much he knew: she might have worn a dress, but was as scrappy as he; might have had long, lush hair and soft, womanly skin, but was as full of fight as any man—might have possessed a body designed to give birth and suckle, but inside it beat the heart of a warrior, a lion. One look into those black eyes was enough to ensure him that if it ever came down to it, the only way the Germans were going to stop her was to kill her.

It was right then and there, not thirty minutes after meeting her, that he began falling in love with his best buddy's girl.

But as clear as this was in retrospect, at the time he didn't see it. At the time his mind was elsewhere. Suddenly, and from out of nowhere, a sword had been thrust into his hands, a chance to be a man again. Not that the call to action turned out to be as warlike as he'd hoped. He soon found to his disappointment that his new comrades-in-arms didn't do any actual fighting. Unguarded trucks and small storehouses were what the

Shomeir raiders were looking for, and anything else the Nazis happened to leave unattended.

Which wasn't to say, even without guns and pitched battles, that playing hide-and-seek with the SS wasn't as dangerous as it was exhilarating. It was only doable when there was no moon, and even then it bordered on the suicidal. Should they be spotted that would be it, they'd be killed, and some of them did wind up paying that price. But aside from the good their plunder did their downtrodden people, for most of those bravehearts who dared to defy the curfew it was worth risking their lives to harass the detested Germans.

No one was more fearless than Roza, or more effective. It had been her idea to lure the guards from their posts by disturbing the night stillness a street or two away. Sometimes a soldier would stay behind while the others ran off to investigate, sometimes one wouldn't. If this last, the Shomeir watching from the shadows would swoop in and grab what they could. More often than not, it was she who volunteered for the role of decoy, and had more than a few close calls eluding her pursuers.

As time went on, she began to talk of hitting the SS harder. In the course of their raids, the Shomeir had succeeded in acquiring some munitions, a handful of guns, a supply of ammo, even a crate of hand grenades. It was Roza who suggested they turn the Nazis' weapons against them. She was tired, she said, of seeing only Jewish blood spilled.

Upon her petitioning them, the elders of the ghetto gave it some thought, but in the end voted her plan down. For one, its opponents argued, it would be self-defeating. The SS had a standing order stating that for every German soldier killed at the hands of partisans, a hundred Polish civilians, Jews and Gentiles alike, would be rounded up and shot. For another, if the Nazis even suspected it was Jews who were gunning them down, who knew what they would do? They might massacre the entire ghetto.

Acceding to the logic of this, she backed off, but continued to stew all the same. Her hatred for the enemies of her people was equaled only by her frustration at being unable to right their wrongdoings. She raged openly at not only the Germans but her own powerlessness, as if she was partially to blame for the crimes that kept accumulating. It particularly ate at her that she couldn't even protect her own family. Her parents lost their life savings, confiscated by the Nazis. Her brother Israel, two years younger than she, had always been a sickly child, and life in the ghetto hadn't helped. The cough he'd developed lately wasn't going away.

It was what she had to watch her older sister endure, though, that galled her the most. She and Shoshonna worked together on a forced-labor squad outside the ghetto, helping demolish Jewish homes to be rebuilt for the German colonists streaming into the area. This was degrading enough, as if the taint her people had left behind was too dirty and deep to be scrubbed out or painted over. But to see the delicate Shoshonna, the beauty of the family, bending beneath her load of bricks, struggling not to fall, her dress sodden with sweat, their guards all the while leering and even pawing at her—this was too much for Roza. She was hard put to restrain herself, though if she had stepped in, it probably would have been the death of both of them.

No one felt sorrier for her, or was more sympathetic, than Noah. By then both his love and admiration for her had taken root and grown. She was the woman he'd always dreamed of but never thought he'd find, had given up looking for out of wondering if she even existed. She was a glorious anomaly, feminine in all of the appropriate ways—nurturing, compassionate, physically voluptuous—but refusing to confine herself to society's expectations of her, also outspoken, uncompromising, indomitable.

She was, in short, the perfect match for him, only now that he had by luck alone found her, she was someone else's. And not just someone's; he and his unwitting rival had been friends since their teens.

That both Godel and Roza suspected nothing was no accident. Noah was determined to keep his love a secret. To do otherwise would have been not only unseemly but unprincipled, as well as in all probability doomed to failure. His two friends had fallen quite obviously in love, were as happy a couple as any he knew. Far be it from him to intrude on their idyll. In fact, despite the pain bred of his thwarted desire, he was genuinely glad for the both of them and never breathed a word of the ache in his heart. To bask in the sun of Roza's presence, to be rewarded with a smile, the occasional sisterly hug, was the only satisfaction he allowed himself in the matter. They were crumbs, but he was a starveling and would take what he could get.

He did avail himself, however, of every opportunity to be near her, and not just out of love. As plenty of others could affirm, to be in Roza's company was to feed off her strength. Her courage made them braver, her tenacity them more determined. Confidence wafted from her like some medicinal vapor. When she spoke, one's doubts and fears melted into the air. Noah especially enjoyed hearing her belittle the strutting SS.

"They aren't supermen," she would say. "Hell, they aren't even men. You want men? Look at the Wehrmacht, the regular German Army, doing battle with the Soviets on the Russian front. And who are the big bad SS waging war against? The unarmed civilians, the women and children of the ghettos. They aren't soldiers, they're murderers, shameless cowards all, and one day as sure as sunrise they're going to pay for their crimes."

Noah's contempt for their new masters mirrored hers. On only one point did they differ, their respective attitudes toward what the Germans ultimately had in mind for their people. Roza was fatalistic, subscribing to much of the more sensational talk, while he continued to have difficulty believing such things possible. Whatever future the Nazis envisioned for the Jews, however, both had no problem agreeing that it wasn't going to be a pretty one.

Look at them now, he mused as he surveyed the packed cattle car. They may not have been on their way to their deaths, but they *were* being freighted like so many animals to a destination unknown, to work somewhere as slaves without regard to their comfort or even health. If this was how the SS saw fit to treat them en route, what could they expect at the end of the line? Forget talk of comfort—were they to be deprived of the barest necessities while being worked half to death? Perhaps one day they would look back on the ghetto with fondness.

Dawn was about to break. Noah could see the first feeble gray of it through the cracks in the walls. He noticed, too, that the train was starting to slow. A while more, brakes squealing, and it came to a halt, causing those on the floor to rise to their feet. A sudden excitement filled the wagon. They'd only stopped three times before, once to take on water for the engine, once to add more guards, and again, God knew why, for half a day at some siding outside of Wroclaw. Was this it, the end of their journey at last? The only thing anyone could see, even those at the ceiling window, was a barren landscape of yellowish earth and some scattered clumps of trees.

They could certainly smell something, though, and had for some time, an odor as unrecognizable as it was unsavory, strong and getting stronger with each passing mile. It smelled like something burning, something animal, oily; one could almost feel the grease in the air. It was as if someone was incinerating fat, an ungodly amount of it, but who would do such a thing and why? No one knew what to make of it.

After a few minutes, the train started moving again, but at no more than a crawl. Leaving the main track, it veered to the right, and those at the window reported a thick woods. From the other side of the car, meanwhile, what appeared to be urgent news had begun to filter back through the crowd. Those able to peer through the cracks had spotted something, and it had them all abuzz. Noah saw one of the shtetl Jews turn around and mumble something to Pinchas.

"What'd he say?" he asked his brother. "What's going on?"

"A station. We just passed a station house, a fairly good-sized one, too. Which means a good-sized town. Looks as if this might be it."

"What was the name of the station?"

"Auschwitz," Pinchas answered. "The man said it was called Auschwitz. He's never heard of it, no one has, but…. Noah, tell me, that stink. What do you think it is?"

He had no idea, couldn't even guess. The farther the train went into the woods, the more invasive the odor grew. Already it overpowered even the reek of their latrine. He wished Roza was here. Not that she would have known what it was, either—but he just wished she was here.

In the confusion at the railroad platform four mornings ago in Ciechanow, the Robotas and the Silvers had become separated from Noah's family. He thought he saw them board the same car, but couldn't be sure. If they did, then at least Roza and Godel were together. At least they had each other at this uneasy moment.

That was good. That would suffice. That was going to have to do. Noah would have felt better, less anxious, if it had been the three of them, but was glad for the two. As the train crept slowly deeper into the forest, into the smell, he tried to pretend a girl standing next to him was Roza, but it didn't work.

*   *   *

Shoshonna Robota huddled with her sister against the raw November wind. "Roza, where are we?" Her voice was shaking, her eyes round. "What—what kind of place is this?"

Roza didn't answer. She was trying to make sense of the whole thing herself. Beneath their feet spread the unloading ramp, concrete, enormous, so big not even the four thousand of them filled it. They were in some sort of line, the women and younger children, inching their way toward a cluster of SS. Their men formed a parallel line some meters away. Roza kept looking for her father, her brother, Godel and his father, Noah, too, but for some reason couldn't find them. They must have ended up farther down, toward the rear.

To her left stood another, less tenuous queue, that of the cattle cars they'd just vacated. Despite the torment they'd endured in those dungeons on wheels the past few days, she looked at them now almost with longing. Never in her life had she felt so menaced by her surroundings, not on her worst day in the ghetto, not on the labor gangs recruited there and guarded by drunken soldiers, not even on those midnight raids outside the ghetto walls. It was as if the people of Ciechanow had been transported to not merely another part of the country, but another world. The air was an uncanny, surrealistic green, the sun unable fully to penetrate what could only be described as a river of smoke flowing overhead. Feeding this river were a number of fat, black columns boiling skyward, big and close enough to take up half the southern horizon, but their origin obscured by forest. The inexplicable, greasy stench that had been plaguing them for miles was so intense here as to make the eyes water.

As soon as they'd got off the train, their bundles had been snatched from their hands by a collection of living scarecrows in filthy blue-and-white-striped burlap. Stinking to high heaven, impossibly thin, these moved with an odd mechanical gait, eyes bright with hunger.

"*Warum*? Why?" Roza had asked one of them in German as he walked away with her suitcase.

"*Verboten*," the creature had croaked, tossing it onto one of many rapidly growing piles.

Corpses lay near the train in short, orderly rows, casualties of the trip, some already bloating. A pack of stray children careened by howling like wolves, behind them some scarecrow men in pursuit. A barrage of unsettling noises filled the green air: the barking of fierce dogs straining at their leashes, the even angrier snarls of the Germans as they ordered the scarecrow men about, the wailing of families freshly torn apart. It hadn't been easy separating the sexes. Blood had been spilled. In the turmoil, Roza was knocked down and lost sight of her father, her brother, Godel.

She had seen this, though, on the ground not far from her: a middle-aged couple clinging frantically together, their fingers digging into each other's flesh, the man holding onto the woman's clothing with his teeth. She for her part was crying hysterically, her face a bright purple. The two soldiers trying to pry them apart finally gave up, and cursing, reached for their nightsticks. Several blows to the head later, killing blows from the look and sound of them, and the two were dragged off like so many sacks of cement.

What kind of place indeed. After a moment, Shoshonna repeated her question. Roza turned to her and in a voice loud enough for them all to hear—her mother, her grandmother, her aunt Sara, the Silver women—said with as much conviction as she could muster, "Don't worry, Shozhka, everything's fine. We're going to be…. just fine. It won't be long till we're all together again, drinking hot soup."

This was to corroborate what the officer had said, the one who'd just strolled imperiously past them. "*Frauen, bitte*," Roza had heard him croon, her German having improved much the last three years. "Ladies, please…. keep moving. There is no need to be frightened. Tea and soup are waiting; the sooner we finish here, the sooner you can start setting up house."

Though she'd loathed his peacock airs and phony goodwill, she was grateful for the soothing effect his words seemed to have on the others. Her mother, her aunt, even Shoshonna were noticeably less ill at ease after his passing. One thing this strange new world had in common with the one they'd left behind was its godlike pantheon of SS officers swaggering about. In their splendor, their regal self-possession and pomp, they paced the ramp as if somehow detached from its meanness and squalor. Immaculate in full battle dress, insignia glittering, boots gleaming, they appeared only reluctantly to condone the brutality shown by their subordinates, the surliness of the scarecrow men. Brandishing thin, flexible little whips in the best Prussian tradition, they radiated a military propriety, a civilized urbaneness that made one want to believe that here were men who could be trusted.

Not that Roza did, not for one second. She hadn't trusted the apes for years, nor from what she'd seen of it was this the place to start. Having dismissed the officer's glib reassurances as soon as she'd heard them, she'd returned to the thing that was bothering her the most. Such smoke, such a fire, such a godawful odor—what on earth were the Germans burning? The prevailing opinion was that it was garbage, or so she kept hearing. It was certainly foul enough to be, but what kind of garbage? For the first time, she could detect a faint undertaste to the smell. She hadn't picked up on it before, but here, closer to the source, it was impossible to miss, nor was there any mistaking where it came from. It was the distinctively acrid, burnt-metal stink of scorched hair.

Suddenly, up ahead, a new commotion broke out, nor did it sound good: wild weeping, shocked protestations, the deep, rumbling cough of big trucks starting up.

Until that moment, Roza hadn't noticed the trucks. For a while, though, she'd been aware of what looked to be a kind of selection taking place, up ahead where the gathering of SS men stood. One of them, an officer—and presumably a doctor as well, as he was wearing a white armband emblazoned with a blue caduceus—was directing part of the women passing before him to a group on the right, and the rest to a much larger one on the left. Now these latter, to their and their families' despair, were being loaded onto open trucks and driven away.

A groan went up from the women in line. Shoshonna would have crumpled to the ground had not Roza held her up. Their Aunt Sara was beside herself. "They're doing it again!" she shouted. "Splitting us up! I won't let them—I won't! I'm not giving up my children!"

This time Roza didn't know what to say. The last thing they needed was to lose their composure, yet how to explain away what appeared to be happening? To her relief, her mother Faige rose to the occasion.

"Sara, calm down!" she cried, taking hold of her sister's arm. "And for heaven's sake, open your eyes! Look there, up ahead, and tell me what you see."

"What do you think I see? People crying and tearing at their hair as their loved ones are trucked away, to who knows where! I tell you, I'm not—"

"And who do you see going on those trucks?" Faige demanded. "Children and their mothers, and the obviously sick and crippled, and of the others not a one under forty. While those staying behind are all young, the healthiest and strongest. What does that suggest?"

At the words "children and their mothers", Sara looked closer and could see it was true: no child under fifteen, sixteen had been separated from its mother. Her face brightened instantly. The two with her, her youngest sons, fell well under that demographic.

Still, she hadn't a clue what her sister was driving at, and this annoyed her. "No, Faige, tell us," she said. "What does it suggest?"

"That the Germans are dividing us according to our capacity for work. Did you expect anything less of them, less efficient, I mean? To us middle-aged, I would think, in addition to some lighter duties, will fall the care of the ill and handicapped, the young and very old. This will free up the fittest for the heaviest labor."

She laid a hand on each daughter's shoulder. "I'm sorry, Roza, and you, Shoshonna—and you, Mrs. Silver, for your Godel—but it looks as if you might be marching off to work this very day, with the rest of us riding those trucks to our new homes. I know we were all hoping to get a respite after our miserable journey, but it's not to be helped. We remain in cruel hands.

"But don't worry, children," she added, "when you get back tonight, we'll make you as comfortable as possible. By then, as the young officer said, hopefully we'll have made a good start at setting up house."

Desperate as they all were for such an explanation, her words fell on receptive ears. "But why trucks?" Shoshonna asked. "How far away could these new homes of ours be?"

"Who's to say?" replied her mother. "For all we know, it's a few miles. Once again, German efficiency. Would you expect Gemmy here, or that woman there, or that one on crutches, to be able to walk even a mile, especially over broken ground?"

Gemmy was what everyone called Roza's and Shoshonna's maternal grandmother, and had for so long that neither girl was sure of her real name. She hadn't done well on the train. Her lungs being as brittle as the rest of her, she'd passed out more than once from a lack of oxygen. She was doing better outdoors, however. With Faige's and Sara's help, she was walking, each taking turns providing an arm for her to lean on.

"But I don't want you to go, mama," Shoshonna pleaded. "I'm scared, not just for myself but all of us."

"Don't be, dear," she said, embracing first her and then Roza. "There's no need to be. Tonight when I see you again, I'll give you both an even bigger hug."

Roza's admiration for her mother was as great as her love for her. It wasn't solely at the hands of the H'Shomeir H'Tzair that as a girl she'd learned to take pride in her Jewishness. As a young woman, Faige Robota had been a pioneering Zionist, one of the movement's early adherents, and even after starting a family had remained active in the cause. As they got older, she would regale her children with not only stories of those days but tales from the Bible of fierce prophets and proud kings. And it was she, more than their father, who'd steered them in the direction of the Shomeir. Intelligent, courageous, and in the eyes of many a beauty still, her mother was the kind of person Roza had always wanted one day to be.

But though she would have liked without reservation to believe everything the woman had just said, and there was a part of her that did, there was no faulting Faige's reasoning, a voice inside her kept whispering that the Germans were up to no good.

What with the racket of the trucks and the unnerving lament of those families being divided, conversation became a chore, prompting the women to walk in silence the rest of the way. Not that by then they had far to go. The closer they came to the SS doctor the faster the line moved, until suddenly it was they who found themselves standing in front of him.

Roza hadn't expected him to be so young. He didn't look all that older than her boyfriend. Aside from that, though, he was no different from the other officers, all spit and polish, his uniform dazzling, with the kingly demeanor endemic to his kind.

He also, to her uneasiness, looked to be enjoying himself. Why this should have bothered her, she didn't know. His hat rested at a rakish angle atop his head, his posture jaunty, arms akimbo. There was a smile on his lips, but it was cold as a crocodile's, and smug, as if he knew something they didn't, was in on some joke about to be enacted at their expense.

Sara and her sons were first. He took in the three of them at a glance. "And how old are *you?*" he asked the children, his voice not unkind. "Eleven" and "Thirteen" came the answers, whereupon he nodded as if to say "Good boys" and pointed them along with their mother to the left. Wordlessly, he waved Faige and Gemmy the same direction, then Roza and Shoshonna to the right.

The whole thing hadn't taken thirty seconds. Shoshonna was crying, still set against leaving their mother, but her sister insisted, shoving her along. She would have liked to cry, too, it was impossible not to feel tears, but someone had to be hard or they weren't going to get through this.

The women managed to keep in eye contact across the gulf that separated them. Roza was all smiles and thumbs-up, but it was nothing more than a charade; all kinds of alarms were going off in her head. The Germans might be pretending as if they cared what happened to them, but their actions told a different story. The purgatory of the train ride; the middle-aged couple's casual murder on the ramp; what was looking more and more like the plundering of their possessions, which even now the scarecrow men appeared to be ransacking; the strange, fetid smoke with its tincture of burnt hair; the dogs, the machine guns, the breaking apart of families, the enigmatic malice behind the SS doctor's smile—all of it made her wish her mother wasn't on the verge of boarding one of those trucks, though even now she couldn't be sure that her imagination wasn't getting the better of her. Maybe that couple earlier had been beaten merely unconscious, not killed. Maybe it *was* only garbage burning (what else could it be?). Maybe her mother was right, and they were being admitted to this place separately, and at the end of the day would be reunited. A reasonable argument could be advanced opposing each of Roza's misgivings. Was it possible she was being premature, or paranoid, or both?

Her question was soon answered. It was Shoshonna who noticed the woman first.

"Roza, isn't that Mrs. Wojowiecz?" she said, wiping the tears from her eyes. "What is she doing?"

A young woman was heading toward them from the group consigned to the left. She walked hurriedly, head down, arms swinging at her sides. They knew her from their father's store; she used to come there with her plumber husband. They had a daughter, an angel of a child, three, maybe four, with pudgy red cheeks and curly blonde hair. It was she who toddled after the woman now, trying but failing to keep up.

"Wait, mama, wait!" the girl cried, stretching out her tiny arms.

Everyone was watching. "Take care of your child, woman!" one of the scarecrow men shouted.

"It's not mine, sir!" she shot back, covering her face with her hands. "Not mine, I swear!" She began walking faster, as if desperate to reach those who'd been pointed to the right, to reach then lose herself in the group that wasn't going on the trucks.

But the little girl kept running after her, sobbing now, frantic.

"Don't leave me, mama, please! Please, mama, stop!"

The woman removed her hands from her face and clapped them over her ears. "It's not mine, I tell you! Oh, God help me, it's not!"

Head still down, she never saw the blow coming. An SS-*Schütze* intercepted her, and with a sickening thud knocked her out cold with the butt of his rifle. Two of the scarecrow men scooped her up, ran her to a truck, and heaved her in. Another followed with her daughter, screaming now at the top of her lungs.

Roza and Shoshonna looked at each other in disbelief. Whether or not her sister understood the implications of what they'd just witnessed, she didn't know, but wasn't about to share them with her. That Mrs. Wojowiecz would have gone to any lengths to escape the trucks was clear, but why? Her own child, Roza fretted.... what could have driven a mother to such an act? It could only be one thing: fear, and an overriding desire to save herself. She was young, she was pretty, wanted so much to live, had panicked and as impulsive, as ignoble as it may have been, the instinct of self-preservation had triumphed over the maternal one. The question remaining was what had convinced her she was in peril in the first place, and Roza, in a quick calculus, again could think of but one answer.

Somebody, one of the scarecrow men, must have told the woman something, either in response to a query of hers or on his own. And that something had frightened the motherliness right out of her. Nor was it likely the mere suggestion of danger could have made her or any parent abandon her child. No, she'd learned for a fact somehow what being sent to the left meant, that the people getting on those trucks weren't coming back, ever.

It had to be that, couldn't be anything else, and if so, then everything from the nauseating black smoke to the excesses on the ramp suddenly made sense. The vague suspicions that had been deviling Roza since even before she'd exited the train had in a flash become hideously real. It wasn't resettlement, it was mass murder. The German people had gone insane. The awful stories that had arisen the past year were true after all.

She had once given credence to these, warning of catastrophe if the Jews didn't start resisting. The more she'd pondered them, though, the more far-fetched they'd seemed, if for no other reason than from an operational standpoint. Supposing even Nazi bloodthirstiness capable of rising to such heights, did the Germans, or for that matter any nation, possess the technology and skill required to wipe out an entire race of people?

She hadn't thought so, but just like that here it was, right there in front of her, or the possibility of it anyway. Yet what could she do? To motion her mother over to what must be presumed was the side of the living would be to watch her clubbed down as Mrs. Wojowiecz had been. She could only look on in impotent anguish as she and her grandmother, her aunt and her cousins, climbed aboard one of the trucks and were hurried away.

She might have broken down then and there, Shoshonna or no, had not a pair of emotions come to the fore to sustain her. The first was born of a natural response to the vile secret she'd just deduced, and consisted of the hope that maybe, just maybe, she was wrong. Her gut told her differently, but there was always the chance that the poor, pitiful plumber's wife had acted on a hunch only. This was doubtful, but hope died hard, even on the threshold of hell.

But though she didn't know it yet—couldn't say with any accuracy where they even were, really—it wasn't only on the threshold but well inside the hell that was Birkenau, the *Vernichtungslager*, the extermination camp, that the second emotion helping now to steel her was going to come in handy. And in that respect, she was ahead of most people left on the ramp, for while hope still puttered lamely at the periphery of her consciousness, hate overran it, consuming her like a fire devouring dry tinder. At that moment, she began to hate the SS as never before, their haughtiness, their lies, their despicable black hearts, and it was this hate, more than some improbable hope against hope, that not only kept her from falling in a despairing heap to the ground but would see her through the long months of her nightmarish new life.

An hour or so later and the morning's business was done, the last truck bouncing springily out of sight into the trees. Or rather, the last truck intended for people. There was other cargo to cart away, and the scarecrow men were hard at it. Roza watched as they piled one suitcase and footlocker after another onto the beds of more trucks, all the while stuffing their mouths with whatever food they could find.

The only deportees on the ramp now were those who'd be walking, and in short order they were, beginning with the men. These, who had for some reason undergone a second selection, were marched off in a formation five abreast, with the exception of forty or fifty who were kept behind. She stood on tiptoe and scanned both groups for signs of the men of her family, but again met with no success. The attempt wasn't lost on her sister.

"I don't see papa or Izzy, either," Shoshonna said. "What do you think could have happened to them?"

"Nothing," Roza said, trying to sound nonchalant. "They're either among those there," she said, nodding toward the two groups of men, "or else they went on the trucks. You heard what mama said, Shozhka, we'll be seeing them soon enough. How about we just worry about ourselves for now, okay?"

Then it was their turn to be led away, also in a column of fives, escorted by soldiers with faces as hard as their helmets. A limestone road took them from the unloading ramp into a treeless field. Ten minutes more and this road skirted a small rise to reveal a sprawling barbed-wire fence half a mile or more long. They could see the white ceramic conductors dotting it, meaning it was electrified. Parallel to and outside this fence, a line of crude wooden watchtowers receded into the distance, each manned by a soldier with a machine gun, while behind it stretched row after row of flat, rectangular gray huts, nestled in a pestilential sea of churned mud. Roza eyed these buildings nervously, searching for signs of life.

She would have been better occupied paying closer attention to her feet. If she had, she could have stopped deceiving herself with even the illusion of hope, and unencumbered by same, sought a greater degree of both solace and resolve in the purgative furnace of her hate. For scattered among the pebbles and crushed limestone she was walking on were bits of bone, tiny, semi-pulverized, but unmistakably human.

*   *   *

Zalman Leventhal lay on his bunk smoking a cigarette, sluggish with schnapps. It hadn't taken many swigs of it to get him that way, either. Despite a full head of reddish hair, unusual for a Jew, and which had earned him the nickname "Irish" growing up, he'd never been much of a drinker, certainly not to the extent the real Irish were said to be.

Through a window, he watched a light snow flutter down. The weather had taken a turn for the worse since his arrival at the unloading ramp four days ago; a large coal-burning stove, however, kept the room warm. Their snug accommodations had him as at a loss as the next man. Clean, spacious, well appointed, it was a place a platoon of SS would have been happy to call home. The floor was dark linoleum, the walls a white stucco, at one end of the room an enormous oaken table at which to eat. Each man had his own bed complete with pillows and clean linen. From the ceiling, fluorescent lights dispensed a uniform white glow, while at the other end of the barracks was a three-toilet, white-tiled beauty of a bathroom. What could the Germans be up to? It didn't make sense. There wasn't a man among them who could figure it out.

There were fifty of them, all from the Ciechanow transport, all in their twenties or late-teens. They'd been selected, they were told, on the basis of their ages and physiques, for a permanent work detail—in the *Sonderkommando*, or Special Squad, whatever that was—which their keepers assured them meant they'd be well cared for. Nor for once were the Krauts lying. Not only had they wound up in this three-star hotel of a hut, but been issued fine coats, boots, and other civilian clothing. And the food was the best and most abundant Leventhal had seen in years: cured meats, bread and jams, pickled vegetables, various cheeses. Following the privations of the ghetto and then the cattle car, it was all very mysterious. They were even, in addition to cigarettes, provided liquor of all things, and though he'd been reluctant to partake of the stuff, in the end he had, if only to take the edge off his anxiety.

For while he and the others for whatever reason lacked for nothing materially, news of their families was denied them, no matter how much they begged. The SS, in fact, weren't telling them much of anything, not even what it was that was so special about the Special Squad. But by now, of course, it was all too obvious they were in a concentration camp, and could only guess what their loved ones were going through. Leventhal's two sisters had seven children between them, and his mother wasn't in good health at all. To think of them in this place of punishment was as painful as it was unimaginable. Children in a concentration camp! It defied comprehension.

Then there was the prisoner from Danzig, an enigma indeed. He'd been all bluster and brass, barging in on their evening meal two nights before as if he owned the place. How he got past the guard posted day and night at their door no one knew, but unlike the scarecrow men on the ramp, his stripes were starched and creased, the flesh beneath them ample.

"The name's Witek," he'd announced, "and I'm looking for a Noah Zabludowicz. We met in Danzig, though he hails from Ciechanow. Any of you yahoos know if he was on this transport?"

Several said they'd seen Noah marched away with the other men on the ramp. "And how did you get in here, friend?" one of them asked. "We've been locked down since we got here. No one in or out."

Witek reached in his coat and tossed a pack of cigarettes onto the table. "Currency of the realm, my man," he said with a hearty laugh. "The SS are easily bribed, especially the lower ranks. Six cigarettes a day is all that they're rationed."

"So how did you come by so many?"

"The same way you got yours, and those warm clothes, that tasty-looking smorgasbord there. From the transports, where else? Everything comes from the transports. You'll find that out soon enough, when you start working."

"And what kind of work is that?" burst from half a dozen throats.

He thought for a moment, then frowned and shook his head. He picked up the pack of cigarettes and slipped them back in his pocket. "I could tell you," he said, "but I wouldn't want to be the one to spoil the Germans' surprise. I can promise you they wouldn't take kindly to that. Now, let me get this straight: you sure you saw Noah leaving the ramp on foot and not on one of those trucks?"

Of course they were sure, and two of his brothers with him. The Zabludowicz family was well known in the ghetto.

"Good," said Witek. "That means he's still alive then. Being the fine physical specimen he is, I thought I might find him in here with you fellows. But, oh well, at least it wasn't the trucks for him. I'll catch up with him sooner or later."

One of them spoke for them all when he asked, "What do you mean he's still alive? What does getting or not getting on the trucks have to do with that?"

Witek turned and faced him. "You're joking," he smiled.

Silence, the seconds crawling by like snails.

"You're not joking," he said at last, the smile disappearing. "Good grief, what a bunch of blind yahoos you are! The smoke, that smell…. where in blazes do you think you are? This is Birkenau, boys, not some Tatry ski resort. Did you think the SS were throwing some kind of giant cookout for everybody?"

"What are you saying?"

"That anyone taken from the ramp on one of those trucks is a goner. *Alles kaput. Touts finis.* Frizzled away into ashes. Gassed and then cremated in open pits, the lot of them."

They didn't believe him, of course. Wouldn't let themselves believe him. Couldn't imagine why he would say something so bizarre in the first place. They tried to argue with him about it, but to no avail—having got what he came for, he left shortly after with a sarcastic wave goodbye and a disgusted look on his face.

They stayed up half the night arguing instead among themselves over what he possibly had to gain from frightening them so. In the end, they could arrive at one conclusion only: this Witek was a scoundrel who'd been taking advantage of their greenness to have a little sadistic fun at their expense.

Leventhal shifted in his bunk and contemplated lighting another cigarette. Outside, the snow had stopped, the sky looking as if it might clear. Despite the condemnation he'd helped heap on their visitor that night, he wasn't so sure anymore. An evil feeling had been growing in him since, and no matter how much schnapps he drank it wasn't going away. Could the man have been telling the truth after all? As absurd, as utterly impossible as this was, it would certainly explain that peculiar smoke people were having trouble rationalizing. And the cocky Witek had been correct about one thing; whatever was going on here, Birkenau was no playground. The electrified fences, the watchtowers, the heavily armed SS…. it was a concentration camp all right, regardless of the lenience unaccountably shown them so far.

He decided against the cigarette, opted instead for a nap. He dreamt it was summer and he was at a lake, swimming. He hadn't been swimming in years but missed it, was good at it, had the body for it: slender but strong, loose-limbed as a seal, lanky. But there was more to it than that, and always had been. Even as a child he'd liked the aloneness of it, just him and the water, the way it insulated him, if only temporarily, from the world and its complications. From dry land and its demands. In his dream, the sun reflected diamonds on the surface of the lake. He was knifing through the water, through diamonds, it was so beautiful, so peaceful, when suddenly—

The door to the hut slammed. Loud as a gunshot. Instantly awake, he jerked upright in his bunk to see a thirtyish bear of a man, a stranger, plunk two heavy brown bottles down on the oak table.

"Okay, lads," the man bellowed, "listen to me! The name's Kalniak, and I'm to be your kapo, or foreman. One last schnapps then we're off to do a little work. It's about time you lazy sods started earning your keep."

Without a word, as if awaiting this very order, the men pulled on their coats, and in anticipation of the cold everyone downed a shot before filing outside. The frosty air seized them by the nose, bit into them. The late-morning sky was like a sheet of metal, its overcast sun shedding an aluminum light. Quickly, they formed a column and headed out, two soldiers on either side of them. They sloshed after their kapo through the muddy snow without speaking, each nervous as a cat; the time had come at last to learn what the Germans had been saving them for.

Once past the main gate, where they were counted and the number recorded, they were led toward a growth of trees from which billowed three pillars of smoke. It was the same woods they'd seen in the distance from the unloading ramp four days ago. A murmur of relief rose from their ranks—they'd been assigned to tend the fires that were burning the camp's garbage. That didn't seem such a bad job. "At least we'll be warm," Leventhal heard someone say.

Upon entering the wood, the road they were on turned into a snake, winding this way and that through the trees. After half a mile, it emerged into a clearing, where a long, single-story wooden building stood. An SS officer appeared from out of it and ordered the column to a halt. After conferring with the *Sturmmänn* in charge, he picked five prisoners to accompany him. As these set out for the building, Leventhal overheard part of his orders to them: "Underwear in one pile, shoes in another, coats and all other garments in a third, *verstanden?*"

Through the open double doors of the place, he saw clothes hanging from hooks the length of one wall, others strewn on the floor beneath. But where were the people these belonged to? And why out here, in the woods, had they been made to shed them to begin with?

The answer to both questions lay a short way down the road. Another clearing, another building, an arrowed sign nailed to a tree: *zum Baden*, to the baths. That explained it. Upon entering Birkenau, Leventhal had had to undergo a shower and delousing himself. With so many people crammed into so small an area, pest-induced epidemics must have posed a constant threat.

The bathhouse, like the undressing barracks, was twice as long as it was wide, though instead of wood it was built of brick and roofed with red tiles. There were no windows. A large door stood agape, as broad as it was tall and made of heavy wooden beams. An older *Scharführer* leaned next to it, his back against the brick, smoking a cigarette. At their approach, he stood erect and broke into a smile. With a sweep of his arm, he invited those in front to have a look inside. Leventhal was among these, but what with the sun having by now broken through the clouds, and the glare off the snow blinding, the doorway was an opaque black square cut in the brick. It took his eyes a few seconds to adjust to the dark interior—and a few more to convince himself that what he was looking at was real.

The room was filled with dead bodies from the floor almost to the ceiling, men, women, and children in a snarled, naked mass. Arms and legs were twined together as tightly as woody vines. From just inside the door, the open eyes of a girl seemed to be staring reproachfully into his, as if to say, "Look, look at me…. I'm only *fourteen*."

With a cry, he stumbled backward, his terrified gaze falling on the *Scharführer*, who clearly couldn't have been enjoying the moment more. He was grinning like a wolf, his eyes darting from face to face, feasting on the shock and bewilderment he found there. After he'd got his fill, he waved their kapo over.

"You, Kalniak, listen up. I want *this* trash out here," he said, pointing to Leventhal and the others, "to take *that* trash in there around to the back where it belongs. And I want it done fast. Looks like we're in for a busy goddam day."

The next thing he knew, Leventhal was standing among corpses, the air in the death room sodden with the stench of excrement and vomit.

He didn't know what to do. WHAT WERE THEY SUPPOSED TO DO? Some of the bodies lay helter-skelter on the floor, but most were piled high in knotted heaps as tall as he was. He took a woman by the arms and pulled, but she remained stuck where she was. He'd never touched a dead person before. The flesh was wet, still warm….

When he woke up, his first thought was that he'd been having a bad dream, but a quick look around and he remembered where he was. What he didn't understand was how he'd come to be sitting down, his back to the wall. Nor why the burly Kalniak was bending over him.

"You've fainted, boy," the kapo said, "but you've got to get up. C'mon, up!" he repeated, tugging Leventhal to his feet. "They'll kill you if you don't."

The man hustled him to the door, made him take some deep breaths. "Good, that's better. Now let's to it," he said, pulling him back inside. "You've got to keep working or…." He drew a finger across his throat. "Don't look at their faces, it makes it a lot easier. It also helps to start at the top of the pile and work your way down. Got it?"

Leventhal nodded, and bracing himself, was reaching up for a pair of ankles when he noticed the showerheads hanging from the ceiling. Wait a minute, he thought, then looked down at the cement floor and saw it was dark with water, even puddled in places. Could it be that these people had been run through a shower after all? But why do that and then kill them? It didn't gibe.

"Quick, here comes the *Scharführer*!" Kalniak hissed. "Get to work!"

He grabbed the ankles and yanked the corpse down, its head hitting the floor with a crack. Someone else seized its wrists, and together they lugged it out the door. The Germans were waiting for them with curses and clubs, and off they hurried in the direction they were driven, their grisly burden bouncing between them.

He tried not to look at either his co-worker or the thing they were carrying, but kept his eyes fixed on the back of the man running in front of him. Not once did he so much as glance at his partner. His shame at being a participant in mass murder, even if it was only at gunpoint and after the fact, wasn't something he wanted to see in another's face.

A fresh dreadfulness awaited them at the rear of the building. The room from which they'd come was only one of two apparently, for another contingent of wretches was dragging corpses out a second door in back and laying them out in rows. There were hundreds of dead thus arranged, among which yet another commando of prisoners moved, some cutting the hair off the heads of the females and shoving it into sacks, others using iron bars to pry open mouths. After a quick search, bloody pliers would start ripping out teeth. Leventhal didn't understand, until told those were gold teeth they were dropping into their tin cans. More sickening yet, he saw that body cavities were being mined for loot as well, an indecency not even the children among them were spared.

A narrow-gauge metal track bordered the far edge of the yard, atop which a line of open trolleys waited. Still other groups of prisoners were working this station, filling the lead car with bodies and pushing it out of sight into the trees. From behind these, the black smoke continued to gush.

He made over twenty trips from the death chamber, running both ways, too tired and stunned to think. But then that was good, might even have saved his life, for to think about what one was seeing, what one was doing, was to risk giving up and collapsing in despair into the snow. The way was littered with those who appeared to have done just that, their nightmare ended by an SS bullet to the head.

One thought, however, refused to be silenced, and it took him a while to answer the question it posed. How in God's name had the Nazi monsters done it, managed to kill so many people all at once, and with no blood? The only blood he could see on any of the bodies was an occasional trickle from the ears and nose, and that oozing from various scratches and scrapes, as if they'd been in some kind of fight. Many also had a peculiar bluish tint to their hands, feet, and faces, though for all he knew, their being naked, this was caused by the cold.

Then, with a start, he remembered what the man Witek had said.

Of course, he shuddered, what else could it be? Apart from explaining the absence of visible wounds, gas—poison gas—was the ideal solution, not only effective and efficient but from the standpoint of the SS neatly in sync with their ideology. For years they'd been vilifying the Jews as parasites, vermin, and how better to get rid of vermin than to fumigate?

He was able to confirm this, however, only after the room had been emptied and he was sent in as part of the crew to "clean it up for the next batch", as the *Scharführer* put it. This involved wiping the blood and excrement off the plaster walls, digging the fingernails out, hosing the floor down, and sweeping the offal out the door and down the path into a drain. It wasn't until he began sweeping that he noticed the blue pellets scattered at opposite ends of the room.

They lay in two patches at the base of the walls, above each patch a narrow vent cut into the plaster. It was easy enough to piece together how the deed had been done. The Germans had poured the pellets in through the vents from outside, where they must have reacted with the air to produce the deadly gas. The showerheads were dummy, meant to deceive. As for the wetness he'd encountered before, later that day he would learn that the bodies, too, were given a posthumous hosing, moisture rendering the blue pellets inert, along with any remaining gas.

He was to discover many such things, unspeakable things. Why in their death struggles, for instance, the victims ended up in piles: the gas spread at ground level, then slowly rose. In their terror, their mindless panic, the people climbed atop each other to try and escape it, the strong crushing the weak beneath them. Judging from some of the injuries, the fighting had to have been fierce.

But this and other revelations lay in Leventhal's future, which at the moment he couldn't help feeling was problematic. What were the odds of the SS allowing him and the others to go on breathing, they who'd seen with their own eyes the Nazis' abominable secret? The only thing that could save them was if the Germans continued to need them, and that was going to require a steady supply of corpses. A ghoulish prospect to be sure, nor was this just a figure of speech. It hadn't taken them long to realize that their survival, like that of the cannibalistic ghoul of myth, was dependent on the ready availability of dead flesh.

When the work cleaning the chamber was done, a squad of *Schützen* marched the men into the woods. Some thought this was it, that they were about to be shot, but their guards merely wanted them in their bloody clothing out of sight until they were needed again. One informed them that the last of the transport was even now at the undressing barracks, and they'd better rest while they had the chance.

Leventhal lay on his back and stared up at the trees towering above him. It felt good to lie down, and not just because he was bone-tired. He was thinking how easy, how inviting it would be to keep lying there after the order came to get back to work. With what he'd been privy to today, it was no longer dying that scared him but living. Survival as what, a craven accessory to the slaughter of his own people? A future doing what—mopping up the gruesome messes of the blood-crazed SS? Given what he knew, he was destined to die anyway, if not sooner then later. To do so now would spare him much, as there could only be more horridness ahead.

Just because it would be easier, however, didn't make it right. He'd decided already that suicide wasn't an option, and never would be. As tempting as it might be never to get up again, he had an obligation to live, live and bear witness to a crime whose traces the Nazis were sure to try and obliterate one day. How he was supposed to accomplish either he had no idea, though of this he was positive, and had been from the moment the dead teenaged girl's accusing eyes had met his: whatever it took, however long it took, he wasn't about to let these murderers of children get away with it. Somehow, some way, he would tell the world what he'd seen, and the world, whether it wanted to or not, would have to listen.

The sky showing through the gaps in the treetops was busy with smoke. He watched it race from east to west like so many dead souls departing this earth. Before the war, he'd attended a *yeshiva* school in Warsaw. He knew his Bible and recalled it now, and the accursed valley of Gehenna, where during the reigns of the evil kings Azah and Masseneh, the children of Israel were sacrificed then immolated on the altar of the pagan god Moloch. Now, incredibly, Gehenna burned again, somewhere out there at the end of the German trolley tracks. He attempted to picture what such an inferno might look like, but mercifully stopping himself, closed his eyes and tried not to think of anything at all.

*   *   *

From the top of the rise overlooking it, SS-*Oberscharführer* Otto Möll surveyed the burning meadow and smiled. It was a clumsy smile, unpracticed, but he was getting better at it; things were going so well for him lately, there hadn't been much call for his usual scowl.

Half the meadow looked as if it was on fire, though in reality there were only three stacks of corpses burning. Still, that was enough to make the *Oberscharführer* happy. Möll cut a striking figure as he stood alone on the ridge, nor was this by chance. He was an inveterate poseur, and made it a point at all times to appear as grandiose as possible. In truth, he felt he had to, knowing all too well he was far from the Aryan ideal physically.

Stocky and rather short, heavily freckled, with hair the color of wet sand and already thinning rapidly at the age of twenty-eight, he didn't come even close to the tall, blonde Viking archetype. One of the beauties, however, of the dashing SS uniform was its ability to make its wearer more imposing than the sum of his parts. Thus his habit of always decking himself out in full dress, every button and bar gleaming, leather buffed to a shine.

To complete the picture, he liked when possible to have his dog Hannibal at his side, a magnificent silver and black German Shepherd of formidable size and exquisite markings. The dog stood on the alert beside him now, the perfect accessory, though today and for the first time (but, he'd already decided, definitely not the last), the beast was trumped by an even more impressive embellishment to his master's person.

It had been presented to him just yesterday in a ceremony attended by none other than the camp commandant, *Obersturmbannführer* Höss. He reached up and fingered it gently, as if to make sure it was real. It was the *Kriegsverdienstkreuz*, the War Service Cross, one of the most coveted medals the Third Reich could bestow. The *Führer* himself had to authorize its giving, and it was awarded only to those soldiers who'd done something exceptional. Now here it was for all to see, hanging improbably from a ribbon round the neck of an ex-ditchdigger from the German hinterland.

His eyes abruptly narrowed, his smile disappearing. What the bloody hell! Could those idiots down below be screwing up again? One of the fires dotting the meadow wasn't burning properly all of a sudden, might even from the look of it be sputtering out. Off he scurried down the hillock, Hannibal trotting ahead of him. He would show them what's what, the damn cowheaded kikes.

Möll's rise in the SS, if unmeteoric, had been steady. After serving a year and a half in two different concentration camps, first at Gusen, a subcamp of the Mauthausen system, then the larger one at Sachsenhausen, he was promoted to *Unterscharführer* and in early 1941 assigned to the growing Auschwitz complex in Poland. Before the war, his parents unable to afford an education for him, he'd had to make a living as a landscaper, hardly a source of pride at the time, but fortuitous later on as it ended up being his ticket to Auschwitz, a posting he'd dreamt of since first hearing of the place. His foot in this new camp's door was as *Kommandoführer,* or SS supervisor, of its groundkeeping department.

But both his ambition and talents went far beyond that, a fact soon recognized by his superiors, who sought to put him to better use. By summer, he found himself in charge of the notorious penal commando, a punishment detail in which troublesome prisoners were prescribed half rations, the hardest labor, and the most sadistic kapos. As often as not, it was a death sentence to any who found themselves there.

Möll flourished in the role. It was here that he invented the game of swim-frog, which would go on to become an Auschwitz tradition. Numerous fishponds occupied the camp grounds, a prime source of SS food. In swim-frog, the prisoners were made to paddle to the middle of one of these ponds and remain there, treading water, while croaking like frogs. Before long they would tire and attempt to reach the shallows, but their guards would repulse them with pistol shots and long poles. It was only a matter of time before they sank below the surface and drowned. The sport, as the Germans saw it, was to keep them croaking to the end.

It wasn't only the inmates who were deathly afraid of Möll. His brother SS, too, particularly those who served under him, avoided him if at all possible. He brooked no nonsense from either group; with a temper to match his gingery hair and ruddy complexion, he was a tiger to both. He only had one good eye, the other being glass, leading to the perhaps inevitable moniker "the Cyclops".

For almost a year, he was the terror of Block 11, that prison within a prison where the penal commando was quartered. Even this, though, his superiors realized, wasn't utilizing the man's potential to the fullest. By late-spring, with the completion of the nearby Birkenau camp, slated to be the killing adjunct to Auschwitz, Hitler's Final Solution to the Jewish problem had begun in earnest. Not only were two confiscated Polish farmhouses converted into provisional gas chambers, together able to snuff out two thousand people at a time, but construction about to commence on the four permanent Birkenau crematoria, modern state-of-the-art murder machines capable of "processing" twelve thousand at once. All this was in addition to the original crematorium at Auschwitz, a smaller installation whose morgue had been converted into a 700-person gas chamber the year before.

It was to be a glorious campaign against the detested *Rassenfiend*, the devil race, and Möll was determined to be in the thick of it. It was a Jew who'd taken his eye out, but that wasn't why he hated them. The man, after all, had been fighting for his life, and though he lost, at least he'd fought. Möll bore neither him nor his kind any animosity for that. On the other hand, as everyone from the *Führer* on down knew, for a thousand years the Jew had been the mortal enemy of the German *Volk*. Recent history had confirmed this. The shameful armistice of 1918 to end the Great War, the humiliating Treaty of Versailles that followed, the divisive Weimar socialist government foisted upon Germany, the rampant hyperinflation that had stolen what little wealth the young Möll's parents did have—all were the doing of the insidious global Jewish conspiracy, and for these and countless other crimes they deserved to be erased from the map of the new Europe. An SS doctor had explained it to him quite eloquently once, using an analogy from his trade. "The Jew," he'd said, "is the gangrenous appendix in the Aryan body politic. Once the appendix is removed, the body will be healthy again."

Möll requested and received permission to transfer from Block 11 to the two gas chambers hidden among the groves of birch trees for which Birkenau was named. There he toiled for three months as transport after transport rolled in, until by August's end 110,000 of the Chosen People lay buried in the forest meadows nearby.

This, however, came to pose a problem as unforeseen as it was unpalatable. Under the relentless beating of the summer sun, the ground these victims occupied began first to swell, then turn color from dirt-brown to an alarming dark red. A network of widening cracks then appeared, out of which was soon seeping a black, evil-smelling sludge that not only stank for miles but threatened to contaminate the local groundwater. Chlorinated lime was spread on the surface, but had no effect.

The decision was made to exhume the corpses and burn them. The first knot in this plan was that no one wanted the repugnant and technically difficult job of supervising such a mess—no one, that is, but a certain barrel-chested, one-eyed, strawberry-blond *Unterscharführer*. Hungry for acclaim, Möll jumped at the chance, and while others scoffed at his foolhardiness, assembled a Sonderkommando of a hundred and fifty mostly French Jews and went to work.

Nobody, not even the Cyclops, was prepared for what awaited them below ground. The shovels hadn't gone a foot down when an odor gushered forth that knocked most of the Frenchmen to their knees. There they would remain for some minutes, vomiting loudly, along with many of the SS, who temporarily themselves were in no condition to bully them back to their feet. It was a smell such as the senses weren't built to withstand, incapacitating both slave and slave driver alike.

When the digging did resume, it didn't take long to reach the appalling stink's source. Another foot into the red soil and the bodies began to appear, blue-black, disintegrating, crawling with maggots and other worms, stacked in descending layers, how deep no one knew. As much as Möll despised all inmates, in particular that social virus, that racial parasite the Jew, one glance into those suppurating, months-old mass graves was enough to elicit a sort of sympathy from even him. How did the wretches manage to keep going, he wondered, those down there in the muck, up to their ankles in corpse soup, their clothing, their skin, their faces smeared with it? That first day, thirty of them were shot for refusing to keep working, and had to be replaced. Möll, his inchoate sympathy aside, would have liked to have made a better example of these than simply shooting them, but to his irritation time wouldn't permit.

The second part of the operation, too, went far from smoothly at first. His orders were to cremate the corpses on tall wooden pyres, but this had presented problems. These tended to burn unevenly and too fast, leaving a good portion of the dead intact. His idea, his brainstorm, was to concentrate the fire by partially submerging the pyre in a long, rectangular open pit. After a few days trial and error, it was found that an excavation measuring two meters deep and eight wide burned the hottest and longest. By arranging the corpses in alternating tiers between layers of kindling, and setting the length at forty meters, twelve hundred could be disposed of in less than six hours, including the removal of the ashes.

What Möll had done, if not invent the fire pit outright, was refine it to the standard used thereafter. By the middle of October, to the delight of those who'd given it to him, the job was completed, his final order being the liquidation of the entire Sonderkommando involved. Then came the Kriegsverdienstkreuz and his almost as startling promotion two full grades to the rank of *Oberscharführer*. He was reassigned to the birch groves, this time as director of the new open-air incineration program.

It was clear to Möll what was wrong with it even before he reached the malfunctioning fire pit below. Although a few prisoners continued to stoke it with their long iron pitchforks, those whose job it was to ladle the kerosene onto the problem areas of the fire lay sprawled on the ground, their scoops at their sides.

"What the hell are you fucks doing?" he roared as he approached. By then he had not only Hannibal but several *Schützen* in tow. "Why aren't you feeding that fire?"

Everyone sprang to attention, the stokers dropping their forks. All were afraid at first to speak.

"*Answer me!*" Möll screamed, his face approaching the color of the coals in the pit.

"*Herr Oberscharführer,*" one said finally, his voice small, "we ran out of fuel. Kapo Bronski went to get more."

"And when was that?" he demanded, pacing up and down in front of them.

"Half an hour ago, *Herr Oberscharführer*. We—"

"Half an hour, you say?" Möll's face seemed to get redder. Abruptly, he stopped pacing and wheeled on the soldiers behind him. "Find this Bronski," he ordered, "and bring him to me. On the double!"

They were back in five minutes, with the kapo and the kerosene. "He was with a woman, sir," one of them reported, "in the shed behind the fuel dump."

"Oh, he was, was he?" Möll said, unexpectedly breaking into a smile. He circled the kapo slowly, hands clasped behind him. "Is that true, Kapo Bronski? Were you with a woman?"

"Y-yes, sir," the man stammered in competent if quaking German. "But we were just talking, I—I swear. And I lost track of—"

"Just talking, you say. My, how virtuous of you." Möll stopped and faced him, not a foot away, still smiling. "And in the course of this.... conversation, you lost track of the time. Quite understandable. It could happen to anybody. But what about my fire? It's looking rather anemic, and as you can see, the sausages aren't done yet. How do you propose we get it going again? What kind of fuel would you suggest that we use?"

The kapo's eyes were big with fright. "Why, the kerosene, sir. It's—it's what we always use."

"Ah, yes, the kerosene. The same kerosene that should have been here half an hour ago. I have a better idea, though, an even more fitting fuel to start with. And you can help me with that, Bronski." He turned to the guards. "Seize him."

Two of them took hold of the kapo and followed their sergeant to the edge of the fire pit. "Whew!" Möll exclaimed, shielding his face from the heat. "It's rather warm over here, isn't it? And about to get warmer—for you anyway, kapo."

He motioned toward the fire and nodded once to the soldiers, who proceeded to pummel their victim to the ground, grab him by the arms and legs, and fling him into the middle of the smoldering pit.

He tried to scramble out, but quickly sank to his waist in the glowing coals and began screaming. Thrashing crazily about, he was soon knocking charred wood and body parts everywhere. With a curse, Möll drew his revolver and put an end to the kapo's agony. He'd wanted it to last longer, but the man was in danger of busting up that whole part of the pyre.

For all of its functionality, the concept of the incinerating pit did possess one drawback. The fact that two meters of the fire were below ground meant that the flow of oxygen to it was restricted, a situation exacerbated once it began to settle. Constant stoking helped, but it wasn't enough; liquid combustibles were needed to keep the thing burning. This worked, but was expensive. What with the hostilities in Russia, methanol, kerosene, and especially gasoline were not only costly but hard to come by at any price.

Möll was well aware of this, and in theory anyway had arrived at a possible solution. He'd noticed that as the corpses twisted and sizzled in the fire, they exuded a considerable amount of liquid fat. This did succeed in nourishing the flames some, but most of it was lost in the ground. Now, if this bounty of more than sufficiently inflammable fluid could be harvested somehow before it was lost, then *ipso facto*, dilemma solved, and less the need for synthetic fuels.

He didn't lack for ideas on how to implement his theory, but realistically speaking, was it worth the trouble at this stage to try to fix things? The four Birkenau crematoria, with their forty-odd ovens, were promised any month now, and then the point would become moot. Why bother with fire pits when one had that many cast-iron ovens at one's disposal, designed and manufactured specifically for cremation? That would certainly be enough to take care of any and all Jews the SS were likely to get their hands on.

The new *Oberscharführer*, therefore, chose not to vex himself with the problem. The system for now was good enough as it was. Instead, he devoted much of what time he could spare to basking in not only his recent triumphs but the satisfactions of the job at hand, content in the knowledge that he was doing something important with his life. No, not just important, earthshaking, historic. Something men would remember, would marvel at, for centuries.

Jewish lore held that at the time of Moses and the Egyptian captivity, God unleashed a final plague to break Pharaoh's will. This plague took the form of the merciless Angel of Death, its mission to kill every first-born Egyptian male. The Israelites called this frightful entity Mal'ach H'Mavet.

Möll's fantasy, his conceit—or as he would have it, his destiny—was to be a latter-day Mal'ach H'Mavet, only this time in reverse, with the Jews at not only their fickle God's mercy but his. Whenever he indulged in this fantasy, he had to smile at the irony of it: he, Otto Möll, an agent of the Hebrew God! On the surface a notion so cockeyed as to be nothing less than laughable, yet incongruous enough to seem somehow, if perversely, almost plausible.

The great thing, the truly wonderful thing, the thing that got his adrenaline going every time he thought about it, was the fact—he'd looked it up before coming to Auschwitz—the fact that there were eleven million Jews trapped within the current borders of the Reich.

If that wasn't the opportunity of a lifetime, he didn't know what was.

1943

Winter

There was a break in the weather going on three days now. Long enough that people were grateful for it, but at the same time already cursing its end. Then again, in the month of January, in this part of the world, even one day with the thermometer struggling past forty—with no ice and no wind, no flying needles of snow—was like a blessing from on high, a gift from heaven. Noah Zabludowicz scanned the sky for some hint of change, an opening or other irregularity in the featureless gray overcast. To his relief, there was none. It was as if a great bowl had been inverted and placed atop their little swath of countryside, shielding them from the storms raging on the other side of it.

As they neared Block 16, Noah kept his eyes peeled. This was the trickiest part of the operation; more than once they'd had to abort because of SS nearby. Not that it happened all that often. Oddly enough, one seldom ran across the Germans inside the camp. Still, it was best to be vigilant. Overconfidence could get a body killed as quickly as anything.

This evening, the coast was clear. Two pairs of men carrying four kettles of soup slung from poles borne on their shoulders scuttled through the open back door of #16 and set their loads down. There the four pots would remain until the residents of the hut got back from their day's work. The *Blockälteste*, or barracks elder, and his assistants were bribed.

All but a few of the prisoners quartered here were from Ciechanow, and thanks to Noah's audaciousness, had been enjoying double rations for a month now. It was only *lagersuppe* to be sure, mainly turnips and cabbage, the color and consistency of dirty dishwater but food nonetheless, and as such precious beyond price. Nor were his friends and ex-neighbors the only beneficiaries of Noah's largesse. He was also running a ring that distributed stolen food to the starving. Some of the inmates had taken to calling him the Messiah of Bread.

As resourceful as he was, though, he'd also been blessed. After their time in quarantine, he and his brother Hanan were sent down the road to the *Stammlager,* or main camp (Pinchas was kept behind in Birkenau, where electricians were needed), and ended up in the Bauhof *Kommando* pouring cement. It was hard work, outdoors, the weather bitter cold, and to make matters worse, their kapo a particularly brutal one. Most kapos of the regular labor gangs weren't only hardened German and Polish criminals, but the worst those countries' penal systems had to offer. Nor was this by accident. The SS encouraged—no, required—a daily attrition rate among their slaves of twenty percent more or less, how the kapo managed this was his or her business. Noah's and Hanan's, an ex-boxer who'd dabbled in loan sharking, practiced an assortment of methods, but his favorite was to throw whomever had displeased him to the ground, place the heavy cane he always carried across the man's throat, then stand on it and rock back and forth until the neck was a pulpy mess. It was all in a day's work for a three hundred-man squad of the Bauhof to go to work in the morning, and two hundred and fifty return bearing the bodies of their dead comrades.

Then one night, the men from Noah's block were rousted from their bunks and put through a surprise selection, common enough during the day but rare after sundown. Fifteen of them were singled out, including the two brothers, and told not to report to their work details tomorrow. This didn't bode well for them, and they knew it. Few were to sleep much that night, their thoughts unable to stray for long from the all too nearby crematorium.

In the morning, however, their fears proved unfounded. After the others were marched off to work as usual to the rousing strains of the camp orchestra, they were taken to Block 25, where the barracks elder informed them they were to be his new *Stubendiensten,* the old ones having been transferred, for reasons unmentioned, to the subcamp at Jawischowitz. A *Stubendienst* was a lower-level assistant to the elder, responsible for keeping the hut clean, bringing food and supplies, lice control, security, and other such duties. Most barracks employed two or three of these at most, as both the place and the prisoners were meant to stay filthy and under-provisioned. Block 25, however, was one of two that housed the camp *Prominenz*, or prominents, the cooks, doctors, tradesmen, clerks, and other prisoner-functionaries without whom no lager could operate. Theirs was more dormitory than hut, as well appointed as it was scrubbed, with its own bathrooms and showers, wood floors instead of dirt, one person to a bunk rather than the customary several. And what bunks they were! With sheets, pillows, clean blankets, real mattresses even, not the usual shapeless sacks of straw most prisoners had to contend with, so thin it was as if one was sleeping on the wood slats beneath.

It was easy to spot a prominent. He might be wearing the standard striped burlap, but it was cut to fit and regularly laundered. He would also have proper shoes, not the broken, ill-fitting, blister-causing clogs issued the ordinary inmate. The men of Block 25 enjoyed many luxuries, enough that it took fifteen Stubendiensten to attend to them. One chore, though, was never demanded of these, the fetching of the hut's daily ration of soup from the kitchen. The soup wasn't needed. Such was the power and wealth of the Prominenz that they were able to buy their own food, either on the black market or from among the ranks of the SS. A gold tooth or diamond ring could go far in that respect.

Thus were Noah and Hanan delivered from the cement commando and its lethal kapo, though as it turned out, this wasn't to be their only piece of luck. Their second day on the job, one of the prominents came up to Noah and wrapped him in a bear hug, a big grin on his face. He, in self-defense, broke free of the other's grasp.

"What, you don't recognize me?" the man said. "I'm Witek, from Danzig. I owe you my life, Noah Zabludowicz, and though it's been a long time, I haven't forgotten my debt."

Actually, as Noah was to learn later, luck had nothing to do with getting him and Hanan out of the Bauhof. Witek, having asked around, eventually traced them to Block 16, and succeeded in bribing his block elder to recruit his new Stubendiensten from there. Part of the deal was that the Zabludowicz brothers be on the list.

Noah couldn't believe his good fortune. To find this man here, in Auschwitz, and a prominent no less! Five years ago it had been, or was it five hundred? Yet he remembered the day well. He was in Danzig on business, dropping off a truckload of steel parts for the Silvers. It was a gray March morning, a considerable fog still in the air. He looked up from his work on the unloading dock to see a man crossing the street. The fool was reading a folded newspaper and didn't see the truck barreling down on him, nor because of the fog perhaps, did the driver appear to see him.

Noah, being Noah, sprang into action. He jumped from the dock, dashed in front of the truck, and with a flying leap slammed the man out of harm's way. But the bumper just caught Noah's lower leg, and it was to the hospital for him. A simple fracture, relatively minor, but Witek was right there and effusive in his gratitude. He visited his rescuer both days he was in the hospital, paid all his medical bills, and after that—every birthday, every Hanukkah for three years—kept paying with presents and sometimes even cash, delivered in the mail to his apartment in Ciechanow.

Then one day the gifts stopped, and Noah figured that was that. He was fine with this, too, seeing as how he'd never asked for anything in the first place. It wasn't until now that he discovered why they stopped. In 1940, the Gestapo arrested Witek for dealing in smuggled goods and sent him to what was then the brand-new Auschwitz lager, where he not only survived conditions even harsher than they were now, but wound up prospering. Within a year, he'd finagled his way into the camp kitchen, where he was working as a cook when he tracked the brothers down.

Now, to know a *cook* at Auschwitz was an advantage not to be underestimated. To know a cook meant life, though Noah wasn't so crass as to be thinking in terms of himself only. He soon made a deal with Witek for the disposal of "excess" food, and it was from here that his reputation as the Messiah of Bread began. Every day he and three others would go to the kitchen and pick up the soup ration for Block 25, but take it instead to the Ciechanow hut. In addition, twice a week he'd make off with a princely quantity of bread, a good half a cartful. Bread served a dual function at Auschwitz, both as food and as the principal unit of currency in the camp. Everything from shoelaces to sex could be purchased with bread.

But Noah wasn't out to enrich himself any more than he was to save just himself. Instead, he and his confederates would speed their windfall from the kitchen to some predetermined hiding place, from where it was distributed to those in direst need of it, that caste of prisoners known in camp jargon as the *Muselmänner*, or Moslems.

They were called this because of their resemblance to the fragile, famished beggars of Calcutta, and were and always had been the rule in

Auschwitz rather than the exception, especially among the Jews. They were those who'd given up, who no longer cared, no longer hoped, no longer thought much if at all, those so debased by overwork and hunger that in a sense they could no longer be considered fully human. A man performing moderate physical labor requires four thousand calories a day; the ration for Jews at Auschwitz-Birkenau was normally eight or nine hundred, at times even less. This was the amount calculated to keep a prisoner alive and working for approximately three months, which in the economic scheme of things was quite sufficient for the SS.

The Muselmänn was a creature as painful to look at as contemplate. Open sores broke out all over him. The lack of albumin and other proteins deprived him of all energy; it became an effort for him to walk, or even roll out of his bunk. His eyesight and hearing deteriorated, as did his mental faculties—confusion, loss of memory, and a general apathy are all symptoms of a shortage of vitamin B. Slow in comprehending orders, he was beaten hard and often for what was mistaken as defiance. The eyes were empty, the face expressionless, the brain fixated on two things: how to avoid further beatings.... and food, always food, all he talked about was food, and how and where he might find more. Crawling with lice, unsteady afoot, his body and uniform indescribably filthy, he shambled about like something out of a horror movie, a constant discharge dripping from his nose, the *Durchfall*, or starvation-induced diarrhea, from another aperture. Once he'd reached that point, the game was all but up. Once the Durchfall appeared, the gas chamber wasn't far behind.

Noah, too, had known hunger. Before they could be admitted to either Auschwitz or Birkenau proper, all new prisoners had to spend a month or so in quarantine, also known as the visa, a sort of boot camp to train them in the grim realities of their new lives. The word visa came from the Latin *visere*, meaning to investigate or look into, which was what Q-Camp was for: to determine if the choices the SS doctors had made on the unloading ramp were correct, that those not put on the trucks were indeed strong enough to serve out what life was left them as slaves of the Reich.

There was no work in quarantine, so the rations were poor. The dreaded nettle soup was common, a noisome concoction of milky-looking fluid bubbling in its cauldron, orange rings of margarine floating on the surface, at the bottom fibrous stalks of chopped nettles and other weeds that not only looked inedible but smelled even worse. Nor was the "bread" any better, dry, crumbly, and fashioned largely of wild chestnuts and sawdust.

Death by malnutrition is one of the more agonizing there is. Essentially, it comes from the body feeding on itself, first its reserves of fat, then muscle and other tissue. In Q-Camp, Noah had begun to feel this very hunger, not that of a missed meal or even a day or two of meals but a silent and continuous scream from the body, a tortured cry every waking minute from every slowly dying cell, a demand that never ceased nor gave surcease from pain. It was the hunger that in its terrible, self-predatory alchemy transformed men into obscenities, into something not men.

He still wasn't sure how he and his brothers made it out of the visa alive. They'd entered it that first day after leaving the ramp, having been clipped of every hair on body and head to curb lice, and issued the repulsive rags and impossible clogs that were henceforth supposed to serve as their only clothing. Around midnight, as they lay a comfortless five in their box-like *koje*, or bunk, their sole cover a single blanket fetid with mold and urine, they were awakened with shouts and blows and made to assemble in the freezing yard. It was their first *Appell*, or roll call, and only in Q-Camp was it done at night. They were out there a full hour, during which their kapo and his assistants, after lining them up in rows, strode among them with jeers and clubs, lashing out at their whim. They would face another, longer Appell at dawn, and another at sundown. Sandwiched in between was a typical day in quarantine.

Breakfast was a cold half-liter of something euphemistically called coffee. Then it was off to the latrine, a few planks thrown across a ditch. Jammed together on these, so close they couldn't help but soil each other, the prisoners were given less than a minute to do their business, without so much as a scrap of paper with which to clean themselves.

Then it was back to the *Appellplatz*, not for counting this time but drill. Here they were taught how to march with the proper precision and snap, moving as one in tight formation, backs rigid, heads high. Hours were devoted to training them in how to remove their caps in unison, the kapos not satisfied until the sound of their arms slapping the caps to their sides consisted of a single sharp crack. The inmate slow to learn this, or who had trouble keeping cadence while marching, or maybe the kapo just didn't like the cut of his jib, was beaten. To death more often than not.

The activity known as *sport* was a staple of the visa. A kapo would pick out ten or twenty or more prisoners, sometimes at random but usually those who'd wound up on his bad side for various reasons, and run them through a rapid-fire series of exercises, he and his henchmen raining blows on them throughout. "On the ground! Now get up! Run! On the ground again! Crawl! Up again, on the double! Jump!" After ten minutes, men started to drop from exhaustion, and if unable to continue, bludgeoned to death where they'd fallen. Sometimes the kapo would leave one or two of the group alive, sometimes he wouldn't.

Another tradition was "the 25", a disciplinary measure considered comparatively light and practiced not just in quarantine but camp-wide. The transgressor was made to drop his pants and lie on his stomach across a bench, baring his buttocks and thighs. Twenty-five strokes were then administered using a heavy wooden club sawed in half lengthwise, the recipient usually forced to count each wallop aloud. If he missed one or confused the count, his assailant had the option of starting over from the beginning. The man punished thus often had trouble walking for a while, much less marching to his kapo's standards. Or else the skin having ruptured during the beating and become infected, it was off to the gas chamber for him, the cure for just about every malady in Birkenau.

There were a hundred ways to die in both Q-Camp and beyond, but somehow Noah and Hanan—and as far as they knew, Pinchas—were among the living still. Not so their younger brother, poor innocent little Mendel, nor their just as innocent parents, nor any who'd ridden those trucks into the woods that first day. Few had believed it when told of the deaths of their families, but gradually the truth of it sank in, there could be no denying it, and in short order they came to know not only when and where the killings had occurred but how.

He would find out that his sister Deborah was gone, too, a victim of the great Hanukkah selection of December 5th as one of two thousand women from Birkenau's *B1a* lager trucked naked to the gas to make room for an unexpectedly large wave of deportees. The Germans tried when possible to coincide such actions with the bigger Jewish holidays. It was a practice born of the same mean-spirited humor written in steel atop the main gates into both Auschwitz and Birkenau: *Arbeit macht frei*, Work will make you free." And so it would—free of this world, of one's body, one's life. Work here, as the Nazis enforced it, was designed to kill.

But with Witek, Noah had been fortunate. Most were who'd made it as far as he had without becoming Muselmänner. Again, though, it was more than about saving himself, or truth be told, anyone else. Beyond even that, he wanted as he always had—in the ghetto, before the ghetto, before the war even—to fight back, not to let those who persecuted him and his people go unpunished. He hadn't made his arrangement with Witek out of philanthropy alone. The stealing (or as he preferred, the redirection) of food was also an act of resistance, a subversion of the bestial *Disziplin* the despotic SS had established in this little kingdom of theirs between the Sola and Vistula Rivers.

Yet he ached to do more, to take his subversion a step further, and to that end began making inquiries to those he thought could be trusted. There was talk, vague, circumspect, and maddeningly bereft of details, of a secret organization of prisoners within the camp that worked in opposition to the Nazis. No one could tell him the name of a single member of this group, or how it operated, but its existence was taken for granted and provided a ray of hope for many.

Many, but not all, as he was well aware, which was why he had to be careful whom he approached on the subject. An informer could be bought for a loaf of bread, or a kapo or other functionary be more than happy to rat on a man in order to ingratiate himself with his German masters. Caution, however, was getting him nowhere. Not even the veteran Witek could help him, had warned him, in fact, that it might be in his best interest to stop snooping around.

Then just this evening, after the four urns of soup had been disposed of, the prisoner Erich Kulka—also from Ciechanow, though Noah knew him only in passing—appeared at Block 25, and once they'd exchanged pleasantries, told him that a certain Bruno Baum wished to meet with him.

"Tomorrow, 9:00 a.m.," Kulka said, "at *Ka-Be*, Block 20." Then handed him a pass for that purpose in case the SS stopped him.

Noah had heard of Bruno Baum. He was an important personage in the camp, a Marxist *and* a Jew, but despite this dual liability, kapo of a convalescent ward in the inmate hospital complex, the *Krankenbau,* or Ka-Be.

Baum's fame as a writer and politico under the Weimar Republic had preceded him here. Word had it he'd once served in the German *Reichstag* as a member of the Communist delegation. Noah wondered what he'd done to attract the attention of such a luminary, and immediately thought of Block 16 and the scam he was conducting. Had he run afoul of some kind of protocol regarding such things? Was today's delivery to be his last, or almost as bad, its frequency in danger of being reduced? He would certainly have something to say about that, but knew if push came to shove he was hardly in a position to defy the Prominenz.

It was a smiling Kulka who met him at the appointed hut the next morning and led him inside. A prisoner he guessed to be in his mid-forties sat at a desk in a small, bare room, poring over a stack of papers. Even with him sitting down, one could tell he wasn't a tall man. Every part of him seemed slightly miniaturized, his ears, his nose, his hands, the arms and shoulders slender as a woman's. Like Kulka he wore the starched stripes of a prominent, nor was his scalp shorn like an animal's pelt, but shaved fashionably to the skin with a razor. The face below it was tired—no, sorrowful was the better word, as if weighted down with grief, with all the woes of the world.

"Noah Zabludowicz, Bruno Baum. Bruno Baum, Noah Zabludowicz," Kulka said and then left, shutting the door behind him.

Baum rose and shook Noah's hand, offered him a seat. Noah got right to the point, or what he figured was the point. After thinking about it all night, he'd decided that the best defense was a good offense.

"Listen, Herr Baum, I'm not sure why you wanted to see me, but I've a sneaking suspicion it's something to do with the men in Block 16 and the double rations they've been getting. Now, I didn't mean to step on any toes. The last thing I'm looking for is trouble, and if I'm going about it the wrong way—the extra soup, I mean—I would hope you'd tell me. But those are my friends in that hut, my townsmen.... my *landsmanschaft* as we say in Yiddish, and it's going to take a lot to convince me to stop doing my damnedest to help them."

Something almost a smile flitted across the older man's face. "I see," he said, picking up a pencil and twirling it slowly between two fingers. What followed wasn't only in a more than serviceable Polish but delivered in a deep, velvety bass that belied its speaker's build.

"Fortunately, my dear Zabludowicz, in view of your obvious determination, that is not why you are here. We know all about Block 16, and your bread program as well, but those are your affairs, not ours. Though we do find your—how do you say it? Your initiative to be commendable. And that *is* why you are here, because we feel you can be of help to us. That and the fact you have been trying hard, and most carelessly I might add, to reach us."

"Us?" asked Noah not a little sheepishly at having jumped to the wrong conclusion.

"Yes, *us*, the underground, Battle Group-Auschwitz.… the international resistance movement here and in Birkenau, working in concert with the *Armia Krajowa*, the Polish Home Army. We are the people you have been looking for, and now you have found us. And we you. We look forward to you joining us in our fight against the SS butchers."

So it was true, there *was* an underground! Though he hadn't at all seen this coming, Noah didn't hesitate. "Sir," he said, leaning forward in his chair, "consider me at your service when and wherever you need me."

Baum nodded once, then got right to business. "I will be your only contact, at least at first. The fewer operatives you know the better, both for them and you. Do not write down what I tell you, ever—memorize it instead. You will soon be transferred to a commando that goes to Birkenau every day, where your mission will be twofold. Are you aware of what the Germans are building in Birkenau?"

"A new crematorium, or that's the rumor anyway."

"Four new crematoria, each several times as large as the makeshift one here. The SS have…. ambitions that curdle the blood. When those factories of death are finished, which will not be long now, you are to establish contact with a certain kapo of the Sonderkommando and report to us daily on how many transports of Jews are arriving, with how many people, and how many of these are being gassed. We will give you the name of the kapo later. Any questions, Zabludowicz?"

Noah shook his head. He was surprised any of the Sonderkommando should be part of the resistance, but said nothing. He'd assumed since first hearing of them that they were the vilest of collaborators, willing to work hand in murderous hand with the Germans.

"The second part of your assignment," Baum continued, "is more immediate. There is an ammunition manufactory, a subsidiary of Krupp, located not far from here. It is called the Weichsel-Union *Metallwerke*, and employs slave labor of both sexes. Of interest to us is the room where the gunpowder is stored, portioned out, and injected into the detonators of the bombs and shells. It is staffed by female prisoners only. As you may have surmised over the years, the Nazis are embarrassingly provincial in their attitude toward women. They regard them, for instance, as incapable on their own of sabotage and other mischief. When they do transgress, or so the SS would have it, it is only because they have been led astray by men. This is why, not counting the German *Meister* in charge of it, they allow only women, and precious few of them, anywhere near their gunpowder. And why they are so strict about keeping those few segregated from the male population.

"We want that gunpowder, Zabludowicz, we need it—you will be told why later—but we cannot get to the women handling it. Two of our agents have been trying, but have yet to come even close. You, however…. you came on a rather large transport, did you not?"

"From Ciechanow, yes."

"Perhaps you know of a woman from that same transport and presently in Birkenau who would be willing—and smart enough, and above all, brave enough—to establish a cell in the Union *Pulverraum* and oversee the regular delivery of some of its inventory to us."

Noah almost jumped from his seat. "I do know such a person, yes! The perfect person, if she's still alive. She's an…. old friend, and even if she isn't in a position to help, I can't tell you what it would mean to me to find her. My brother, too, holy God! How much freedom of movement would I have at Birkenau?"

"As much as you require. That can be arranged. But first, I must ask this." Baum measured him with narrowed eyes, like an artist a model. "Can this person, this woman, this friend of yours be trusted? More than you can imagine is riding on this remaining a secret."

"Trusted? I'd stake my life on it," Noah said, "and those of my brothers. And if I may be so bold, Herr Baum, yours, sir, as well. I must get to Birkenau. When can I go to Birkenau?"

That evening Baum requested a meeting with his superior in the underground, its recognized leader, Josef Cyrankiewicz. They scheduled it for the latter's chambers, as private a place as any, for he was Blockälteste of a barracks and had his own room at one end of it. Baum knew this room well. A large, hardwood table took up a quarter of it, its polished rectangle bordered by six matching high-backed chairs. It was the only elegant item of furniture Cyrankiewicz allowed himself; the rest was a hodgepodge of battered pieces. There was a small kitchen area, however, and an even tinier bathroom. Such were the privileges accorded a block elder.

He found his chief sitting at the familiar table, head in hands, lost in thought. A single lamp bathed the room in a dim light. Such was the stature of the prisoner Cyrankiewicz, and the reach of his Battle Group-Auschwitz, that he also commanded the Home Army, issuing his orders to the partisans outside the wire via those working undercover as civilian laborers inside it. The SS were harboring one of their biggest nemeses in their midst and didn't know it.

"Hello, Bruno," he said, rising to shake his visitor's hand. He was a large man, well over six feet tall, with the flattened nose and square, jutting jaw of a prizefighter. Baum's hand in his looked like a child's. "What was it you wanted to see me about?"

Baum took a seat across from him. "I recruited that Zabludowicz fellow today," he said. "I think he is going to be a good man for us."

"How so?" Cyrankiewicz said. "Would you care for some hot tea?"

"Thank you, sir, no. Well, for one thing, it is possible he could be of use right away. He might already have a contact who can help us crack the Union gunpowder room."

"Ah, that again," Cyrankiewicz said, "hard-headed Bruno's beloved gunpowder. I thought we decided last week we weren't going to be requiring it after all."

"Pardon me, sir, but nothing was decided. If you will recall, I disagreed most strongly with the Steering Committee's recommendation, and the matter was put on hold. And I still disagree. I believe it imperative that we at least have the gunpowder on hand should the situation arise in which we find ourselves in need of it."

"And that situation, I suppose, would be the general uprising you've been pushing for. Followed, correct me if I'm wrong, by a mass escape."

Baum's silence spoke for itself.

Cyrankiewicz got up from his chair and made his way to the window, where he stood for some time staring into the blackness. There was no moon that night, but every few seconds the white sweep of a searchlight lit up his form.

"Did you know," he said finally, his face still to the window, "that just this morning the city of Stalingrad fell to its rightful owners? Field Marshal von Paulus and the entire German Sixth Army are in Soviet hands."

"Great news," Baum said, "but not unexpected. The Sixth Army has been surrounded and cut off for weeks now."

Cyrankiewicz returned to the table, but remained standing. "I suspect," he said, "that this just might be a turning point in the war. The Wehrmacht is not only reeling but depleted, perhaps irreparably. Soon it will be the Russians who are on the offensive, and Herr Hitler isn't going to have the men and matériel to stop them. All of which makes your notion of an armed uprising less attractive. Better to wait for liberation than risk a slaughter trying to make a run for it."

"Better for whom?" Baum shot back. "The walking dead of the Sonderkommando? The tens of thousands of Jews here and in Birkenau? Only a fool would believe that the SS are going to leave a single one of them alive."

"The Sonder, Bruno, are what—a few hundred men at most? And the Jews, despite their numbers, but a percentage of the inmates. It is our responsibility to look after the well-being of *all* the prisoners, and I hardly think an attempt at a mass breakout would be honoring that responsibility. Do you realize how many could die in such a venture, not to mention from the reprisals sure to follow against those left behind?"

"But what of the Möll Plan, commander? Our intelligence has confirmed not only its existence but that the SS have adopted it as official policy."

Cyrankiewicz fell back in his seat with a sigh. "*Oberscharführer* Otto Möll…. the man's starting to make quite a name for himself, isn't he? Frankly, though, I'm surprised the Germans would sign off on such a plan. How does it read again?"

In response to a general request from the camp administration about what to do with the inmates in the event the Red Army should ever draw near, First Sergeant Möll had submitted his idea, and to the surprise of him and others, it had been accepted. What had won it this honor, aside from its ruthlessness, was the attention to detail he had put into it: the logistics, the numbers, the coordination and timing, exactly how the thing could be done and by whom.

Both Auschwitz and Birkenau, Baum informed Cyrankiewicz, were to be surrounded by tanks and artillery, and with the help of bombers from above pounded into rubble. The infantry would go in after to ensure there were no survivors.

"Really, Bruno, doesn't that strike you as something of a reach? I'm not even sure why you bring it up; I thought we'd resolved that last week as well. With the Russians having fought their way this far into the Reich, would the Wehrmacht and Luftwaffe be able to spare that many tanks, guns, and bombers? I don't see it, and more than one of your brother officers is with me on that."

It was Baum's turn to sigh. "I have to admit, it would seem to have its inconsistencies, but I still feel it unwise to discount it entirely. For argument's sake, let us drop it for now, as long as you give me your take on Mexico instead. Please, sir, if you will, explain Mexico to me."

Cyrankiewicz didn't follow. "Mexico?" he said.

Baum had been careful not to bring this up last week. He'd been saving it, as the Americans would say, as his ace in the hole. "That is what the prisoners have taken to calling the tenth and newest lager in Birkenau, still under construction but due to the crowding in the other nine, inhabited all the same. Conditions there are catastrophic. No electricity, no water, a good part of the huts without even roofs. So regular are the transports these days, and their number growing, that though two-thirds of their cargoes are being sent straight from the ramp to the birch groves, enough are being admitted into Birkenau to cause its landlords concern. Forget quarantine—a lot of the new arrivals are going directly to Mexico, some with blankets as their only protection against the elements. Hence the name of that tragic place; those condemned to it resemble nothing so much as Mexican Indians bundled up in their serapes."

"I'm all too mindful," Cyrankiewicz said, his irritation plain, "of the disaster brewing in the *B3* lager. I've just never heard it called Mexico of all things."

"My point, sir, is this. *B3*, when finished, will be as large as the other nine lagers combined. Even if the transports were to double, that would still be larger than needed. But they are not going to double, they cannot, there are not enough hours in the day to admit and process that many, even with four crematoria." Baum moved to the edge of his chair. "For whom then are the Nazis building this new annex of hell? Which is to say, building it so huge. And why, as our intelligence has also established, have they drawn up the blueprints for four *more* crematoria, which would bring the total to a mind-numbing nine?"

Cyrankiewicz knew of these blueprints, of course, but had thought them no more than empty Nazi hubris. Since informed of them, in fact, and as irresponsible as he felt about it now, he'd forgotten all about them.

"The answer to both questions," Baum continued, "is as unavoidable as it is horrifying. Apparently, Hitler has plans beyond the eradication of the Jews. Once they are no more, it will come the turn of others—the Poles, the Czechs, the Russians, maybe the Slavic peoples as a whole, any and all of the 'inferior' races standing in the way of German expansion. It is a mad dream, a nightmare, but what is Hitler if not a madman? There are no lengths to which he would not go to secure his Thousand Year Reich.

"Nor should one make the mistake of assuming the arrival of the Red Army an inevitability. It could be argued that a total defeat of the Germans is as unlikely as total victory for them now. The Wehrmacht could dig in and hold, the lines stabilize, become static as they did in the last war. A truce could be proffered. And if it was, and Hitler accepted it, which he would have to, the SS would be ready with their new and expanded Birkenau, even further removed from the reach of the Allies than now."

"So what are you proposing?" asked Cyrankiewicz. "That we just up and assume the Soviets aren't coming, aren't ever going to come, and following through with our plans, unpromising as they are, blow up the cremos and make a mad dash for it?"

"Well, not *we* exactly, sir. Not we at all. I have been thinking more and more of late that a double breakout might not be the way to proceed. Auschwitz is two miles from Birkenau; an uprising in both places simultaneously would be all but impossible to coordinate, and the Home Army, whose assistance I need not tell you is vital to its success, would be spread so thin as to endanger the entire operation. And what of Auschwitz

III, the Monowitz facility, where Siemens, Bayer, I. G. Farben, and others have set up factories? There are twenty thousand slave laborers being worked to death in Monowitz. How would we go about extricating them?"

Suddenly, shattering the stillness of the night, came the staccato pop of gunfire nearby, like a string of firecrackers going off. Then another string, then quiet. Baum paused for a long moment to make sure it was nothing before picking up where he'd left off.

"No, what I propose is that we target Birkenau alone. This would benefit, I believe, both us and the prisoners trapped there. First, it would solve the problem of conducting a double or even triple-pronged engagement. Second, all but a minority of its inmates are Jewish, destined to die anyway, whether the Russians come or not. An escape would afford at least some of them a chance at survival. And with Auschwitz having kept the peace and stayed out of the fight, SS retaliation would almost surely be limited to Birkenau, or maybe even to the Sonderkommando alone, once discovered it was they who led the rebellion.

"This we have already agreed on. No demographic in camp is better suited than thc Sonder to spearhead an attack. They are the healthiest, best fed, and possessed of the most resources, not to mention the motivation: as its victims, none are more aware than they of German diligence in eliminating them periodically as eyewitnesses to their great crime.

"Yes, I can see the Sonder bearing the brunt of the blame, their guilt compounded should they succeed in dynamiting the four crematoria that will be in service by then. This, of course, as you just alluded to yourself, remains essential to the plan, and why I recommend the gunpowder, most of it, be committed to the Special Squad. Whether they or anyone succeeds in escaping, if nothing else the killing machinery will have been put out of action. Nine death houses, Josef.... we cannot let that happen."

Cyrankiewicz, chin in hand throughout Baum's disquisition, said nothing for a moment. Finally, "Your point is well taken, general, several of your points. We, you and I, will raise the question with the Committee again day after tomorrow, but I suggest that in the meantime you proceed with—no, expedite—the penetration of the Union works. Mind you, I'm not guaranteeing an insurrection in Birkenau or anywhere. But as you said, it can't hurt to be prepared."

"Thank you, commander. Day after tomorrow then."

"I am concerned, though, as always" he added, "about the Sonderkommando. Should it be approved, putting together a project like this is going to take time. I have no idea how much of that remains to this squad, but with an eye to it, how desperate are they, the poor devils?"

"The 8th Sonder was liquidated just ten days ago," Baum answered, "leaving only those skilled in cremation and such. That means the 9th has almost all of the four months usually allotted the squad, perhaps more if the transports continue arriving in the numbers they have been. But none of that need matter, not after we offer them the help of the Home Army. Once they learn that the Armia will be behind them, prepared to fight alongside them—when the time is right, of course, meaning when we say it is—you can stop worrying about the Sonder forcing the issue on their own. If indeed that is what you are getting at, sir."

Cyrankiewicz stood once again, signifying the meeting was over. "Thank you, Bruno," he said, engulfing Baum's hand in his. "Please don't take this wrong, but I must say I've always congratulated myself for insisting that you, a Jew, be admitted to the Committee. Your advice, your dedication, continue to be indispensable."

As Baum made his way back in the dark to his barracks, the words wouldn't leave his head. You, a Jew, the man had said, as if that was some flaw to be overcome. Not that Baum had taken offense, for there'd been none to take. Not one administered on purpose, that is. Most Poles, even the best of them, as suckled on anti-Semitism and from as early an age as the Germans, were incapable of looking at the Jew as an equal.

Still, he had to wonder how many of his people had perished that day, or for that matter since he and Cyrankiewicz had sat down to talk. A dull, orange glow still pulsed above the tree line to the north; the last of the new *Oberscharführer's* fire pits were dying out for the evening. Granted, a little unintended bigotry or even the occasional racial slur was something to be expected, and certainly no cause for high dudgeon. But to what extent, one had to ask, had such seemingly innocuous behavior led to the slaughter of children and the emergence of creatures such as Otto Möll?

On the brighter side, there was Noah Zabludowicz. He'd been impressed enough with what the man had done already on his own, but upon meeting him was further taken by his loyalty to his friends, his eagerness to act, his whole demeanor. He sensed both a strength and a fire to this Zabludowicz that made him one to be not only relied on but reckoned with. Which was why he'd had no compunction against handing him so critical a first assignment, and more in the future if he had anything to say about it.

At the same time, he was curious about his new recruit's possible contact in Birkenau. What kind of woman would a man like that be so quick to stake his and others' lives on? She must be something special to have earned such an endorsement. Perhaps this "old friend" of his, as Zabludowicz had called her (the light that had appeared in his eyes at mention of her spoke of something stronger than friendship), perhaps she, too, would end up proving of value to the Resistance, both now and later.

If, as Zabludowicz had said, she was still alive. And that, Baum told himself, as he had so many times about so many others, was a big if.

*   *   *

The icy wind tore at Roza Robota like a living, angry thing. It tried to knock her off her feet, sought to possess her, get inside her, drove the snow up the sleeves and down the collar of her tunic in search of the vulnerable flesh underneath.

The storm had been howling for half an hour now, and wasn't close to letting up. If anything, it was growing stronger. She stopped swinging her pickaxe and made for the woman working nearest her.

"It's getting worse, I think, Trina!" she yelled above the wind. "Have you seen the guard lately? Where is the guard?"

"In there!" the woman shouted, pointing to a small barn barely visible through the blizzard. "I watched him duck inside a few minutes ago!"

"That does it then!" Roza told her. "Help me get the others!"

Soon, all five of them were huddled behind the fragment of wall that still stood. Mercifully out of the wind, they squeezed together to feed off each other's body heat. Theirs was the misfortune to have landed, as most did after Q-Camp, in an *Aussenkommando*, an outdoors work gang. They were part of a crew assigned to demolish certain inconvenient Polish farm buildings for the construction of a new clinic for the SS. It was the same work Roza had been forced to do in the ghetto, but here, on starvation rations and without the protection of a coat, it was only hastening her, as she knew, to her grave.

"What if he finds us here, the guard?" one of them said. "He'll put us on report, which means a thrashing later."

"Beats turning into five Jewish popsicles," Roza said. "Besides, he's inside that building over there, and not likely to be leaving it anytime soon. Would you stick your nose out in this if you didn't have to?"

They held onto each other wordlessly after that. It was better behind the wall, but not by much; Roza wouldn't be feeling her feet again anytime soon. Should the storm last, they were going to be in big trouble. Even if they didn't freeze to death, it could cost them some toes, maybe a few fingers, either of which probably meant a trip to one of the bunkers.

But while the gas chamber was never far from most prisoners' thoughts, theirs weren't only somewhere else at the moment but tuned in to the same thing. It was what they started thinking of at about this time every morning, though none was so careless ever to think it aloud.

Until to their shocked disapproval, the newest to the commando, a seventeen-year-old from Krakow, did just that. "How much longer until noon, until the soup?" she moaned weakly. "I'm so hungry. So hungry...."

They frowned, but let it go. She was new and didn't know any better. Their silence, however, was as arctic as the weather. Recognizing it for the reprimand it was, the girl, too, went quiet. But not for long.

"Chicken and dumplings," she blurted from out of nowhere, half dreamily, half defiant. "My grandmama used to make them. She'd put a whole chicken in, and the dumplings as big and white as this," she said, scooping up a handful of snow.

And with that, there was no resisting the temptation. "Potato pancakes," another chimed in, "with onions and lots of flour. Golden-brown at the edges, spoonfuls of applesauce on top."

"Apples yes, but in a cobbler, fresh from the oven. Bubbling in its pan, all shiny with sugar."

"Roast leg of lamb", "lemon meringue pie".... and so on and so on, a pathetic litany of favorite recipes, more torment than joy but insuppressible all the same. Only Roza abstained, though unable to keep at bay entirely the image of her mother's pot roast swimming in tomato gravy. For weeks now, she'd watched those around her indulge more and more in this little game, though to her it was far from harmless, more a symptom than a pastime. They were obsessing on food because they were starving to death, as if having the words of it in their mouths, pictures of it in their heads, was compensation somehow for the physical absence of it.

Which wasn't to say they weren't exhibiting more conspicuous signs of hunger. All but the new girl looked decades older than they were. Their faces were sunken, the skin gray, noses turned into beaks, their eyes those of hunted animals, bewildered, afraid. Mysterious, oozing sores had broken out on their cheeks and foreheads. Their breasts were going fast, their periods gone already, causing their feet, lower legs, and abdomens to swell. They'd been at Birkenau for two desperate months now and were showing it. Their filthy uniforms swallowed them, the bones of their shoulders and hips as sharply protuberant beneath the cloth as metal pipes. The flesh was stretched so tight over their wrists, elbows, and knees that it was red, as if burned, and painful to the touch. Anyone with eyes could see they were dying.

Though she missed them with an ache that was never going to abate, in a way Roza was glad that her father, mother, little brother, and the rest of her family had departed the unloading ramp that first day on the death trucks. The same part of her that felt this hoped Godel was out of his misery, too, for by now she'd come to understand why they'd been brought to this place: to perish, every last one of them, there was no getting around it, by one means or another the Germans were bound and determined to kill them all. Better to go quickly before one had time to suffer, before the pickaxe, the cold, the sores, and the lice, the crippling hunger that made each minute, each movement an ordeal.

Shoshonna was gone, too. She hadn't lasted two weeks. For the longest time, Roza had blamed herself for failing to save her, but now, if she had it to do over again, she'd have sent her on the trucks with the other of her loved ones.

In retrospect, actually, she saw that her sister had died that first day as well, or rather that was when the poor girl had begun to. After leaving the ramp, their guards marched the three hundred-plus women remaining from the Ciechanow transport into the camp and a large room devoid of all furnishings but for two long metal tables placed end to end. There they were ordered to remain standing at attention, and left alone. With the doors bolted from the outside, they waited nervously for something to happen, but after an hour passed and nothing had, all but a few were curled up on the cold concrete floor.

Suddenly, the doors crashed open and in swung three large, mannish women, big-boned, square-jawed Czechs, clad in the same stripes as the scarecrow men on the ramp, but wearing jackboots and waving clubs. They screamed the women to their feet and toward the tables, where they were told to leave what possessions they still owned, wallets, jewelry, eyeglasses, everything. They were then ordered to strip to the skin and be fast about it, clothing in one pile, shoes and belts in another. At this they hesitated, but the clubs of the three quickly had them tearing at their clothes. Once naked, they were driven out into the mud and the chill and into a second hut.

This barracks, too, was bare save for a row of three stools at one end, around which a dozen young *Schützen* were gathered. Some were drinking from a bottle of vodka. As the nude women and girls poured through the door, a chorus of jeers and wolf whistles greeted them.

Though the new internees couldn't know it, typhus had once been the curse of the camp and raged intermittently still, endangering both prisoners and SS alike. Since the lice that spread it lived in people's hair, shaving was mandatory for those entering Birkenau and at regular intervals thereafter. Behind each stool stood a prisoner-barber, all of them male. One of the Czechs led three of the women to the stools and had them sit. The barbers then proceeded to scissor as much of the hair off their heads as they could before resorting to electric clippers to buzz it close to the scalp. Following this, they were directed to get up again, reach for the ceiling, and the hair under their arms removed. This elicited a few sniggers from the *Schützen* looking on, but it wasn't until the women were told to climb atop the stools that the SS men's fun really began. Once there, they were made to stand legs apart, thrust their hips forward, and in front of their expectant audience present their genitals to the clippers.

At this, the Germans erupted in lascivious glee, their laughter and lewd comments filling the room. A despairing groan rose from the women waiting their turns. Roza felt her sister, who'd done all right up to this point, sag as from a blow.

"Oh God, no!" Shoshonna gasped. "Roza, I can't, I won't!"

"But you must!" she said. "You can and you will. You've got to or those Czechs—"

Two of the latter wheeled on their charges. "Quiet, all of you!" one of them roared. "Stupid sacks of Jewish shit! You'll be quiet or you'll be sorry, I promise you that!"

"Those damned Czechs," Roza whispered, "aren't playing around. Pull yourself together, big sister! You can do this!"

Shoshonna shook her head with a vengeance. "No, please, I—"

Roza cupped her sister's face in her hands and held it to hers. "Listen, Shozhka," she said, their noses almost touching. "Listen to me: they'll hurt you if you don't do what they say, hurt you bad. I've seen it today already, this morning on the ramp. You're going to—look at me!—you're going to have to try to distance yourself from it. Just get up on that stool and shut your eyes, close your ears, imagine yourself somewhere else, and it'll be over before you know it. It's not as if they'll be doing you any harm physically up there, but they will if you resist. You want me to tell mama and papa that you were put in the hospital, or worse, for defending something as meaningless as your modesty?"

Shoshonna said nothing, but the refusal in her face began slowly to soften. Despite the impossibility of doing what she was being asked to, it was difficult to argue with what her sister was saying. When at last it came her turn, she went without a fuss, but no sooner had she sat on the stool than she started softly to cry.

Roza, preceding her, had stared her tormentors down, holding her head high throughout the procedure. As a result, she wasn't nearly as much sport as her sister, who by the time she'd ascended the stool was bawling like a baby. This only goaded the Nazi hooligans on. When a moment later, the barber was done and she hurried away to join the others, the soldiers gave her and her "*rosig klein Muschi*" a loud, mocking farewell.

Shoshonna wasn't the same after that. They all looked different, even comical, with their ridiculous shaved heads, but Roza sensed that her sister had lost more than just her hair. Through the shower, the delousing by powder, the issuing of the malodorous stripes, she moved as if sleepwalking, indifferent to her surroundings. Upon their finally reaching Q-Camp in the late afternoon, she still wasn't herself, though Roza had every confidence she would snap out of it eventually.

By the end of the third day, however, she'd withdrawn even further, especially after learning of the murder of their family. This seemed to take the last of the wind out of her sails. Roza had to watch her constantly, to make sure that she ate, to babysit her during drill, and scariest of all, to keep her from sneaking off to the electrified fence. She intercepted her twice heading suspiciously in that direction, but though she denied it both times, Roza wasn't convinced.

Then one day she was called away to help carry the soup from the kitchen and was forced to leave Shoshonna in the care of some friends. When she returned, she had but to look at their faces to know that her sister was dead. They'd tried to restrain her, the women insisted, but she'd broken free and run, like a crazy person she'd run, screeching for her mother and father all the way to the barbed wire.

But for her Godel and Noah, who could well be dead by now, too, Shoshonna was her last link to the past. Now with her gone, Roza had nothing left to lose. Everything that could be taken from her had been, her family, her dignity, the clothes on her back, even her hair. Or so she thought. A week and a half later, she was to find out differently when the last thing she possessed was snatched coldly away, something she hadn't figured it possible to steal.

It happened on her next to last day in quarantine camp. Following the morning roll call, she and the rest slated for "graduation" were lined up alphabetically and marched to the camp registry. There they had to file past a prisoner-clerk (so clean, so fastidious in his pressed blue-and-whites!) and give their names, ages, ethnicity, and places of origin, which were typed onto index cards. In return, each received a strip of cloth stenciled with a five-digit number. Other trustees hurriedly sewed these onto their tunics. They were then passed a dozen at a time into a smaller back room where two tables and twelve empty chairs awaited them. On the other side of the tables sat prisoners equipped with what resembled over-large ink pens. Upon sitting, the women were instructed to roll up their left sleeves, stretch their arms out in front of them, inner forearms up, and on these were tattooed the numbers sewn to their chests.

It wasn't overly painful and only lasted a few seconds, but its psychological impact, its implications were dire. Later their block elders would tell them these numbers were to serve from this day as their only permissible names. They might as well forget their old ones, for like their lives before the camp, these no longer existed. Each would be addressed as number such-and-such, and announce herself as same. *That* was to be her name, now and forever.

To Roza this was the final and most sinister insult. Having been deprived of everything, now even her name was no longer hers! What kind of person had no name? The answer was simple: someone who wasn't a person, less than a person, inferior, subhuman. With this theft of one's identity, the progression from *Mensch* to *Untermensch* was complete and the victim ready to join the general population. Once again, the inescapable analogy of the cattle car; they weren't women anymore, they were livestock, so much meat on the hoof, soulless commodities to be herded into pens and treated, or mistreated, as their handlers saw fit.

The tattoo to her wasn't so much a means of identification as an augur of impending extinction. But if she *had* been marked to die, if this thing on her arm was but a prelude to that, this much Roza vowed on the very day she received it: unlike her poor sister's, her death would be neither a capitulatory nor solitary one. How she was supposed to do this she didn't know, but if at all possible, and by any means possible, she promised herself she was going to take someone with her. An SS *Schweinhund* ideally, or failing that a stinking kapo, but someone, anyone with Jewish blood on his hands.

In the weeks since, this had given her life purpose, sustained her in her despair, kept her from even contemplating succumbing to the torpor that had killed her sister. It helped get her through not only the terror and backbreaking slavery of the day but what awaited the prisoners back in camp when their work was done. The first of these tortures was the evening roll call, where no matter the weather, the inmates had to stand at attention while they and all those who'd died during the day, or been sent to a hospital barracks or the punishment block, were counted. And if the numbers didn't tally, recounted until they did, no matter how long it took.

Then it was off to the latrine, in its way worse an ordeal. One didn't have to be close enough to see the latrine to smell it. Occupying a hut down the center of which ran a long concrete trough, a double line of slightly cantilevered beams parallel to each other bisected the length of this ditch, against which those using it were expected to lean their backs while squatting. No provisions were made for either privacy or paper. Since there was never more than a trickle of water to keep this sewer flushed, and thousands of women, many of them diarrhetic, seeking relief all at once, the area around the trough was generally awash in a nauseating brown sludge.

Upon entering their barracks afterward, each was handed her supper, a few ounces of grayish bread sometimes smeared with a margarine consisting mainly of lignite. Though finally out of the wind and snow, they faced a new discomfort inside. With the deportees arriving in greater numbers each week, the huts felt as if they were shrinking, their original capacity of two hundred and fifty having become ancient history. At night, the narrow aisles between the vertical tiers of bunks were quick to jam with traffic, the air to thicken with dust from the dirt floor and the reek of unwashed bodies. One didn't have to be claustrophobic to find it difficult to breathe, to feel the walls closing in, the crush of flesh from all sides.

Still, but for a few minutes over soup at lunch, for most it was the only time of the day they were able to socialize—to mingle, talk of home, of the camp, the latest rumors, tend to each other's throbbing, bleeding feet, casualties of their ill-fitting clogs. There was always business to conduct, too, in those bustling aisles, the bartering of goods, the exchange of favors, the trade in services, the collecting of debts. Then ready or not it was time for bed, the lights blinking once before going off for good five minutes later at nine o'clock.

Far from providing a respite, however, from the afflictions of the day, sleep also had its thorns. To begin with, the rough wooden kojen were barely big enough for two people, much less the five or six regularly crammed into them. It didn't help that a prisoner's shoes and any other possessions had to be taken to bed with her to prevent their being stolen.

When finally she did manage unconsciousness, after all the shoving and shifting for position and fighting for a piece of the blanket, then came the dreams, most of them about food. In these they not only saw whatever delicious dish they'd conjured, but held it in their hands, raised it to their lips, smelled the aroma of it and were just about to bite into it when suddenly it was ripped away, or something else intervened to prevent its consumption. It was the Tantalus myth brought to terrible life, and as often as not Roza would wake from it to find her face wet, the saliva running down her chin, tears down her cheeks.

They shared other dreams, too, these forgotten women of Birkenau, formless phantasms, as from a fever, of angry orders shrieked, vicious slaps to the face, naked bodies alive and dead, the unending, ice-laden Silesian wind. That the majority of their dreams should be nightmares, of course, was but a reflection of their violent, nightmarish days. It was as if the camp itself was alive, a malicious entity in its own right working in concert with the SS, the one harrowing its helpless victims by day, the other continuing the abuse at night by poisoning their slumber with its Grand-Guignol dreams.

Looming over it all, especially in those hours after midnight, was the specter of the reveille bell, its long, electric burst at 4:00 a.m. seldom finding many fast asleep. The anxiety arising from its approach, and the fresh day of pain it presaged, was too great to leave even the deepest repose undisturbed; most prisoners lay half-awake in anticipation of it, and even without watches were able to predict its ringing almost to the minute.

And with that there was chaos, hundreds of people falling out of their bunks all at once, hurrying to make their vacated "beds" to the exact specifications of the Germans, hurrying to exit the barracks ahead of the curses and kicks of the hut-sweepers, running to stand in line for cold coffee, running to stand in line at the latrine, running to stand in place and at attention for an hour or two of freezing roll call.

Then the work squads were formed and the march out of camp begun, passing on its way the bodies of those who'd died during the night. If not before. There were always piles of naked corpses lying everywhere in Birkenau, and what with the air being conveniently refrigerated at this time of the year, and the transports so many as to keep the fire pits filled, the dead from the camp might be allowed to stack up for days. Apart from its ugliness, not to mention the glimpse it gave the prisoners into their own futures, it was a situation made to order for the swarms of rats infesting the camp. Invariably, the piles of dead crawled with these creatures. So abundant were they, and as a consequence so emboldened by hunger, in the hospital barracks they often didn't wait for their prey to breathe their last, feeding on those still alive but too far gone to move.

The work squads left by way of the main gate every morning to the lively tunes of the camp orchestra, composed itself of inmates. They played mostly German marching songs, with which those heading out were required to keep in step. By then—actually, soon after climbing into their shoes at reveille—the blisters on the women's feet had reopened. To stay in rhythm, to march as expected, they had to ignore the electricity shooting up their legs at each footfall and try to subsume themselves in the music, lose themselves in it, letting it fill them to the exclusion of all else.

To the woman once known as Roza Robota, now prisoner 73476, even more excruciating than the pain in her feet were the conceited faces of the SS always gathered at the gate. A few came here every morning to watch, to gloat at this fascinating thing they'd created, this synchronized mass of gray men and women moving as one against their will to the war songs of the Fatherland. Moving *without* will, without emotion, without thought, the beat of the drum and clash of the cymbals propelling them forward. More than just slaves, they were an army of mindless automatons, thousands strong, subjugated to their cores by a handful of Aryan elite. So powerful was this elite's perception of itself that it wasn't content merely to fulfill its prime directive, which was to kill. First, it had to annihilate the ego, the very soul of its victim, and this musicalized ritual, this dance of the doomed that waltzed the Aussenkommandos out of camp in the morning, was one of the more theatrical, therefore enjoyable manifestations of that annihilation. To the Germans congregated at the gate, it was visible proof of the completeness of their victory over the Jew.

Yet as low as this laid her, Roza had no choice but to abdicate self-respect and keep up with the others; to rebel would be asking for worse than trouble. As children, she and her siblings had been teased relentlessly because of their last name. That had stung, but now, with a hurt that burned fiercer than the fire in her feet, she had to endure the immeasurably greater shame of having been turned into a robot in more than name only.

Shame, however, had never killed anyone. Nor its cousin, degradation—these were crosses, that though bitter, one could bear. What one had to worry about at Birkenau were those things that did kill. The morning of the blizzard, for example, as she and the rest marched out of camp, Roza was focused less on the self-congratulatory faces of the Nazis and the brassy blare of their hated music than on the dark clouds building to the north. Soon they would be here, shoving aside the sky, uncaringly disgorging their frozen tons. Sure enough, her squad hadn't been at its work site for an hour before a light flurry began to fall. In twenty minutes, the snow was blowing horizontally, the wind loud as a train.

Pressed against each other as they were now, though, behind the remnant of wall, it wasn't nearly as bad. The teenager from Krakow, despite knowing she shouldn't, was on the verge of again asking how long until soup, when suddenly a shout burst from out of the snow.

"*Mein Gott*!" it roared above the wind. "What the hell is *this*?"

Their heads jerked up as one to the sight of their guard almost on top of them, gun leveled. So furious was the storm, they'd neither seen nor heard him coming. Four of them leapt up and scampered for the concealing white. "Stop, you! *Halt*!" he commanded, but the next second they were gone. The one who remained, though she'd risen to her feet, clearly wasn't going anywhere. Her eyes weren't looking to either side for a way out, but straight into his.

It was Roza who stood her ground. Exactly why, she couldn't say. Out of stupidity? To retain some dignity? At this point, it didn't matter; all she knew was that her brain had ordered her legs to stay put. She could no more have run off than sprouted wings and flown away.

He was young, this *Oberschütze*, maybe even younger than she, but judging from his abusive manner earlier in the day, no less hardened than any Nazi. "*Was ist los, Jude?*" he shouted. He moved slowly toward her, rifle still leveled. "Why didn't you light out with your bitch friends?"

She didn't answer, her eyes glued to his. This in itself was a crime, not to come to attention, head bowed, when addressed by the SS. He was aware of her insubordination, too, of that she made sure.

"Well, what have we here?" he said, stopping ten feet from her. "A Jew with spirit, with a backbone? I didn't think there was such an animal."

Roza glared at him, not attempting to hide her hate.

"Still," he said, "there are rules here, and you appear to have broken two of them. The question becomes then, should I shoot you for daring to stare at me like that, or for sitting on your butt instead of working like you were told to?"

Having leaned on the shaft of her pickaxe in getting to her feet, she suddenly found herself holding it in front of her with both hands. In that instant, with a fanfare only she could hear, it all came together for her: not only was this it, the chance she'd been waiting for, but why she hadn't hightailed it out of there with the others. Somehow she'd sensed her moment had arrived, that this German, this boy, was the one she'd been seeking, the sacrifice to be offered on the altar of her vengeance.

Closer, she implored him under her breath, come a little closer, you dog, and I'll have you. If she rushed him now, he'd shoot her down before she could get to him, but any nearer, if she was quick enough, she could bury the axe in his chest. He'd shoot her still, but she didn't care. She was halfway to the grave already, and with Shoshonna dead, and her little brother, and her mama and papa and probably Godel, what did she have left to live for? At least this way, she'd get to take one of the baby-killing bastards with her.

But he didn't come closer. On the contrary, he backed off a little, having seen something in the face of this evil-eyed Jewish skeleton that moved him to caution. He tightened his finger round the trigger of his gun.

"So, Jew, unafraid Jew, lazy pig of a Jew, before I do anything, I'm curious: what made you think you could stop working? Was it this storm, you damned filthy whore, or because you just didn't want to?"

At this, Roza lost it. Between her intended victim's invective, the fact that he was now definitely out of reach, and all the frustration and anger that had been building in her for months—she went berserk. She whirled on the ruin of the wall behind her and lit into it like a madwoman, hacking at it with the pick, screaming with each blow, tearing off large chunks of masonry one after another. The private let her have at it, the face beneath the steel helmet unreadable. He stood there watching in silence until she was done, until the wall was no more. In her frenzy she'd obliterated it, then collapsed on her back in the snow.

Only then did the German act, taking a pad and pencil from his coat pocket. "What is your number?" he demanded. "Let me see your tattoo number."

She rolled to her right so he could read the strip of cloth sewn to her shirt. He wrote the number down. "You will present yourself to your Blockälteste tonight after the Appell. She will have been notified of this and be expecting you. I would suggest for your sake that you don't fail to report."

Later, back at camp, after filing into their hut for the night, her friends gathered round her. "You're lucky he didn't shoot you right then." "Now it's the 25 for you for sure." "Or worse, the penal commando." "Or worse yet…." This needed no finishing.

Roza was disconsolate, but only because she'd let her *Oberschütze* escape. She'd missed a golden opportunity, nor was a better likely to come along. That she'd have been killed in the process was of little import, just as the punishment awaiting her didn't matter much, either.

"Stop your bellyaching, please," she begged of the women. "I appreciate your concern, but whatever's going to be is going to be. There's nothing I can do about it now."

"Not now, no—but what the hell were you thinking then?"

"In such seconds you don't think, you do what fate wants you to. Not that I would change it if I could, not any of it. At least I got to hold my head up, look one of that scum right in his mangy eye."

She didn't have to search out their *blockova*. The woman sent a Stubendienst to bring Roza to her room, where to the growing consternation of her friends she remained for a while. When finally she emerged, it was with a small bundle in her hands and a big grin on her face.

"What happened?" they cried all at once. "Why on earth are you smiling?"

She had them follow her to a corner of the hut. "Did any of you know," she said placidly, still smiling, "that there's a commissary for prisoners in this rat's ass of a place, and that the kapos have leave to hand out coupons redeemable at that commissary?"

They could only stare at her blankly.

"I had no idea, either, but guess what I just got for throwing my little tantrum today: not time in the penal squad, not a beating, not even a slap on the wrist, but a coupon worth the equivalent of one German mark. For doing good work. Exceptional work, the blockova said. Maybe I should have gone looking for a second wall to vent my spleen on."

Laughter wasn't a frequent visitor to *Frauenlager B1a* of Birkenau, but it rose now from half a dozen throats, partly from relief, partly at the wacky unpredictability of life.

"So show us," said one of the group. "What does this coupon of yours look like?"

"I don't have it. I gave it back to her, as a gift. Which explains what I do have, here in this sack." She opened it to reveal a mess of boiled potatoes in their jackets. "And this," she said, producing a jar of orange marmalade from her shirt. "This she just handed me, on my way out. I didn't even have to ask for it."

Roza paused to let them take in the wonderment of the potatoes.

"Was I right," she said finally, "or was I right? Sucking up to her, I mean. What was I going to buy with a single mark anyway? Certainly not something as valuable as the goodwill of a block elder. I told her she could probably make better use of the coupon than I. She thanked me and smiled—yes, *smiled*, that foul-tempered brute of a Czech—then asked me if there was anything I needed. 'Food, if that's permitted, *Frau Älteste*,' I said. 'A few potatoes would be nice.' So she gave me some. As for the marmalade, who knows? I think my 'generosity' must have caught her off guard."

The women were in awe. "So what are you planning to do with all this, Roza?"

"Why, it's for us, silly, the six of us. The SS may call us pigs, but that doesn't mean we have to act like one." She unscrewed the lid on the little jar of jellied gold. "Anyone hasn't managed to organize a spoon yet, feel free to use mine."

To organize was camp lingo for acquiring something of value, either by barter or theft. The Germans provided nothing, not even spoons for their prisoners' soup. There was a Stubendienst in Block 12 who hand-made them, but she charged two whole rations of bread, a steep price. Roza had given her one ration and a small spool of thread she'd stumbled upon, and considered it well worth it. Scarce were their masters who didn't delight in watching them lap up their dinner like animals.

The next morning after roll call, she was pulled from her work crew and ordered back to the hut. Not especially to her surprise, but most assuredly her unease, her benefactress from the night before was waiting for her.

"I have a cousin assigned to the clothes-sorting warehouse," the woman said. "This morning she told me they were in need of another person. The work is light and indoors. Though you're not Czech, I thought of you. You've got to hurry, though, before the spot is filled. I must have an answer now."

Roza thought for a few seconds. "But what about my friends?" she said. "I can't just—"

"Yes, you can, don't be a fool. Many are the riches that pass through the *Bekleidungskammer*; the Jews like to hide their valuables by sewing them inside their clothing. You can help your friends best from there. All you can do here is watch each other die. I'm going to ask you once more, which is it to be: the warehouse, indoors, folding clothes, or the pick and shovel?"

*   *   *

Noah Zabludowicz's heart thumped like a triphammer as he waited outside in the snow. It had taken him a while to find out if Roza was alive, and a while after that to track her down. He'd had to bribe more than a few individuals in the process, the final one the *Schütze* posted at the entrance to the clothing depot.

His joy at learning of her survival was matched only by his admiration at her having landed a job in the Bekleidungskammer. The position wasn't only out of the weather but potentially very lucrative, and not easy to come by. The sorting and folding of clothes was incidental to the commando's real purpose, which was to hunt out the wealth the Jews had concealed in the linings and shoulders of their garments. Up to a hundred women per shift inspected every inch of these, looking for suspicious bulges. The items to be searched came from the undressing barracks in the woods. Once valuables were discovered, the SS officer on duty entered them in a ledger and deposited them in a large, open box. But though guards circulated among them as well as watched from catwalks overhead, it wasn't impossible for a worker to pocket the occasional diamond and sneak it back to the barracks.

The clothes-sorting commando was a part of what the prisoners called "Canada", that multi-tentacled monster of a network that expropriated the goods brought in on the transports and redistributed them into German hands. At first, Noah hadn't understood the reason behind the name, but would learn it was known as Canada because of the riches associated with that country. Everything from furniture to pharmaceuticals was stored in warehouses within the camp until it could be packaged and shipped off by train to Greater Germany. The same cattle cars that arrived crammed with people often left stacked to their roofs with the worldly goods of those from earlier transports. Noah had been witness to it time and again: if anything could be said to rival the Nazi thirst for Jewish blood, it was the Nazi hunger for Jewish treasure. The SS were no less acquisitive than they were cutthroat.

Which wasn't to say they couldn't turn around and be generous after a fashion, too. Much of the booty was dispensed gratis to those on the home front to alleviate shortages and keep up morale. Of course, the more prized merchandise—the diamonds, the currency, the rarer stamp and coin collections, the gold—the government kept for itself, hundreds of pounds of it a month trucked by armed escort from the coffers of Auschwitz-Birkenau to those of the *Reichsbank* in Berlin. And though much of this was dental gold or came from the unloading ramp, a good amount of it originated in the Bekleidungskammer, secreted until then in the seams of Jewish clothing.

If he hadn't known it was Roza that he'd sent the guard to fetch, Noah wouldn't have recognized the woman who emerged from the building. She stepped into the morning sunlight and stood blinking on the wooden landing, both her luxuriant head of hair and bountiful figure gone. He was shocked at how wasted away she was. He knew she hadn't been on the job for long, less than a month judging from what her Blockälteste had told him, but he hadn't pictured her being so emaciated still.

She didn't recognize him at first, either; the glare of the sun off the snow was blinding. When after a few seconds her eyes adjusted to it, she let out a yelp and went bounding toward him.

"Fifteen minutes!" barked the guard. "And I'll be watching!"

She threw herself into Noah's arms, her own enclosing him as tightly as the shell its nut. Neither said a word at first, too overcome with emotion to speak. She was smiling and crying all at once, nor were his eyes exactly dry.

"Roza, you look lovely," he said at last, holding her at arm's length.

She rolled her eyes and laughed. "Oh yes, lovely, a regular beauty queen. But a lot better than I was looking a month ago, let me tell you."

"So how did you wind up here, in this commando? Not that I'm surprised, but…."

"Ah, so you know about this place," she said, crooking her head toward the block at her rear. "How did I end up here? I got lucky, Noah, that's all, so very, ridiculously lucky. One day I was dying—then the next, saved. I'm still not sure why or even how it happened. When we have more time, should we, I'll tell you all about it. For now, though"—she made a show of feeling the muscles in his arms—"how have you come to stay so nice and fat? Did you get lucky, too, or did you battle your way, you fighter, into those clean stripes?"

"You need luck here," he said, "I don't care who you are. Luck and an instinct for survival, an animal's instinct. Sometimes I think the best of us, the more civilized, died early. Welcomed death rather than live in such a place."

At this, the smiles faded from their faces. The dark-gray of the Bekleidungs warehouse rose mute and somber behind them. "Noah, there's something you should know," Roza said. "Your sister Deborah—"

"Yes, I heard. My brother Pinchas told me. He's here in Birkenau, too. The Hanukkah selection, that part of it from the women's camp—Deborah, it seems, was taken with the two thousand. I still have two brothers, though, thank God. You remember Hanan; he's with me in the main camp. As for the rest of the family...." His silence was loud.

"But what of *your* peo—" He started to say "people" then stopped, but it was too late. *Idiot*! he spat at himself. *Moron*! How could you be so clumsy? Based on their ages alone, and her brother Israel's ill health, he knew that most of Roza's family wouldn't have made it past the unloading ramp. "Shoshonna, I mean," he added lamely. "What of Shoshonna? How's that beautiful sister of yours?"

Roza's gaze had fallen. When it met his again, the eyes were flint.

"Enough of the dead," she said. "What the hell good does it do to talk about them? Besides, we've no time for that." She squared her shoulders, forced a smile. "What I want to know, Noah, is how you come to be standing here. You said you were living in the Stammlager. In Auschwitz. What, have you gone and joined the SS? Look at you, gallivanting from camp to camp as if you owned the place."

In spite of his having put one of his size-twelves in his mouth, and what he'd just learned about poor Shoshonna, her remark nearly brought a smile to his face as well. "No, Roza, not the SS, but I have joined something. You're talking to an agent of Battle Group-Auschwitz, the camp underground. That's how I come to be here, and other than to see your wonderful self again, also *why* I'm here. Once, long ago, you gave me the chance to strike back at the Germans. Remember when we first met?"

She nodded, her eyes two perfect circles of expectation. Was it possible Noah was about to ask her what she hoped he was going to? She'd heard of the underground, but had suspected it, like so many rumors, mere talk. Now all of sudden.... "The Yellow Rose. I remember, I remember."

"Well," he said, "I'm returning the favor now. The Resistance sent me here to tell you we want you one of us."

She let out a gasp, took hold of his arm as if to steady herself. "No!" she shouted in disbelief. "Wow, I—I'm—wow!" The brown eyes flashed to black, the words tripping over each other in their rush to get out. "When can I start? I'm ready right now! You just tell me what to do and I'll do it, anything!"

"I figured that'd be your reaction," he grinned. "Would have been shocked if it wasn't. But I do have to warn you, before we go further—"

"Yes, I know," she broke in, "I know it'll be dangerous. But I don't give a flip, all I want is to help. Talk to me, Noah, how can I help?"

He couldn't imagine being prouder of her than he was at that moment. Or more in love. It was as plain as the nose flaring on her pretty face: she was panting for a fight, to get back into action.

"I'll tell you how," he said, "and you can bet it'll be dangerous. But what I was trying to say was that it's got to be kept on the q.t. No revealing it to *anyone* but those directly involved. These you will recruit yourself from a very specific group of prisoners. Have you heard of the Weichsel-Union ammunition factory?"

Her mission was as follows: to establish a cell among those women working in the gunpowder room of the Union factory for the purpose of stealing regular quantities of the explosive. This, most of it, would then be smuggled to her, she in turn passing it on to the Sonderkommando. That she would see to when they brought the clothes of the dead in a cart from the undressing barracks in the birch groves—or once they were operational, from the new crematoria—and unloaded it at the Bekleidungskammer. It would be arranged for her to be a member of the work party in receipt of this clothing. The cart would have a false compartment in which the contraband could be stowed. Some of it will have been diverted to Battle Group-Auschwitz, but all save that fraction was to find its way to the Sonder through her.

None of this, Noah cautioned, was going to be easy. The Pulverraum was actually two rooms, a large one where six prisoners a shift worked the pressing machines, and a smaller that served as the German Meister's office and housed the safe in which the powder was stored. The job of the Meister, a civilian, was to allocate and inventory this most precious material, as well as supervise production. He'd been given a female prisoner to assist him with the latter, also German and as watchful as he, which meant two pairs of eyes on the alert for any funny business. The women Roza recruited here would have to be more than careful.

But the stealing of it was just the beginning. A system needed devising that was artful enough to funnel the gunpowder to her so as not to arouse curiosity. Finesse would be required, too, when transferring it to the Special Squad; she should never assume that the SS guarding the women unloading the clothing cart weren't watching her every move. Above all, again the strictest secrecy must be maintained. Not only did the success of any attempt at a breakout depend on it, but the underground itself might be endangered if the thievery was discovered and an investigation launched.

"A breakout?" Roza said. "From the camp? Is that what this is about?"

"That," Noah replied, "and the destruction of the four coming crematoria. Thanks to Bru—well, thanks to a certain person, the two tie together. I was given discretion on whether to tell you what the explosive was to be used for, though I would have even if it hadn't been given. The Sonder will be spearheading the attack, but if this even makes sense, I guess you could say you'll be spearheading the Sonder. Without you, it isn't going to happen, not the way we want it to. I thought you ought to know that. Would want to know."

She couldn't believe her ears. This was too good to be true. Where before she'd been hoping to rid the world of an SS man or two at most, now she'd been handed the opportunity of being instrumental in the killing—no, the justifiable execution—of who knew how many. And the dynamiting of their infernal death factories along with them. From the Bekleidungskammer, she had an unobstructed view of one of the nearly completed crematoria, and it was an evil thing to behold, forbidding, immense, its heavy brick smokestack dwarfing the watchtowers nearby. And this was only that part of it the eye could see. A broad bank of concrete steps led below ground; how big this subterranean level was, there was no telling. Soon thousands at a time would be descending those steps and leaving through the chimney. She could hardly look at it without wanting to cry.

But there was no need for tears now. Not anymore. Thanks to Noah, no longer would the sight of it sadden so much as motivate her, knowing that she was working to destroy the vile thing.

"So, what do you think?" he said, though he knew the question a formality. "Are you with us, Roza?"

"To the end," she swore, her voice even deeper than normal, "and let the devil himself try to stop me."

"Time's almost up!" yelled the soldier from the landing. "Start saying your goodbyes."

Noah instinctively glanced at his watch, only to realize he'd done it again. Instead of the familiar white dial with its twelve Roman numerals, the number 73982 stared tauntingly back at him, tattooed on his forearm, tattooed on his soul. His watch was long gone, but three months later he was still searching it out, not as frequently as before, but as ugly a reminder each time of the nameless piece of property he and every Jew here had become.

When he looked up he did a double take, for it was to find just like that a whole different Roza staring back at him. The determined, eager face had deflated as quickly as a balloon. With the guard's warning, she'd gone from struggling not to shout her excitement to the sun, to looking as if she wanted to crawl into a hole and pull it in after her.

"What's the matter, Roza?" he asked, though even as he did he knew the answer, and it had nothing to do with the guard. He'd been waiting for this, waiting in dread of it. Praying that somehow it wouldn't come. "Was it," he attempted, the words sticking in his mouth—"was it something I said? Something I…. didn't?"

"Yes, that." Her voice was tiny. "Something you didn't. But I'm afraid to hear what it might be, have been since I saw it was you standing out here." Abruptly, she set her jaw. "But I do have to know. Yes, I must know." She looked him hard in the eye, as if to will the desired response from him. "Is Godel…. is he all right? Is he still alive?"

On the road back to Auschwitz, Noah chided himself for the cad, the selfish brute he was. It wasn't that he intended on not telling her that Godel Silver was alive and well, safely ensconced in the Ciechanow block of the Stammlager, just that he wanted to see if she was going to ask about him herself. What a contemptible creature he was! Admit it, he told himself, you were hoping she wouldn't mention Godel at all, that maybe something had happened these last death-filled months to change her feelings for him, or at least relegate them to an emotional back burner.

Contemptible *and* blind! Made so by love, yes, but blind all the same. Just who, he continued, do you think you are, Noah Zabludowicz? Certainly not Roza's, nor will you ever be. She belongs to Godel and he to her, and that's the way it should be, to hell with your pathetic, delusional self. Would you in all honesty have brought his name up if she hadn't? That was a question that would haunt him for some time to come.

He'd realized the wrongness, the absurdity of his conduct as soon as he saw her face at hearing him pronounce Godel well. Her eyes had lit up like a kid's at the circus, and he knew then and there not only the shabbiness of his sin but how, right now, he was going to atone for it.

"Oh, Noah, thank you," she'd said, hugging him, "for so many things. For giving me a mission. For giving me Godel. For—for bringing more good news than a body can stand. If I can ever—"

"Hush, Roza, hush, there's no call to thank me. Not for letting you know about Godel any more than for asking you to put yourself in harm's way. It's you who's doing us the favor by accepting this assignment. If you feel you must show gratitude, show it for this: I'll be back in five days for a full report on what you've done, the progress you've made, only this time I'll be bringing a certain Mr. Silver along with me."

Her mouth dropped open, and against his protestations she'd wrapped him in another hug. "Come back in five days, Noah, and I promise on my family's graves that I'll have a good deal to report, a good deal and more. Until then, goodbye and God bless, my best and bravest friend."

Some friend, he thought as he walked the limestone path back to Auschwitz, but he'd already made up his mind never again to let his love get the better of his loyalty. From now on, he'd comport himself as the man of principle he liked to think he was.

He'd decided a while back to approach Godel about joining the Resistance, a decision that would now have to be effected pronto if the lad was to accompany him to Birkenau in five days. What with events to come, he wondered if he shouldn't try to secure him a regular posting there; they'd soon be needing all the operatives they could get in that camp. He'd better talk to him first, however, before running it past Baum. There was always the chance Godel would say no to the whole thing, though Noah knew him well enough to know also what his answer was going to be.

For a moment, Roza's face intruded on his train of thought, the same face she'd assumed upon learning the reason for his visit—the eyes as gleaming-black and unyielding as obsidian, but as if to contradict their ferocity, that rascally grin of hers, like that of a schoolgirl contemplating a prank. It was this face that had drawn him to her as forcefully as any of her charms, and always would. He savored it for a while as one might a lost love's, then banished it from his mind for the indeterminate future.

Spring

S tanislaw Kaminski never tired of telling the story of how a jar of pickled herring had once saved his life. Upon coming across someone who hadn't heard it before, he usually managed to work it into the conversation. His fellow Sonderkommando, of course, were subjected to it ad nauseam, but never complained. Such was their fondness for their garrulous kapo that this was but one of the indulgences they allowed him.

They did know the story by heart, though, and it went like this. It was June 1942, and Kaminski just another new and disoriented internee. He'd only recently arrived on a transport from the city of Bialystock and was still in quarantine camp, fortunate to have made it that far. He almost didn't pass the selection at the unloading ramp; though not yet forty, most of his hair had gone gray. He was also, however, a thick-chested bull of a man who looked as if he'd have no problem lifting his weight. The SS doctor on the ramp had studied him for some seconds before pointing him to the right and the privilege of working himself to death for the Reich.

One morning in Q-Camp, sent to return the coffee urns to the kitchen, on his way back he spied something shiny in the mud. He walked over and picked it up—almost to drop it in shock. It was a small jar of preserved herring, its silver lid gleaming in the sun. How this treasure had got there and gone unnoticed till now he couldn't imagine, but to a man who'd been living on nettle soup and sawdust bread for two weeks, it was no less miraculous than the biblical manna from heaven.

Since the rags he'd been given to wear had no pockets, there was only one thing to do with his find. Hiding behind a corner of a hut and making sure no one was watching, he wolfed the thing down, then buried the empty jar in the mud to hide the evidence.

For an hour or so, he felt almost human again as his body absorbed its bonanza of protein, but eventually it rebelled at the unexpected richness, and he found himself with a case of the runs. Somehow he succeeded in holding it in until the midday soup break, his best opportunity to sneak off to the latrine. To be caught relieving oneself out in the open was a grievous offense. Sometimes, as he'd witnessed once already, a capital one.

As it turned out, he never made it to the latrine. Nor notice that his kapo had seen him slip away and was following at a distance. Unable all of a sudden to keep it in any longer, he sprinted from the path to as isolated a spot as he could find, dropped his pants, and squatted down.

His relief was short-lived. The last thing he remembered before the explosion in his brain was the sound of running feet coming up on him from behind.

When he awoke, he was lying on his back on a concrete floor, his head pounding. He touched his right temple and drew back fingers wet with blood. There was blood all over him, his shirt, his pants, his shoes, and hovering above him an SS man in an officer's cap.

"Well, well," the Nazi smirked, "enjoy your little nap? I hope so, because shortly you're going to be needing all your strength. Your kapo told us what you did—what animals you Hebrews are! He was within his rights to kill you for your disgusting behavior, but instead he brought you to us. Perhaps upon seeing what we have planned for you, you'll wish he had done you in. Now get on your feet."

He and another prisoner, also bloodied, were hurried to one of the meadows in that area of forest where the Germans were burying bodies. These were arriving, piled high and naked, on a steady stream of trolleys pushed along by other prisoners. With a blow almost as felling as the one he'd just taken, it was from them that he learned of the gas bunkers in the woods.

For the rest of the afternoon, he and a few dozen others wrestled with the dead, dragging them from the trolleys down into the funeral pit. The day was a scorching one—he'd smelled the meadow before laying eyes on it—and the SS in a rage, keeping them at a constant run with bullwhips and threats. By sundown, there wasn't a prisoner not covered in a noisome paste of mud, blood, sweat, and powdered lime. On the truck taking them to their new quarters in Auschwitz, they were too exhausted to talk. Not that he or any of them, after what they'd seen, would have had a clue what to talk about.

Thus did Kaminski, despite his age, come to join the predominantly younger ranks of the Special Squad. But for getting caught literally with his pants down, he probably would have found himself in an Aussenkommando after Q-Camp and been history by now.

"I can't claim it the most satisfying shit I ever took," he liked to say, "but it was certainly the luckiest. We may be living in a hell on earth, boys, but for what it's worth, at least we're living."

To keep them and the details of the slaughter away from the other inmates, and with their numbers still small, the Sonderkommando weren't housed in a barracks but Block 11, the punishment block. Conditions were severe. Seven or eight men were made to share a cell, with little sunlight, less ventilation, straw mattresses on a concrete floor, their only toilet a large metal bucket in a corner. All they could hope was that their inevitable deaths be quick but not soon, yet as witnesses to murder, knew any hour could be their last. True, they were provided sufficient food to enable them to work. And decent shoes for the same reason. And regular showers and access to medicine so they wouldn't get sick; working in proximity to them every day, the Germans didn't want to risk catching a disease.

But the bunkers and the pit were the price they paid for these luxuries, and before long something else that would prove worse than either. One day in early autumn, thirty of them, Kaminski included, instead of being trucked in the morning to the meadow were marched to the crematorium—not, as they feared at first, as fodder for the gas chamber, but to be taught how it worked, the techniques of mechanized mass extermination and incineration. They'd been selected on the basis of their performance as the first of the hundreds of extra Sonder who'd be needed when the four death factories under construction in Birkenau opened. Which meant not only learning how to operate and service the ovens but in addition to handling corpses and cleaning up after them—this differing little, admittedly, indoors from out—how to deal with the living now as well: greeting the victims as they arrived, reassuring them, keeping them calm, keeping them moving…. listening from the next room to their screams as they died.

It was Sonderkommando school, graduate or be killed yourself. And their professor, with the assistance of the few already proficient at the ovens, was the non-Jewish kapo of the crematorium, a Pole named Mietek Morawa. Though only twenty-three, Morawa had long been known for both his cruelty and foul temper. Kaminski and his new kapo took an instant dislike to each other, but because of the prestige the elder had garnered in the meadow through both the bigness of his character and the strength of his work ethic, the other was unable to squash as he had so many before.

Kaminski had tumbled from the start to the fact that anything less than total compliance with the orders of the SS was to court an early death. Never once working the burial pit did he show hesitation or weakness, giving the impression that to him neither the gruesome nature of the labor nor its frenetic pace was anything but routine. More than that, he made every effort to do the work of two men. Where the others paired up in hauling a single corpse to the pit, he never failed to manage one by himself, sometimes even two, one slung over each shoulder.

As might be expected otherwise, his companions didn't take offense at his industriousness. Kaminski was a man of great charm, able to make friends with almost anyone. Perpetually florid-faced and raspy of voice, he wore his emotions for better or worse on his sleeve. He, too, had a temper and could be dangerous if provoked, but unlike Morawa was good at heart, tolerant, even tender toward those suffering or in need. He had a knack for defusing the tensest moments, for saying the right thing at the right time, imparting his coolness under pressure to those around him. His self-confidence was contagious, if sometimes bordering on the arrogant. He appeared in control of himself and the situation no matter what.

In short, he was a born leader, commanding the affection and admiration of all. The Sonder knew he despised the Nazis as much as they, and recognized that the hustle he showed in the course of his duties was less an expression of submission than defiance. Sure, there was no denying that he was insinuating himself in their overseers' good graces as a means of bettering his chances of survival, but it could also be said that by doing more than the Germans asked of him, he was *being* more as well, showing them that a Jew was as capable, therefore as human as anyone.

Nor did he slow down upon entering stoker training. In no time, Kaminski knew as much about mechanical incineration as his teachers, everything from how many bodies and what kinds could best be burned in a single load, to how and when to "clinker" (clean out) the ovens, replace the fire bricks in the chimney. As nightmarish as the work was, he shrank from none of it, passing himself off to the SS, as he had at the pit, as someone not only ready but eager for whatever they could throw at him. He hopped to every order, he didn't care how horrendous, never letting the repulsion with which it filled him show.

Some of those chosen for the squad couldn't, had trouble even believing what they were seeing, much less joining in it. These were either shot on the spot or ended up at the Black Wall. This was a structure constituting the back end of a courtyard between Blocks 11 and 10, this last serving as the quarters for those women, those wretched, condemned to the bizarre vagaries of Nazi medical experimentation. (It was no accident the Black Wall was situated where it was, both buildings providing it with a steady succession of victims). Brick underneath, it was covered with a thick layer of black cork put there to absorb bullets, an expanse of sand stretching from its base to sop up the blood. The Black Wall had been a fixture at the camp from the beginning. Thousands had perished there, were perishing still.

Kaminski was certainly in no danger of such. His stock, as it were, was spiraling upward, not least in the eyes of the Germans. Particularly beneficial was the high opinion in which *Hauptsturmführer* Hans Aumeier held him. Aumeier was in charge of the main camp at the time, one step below Rudolf Höss, the overall commandant. The SS captain had acquired a grudging respect for the new stoker, who though much older than the other Sonder, twice as old as some, regularly left them in his dust at the workplace.

It was because of Aumeier that Kapo Morawa was hesitant to do harm to this man that the young blond Pole had quickly sized up as a rival. Prevented from striking at him directly, therefore, Mietek, true to his mettle, went after those close to his competitor, circumspectly at first, but with an escalating violence that threatened to turn lethal.

Upon discovering he had a patron of sorts in the *Hauptsturmführer*, Kaminski confronted his kapo and told him to back off. Not content simply to safeguard his friends, he applied himself from then on to countering Morawa's excesses against the rest of the squad, becoming a champion to them in the process. Accordingly, as his standing in the commando grew, so did the other's jealousy-fueled hatred of him.

With the number of crematorium trainees increasing weekly, the punishment block was soon unable to hold them. Having anticipated this, the SS had a home ready and waiting for them in Birkenau's *B2d* lager. Block 13 was a barracks unlike any other. The Germans had enlarged it to twice the normal size, then constructed an eight-foot wooden wall around it, the only entrance a door guarded by a prisoner with a club whose function was to keep the inquisitive away.

Nor was that all. After enduring the conditions at Block 11, the Sonder felt as if they'd moved into a rest home. Each man was assigned his own bunk, complete with linen that was regularly laundered. They also had their own showers and real toilets, and within the confines of the wall, unsupervised and glorious freedom of the yard. For the first time in months, Kaminski was able to indulge in the beauty of the night sky, enjoy the night breeze. Neither was it possible, wall or no wall, to segregate the detachment completely. Courtesy of the eminently bribable prisoner at the door, the more aggressive of the black marketeers were regular visitors. They brought food, cigarettes, alcohol, and other items in exchange for the cash, diamonds, and gold the Sonder had learned to retrieve from the bodies and clothing of the dead. They'd succeeded in purchasing such before, of course, but given the strictures imposed by the punishment cells, on a hit-and-miss basis only.

The grandness of its new residence wasn't the only surprise awaiting the squad. Once settled into it, they found themselves bunking with men who'd never known Block 11. Though not restricted to them, the majority were those Sonder from Ciechanow culled from the unloading ramp the month before. There was confusion on both sides. "But the Nazis have been allowing us all this stuff since we got here," the latter said. "And you've been living on lager food and sleeping on stone floors? That doesn't make sense."

Kaminski thought he had an explanation. "Just another case of one hand not knowing what the other is doing," he proposed. "It's like that in any big outfit, be it the SS or the Red Cross. My guess is you people just lucked out, is all. The Germans may be pros at this, but that doesn't make them infallible. Witness our boy there on the other side of the wall with the big stick…. and even bigger pockets," he added with a grin. "You'd think the Krauts would want one of their own at that door to make sure those in on their little secret were in no danger of blabbing it to whoever had the price of admission."

It so happened that he was wrong. Beginning that winter, the Germans' coddling of fledgling Sonder was a calculated shift in tactics designed to buffer the shock of their barbarous new lives by distracting them with alcohol and other comforts. It was a way of getting them to work, and more to the point, continuing to work as opposed to giving up and opting out for the Black Wall. Why this strategy wasn't applied to the men preceding them in the commando was because these had become inured to their harsh existence and were producing just fine despite it.

Not that it mattered, really, if Kaminski was right or wrong, on this or just about anything. What with his irrepressible sangfroid and infectious good humor, not to mention the fact he was the oldest man in the squad, he soon became a magnet for the others' questions and concerns, especially the younger among them in aching need of a father, who'd seen their own trucked away never to return. But for the change in their living arrangements, this could never have come about. With the detachment sleeping under one roof now, not only did Kaminski have the ear of some of the Sonder during the day, but as opposed to being shut away in a small cell at night, could interact with them then in their entirety. It was an opportunity that both he and they took full advantage of. As the launching of the Birkenau crematoria drew near, the number of men housed in Block 13 swelled into the hundreds. In that the elitist Morawa continued to billet with his friends in Block 2, a Prominents hut, Kaminski had these hundreds to himself, and quickly emerged as their de facto leader.

But Morawa, too, had his backers among the SS, notably the distinguished *Untersturmführer* Max Grabner, head of the camp's Political Department, a euphemism for the Gestapo. So a compromise was reached. Both factions conceded that Morawa and Kaminski were the frosting on the Sonder cake, and their talents utilized best in Crematorium II, the largest and potentially most productive of the four. (Number Three had the same layout and dimensions as Number Two, but due to electrical and foundation problems was lagging far behind in construction). Instead of raising one man above the other, however, the Germans decided to make each a subkapo—Morawa in charge of the cremation room, Kaminski of the undressing and gas chamber areas—and bring in a third party as Chief Kapo, the German inmate August Brück, veteran of a long line of prisons and concentration camps. Brück's position was to be in essence a titular one. His assistants would be the ones running the operation.

The three were informed of this on March 10th, three days before Crematorium II was scheduled to open. Morawa was angry at what he perceived as more of a demotion than a promotion. He'd always assumed he'd be appointed head of whichever crematorium opened first, in fact had been promised as much by the powerful Grabner. Then this usurper, this middle-aged old windbag of a Jew! Still, there was no use fighting it, so he accepted it—but never forgot it. He made a show of welcoming Kaminski into the ranks of the kapos, but that was all it was, show. Secretly, he vowed to have his revenge one day, and was willing to wait patiently until that day should come.

Beginning on the 13th, however, both men had other, more urgent things to occupy them. Until then Kaminski thought he'd seen it all, but was mistaken; the progress the Germans had made in the science of mass annihilation was frightening. The new crematoria came with more than a few technological advances to be sure, and these were impressive enough, but it was the *scale* at which the slaughter was to be conducted now that turned the blood to ice, that made one see how a people might realistically think they could wipe an entire other from the face of the earth.

The night of March 13th, Crematorium II: the first transport to descend the steps into the underground jaws of this beast was from Krakow, and consisted of 1,492 men, women, and children selected from a shipment of 2,000. The women entered first, followed by the men. Kaminski watched them stumble out of the blackness above into the large rectangular undressing room, wave after wave of them blinking in the white light of the fluorescents.

"Sir, what is going to happen to us?" Their voices were strained, their eyes questioning. "Please, sir, where are we? What is this place?"

The Sonder were encouraging. What else could they be? To say that at this point these innocents from Krakow were beyond rescue was not saying enough. Two squads of soldiers had followed them down the stairs, machine guns at the ready. What good would it have done to tell them the fate that awaited them, to fill their waning minutes with needless terror? Better they remain in the dark as long as possible. Besides, for the Sonder to do so would be to sign their own death warrants, and for what? So that the people might panic and be gunned down rather than gassed?

So they did what they had to do, what they'd been trained to do, convince the skittish crowd that there was nothing to worry about, that everything would be all right, directing them all the while toward the line of benches running the length of each wall. Above these stretched two rows of numbered wooden hooks. In the courtyard prior, they'd been told they must have a shower before entering the camp. A permanent sign affixed to the crematorium entrance proclaimed in German, "To the baths and disinfecting rooms", while a portable one below it announced the same in Polish. Inside, on the walls and thick columns supporting the ceiling, were numerous other signs in various languages: "Cleanliness means life", "One louse can kill", and so forth. A couple of Sonder went among them handing out pieces of soap.

Presently, an SS officer stood on a chair and repeated the order given in the yard. "*Achtung, alles achtung!* It is required that you take a shower before proceeding further. This is not meant to inconvenience you, but to prevent the spread of disease. We did not bring you all this way only to have you carry typhus into the camp, or die of it yourselves. Everyone, therefore, must get undressed now. We regret any embarrassment this might cause, but it has to be done."

Those who could speak German looked up at him in amazement, as if just told to do somersaults or stand on their heads. Again he gave the order to undress, and still no one moved.

"Ladies and gentlemen, please, the sooner you take your shower the sooner you will get to your new homes, where hot soup is waiting. If your shoes have laces, tie them together and hang them and your clothing from the hooks on the walls. And remember your hook numbers. This will make it that much easier to reclaim your belongings later."

The Sonder moved among them, translating. People stared dubiously at them and each other. Parents strip in front of their children, sisters in front of brothers? Are you sure that's what the young officer said?

Some of the soldiers in the room, their own nerves stretched thin, had had enough. "Undress, do you hear?" they yelled. "*Alle Kleider!* Everything!"

Slowly, the people began fumbling at their clothes, but not enough of them, nor fast enough. Without warning the soldiers attacked, wading into them with truncheons and the butts of their rifles. Within minutes, all were naked and not a few of them bloodied, covering themselves with their hands as best they could.

With the SS hard on its heels, this dazed and defenseless mob—the younger children hysterical, many of the women and even men weeping— was herded down a short corridor that broadened into a spacious anteroom. Through a curiously stout open door, they could see a long, electrically lit chamber, thirty meters deep and seven wide, whitewashed from floor to ceiling. To their relief, a double row of flat, circular showerheads hung from that ceiling, though if they'd looked closer, they would have noticed there were no drains in the cement floor.

It was into this room that the phalanx of soldiers pressing from the rear drove them, and once all were inside, the thick, rubber-sealed door shut and hastily secured with screw-in bolts. By then Kaminski and his team had gathered their equipment and hooked up their water hoses and were waiting anxiously in a storage room for the grisly task that lay ahead. It was their job to clear out the gas chamber once the deed had been done. But it was more than just this that had them on edge. Ahead of them, too, lay the sound which must accompany the deed, that bloodcurdling farrago that as many times as they'd heard it never failed to horrify. It was the worst sound in the world, the worst sound possible, and the atmosphere in the little room was taut in anticipation of it.

They didn't have long to wait. Above them, jutting from the grass that covered the roof of the underground gas chamber, were what looked to be four miniature concrete chimneys. A pair of SS non-coms, the *Disinfektoren*, stood at two of these, gas masks in place, waiting for the order from below to begin. Upon this reaching them, each removed the heavy lid from the structure in front of him, opened one of the flat, round tins at his feet, and dumped its load of deadly pellets down the shaft. After replacing the lids, they moved to the remaining shafts and repeated the process. Inside the gas chamber, these induction columns, anchored to the floor, were protected by a double layer of wire mesh. An upright cone at the top of the column's core ensured the equal distribution of the poison. Later, this core would be taken out and the used pellets discarded.

This was a much safer and more efficient method of delivery than existed in either the main camp's crematorium or Bunkers 1 and 2. There, each *Disinfektor* had to balance on a ladder while opening his tin, then carefully pour the contents through a narrow, flap-covered vent in the wall. A pair of gas-masked Sonder stood near with buckets of water in case of spillage.

Zyklon-B, a hydrocyanic, was the German trade name for this gas, an acronym of its main ingredients: cyanide, chlorine, and nitrogen. The B stood for *blau*, from the brilliant blue color of the granules in which the poison was locked. Originally used to fumigate the lice-infested clothing of the prisoners, it was harmless until exposed to oxygen, and only achieved optimum utility at a temperature of 81° or higher. During the winter, a stove filled with coal burned in each of two corners of the older gas chambers, but even with these and the body heat of the hundreds packed inside, it could take up to thirty minutes to reach the requisite warmth. Crematorium II, however, came with a forced-draft ventilation system that channeled hot air from the ovens and chimney directly into the gassing room.

Zyklon-B killed by paralyzing the muscles of the lungs, causing its victims to smother to death. It was the devil's own brew in every sense of the phrase. Upon hitting the ground, the pellets would begin violently to hiss, like a thousand angry snakes—or on the night of the 13th, after rattling down the induction columns of this new layout, more like two thousand, as the dosage had been doubled to deal with the larger payload.

The Sonder in their holding room tensed at the ominous sibilance, for they knew what was next. It was the sound they'd been dreading, waiting in fear of, the screams of those in the gas chamber once they realized what was happening. It was a sound few but them had ever had to endure, a mix of shocked disbelief, bellowed outrage, and desperate pleading, torn all at once from fifteen hundred throats. Of special hideousness were the high-pitched shrieks of the women and children. This was how their own mothers, wives, and babies had died, in agony, alone, feeling abandoned by their sons and husbands, they who were supposed to be their protectors. The thought of it was enough to break the heart, sicken the stomach. Some of the Sonder clamped their hands over their ears, knuckles white with the effort. Some wept softly, a few mumbled prayers. All of them kept their eyes riveted to the floor, unable to look one another in the face.

After what seemed like minutes but was only seconds, the cries gave way to coughing and a convulsive gasping for air, as if fifteen hundred asthmatics were having a seizure all at once. Was this a harder sound to bear, more devastating than the screaming? One might as well have asked which was worse, dying of pneumonia or typhus.

As the gasping grew fainter, so did the banging on the death-room door. This pounding had been as furious as it was continuous at first; now only the occasional weak thump challenged the massive door's impregnability. Then all was quiet, less than ten minutes after the snakes of Zyklon-B had hissed their arrival, though the SS doctor in charge would wait ten more to be certain.

At which point the mechanical de-aerator was switched on to rid the chamber of its fumes. The Sonder team, already in the anteroom, buckled their gas masks, hoses ready, chests pounding at what they were about to face. When the bolts to the door were unscrewed, it swung open by itself, propelled from behind by the crush of bodies spilling out. There was always a mass of corpses jammed up against the door, and their first task was to untangle these and move them out of the way. Once a path had been cleared, the larger hose was brought up and the inside of the chamber thoroughly drenched. This was to negate any isolated pockets of gas that might remain under the bodies.

Kaminski, as always, led the way into the stifling room. Though a kapo now, he had no intention of resting on his laurels and dishing out orders without participating himself. The dirtiest, sweatiest part of the whole business was tearing down the piles of bodies. The stench was overpowering: blood, excrement, vomit, urine, and a pungent medley of body odors, their effect intensified by the wet, steamy heat. Worst of all was the excrement. There was shit everywhere in the gas chamber, on the dead, on the floor, smeared on the walls. Gassing, like hanging, often produced a last evacuation of the bowels.

The Sonder carried an assortment of tools. Heavy iron rods were used to pry the dead apart, in the process breaking bones, splintering ribs. Some wielded meat hooks, others picks, while all had leather loops attached to their wrists that they would slip over hands or feet in order to yank the bodies free. They never ceased to wonder at how compact these heaps were, how intricately the dying had twined themselves together. In their madness to escape the gas rising from the floor, they'd trod each other underfoot, clawing and scratching their way to the ceiling. In the process, they created little mountains of flesh as snarled as antiquity's Gordian knot, legs and arms interlaced as if crocheted together, hands clutching bone in frozen death-grips of steel.

As these were broken down, the dead were hauled into the anteroom, where a second team arranged them face-up in rows. Here the females' hair was shorn and stuffed into bags, and all spectacles, artificial limbs, and jewelry removed, the search for this last extending to body cavities. An SS officer collected all valuables in an open briefcase. A third team of Sonder busied themselves with dragging the plundered corpses to the elevator and sending them to the ovens on the ground floor, twenty-five at a time. There, prior to incineration, a tooth-pulling commando would inspect their mouths for gold.

Kaminski was always preaching to his men the necessity of disassociating themselves from their work, to think of what they were trafficking in not as people but so much meat. This, however, was something easier said than done, especially when dealing with the children. Being smaller and lighter, these were less trouble to handle, but came with a psychological weight that made grappling with the corpse of a full-grown man or woman infinitely preferable. Even Kaminski's impassiveness was tested where children were involved, as happened that night, when at one point he stepped from the death chamber holding by their heels the bodies of three infants like so many dead chickens. The Sonder who accepted this burden from him saw the tears staining his cheeks—by then he'd shed the cumbersome gas mask—but pretended not to and said nothing, recognizing it as not the reaction of a hypocrite but a man.

It took over two hours to empty the gas chamber, and another to clean it and dispatch the last of the bodies upstairs. The rest of the hoses were brought in, the blood and filth scrubbed off the walls, and the mess swept into the large grated drain in the anteroom. As a final touch, the walls and floors were slathered with a fresh coat of whitewash. In the silence that followed, as the Sonder waited to be led back to their barracks, they could hear the muffled roar of the furnaces overhead.

There would be no more transports that night. This had been a test run, and any glitches were to be addressed the coming week. Tomorrow, a Sonder detail would collect the clothes in the undressing room and take them by cart to the Bekleidungskammer. In the course of this, nimble fingers would ply the garments for valuables. There was a patdown by their guards later, but it tended to be perfunctory, making it possible to conceal diamonds or even cash on one's person if one were careful. The Sonder had no compunction against taking from the dead. The way they saw it, as Jews themselves, they were the rightful heirs of that dead. It wasn't as if they didn't know where any loot they might fail to preempt was headed, and better they should end up with at least a portion of it than have it all fall into Nazi hands. That the Germans should get hold of any of it was bad enough, as egregious an instance imaginable of adding insult to injury.

Back at Block 13, Kapo Kaminski couldn't sleep. As tired as his body was, his mind was refusing to cooperate. Giving up finally, he exited the barracks and began walking the yard, head lowered and deep in thought, thoughts as black and cold as the chilly March night. Today's had hardly been his first gassing, true. He'd been a party to plenty of them, seen things and done things no man was ever meant to. The gas chamber in the original crematorium held seven hundred. How many thousands had he helped connive into that room, or stuff into ovens and burn to ashes afterward?

This last 1,492, however, had been different. Gone were the haphazardness and improvisation that had characterized operations before. The two converted farmhouses in the woods, the fire pits, even Crematorium 1, all were the products of expedience, temporary solutions to the problem of how to rid Europe of its Jewry. Crematorium II, on the other hand, was the permanent answer to that problem, a mechanized, specialized, seamless assembly line of death designed from the outset, unlike its predecessor, as not merely a place to burn bodies but as an engine of pure destruction, as ravenous an eater of people as any dybbuk in Jewish mythology. The 1,492 were only the beginning. Three thousand at a time could be crammed into this monster's gas chamber, then reduced to powder, in rain or shine, in a matter of hours.

And that was but the tip of the iceberg. That Number Two would soon be joined by Numbers Three, Four, and Five was as big a reason as any that he was having trouble sleeping.

But it wasn't the only one. Something else was bothering him; the SS, it seemed, had been a bit off in their counting. It hadn't taken long for the pregnant woman to catch Kaminski's eye in the undressing room. Actually, though about as pregnant as a body could get, her belly impossibly distended, she was more girl than woman, nineteen, twenty at the most. She was also as pretty as he could remember seeing, a true daughter of Israel, the strong yet graceful Semitic nose, the large, limpid eyes of a desert antelope, skin the warm, golden color of fine olive oil.

It wasn't this, however, that had turned his head, set her apart from the others. No—somehow she wasn't fooled. He could see it in her face, in the way she looked at him as he was explaining the necessity of a shower. She knew what lay ahead, maybe not its specifics, not that it was gas, but most definitely that it was the end for her and her unborn child. How she knew, this random girl, this little more than a teenager, he had no idea, but there it was in her expression, the resignation, the reproach. The proud refusal to be suckered by yet another Nazi falsehood.

She held her chin high and stared him in the eye, her own not without fear, but at the same time as inflexible in its disapproval as iron. He could feel her staring at him even after he'd turned away, feel her gaze on his back, boring through his sham reassurances like a drill. It didn't happen very often, but he always hated it when they knew, when somehow they sensed their minutes were numbered. To her credit, this one at least kept it to herself, no tears, no hysterics, probably to keep from alarming what family was with her. For that, he couldn't help doffing his hat to her courage.

It was never easy enduring that recriminatory stare, to be acknowledged by the victim of one's complicity for what one was, an accessory to murder. A helpless one, to be sure, but guilty all the same. Quickly, he slunk himself and his despicable spiel to the other side of the room, though even as he did he was aware of the futility of such a move. One way or another, alive or dead, odds were he hadn't seen the last of this girl.

And so he hadn't, coming across her an hour later inside the gas chamber, not buried in one of the piles but among those corpses scattered on the floor. She was on her back, her spine arched, which made her belly look even bigger, when in fact it should have grown noticeably smaller. It should have been smaller because there it was, plain as day, its lifeless face turned toward his, the head of her fetus poking from between her open legs.

He'd encountered this before in Crematorium I, but had never grown used to it. There was something disturbingly unnatural, something not of this world about it, like the two-headed animals preserved in formaldehyde one paid half a zloty to gawk at back home when the carnival came to town. Never had this gas-chamber grotesquerie affected him, though, as it did now with this brave and beautiful womanchild from Krakow. She deserved better than this, better than to be on display like some monstrosity in a sideshow, her and her baby stripped of not only life but all dignity.

Yes, the Germans to their everlasting ignominy had miscounted. It should have been one thousand, four hundred and ninety-*three* dead, not two, and the discrepancy wouldn't stop eating at Kaminski. Didn't this little one who would never see the light of day, yet had lived on this earth for nine months in the womb, didn't he or she deserve to be counted, to be judged a human being along with the others? As trivial, even whimsical a detail as he had to admit this was, he couldn't get past it, stop thinking about it, just knew it was going to haunt him for the rest of the evening. Together with the image of that unborn, bloody head.

But the goblins of this evil night weren't to disappear with the rising of the sun. Indeed, they would continue to torment him all through the next day, so that night once again found him alone in the yard of Block 13. Why should this one nineteen-year-old and her aborted baby, out of the hundreds of dead to cross his path the night before, refuse to go away, fade into the background? It was as if they were hanging around for a reason, waiting for something to happen, something they wanted to make sure he didn't miss.

Standing in the yard, absorbed in the black stew of his thoughts, he'd been gazing at the stars without really seeing them. There was no ignoring, however, what greeted him upon his turning around. A full moon had snuck up on him, just now risen above the treetops, but such a moon as to cause his lips to part in surprise. In place of its usual pallor, it shone a startling, flamboyant scarlet, a red as rich and velvet as the petals of a rose. He'd never seen anything so cosmologically lovely or out of the ordinary; it was as if Mother Nature had grown bored and decided to put on a show. For some moments, he succeeded in losing himself in its rare beauty, his dark mood forgotten—when without warning it hit him, a shock of recognition like a fist to the stomach. With a grunt, he crumpled immediately to his knees.

There was no escaping it: the moon was the dead baby's head all over again, an almost perfect facsimile. Not only was it as round but as red, as if dipped in blood, the aghast, open-mouthed expression of the proverbial man in it identical to that he'd beheld on the tiny face yesterday.

He was on his knees for a while, unable to move, the withering stare from the thing above pinning him like a bug to a board. Nor would he allow himself the relief of averting his eyes from it, small punishment for his role in the tragedy it had chosen to mime. The more he did look at it, though, the more he began to wonder if maybe this charnel moon wasn't trying to punish him so much as shake him up, get his attention, tell him something. After that it took him no time, and with a little gasp when he did, to realize just what that something was.

Though not fully formed until then, it was a thought that had been nibbling at the edges of his brain for a month, ever since a certain kapo from the main camp's Ka-Be had strode into this very yard to lay some extraordinary news on him. How Bruno Baum had managed to penetrate the Sonder compound, Kaminski could only guess. The prisoner posted at the outer door may have been brazen in his greed, but he did have his limits. Even the better supplied of the black marketeers, able to offer the biggest bribes, had no choice but to conduct their business from outside the wall.

It was late in the day, the sun a blazing, orange ball of cold fire balanced atop the snowy tree line. The two of them had retired to a corner of the yard. Never had he seen a face as mournful as Baum's, a face so limned in pain, not even among the wretches he worked with. And yet there wasn't a trace of surrender in that face. Physically, he was as unprepossessing as they come, a short, slender man with round, girlish shoulders, arms and legs spindly as a child's. But Kaminski could tell from the proud bearing of those shoulders that here was a man who hadn't stopped battling, a prisoner to be sure, as captive as any other, but one it would take more than the SS to break.

"I come here, Herr Kaminski, with a proposal," Baum said, the voice a sonorous bass that didn't at all fit the slight body. "You have been recommended by reliable people as reliable yourself, but more than that as a man capable of leading other men. We would like you to join us in making history, you and your comrades."

"Oh, we would, would we?" said Kaminski. "And just who is this *we*?"

"The Resistance, the camp underground. Battle Group-Auschwitz…. you are aware, I presume, that it exists."

"I've heard tell of it, all right, sure—Battle Group-Auschwitz, I like the sound of that—but can't say as I know a whole helluva lot more. Since Q-Camp, I've been…. excluded, you might say, from much of what goes on out there."

"Understood," Baum said, "but believe me when I tell you we are a force in the camp, well-organized and determined. This is our proposal: we are planning an insurrection that will take place in Birkenau, a mass escape of as many prisoners as we can get out. And we want—no, *need* the Sonderkommando to be in the fore of the attack. Do not ask why we deem a revolt advisable, but we do. The SS have their own plans for our future, none of which, as you might imagine, is born of the milk of human kindness."

Kaminski let out a slow, appreciative whistle. "An escape? From this place? You're pulling my leg."

"I assure you, my good fellow, I have no designs on your leg, or any other part of you. I could not be more serious. We have come up with a plan, a battle plan, we think could work. And you play a large part in it, you and your men."

"Nice of you to tell us," Kaminski said, struggling to take it all in. "But what I'd like to know, among other things, is why us, why the Sonder? To lead the attack, that is." Then, unable to resist, "I mean, after all, what makes us so…. special?"

"Because you are in better—"

Baum stopped himself in mid-sentence. A shadow of a smile crossed his face, his way of saying that he'd got the joke. But as rapidly as it appeared, it was gone. "Because you are in better health, therefore stronger than any other group of prisoners, and have access to the wealth of the transports for the purchase of guns, ammunition, and such. In this, I am afraid, you would have to rely on yourselves; the Home Army at present, engaged as it is at Wars—well, engaged as it is, needs every weapon it can get hold of. One of our operatives, however, will be able to supply you with regular quantities of gunpowder, much of which you will be asked to set aside for a specific purpose."

A smile, actually, was all that Kaminski had wanted. He found it difficult to trust a man as self-righteously solemn as this one had seemed. "And what purpose is that?" he asked.

"The dynamiting of the four soon-to-be-completed crematoria." Baum paused for effect. "This is another reason your people were chosen to head the assault. The destruction of the four is integral to the operation, and must be carried out simultaneously. It will be the signal to the rest of us that the rebellion has begun."

Again he paused, searching Kaminski's face. "So what do you think, kapo? Your first impression…. and please, no holding back. I prefer you be honest."

"Honestly? I don't know what to think. It's all pretty overwhelming. A hundred questions come to mind, the first being, I guess, when is all this supposed to go down?"

"Questions may be difficult to answer at this point, everything being in the formative stages still. What I would like you to do is just sleep on it for now. Give it some thought, hash it over with your comrades. Discuss it with them, those you feel are discreet. When you are ready to talk again, I will be ready to listen, and hopefully by then I will have more to tell you."

"Fair enough," Kaminski said. "How do I get in touch with you?"

"You do not, nor will I be back." Another phantom smile. "My duties at Ka-Be don't warrant frequent excursions to Birkenau; my presence here can only attract the wrong kind of attention. One of our top agents, though, will serve as liaison between you and us, a fellow named Zabludowicz, as dedicated a Jew as he is able a soldier. He will be our mouthpiece to you, and yours to us. When you need him put a brick atop the wall on each side of that door over there. He is quartered in the Stammlager, but is in Birkenau almost daily."

"There is one question you can answer now, if you would," Kaminski said. "Are you, like me and this Zabludowicz, by any chance Jewish also?"

Baum blinked in surprise. "Yes. Why do you ask?"

"Oh, nothing, just curious." Kaminski held out his hand. "I must admit, sir, I'm intrigued to say the least. An armed revolt, you say? The gall of it alone…. it's got this old tree's sap flowing, that much I do know. I'll do as you ask and talk it over with my men, see what they think. Thanks, Herr Baum, and if there's nothing else, have a safe trip back."

Baum, having taken the extended hand in both of his, didn't let go. "There is one more thing. I want to make sure you understand the consequences likely to come from such an undertaking. There will be casualties, perhaps many. Perhaps no one will survive. The whole enterprise could turn out to be a disaster. The risks are as huge as the odds against it being an even partial success.

"But what should that matter to the men of the 9th Sonderkommando? Your fate has been ordained already. Witness that which overtook the eight squads that came before you, and when you are gone, those to come after. We are offering you the chance to save not only yourselves but others, or failing that, to die fighting, like men. There will be casualties all right, but not all of them ours. What would you not give to find a gun in your hands and a German in its crosshairs? You might live a while longer, if you want to call it living, by sitting on those hands and continuing to do nothing, but how much of that time would you be willing to sacrifice to be able to take some SS with you, the murderers of your women, your children, your race? Tell that to your men when relaying our proposal. Ask them how they would feel avenging their families, taking the battle to those who have taken their loved ones from them."

Though Kaminski had been sincere in his enthusiasm—a revolt, guns, dynamite, *escape!*—the longer he ruminated on it, the more this began to dim. Baum had seemed sincere enough, at the end even emotional, but Kaminski wasn't so unfamiliar with the underground not to be wary of any aggressive posturing on its part. The Resistance, from what he'd pieced together over the months, was by nature a defensive organization, set up to protect the inmates from the worst depredations of the Nazis. If anything, its mission was to keep the peace, not disturb it, to make sure that the applecart remained upright, not upset it. Out and out rebellion, by force of arms no less, wasn't something he'd have figured to be up its alley.

Plus, its members were almost exclusively Polish. The Poles had been at Auschwitz since its founding in 1940, their positions in the hospitals, the clerical offices, the kitchens long entrenched. And just as the power they enjoyed often approached that of the SS, so too did their anti-Semitic sentiment, their racism. He knew all about that racism; he'd been a target of it for as long as he could remember, since boyhood. Why, he wondered, should this confederacy of Poles risk everything, their jobs, their privileges, their lives, to liberate Birkenau, the population of which was growing more Jewish with every transport?

The individuals he informed of Baum's visit echoed his concerns. The underground couldn't be trusted; it was all talk and no action; the Poles weren't about to stick their necks out to try and save a bunch of Jews. There were some among the Sonder who argued otherwise, of course, who maintained that they had an obligation to themselves as well as others to rebel against the slaughter, to stop aiding and abetting the kill-happy Germans. But at this early stage anyway, these were in the minority. On the whole, it appeared that skepticism ruled the day.

There was something else, their kapo suspected, giving his men pause, not that any among them would have admitted to it. Each secretly harbored a last desperate shred of hope that the war would end before long, or the Russians bomb the crematoria, or that he'd be one of the lucky few to slip through the cracks somehow, to be overlooked when it came time to pay the pitiless SS piper. In the Vernichtungslager, everything was either ass-backward or a corruption of itself. The Ten Commandments were turned on their heads—thou *shalt* kill, thou *shalt* steal, thou *shalt* covet—the Golden Rule nonexistent. Here, the weak were at the mercy of the strong—the lame, sick, and feeble treated not with kindness but contempt. Here, nothing was less valuable than the life of a human being; a crust of bread, a pack of cigarettes, a needle and thread were worth more. Women with children and the elderly were the first to die, not the last. Here, people went to the hospital to be killed, not cured.

And so it was with hope. In the annihilation camp, hope was neither balm nor beacon, but an enemy. It was hope that led people unresisting from the undressing room to the gas chamber, that made men stand idly by while children were murdered. That prompted people to sink to just about any low for one more day of life, one small but essential step on the road to eventual liberation.

It was hope that helped make even the Sonder, men certain to die, men who found themselves up to their waists at times in the corpses of their own people, unreceptive by and large to Baum's invitation to action. In that sense, their knees were as weak and their apathy as strong as they argued that those of the men in the underground were. An observer of

Block 13 would have been hard-pressed to ascertain where caution ended and hypocrisy began.

Kaminski was among those who remained undecided. Common sense told him that any notion of a mass breakout was folly. From Noah Zabludowicz he'd learned some of the particulars of Baum's battle plan, one of them that the underground, being in contact with the Home Army, had enlisted its aid in not only providing firepower for the breakout but in escorting any escapees to safety. Which was all fine and good, except the forces who'd be chasing them were hardly those of Pharaoh's chariots in pursuit of the Chosen People fleeing Egypt. The Nazis had automatic weapons, artillery, even access to airplanes. What kind of safety, and where, did the partisans have in mind, especially should they find themselves responsible for who knew how many thousands?

Yet who could not applaud the opportunity to fight back, to give the killers a dose of their own medicine? Or as Baum had put it, if not by chance to live, then at least to die like a man, with a gun in one's hand. Though the allure of this wasn't lost on Kaminski, still he wavered. He knew full well what had befallen the 8th Sonderkommando, of which he'd been a part; two hundred of them had been tricked into an airtight room and gassed. What with the number of transports beginning to stream in, however, the 9th wouldn't have to start worrying for a while. Maybe a long while. How in good conscience could he be expected to rush men into risking what little life was left them by embarking on a project all but guaranteed to fail?

Though having taken an instant liking to him, he managed for weeks to string both Noah Zabludowicz and his organization along, telling him, not entirely untruthfully, that before he could commit them he needed more time to bring the Sonder to a consensus.

All that changed, though, on the transformative night of March 14th, when on his knees in the dark of the Sonder yard, unable to move, transfixed by the gory face of that accusing red moon, he saw what he hadn't before, with a clarity that shook him to his bones. Despite the emphasis Bruno Baum had put on escape, that wasn't what the uprising was about at all. And Baum knew it wasn't. Of much more importance, of paramount importance, was the razing of the crematoria, those four insatiable demon sisters poised even now to gobble up uncounted thousands, hundreds of thousands. This was Baum's real objective, the end to which any talk of forcing their way out of this place was merely the means. He'd been clever to dangle the twin incentives of escape and revenge so prominently while keeping talk of the cremos to a minimum. Kaminski knew, though, that bottom line, Baum didn't care whether a single prisoner made it to freedom as long as those four devourers of men were put out of action.

Not that getting rid of them would put a stop to the slaughter. Nothing could do that. It was clear that the SS were and always would be positively messianic in their bloodlust. It would certainly go far toward slowing that slaughter down, though, perhaps keeping it at a level that might see the war end before the Nazi dream of a Jew-free Europe was realized. The transports were arriving from all over now, from as far away as Greece and the Mediterranean. There was no way the two makeshift bunkers in the woods, or the even smaller and decrepit Crematorium I, which was forever breaking down from overuse as it was, could be expected to dispose of what might very well end up being a quarter or even more of the continent's Jews.

The moon was trying to tell him something all right, and he would have been both a fool and a coward not to listen. By putting on so ghastly a face, it was doing no less than adding its entreaty to Baum's, one as tacit as the other but no less urgent for it. Somehow these mammoth new additions to the machinery of death had to be put out of commission; not only exigency but simple decency required it. Even the night sky was demanding a stop to the butchery.

Later, after lights-out, Kaminski lay awake in his bunk. Two emotions had him on fire, keeping sleep away: a white-hot shame at having acted diffidently toward Baum's proposition, and a commensurate desire to make amends for that diffidence. What in the hell had he been thinking? The answer to that was he hadn't been, not for himself at any rate. He'd been listening more than he should have to the wishful thinkers, the timid, and to that selfsame little mouse that cowers somewhere inside every man, even the boldest.

Starting tomorrow, things would be different. Morning couldn't come fast enough for him. He knew there were plenty in the Sonder more than eager to fight, men such as Zalman Leventhal, Zalman Gradowski, Leyb Langfus, and Yankel Handelsman to name but a few. These he would assemble at the first opportunity and discuss how best to proceed, specifically how those either unsure of or opposed outright to rebellion might be persuaded to change their mousy minds.

As the perceptive Baum had foreseen, the word escape was the first requisite for attracting conspirators. Not even the most militant of the Sonder could be expected to agree to a suicide mission, to blowing themselves up along with the crematoria. But to make any talk of escape meaningful, he knew he would have to convince his men that the underground would be behind them all the way, if not as combatants then as providers of material and logistical support. The latter meant mainly that there be an adequate deployment of partisans waiting in the woods to assist the rebels in their fight, while the indispensability of the former could be reduced to a single word: gunpowder. And lots of it. It was vital that the Resistance follow through on its promise to supply the Sonder with gunpowder, and not solely for the purpose of demolishing the crematoria. They would need it for the construction of dynamite to clear a path through the electric fences, that and some kind of hand grenade to use in battle. Until the day he held a pouch of the stuff in his hands, with the certainty of more coming, he wasn't going to permit himself the luxury of getting his hopes too high.

But he knew that day would come, if for no other reason than Baum had said it would. At their meeting, he'd asked his visitor if he, too, was Jewish. His answer in the affirmative helped to buttress what Kaminski suspected, that he was the driving force behind the decision to blow the cremos. That he occupied a high position in the underground had to be assumed, and it was difficult to see the Poles, many who'd no doubt looked with approving eyes on the smoke boiling from the crematorium's chimney, insisting on such a measure. A Jew, on the other hand, with the clout to push it through….

Yes, if this Baum, this Jew, had anything to say about it, the Sonder would be getting all the gunpowder they could handle. Clear now was the reason for the metal in the man's voice when he'd said the destruction of the gas chambers was "integral to the operation."

As the night of March 14th eased into the morning of the 15th, Kaminski still couldn't sleep. A key component of what he wanted to say to Leventhal and the others was eluding him, but what? If the revolt were to appeal to those willing to gamble their lives on it, it would have to have trappings as well as substance, a little window dressing. Like that of the underground, or so the name Battle Group-Auschwitz implied, Sonder activism could only benefit from a military touch: a rigid chain of command, a commitment to the giving and taking of orders, discipline yes, and devotion to duty, but also that soldierly swagger, the camaraderie of men-at-arms. But before it could acquire these, it had to have an identity, something as basic yet unifying as a name. Battle Group-Sonderkommando? Not very original, he had to admit, but suggestive of affiliation with that other, older group. And it did accomplish what it was supposed to. In order to create esprit de corps, one must first establish a definable corps.

But it wasn't enough. There was something he was overlooking, something more…. inspirational for lack of a better word. Or maybe that was the word. What, after all, was he searching for? A way to *inspire* the fence-sitters in the Sonder, as the moon had inspired him, to get off their butts and start behaving as if they had a pair. And where should a Jew seeking inspiration go? Why, to the Bible, of course, and though he'd never been much of a one for religion, to the Bible he went.

As a child he'd been taught all the old, familiar tales, and commenced in his mind to thumb through them now as if he had the Testament in front of him. He didn't have to go far. Upon arriving at the saga of the fall of Jericho, a smile began to play at the corners of his mouth and would only keep growing, as gradually it dawned on him that maybe he might have found just what he was looking for.

Everyone knew the story of the battle of Jericho. The Israelite army, under its leader Joshua, successor to Moses, had encircled the heavily fortified city, its walls higher and thicker than any in all of Canaan. The people behind those walls, confident they could never be breached, hurled insults along with the occasional projectile at their besiegers. The Israelites, however, had a secret weapon, their God, Who directed Joshua to assemble a procession bearing the Ark of the Covenant which was to walk around the city once a day for six days, trumpets blaring. On the seventh day, they were to repeat this circuit seven times, the final sounding of the trumpets to be accompanied by a great shout from all the people. Then would the walls of Jericho come crashing down.

And so according to legend did it happen. The city was taken and put to the sword. Kaminski, being the pragmatist he was, had never given much credence to this or any other biblical stretch of the imagination, but whether he did or not was immaterial. What mattered was that he could use the hyperbole and very real audacity of the old battle to light a fire under the Sonder and win converts to the approaching new one. Just as the heroes of yesteryear had leveled the walls of the enemy with their trumpets, so would the heroes of today reduce the walls of the crematoria to rubble with their dynamite. Except this time around, it wasn't just the conquest of a city at stake but quite possibly the future of the Jews as a people.

The trumpets of Jericho, the gunpowder of Birkenau—the two were one and the same. And so it would be said for all time of the warriors who'd wielded both, unless this Special Squad proved itself unequal to the challenge and let history roll over it as all previous had.

Kaminski, the newly galvanized, the stick-at-nothing-now Kaminski, wasn't about to let that happen. He was as determined to take charge and set the wheels of rebellion in motion as he was to see the operation through to its end, good or bad. Come dawn, he would put up the pair of bricks that summoned Noah Zabludowicz to learn what progress Auschwitz had made on its plan.

After that, he meant to get with the two Zalmans, Leventhal and Gradowski. He thought it might be best to test the waters with them as he pretty much knew how they'd react. Not only were both vocal about fighting back somehow but had already put their money where their mouths were with their pens. For some weeks they'd been writing, much to their peril, a record of all they'd seen since the ghetto, plus what life was like in the commando of the living dead. Gradowski, at the kapo's request, had shown him something of his, and he'd been both taken by its truth and surprised by its poetry. "The dark night is my friend," he'd read, "tears and screams are my songs, the fire of sacrifice my light, the atmosphere of death my perfume. Hell is my home...."

The pair intended to seal these and future compositions in moisture-proof containers and bury them in the yards of the different crematoria. If caught they'd be killed, and not quickly, with a bullet. The SS had let the detachment know that anyone found divulging the secrets of *Sonderbehandlung*—special handling, the euphemism for mass murder—to either its chosen victims or other prisoners, would be bound hand and foot and thrown alive into one of the ovens.

Neither Zalman gave a damn. They were the bravest of the brave. They'd surmised that should the Germans end up losing the war, the area in and around the death houses would be seen as fertile ground by historians and others seeking evidence of Nazi crimes. And they meant to provide some of that evidence with eyewitness accounts of the horrors. They weren't going to survive, but their testimonies would. Though bigger and stronger and wiser to the ways of the world than either, Kaminski felt puny in their presence. Their valor dwarfed him.

Sleep came late that night to him, but it did come. It was while honing his "trumpets of Jericho" peroration that he finally dropped off. When he awoke in the morning, to his relief he hadn't dreamed, or just as welcome didn't remember any. This was always a plus. He'd learned from experience that the dreams of a Sonder man weren't things one wanted to carry around with one all day.

*   *   *

It was a chilly mid-April afternoon, the sky a bleached, bird's-egg blue, the sun so blinding white one didn't have to look directly at it for it to sting. Every shadow stood in sharp relief against last night's fall of snow, which had been unexpected but would also be the season's last.

But for the incandescent, orange cherry of his cigarette, the man loitering in the shadow of the crematorium was invisible. Even without shade, he might have been hard to distinguish from the dark brick he was leaning against, for his entire body was covered in a greasy black soot, his hair, his face, his clothes. He could have passed for someone who'd been working in a coal mine all day instead of up to his elbows in dead bodies.

Crematorium V had been in operation going on two weeks now, and Zalman Leventhal had been a part of its crew from day one. His station was the incineration room, where two Mogilev-style furnaces housed four ovens each, all fueled by coke, or refined coal, which would explain his appearance. Why he should have been absent from work in the middle of a shift had its own explanation, part of which lay in the make-up of the death house itself.

Unlike much of Crematorium II and the still uncompleted III, none of Number Five extended below ground. This was but one of the differences between them, all adopted (as they were in V's identical counterpart,

Crematorium IV) with an eye to cutting costs. Though each could claim the same gassing capacity as Number Two, when it came to cremation, Four and Five were only half as productive. Leventhal knew this because he'd worked Two right after it had opened, briefly but long enough to be impressed by its sophistication.

In contrast, Crematorium V resembled less its bigger, more modernized sister than it did the site of his first assignment in the Sonderkommando, Bunker 2 in the birch forest, where he and the rest of the hapless young conscripts from Ciechanow had received their first taste of the SS mania for destruction. As with that farmhouse turned slaughterhouse, Number Five had neither Two's forced-draft heating capability nor de-aerating system; its gas chamber was warmed to the required 81° by a pair of coal-burning stoves, its poison extracted by the natural draft that came from opening its two gas-tight doors. What was more, the Zyklon-B pellets were introduced in the same awkward fashion as in the bunkers, through vents in the walls near the ceiling sealed with movable flaps.

And then there was its floor plan. The building was almost six times longer, seventy meters, than it was wide, a spacious undressing room in the center separating the gas chamber at one end and the crematory at the other. The corpses had to be hauled from the killing chamber back into this central room to have their hair cut, their jewelry and such collected, then dragged the rest of the length of the building to the ovens. When these already had more than they could handle, there was no choice but to leave the bodies stacked in the undressing room to wait their turn. This, of course, tied up that area, putting pressure on the Sonder working incineration to increase output. As a result both the men, but even more detrimentally, the machinery were taxed, this last exposing the principal flaw in the design of these smaller crematoria.

This resided in the arrangement of their ovens. Originally drawn up for a low-budget cremation facility deep in central Russia to assist with the disposal of the millions murdered there (but never actually built), the Mogilev system was at far greater risk of breaking down, if cheaper to install, than the configuration existing in Crematoria II and III. The problem was the overly centralized structure of the two furnaces that contained the eight muffles, or individual ovens. The four muffles closest to the electric generators that ignited the coke and kept it burning tended to get hotter than the four that were farther away. This distortion gave rise to tensions in the fireclay, which after a while began to buckle and split apart. After less than two weeks of admittedly heavy usage, both furnaces in Crematorium IV developed large cracks. These were filled in with rammed earth and cement, but eventually reappeared. And kept reappearing, no matter what the Germans did.

To prevent the same from occurring in Number Five, they did manage—as they had in Four, if too late—to reposition the two generators and install protective ducts along the edges of the inner muffles. This allayed the defect somewhat, but didn't dispense with it entirely. Caution had to be taken from then on when dealing with its ovens, while those of Number Four were rarely again at full service. It was this that had brought Leventhal out of the darkness of the furnace room into the bright light of day. Though the sun was still high, the Sonder were on their second transport of the day, and had been warned there might be another on the way. With the oven and undressing rooms hopelessly backed up as it was, his kapo had pulled him off the line.

The anxiety in the man's voice was detectable even above the roar from the ovens. "I need you to drop what you're doing and get your ass next door."

"Where, Number Four?"

"Goddammit, where else? Find out how they're doing, see if they can't help us out. I need to know if—"

"Why not just call them on the phone?" Leventhal said with a smile, enjoying his boss's frustration.

"No one's answering the goddam phone! It's probably not working any better than anything else over there! Just do what I say and get going. I need to know if they can take some of these stiffs off our hands."

Leventhal's SS escort was drunk. He didn't walk so much as weave his way to their destination. What with the prospect of another transport facing him, he was more envious of the man than anything, a feeling fortified by what he discovered at Crematorium IV. Only five of its ovens were functioning, and one of those not fully; no way could its crew handle any more business today. Indeed, it looked as if it might take them until tomorrow at the earliest to get rid of the dead they already had.

Upon returning to his own compound and shedding the guard, he was in no hurry to get back to work. For one thing, he wasn't looking forward to telling his kapo the bad news. For another, it was such a beautiful, crisp, crystalline day, a heaven to the scorching hell in which he'd been slaving. He decided to take a break, smoke a cigarette, hide out a while. Seeking cover in the shade of the house of the damned, he reached in his coat pocket for his pack and lit up.

Hardly had he done so than he heard them, approaching from the south. Deportees on the march, large numbers of them, had their own sound. The shuffling crunch of their shoes on the road, the insistent wailing of small children, the deeper flux of adult voices a tense, weary murmur—Leventhal could tell it was another transport all right. He shook his head half in disbelief, half in disgust.

Shortly, they emerged from the greenbelt of trees meant to hide the crematorium, a long column of people flanked on both sides by soldiers. Like the two preceding it, this one looked to be a shipment of Greek Jews. This was clear from their dress and the desperation in their faces. Not that Greeks were inherently more prone to despair than Czechs, say, or the French. As he'd learned long ago, it was all about water, or rather the lack of it. The lengthier their journey, the greater the thirst of the new arrivals, and the greater their thirst the more distracted they were. And the easier to manage. The SS on the trains weren't denying their cargoes water just to be cruel. It was a deliberate ploy to reduce both their will and ability to resist, to so disorient and demoralize them that all other considerations took a back seat to wetting their parched throats, their swollen, cracked lips. It would take the Greeks a good week or more to make the trip to Poland, depending on what part of that islanded country they came from. By the time they got to Birkenau, they would have run off a cliff if the Germans told them there was water at the bottom of it.

He watched as the bolder among them would attempt to break ranks and scoop up a handful of melting snow, only to be chased back into line by a snarling SS. As they neared the barbed-wire perimeter of the yard, however, the people seemed to forget for a moment the demands of the flesh, and those in the back craning their necks for a better look, turned their attention instead to the curious building looming in front of them. The Germans had rigged the crematorium to look as unthreatening as possible. Red brick trimmed in white gave way to a gabled roof; windows thick with drapery sported white flower boxes. There were wrought-iron lampposts, a grass lawn, even a white picket fence enclosing more flowers. A decorative flagstone path wound among a few pine trees. The effect was of a well-to-do family's country home.

Except for two things: a low, white-plaster annex resembling an outbuilding, windowless but for three rectangular vents in the wall; and a pair of oversized chimneys at the opposite end of the complex, the Mogilev set-up requiring two smokestacks in contrast to Crematorium II's one. What the Greeks might have made of these anomalies, and the smoke pouring from the latter, Leventhal couldn't say, though he doubted any suspected the true purpose of either. What he was waiting to see was what the SS were going to do now. With hundreds of dead piled like logs in the undressing room, how were those about to join them supposed to get ready for their "bath"?

He got his answer soon enough. After all had entered the compound and the gate was closed behind them, the officer in charge gave the usual speech about the necessity of a shower, then ordered them to strip right there in the yard. Leventhal would have expected at least some resistance to this, but there was none. Despite the nip in the air, and the lack of even the meager privacy afforded by four walls, after a moment's hesitation the Greeks began to undress, obediently and as one, with little sign of the reluctance the order so often inspired. Apparently, not even the compulsion to modesty was a match for the prospect of water, any water, and the chance to douse, even if it was from a showerhead, the fire smoldering in their gullets.

And with that, he was out of there. He knew what was coming next and had no intention of sticking around. It wasn't just because of the audible part of it, either, the screaming and the rest that accompanied a gassing. As disturbing as that was, there was something else in its own way just as bad. Number Five's gas chamber was divided in two, the bigger room large enough to hold two thousand people, which was about how many were getting ready to file into it. More than once he'd watched, mouth agape, as a chamber similarly packed had seemed to rock on its foundation from the upheaval inside. How much of this had been his imagination he wasn't sure, but it wasn't a question he had any desire to settle now or anytime.

Blanking his mind, therefore, to the tragedy about to unfold, as only a Sonder could do—as a Sonder had to do if he wanted to stay sane—he turned his back on the increasingly naked two thousand and headed to work, toward the door that led to the flames and the smoke. A sign reading "Abandon all hope ye who enter here" would not have been inappropriate tacked above that door, for like Dante forsaking the friendly sun for the inimical gloom of hell, he, too, was leaving the light and fresh air for the toxic black murk of the cremating room, the inferno.

It took his eyes half a minute to adjust to the dark, though there was no getting used to the noise or the suffocating smoke. When the ovens were as busy as they were now, it felt as if there was more smoke in the air than oxygen, the sweetish, cloying smoke of burning human flesh. In view of its importance, it wasn't an especially large room, twenty meters long and half as wide, and was made even more cramped by the two brick furnaces taking up the middle of it. The walls, too, were made of brick and permanently blackened, as was the low ceiling. There were two windows on each side, but so soot-stained as to be all but opaque; the light that did leak through them was gray. A short, wide corridor separated this room from the undressing hall, while acting as a further buffer against the din and the heat was the kapo's office, a bathroom, a small storage area, and the coke bin.

The blanket of hot air blasting from the nearest of the two furnaces wrapped itself around Leventhal as soon as he walked in, but hardly had he started to perspire than his kapo was on him.

"Glad you could make it back. How was the movie?"

"Sir, it was the guard. He'd been drinking and…. well, he wasn't in any hurry."

"Sorry lying rotter," the other growled, but less angrily than he should have. Of more concern to him at the moment was what he'd sent his stoker to check on. "So, what about Number Four? Can they help us out?"

Leventhal had considered qualifying his report in hopes of tempering the kapo's wrath, but decided it best not to. He wasn't about to tell him, though, that the third transport they'd been fearing had arrived. "Number Four, I'm afraid, could use some help themselves. Only half their ovens are working, and—"

"Blood and thunder!" the man yelled. "Did they say when they might—oh, never mind!" He glanced at the corpses heaped high in the dental station and threw up his hands. "The fire pits full, Number Four next to worthless, and Three still unfinished! That means we're on our own, us and Number Two. Which also—son of a *bitch!*—means express work, it looks like. If the ovens can even take it. Let me find that prick of a *Kommandoführer* and see what his lordship wants to do."

He started off, then abruptly pivoted on his heel. "You, meanwhile," he snapped, "back on the job! And don't let me catch you loafing again!"

As soon as he'd seen there was going to be another transport, the first words to pop into Leventhal's head had been "express work". It was only after his kapo spoke them aloud, however, that the reality of them hit home. Express work was used as a last resort only. The SS were no fonder of the tactic than their slaves, as it put a strain on the entire system, the ovens, the furnaces that held them, the generators, the chimneys, that none of those components was designed to withstand. For the Sonder it meant not only more work and at a faster pace, but worse, the necessity of having to pay closer attention to the dead, to appraise and group them according to age, sex, and physical condition.

Each oven had a manufacturer's recommended limit of two corpses per half hour. Seldom, however, was this limit adhered to. The usual rate was three every twenty minutes, though when the gas chamber was going full tilt and the flow of bodies became a cataract, the figure was upped to five every twenty-five minutes. From the rows of bodies stacked face up at the tooth-pulling station in the oven room, the Sonder would mix and match, combining the different physiques in such a way as to enhance combustion. For example, two children and a Muselmänn might be thrown together with a well-nourished man and woman. Or two Muselmänner, a child, and two overweight women—every Sonder team had its own array of formulas, though each was predicated on the common denominator of fat. During express work especially, body fat was the oil that kept the engine of extinction running; the bonier the corpse, the more it needed another's fat to burn. Seeing as how nature had endowed their sex with an extra layer of the stuff, the bodies of women, especially those fresh off the trains, were particularly prized. Where in happier, less hallucinatory days, the men of the Sonder might have competed with each other for eligible females, now disputes often flared up among them over the rights to those same females' cadavers.

From the expression on his kapo's face when he returned twenty minutes later, Leventhal could tell what the *Kommandoführer's* verdict had been. Express work it was, there was nothing to be done about it. Now they would be forced to get intimate with the dead, to assess, to assort, to scrutinize their persons instead of trying not to look at them as they slung them about. He wasn't the only Sonder to feel sorry for those in the dental commando. It wasn't uncommon to see one of them reach over and close the eyes of his corpse before inserting the crowbar into its mouth and forcing its jaws open.

After the pliers had done their work, the dead were dragged nearer the furnaces and arranged in the four apropos piles: adult males, adult females, children of both sexes, and from the camp the Muselmänner, always the Muselmänner, there was never any shortage of those lying around to dispose of. From these piles, the oven-Sonder, with the help of bearer-Sonder, would collect what they needed and haul them to their stations. There they were placed in accordance with the chosen formula into a contraption resembling a stretcher, an open-ended metal trough with a pole running the length of each side. With a loud rattling, the heavy iron door of the oven was cranked open not unlike a theater curtain rising, the fierce heat that gushed forth withering everything in its path. When fully drawn to reveal the fire raging inside, two pairs of Sonder picked up the poles, laid the leading ends atop the two rollers astride the oven door, and shoved the whole thing in. When the stretcher was extracted, an iron fork was pushed against the bodies to keep them in place. The door was then lowered shut, but partially raised twice more to allow the stokers to "stir the stiffs", as Leventhal's kapo liked to say.

Air from the motor-powered Exhator ventilators, one to an oven, assisted the flames, which burned two wheelbarrows of coke per cremation. After every three or four of these, the ashes were removed from the bottom of the muffle along with any unconsumed bone. This was to prevent them from clogging the flues under the floor which channeled the bulk of the heat and smoke from the furnaces to the chimneys. The fiery tempest beneath one's feet not only caused the room to tremble (nor could Leventhal in this case ascribe it to his imagination) but forced one to shout to be heard above the locomotive roar, not to mention the lawnmower racket of the Exhators. It was Pandaemonium in its original, most fearsome sense, as the poet Milton had called his capital city of hell—what with the deafening noise, the flames and smoke, the mutilated bodies of the dead everywhere, Leventhal was pretty sure that after the ovens, the real hell was going to hold few surprises for him.

That he was to be forever damned, he had little doubt. As a cog in the SS murder machine, he expected nothing else from the afterlife, no matter that his reason for choosing to go on living was to do everything in his power to get the word on that machine out to the rest of the world. He'd made that promise to himself his first day on the job, that eye-opening day almost five months ago when he'd been marched, unsuspecting, to Bunker 2 in the woods and learned firsthand what the Nazis were up to, what those baffling columns of black smoke meant, that oily stench in the air. And though he had no idea at the time how he was going to fulfill that promise, fortune had seen fit to show him a way.

It came in the person of his friend and namesake Zalman Gradowski, whom he'd met in Block 13. Gradowski came from a small town in Poland near the Lithuanian border. The thing that first struck Leventhal about him was his methodical nature; even here, in the muddy slaughter pen that was Birkenau, he was a man of fastidious habits. His bunk area was never anything but military-neat, the nails atop his childishly stubby, pudgy fingers always trimmed and cleaned. A clerical worker by trade, he'd aspired to be an author and had had a few minor pieces published, but the German invasion forced him to set any thought of that aside. The war ended up crushing another dream of his as well: an ardent Zionist, he'd been making ready to immigrate with his family to Palestine in the summer of 1940. Instead, it was the ghetto for them, and eventually the death camp.

Physically, the two men couldn't have been more different. Where Leventhal, the redhead, was fair-complected and thin, Gradowski was broad in the beam and on the swarthy side, his coloring more typical of the desert Jew of the Bible. They differed in temperament, too. Leventhal was an introvert who'd never mixed well with others, a shy oyster of a man who until the ghetto made it impossible had spent much of his life avoiding people. Gradowski by contrast loved a good party. He genuinely enjoyed the company of his fellow man, and when so moved could talk a blue streak. They also didn't see eye to eye on religion. The miseries of ghetto life had failed to impact the faith of either, but after Birkenau, Leventhal's had taken a serious beating. Argue as he felt compelled to as a friend, however, to dissuade Gradowski from his and the enervating hope it fostered, he'd met with only sporadic success.

In spite of these disparities, the two had bonded from the start. It wasn't like the unsociable Leventhal to make friends so effortlessly, but upon their discovering they'd each been gifted with a classical education, it wasn't long before they were talking books, philosophy, history, and yes, religion. Sadly, they had more than just this and their first names in common; both of their families lay in ruins as well. While Leventhal's maternal grandparents, his parents, a younger brother, both sisters, and seven nieces and nephews had gone to the gas, Gradowski lost his wife, his mother, also two sisters, a brother-in-law, a father-in-law, and three little nieces. Due to these mutual tragedies, they also shared an unquenchable thirst for retribution, a determination to avenge the murders of their beloved somehow.

They knew at the same time, of course, that vengeance, if attainable at all, would have to wait. The Germans were too powerful, they too utterly helpless. Leventhal was content at first merely to observe, to remember, and on the chance he might survive the SS whirlwind, bear witness one day. It was Gradowski who suggested the more audacious approach of keeping written accounts of what they'd been through and seen, and burying these in the crematoria yards. His reasoning was twofold, and hard to refute: only a fool would bet on the Germans leaving a single Sonder alive; and what with the news filtering in from the Russian front these days, it was looking less likely the Nazis would win their war. Meaning untold numbers of truth seekers would one day be scouring the cremo grounds for clues to the greatest crime in the twentieth if not every century. If they were to unearth eyewitness documents detailing the particulars of that crime, it would make it that much harder for the SS specifically, and the German nation in general, to deny responsibility, or go so far as to maintain such outrages never happened.

Already, each had bottled up one of these rough time capsules and planted it, Leventhal's a few meters to the rear of Crematorium V, Gradowski's at Number Two. To help corroborate what they'd written, lest their intended audience find it incredible, they'd also scattered numerous teeth at both places. If there was one thing there was no shortage of at Birkenau, it was skulls.

Gradowski worked in the undressing room and gas chamber of Crematorium II under Kaminski. It was at his kapo's invitation that he'd buried his document there, but beyond that, he'd given the pair of them something for which they were even more grateful, a chance to be men again and not cattle. It was Kaminski who'd informed them of the revolt that was brewing, and asked them to be a part of it. Nor did he have to ask twice. If Leventhal was indeed docketed for everlasting perdition, he wasn't about to pass on taking some SS with him.

He labored into the evening that day burning the Greeks, his kapo making him work overtime for his tardiness earlier. Upon the arrival of the night shift, he was put to assisting them as a bearer of both corpses and coke, this last, what with express work in force, virtually without interruption. By the time the new kapo took mercy on him and relieved him for the night, it was all he could do to drag himself to Block 13, his body as beat up as it was caked with sweat and coal dust.

Though Gradowski had already washed the gore of the gas chamber away and changed into fresh clothes, he embraced the begrimed Leventhal as was their habit. Once he, too, had showered and sat down to eat, Gradowski joined him at the long communal table in the middle of the hut. "The Greeks again?" he asked in response to his friend's silence.

Leventhal nodded.

"Us, too, and more on the way tomorrow, or at least that's the scuttlebutt. Any word on Number Four?"

"Good news and bad," the other replied, looking up from his plate. "The bad is that only half of its ovens are working. Which is, of course, also the good news. Judging from the smoke rising to the north all day, though, it looks as if Sergeant Möll's fire pits are doing their best to pick up the slack. Who knew there were so many Jews in Greece of all places?"

"You'll excuse me, Zalman, if I swap your question for a better one," Gradowski said. "How many are liable to be left six months from now?"

Leventhal, frowning, went back to his food. Neither spoke for a time. It was Gradowski finally who attempted to lighten the mood.

"Speaking of good news," he said, "there's an interesting fellow joined our ranks a while back, works with me in Number Two. Tall, black curly hair, thick black glasses, around thirty—you run across him yet?"

"I don't think so. What's his name?"

"Langfus. Leyb Langfus."

"Leyb *Longfoot?*" exclaimed Leventhal, who'd perfected his Yiddish at the yeshiva school. "That's a peculiar name."

"He's a peculiar individual. Believe me, if you'd met him, you would remember. There's something, I don't know, a weird energy about him, a light in his eyes, as if he was looking past this world into a whole invisible other. If he was here I'd point him out, but…."

Gradowski half-rose from his chair, looked around, but no Langfus.

"Anyway, he's quite religious, to the extent it's this, you could say, that defines him. Though like us, he lost family to Birkenau, a wife and infant son, unlike us his faith, or so I'm told, hasn't dimmed for one second. But then word also has it he was the *dayan* of the Makov-Mazovietsk ghetto. And when the rabbi there fled to Warsaw ahead of the Nazis, Langfus took over his duties."

Dayan, Hebrew for judge, was the title of a person versed in Talmudic law whose advice was regularly sought by the rabbi and others. Leventhal was impressed. To have been a dayan before the age of thirty, then a rabbi, was unusual. But he was leery at the same time of that weird light in the man's eyes, or however Gradowski had put it; the phrase "religious hysteric" had grabbed hold of him and wasn't letting go. "Sounds…. interesting, this Langfus of yours," he said disinterestedly.

"Wait, there's more," Gradowski said, "listen to this. Though assigned to the Sonderkommando, he refuses to do the work. The most he'll concede is helping the sick and the old in the undressing rooms. And janitorial work and such. As for the gas chambers and ovens, he won't set foot near them."

Leventhal's brow knit in surprise. "And the Germans haven't shot him yet? How can that be?"

"I don't know. No one does. It defies understanding. I asked Kapo Kaminski what was what, and he seemed as puzzled as anybody. He did say *Oberscharführer* Muhsfeld once approached him about it—Muhsfeld that butcher, who kills as if he's swatting flies—and asked what was going on. Kaminski lied and told him Langfus was recovering from pneumonia, and wondered if maybe there wasn't something less physical the man could do for now. Strangely, miraculously, the *Ober* thought for a moment then said that there was, and put the dayan in charge of collecting and burning the incidentals the dead are always leaving behind. You know, the passports, the birth certificates, the photographs, the cheap children's toys, all that the SS regard as nothing but rubbish.

"He tends his fires, reads from the Talmud and the Haggadah, recites the prayers for the dead all day, and the Nazis leave him alone, let him do as he pleases. I've never seen anything like it. It's as if even the Krauts aren't sure what to make of him and his otherworldly ways. Did I mention he eats only bread and onions, the camp soup when he can get it? He won't touch a thing that comes off the transports."

"Quite the individual," Leventhal said, "but I'm afraid I don't follow. What does all this have to do with the good news you said you had?"

"I'm just coming to that. This Langfus isn't one of those who wraps himself in a prayer shawl and rocks on his butt mumbling Scripture for hours on end. Turns out he's that rarest of Jews, both ultra-devout and, get this, a scrapper. I've talked to a couple of people from his village who say that prior to their deportation, he argued against meekly boarding the cattle cars in favor of trying to break through the German cordon at night and making a dash for the forest. He may be as spiritual as they come, but unspirited he isn't."

"Go on."

"Yesterday," Gradowski said, lowering his voice, "he takes me aside and says we should be working together. I told him I thought we already were, and he says no, not crematorium work, the work of the devil, but the holy work of keeping a record of Nazi crimes. I asked him how he knew about the jars that we buried, and he said Kaminski told him. In fact, it was Kaminski who sent him to me. I questioned the kapo about this later, and he assured me the dayan could be trusted, was one of his best men, in fact, as committed as anyone to making the revolt a reality. Who'd have thought him the type? I never even considered recruiting him into the plot, and there he was, in on it all along.

"And now he wants to stick his neck out even farther and help you and I assemble our little narratives. Anyway, I figured you'd be glad to hear we were three now instead of two."

Leventhal pushed his plate away. "Glad? Yes, of course. We need all the volunteers, all the help we can get. And in the end, a third diarist can only add credibility. But as far as news, I was hoping for something, I don't know, meatier. Have you any idea, for example, what progress the

Battle Group has made? In its hunt for weapons, I mean? I've noticed you and Kaminski together a lot lately—I thought he might have told you something."

Gradowski made a face. "Ammunition, yes, from the military salvage yard outside the camp; it isn't coming cheap, but it is coming. So far no guns, though. Guns, I hate to say, don't look promising, not at present. Gun*powder*, on the other hand.... One of the underground's operatives has been feeding it to us regularly, with the result that our supply of dynamite is growing. From what I hear, this person is female, out of the Canada commando. Makes one proud to be a Jew, doesn't it? That we as a people can claim such women. May God continue to protect and watch over her."

"God?" Leventhal said. He had a feeling this was coming, what with all the foofaraw just made over this Langfus character. "What, my man, are you backsliding on me already? The last time we talked God—when was it, two weeks ago?—you said you were back to having serious doubts about Him."

"Yes, I know," Gradowski sighed, "but now I'm beginning to doubt my doubts. It's the dayan; he can be most convincing on the subject."

"I can only imagine."

There was no missing the derision in Leventhal's voice, but Gradowski let it go. The last thing he wanted at this hour was to get into another argument about religion of all damned things. It had been a long enough day as it was. "Anyhow," he said, half-feigning a yawn as he rose from the table, "I'm pretty beat—think I'll hit the sack early, if you don't mind. You should do the same, Zalman. You've got to be exhausted."

And so he was, but sleep wasn't in his plans. Not yet anyway. He'd decided just this morning to write another witness, and knew with what he was going to begin it. The incident he'd chosen had been tugging at him for days, demanding to be written. He'd put it off, frankly, because he was loath to revisit the awful thing, but the time had come to set such selfishness aside.

It was something he'd seen in the morgue abutting Number Two's incineration room. This was an area where the freshly killed were temporarily stored when the ovens were backed up. At other times, it served as an execution site for groups too small to warrant the use of Zyklon-B. For the most part, these consisted of people from outside the lager, either locals who'd somehow run afoul of the Nazis, or Jews who'd managed to escape their villages or towns and gone into hiding in the forests. The Gestapo hunted down these runaways with tracking dogs, and after amassing a sufficient number, trucked them to Birkenau.

A freestanding wall six meters long had been erected in the morgue. Five or six victims at a time would be led inside, naked, while the rest waited their turn. Made to face the wall, each was held there by a Sonder while an SS officer went down the line with a pistol, shooting them in the base of the skull; some required the Sonder to position the head at just the right angle for the kill. The bodies were then drug behind the wall and the next batch brought in. Only after all were gone would the gunman move among the fallen, administering the coup de grace to those still alive.

As short-lived as his stay at Crematorium II was, Leventhal wound up working two of these small-scale murder sessions. One of them, however, in its villainy, its heartbreak, stood out above the other. It was this, tired or no, he felt the need to record tonight, to set down while he could on the chance, the same chance every inmate ran, something happen to him tomorrow. It was vital it be preserved for some future day, so those dwelling in that future gain some insight into the Nazi mind, see not only what the SOB's were capable of but that they knew, deep down they knew what they were doing was wrong.

He made for his bunk soon after Gradowski, not to sleep, but to lie there waiting for lights-out. For secrecy's sake, it was better to hold off until lights-out before one began to write. As much a non sequitur as this sounded, there were always a few men who weren't done with their reading and would burn a candle or flashlight in bed. Leventhal would make a sort of tent of his blanket and scribble away under there. Aside from the freedom to stay up as late as they wished, that they had access to books at all, much less pen and paper, wonders undreamed of by the average prisoner, was as good an indication as any of the latitude allowed the Sonder. Like most of their luxuries, of course, these came from those inexhaustible horns of plenty, the transports.

He had no trouble recalling the events of the day in question. The Germans had herded about fifty people into the area outside the morgue. Beyond filthy, bedraggled, some with twigs and bits of leaves hung in their clothing, all were clearly from the forest. And all perfectly aware their final hour had struck. Leventhal watched a young mother, at the order to disrobe, remove her shoes and stockings before starting to undress her four-year-old. He heard the little boy say, "Mama, why are we taking off our clothes?"

"Because we have to, darling." There was a catch in her voice.

"Is this the doctor's?" he asked as she was unbuttoning his shirt. "Is he going to look at me and make me not sick anymore?"

"Yes, my precious boy, soon you'll be feeling much better." The mother was struggling to hold back her tears. "And we'll be with your daddy again, just like before, only happier."

Leventhal remembered not wanting to hear more and heading back into the morgue. The woman entered in the sixth group, her babe in her arms. To his relief, it fell to another Sonder to lead her to the wall. The shooter that day, the ill-tempered if normally adroit *Oberscharführer* Voss—a tall, lean man in his mid-thirties, with a sour, pinched face— started with her and immediately bungled it. Instead of doing away with the mother first, he sought to position himself for a shot at her son, to which she reacted by frantically twisting and turning left and right so as to keep her body between the child and the pistol.

Refusing to acknowledge his mistake, probably because he'd been drinking, Leventhal could smell it on him, Voss kept stubbornly after the little boy. "Hold her!" he snapped at the Sonder assigned her, but she wouldn't be held, nor stop her desperate maneuvering, until suddenly the gun barked and the toddler let out a shriek.

What happened next stopped Leventhal in mid-breath. Red with the blood of her dying son, the woman wheeled and hurled the body straight at his killer's head, the startled Voss taking it literally on the chin. With an animal scream, she then launched herself after it, but the pistol exploded twice more, and she fell at the sergeant's feet.

Voss looked shaken to say the least, but it wasn't until he reached up to wipe his cheek and drew back a hand dripping with the boy's blood that he lost it altogether. His face an instant white, he let his gun clatter to the floor. For several long seconds, he stared slack-mouthed at the offending hand, then lurching for the door yelled at his SS assistant to take over, that he'd had enough for the day.

The way Leventhal saw it, the encounter was remarkable for two reasons. Why the mother should have used her child as a projectile like that was beyond his comprehension. But then who was to say in a similar situation what one would do, with the light of one's life, the flesh of one's flesh expiring in one's arms, his blood splashing one's feet? Was it temporary insanity or defiance that made her do what she did—a cognitive breakdown in the face of the horror of the moment, or a deliberate attempt even in the midst of that horror to distract Voss so that she might exact some revenge with her fingernails? He would never know the answer to this, though had no doubt which scenario he would have liked to believe.

The meaning of the second act of the tragedy, however, was plain. Voss had self-destructed, but why? If the Jew was indeed a bloodsucking leech, the subhuman and eternal enemy of the German Volk, the only emotion elicited by his elimination should have been one of satisfaction at a job well and rightfully done. Having a dead baby flung at him, admittedly, was neither routine nor to be expected, and certainly nothing Voss would be forgetting anytime soon. But Leventhal could tell it wasn't this that had caused him to drop his gun and desert his post, not on its own anyway. His baptism in that baby's blood was what had done the trick; one look at the man's face after he'd discovered it on his cheek was enough to affirm that what had unhinged him was the crimson mark of Cain staining that face.

Which meant that at a gut level, beneath the veneer of ideology and blind loyalty to the Fatherland, lurked the recognition on Voss's part that he'd just committed infanticide. Not disinfection, not deverminization, nor the dutiful removal of a future threat to the Aryan race, but the cold-blooded murder of a fellow human being, a child.

No wonder the SS drank. The privilege of playing God came with a price, an assault not on the ego so much as the superego, the conscience. As opposed to mitigating the offense, though, the occasional pang of remorse they exhibited only augmented the Germans' guilt, added to their crimes. They deserved to be doubly condemned, not only for the physical act of killing but for refusing to listen to that inner voice that kept trying to tell them it was neither necessary nor laudable, but an atrocity.

As for the actual God, He Who didn't have to play at it, the God of their forefathers, the almighty Yahweh—Leventhal didn't know what to make of Him anymore. It was a question that continued to vex others as well: what kind of God would allow a Birkenau to happen? Could it be the same God Who'd established a supposedly eternal covenant with the Jews, went so far at one time as to form a speaking relationship with them, watched over them and shepherded them down through the ages to the point where even the Gentile referred to them as His Chosen People? It didn't make sense. Millennia of history had come to nothing. With Birkenau, the divine rug had been pulled out from under them.

It wasn't as if he'd stopped believing in God. One might as well doubt the existence of the mountains, the sky, the oceans. To say that He didn't exist simply because Birkenau did wasn't only selling God short, it was letting Him off the hook. Leventhal did, however, feel he could no longer trust Him, particularly after learning of the death of his family. With that had come the realization, sickening, abrupt, that most of the theological pablum he'd been fed over the years, from earliest childhood to his studies at the yeshiva school, was a lie. God wasn't the loving father he'd been brought up to believe, the stern but fair father, Who though He could be demanding, was concerned above all with the welfare of His children. He was the father Who abandoned His children, blithely left them to the wolves without so much as a fare-thee-well.

God had either gone insane, or worse yet, lost interest. Why would He take the trouble to rescue the Jews from the Egyptians and slavery, keep them intact under the conquering Babylonians and Assyrians, keep them alive before both the fury of the ancient Rome of the Caesars and the New Rome of a Christian Europe, only to stand idly by now while they were ushered into extinction? What could have prompted this Yahweh to forsake His people, to change from God the protective, the nurturing, into God the aloof, the callous, the criminally indifferent?

Leventhal hadn't a clue, but this much he did know: whenever God entered his thoughts these days, sorrow and betrayal weren't far behind. For this reason, he tried to avoid thinking about Him at all, but there were times, such as today, when this proved impossible. He had yet to meet this Leyb Langfus, but already didn't like him. Was he being hasty? Perhaps. Having never met him, he could hardly presume to speak ill of the man, especially given not just his offer to add his testimony to theirs but the courageous picture Gradowski had painted of him. From that alone, there wasn't a lot not to like about the Makover dayan.

He couldn't help resenting the fact, though, that all this blather of him and his unshakeable faith, a faith he appeared to wear like some sclerotic suit of armor, had forced Leventhal to contemplate his capricious God again. As was likely to happen whenever their paths did cross. Judging from Gradowski's precipitately improved attitude toward the deity, Langfus wasn't only a persuasive proselytizer but an aggressive one.

He lay in his bunk with his face to the wall, rancor eating at his brain, loss at his heart. Everything he'd held dear had been stolen from him: his life in Ciechanow before the ghetto, the few friends he'd had, his family, and finally with this last theft, his God. He'd always, as both a child and a man, been devout, feeling a genuine affection for his father in heaven at the same time he leaned on Him for sustenance and support. Now this pillar of support, this last love was gone. God had fled the field and left the devil in charge.

"So be it," Leventhal whispered to the plaster wall in front of him, "let the devil have it then. Let him have the whole thing. Let the world be as bleak as this Birkenau that inhabits it. But in return, let the dayan keep his piety to himself or so help me I'll shut that damn mouth of his for him."

At that moment, as if holding back until he arrived at this conclusion, the overhead lights blinked off and on as a warning that soon they'd be extinguished. He reached under his blanket and felt for the sheaf of paper he'd smuggled into bed. He had his flashlight ready, his pen and ink, and was anxious to start writing, to get his brain off what it had no business being on to begin with.

While he waited for the dark, and to get his thoughts in the place they needed to be, he directed them back to that day in the morgue, recalling with a smile that wasn't a smile, with something more like the rictus on the face of a corpse, *Oberscharführer* Voss showing up the morning after his poor performance in a good, one could even say a jovial mood.

*　　*　　*

"Godel. Godel, sweetheart," Roza breathed in her lover's ear. "Are you awake, precious? You awake?"

A low, luxurious moan told her he'd rather not be. She kissed him softly on the cheek and lay back in their makeshift bed. After a moment, she raised a hand to her face, sniffed her fingers and smiled—it was the

132

odor of sex, of animal rut, of wild, sweaty abandon. Of male and female, Godel and her, mixed all together. She lingered over them until there seemed to be no more smell left, her fingers as leached of fragrance as if she'd licked them clean.

Though not much time remained them, she didn't begrudge her man his nap. There was no denying he'd earned it, that she'd put him through quite a workout. That she was as energetic a lover as she was worldly a one was hardly a fact lost on her. Nor was this a source of either pride or shame, it was simply who she was. It wouldn't have been easy to be more reserved, more "ladylike" (how she despised that word!) even if she'd wanted to.

She stretched like a contented house cat, let her eyes wander their little love nest. It was dark but for some shafts of sunlight poking through a couple of cracks in the wall. They were in a utility room in a seldom-used corner of one of the Canada warehouses, locked inside by an amenable kapo. In thirty minutes or so, he would be making his way back to let them out, having been paid as usual for his cooperation. It was an arrangement that assured the pair of their privacy. They would never be discovered here, he told them, adding with a grin, "Provided you two don't make too much noise."

Motes of dust floated in the angled wedges of sun like lazy insects. A large, three-basin metal sink took up a good portion of the room, flanked on one side by an assortment of brooms and mops. A squad of disconnected water heaters stood at white attention in the shadows; it was behind these that she and Godel hid their mattress and blanket when they weren't there. It may not have been much to look at, this dreary, musty room, this glorified closet, nor conducive to fostering romance. But to her it was as titillating, as libidinous as any bridal suite. It happened every time: as soon as she set foot in it, before Godel even touched her, her heart would begin to race, her juices to percolate.

But there was a further allure to this shabby room other than as the setting for her and Godel's lovemaking. It was the only place in the camp that she could be alone, or as alone as she wanted to be. Everywhere else, she was surrounded always by people—at work in the Bekleidungskammer, twice daily at the Appell and latrine, jammed together at night in the noisy, busy barracks. The human organism has a need periodically to be apart from the crowd, removed from the hurly-burly. One would think this need might be met once one was in bed after lights-out. But even then, in the dark, in addition to one hearing, smelling, *feeling* the weight of humanity in the hut pressing in from all sides, from above and below, there were the bunkmates, always the bunkmates, those annoyances, those adversaries with which one was forced to fight throughout the night for space and a share of the blanket.

Rarely if ever did a prisoner find herself alone in the anthill that was the Vernichtungslager. Solitude and its fair-haired child, uninterrupted thought, were luxuries there, yet another reason for Roza not to resent her Godel his nap.

She pulled her blanket to her chin, snuggled her nakedness against his; it wasn't an especially cold day, but neither was it warm. With a satisfied sigh, she let her mind drift. Much had happened the past two months. The mission with which she'd been entrusted was going well, nor had she wasted any time justifying that trust. After Noah had re-entered her life that blessed day outside the Bekleidungs warehouse, bringing the double miracle of the underground and its gunpowder proposal with him, it hadn't taken her three weeks to get the operation up and running. Not that she'd accomplished this on her own, nor could she have in so short a time. Indeed, if it hadn't been for Marta, she might not have accomplished it at all.

Maybe that was putting it too strongly, she told herself. She would have got it done somehow. But it was certainly no exaggeration to say that her friend and fellow Jew, Marta Bindiger, had sped things along. She'd met the slightly younger Czech at the Bekleidungskammer, where they worked the same table. Marta, who spoke a more than passable Polish, had preceded her there by six months, and impressed by the new girl's clear disdain for their SS masters, had taken her under her wing. She taught Roza how best to locate the jewels and cash hidden in the garments that passed before them, and more importantly, how to sneak some of it for oneself from under the Germans' noses. The two women lived in different barracks, but saw each other daily at work, and before long were fast friends.

Marta had the kind of sly, puckish good looks that made one like her at first sight. A smile that would fill her face was never far away, the playful, brown eyes permanently crinkled at the corners from it. Her nose was gently flattened and just the slightest bit crooked, as if broken long ago, but the imperfection of it only made her the more endearing. Adding to her elfin air, she was shorter than most, and had a habit of cocking her head to one side when she talked.

Underneath, however, she was more a Cordelia than a Puck, as forthright as she was upright, forgiving when virtue called for forgiveness, but adamantine in sticking to the standards she'd set for herself and others. When she spoke of the SS it was with open contempt, nor did her fellow captives get a free pass; as profligate as she was with her smile, she didn't bestow it indiscriminately. She could sniff out a liar or a bully in a heartbeat and had no patience with either, was quick to call them out when they offended. She was going to make a good mother some day, if she lived—indulgent as a rule, stern when she had to be.

At their soup break one morning, Roza asked her if she happened to know any prisoners assigned to the Union munitions factory nearby. As luck would have it, she did. "Two, in fact," Marta said, "sisters. Both from Warsaw, by way of the Maidanek camp. Why?"

Esther and Anna Wajcblum, twenty and fifteen years old respectively, hadn't stayed long at Maidanek, an extermination facility, but having failed the selection at the unloading ramp, their parents would remain there forever. After a month in the camp, the sisters were bundled back onto a train and shipped off to Birkenau, where they were eventually housed in Block 8 of the *B1a* lager, the same barracks as Marta.

It was here that the three struck up an acquaintance, in large part because of Anna, whom out of a mixture of fondness and deference to her youth, everyone knew as Hanka. Not only was she so very young but highly emotional, and given what she saw at Birkenau, once she had to admit finally that her father and mother were dead, she took it hard. So hard that her older sister, afraid she might try to end her grief by running to the electric fence, asked Marta to help her keep an eye on the child.

Marta only too happily agreed. Hanka reminded her of her best friend when she was growing up in Czechoslovakia, while in Esther she recognized a refusal to grovel before their captors on a par with her own. The elder of Block 8 was one Edith Weiss, a Sudetenland Jew, and providentially through marriage a distant relation of the Bindigers. It was she who'd got Marta a job in the clothes-sorting commando, and now the recipient of this favor sought another, though not for herself.

She asked the blockova if maybe there wasn't some kind of indoor work available for two of her friends, if not in the Bekleidungskammer then elsewhere, anywhere, it didn't matter. Within the week, both Esther and Hanka, who'd been breaking their backs unloading truckloads of coal from the Fürstengrube subcamp, were transferred to the newly opened Union Metallwerke. Excelling in first the stock room then quality control, Esther was promoted to the gunpowder detail, where she worked the day shift.

Roza almost dropped her bowl of soup when told this. "You mean you know someone who actually works in the Pulverraum?" she asked in amazement.

"Esther Wajcblum, yes. I talked with her just a few days ago."

"And how difficult is that?" Roza wanted to know. "Meeting with her, I mean."

"Not as easy as it used to be," Marta answered, "but also not impossible. Shortly after the two started their jobs at the Union, all the women who worked there were collected from the different barracks and relocated to Blocks 2 and 3. As the Germans are always worried about sabotage and theft—especially, one would think, among the workers at a weapons factory—this was done to isolate them from the rest of the prisoners to deny them a market for stolen goods. The guards at these two blocks are under strict orders barring visitors, but as you're aware," she added with a wink, "there are ways around strict orders."

Pausing, she frowned. "Not always, however. Sometimes their orders outweigh the soldiers' greed. Such would appear to be the case at the Union women's barracks; for some reason, they remain off-limits to any and all male inmates, no matter what the guards are bribed. I remember Hanka telling me a while back about two men who tried for weeks to gain entrance, but to no avail. I've since puzzled over those two, why they should have been so persistent."

"I know of those men," Roza said. "They work at the Union factory, too, but never succeeded in getting near any of the women."

"But why would they want to?" Marta asked. "And how do you happen to know about them? You're up to something, you Polish fox, I can smell it. You might as well get it over with now and tell me what it is."

Roza thought for a moment, then proceeded to bare everything, from the underground's plan to steal the Union gunpowder to what it was being stolen for. She figured if she couldn't trust this one, whom could she? Marta was ecstatic, asked how she could help.

"I need to talk to this Esther Wajcblum, and as soon as possible," Roza said. "If you could arrange *that*...."

The two set out that night, keeping to the shadows until reaching Block 2. Marta walked up to the *Schütze* at the door and handed him a pack of cigarettes. He took it, but didn't budge. "*Ein mehr*," he said. "One more, for your friend."

She'd anticipated this and produced another pack. The soldier stepped aside, and just like that in they went. Roza's first impression was how uncrowded it was, as large as her barracks but with not nearly as many occupants. It smelled better, too. Later, she would learn there were showers on the Union grounds. A good number of civilian Meisters was needed to oversee the place, and it wouldn't do for them, not to mention the SS on duty, to be exposed to the germs dirt can generate. They also ate better, this commando: lager soup and the hard, gray bread, but a little more of it. The Pulver women even received a glass of milk every day.

She felt self-conscious in her comparative grubbiness as they moved through the hut, but no one seemed to notice, or even that she and Marta were unfamiliar faces. Presently, they stopped at a set of kojen indistinguishable from the others, a three-tiered affair rising almost to the ceiling. On the bottom mattress, two prisoners sat facing each other, holding hands.

"Esther, Hanka," Marta said, "I've brought a guest."

Despite their shorn scalps, Roza could see right away that one was disarmingly pretty, one no more than a child. Hanka's ears stood at nearly right angles to her head like those of a cartoon mouse, while her sister boasted the oval face, bee-stung lips, and almond eyes of a film star. It was she who spoke first.

"Hello, I'm Esther. And you are—?"

"Roza. Roza Robota. Sorry if I'm intruding, but if you don't mind, Esther, I was wondering if you could spare a few minutes of your time." She took Hanka's hand and shook it. "Hi, I'm Roza," she repeated. "Would you object, dear, to my chatting with your beautiful sister for a while?"

Marta stayed behind to keep Hanka company, Esther leading the way to an empty bunk. She seemed to move with the grace of a movie star, too, or an athlete or dancer. Though not much taller than Marta, and delicately built, her step exuded confidence and the spine to back it up. She'd been through some things, this one, Roza could tell, would have thought twice before mixing it up with her.

Their conversation was brief. In five minutes the deal was closed, sealed with Roza's promise that if Esther did choose to plant the seed of theft in the gunpowder room, the fruit of this seed might be a chance at escape all right, but also, and perhaps as much to her liking, SS fatalities, the destruction of their crematoria. She took this tack because she saw in Esther's eyes the same hate she'd been told burned in hers at mention of the detested Germans. Like her, the girl ached to see the murderers of her family bloodied, the would-be annihilators of her race thwarted in their unholy pursuit.

"But can what we're asking of you even be done?" Roza had been sweating this for days. "I'd think that while you're working, every move you make is watched."

Esther's smile was dismissive. "There are at most two pairs of prying eyes in the Pulverraum at any one time," she said, "the Meister's and those of his assistant, a female prisoner, also German. They're watchful enough, but not very bright, either of them. Nor are both always present. Can it be done? Yes. It won't be easy, but yes."

"And what of the other women on your shift? How many of them might be interested, and more important, trusted?"

"One for sure, maybe more. I'm going to have to sound some people out. Then there's the night shift; I know of two there who would jump at the invitation."

"Let me come back in a couple of days then," Roza said, "and see what you've done. And be careful, Esther, please. If any of this were to reach the wrong ears...."

"Don't worry, I'm not approaching anyone I'm not absolutely sure of. You can rely on that, just as I'd like to feel I can rely on you. And by that I mean do you really, in all honesty, in your heart of hearts, believe there's a chance of any of us escaping this death trap? My little sister, she's all I have left. I don't know what I'd do if she were to die."

"She's not going to die. Nor are you and I. One day soon, we'll all be sitting around a partisan campfire. And then home."

As essential as having an operative in the gunpowder section was, recruiting Esther wasn't the only thing on Roza's to-do list. Just as important was establishing a network of smugglers, not only to deliver the powder to her but to make its trail as confusing as possible. She, of course, was to be the terminus for every gram of the stuff, except for that bit of it reserved for the main camp. But to make sure it wasn't intercepted before it did reach her, its route would have to be as convoluted as it was efficient.

Which meant a working knowledge and intimate understanding of Union factory personnel and procedure, a knowledge she lacked and couldn't be expected to acquire. A Union insider was needed, preferably someone with both a little authority and mobility. Hanka was too young and wanting in credentials for the job, and Esther too confined to the gunpowder room. Roza did know two male prisoners employed at the factory, Israel Gutman and Yehuda Laufer, the same men Marta had mentioned. As agents of Battle Group-Auschwitz, they'd been inserted into the Union works to try and infiltrate the Pulverraum, but after the failure of their mission remained as intelligence plants, and should it get started, to help with the smuggling effort. They'd showed up one day and briefed her on various particulars, but their usefulness to her ended there. Men weren't, nor could they be, the intermediary she was looking for. Since the stolen gunpowder must perforce start out in the hands of women only, it could only be passed to other women, for even on the factory floor the SS were careful to keep their male and female slaves separated. There were times, at the changing of the shifts or during restroom breaks, when the paths of the sexes might cross, but these were as fleeting as they were haphazard and couldn't be counted on.

No, Roza needed a woman to set up and oversee her ring of smugglers, and unpromising as such a search may have appeared, she had a hunch, or at least a hope, who that person would end up being. Marta wasn't the only contact she'd made at the Bekleidungskammer. She'd also come to know a Jewish prisoner in her mid-twenties from the nearby town of Bedzin. Ala Gertner possessed a beauty to rival Esther's. Though she towered a good head above the rest of the women, like Esther she moved with that easy languor peculiar to the truly attractive; tall she may have been, but there was nothing gangly or clumsy about her. Her features were sharper, less rounded than Esther's, but glamorous all the same—hers was the fierce, aquiline beauty of the hawk, head proudly lifted, yellow-green eyes never still. Beneath the elegance with which she carried herself, and like the bird of prey she embodied, there was a restiveness to her that seemed subject to the laws of gravity only in so far as she chose to let it be.

As with most of the inmates Roza found herself drawn to, Ala didn't hide her hatred for the Nazis. And she had reason to hate. One time at work in the clothing warehouse, Roza asked her about the middle finger on her right hand, which was missing mid-knuckle. In fact, the wound didn't look to be quite healed. Ala told her this story:

Upon her arrival at the unloading ramp, while standing in front of the SS doctor, she'd had her baby daughter, Rochele, ripped out of her arms and handed to an old woman standing behind her. This woman was then pointed toward the group of deportees on the left, and Ala to the right. Not only did she refuse to go as directed, however, but proceeded to raise a ruckus, howling like a hellcat while attempting to fight her way past the guards in pursuit of her kidnapped, terror-stricken child. It took three soldiers to restrain her, and not even they could get her to stop screaming, until one of them pulled a knife and cut off her finger. As if they knew the effect this would have, as if they'd done it before, her frantic shrieks subsided to a whimper, and she was dragged to the group on the right.

"From this hand, they tore my baby Rochele," she told Roza, holding the injured part up, "and for screaming so loudly, cut off a finger. I fought for my daughter, but they were stronger and took her. And that's the last I saw of her, or ever will see. But I won't forget. Never will I forget, and some day, somehow, I'll have my revenge."

Not long after this conversation, a team of German civilians in white lab coats entered the clothing depot one morning and began picking out the strongest-looking prisoners. These were then led away and reassigned to the Union factory. Ala was among them, and Roza hadn't seen or spoken with her since. She didn't find out where she'd been taken until Gutman and Laufer recommended her as someone at the Union who might be of use.

In the course of their talk the night she met Esther in Block 2, Roza asked her if she knew Ala, and if she perhaps was there now. Esther said she did, but hadn't seen her all evening, which meant she was working the night shift. She would try, though, she promised, to have her present when Roza returned.

And so she was, and Esther beside herself with excitement. When she spotted Roza, she practically ran to meet her. "Guess what happened!" she blurted, her expression deadpan.

Roza tensed. "I wouldn't even want to try."

"Answer me this then. How much is two plus two?"

Roza shot her a baffled look. "Uh…. four, last time I checked. Don't tell me that's what has you in such a dither."

"No," Esther beamed, unable to suppress it any longer, "but it is how many Pulver girls I've found who are eager to put a bad case of sticky fingers to good use. Isn't it wonderful? Can you believe it?"

Roza, excited herself now, scooped her up in a hug. "Yes, I can, Estusia! I knew you wouldn't disappoint!" Then letting go of and looking past her, "And I see you've brought someone with you. Hello, Ala, remember me?"

"Of course I do. And I can't tell you how grateful I am that you remembered *me*."

"So, I take it you know. Why I wanted to see you, that is."

"Esther here told me everything. And I have just one question."

"Yes?" Roza said.

"When do we start?"

Ala had performed so well at the Union factory, she'd been promoted to assistant *Vorarbeiterin*, or forewoman, of quality control. This gave her access to all but a few restricted areas. Roza couldn't have asked for a better chief of operations, and in the course of the night's meeting, much of the groundwork for the venture was laid.

Things moved quickly after this. In less time than she would have thought possible, the business of relieving the Nazis of their gunpowder was running like clockwork. The only complaint that might be made lay in the quantity the conspirators were able to move. To keep from arousing the Meister's suspicion, only a small amount could be taken from the Pulverraum each day. Also hampering the smugglers' efforts were the searches conducted by their guards, often without warning, forcing them to dump the day's take onto the ground at their feet. Though these tended to occur when the prisoners were entering Birkenau at the end of their workday, they might happen at any time. It became even more difficult to dispose of the evidence when it came not in the form of powder, but as it often did, in tiny pear-shaped disks, which had to be ground up by hand before being stomped into the mud. And this with the SS swarming their ranks.

As elated as Roza was at the success they'd enjoyed so far, she was also surprised that no one had been caught yet. Some weeks ago, Israel Gutman told her of an incident that made her wince. Thanks to the freedom Ala Gertner had as a forewoman to circulate among the Union workers of both sexes, she'd started slipping packets of gunpowder to the German-born Gutman and his Czech friend Laufer. This was that part of the dynamite consigned to Battle Group-Auschwitz; unlike the women, who were based out of Birkenau, the men of the Union were quartered in the Stammlager. One evening, as these were lining up in the factory yard prior to marching back to camp, the order rang out: *"Mutzen ab!* Caps off! Stand at attention and don't move!"

It was a search. Already their guards were moving among them, together with some officers who'd appeared from out of nowhere. Laufer leaned toward Gutman and whispered that he had yet to transfer the gunpowder he was carrying to his shoe; it was still in the empty cigarette pack between the waistband of his pants and his stomach.

Gutman went white, began shaking. This was it, they were lost. It was too late for the Czech to try and transfer his stash; the Nazis even now were searching the prisoner in front of them. When Gutman's turn came, one of the soldiers noticed his distress and patted him down extra thoroughly, looking inside his shoes, his cap, even his mouth. Upon finding nothing, he swore in disgust and waved him on, subjecting Laufer, who'd managed to maintain his composure, to only a cursory examination before moving to the next prisoner.

It had been too close a call, and made them rethink their strategy. They had a tinsmith friend of theirs create a food bowl with a double bottom, inside of which they would secrete the gunpowder upon receiving it from Ala. There were always several prisoners who would save some of their soup from the day and carry it back to their barracks to consume later on. Gutman and Laufer were soon following their example, as the SS, even during a search, would but glance at the half-filled bowls.

Roza thought this most clever, and asked them if they'd be able to come up with other such bowls. Additional improvements to their thievery were devised as well, by far the most productive a ruse the daring Esther had hit upon. The Meister of the Pulverraum, the elderly Paul von Ende, though in earnest about his duties could also be absent-minded. And that was putting it mildly. The main room of his little realm measured ten feet by twenty and occupied the plant's southwest corner. Its only furniture consisted of a long metal worktable and an assortment of folding metal chairs. Atop this table, amid a clutter of large aluminum trays, miniature scales, various utensils, cups, and other odds and ends, stood six devices resembling small if elaborate kilns, each festooned with a panoply of gauges and dials. These were the pressing machines that injected the gunpowder into the *Verzögerungen*, or detonators.

The two exterior paneled walls, like the rest of the building, were windowless, while the one facing the factory floor was made of glass from top to bottom. The fourth adjoined an even more compact room that served as von Ende's office. There was only space enough in there for a cheap metal desk, a small sofa, and the imposing floor safe he kept his gunpowder in. From this safe, he would dispense it to his girls, carefully weighed and measured, a precise half-cupful at a time per prisoner. In this way, he knew how many Verzögerungen they were supposed to fill, and could compare this to their actual output.

His high position at the factory made von Ende a busy man. He was often called away to attend to some matter elsewhere, leaving his assistant Elsa in charge. There were times, though, when he'd have to go when she was off somewhere already, on business herself or on a break. This left their six prisoners unsupervised. As if that weren't careless enough, he didn't always take the key to the safe with him, or even more astounding, would leave it unlocked. More than once, Esther had seized the moment, slipped into his office, and pilfered the gunpowder at its source, thereby circumventing the weighing process and its burden of accountability.

Normally, however, the three day-shift *Pulverfrauen* now involved in the plot, Esther, Rose Greuenapfel, and Genia Frischler, had to practice their sleight of hand with two pairs of eyes on them. (Their night-shift accomplices, Mala Weinstein and Ilse Michel, had to contend with only one sleepy kapo). Theirs was no easy task. The detonators were the size and shape of a checkers piece, with a cavity in the middle a quarter-inch in diameter. Each woman, using a tiny spoon, would fill half a dozen of these with a heaping amount of gunpowder, then load them into her pressing machine. Thirty seconds later, out they would come with the powder compacted into a solid mass, all but for a scattering of residue. This leftover material was called the *Abfall*, and being dispersed by the action of the press, was so degraded by the machine's heat as to be unusable.

The trick was to collect the worthless Abfall and substitute it for the real thing, secreting the latter to the side. As soon as one of the conspirators noticed neither of her overseers looking, she would scoop the gunpowder she'd amassed into either a matchbox or pouch fashioned of paper or cloth, and return it to its hiding place. Once it could hold no more, she would wait until the striking of the hour to ask to use the bathroom, where either Ala or one of her agents would be posted as pre-arranged.

The problem was that after the detonators emerged from the press, von Ende would test them to make sure they were functional. From the metal trays like cookie sheets upon which they were arrayed, he would select some at random and measure their explosiveness. A couple of bad ones and he might let it slide, but any more and he would fly into a rage, beating those he assumed weren't doing their jobs properly and later withholding their rations. Of greater concern to the three than missing a meal, though, was that he begin to suspect something more than mere negligence, and either grow more vigilant or replace them with a new set of workers.

Fortunately, the Meister, among his other idiosyncrasies, was a man of rigid habits, a foible exploited later by the Jewish forewoman of the Pulverraum, the just as seditious Regina Safirsztajn. Having deduced after a while that something was going on, she insisted she be included in the plot. One of her official duties was to collect the Verzögerungen and arrange them on the cookie sheets for von Ende's inspection, and she'd noticed long ago that his selection of the things wasn't random at all, but followed a pattern that didn't vary from day to day. In collusion with Esther, Rose, and Genia, therefore, she made sure to place the defective pieces where he wouldn't pick them; as they watched him choose from the same rows over and over again, it was all the four could do to keep from laughing.

Thus was the contraband obtained, teaspoons at a time, and from the launching point of the bathroom started on its circuitous route to Roza. In the process, it would be passed from one set of hands to another, or maybe stashed somewhere and left until the shift was done, when it would be picked up before changing hands once again and taken by shank's mare the two-odd miles to Birkenau. There Ala might reclaim it, or Marta Bindiger, or Esther or Hanka or any number of women before it found its way to Roza, the penultimate link in the chain. From her it would ride to the crematorium in the empty clothing carts of the Sonderkommando, and from there eventually to the safety of their barracks.

Once Gutman, Laufer, and another man in on the game got their quantity of it back to their quarters in the Stammlager, it was delivered to Battle Group-Auschwitz in the same roundabout fashion. Roza suspected her own Godel of being involved in this, and was almost positive Noah was, and worried for them both. She came close to asking Godel about it once, but in the end decided not to. For her to know would be to put him in harm's way if she were ever caught and interrogated, though she couldn't imagine a torture terrible enough to pry his name from her.

But it wasn't just Godel and Noah that concerned her. She worried for all the brave men and women who'd chosen to put their lives on the line to help arm the rebels. Happily, the risk was ameliorated by the utter stupidity of the Germans. Marta was right to harbor so low an opinion of the SS; why the Pulver women weren't frisked whenever they left their machines instead of at the end of their shifts only was beyond Roza's comprehension, nor did Nazi ineptness end there. It became evident before long that during their periodic searches, the Germans weren't on the watch for gunpowder at all, but rather other, bulkier items—small tools, bars of soap, work gloves and such, anything that might fetch a price in the camp. Once this was discovered, it made hoofing the powder that much less slippery a business, as one could hide the bundle in one's armpit, in the crotch of one's underwear, the bottom of one's shoe and be credibly assured of it not being found. As a result, more began to get through instead of being dribbled in panic on the ground.

Such were the thoughts, together with the blanket under which she snuggled and the heat of the man sleeping next to her, that kept Roza warm as she lay on the utility room floor, ticking off the triumphs of the past weeks. The twin cocktails of success and righteous vindication coursed through her like a drug, not only warming her but causing her open eyes to shine at this bold and beautiful thing she and her fellow conspirators had wrought. To be a soldier at last, finally fighting back!

Engaged not in the token resistance of the ghetto, or that practiced in small, feckless doses in the lager, but in something much more serious, something decisive, something meant to deprive the high and mighty SS of first, the crematoria, those factories of death and pain of which they were so proud, then hopefully their lives as well, a good number of them anyway. Against odds too high, too discouraging to calculate, it was *Jews* who were rising up, *Jews* who were waging war on those gangsters, those preening goons who'd tricked them to this necropolis, this city of the dead and the living dead, this graveyard that had already claimed their families and where they, too, were meant one day to lie.

So far it was but a secret war they waged, silent, undercover, but it wasn't going to remain silent forever. One day the quiet of Birkenau, that eerie, encompassing hush born of mud, disease, and slow death, would erupt in shouts, gunfire, explosions, in roofless, burning buildings and barbed wire fences trampled in the earth. Soon those swallowed by the Nazi monster, buried alive in its monstrous gut, would no longer be entombed, but dashing for the concealing forest and its army of partisans.

Roza lay on her back staring up at the plaster ceiling at this image of a mob of people, a mob of thousands, running for their lives, running to freedom, scared out of their wits but at the same time exultant. And she and Godel would be among them, fleeing hand in hand, she and Godel and Noah along with all the others. There on the ceiling, she watched the three of them reach the trees, disappear into the trees, and what they would do then. They'd run a while longer, until deep into the woods, then after stopping to catch their breaths they'd look at each other and burst into tears, laughter and tears all at once, overcome at the impossibility of what had just happened. Behind them the battle would still be popping and crackling, but not nearly as close, while ahead lay the forest, and beyond that the river—and beyond that, after the damned Germans lost their damned war, Eretz Israel, the Promised Land, the home of their fathers.

Suddenly a voice, his voice, snapped Roza from her reverie. "You know how beautiful you are when you smile?" Godel said.

Her gasp of surprise melted into a giggle as she turned her head to face him. "You spoil me, sir. Beautiful? With this hair, these skin and bones? If you need glasses, you know, I could probably organize you a pair."

"No, thanks," he laughed, "my eyes are just fine. And you can say what you will: you're the most beautiful woman I've ever known, inside and out."

"So how long, you naughty boy, have you been watching me? Quiet as a mouse, too. Was I really smiling?"

"Not long. And you weren't just smiling, you were glowing, your face as lit up as a Shomeir bonfire. What on earth, love, were you thinking about?"

Roza didn't answer right away. "The future," she said finally, "our future, the near and not so near. In fact, I was just getting to the part when we…. Oh, please tell it to me again, Godel, how it's going to be. I love it when you tell me. You know how I love it."

He turned on his side and held her to him, his cheek pressed to hers. He enjoyed saying the words as much as she did hearing them. "Well, let's see, first it's to Palestine, probably by refugee ship. Nor will we lack for company; hundreds will have scrambled to get aboard. After the war, after Hitler and the camps, who's going to argue with the Zionists then? I'm guessing it'll take us a week or more at sea. We'll get married before we leave and make that our honeymoon."

She closed her eyes and envisioned a ship, a big one, its open deck crowded with people. Every face is turned east, gazing east to the horizon. No one is looking back. There would be no looking back.

"And once we're there, we'll get some land," he said, "I don't know how, but we'll get it. And farm it, grow things. Melons, lettuce hell, rutabagas, who knows? Maybe even a vineyard. I think I might just fancy owning a vineyard."

Roza, having never seen a vineyard, tried to imagine one.

"And while we're at it," he went on, "we'll grow babies, too, lots of babies. How many little Silvers did you say you wanted to have?"

"Four. I want four, two boys and two girls."

"Four it is then. And we'll name them—I've been giving this some thought lately, Raizele, tell me what you think—we'll name them, each and every one of them, after the dead. I like that idea. I think it'd do both of us good. Maybe the dead won't feel so dead with their names on our lips again."

This was news to her. She raised herself on an elbow, and embracing him with her eyes, cupped his chin in one hand. That he would wish to name their children thus brought a lump to her throat, a swelling in her heart. Not that she needed reminding, but such was the goodness, the moxie of which this man of hers was made. Should she indeed find her life gifted with two daughters one day, the names Faige and Shoshonna would live again.

Leaning forward, she kissed him lightly but lingeringly on the mouth, then began to walk her own ever so slowly down his body. When she came to his right armpit, she stopped and let herself hover there, a dreamy look on her face. With soap all but nonexistent, and the taps in the washrooms not always working—and even when they were, the liquid that dribbled out a disconcerting brown—bathing as they'd once known it, with plenty of suds and hot water, was an extravagance unheard of for all but a few prisoners. But though Roza would have been the last to deny either the necessity or pleasures of a good scrubbing now and then, she had to admit, in one regard anyway, that life without a bathtub wasn't entirely to her unliking.

She'd felt the allure of the body's natural perfumes since adolescence, and on many an occasion during their more intimate moments in the ghetto had shared her taste for them with Godel. He for his part had always loved it that unlike some foolish and misguided girls, she didn't shave under her arms. Not only had the ostentatiously sexual fur that flourished there turned him on visually, but he'd called the two black, bushy tufts she'd once cultivated her little powder-puffs, in that they helped to disseminate, as he put it, that mouth-watering scent of hers. Now, of course, they were gone, as were his and every prisoner's, casualties of that monthly denuding that was lice control.

Irrespective of when it had begun, it was here in Birkenau, more even than before, that Roza had come to relish the distinctive aroma of the not entirely unwashed but certainly undeodorized armpit, both Godel's and her own. Not only was there something thrillingly animal about it, primal, something that fanned the flames of her unapologetically strong libido, it was also an old friend, a smell from a time before Birkenau, when the world, if not perfect, was at least not insane. It was a spice, familiar yet exotic at the same time, that triggered memories, brought back feelings of happier days, of growing up, growing fecund, discovering sex, becoming a woman. Though she much favored her lover's, his visits were infrequent. But again, even if only her own underarms, at least she was able to treat her nostrils to the sweet stink of life when so moved instead of the death-stench of burning flesh that permeated the lager.

Besides, it was only May, the sticky heat of deep summer still weeks away. And seeing as how the underground had wangled Godel a job as a locksmith (an occupation propitious, too, in that it didn't restrict him to Auschwitz), he, like she, was spared heavy physical labor. Consequently, they were able to keep themselves, even with the camps' woeful washrooms, if not civilian-fresh then clean enough for each other.

After getting her fill of his pungence up top, she resumed her leisurely descent down his body, dallying at his nipples, briefly tonguing his navel, before moving on toward that part of him that was her ultimate destination. When shortly she did arrive there, it was to do nothing at first but nuzzle into his manhood as she might into a pillow. And though her mouth was soon enthusiastically working its magic, she didn't stay down there for long. That was only meant to revive him, snap him back to attention. The next minute she was squirming, impaled, on top of him, then riding him like a horse, riding him bareback, her frantic bouncing loosing a desperate keening from her throat along with several rivulets of sweat down her back.

Time as the two knew it ceased to exist. For an eternity of a moment they lived for that moment alone, adrift in its deliciousness, lost in its splendor—until finally, simultaneously, they collapsed into a wet heap, shiny with perspiration, panting like dogs. For some time, they lay there too spent to move but for their hands feebly stroking the other, the occasional chaste kiss.

It was Godel who broke the silence, and with it the spell. "I'm not sure," he whispered into her ear, "and it pains me to say it, dearest, but I think our time's about up. Shouldn't we be getting dressed?"

"Oh please, no, not just yet. Can't we lie here a little longer? You feel so good, and it's going to be a while, a long while I'm afraid, before we can do this again."

So there they remained until it was almost too late, until their complicit kapo's footsteps sounded in the hall. Given the risk he was taking generally, and his exposure at that moment specifically, he would be angry if they weren't ready to leave on the instant. They barely had time to jump into their clothes before his key was in the lock and the door swinging open.

Summer

Kapo Kaminski had to have one last look at the three "potato mashers", as if to verify that they really existed. A hole in the drywall near the baseboard waited to receive them; once the grenades were inserted, the hole would be plastered over.

He opened the canvas sack and peered inside. The miraculous little bombs glinted dully back at him in the light from the electric bulb overhead, three German army-issue beauties of the sort used in combat, their long stems attached to heads the size and shape of tin cans. It was still hard to believe that Battle Group-Sonderkommando could claim them as its own.

After a few seconds, he knotted the bag and shoved it into the hole. It was only through dumb luck, of course, that they'd fallen into Sonder hands. Though Kaminski wasn't there, he learned later how it happened. The word had been out for a while that Crematorium I in the main camp was about to be closed permanently; since the transports had increased starting the summer before, it had had to be shut down more than once anyway, at times for up to a week. Built as it was in the camp's earlier, less homicidal days, it wasn't designed for such heavy use. The main problem was the smokestack. The firebricks composing its inner lining kept crumbling, not only blocking the flue but threatening the entire structure with collapse. Though these were replaced by a new layer of brick, this also proved inadequate, and the problem persisted.

With the completion in June of Crematorium III (Kaminski not unexpectedly having been appointed its Chief Kapo), and all four of the death houses finally on line, the Nazis deemed the original more trouble than it was worth. Its ovens and related equipment were dismantled, crated, and shipped west to the Dachau camp, for use in a crematorium

150

in the planning stages there. Even before this dismantling began, the eight Ukrainian ex-Red Army soldiers that made up its guard, who sharing their people's hatred of both Stalin and the Jews had volunteered for the SS after the Wehrmacht's invasion of Russia, suspected that because of their nationality, they, too, might be considered expendable. Attempting to flee, they were overtaken, and in the brief battle that ensued all eight were killed. Their remains were trucked back to Crematorium I, where ironically theirs were the last bodies burned in its ovens. The two gas bunkers in the birch woods were decommissioned as well, the smaller one and its undressing barracks demolished for their brick and lumber. The Germans were confident that their bigger, better, newer death machinery would be more than sufficient for their purposes.

Prior to their incineration, the bodies of the eight Ukrainians were searched by the Sonderkommando for cigarettes, and the three grenades discovered in their clothing. Within the week, these had made it to Birkenau and Crematorium III.

Yankel Handelsman pulled up a chair and sat across from Kaminski, who was by now lying fully clothed atop his bed. It wasn't long before lights-out. "They're a sight for sore eyes, aren't they?" he said to his kapo.

"What, the grenades?" Kaminski didn't look at him, his gaze fixed instead on the bottom of the bunk above. "I suppose so," he sighed, "but in a way I would rather it a sight these sore eyes had been spared."

"I'm.... afraid I don't follow," Handelsman said.

"Think about it, Yankel. This is our biggest haul since we started shopping for weapons, three lousy grenades! Don't get me wrong, I'm more than happy to have them, but they also drive home the point how little progress we've made."

This was true. The search for arms had so far been a frustrating one. Aside from the grenades, all the rebels had to show for their efforts was a single pistol, that and assorted calibers of ammunition should they in the end wind up with the guns to match. Both the pistol and bullets had come from the military salvage yard located just south of the Stammlager. It was there that the Luftwaffe and Wehrmacht sent wrecked aircraft, trucks and other personnel carriers, even disabled tanks to be cannibalized for usable parts and materials. The machinists dismembering these, clad in the striped burlap of the camp, were no more immune than any group of prisoners to the temptations of the black market. Most of what they smuggled out and sold were various metal parts and fittings, but had been known to chance upon ammo and even small arms hidden in the wrecks.

Thus had the Sonder come by their Luger. "But what of our alleged brother insurrectionists in the main camp?" Handelsman asked. "I still don't understand why they haven't been of more help."

"It would appear," said Kaminski, "that we have two friends with any pull, and two alone, in Battle Group-Auschwitz: Bruno Baum, and to a lesser extent, his emissary Noah Zabludowicz. And neither has been able to persuade the Poles in the Resistance to share what weapons they do have at their disposal with a bunch of Birkenau Jews. We can thank our stars for our brothers and sisters at the Weichsel-Union factory, and those brave souls helping them. A good amount of gunpowder, as you know, professor, continues to reach us, but as you of all people are also aware—"

Handelsman finished the sentence for him. "We have yet to find a way to make a serviceable hand grenade. Dynamite, yes, for the blowing up of the crematoria, but in the fight to follow we're going to need grenades. Nor, I regret to say, do I have anything new to report on that front."

As one of Commander Kaminski's top aides in the Battle Group, Handelsman had been put in charge of developing a proper hand grenade, only to find the squad bereft of anyone with the least idea how to go about constructing such a thing. Though just turned thirty and possessed of a face that looked even younger, he was already balding heavily in both front and back. It was a face shared by a good many Poles: high, chiseled cheekbones, a thinly bridged nose, the lips perpetually pursed as if in disapproval or awaiting a kiss. The dark eyes were shrewd as a weasel's, yet there was a gentleness to them also. One could tell by listening to him, from his diction and vocabulary, that he'd been blessed with a first-rate education, a pair of round, wire-rimmed spectacles reinforcing the impression. In addition to committing the crime of having been born a Jew, he was also political. A Communist labor organizer by trade, in 1939 he'd escaped Poland for France, only to have the Nazis catch up with him a year later. Slow to anger, fast with a smile, he was liked and respected by all; everyone from Kaminski on down addressed him affectionately as "the professor." It was an epithet in which, though he'd never have admitted it aloud, Handelsman took a sneaking pride.

"It seems to me," his kapo went on, "and possibly you as well, that our best hope for help might lie outside the wire."

"You're referring, I suppose, to the partisans."

Kaminski nodded. "And the drop they made the other night, lacking as it was."

For some weeks now, Soviet bombers had been making forays into the area at night, their targets the industries concentrated at Monowitz. In the air-raid alerts that resulted, once the sirens started wailing, all but those Sonder dealing with live deportees were taken to whatever gas chamber wasn't in use. These had been picked to serve as the squad's bomb shelters.

This wasn't easy on the nerves, nor was it the threat of bombs raining from the sky that had the men in the chamber on tenterhooks. It would have been a simple matter for their guards to bolt the door, and with a tin of Zyklon-B put an end to this 9th Special Squad. It had long passed its allotted life span as it was, and though its members knew the Nazis were loath to eliminate the technicians among them, this did little to allay their fears. They also knew that the SS could be both erratic and lazy, and how better to safeguard their foul secret yet again than to do so during one of these air raids, with all of their cats, so to speak, in one bag.

For the Sonder, therefore, every minute of one of these alerts felt like twenty, and they often dragged on for hours. The most recent had lasted three, after which they'd been escorted either back to work or their barracks. In the morning, however, a surprise was waiting for them in the farthest corner of one of the crematorium yards. During the blackout, a group of partisans had penetrated Birkenau's outer and inner cordons all the way to the wire enclosing Number Five. This, these men, these fearless, then proceeded to cut, leaving a cache of gifts for the Sonder to find: a two-way radio, a pair of field glasses, two compasses and some maps, plus a well-intentioned if superfluous offering of food, clothing, and medicine.

"But no guns," Handelsman said. "Or weapons of any sort."

"No," said Kaminski, "but if I can get Noah to petition his superior Baum to use his powers to convince the Armia to leave something more substantial next time, then we might be in business. Anyway, it's worth a shot."

Alas, it was not to be. The Home Army took its orders from Cyrankiewicz, not Baum, and he was in no hurry at this point to increase the Sonders' firepower. The incident at the wire, though, had given Kaminski an idea. His men had become adept at supplying themselves with more than enough to eat, nor did they want for clothes. And their pharmacy, thanks to the transports, was equal to that of the SS. The question begged itself: what then to do with the partisans' munificence?

On the other side of the road bounding the southern edge of Crematorium II's courtyard stretched the *B1c* lager of the huge tripartite women's camp. Occasionally, the Sonder would catch a glimpse of its occupants from afar, and after the distribution of the women's bread at night, the rise and fall of their bird-like chatter would often waft toward them on the breeze. Many were new arrivals, these prisoners of C Camp, fresh from quarantine, still in shock at their surroundings, still in denial, some of them, that the Grim Reaper's scythe had cut a swath through their families. That they, too, would soon be dead of starvation and disease—of pulling plows and building roads on eight hundred calories a day—they had yet to realize, though by the time they did they wouldn't much care. By then they would be well on their way to becoming Muselmänner, mindless, cringing caricatures of their former selves. By then it would be too late for anyone short of God to help them.

But it wasn't too late now. If they chose to, the Sonder might make a difference to some. And he, Kaminski, decided to do just that. Starting posthaste. What was more, he knew how he was going to do it.

The hard part was gaining access to C Camp in the first place, no easy trick for a gang of men. During the day, though, and even at night, construction crews still frequented its grounds, putting the finishing touches on what was the last exclusively female lager to be built. It shouldn't be that difficult, or so he reasoned, for a dozen or more Sonder to enter posing as one of those crews. By bribery if nothing else, if that was what it took. Nor would the sacks they'd be lugging at their sides contain tools, but rather the food and medicines the partisans had left them.

Once inside, they would locate the more lenient block elders and other functionaries—there were always some who took pity on their charges—and arrange for the wealth to be distributed among the inmates, either by appealing to the elders' humanity, or again if necessary, by greasing their palms.

It worked, too, like a charm. Everyone from the *Rottenführer* commanding the *B1c* guard gate to the blockovas inside the camp had from the first, if for a price most of them, been more than cooperative. And continued to be, the Sonder having elected, with a little push from their kapo, to make the charity permanent by donating some of their own stores. Not that the stunt was attempted every day, or even every few days, but often enough to alleviate much misery, and as time went on, for attachments to form between some of the female prisoners and their Good Samaritans. In light of the biological imperatives that drive men and women, this was to be expected. But it wasn't just about sex. Of greater motivation to those men seeking to ease the suffering in C Camp was the desire to have someone to care for again. Severed from their families forever, alone in the affectionless vacuum of the Vernichtungslager, each needed a person to feel tenderly toward him and on whom he could lavish tenderness in return. Having failed to protect their own wives, mothers, sisters, it was important they have someone they could look after now.

None of this came cheap, of course, but Kaminski didn't care. He would have spent twice as much. Not that his motives were entirely humanitarian; there was a selfishness to them, too, an attempt at atonement. Engaged as he was in the obliteration of his race, he felt the need to offset this by doing what he could for those of his people still living. He might be reducing to ashes those they loved most in the world, but if he could contribute to even one of these women surviving, at least some of the debt that was his complicity would be paid.

The Sonder assembled their formidable riches from a variety of sources. The dental commandos that worked the oven rooms pocketed their share of gold teeth at the job site. Those of the squad chosen to gather the clothing of the dead bound for the Bekleidungskammer each sported a penknife, with which, when their guards weren't looking, they would investigate any unusual bulges in the garments. Often these yielded diamonds and cash.

An even greater wellspring of Sonder wealth was a room on the ground floor of Crematorium III. One of the more restricted areas in the camp, a sign on its door prohibited entry to not only prisoners but all SS who had no business there. This *Goldarb*, or gold foundry, had been moved from Auschwitz to Birkenau just this summer, no doubt to be nearer its source of supply. Manned by two Jewish goldsmiths from the Stammlager and one from its new home, the articles laid before the three consisted in the main of the gold teeth of the slain. These were soaked in tubs of hydrochloric

acid to dissolve any remnants of flesh and bone adhering to them. Using
blowtorches, the smiths then melted the gold and cast it in either ingots
of up to a kilogram in weight or round disks an inch high and two across.
These tipped the scales at one hundred and forty grams, or five ounces.

It wasn't just teeth, though, that were mined for their metal. Everything
from jewelry to timepieces to gold cigarette cases and lighters were brought
to the foundry in Number Three and melted down. With the spike in the
number of transports so far this summer, it wasn't uncommon for this
workshop to crank out fifteen or even more pounds of ingots and cylinders
in a single day.

Kaminski knew this because one of the goldsmiths had told him
as much. Though not even his status as head kapo of the crematorium
allowed him into its Goldarb, it did make it easy to approach the three
metallurgists after their day was done, in one of whom he saw a potential
collaborator. The man's name was Karolyan, a young Jew from Krakow
whose wife and child had perished in the bunkers. Short of revealing that
an armed uprising was in the works, Kaminski told him that any gold he
might be able to put at the disposal of the Sonder would sooner than later
have dire, even lethal consequences for those who'd murdered his family.

Karolyan was all for this. Soon Kaminski was in regular receipt of a not
inconsiderable number of the five-ounce gold cylinders. Both convenient
and precise, this "coin" would prove the perfect unit of exchange on the
black market. The larger ingot was too pricey for most purchases, while
the gold teeth from which both came, though long employed as currency,
weren't only inexact but affronts to the eye.

Not that those in the Special Squad were the only ones engaged in
plundering the Third Reich of its ill-gotten gains. The individual SS could
be just as larcenous. More than once, Kaminski had caught them rifling
the clothing left behind in the undressing rooms. Zalman Leventhal could
cite a far more egregious example, witnessed months ago while he was
working one of the gas bunkers in the woods.

"We were resting, my squad and I, at the edge of the trees behind
the death house, waiting for the next group of naked to appear. A few
of us noticed an officer we'd never seen before, a handsome young
Untersturmführer busying himself among the rows of dead lying on
their backs. At first we thought he was checking up on the tooth-pulling

156

commando to make sure it had done its work properly. Upon watching further, however, we saw that he had a pair of pliers and was wrenching the teeth out himself, depositing them in a coffee can on the ground beside him."

Leventhal would smile sadly then. "It was obvious he planned on keeping these for himself. After a while, his progress brought him near us, whom he seemed to see for the first time. Turning to face us, and with a grin somehow conspiratorial and contemptuous at the same time, he held the can out in front of him and noisily rattled its contents. He then went back to his pliers, as if we weren't there."

But again, though outrageous, that was but one individual's avarice, as nothing to the concerted and collectivized greed exhibited by the Germans in their quest to profit from mass murder. As much as any blasphemy he'd observed or been a part of, Kaminski was shaken to his core by the exploitation of Jewish corpses for industrial and commercial purposes. The killing of innocent people was unacceptable enough, but to violate their persons afterward both shouted a cynical disregard for the dead as well as underscored the Nazi tenet that Jews weren't fully human to begin with.

Though the harvesting of dental gold was by far the most lucrative of these endeavors, the SS didn't stop there. Those bones not completely incinerated were broken into fragments and mixed with crushed limestone with which to pave roads. The mountains of ash that were once people served an aggregate of uses: as insulation in construction, as fill in the reclaiming of bogs and other lowlands, even as fertilizer for the gardens and croplands of the camp.

Of all the raw materials reaped from the bodies of the dead, however, none was utilized in as many different ways as human hair. This was sold by the ton to German industry, where it was employed in the manufacture of felt, yarn and other threads, and certain fabrics. Mattresses were stuffed with it, as were pillows and quilts, and it helped to strengthen rugs and carpets. The military also coveted it. The heavy ropes used on ships consisted in part of hair, and since it expands and contracts uniformly in conditions of extreme humidity, it was packed into the business ends of submarine torpedoes and delayed ignition bombs. Odds were that some of the U-boat crews firing those torpedoes were wearing socks into which the hair of dead Jewish females had been woven.

Kaminski, of course, could know none of this, though he would have had to be blind not to take note of the diligence the SS showed in their pursuit of what they clearly considered a prized resource. Few were the corpses he'd burned or seen burn with hair longer than a few inches. He was reminded of the Nazi preoccupation with hair one day when the *Kommandoführer* of Crematorium III, SS-*Oberscharführer* Muhsfeld, ordered him to square away the attic of the building for its role as the site of what was to be a permanent operation.

"We'll call the men working it the *Reinkommando*," Muhsfeld said, "the cleaning squad."

As part of his strategy for survival, Kaminski had taught himself a rudimentary German. "And what, Herr Sergeant, are they to clean?"

"Women's hair."

Kaminski stared at him, blinking. "Excuse me…. did you say hair?"

"*Women's* hair, that taken from the living as well as the dead. You find that surprising?"

"Now that I think about it, sir, no."

Muhsfeld made an impatient clucking noise. With his pencil-moustache, cropped scalp, and trim build, he was the picture of the Prussian military man. He drank, and heavily, but was never sloppy about it, his uniform always perfect, his posture board-rigid. He was dangerous in that he was unpredictable; he could be almost sociable with a prisoner one minute, turn around and shoot him dead the next. Kaminski had seen him do it.

"As you shouldn't," the sergeant snapped. "There's a lot of money to be made from hair. Why do you think we've had you people collecting it all this time?"

From Muhsfeld's expression, he thought it best to keep quiet.

"Anyway, the men of the Reinkommando are to wash, chemically treat, and dry the hair given them to prepare it for shipment by rail. You will be told the details later. Your job once the attic is in order is to assemble the squad, and in that you are free to choose anyone you wish. My only stipulation is no idlers or kids. Remember, you as kapo will be held responsible for the operation's success."

Though located in Crematorium III, every member of this new command but one wound up coming from outside the Sonder. Nor was this by chance. For several days, Kaminski made regular visits to the unloading ramp bearing a pass signed by the *Oberscharführer* permitting him to select and take with him any deportee he desired. By week's end, he'd gathered a group of older men only, many in or near their seventies, and all of them either rabbis or dayans.

As with the help he was still extending to the women of C Camp, his reasons for rescuing these aged holy men from the flames weren't solely altruistic. Though not observant himself, he sensed the necessity of keeping the Jewish religious tradition alive, and if in a small way, saw in the Reinkommando an opportunity to do so. The work itself would be neither strenuous nor time-consuming, allowing his rabbis to devote themselves to the study and interpretation of Scripture, the recitation of prayers, and the perpetuation of Mosaic law and belief in their ancient God. Hadn't the prophets promoted the same agenda during the Babylonian exile and the Assyrian conquest? As far as he was concerned, if Ezekiel and Isaiah had viewed the preservation of the Jewish faith as imperative, that was good enough for him.

Muhsfeld, while initially disapproving of Kaminski's choices, soon found the whole thing humorous, and a chance to have a little fun at his kapo's expense. "Graybeards in the Sonderkommando!" he would jeer. "What's next, Kaminski, women?" Or: "We build a crematorium and you try to turn it into a synagogue." Or: "I've finally figured out why you insisted on stocking your attic with senior citizens, kapo. So you wouldn't be the oldest man in the squad anymore."

Crematorium III now had two workplaces to be found nowhere else in either camp. But though the hair-drying room, unlike the gold foundry, was not a restricted area, it didn't get many visitors. Situated at one end of the spacious attic, it was a spooky place, ill-lit and claustrophobic. Most of it was taken up by an impossible tangle of clotheslines, a crisscrossing skein of drooping cords from which hung long knouts of hair in a hodgepodge of colors, from purest white to raven black. It was a maze as difficult to look at as it was to navigate, inviting comparison to an image from the American Old West: strings of scalps hanging in the teepee of a wild Indian war chief. Even the floor was covered with hair, row after row of it laid out to dry in the heat rising from the ovens. Each stolen tuft told a different sad story, the grandmother's salt-and-pepper, the wife and mother's long, lush mane, the curly ringlets of what was once a bouncing little girl. Kaminski never went upstairs any more than he had to, and invariably left this macabre loft with a heavier heart than when he'd entered.

The lone exception he'd made to the advanced ages and outsider status of this new detachment was, for two reasons, a logical one. Its only member to come from the Sonderkommando was the dayan Leyb Langfus. That the man's faith was as unassailable as the most pious of the older rabbis, there was no disputing. And by choosing Langfus, Kaminski was safeguarding one of his ablest warriors. Having in a rare moment of benevolence given the dayan the job of burning the "trash" from the transports, the fickle Muhsfeld could just as easily decide to rescind the offer and have him shot for refusing gas chamber and crematory duty. Sequestered in Number Three's attic, however, he would for all practical purposes be out of the *Scharführer's* reach.

It coming as no surprise to his kapo, Langfus quickly assumed leadership of the group of newly arrived rabbis, all of whom were still in shock at the waking nightmare that was Birkenau. It wasn't just this, though, that gave him the advantage. He may have been younger than they, therefore lacking in the astuteness only the years can bestow, but did possess attributes that in the context of this time and place were seldom found in anyone, of any age. As evidenced by his refusal to do Sonder work or eat Sonder food, his moral fiber was without peer, his principles carved in granite. But when it came to offering what comfort he could to those around him, be it a deportee in the undressing room or one of his own in despond, his heart was softest soapstone. Unimpressive in appearance, if not downright comical—tall, ungainly, he walked with a slight stoop, his thick black glasses forever threatening to slide off his nose—he was nevertheless blessed with the gift of oratory, his deep voice made the more mellifluous by the power of its conviction. He was a natural speaker, and could be a passionate one, though his words generally had the effect of calming rather than exciting. One might disagree with or tire of him, especially when he got on his religious high horse, but it would have taken a real *schmuck* to shut one's eyes to his good points.

His value to Kaminski, however, lay elsewhere. This Langfus may have been a man of God, but he was also a man of action, not at all the sort to hide behind his Bible, content to let that God do his fighting for him. He was as insistive of armed revolt as anyone in Battle Group-Sonderkommando, as Leventhal, Gradowski, Handelsman, Warszawski, and like them not only did everything his general asked of him to further it but never quit pestering him as to when it could be expected.

He'd done so just the other day. Having noticed the dayan acting out of character of late, standoffish, if not out and out sullen, Kaminski took him aside and asked him what was wrong.

"You know as well as I do what's wrong, kapo," he said. "Is that mutiny we were promised still in our future, or was that just a lot of talk? Our so-called allies in the Stammlager may be saying all the right things, but they don't appear in any hurry to turn their words into deeds."

"The underground, yes." Kaminski frowned in sympathy. "It's frustrating, I know, I won't say it isn't. But you could also make a case that it's still early. We've got what—a single pistol, three grenades, a little dynamite? How far are those going to get us? Not past that barbed wire, that's for damned sure."

"But Auschwitz has yet to come up with a plan even!" Langfus cried, spreading his arms in exasperation. "There has to be a plan, a strategy of attack. Something, and in detail, for us to familiarize ourselves with and prepare for. Have they told you *anything* about how they intend to pull this off?"

"Some, yes, but—"

The dayan cut him short. "I saw something. Last week," he said, letting his arms fall and his voice with them. "I've seen a lot of things, we all have. Terrible things. This, though…." He looked away. "This was unforgivable."

"What was?" Kaminski asked. "Tell me what you saw."

"Children, a couple of hundred of them. From…. Greece, yes, they had to have been. But—but I can't—With my own eyes I saw it, what the SS did to those children, but I still can't believe it. Still can't believe it."

Kaminski laid a hand on his shoulder. "Tell me, Leyb, what was it?" he said, though he didn't want to know. Was dreading to know. "Why keep it bottled up? Maybe it'll help to talk about it."

"It won't help. And you know it won't. Nothing's going to help, nothing short of us putting a stop to the madness ourselves. We've got to put a stop to it, and we've got to do it soon. I mean, these were *little* children, kapo, none older than eight or nine. What's wrong with people that they could do such a thing to a child?"

Good question, a goddamned good one, Kaminski told himself later. But a question without an answer—or perhaps too many.

The dayan never did tell anyone what he saw. Nor was it because by recounting it he'd be forced to relive it. What was sealing his lips was a certain misgiving the incident had raised, a kernel of doubt that had taken root in him where none had before, not even upon his learning of the murder of his own wife and baby boy.

Though Langfus wouldn't have dreamed it possible, this doubt was directed at his God. Not that he dared question the Divinity's existence or His dominion, but rather whether He possessed an acceptable quantum of mercy. Was He in fact the loving God the dayan had been raised to believe, or an indifferent, even a cruel One? If those last, that would make Him no less powerful and omniscient, but certainly less deserving of man's love in return. It was one thing to surrender adults to an agonizing end, quite another to permit children to suffer such a death. The gas chambers, granted, claimed their portion of younger victims, as they'd claimed his precious son, but to watch them die as they'd died in front of his eyes the other day, to watch them die like *that*, left him at a loss for words. Except for one: why?

He found himself in uncharted territory. A crack, the thinnest hairline but a crack nonetheless, had appeared in the foundation of the monolithic temple that was his faith. And if what he'd had the misfortune of witnessing that morning had caused him, the Makover dayan, the champion of his God, to call into question that God's infinite goodness, how might his repeating of the tale affect those less devout? The last thing he wanted was to further damage the already soured religious sentiments of his brother Sonder. Which was why he'd chosen to keep the episode to himself, and counted himself fortunate that no one had been there to see it with him.

Except, of course, for the twenty or so Sonder dragooned into working it. And there was nothing to be done about them beyond not adding his voice to the ugly story he was sure they'd be bringing back to the barracks with them.

He needn't have worried. He never heard a word about the matter, then or later. Curious, he approached one of those forced to take part in the massacre, someone he knew from his hometown, but the man not only refused to discuss it with him, he got angry almost to the point of blows that Langfus had asked him about it. Clearly, the twenty present that awful day were either too traumatized or shamed, or both, to admit their involvement. As far as the dayan knew, to a man they kept their mouths shut about it.

It was understandable that so many of the Special Squad should have turned their faces from God. Made to escort an endless parade of the naked and defenseless into gas chambers, then burn them afterward like so many bags of garbage, most found it hard to retain either their belief in a Divine Being, or conceding that, their continued respect for Him. The word guilt wasn't strong enough, nor betrayal, nor disgust; a new vocabulary was needed to describe the forces at work on the Sonder as the days and the bodies and the tears piled up, and still the people kept coming as if they would never stop.

But as distressing as he found this erosion of their faith, Langfus was careful never to bring religion up. Seeing as how he was spared most of the obscenities heaped on them, he didn't feel he had the right to. He didn't shy, however, when they broached the subject themselves, from taking a position that argued on the side of the angels.

Not long after talking to Kaminski, and upon making his way one morning to Crematorium III, he ran into the last of Sonder Squad 57B, the night shift, returning from work to Block 13. Even in the half-light of dawn, he could see the blood on their clothes.

"Well, look here," said one of the group of half a dozen, a short, muscular boy named Menachem not yet out of his teens. Langfus recognized him from the barracks. "If it isn't the prophet on his way to the mountaintop. How's the view from up there, holy man? Any windows in that attic?"

The rest snickered at the sarcasm, which drew a smile from Langfus, too. "Not the part of it I work in, Menachem. Which is just as well, wouldn't you say?"

"Yes," said the boy, "I suppose it is. So how'd you sleep last night, rabbi? Pleasant dreams, I hope."

"No.... no dreams, thank God."

"That's even better, is always better. Guess I don't have to tell you what we were up all night doing. More women and children than usual, or so it seemed, didn't it, boys?"

A few nodded, every face somber again.

"I'm so sorry, son," Langfus said, "but what choice did you have? God will understand."

Menachem leaned to his right and spat. "There's that name again," he said, wiping his mouth with his sleeve. "Refresh my memory, will you, rabbi? Who the hell is this *God* you keep mentioning?"

Langfus responded as if to a legitimate question. "The one true God of our fathers. The God of Abraham and Moses."

"Oh…. Him," Menachem said. "Yes, I remember Him. He went away a while back, didn't He? For good it looks like, too. But He did leave a message, want to read it? It's written right here."

The boy pulled up his sleeve to reveal the five-digit tattoo.

Langfus looked at it, then back to the unsmiling face above it. "Yes, I, too, bear the Gentile's blasphemous mark," he said. "But I'm afraid you're mistaken if you think God went away. We're hardly the first—"

"Mistaken, you say?" He stretched a hand to the horizon. "Take a look around, why don't you?"

The dayan, feeling his pain, wished only to alleviate it. "We're hardly the first Jews in history," he began again, "God would seem to have abandoned. How many times in the synagogue have I read aloud from the Book of Esther, which tells of the Persian Empire's attempt to annihilate its conquered Jews? And what of our three-hundred year bondage in Egypt, or the generations of Babylonian exile? On all three occasions, God, to Whom the centuries are but seconds, delivered us from the oppressor."

"Well, He'd better hurry this time," Menachem said, turning with a grin to the others, "or He's liable to wake up one day and find no one left to deliver."

Far from taking offense, Langfus smiled himself while waiting for the laughter to die down. "Tell me," he said then, gazing at each in turn, "would you consider yourselves enemies of the Germans? Do you not loathe the very ground they walk on?"

A murmur of affirmatives.

"Let us not talk then of God abandoning you, but of you abandoning Him. Don't you see what you're doing? Exactly what the SS want you to. To lose one's faith is a kind of death in itself. The Nazis would kill you twice, first your soul, then your body. Before they steal your flesh, they must rob you of your heritage, that is how arrogant, how enamored of their power they are. They've slain your families, your friends—would you allow them the victory of murdering your God, too?"

There were a few smirks, but his question went unanswered.

"God has not deserted us. He has designs beyond our vision, beyond the scope of our understanding. To dust off the old adage, He works in mysterious ways. Look at it like this: forget the three hundred years in Egypt—our people have been denied their homeland for almost *two thousand* years, scattered to the winds after the Roman legions destroyed Jerusalem and the Second Temple. Yet we have not been extinguished. God will not let us be extinguished. He has a plan for us still, a purpose, the particulars of which we're simply unaware."

Another stepped forward, a boy little older than the first. "Rubbish," he said. "Menachem is right. We're dying by the thousands every day, the tens of thousands every week. And that at this one camp alone. How can God's purpose for us be served if the Jewish race is wiped out, if none remain to carry it through?"

"Which is why we won't be wiped out," Langfus said. "Again, God won't let us be. Throughout history, my brothers, there have been pharaohs who would exterminate us. As we've managed with God's blessing, praise be the Most Holy, to survive until now, we will survive this as well, this latest holocaust. Jewish suffering is not new. But for its brutish technology, Birkenau is not new. The Bible, if you'll recall your Ecclesiastes, is most precise on this point: 'What has been will be again, what has been done will be done again; there is nothing new under the sun.' One of the main lessons, in fact, to be learned from the Bible is that what happened to the fathers is often visited on the sons."

"Does that mean," the new boy sneered, "that because the Egyptians and Persians and who knows how many others persecuted us, it's all right for the Nazis to?"

"Of course not." The dayan remained serene, his voice genial. "There can never be a justification for the slaughter of the blameless. All I'm saying is that the Bible should not be read as mere yesteryear, as a tale from the past, but as a guide to the present, something to help us in the here and now. Just as our forefathers persevered in their travails, kept the flame of their faith going, their trust in God alive, so must we also. And as in the end their descendants were rewarded for that perseverance, so will ours

165

be. When our people are in peril as they are now, the Talmud commands that each of us must think of himself not in contemporary terms, but as a Hebrew slave in Pharaoh's Egypt. If that slave and his countrymen had angered God by despairing of Him and renouncing their faith, there would have been no Moses, no Exodus, no gift of the land of Canaan. Are we to risk by our short-sightedness denying our children whatever recompense for our suffering God might have in store for them?"

"Children?" This from a third Sonder, older than the rest. "Which children, rabbi? The ones I lost the first day here, my two little girls, or the dozen I carried out of the gas chamber last night?"

"My poor man," Langfus said, wanting to embrace him but unsure if he should. "I, too, lost a child, along with his mother, but—"

"And why suffering?" the man persisted. "Why must we Jews always be suffering? We were doing just fine until the Germans came along. Is your God such a sadist that He would make His people bleed before giving them back what He took from them in the first place?"

Langfus looked skyward, as if searching there for an answer.

"Perhaps it is not God's intention," he said finally, "to restore the status quo, to make things as they were. Perhaps in His omniscience, His knowledge of the future, He's deemed our situation needful of change, radical change, so that in the end we may prosper as never before. Perhaps only by suffering to the degree we are now can this change come about. How can we know what the future holds? But God surely does, and maybe in light of it our present anguish is necessary.

"This, though, we can know, and summon much hope from: after our fathers fled Egypt, after proving themselves there, and with a couple of lapses, in the Sinai, God led them into Canaan, invited them to take the land of milk and honey as their own. Could something similar be awaiting us after the black night of Birkenau? Provided we remain steadfast and not renege on the covenant God forged with Abraham, might not our agony in the camps be our ticket to a new Canaan, perhaps even a return to Eretz Israel itself?"

He paused as if expecting this last to be met with jeers. But for the distant shouts from the Appellplatz of roll call, however, all was silence.

Encouraged, he plunged ahead. "Who can presume to understand God's plan? Who can penetrate His all-knowingness? If on the other hand, there is no plan, if He has in fact forsaken us—if you are right and I am wrong—allow me now in all humility to beg your forgiveness. For then God will have proved Himself a fraud and unworthy of us, and I as His cat's-paw will have done you a great disservice. False hope, as you know, as you've observed it in those walking meekly into the crematoria, can be more destructive than no hope at all.

"It'd be foolish, however, to give up on Him now, at this the eleventh hour. One way or another, it would appear that our future, our fate is about to be decided, either at the bloody hands of the Gentile or by the saving hand of God. After two thousand years of oppression and exile, why chance displeasing Him at the last minute? Remember, though protective, He is also a vain God, and jealous of our attention."

He turned to the third Sonder who'd spoken. "Yes, our children are gone. Nor is there any bringing them back. Some of us, however, maybe not those of us present, but some are going to have children again. There will be survivors, the SS can't kill us all. It would be a shame—no, a crime, would it not?—to deprive those children of their patrimony by incurring God's wrath with our rejection of Him. Just as it would if the dead were to end up dying for nothing."

Afterward, the dayan was philosophical. He hadn't convinced them, knew he hadn't, but that hadn't been his intention. He wept for the men of the Sonder, especially those of them not yet men, those little-more-than boys made to wade in the gore of the death house. In deference to their lot, whenever they obliged him to bring religion to the fore he made it a point to lose neither his solicitude nor poise. By approaching them in this way, not as a preacher or pontificator but as an equal, a friend, he could be forceful yet still come off as supportive, as someone who genuinely cared, a combination that tended to console them if not win them over. His words, while seldom changing their minds, did seem, by bringing their anger and pain into the open, to blunt the cutting edge of both. In spite of the emotions this stirred, his was an influence more anesthetic than anything, a balm on their psychic wounds, and that was all he ever really wanted in the first place. That and maybe to make them at least question their apostasy.

In the end, the six Sonder bid him what sounded like a sincere good day, which in itself was a victory considering the antipathy with which they'd greeted him. He could tell from this that maybe they weren't only a little less sure of their position but appreciated his attempt to buck up their spirits.

Not that they were the only ones to have gained from the exchange. Langfus, too, had benefited. Airing his convictions aloud had helped to clarify them in his mind, reinforce their validity, begin the process of restoring some peace to that mind. The *Sonderaktion*, or special action, taken against the Greek children, though appalling in its savagery, was made somewhat more explicable by the very arguments he'd advanced to the Sonder. That there was nothing new under the sun meant it wasn't the first time Jewish or any children had met so abominable an end. Horrendous as it may have been, it wasn't without precedent.

Nor was God necessarily to be blamed for its cruelty. Birkenau, though not novel in its bloodthirsty intent, remained as pitiless a killing ground as the world had ever seen. Excesses were bound to happen, but one had to remember: at Birkenau it wasn't God in the details, but the devil. It was the nature of the place that it should spawn such barbarisms as the one weighing on him now. If this offense against humanity had occurred anywhere else, in any other time, it would have caused the rocks to weep, the heavens to blacken. But here it was all in a day's work, hardly commonplace but not that out of the ordinary, either. If God did have a plan for His people requiring a good part of them be offered up for sacrifice, and if this and the other camps were the altars upon which that sacrifice was to be enacted, then such a fate as that which had overtaken those poor children was to be expected. God was no more responsible for it than the victims themselves. In a sense, He, too, was a victim in that this product of His love, this being He'd created, this Man, should be capable of such an enormity, such evil.

But while all of this may have gone a long way toward mending the dayan's fences with his God, to repairing that crack in the foundation of his faith, it did nothing to dispel the corrosive memory of the day in question. He could recall the Aktion in its every detail, both awake and in his dreams, and would continue to if somehow he were to reach an old age.

It had rained two nights prior to it, a dense, drenching rain, revealing some leaks in the crematorium roof. Not many, but enough—any stray water in the hair-drying attic was too much. As the youngest by far of the

Reinkommando, he was drafted to scale the roof and patch it. With two of the oldsters holding the ladder secure, he rose into the mid-morning sun with a bucket of tar and a brush.

He hadn't been up there thirty minutes when something below caught his eye, something peculiar, a convoy of open trucks lumbering from the direction of the unloading ramp toward a pine woods just east of the camp perimeter. This was unusual because there was nothing in that wood, nor even a road leading to it. The five trucks were bumping across an ungraded, grassy field. Four were heaped with corpses like so many broken dolls, two hundred of them if he were to guess, heads flopping in unison with every jolt, eyes wide-open and unblinking in the sun.

Even odder, these dead were fully clothed, something one never saw, but then he realized they must in fact have come from the ramp. Which, given their numbers, meant also that they'd arrived from somewhere far away, probably Greece. Those transports from distant climes, Greece in particular, often arrived with a good amount of their passengers dead already from thirst and overcrowding. He'd heard of one from the island of Crete, after three unimaginable weeks en route, showing up with *nobody* left alive but for a handful of the semi-comatose.

But why was this load of corpses being rushed to empty forest? The crematorium beneath him was still awaiting its first comers, and the fire pits nearby even more convenient.

It was then that he noticed the bodies seemed to be those of children only, very young children from the size of them. This was strangest of all. If fresh from the cattle cars, they should have been mixed all together, children with adults, young with old. Yet as far as he could tell, there wasn't a one much above the age of ten. Had they been brought here together in a group, and if so, from where—some boarding school, hospital, orphanage? Or perhaps the Nazis *had* culled them from the dead at the ramp, but for what purpose?

His curiosity getting the better of him, he climbed to the top of the roof and sat astride it. From there he could see for miles. He watched the trucks enter the trees and disappear under the foliage, then emerge after a hundred meters into a clearing and stop. From his perch, they weren't only plainly visible but within earshot.

Also plain all of a sudden was why they were there. A pair of small fire pits scarred the clearing, already stacked with kindling, though never had he seen any like these two. Instead of rectangular and deep, they were circular and fairly shallow, about ten, maybe twelve meters in diameter. Why the Germans should have gone to the trouble of having new holes dug was a mystery. Weren't the crematories they'd managed to contrive so far, both indoor and out, sufficient to dispose of these few remains? The new death factories did boast forty-six ovens between them.

Upon the convoy coming to a halt, from out of the fifth truck tumbled a squadron of SS and twenty Sonder. Instead of unloading the bodies and stacking them atop the pyres, the twenty immediately lit the latter, then sat down to wait. This only deepened the mystery, departing as it did from the usual sequence. Their guards, meanwhile, had begun to drink. Langfus could see the bottles passing back and forth between them, hear their voices grow louder as the liquor took effect. Later, he would learn that duty at a Sonderaktion, an operation outside the pale of the routine, typically entitled each volunteer to not only an extra ration of cigarettes but a half-liter of schnapps.

After ten minutes, both fires were blazing, though why he'd stuck around that long he had no idea. It wasn't as if he hadn't seen corpses burned before. Having ended up a while back on one of the labor details sent to dismantle Bunker I and its undressing barracks, he'd had to pass close enough to the fire pits to observe bellies bursting open from the heat, arms and legs slowly contorting as if their owners were still alive. It was a sight he'd vowed then to avoid in the future, yet that morning he remained a rapt audience, as alert at his roost as a sailor in his crow's nest.

Once the fires had crested then subsided a bit, the wood in them just starting to glow red at the tips, the order went out and the Sonder jumped to their feet. Working at a run, driven by the blackjacks and imprecations of the Germans, they lowered the gates of the trucks and began hauling the bodies out and dragging them to within tossing distance of the flames. From there they heaved them, still clothed, into the pits. The dayan watched for a minute before deciding he'd seen enough after all, and was heading back down to where he'd stopped working—when something froze him in his tracks, a sound to make the blood run cold, a broken, tormented wail that he thought at first torn from the throat of some animal.

As a young child, he'd come across a group of boys, thuggish, older boys, torturing a cat to death. He'd run from the scene horrified, but not before the unfortunate creature's yowl seared itself into his memory. That same sound assailed him now from the clearing below. He clambered back up top and shaded his eyes against the sun. Was that something moving? Yes, there in the farther pit, something was struggling to lift itself up.

It was a little boy, no older than four or five, every time he tried to raise himself he would fall screeching down again. He wasn't the only one, either. Soon other shapes were floundering and thrashing in the flames, other voices adding their shrieks to the original.

Langfus grew suddenly dizzy. He had to grab hold of the rooftop or he would have lost his balance. They weren't dead, these wretched children, not all of them anyway. Some were merely unconscious, survivors of who knew how many days in the stifling cattle cars.

That they were from Greece, there could now be no doubt. From his studies of the Septuagint, the Greek translation of the Bible, Langfus recognized the occasional word in their piteous cries. He also couldn't help noting that none were calling on their fathers and mothers to save them, but were pleading instead for the intercession of a Father Andros, a Sister Helena. Later, he would put them at having come from an orphanage.

But that was later. At the moment, his brain was reeling at what it was being asked to take in. Most of the children still alive when thrown into the fire were either too small or weak to do more than lie where they landed, arms flapping, legs kicking, screaming their little lungs out. Some of the older ones, however, succeeded in scrambling to the edges of the shallow pits from where they were attempting to hoist themselves out. But the Germans, experienced hands at this apparently, were ready for them. Two soldiers with long poles patrolled the circumference of each pyre, shoving these already badly burned children back into the conflagration. A boy of about seven, his clothing ablaze, did manage to get out and run howling from the inferno, only to lurch blindly for the second pit and plunge in headfirst, his fatal pratfall eliciting cheers from the drunker SS.

How long the tears had been coursing down his cheeks, Langfus couldn't say. All he knew was that they hadn't sprung from grief alone. There was anger behind them, too, a rage made the redder by his powerlessness to intervene in the crime happening right in front of him. If this outrage against the innocent wasn't enough to move one to defiance, to wanting to grab a gun and blast the laughter off its perpetrators' faces, then one was made of stone and not flesh. The Nazis were smart to finish the job begun in the cattle cars where they did, out of sight in the woods; if at the regular fire pits, there was no predicting what kind of storm it might have sparked.

After what felt like an eternity but was only minutes, the screams from the clearing grew fainter, then ceased. The blackening stumps that once were toddlers sizzled mute and unmoving in the fires. The Germans began to load their gear and start up the trucks. Two of these would return later to remove what evidence remained. Here and there, the dayan saw a Sonder bent double, vomiting into the grass. The rest stood in abject silence, waiting for orders, making sure to keep well away from each other. A Sonderkommando himself, he could relate to this; even if some had been disposed for whatever reason to conversation, what could they have said? Words, any words, would have rung worse than false.

He didn't remember finishing what had brought him to the roof, although he must have. It rained again two days later without further leaks. For one whole week, he wouldn't have anything to do with anyone, working in silence, eating alone, avoiding all overtures but for the one from Kaminski. He was both there and wasn't, like some will o' the wisp, some ghost flickering in and out of sight. A dozen times a day he would stop what he was doing and just stand there, staring into space as if lost in thought.

And so he was, laboring to reconcile what he'd seen from the crematorium roof with all that he'd been taught to value, to hold dear in life. Then came his dawn encounter with Menachem and the others, after which he began rapidly to come around, to be his old self again, his faith renewed. One of the first things he did upon reaching this point, having run out of both, was scare up some ink and paper.

Weeks before any of this, he'd sat down with the Zalmans Leventhal and Gradowski, and they'd agreed to work together at the business of holding the murderers accountable. He'd found a waterproof glass jar and in it had enclosed a log he'd been keeping since the ghetto, along with testimony from a fellow Sonder who'd spent time at Belzec. After burying it in the yard of Crematorium III, he'd felt like more of a man than he had in years. At long last he was fighting back, inflicting real damage on those who'd been molesting him and his people for so long. That this damage wouldn't be effected until the war was over and he was dead didn't matter. Planting that jar in the defiled soil of the crematorium was like planting a hundred daggers in the chests of as many SS.

He was hot to have another go at it. Indeed, as spokesman now for the dead, felt he had an obligation to. He also knew what his next effort was going to be about. How better to illustrate the utter heartlessness of the executioners than by recounting what he'd had the evil fortune to spy that day from the roof?

Though he'd taken an instant liking to Gradowski, he didn't know quite what to make of his pal Leventhal. In the redhead, he sensed an animosity he'd done nothing to provoke. He'd given some thought to confronting him about it, but in the end chose not to. As long as it didn't get worse or interfere with their new partnership, he was willing to ignore it. Personally, he admired the man. Both men. Unlike some others, each had retained his humanity in the face of great loss, and their actions since proof that no one was braver or more dedicated than they to waging war on those responsible for that loss.

It was important, they told him, that each man sign his depositions. The more traceable witnesses who came forth, the more believable their claims in what they were hoping would one day be the court of world opinion. Langfus had given much thought to this signature. He wanted it above all to reflect his militancy, his refusal to bend to the German tyrant. To that end, in his initial offering and as he would in those to come, he hadn't used his Yiddish but his Hebrew name, Arye Yehuda Regel Arucha (the last two words translating to "long foot"). But in what he'd be the first to admit was a stroke of whimsy, he decided also to make the finders of his testaments work a little harder in establishing their origin—which, incidentally, should they find them first, would make it more difficult for the SS as well. He elected, therefore, to adopt the acronym of that name as his signature, giving the historians of tomorrow a chance to play detective.

Less lighthearted was the request he'd be including in each jar asking those who discovered these time capsules after the war to gather the entries inscribed with the name A.Y.R.A. and print them together under one title.

He saw no reason to bandy words. It was his wish the collection be called "The Horrors of Murder."

*   *   *

As surprised as Noah Zabludowicz was to find his cousin Shlomo Kirschenbaum at Birkenau, he was even more taken aback to see him a member of the Sonderkommando.

Though they'd only met twice, and that when they were children, he remembered Shlomo well. He'd been a cheerful boy, big on cracking jokes, as quick to smile as he was to make others do the same. He was also a scrawny kid, nor had the years beefed him up much. No way would Noah have figured him for Sonder duty. In fact, one of the first questions he'd asked him, knowing the SS would never have picked him for his physique, was what breach of the rules had landed him in the Special Squad.

"Nothing," he'd replied, "I didn't have a chance to do anything. The Germans plucked me and some others straight off the unloading ramp, and the next thing I knew, I was emptying carts piled with corpses."

The two men had grown up in different countries. Noah's Aunt Alicia had married a German-Jewish businessman when she was young and gone to live with him in Heidelberg. It was there Shlomo was born. Twice they'd returned to Ciechanow to visit, once when he was nine, then again at fourteen. After Hitler came to power, the family fled to France, where eventually the Nazis and their war machine followed. By then Shlomo had a wife and child of his own, a baby boy. For two years, they lived under the German occupation, the last few months of it in the transit camp at Drancy. One day he was picked out of a line, hustled onto a cattle car, and shipped east. Petrified as he was for both himself and his family, he took some comfort in knowing they were safe at least. And if there was a God, would remain so.

It was a different cousin than he remembered that greeted Noah at the entrance to the Sonder compound. Kapo Kaminski had summoned him to Block 13 by placing the two bricks atop the wall, and there waiting at the gate with the kapo was Shlomo. Having got them together, Kaminski granted them their privacy and left.

"So," Noah lied, "you seem to be doing…. all right."

In truth, he could tell something wasn't right at all. Shlomo struck him as more mannequin than man; the eyes were open but empty, the face human but not. Gone was all trace of the light-hearted child, in its place the pathetic wreck of an adult with not only what looked a permanent frown but a voice bereft of life, a dry husk of a voice, that instead of the emotion a reunion of long-lost relatives should have kindled, possessed all the enthusiasm of someone reading from a grocery list.

"Doing all right?" If he hadn't forgotten how to smile, Shlomo might have here. "If you say so," he muttered, the frown carved in marble.

Not that Noah found his unapproachability odd. In the crucible that was Birkenau, one had to expect as much, especially from someone condemned to the commando of the living dead. It wasn't, however, exactly conducive to conversation. For a long, painfully long quarter of an hour, each in his way made an effort at this before having to admit defeat. But when they did part, it wasn't without embracing, though even Shlomo's hug lacked sincerity. It was as if he was going through the motions only, incapable anymore of showing real feeling.

Later, Noah was to discover why. During his second week of working the burning meadow, by the bitterest of coincidences he came across his wife and child among the heap of corpses in one of the trolleys. Word had it he'd carried them to the fire pits himself. It was also said he tried later to commit suicide by overdosing on some sleeping pills. The SS, however, informed of the attempt by his kapo, had his stomach pumped, and upon his waking the next day told him it was they who would decide when he was to die, not him.

Noah had trouble digesting such a horrific tale. No wonder Shlomo was but a shade of his former self. Something had died in him that day in the meadow, some flame been extinguished. Noah couldn't be sure how he'd have reacted if faced with same (he tried to imagine having to burn the corpses of his parents and little Mendel), but didn't think he'd be able to smile much afterward, either. Or in keeping with Shlomo's first impulse, if he'd even have allowed himself an afterward.

Despite their initial awkwardness, the two got together frequently after that, if not so much as surviving members of a decimated family—in the Vernichtungslager, one was careful never to bring up family—then as brother members of the underground. True to his original mission for Battle Group-Auschwitz, Noah continued to collect data on the number of transports coming in, the amount of Jews in each, and how many of these were sent straight to the gas. Much of this information came from Kaminski, but the man couldn't be everywhere or know everything. With a trusted cousin in Number Four, Noah now had a reliable contact in each of the new crematoria.

Indeed, Shlomo had contributed by adding a whole new dimension to the count. Where the underground had overlooked the victims of selections inside the camp, he said these could be considerable and were comprised mainly of Jews. Normally running in the hundreds or less, during large-scale selections they could reach into the thousands. And what with the transports rolling in night and day now, packing the barracks with their surplus, these last were being conducted with increasing frequency.

Noah was all too familiar with the in-camp selection. He'd been through several himself, witnessed numerous others. On a smaller scale, they were ubiquitous, as much a part of camp life as the hunger, the mud, the fulsome stink of the chimneys. Most of the inmates endured no less than two of them a day, once when they were marched to work in the morning and at night when they returned. Those SS gathered at the gates to gloat over their slaves parading by were also there to weed out any who looked hobbled or likewise unfit. These were forced onto trucks and never seen again.

Similar triages were conducted on a regular basis in the medical blocks. Every prisoner knew to avoid the hospital if at all possible; death in the form of an SS doctor was a regular visitor there. Accompanied by an inmate-physician, he would "examine" each patient, this consisting of a quick glance at the person and then at an index card on which was written the prisoner's medical condition, and whether or not he or she was Jewish. The cards ended up in three stacks, one for those deemed well enough to return to their huts, one for those who were to remain in the hospital, and the last a pile of one-way tickets to the crematoria.

The mass selection was a different animal. Noah would never forget his first. It was early December, a part of the same Hanukkah purge that took his sister at Birkenau. At the main camp, the Polish word *Selekcja* was suddenly on everybody's lips, nor to the general angst did anyone seem surer of its coming than the more experienced prisoners. He didn't know what to make of any of it, but sensed a tension in the air as thick as the stench from the fire pits. These had been sending a solid wall of black smoke skyward for days. *Something* was going on over at Birkenau, and it didn't bode well.

Rumors abounded, but later he was to learn this was always the case prior to a large selection. Someone said they heard their Blockälteste promise that things would be different this time, and those chosen were to be sent to a convalescent camp. A Czech younger than he, but already an old Auschwitz hand, guaranteed—if refusing to divulge his sources—that this selection was to be overseen by the International Red Cross. Others said it was to be aimed at only the older among them, or that German Jews would be excluded. Or the low tattoo numbers, those who'd been interned the longest. All Noah could tell for sure was that everyone seemed as skittish as a spooked cat, their nervousness making his more pronounced by the day.

Not that he was all that afraid for himself. That he could deal with—it was his brother Hanan who worried him. Trapped in the punishing Bauhof commando, lugging bags of cement around all day, starving to death, both men were in sorry shape, especially Hanan. Skinny to begin with, he was wasting away rapidly. His cheeks had started to sink, his eyes to hollow, nor was the diarrhea he'd developed showing any sign of dissipating. He'd also injured himself on the job, breaking a toe, and although the limp this caused was slight, it was discernible. The day the Germans caught sight of it could well be his last.

Even more treacherous was his state of mind. It was this more than anything that had Noah concerned. Each day brought Hanan closer to throwing in the towel, to quit struggling against what he'd begun to perceive was his inevitable death. Noah could tell he was thinking this from the way he commenced to drag himself about, suddenly indifferent to his surroundings, to the hunger twisting his belly, the pain pounding in his foot. He no longer complained about either, had ceased to talk much at all. Noah didn't want to admit it, but there was no denying it: his kid brother was turning into a Muselmänn in front of his eyes.

Frightened, Noah took him aside. "You're not going to die on me," he told Hanan at their soup break one day, "because I'm not going to let you. What you *are* going to do is gut it up, square those shoulders of yours, get mad. I want you to get mad and stay mad, or I'm going to be mad at you."

"What are you talking about, Noah? Get mad at whom?"

"Why, the Germans, who else? It's they who would steal the very breath from your lungs, just as they did to mama and papa and Mendel, and for all we know, Deborah and Pinchas by now as well. It makes it easier for them, you know, when they see you've given up. I won't let you make it easy for them. I won't let you give up."

177

"Just leave me be, big brother. Can't you see I'm trying to drink my soup?"

"*Put the soup down!*" Noah yelled. Those prisoners squatting near looked up for a second, then went back to their lunch. "The soup can wait, Hanan. This is important, this is about saving your life. They say there's a selection coming, and I believe them. One involving the whole camp. I've heard how these things are run, and seeing as we're both skin and bones and you with a bad foot, it won't be easy to survive it. But it can be done. There are precautions we can take to help us get through it. Would you like me to share some of them with you? Tell me you would."

"Noah, I really don't feel like—"

"Good, let's go over them then. Stop me if you have any questions."

Many of the veterans of the camp swore to the efficacy of managing a freshly shaven face on the day of a selection. It might cost half a ration of bread for the use of a razor, but the consensus was that it was a price well worth paying. Not only did it make the older prisoners look younger, but everyone cleaner, therefore fitter in the eyes of the SS doctors.

Another trick was to prick a finger so as to draw forth some blood, then apply it to the cheeks to create the illusion of health. So many of the inmates, Noah and Hanan among them, wore the grayish pallor of impending death. It was also important, those in the know said, to keep one's muscles taut when parading naked in front of the doctors, head erect, chest thrust out in as military a bearing as one could muster. Above all, one mustn't stumble, nor God forbid, fall. A firm and steady step was as important as anything.

"And that's why I need you to get mad," Noah said. "Broken toe or no, you can't be limping in front of the selectors, it'll be the gas for you then for sure. You're going to have to walk normal, to endure the pain as if there wasn't any. How? By becoming so angry that the pain ends up as nothing to that anger, nothing to what you're feeling toward those forcing you to go through this. You following me so far?"

Hanan didn't answer, continued staring at the ground in front of him.

"You're going to have to fill yourself," Noah persisted, "fill yourself with rage, to the point where there's no room for the pain or anything else. You've got to despise that Nazi doctor like you've never despised anybody, at least for the few seconds you'll be marching past the bastard. It'll only be a few seconds. You can do it, Hanan, you can. I'll help you, you'll see. Together we can beat this."

Hanan shook his head. "I don't think I can get that mad, Noah, not anymore. Not after these last four years. I'm done, worn out, finished. Let the SS do their worst. I—I don't have it in me to keep on fighting them, I just don't."

"Oh, you don't, do you? I see." Noah's voice went cold. "To be honest, I'm not surprised. If you want to know the truth, I never thought you did. Have it in you, I mean."

"What are you trying to say?"

"I've always admired your smarts, Hanan; it was your backbone, your manliness I'm afraid I found suspect. You may look grown up, have hair in all the grown-up places, but in a lot of ways you're a little boy still. A spoiled one at that."

Hanan glared at him. "Now you're just being spiteful. Why do you have to do that?"

"Spiteful? You want spiteful? Here, I'll show you spiteful." He reached across and cuffed his brother's chin, not hard but not playfully, either. Hanan's jaw dropped in surprise.

"What was that for?" he said

"Nothing. I did it because I could. Because I knew I could get away with it, knew you wouldn't hit back."

"Screw yourself," Hanan said, returning to his soup.

"Oh yeah? How about this then?" Noah slapped him on the cheek, hard this time. "What do you think of that?"

"Stop it! I know what you're trying to do, but just stop it!"

"Make me," Noah taunted, and slapped him again. And kept slapping him until Hanan had had enough and they wound up grappling in the dirt like a pair of schoolboys. Fortunately, their kapo wasn't present, or that might have been the end for both of them. The prisoners sitting near clutched their bowls to their chests to protect the contents.

These would have been pressed to say which of the brothers ended up the peacemaker, but all of a sudden they weren't audience to grunts and curses anymore, but laughter. Both men laughed until the tears came to their eyes, the struggle to pin the other down having turned into an embrace.

"So you don't have any fight in you anymore," Noah said at last. "You sure about that?"

Hanan's laughter had subsided into a shame-faced smile. "Alright already, older brother, you've proved your point. And I have to admit I love you for it. The question is, will it work? Is it possible to get pissed off enough to block out a broken toe?"

Sunday came. It was an *Arbeitssonntag*, which meant work. Every other Sunday, the prisoners were exempt from their normal labors, but the following one it was work as usual for half a day. After the Appell, soup was dispensed, and the rest of the afternoon devoted to such tasks as cleaning the huts and grounds, the blacking of their clogs with machine grease, the shearing of their heads and bodies, the search for lice, and so on.

This Sunday, though, would be different, beginning with the weather. It was unusually warm for December, hardly balmy but far from freezing. What with their flimsy clothing, this was always a plus for the prisoners. Any benefit, however, was tempered by another chill in the air: the feeling, inexplicable but no less strong for it, the day they'd been fearing was finally upon them. Somehow everyone knew that the selection would be today, as surely as if the Germans had announced it beforehand.

Noah and Hanan were prepared, and after the Appell had hurried to the washroom for an emergency shave. Between them the use of a razor had cost a full ration of bread, a crumb of soap half a helping of soup. Whether these would prove justified, they would have to wait to find out, though not for long. A little after three o'clock, the reveille bell sounded, which in the middle of the day could mean only one thing: *Blocksperre*, or immediate confinement of all prisoners to their barracks. It was a Selekcja, a major one, too.

Their block senior knew exactly what to do. First, he made certain that everyone was inside the barracks and counted, then had all the doors locked and the shutters closed. He then produced a file box filled with index cards on which were typed each prisoner's number, name, nationality, age, and occupation. Everyone was ordered to strip to the skin but for his shoes, and the cards handed out. After that, it was a matter of waiting for the SS to reach their hut.

The Blockälteste returned to his room, but every so often stuck his head out to see that all was as it should be. Most of his charges had returned to their bunks and blankets; it may have been unseasonable for December, but was still cold. Others, oblivious to the temperature, stood about naked and largely alone. Conversation was negligible, each man busy with his thoughts.

Noah was an exception. He held his mouth to Hanan's ear as one would a bellows to a fire, hoping to get the flames of his brother's ire going by leading him on a stroll down memory lane. Every insult, every injustice perpetrated against their family since the ghetto, he recounted in relentless detail, leaving out nothing.

Hanan listened obediently, but showed no emotion. Noah couldn't tell what effect he was having if any, but kept at it. After twenty minutes, he'd barely got them off the train and into Auschwitz when an explosion of voices erupted at one end of the barracks. It was the Älteste and his helpers. With curses and blows, they drove the prisoners from their kojen and the whole apprehensive mass the length of the building toward the quartermaster's office and storage area. This *Tagesraum* measured only nine meters by six and a half, but somehow all four hundred men were stuffed inside and the door squeezed shut. So full of flesh was the room that the boards in the walls creaked outward from the pressure.

Even as they began to be ordered one at a time into the yard, Noah remained at Hanan's ear. He urged him to remember how their mama, papa, and baby brother had died, in the pitch-black of the gas chamber, screams filling their ears, the burning gas their throats.

"Picture," Noah said, "the terror of that room. Of bodies crashing into bodies in the dark, people fighting, trampling each other. Imagine our mother holding Mendel in her arms as both choke to death, suddenly unable to catch their breath."

Hanan listened without saying a word, but Noah could see the moisture brimming in his eyes. He didn't like what he was doing, didn't like it one bit, but if it succeeded in working his brother into the desired lather, it was worth it.

Gradually, the pressure in the room eased as it was emptied man by man, until finally it came Hanan's turn. When Noah was pushed outside a minute later, he stepped blinking into the late-afternoon sunlight to this: an SS doctor-major stood near the barracks' main door, flanked by its elder and quartermaster. He was ordered to walk to this group, then back to the Tagesraum door and back again. He made every effort to emulate an infantryman on parade, step purposeful, head high, chest out, muscles clenched.

(Whenever he chanced upon such a performance later, with the selection limited to a barracks or two and no Blocksperre in effect, the sight never failed to disturb him. To see a living skeleton trying to march like a soldier, naked, pale as a grub, the scrotum swollen with hunger edema swinging pendulously to and fro—there was something obscene about it, a maneuver as debasing to those watching it as those forced to execute it).

Upon completing the test, he handed his index card to the doctor and made for the hut. As he entered it, he looked back and saw the SS man give it to the Blockälteste.

This detail would prove crucial. Each man's fate hinged on where his card ended up. There was a good side and a bad, the issue being which was which, the block elder's or the quartermaster's, it was unclear at this point. Once it emerged, however, that some of the more obvious candidates for the gas had seen the latter take theirs, those who'd noticed where their own had gone were spared the suspense of waiting to know whether they were going to live or die.

Most weren't to find out for a couple of days, though. Masking his anxiety as best he could, Noah had gone straight to Hanan. "Well?" was all he said. To which his brother replied, "My foot feels as if it's been hit with a hammer, but I'm guessing I did all right."

"Did you see where your card went?"

"No, but I think the *Sturmbannführer* might have been more focused on the daggers in my eyes than the limp in my step. I'm surprised he didn't shoot me right there for insubordination. At any rate, thanks, brother of mine, for setting me straight. If it hadn't been for you...."

"Don't thank me yet," Noah said, "until we know you're out of the woods. As for now, let's get our clothes on and have a look at that foot."

Two days later, the numbers of a hundred men were called, and as the rest of the barracks made for the Appellplatz and morning roll call, these were kept behind. Neither Hanan nor Noah were among them—in fact, were twice blessed in that not long afterward they were rescued from the Bauhof by the cook Witek as part of those chosen to be Stubendiensten to the Auschwitz Prominenz of Block 25.

As for the hundred, they were dispatched that morning to Birkenau, though not necessarily to their deaths, which was to say not straightaway. For many selectees from inside the camp, depending on how long it took to build their numbers up to warrant the use of Zyklon-B, the route to the gas chamber involved a layover of up to a few days at a restricted barracks known in lager parlance as the *Himmelblock*, or heaven block. Once, on his way to see Roza in *B1a*, Noah took a wrong road and wound up at an out-of-the-way corner of the barbed wire. There, set apart from the others, was a noticeably larger hut with barred windows and a heavy door guarded by two *Schützen*.

It was the Himmelblock for women, Birkenau's Block 25, his first, and as he was to promise himself, last trip to that frightful place. At each window, a flurry of arms floated out from behind the bars like the tentacles of some monstrous sea anemone. These belonged to those women, who having spotted him, began begging for water, while from behind them wafted an unbroken susurrus of female sobbing and moans. Even from where he stood, the reek of excrement was intolerable, the soldiers at the door having plugged their nostrils with cigarette butts.

What food was given these doomed souls was freely plundered by the kapos in charge of them; it didn't take long for the already sick and decrepit to grow disturbingly worse. Shlomo Kirschenbaum, for the few weeks he was there, had twice worked the detail that received the condemned of the Himmelblocks into Crematorium II. One had been made up of women, the other men, an identical facility for them existing in the *B2f* lager. He told Noah once what this was like, using the former as an example. Even in the man's dessicated monotone, the other felt his heart wilt at what his ears were hearing.

"They entered the death-house grounds packed into open trucks, already naked. Those not weeping loudly looked to be in a state of shock, shivering despite the June heat, eyes big as saucers. We helped them to the pavement, then underground. Not a one of them resisted, knowing it'd be useless. Twelve hundred women that afternoon descended the last stairs they ever would.

"The final load, those unable to walk, arrived by dump truck. These were heaped one on top of the other as if they'd been thrown there. Once it pulled up to the crematorium, its bed began to rise at one end. Groaning, the women clawed at the sides, but it was no use; with a cracking of heads and knees they spilled onto the cement. A few atop the resulting pile managed to untangle themselves from it, and as if drunk, staggered about. The rest lay where they'd fallen. These we had to carry down the steps, careful not to slip in the shit and the blood."

The gassing of Aryans had ceased in April on orders from Berlin. All those selected at the unloading ramp from then on were Jews. But as Shlomo reminded his cousin, while the quantity from the camp paled before these, it could be significant and should be included in any tally. This moved Noah to refine his figures. If it was numbers Auschwitz wanted, he was going to see they got the truest possible.

As alarming as these numbers were, nothing drove the point of the slaughter home more than what he'd chanced upon one morning while making his way from the Stammlager to Birkenau. The dry arithmetic provided him by his Sonder contacts, while appalling, didn't pack half the wallop of what he saw that day. From a distance, it was as improbable a sight as any he could recall coming across. A column of prisoners three abreast, male and female both, approached him on the road, each pushing a baby carriage as if part of some mammoth mass-promenade in a park. As they drew closer, he could see that the carriages, of course, were empty, the strange procession simply a means of getting them from the Canada warehouses to the rail siding and the train taking them to Germany.

As might be expected, few of the prisoners met his gaze as they passed. What did surprise, and sicken him, was the sheer magnitude of this display. All his way to Birkenau the strollers kept rolling past him, a virtual river of them, interminable, relentless. Every color and kind rattled down the limestone road, having originated in a dozen different countries. Nor could there be any doubt what had become of their former occupants. But for the segregated Gypsy and Czech Family Camps, there were no children at either Auschwitz or Birkenau under the age of fourteen. Here was his people's future, or rather the lack of one, made visible. What could be more telling, more chilling than that parade of empty prams stretching to the horizon?

Noah had been witness to this proof of atrocity on his way to meet with the leadership of Battle Group-Sonderkommando. The mission Bruno Baum had given him was to relay to the Sonder, at long last, the plan of attack for the revolt, an announcement sure to raise their hopes, then dash those hopes by informing them that the operation had been postponed. The reason Noah was supposed to give for this was bogus, and he knew it. He'd been ordered to tell them that the partisans, whose contribution to the uprising was intrinsic to its success, were in no position at present to be of any help. Why? Since the world-shaking developments in the Warsaw ghetto in April-May, Nazi military and police activity in all parts of the country had increased to the extent that the Home Army had its hands full looking out for just itself now. There was no hope anytime soon of it diverting the manpower or coming up with the weapons and supplies needed to support a mass escape from Birkenau.

But Battle Group-Auschwitz's reticence had nothing to do with the partisans. It was true that beginning in May these had been pressed to the limit for a time, but SS anger at the humiliation it had suffered in Warsaw had abated much the last three months. Or so Noah gathered from what he'd been able to overhear in Baum's and Cyrankiewicz's offices. The Armia had replenished itself much in those months, to the point that now it had to be more than capable of acting.

What was, in fact, moving the underground to caution was the electrifying, long-anticipated news from the Russian front. He knew this because he'd been present when that news had arrived via courier from Krakow: the Wehrmacht, having launched its third offensive in as many years against the Soviet Union, had been routed at the climactic battle of Kursk in southern Russia. The Germans were even now in retreat, leaving behind two hundred thousand troops dead or captured and the burning hulks of the better part of eleven armored divisions. Kursk was primarily a tank battle, and for the Wehrmacht a disaster. The likelihood of it taking the initiative again in the east was all but nonexistent. From now on, it would be the Red Army on the offensive.

The significance of this wasn't lost on the Auschwitz underground. Why chance a breakout from Birkenau with the Russians on the verge of one of their own perhaps? The Soviets could very well be in Poland before the year was out. Better for the underground and those it was responsible for to wait for liberation than try to force the issue by taking on the SS themselves.

Noah didn't like for one minute what he was being asked to do, hadn't since before even leaving Baum's office. The lone window had been open, letting in the flies and summer heat alike. "So why not tell the Sonder the truth, commander, instead of leading them on? What good does it do to try stalling them?"

"It does two things," Baum answered, "both of them critical. I should think it would be clear to the men of the Sonderkommando that whether the camp is liberated or not, they will not survive the war. The Nazis are not about to let the only eyewitnesses to their crime live. Now if these walking dead begin to suspect that enthusiasm for the revolt is fading, what do you think their reaction will be? What would yours be? Having nothing to lose, they might attempt to make a go of it on their own, and succeed or not, endanger the whole camp by exposing it to SS reprisals. We do realize that the Sonderkommandos of the past have all gone unprotesting to their deaths, but these men are different. Months of inflammatory rhetoric and high hopes have their blood up. But they cannot be allowed to act independently. The risk to the other tens of thousands of inmates is too great. That is why we are sending you, to make them think we are still behind them when…. actually we are not. Not at this point anyway."

Noah got the impression that this wasn't Baum speaking, but came from others. He watched him shift uneasily in his chair, as if what he had to say next agreed even less with him. "If, on the other hand, the situation on the battlefield should change, say the Wehrmacht regroups, and establishing a defensive line, is able to hold off the Soviets indefinitely, then the Special Squad will be there to head the uprising as planned. That is the second reason for leading them on as you so perceptively put it, to have them available should the Russian counteroffensives fail."

Noah looked his chief in the eye. "Meanwhile," he said, "the crematoria continue to kill. I trust the Steering Committee is aware of what its new strategy is going to cost."

Baum rose from his desk and walked to the window behind it, his back to Noah. "Of course we are aware," he said. "It was not an easy decision to make. I personally was against the call to stand down, and still think we might live—or should I say die?—to regret it. Not only does it leave the death houses intact but should the Soviets indeed get close, I fear the Germans would do anything to prevent us, especially those of us Jewish, from falling into their hands."

Here he turned to face Noah again. "However, I also fear the crematoria may have done their worst, that the time to destroy those diabolic mills is past. Despite every effort to err on the side of excess, it would appear we have underestimated their lethalness. In just the last few weeks, the number of transports has dwindled, imperceptibly at first but hard to ignore now. You of all people, Comrade Zabludowicz, should know this, what with the figures you continue so admirably to collect."

"They have tailed off, yes."

"Have you stopped to consider why? I can assure you it is not because the SS have had a change of heart. Nor do we believe it an aberration, some kind of lull. With the exception of Lodz, because of its economic value to the Reich, the great ghettos of Poland have all been liquidated—Lublin, Krakow, Warsaw, Poznan, all drained of their humanity until only a very few residents remain. Likewise Riga, Vilna, and others in the Baltics. The enormous transit camps in France and Holland have been sucked dry as well, and God only knows what death the *Einsatzgruppen* are sowing still in the east. Not to mention the other five Vernichtungslagers in Poland."

"Pardon me, sir." Noah had never heard the word before. "The Einsatzgruppen?"

"Another, I am afraid, in that long line of Nazi euphemisms—'rapid deployment units' will suffice as a translation." Baum returned to his chair, looking older than he had just seconds ago. From the window, a gust of hot wind ruffled the papers on his desk. "In fact, they are SS murder brigades. Four of them continue to roam Russia behind the Wehrmacht lines, their task to round up and eliminate all Jews, political authorities, the intelligentsia and such. Nor is their method as sophisticated, for lack of a better word, as gas. They use guns, machine guns for the most part, certainly in their larger Aktionen. A pit is dug, several pits, and six or seven people at a time lined up naked at the edge of each, where they are mowed down. Families are often butchered together, parents and children, brothers and sisters, holding hands, looking at each other in—what, astonishment? Despair? It is as difficult a scene to visualize as it is to convey."

His expression grew darker. "The SS have been busy in Russia since the invasion of the country in '41. Outside the city of Kiev, thirty-three thousand Jews were shot in two days, with one hundred and fifty thousand eventually to follow. This from Kiev alone! There are almost three million of our people in the Soviet Union, Zabludowicz. That is, there used to be. Now…." He shrugged his shoulders.

Noah was shaken. He dropped into the remaining chair. As if Birkenau and all the rest, all the other camps, weren't enough, now this horror story from Russia. It made one wonder that such evil should occur outdoors, in the bright light of day, and the sun not hide its face in disgust. "But how—"

"I just told you how."

As much trouble as he was having processing Baum's Einsatzgruppen, that wasn't Noah's question. "No, general, not how is it done, nor how can such a thing be, but how in blazes do you come to know all of this? And be so dead sure of it. If you ask me, it smacks of someone's bad dream. Or maybe somebody with an overactive imagination, or even some sort of agenda to push. I won't presume to ask you your sources, but are you positive they can be trusted?"

"We have many sources," Baum said. "Rarely are we at the mercy of a mere one or two. The reach of the Armia Krajowa is long; there is little that goes on in the occupied territories we do not know of. But that is neither here nor there. The point I am trying to make is that I have a feeling the Jewish goose, if you will, is just about cooked. All the Jews in Europe and beyond able to be rounded up easily and unsuspectingly have been. All that are left are those in hiding or otherwise gone underground. It would not surprise me if there were as many who can be accounted for concentrated in the barracks of Auschwitz-Birkenau than in any single country on the continent now save Hungary. And Hungary only because it is an ally of Nazi Germany, encouraged but not required to give them up."

Baum wasn't finished, but here lowered his voice, as if he weren't addressing another so much as thinking out loud. "So which is the better course of action, to sit and wait for the Red Army and risk our fanatical keepers preempting its arrival by slaughtering us in our bunks? Or the even riskier tactic of attempting to liberate ourselves and imperiling those clinging to life here, one of the last remaining enclaves of Jews in all Europe."

He seemed to ponder this a moment, then in a normal voice, "Who can say? So I say this: I am going to follow the orders given me, as you are going to follow yours, which are to deliver to the rebels of Battle Group-Sonderkommando the underground's battle plan, then break the bad news it cannot be implemented for another few months. Whatever you can add that you think might buffer their disappointment, lift their spirits a little, feel free to—except, need I say, anything to do with the actual cause of the delay. Afterward, report back to me with their reaction."

"Yes, sir, as you wish."

Both rose, Baum making it a point to hold his agent's gaze. The tired, cynical eyes had softened somewhat. "It is a dirty business, I know, but we depend on you, young man. Your people depend on you. Always remember it is to them that you owe your first allegiance."

"Yes, sir, I will. And will do my best, as always."

But it wasn't going to be easy. Noah wasn't the lying kind. Besides, he'd developed a real liking for some of the Sonder, the gruff yet bighearted Kaminski in particular. To play so dishonest a game with men who'd come to be his friends, whom he'd laughed with, broken bread with, went against his grain.

Then on his way to Birkenau and Block 13, he ran into that apocalyptic dirge of babyless carriages. Which didn't help his conscience any knowing that as a result of his mission, the four death factories responsible for that ghoulish parade were to be given a new lease on life. He thought about trying to find his older brother and asking Pinchas whether he should return to the Stammlager and decline the assignment, but abandoned the idea as soon as it entered his head. Aside from revealing secrets no outsider, not even a brother, had any business knowing, what in the end could that brother possibly say to dissuade him from his duty? Baum, of course, had been onto his misgivings, and with his closing words had sought to offset them. And the more Noah thought about it, the truer those words rang: however uncomfortable this latest job made him feel, there was vastly more at stake here than his or any man's comfort.

The prisoner stationed outside the Sonder compound barely glanced at him. Kaminski and three of his top men were waiting for him inside the hut. Two of them he knew already, Yankel Handelsman and Yossel Warszawski, and after being introduced to Zalman Gradowski, the five adjourned to the empty Tagesraum.

He wasted no time presenting Auschwitz's plan for their approval, the longer he talked, the livelier his voice. The keys to the success of the revolt were the element of surprise and a high degree of coordination among its participants. Timing would be crucial. The wheels had to be set in motion by late afternoon, no earlier, no later, so that once the escapees reached the woods, and not before, night would have fallen. They would need the light to recognize each other in the fighting, then the dark to cloak them from the pursuing Germans.

It was all to commence at 5:30, a half hour before the change of shifts at the crematoria. The eight SS manning Numbers Four and Five, and the ten whose job it was to oversee Two and Three, were to be overpowered silently and their weapons and uniforms seized. When their relief escorting the night shift arrived, they too would be killed and their arms taken. This would leave the insurgents with a fair number of guns and uniforms, these to be donned by those fluent in German.

Once the pair of guards at the gate of each crematorium were disposed of, again in silence, the men posing as SS would lead the day shift back to its barracks in the camp. On the way, they were to cut all telephone lines. After outfitting themselves with the supplies and munitions they'd stashed, the battle was on. The Sonder were to boil out of their barracks and spread across Birkenau, dealing death to the camp sentries and any soldiers they met while herding those prisoners wanting to join them toward the crematoria. The night crews waiting at these, meanwhile, having rigged the four with explosives, were to blow them at the first sound of gunfire. That would serve as a signal for the partisans hiding in the woods to attack the western section of the outer guard cordon. This was a ring of watchtowers encircling the camp a kilometer and a half from its barbed-wire perimeter. Once the Armia had knocked out enough of these to form a sufficiently wide escape corridor, it was to move against the towers at the edge of the camp. The Sonder who'd destroyed the crematoria would already have engaged this inner cordon from the front, preparatory to taking out the electrified fence.

By the time the first of the fleeing inmates reached the western perimeter, the area should have been subdued, freeing the rebels there, those with weapons, to defend against what was sure by then to be German reinforcements. The Sonder disguised in SS uniforms would be wearing yellow armbands to identify themselves. Their and their compatriots' main concern would be to protect the prisoners making for the gaps in the fence. They were to withdraw only when the last of these had reached the forest, when together with half the partisans, they would serve as a rear guard for the escapees until the other half had finished dividing them into smaller groups and these had scattered. This was meant to confuse the Nazis while dividing their forces as well. Led by their Polish allies, all by roundabout routes were ultimately to converge on the marshes surrounding the Sola River to the south, a Home Army stronghold since the war began.

That was the plan roughed out. It would be polished smooth later with the requisite details. "Any questions?" Noah asked.

Silence at first. It was Kaminski who broke it. "Well, it's as good a way to die as any, I guess. Better than most, I'd have to say, in this damned place anyway."

"I have a question," said Warszawski, balancing his chair on its hind legs. He and Handelsman were friends, had been for years. Both active in the Communist Party, they'd escaped Poland for France together, been arrested there together, and were together still. Apart from the fact they were also both thirty, however, and each committed body and soul to the revolt, they were two very different people. Where Handelsman could be calm to the extent of appearing lackadaisical at times, rare was the moment at least some part of Warszawski wasn't in motion. Though little taller than five feet, packed into this small frame was the coiled vitality of two men. His face was all bone and sharp edges, and he would walk with it thrust forward as if it were in a race to outrun the rest of his body. He talked fast, ate fast, even snored in double-time. Nervous energy radiated from him in all but visible tendrils. There was nothing subtle about him; as with Kaminski, one always knew where one stood with Warszawski. Which, unless it was in favor of taking up arms and killing Germans, wasn't very high. One either showed himself a man or not, there was no in-between with him.

He let the front legs of the chair drop to the floor, on which his own left foot was soon vibrating. "Answer me this, if you will. Those marshes you're talking about aren't exactly close by. I can see a few of us reaching them maybe, if we're lucky, but what makes your bosses, Zabludowicz, think the SS are going to let the thousands you say will be tagging along with us get anywhere near that far? That just seems crazy to me, and suicide for those of us held back to protect them."

"Allow me, please, Noah, to answer that," said Handelsman, "by suggesting we not overrate these Germans of ours. The deeper we get into the woods, the less of an advantage they have. Like us, they'll be on foot, unable to bring any vehicles or heavy guns with them. And keep in mind, the partisans have been living in these forests for four years now. They know the terrain and how to use it, where to lay ambushes, booby traps, the ravines and such to avoid. And what have our captors been doing these past four years?"

"Enjoying the privileged life of garrison duty," Gradowski jumped in, "concentration-camp duty. Getting fat. Getting soft. Staying drunk half the time. I'm with the professor: once we do make it into the woods, if we do, I believe we'll stand a decent chance."

"Oh, we'll make it into the woods," Kaminski huffed, "and there will be battles there. But we're going to win those battles, just like we will have won the one to bust us out of this shitpile. We'll make it into the woods all right, I promise you that, just as I can promise that a lot of those pig-eyed Krauts won't."

Noah nodded his approbation with the rest of them, then turned to Warszawski. "The escapees, remember, Yossel, won't be fleeing in one big mob," he said, "but fanning out in a dozen directions. That's one reason it's so important the partisans be involved; it's they who'll be responsible for shepherding all those groups to safety. Not that this is going to be easy in the dark, but neither will that dark be a friend to our pursuers."

"One thing I would like to know," asked Handelsman, "is how much support we can expect from the main camp. Does the underground have any intention of joining us in the fight?"

"I'm afraid not," Noah said. "All I can tell you—"

"Or at least do something," Gradowski said, "anything, to divert some of the SS from Birkenau."

"All I can tell you," Noah repeated, "is what I've been told. If the breakout is successful, especially if the cremos are brought down, there'll likely be reprisals against those left behind. The Resistance would rather these were confined to Birkenau. Should Battle Group-Auschwitz be implicated in the uprising, not only would the population there be subject to German vengeance but the organization as well, to the detriment of all the inmates. It is enough, think my superiors, that they've stuck their necks out as far as they have by enlisting the troops of the Home Army in the revolt. If the SS were to learn of that...."

He screwed his face up at this, but not because of it. Having forgotten what he was there for, all of a sudden he remembered, and remembering, knew what had to come next. Clumsily, he'd let himself get caught up in the moment, in the excitement, the promise his words had generated. Carried away by them himself, losing his handle on himself, he'd come across as if the message he was bringing would, if not immediately, then soon translate to action. The time had come, though, to disclose the second part of that message. He forced the words out, his ears burning with the shame of them.

"That, I know, isn't what you were hoping to hear. But I bring even worse news. A lot worse, in fact." In a hurry to get it over with, he imparted it rapid-fire. "I've been instructed to inform you, in light of recent events in the Warsaw ghetto, that Nazi pressure has the partisans running for cover, barely able to protect themselves, much less lend a hand to others. Which for the time being anyway—means the revolt has been put on hold."

Asked to define "for the time being," Noah studied his shoes for a moment then came out with it, the sentence as bitter in his mouth as the berry of some inedible plant.

"A few *months*?" Kaminski snorted. "Have your generals lost their marbles? We might not have a few months, not a lot of us anyway."

The others were just as floored. "Do you realize what you're asking?" demanded Gradowski. "That we keep doing this—this work, living this nightmare, for who knows how much longer. Time, as our kapo said, many of us don't have."

Handelsman seemed more saddened than angry, though his tone, too, bristled with accusation. "Your commanders have to know, Zabludowicz, that for every week they delay, more thousands of Jews will be reduced to so much dust. Gone, wiped from memory, as if they'd never existed. What kind of men are they that they can live with such a decision?"

Forced to split his loyalty between his bosses in the movement and his friends in the Sonderkommando, Noah didn't know how to respond. "I'm not sure what kind, Yankel, but I suspect they're no different than you and I, or any other mother's son delivered to this slaughterhouse: desperate, afraid, the grave a step away, their lives dependent on outthinking, outguessing the SS. What kind of men are they? I'd have to say that was for you to decide."

"Cowards," said Warszawski, "that's what they are. And liars to boot. Do any of you buy this claptrap about the Home Army being on the run, forced to lie low? Lie low from what? I'd say it wasn't the partisans who were stretched thin here, but the truth. Why don't you tell us what's really going on, Zabludowicz? The real reason your buddies at Auschwitz have come down with cold feet."

"All right, that's enough!" snapped Kaminski. "I'll have none of that. I'd tread lightly, too, if I were you, Yossel—from what I hear, Noah could whip the bunch of us single-handed. But we're not going to let it come to that, are we, boys? No, we're going to behave like the gentlemen we are and mind our goddam manners."

He stared at each in turn as he spoke. Then on a gentler note, "So the revolt is off for now." Kaminski didn't like what he'd heard any more than the next man, particularly as it related to what Handelsman had said. He wasn't the type, though, to let bad tidings get the better of him. "There isn't a whole lot we can do about that, but when you think about it, we're not ready to take on the SS anyway, are we? Far from it, and at least now we have a plan to build on and prepare for. I say we put it behind us and move on to something more constructive. Or maybe *instructive* would be the better place to start."

He turned to face their visitor. "And by that I mean, Noah, what's this we keep hearing, to use your own words, about 'recent events in the Warsaw ghetto?' And now here you go telling us that's why the revolt has been put on ice. Yossel has a point: why should the Germans choose this of all times to crack down on the Home Army? Enlighten us, sir, please. What the hell happened in Warsaw to get the Krauts' panties in such a wad?"

Noah's eyebrows arched in surprise. "You mean you don't know? How can you not?"

"Again, we've heard talk, but nothing specific," Kaminski said. "Something about some Jews resisting deportation. But then we're kind of cut off over here; the SS don't like us hobnobbing with the general population. Most of the prisoners we do see are too busy getting ready to be murdered to have time to stop and chat about what's going on in the war."

Like a gift dropped in his lap, here was a way for Noah to follow both his orders and his conscience. He hadn't forgotten the license Baum had given him, once he'd deflated Sonder hopes, to try and assuage Sonder disappointment if he got the chance. And here that chance was, a means of softening the blow he'd just dealt them with as rousing a tale of Jewish heroics as any in all history.

"Then let me share with you what we've been told by those who were there," he said, "and prepare to be awed."

There could be no denying it was a story for the ages. Beginning in July of last year, successive waves of deportations to the death camps, mainly Treblinka, had decimated the Jews of Warsaw, at times to the tune of thousands a day. Starvation and disease also took their toll, so that from a high of half a million people, only sixty thousand remained in the ghetto come April. On the morning of the 19th, units of the SS, backed by the Gestapo, moved in to round up this last sixty thousand, it having been determined that the ghetto was to be liquidated once and for all.

Their would-be victims, however, were laying for them, hidden from sight in prearranged battle stations. Having learned at last the truth about Treblinka, that it wasn't a labor but an extermination camp, they'd vowed never again to let themselves be loaded peaceably into cattle cars. For months they prepared. Tunnels and bunkers were dug under the streets and provisioned, weapons smuggled in by bribing the Polish policemen guarding the ghetto walls—mostly pistols, ammunition, a few grenades, and gasoline, this last to go into the making of hundreds of Molotov cocktails. They even managed to get their hands on a heavy machine gun. When the Nazis marched in on the 19th at dawn, all cocky and loud, singing their Nazi songs, they were confident the deserted streets meant that the lily-livered Jews, the same Jews who by the hundreds of thousands the past year had been led like sheep to their deaths, were quaking under their beds waiting to be drug out by the scruffs of their necks.

And waiting they were, but nowhere near their beds. Nor did they have any intention of being dragged anywhere. No sooner had the Germans, four companies strong, filled the intersection of Mila and Zamenhofa Streets than a hail of bullets and explosives tore into them from three sides. Fifty soldiers fell in twenty minutes. As did the tank they'd called to provide cover for their retreat.

As unthinkable as it had been just minutes ago, the mighty SS had been repelled, slinking back the way they'd come with those of their dead and wounded they'd been able to recover. They hadn't expected the Jews to fight, hadn't thought the Jew *could* fight, but impelled now to confront this disquieting fact, returned that very morning in force—at Muranowski Square, where a second tank was destroyed; at the enormous brush factory to the north a full city block long, where fifty more of the invaders died; at the corner of Nalewski and Gesia Streets, the SS attacking from all sides, but after a seven-hour battle failing to gain an inch of ground. By late afternoon, there wasn't a German soldier left in the ghetto. All had withdrawn to the safety of the Aryan side of the wall.

The second day was the same, the Nazis repulsed wherever they tried, every other apartment building, house, store front a fortress. By now the defenders' supply of weapons had grown, taken from the hands of their dead enemies. Women fought alongside their men and with the same ferocity, even children when necessary jumping into the fray. Two weeks passed before the Germans admitted the futility of trying to take the ghetto by storm and chose to adopt a different, less dangerous strategy: burning it to the ground building by building so as to flush the Jewish demons out of their holes.

The infantry set fires and the Luftwaffe dropped incendiaries, and by the time they were done, there wasn't much of the ghetto left. Those Jews who survived the flames were driven underground, yet even then refused to give up. By day the SS used sound-detecting devices and police dogs to sniff out their bunkers and eradicate them, while at night furious skirmishes lit up the ruins. For another month, this war within the war raged, until the handful of guerillas left alive escaped through the sewers into the city proper.

The four Sonder sat through Noah's account without saying a word. Though the disillusionment he'd planted in their faces was still there, he could detect a gleam of pride alongside it now, too. It was the reaction he'd been hoping for, his amends for having had to lie to them about the partisans. Feeding off that pride, and hoping to cement it, he sought to finish with a flourish.

"And so the ghetto fell," he said, his voice rising. "But though the battle had been lost, this was won: despite repeated German guarantees to provide the Jews safe conduct if they laid down their arms, most chose to die fighting. Or committed suicide rather than surrender. Having tasted freedom, if only briefly, they weren't about to eat at the trough of slavery again."

Later, on the road back to Auschwitz, Noah reflected on the meeting. It had, of course, left a bad taste in his mouth, but not as bad as it could have been. Not only had he salvaged some self-respect there at the end, but lightened the heavy load he'd dumped on his audience prior. He liked to think he'd done more, though, than simply lift their spirits. He'd also reinforced the fact that despite their steel helmets, their firepower, their aura of invincibility, the SS were as vulnerable to hot lead as any *mensch* born of woman, could be dished death as easily as they'd been dispensing it all these years.

It was a truism he hoped would resound as strong when the four relayed what he'd shared with them to the rest of the squad. But he was hoping as well he'd given the Sonder something beyond even that, or rather served as the vehicle through whom it was given: a warrior tradition, a *Jewish* warrior tradition, a concept that had lain dormant for eighteen centuries until re-emerging just this spring from the smoldering ruins of the ghetto. No longer could the world disparage Jewish manhood, look at them as spineless, effeminate weaklings. With Warsaw, the Jew as born coward had become a conceit of the past. But this tradition, like most, came with a price, in this case namely the duty to uphold it, to use it when and where its use was required. From now on, the Jew would be expected to fight back. There could be no return to his compliantly accepting his fate, passive and prostrate before the will of his God.

Not that he didn't think this slur against his race overblown, an opinion supported by what he'd come to know of the Vernichtungslager of all places, where on the surface Jewish servility looked to have outdone itself. But for almost five years, men and women had been dying at first Auschwitz then Birkenau, methodically slaughtered without tendering the least resistance. And by no means were all of them Jews. Political and religious activists from a wide swath of countries, common criminals and other undesirables, the Polish intelligentsia and middle class, suspected partisans and assorted other enemies of the Reich—all had been starved, shot, beaten, and gassed to death without lifting a finger in their own defense. Even uncounted thousands of Russian prisoners of war, men trained to do battle, combat their profession, had in the early days of

Auschwitz gone quietly to their graves. Under the right conditions, both physical and psychological, submissiveness to the point of walking obediently to one's death could hardly be called a flaw specific to the Jewish character, but rather a chink in the armor of the *human* character that the SS had become adept at exploiting.

Be that as it may, the martyrs of the Warsaw ghetto having led the way, now it was up to those in like straits to carry the fight forward. Nor could he imagine any group more suited to the task than the Sonderkommando of Birkenau. His faith in this unfaltering, he'd sleep better tonight having made at least the effort to keep the flame of their rebelliousness lit in spite of the cold water he'd had to splash on it. And if, as he knew he shouldn't be thinking but was, that flame ended up burning so fiercely as to ignite this 10th Detachment into acting counter to the designs of his superiors, then so be it. As Baum himself had confessed, who could be positive—and this a question any inmate might reasonably ask—which was the right course to chart and which wasn't? Despite his instructions, despite the Steering Committee, despite even Baum's closing admonition to him, Noah would have been fine with the men of Block 13 emulating their cousin insurrectionists two hundred miles to the north. And that without the consent of their tepid collaborators in the Stammlager.

Not that these, with the exception perhaps of Baum, wouldn't have had his hide for daring to condone such. By the same token, he didn't approve of some of the things they were doing, either. The duplicity of their explanation for the delay of the revolt aside, he'd neglected to tell the Sonder that some of the munitions smuggled into Warsaw in preparation for the upheaval there had been courtesy of the Home Army, the very people Auschwitz claimed had no weapons to spare the Special Squad. Which in truth they might not have, not back then anyway, given what they were sneaking into the ghetto. But the partisans had provided Warsaw with more than just guns. In addition to acting as a link to the outside world, some had gone so far as to join in the fighting. When on the third day, the rebels raised their flag atop their headquarters in Muranowski Square—a blue Star of David on a white field for the Germans, for all the city to see—next to it flew the red and white banner of the Armia Krajowa.

It wasn't, of course, that the leaders of the underground favored one group of Jews over another, nor as demonstrated by the support they'd given Warsaw, that they were opposed in principle to the idea of armed revolt. They merely questioned the advisability of launching one from Auschwitz-Birkenau. Again, with the Red Army on the verge possibly of rolling the Wehrmacht all the way back to Germany, any attempt at a breakout of soon-to-be liberated prisoners made less sense to them than ever.

Actually, when it came down to it, Noah didn't know what to think. It could be argued that it was as hard to fault the Battle Group as it was to praise it. It might even be said that logic was on its side, all the more so since its intelligence arm had discovered a week ago that newly promoted *Hauptscharführer* Otto Möll was on his way out, transferred to another post. Not only did this reduce the chance of the dreaded Möll Plan being employed but if in the opinion of his superiors the sergeant's more than estimable services were no longer needed at this biggest and most productive of their killing grounds, they too must have been convinced, as Baum had put it, that the Jewish goose was cooked, the war against him all but won. Making the destruction of the crematoria less of an imperative, which was to say less a one worth sacrificing who knew how many more thousands of lives for.

Noah shaded his eyes from the heavy summer sun. It had passed its zenith and begun its slow descent, an erratic breeze kicking up swirls of white dust from the road. In the distance, the reddish brick of the Stammlager shimmered in the heat. There was no sign of any baby carriages, nor the small army of prisoners who'd been pushing them. He'd half-expected to encounter these last on his way back, but they were either still at the rail siding or already returned to Birkenau.

He had the limestone road to himself, or so it would have seemed to someone watching. In actuality, he was accompanied by two of his brothers. Not Pinchas, who he'd tried to check up on earlier but failed to find, nor Hanan, to whom he couldn't get back fast enough.

No, it was the twins Ezra and Ehud who tramped at his side, and had since he'd left Block 13. Warsaw had only to come up in conversation for his thoughts to gravitate toward them. Though he couldn't be certain, it was likely the two had occupied the ghetto from the start. They'd moved to the big city after war had broken out to try to earn some money for the family, and no one had seen nor so much as heard from them after the ghetto wall had gone up. For the longest time, Noah had done his best to stay upbeat, but had since ceased holding out much hope for either of them. There were too many ways for a Jew in Warsaw to have died, if not from disease, malnutrition, or later SS bullets and flamethrowers, then Treblinka, always Treblinka. There were no selections at Treblinka. Everyone who got off the trains went directly to the gas.

But not everyone ended up at that terrible place. Maidanek got its share of the Warsaw transports, as less often did Birkenau. He'd kept a sharp eye out for the twins, but so far no luck. He'd always had a soft spot in his heart for those two. As sweet-natured as they were inseparable, he remembered the grief that as children they caused their parents by taking in every animal in distress that crossed their paths, stray cats and dogs, injured birds, even—he had to smile every time he recalled it—a sick sewer rat once. Their decision to uproot themselves and brave Warsaw for the sake of the family had both surprised and impressed him, though he had a little trouble picturing them hurling Molotov cocktails at tanks.

In all probability they hadn't, not those two gentle souls. But then who knew? As if it mattered a fig to him. Whatever they had or hadn't done, or wherever they were, or if they weren't anywhere at all anymore, he missed them and would continue to until he saw them again, be it in this world or the next.

Oh, his poor family, like a house burgled, a home ransacked. First Joseph, grabbed off some Ciechanow street by the Gestapo. Then his parents and little Mendel, Deborah not long after, Ezra and Ehud…. Noah wept for them all, and always would. As soon as he made his report to Bruno Baum, he raced his shadow back to Block 25 and Hanan, where to his brother's perplexity he didn't let him out of his sight for the rest of the day and night until forced to by the undisputable finality of lights-out.

Autumn

But for the mess of paperwork growing like a living thing atop his desk, SS-*Hauptscharführer* Otto Möll sat alone in his office. He dropped his pen onto the desk and rubbed his eyes with the heels of his hands. When he opened them again, the room was the same, nothing had changed. Not that he'd expected it to, of course, but a person could dream.

He saw the shabbiness of this office as but a reflection of the utter wretchedness of his new posting. The desk was a battered metal hand-me-down, its left bottom drawer refusing to open, a smudge of rust here, a dent there. A single ancient radiator hugged one of the cheaply paneled walls, inadequate at a glance for the freezing months right around the corner. A bank of fluorescents flickered uncertainly above, only half the bulbs working. He would have had new ones put in, except this he didn't mind so much—the last thing this place needed was adequate lighting. From the water stains on the ceiling to the cracked linoleum of the floor, there was nothing that would have gained from more light.

The rest of the camp was no better. Fürstengrube, one of the smaller satellites in the Auschwitz cosmos, had with its coal helped build the huge I.G. Farben factory at Monowitz. It consisted back then of one weather-beaten barracks, a smaller one for the guards, a kitchen, a rough latrine, a tiny shack of an infirmary, and an administrative hut built of the same unpainted gray wood as the rest, all encircled by eleven strands of non-electrified barbed wire.

This past summer, however, the overall commandant of the Auschwitz system, SS-*Obersturmbannführer* Höss, had brokered a deal with Farben Industries to dig a second mine that would raise Fürstengrube's inmate population from a hundred and fifty to seven hundred. As a reward for his services to the Reich at Birkenau, Möll was promoted to master sergeant and installed as commandant. Not that he was given so much as a pfennig to upgrade the place. But for the beehive of construction that was the new mine, and the addition of a second barracks, it was the same decaying backwater of a subcamp it had always been.

Even shabbier than his new surroundings, though, was the way he'd been treated, promotion or no. He saw this last for what it was, a sop to mollify him for removing him from the center of the action. The few hundred prisoners he'd been appointed commandant of were less than the number of *guards* he'd had at his disposal at Birkenau. Some promotion that! He would rather have been demoted if it would have allowed him to stay where he was.

What was behind it all was politics, something he'd never been very good at. Diplomacy, compromise, tact were foreign concepts to him; they weren't and never had been a part of his vocabulary. While this wasn't an issue where those prisoners ill-fated enough to be at his mercy were concerned, in his dealings with his fellow SS it worked decidedly against him. With his hair-trigger temper and lack of patience, he tended to rub these the wrong way, be they below or above him in rank, and though he recognized this flaw in himself, he was powerless to correct it. One might as well have told him to start wearing a *yarmulke* and learn Yiddish.

On top of everything, there wasn't an SS man out there who wasn't jealous of his success. The disinterment and cremation of the hundred thousand Jewish corpses a year ago, the performance of his fire pits both then and later, the Kriegsverdienstkreuz—that the 5'7" ex-ditchdigger, a sergeant no less, had triumphed where they had failed or been too timid to try, was too much for all those tall, dashing officers to bear, a slap in the collective face of the whole swagger-sticked bunch of them.

As for the reason given him for his transfer, the discontinuing of the open-air incineration program due to the dwindling number of transports, this was clearly an excuse by which to render him his comeuppance. It was far too premature to start filling in the fire pits. There were millions of Jews left in Europe alone yet to be dealt the just desserts their race's malfeasance had earned them. And once Hitler and the Wehrmacht were on the march again, back on the road to victory, there might be millions more, depending on how much of the world the *Führer* chose to subdue.

And then there was Hungary. Almost a million Jewish renegades continued to hide behind the skirts of the womanly Hungarian government, some having managed to flee there from as far away as Greece and Russia. Though an ally of Germany, Hungary was blind to the Jewish cancer consuming it from within, and up to now deaf as well to all entreaties from Berlin to do something about it. Möll, however, didn't see this deplorable situation lasting forever. Making it a point to keep abreast of such things, he knew that his Chancellery's Jewish Office, under the leadership of the indefatigable SS-*Obersturmbannführer* Adolf Eichmann, was increasing its pressure on Budapest to turn over its Hebrews. Given this, and the power and popularity of those anti-Semitic elements that had proliferated in Hungary since the alliance, it was only a matter of time before Admiral Horthy and the other leaders of the country would have little choice but to agree to the deportation of their Jews.

That was how Möll viewed it anyway, and it worried him sick that he might end up missing out on the big show to come.

On the other hand, if hundreds of thousands of new faces should show up at Birkenau all of a sudden, he knew that though the gas chambers would be able to handle the load, there was no chance the ovens could. There simply weren't enough of them. Without the fire pits to help, the bodies would be backed up for weeks, a less than pleasant prospect made incalculably worse should the thermometer at the time read much above freezing.

This thought brightened his mood some, to the point of wresting half a smile from his lips. To say he'd seen the last of Birkenau wasn't being realistic; just as their "magnificences" the SS brass had depended on him before, so would they again. Plus, it wasn't as if he'd been exiled to Lithuania or someplace. Fürstengrube was only nineteen miles from the crematoria.

At the moment, however, it felt more like nineteen hundred. He missed his old digs as much as he could remember missing any place. Birkenau had a majesty to it, a presence, this rat's nest of a camp couldn't begin to approach; he'd seen interrogation rooms there better maintained than his headquarters here. With a frown, he stared at the mound of paperwork beneath which his desk was buried. To the high-energy man of action Möll fancied himself, this was the ugliest part of not only his new office but job. He picked up a bundle of the confounded white sheets and leafed through them. Regulatory permits, construction invoices, invoices of every kind, guard schedules, guard payroll, purchase orders, requisition orders, you name it, it was there. From exterminating angel, he'd been reduced to full-time bureaucrat; here it was past midnight and he was still shuffling papers around, signing his name to this and that one, filling out forms.

To hell with it, he swore silently, tossing the papers back onto the pile. The blasted things could wait for now. He swung out of his chair and made for the room's one window, four curtainless squares of glass as black as if they'd been painted. In the distance, he could see the lights illuminating the construction site for the new mine, like a sprinkling of stars fallen to earth. Business was good apparently, I.G. Farben hungry for coal. It had insisted its Fürstengrube project be worked on day and night.

Hopefully, this second mine would be an improvement on its predecessor. The original collected water, and its tunnels were always collapsing; the camp's mortality rate, by percentage, was almost as great as that at Birkenau. Not that this was in any danger of moving him to tears. As long as production quotas were met, he didn't care how many inmates were lost. The human material sent here was of very poor quality. The various mines in the region, mostly coal and iron, were considered punishment duty; the prisoners remanded to them were from the bottom of the barrel, those unable or unwilling to adhere to concentration-camp discipline. They were the least palatable sort of Jew, lazy, slovenly, or worse, rebellious. So what if they dropped like flies; it wasn't as if there was any scarcity of them. If there was one thing this part of Poland wasn't short on, it was expendable bodies.

It hadn't taken long for the ex-*Kommandoführer* of Auschwitz's Block 11 to figure out that Fürstengrube wasn't as punitive an establishment as it could have been. The first thing Möll did was cut the prisoners' rations. The expense he saved there, and by abolishing the infirmary, went toward strengthening security. He requested and received more guards, had four watchtowers built, and was awaiting delivery on a pair of searchlights.

These precautions might have been deemed paranoid but for one thing. His first week there, two prisoners had escaped by cutting the wire. It wasn't until then that he learned the camp had a reputation for being porous, three such attempts in the past six months alone. This fourth attempt, he suspected, was the prisoners' way of testing their new commandant, a test he both welcomed and knew he mustn't fail. At the morning Appell following the escape, he strode to the front of those assembled, mounted a crate, and demanded to know where their missing comrades were headed. He didn't get an answer, but then he wasn't really after one. With their silence filling the yard, he stepped down from his perch and unholstering his pistol, strode among the prisoners, shooting them calmly and at random. He didn't stop until he'd left twenty of them splayed in the dirt before sending the rest off to work. When they came back in the evening and as the night shift departed, both groups passed the corpses of the unlucky twenty laid out in neat rows on either side of the main gate. There they would remain for three days, until the capture and return of the two fugitives, both of whom he ordered beat to a pulp before dispatching them to the gallows.

There were no more escape attempts after that. From then on, the inmates lived in terror of their new overseer. With no infirmary anymore, all the sick and wounded were diagnosed as incurable and shot, often by Möll himself. A long list of transgressions, many of them minor, now merited a death sentence as well. He was cracking the whip all right, and not just to tighten ship. Having been railroaded into so humble a command hadn't helped his disposition any.

It wasn't just the place that was galling him, though. As trying as anything was being deprived of the chance to exercise his talents to the fullest, talents he wished nothing more than to put at the disposal of his country. He liked to think he'd been forged for one purpose and one alone, to act as a sword for his people, a blade to cut away the tentacles of the Jewish monster strangling them. He hadn't been put on this earth to sit behind a desk, but to wade hip-deep in the corpses of the enemies of his race, that most pernicious of enemies, that grinning jackal, the Jew.

Yet here he was in an office where he'd been most of the day, not a drop of mud, much less blood, on uniform or boot. He spread his fingers in front of him and shook his head ruefully. They weren't smeared with red as they could have been, by all rights should have been, but with the blue from a leaking fountain pen.

Not that he wasn't grateful for the opportunities extended him up to now. In the unlikely event he were never to lay eyes on Birkenau again, he'd had a great run. He returned to his chair, and tilting it back, appeared to study the ceiling. It had been a glorious summer. The success of the war against the Jews continued to exceed all expectations. Already much of the Reich was for all practical purposes *Judenrein*, Jew-free, including Germany and Austria, what used to be Poland and Czechoslovakia, all of the Baltics and much of the Balkans, with Italy, Greece, France, and the Low Countries not far behind. And most of this in less than a year and a half. But for the Einsatzgruppen in Russia, sanctioned hostilities specifically targeting the Jews hadn't arisen until the establishment of the death camps two springs ago.

When one thought about it, the progress made since was almost too good to be true. Putting aside the iron will needed to see the thing through, the logistics alone for so vast an undertaking were hard to wrap one's mind around. From the sun-bleached islands of the Mediterranean to the farthest reaches of frozen Norway, those Jews under German authority, both urban and rural, had to be registered, rounded up, then moved to embarkation points, either transit camps or ghettos. From there it became a matter of transporting them to the killing centers in Poland, often many hundreds of miles away. The cost for this must have been staggering, never mind the technical complexities involved. Trains, in some cases even barges and ships, had to be procured, assigned routes and timetables, guards and engineers, then make their way through the bureaucratic jungles and rail systems of various countries until reaching their destinations.

And all of this complicated by the necessity of adopting a cloak of deception designed to keep the deportees ignorant of their fate right up to the very doors of the gas chambers. Which had been neither easy nor cheap in their own right to build. What was more, Germany had taken this task upon itself while fighting a world war for national existence against the mongrel Bolshevik hordes and their western/Jewish allies.

No one was prouder of his country for assuming this burden than Möll. From an organizational point of view, it was a project surpassed by few if any in history. The pyramids of Egypt, the Great Wall of China, the towering cathedrals of medieval Europe, the colonization of the Americas—all had taken generations to realize, while in the span of a paltry two years the Third Reich was poised to accomplish its goal of freeing this critical corner of the world of its Jewish pestilence forever, an achievement as lasting and arguably of even more benefit than the rest.

As for the killing itself, the method and equipment employed were paragons of modern German engineering. The apparati of Birkenau weren't much different in function from the Krupp and Siemens factories operating day and night at Monowitz. One was as industrial in form and content as the other; the raw material going into the crematoria just happened to be people, the finished product coming out, death. Not just death, either, but disposal, and in numbers never dreamt of. The Birkenau assembly line was capable of cranking out fifteen thousand "units" of untraceable ash a day, *every* day, for weeks at a time if required. Little muss and less fuss, and no one the wiser. Not until the *Führer*, that is, should deem it expedient one day to let the rest of the world in on the good news.

That was the thing, Möll mused: no country on earth gave so much as a snap of the fingers for the Jews. From the start, the international community, while condemning what it called the cruelty of the Nazis, had no wish to open its doors to any more of that conniving race than it already possessed. Beginning in the 1930's, Hitler had tried to get somebody, anybody to take them off his hands, but had met with nothing but resistance. Germany's initial proposal for the solution of its Jewish problem had been the deportation of that problem *en masse* to either the underpopulated African island of Madagascar or inland to the interior and Uganda. Why these two places, the sergeant had no idea, but when they proved unrealistic a second solution was advanced, a more voluntary emigration. To this end, the Nuremburg Laws of 1935 were enacted, a body of precepts so draconian and degrading that it was thought the Jews would have no choice but to flee and seek residence elsewhere. These laws ran the gamut from the serious to the symbolic, everything from denying Jews access to schools, hospitals, and banks to making it illegal for them to use the sidewalk or keep a pet.

Though it should have come as no surprise, they weren't as effective as hoped. For almost two thousand years, the Jews of the Diaspora, uprooted from their ancestral homeland and forced to settle in countries often resentful of their presence, had weathered many storms. They'd seen the Nuremburg Laws before, if under different names and in different languages, and harsh as these were, they'd been nothing to the blood-drenched pogroms their host peoples had regularly visited upon them. Through it all, though, they'd not only survived but grown prosperous. How? By hunkering down and holding fast, keeping a low profile, bowing their heads and doing as the Gentile commanded, but also never forgetting where their true loyalty lay, to each other and only there. This had served them well for centuries, nor was there any reason for them to think it wouldn't now. This storm, too, would pass. History as they knew it practically guaranteed it.

The flight of those few who saw what was coming, or were simply tired of being bullied and living in fear, didn't in most cases meet with a happy ending. Either for them or the Germans seeking to get rid of them. Ships full of the Chosen People (meaning those, as the joke went, who'd chosen to get the hell out of the country) steamed out of Hamburg and other ports with emigration papers and sometimes the vessels themselves gladly provided by their evictors, only to return weeks later with their cargoes intact, their search for asylum having been rebuffed at every turn.

In every ideology, no matter how uncompromising, there sometimes appeared a crack in the wall of belief, a whisper of doubt as to whether the end justified the means. Not even Otto Möll, the unregenerate *Hauptscharführer*, the Cyclops, the Angel of Death—Mal'ach H'Mavet reincarnate—not even he was entirely immune from this doubt. Alone in his bed, slowly surrendering to sleep, his senses shutting off and defenses down, a question would sometimes creep up on him from out of the blackness: was all this bloodshed, this killing, defensible? Was it even called for? The logic of deverminization aside, it wasn't cockroaches or bedbugs he was helping to eliminate, but people. Or if not exactly people, a species not far removed.

At such moments, his resolve was rendered implacable again by remembering those ships crammed full of German-Jewish émigrés returning, still crammed, to their original ports of call. There wasn't a government in the world that cared a whit for the Jews. Indeed, he suspected most of clandestinely applauding the Germans for having the daring to recognize the Jewish menace for what it was and deal with it. Surely Churchill, Roosevelt, and Stalin knew what was going on in Poland and occupied Russia, if not the exact numbers and other details then the substance of it. Their respective intelligence services were too sophisticated and far-flung, too infiltrated with double agents, not to. It was one thing to succeed in keeping the operations secret from civilians, both at home and abroad, quite another to hide it from the eyes and ears of enemy spies.

So what was the aforementioned triumvirate doing on behalf of the Jews? Continuing to mouth self-righteous platitudes on the radio and in the newspapers about the evils of Nazi racial barbarism, when a few Soviet bombers could have leveled Birkenau's crematoria in five minutes. It was clear that here were men who in their hypocrisy were perfectly content to let Hitler do the dirty work of Judaicide for them. The thought of it was enough to make Möll want to vomit.

With the failure of its emigration program to make much of a dent in its Jewish population, a desperate Germany made one last push in that direction. On the night of November 9th, 1938, the whole country erupted in a spasm of violence, hate filling the streets of every city like lava from a volcano. The object of this hatred? Why, the Jews, of course, their homes, businesses, synagogues looted and burned, hundreds lynched on the spot wherever the frenzied mobs found them, thousands more trundled off to concentration camps. This *Kristallnacht*, or Night of the Broken Glass, though touted as a spontaneous outpouring of popular ill will, was in fact a carefully organized, government-backed demonstration, a dance of death and destruction choreographed at the highest level in Berlin. Möll couldn't be positive, but he suspected that the riots weren't intended so much to terrorize the Jews as to shock those watching from afar into loosening their immigration quotas. If even a little sincere in their concern, this would have been the time for the nations of the world to act.

And so they did, notably Britain and the United States. In the months following Kristallnacht, England capped Jewish entry into Palestine at fifteen thousand a year, a significant reduction, while in America a piece of legislation known as the Child Refugee Bill was put to a vote in their Congress and roundly defeated. It would have allowed ten thousand German-Jewish children into the country every year. Reclining in his chair, Möll had to smile, as he did every time he recalled this last bit of American smarminess. Apparently the invitation inscribed on that famous statue of theirs, "Give me your tired, your poor, your huddled masses yearning to breathe free", didn't extend to the Goldsteins and Greenburgs of the world. Nor their just as unwholesome children.

At any rate, Germany had run out of options. When three years later, the Semitic cabal that owned America manipulated it into the war, Hitler's patience evaporated. He ordered that the third and Final Solution to the Jewish infestation begin, and chose Poland as the site for its enforcement. Möll trusted that when it was completed, and the time was right, the *Führer* would reveal his and his countrymen's gift to the world, and the world, though sure to squawk in protest at first, would in the end be all gratitude.

The Jews, meanwhile, had only themselves to blame. In their greed and lust for domination, they'd amassed a huge debt. Apart from ten centuries of behind-the-scenes scheming and machinations culminating in their ascension to the top rungs of power, not only had they engineered the mortifying German surrender of the last war but started the present one, as Hitler himself had so convincingly argued. What they'd had the temerity to begin, however, the SS were intent on finishing. It had become their sacred mission to excise the Jewish tumor from the European body. Nor could anyone have predicted the success with which they'd met so far.

Of course, the progress of the deverminization wouldn't have been nearly as rapid without the unfathomable cooperation of the vermin themselves. Möll just didn't understand it. Oh, he did, he supposed— if one wanted to, one could boil it down to simple arithmetic. For a thousand years, the European Jews had attached themselves like parasites to host populations outnumbering them hundreds to one. In such an environment, any attempt to expand their influence would have prompted serious retaliation, maybe even a bloodbath. In their quest for sovereignty, therefore, they'd had to be sly, resorting to subversion of all types, bribery, racial and other defilements, and out and out trickery, all under the guise of smiling acquiescence.

As a consequence, both his culture long ago and the individual from childhood having forsworn overt aggression as a way of solving anything, the Jew was no longer capable of fighting his way out of a paper sack, not even to defend himself. In short, he had evolved into a natural coward. Physical resistance was as alien an abstraction to him as that generosity of heart and purse for which the Christian was known. That brief set-to in the Warsaw ghetto these five months ago had been no more than an aberration, instigated and much of it carried through no doubt by outside agitators, namely that partisan rabble that called itself the Polish Home Army.

Still, it never ceased to amaze him how willingly, almost gladly the Jew went to his death. And not a heroic death, but a naked, shameful one. With few exceptions, they followed SS orders every step of the way. When told to register in their native countries at the appointed place and time, they'd registered. When commanded to pack their belongings and relocate to the ghetto, they'd relocated. When driven out of the hovels they'd been jammed into there only to be packed even tighter into cattle cars literally lacking a pot to piss in, even then they hadn't resisted. At the unloading ramp at journey's end, they continued to obey orders and climbed without incident onto the crematorium trucks, and later in the undressing room, having dutifully stripped to the buff, were easily herded to the "showers". Was it possible, what with the smoke billowing from the enormous *Krema* chimney and the stink of roasting flesh stronger at this strange-looking building than anywhere, that they weren't at least suspicious of what awaited them inside? Yet in they'd walked by the hundreds of thousands with nary a whimper.

Möll had managed to stay in touch with several acquaintances from his days at SS training school, some of who had been sent east and ended up in the Einsatzgruppe brigades in Russia. Together, two of these last had stopped to visit him in Birkenau while on leave and en route to Germany, and from them he'd learned much. Apparently, the Bolshevik Jews were as gutless as their European kin. Not only did they let themselves be taken unresisting to the killing grounds, they dug their own graves, then lined up obligingly, almost casually in front of them. What happened then all too often was even less explicable. According to his friends, sometimes those women with children, upon turning to face the guns, would scramble to arrange their offspring in descending order, from tallest to shortest, as if posing them for a picture. This appeared for all the world to be nothing less than a final, maniacal nod to decorum, one last show of propriety.... at the very edge of the pit!

And in a way, so it was. As one of his soldier friends explained to a stupefied Möll, the other looking on in agreement, it was his opinion that those hell-begotten Jewesses, mother hens to the last, hoped that "if we Germans saw how well-behaved, how obedient and polite their children were, we might have second thoughts about shooting them."

Who were these fantastical creatures the Jews? Were they indeed imps of Satan, spawned out of spite by the Father of Lies to vex and otherwise provoke that nobler creation of God, man? That they weren't fully human was axiomatic. No one at death's door would have conducted himself as the Jew did. On and on they'd come at Birkenau from early spring to the end of summer, like waves of lemmings eager to launch themselves into the sea—except, unlike the lemming, whose behavior was dictated by instinct, there was nothing natural about the Jewish fondness for self-obliteration. It wasn't normal for people to walk with such determination to the grave, yet how many times had Möll seen them muscle each other out of the way in their hurry to reach the gas chamber, to be the first ones in?

Granted, the SS took every pain to disguise the true purpose of the death houses. Nor, after so long and dry a journey as most of the deportees had endured, should the enticement of water, even shower water, be overlooked. This failed to explain, however, the reaction of those Jews arriving from the Himmelblocks, none of who could have had the slightest doubt what awaited him. Yet never had he heard of a single one refusing to board the truck taking him there or unboard it when it reached the crematorium yard. All had done as instructed, if not without complaint then certainly with the passive docility of brute animals.

Or maybe that docility wasn't so passive after all. Perhaps passive-aggressive would better describe it, a ploy on the part of the victim, whether calculated or not, to exact if only *post mortem* a modicum of revenge. If so, how cunning the Jew, how terrible his submission! By walking so obeisantly, so lamblike to the slaughter, no dignity remained for his execution. The soldier responsible was reduced to nothing more than a hireling at a stockyard, his proud uniform to a rubber apron, his rifle to a cattle prod, his soldier's daring and dash to a menial's drab routine.

Leave it to the Jew to attempt to have the last laugh, and succeed. By making it too easy for him, depriving the warrior of the glory of the kill, he was in effect stealing not only that warrior's honor but his manhood, and by extension his humanity as well.

It was psychological murder, in its way as ruinous as the physical kind. Nor did one have to look far to see the damage it was inflicting on personnel. Of those two pals of his, for instance, who'd taken the time to come see him, one had the shakes from drinking too much schnapps, while the other admitted to being on psychiatric leave. The first, in addition to the tremor in his hand, never once his whole stay managed to meet Möll's gaze, his eyes darting about like those of an anxious dog. The second revealed an even more troubling symptom. His right arm hung in a sling, not as a result of some wound, but from a partial paralysis of that side caused by what he confessed, after some prodding, had been a "nervous episode". He was quick to add that his doctors had assured him he'd be back up to snuff in no time. Unlike his companion's, his eyes seldom strayed, but not to look *at* a person so much as through him, as at something behind him; that person might as well have been invisible. Möll had a pretty good idea what that something was, too, or did after he heard this story from the poor man.

"Our brigade, Einsatzgruppe B, was engaged in an operation outside the Ukrainian town of Janina. It was my turn that day to man one of the machine guns. The boy was six or seven, no different from the other boys I'd faced that morning, except for one thing. Just as I was about to pull the trigger, a fraction of a second before, he—he did a strange thing. Something I'd never seen, or thought I ever would see."

Möll waited, but the man just sat there, a puzzled look on his face. "What?" Möll said finally. "What did he do, the boy?"

"He waved at me!" the other exclaimed in disbelief. "Raised his hand, and with a little smile, waved goodbye… at *me*! Not the man on either side of me, or anyone else, but at me. I could tell because his eyes were as locked onto mine as yours are now."

For one of the few times since his arrival, he was really looking at Möll, not past him but directly, imploringly at him. Now that he'd done so, he told his confidante, he wasn't sure why he'd brought it up. He hadn't come here to burden Möll with his problems.

"I just can't seem to get it out of my head, Otto," he explained, "waking or sleeping. I still have dreams about that day, and they won't go away. Smiling, that miserable kid, as if I was his friend or something. Can you imagine?"

Yes, he could, yes indeed. He'd seen the same leering smile at Gusen, Sachsenhausen, Birkenau, even here at Fürstengrube. It was a smile of victory snatched from defeat, triumph from surrender, born of the knowledge that by giving up his life cheaply, without a struggle, the victim was taking a chunk of his killer's soul to the grave with him. That a six-year-old should be in on the act, a child not old enough to be doing it on purpose, only demonstrated the depth to which this perverseness had entrenched itself in the Jewish psyche.

As for his visitor who'd owned up to drinking too much, he was far from alone in that. Möll could count on his hands the number of officers and men at Birkenau not driven by their work to consume inordinate amounts of alcohol. And though as a brother SS he commiserated with their frailty, he couldn't bring himself to excuse either the reason or remedy for it. In his view, it stemmed from nothing less than a failure of ideology. One of the pillars of the Nazi *Weltanschauung* was its recognition of the Jewish threat to the survival of the German Volk, and its vow to expunge that threat by any means. If the soldiers chosen to enforce this had to get drunk to do it, what did this say about their attitude toward that doctrine? It was, pure and simple, a repudiation of it, if not in so many words then on a subliminal level.

And these were the SS, the supposedly fanatical guardians of all that National Socialism held dear and stood for! He couldn't decide if such men should be pitied or shot. To him their dipsomania smacked of betrayal. Despite their swagger and the fearsome uniform with the silver death's head on the collar, too many of them at their core weren't cut out for the job. It was one thing to strut about and act the bully toward a bunch of weak-kneed ghetto Jews, quite another to send them thousands at a time to their just reward, particularly when this involved women and children.

One had to remember, however, always remember, that these were no ordinary women and children, but the misleading human forms the subhuman Jews hid behind. Unless he believed this, and without reservation, eventually it could get to a man, cause him to question whether he was purging the Reich of a thousand-year scourge or simply murdering defenseless civilians.

Möll had no such problem. He was unflagging in his belief, and liked to credit it to the fact one was either a patriot or wasn't, loved one's country or didn't, trusted in the values and defining principles of that country or when confronted with a moral or similar dilemma, destroyed oneself with doubt. Prior to joining the SS, he too had drunk his share and more, but even before Gusen had sworn off all such nonsense. From the day he'd first pinned that grinning skull to his tunic, he'd found a purpose in life—more than that, had found *himself*—and as never in all the years before was at peace with both that self and the world around him.

Of course, it didn't hurt his abstemiousness that he took the utmost care always to be on his guard. While many of his comrades concerned themselves only with avoiding typhus, diphtheria, and the other diseases the Jews of the camps carried, he made sure to insulate himself as well from those illnesses originating in the corrupt Jewish heart, the deceitful Jewish tongue, the scheming Jewish brain. Seeing as how they were human in appearance only, whenever he saw or heard anything remotely human from them, a sob, a smile, a tear, any emotion at all, he had to regard it as either a trick or an attack or both, and not only hardened his heart against it but as a rule attacked back. One had to keep on one's toes around the Jew. Any contact, even conversation, could be dangerous.

God, how he despised this degenerate race, this woeful excuse for a people! After living for the past half-dozen years in close proximity to them, what once was strictly business had since turned personal, though the seeds of that odium sown at Gusen and Sachsenhausen didn't sprout until he'd reached Auschwitz and stewardship of the penal squad there. And not until Birkenau had they begun to yield their harvest.

No matter, he reflected from the dubious comfort of his hard chair. He had his feet propped on the desk now, hands clasped behind his head. It might have taken a while for his hatred to mature, but no one could say he hadn't made up for lost time. He closed his eyes in recollection of the recent past, the third smile of the night flitting across his face. As proud as he was of his fire pits and how they'd performed, also fulfilling were his contributions to the success of Bunkers 1 and 2. None of it had been easy, the stress, the long hours, the often messy work, but by the same token the rewards had been considerable, foremost among these the satisfaction of a job not only well but extraordinarily done.

He wasn't just trying to be noble here, either. Having once been motivated almost exclusively by ambition, he'd since turned selfless, dedicating himself without thought of recompense to securing his country's future by doing everything in his ken to exclude the Jew from it. He'd become, as a result, one of that new breed of fighting man, the biological soldier, a role that while entrusting him with racial purification also bound him to refrain from both gratuitous violence and profiting from that task.

With regard to these last, he'd be the first to admit that he was only good for one. While the majority of his SS peers were shameless in their greed, he would have none of it. But for the occasional cut of cured meat or other delicacy that would have been wasted on the Sonderkommando anyway, he refused to take part in the plundering of the deads' possessions. On top of such banditry sullying their cause, it was something, if one thought about it, a Jew might have done.

As for the gratuitous violence…. well, there were some rules that were made to be broken, that it was beneficial to break. Or to put it another way, all work and no play made Otto a dull boy. Take, for example, his own little game of swim-frog, not only a welcome diversion from the humdrum but food for the soul as well. What could be more gratifying than to see the sons and daughters of rich Jewish bankers forced to mimic those amphibians that in the evolutionary scheme of things, some would say they weren't all that removed from?

Möll harbored a particular animosity toward the Jewish elite, the wealthy, the educated, the privileged of their kind. He had a knack, too, for sniffing them out that rivaled his dog Hannibal's for flushing rats and other varmints. He would approach a group of prisoners, single out those he suspected, and ask them their trades. Invariably, he would acquire a quick collection of lawyers, teachers, and other professionals, then subject them to whatever sport appealed at the moment.

Another bit of fun he'd cooked up he called "brick-bashing". For this, he divided his victims into two teams, providing each participant with two heavy bricks. The object was to slam these together until they disintegrated, the winning team being the one to accomplish this first. While its members escaped with no more than bruised and bleeding hands, the losers were ordered to start running, whereupon he would grab a rifle from the nearest *Schütze* and pick them off one by one. He'd learned to shoot while hunting squirrels as a boy, in the process acquiring a talent that bordered on the uncanny. Whether his target was moving or stationary, rarely did he miss, and that without seeming to take the time to aim.

"Walking the plank" was another game. A two-by-six was laid athwart a fire pit that had almost burned out, with only a bed of glowing coals at the bottom. The prisoner would be blindfolded and made to cross the board to the opposite edge of the pit. If he refused, he was thrown into the fire, or if his tormentors saw him so much as touch the blindfold, the board was tipped over. Should he appear as if he might make it across, a gun was set off to startle him into stumbling. If this didn't work and he reached the other side, his prize was a merciful bullet to the brain in place of the agony of burning alive.

He also enjoyed browsing the crematoria's undressing rooms for attractive young women. After culling out three or four, he'd have them brought naked to the incineration meadow and lined up before one of the more dissipated pits. There they'd stand trembling, eyes round with fear, staring into the mess of charred corpses at their feet. After soaking up his fill of this, Möll would start crooning that they were next, all that was needed was his order and into the pit they would go. Even if they didn't speak German, the women got the message, and usually ended up panicking and fleeing for their lives. Waiting for just that, he'd sic Hannibal on them. The dog would leap after them, tearing at their legs and buttocks, until its owner had had enough and told their guards to drag them back.

By then he would have worked himself into a frenzy. Shouting curses at his victims, hysterical themselves now and bleeding, he would line them up again in front of the fire, a growling Hannibal loping back and forth behind them.

"Go ahead," he'd scream, "cry your pretty eyes out! It won't do you any good. In a few seconds, you're going to be frying with those down there!"

Sometimes he would shoot them, sometimes he wouldn't, but after they'd either fallen or been pushed into the flames, always stayed to watch until they stopped thrashing about.

As head of the penal commando at Auschwitz, punishment had been Möll's job, but never had it taken so exotic a turn. Puzzling him at first even more than their flamboyance, however, was the way these torture games of his made him feel. Though it took him a while to identify those feelings, in the end there could be no denying where they came from. The slow build-up of tension as the game progressed, the fevered emotion and loss of control accompanying same, the abrupt sensation of release, of pressure relieved at its completion—each of these responses was unmistakably sexual, and all heightened, he noticed, when the victims were female. At his fire-pit frolics in particular, after toying with the young beauties he'd snagged in the undressing room, once he'd had his fun with them, he'd often sneak off somewhere private, a shed or the like, to masturbate.

If he didn't know better, he'd have suspected himself of being a closet sadist, and not in the loose but clinical sense of the word: someone brought to actual physical arousal by the inflicting of pain. The more he pondered it, though, the more simplistic this seemed. Apart from his having never felt the least pull in that direction, incipient sadism was as common a misdiagnosis as a true case was rare. A more credible explanation suggested itself.

He'd been knocking this theory of his around for some time now. Though seldom spoken, it was widely known that among those SS detached to the Russian killing fields and death camps of Poland there existed, in addition to the alcoholism, nightmares, and other infirmities deviling them, a curiously high rate of impotence. He'd first heard veiled complaints of this while working the gas bunkers at Birkenau, and these had got him to thinking. Eventually, he came to the conclusion that the female body as sexual stimulus no longer existed as such for the biological soldier. It had been transformed into something countervailing and ugly, a suppressant rather than a promoter of desire. The rationale for the camp's existence, wholesale extermination, made this inevitable. The Jews spilling out of the cattle cars came with repetition to resemble nothing more than so much meat in transit, walking carcasses processed and consumed, most of them, the first day. To the SS at their posts, the danger inherent in this perception resided in the female form losing its power to titillate and turning cadaverous, into an object of repugnance, the impression reinforced by the sheer number of women that passed before one's eyes daily. Nudity only magnified the effect.

Those deportees who'd been interned for any length of time were even more unappetizing. Once the very flower of youthful femininity, meticulous in appearance and dress, attentive to making the most of what beauty nature had meted them, they'd been reduced after a few months to gaunt, hollow-eyed mockeries of their former selves, their breasts empty pouches, legs swollen and streaked with excrement, heads shaven like convicts, faces pocked with open sores. The smell that washed from them stank of sea rot, of some brackish tidal backwater, a place of mud covered with a carpet of tiny dead crustaceans that crackled underfoot.

If one defined the sex drive as a prerogative to good health, and the allure of the opposite sex as essential to that drive, then the loss of the latter could be as crippling as any wound received in combat. In its stead, new and different erotic incitements were needed. Doors that normal men in normal times were loath to open became expedient to walk through now or risk having their virility end up a fatality of war. How much say one had in which door to pick was anybody's guess, though Möll's appeared to have been chosen for him. As unprepared as he may have been for the shape it took, that didn't mean he wasn't glad to have it. To be left with nothing, to be less than a man, was not an alternative.

As for what was normal and what wasn't, who was to say anymore? Nothing he'd been engaged in for the past several years could be considered normal, and had only gotten less so over time. With summer having boosted the exterminations to well past a million, the orgy of death in which he was immersed had exposed him to phenomena he doubted many had ever known. He'd marveled at the sights and sounds of a hundred thousand men and women held against their will while ten thousand of them went up in smoke every twenty-four hours. He'd have sworn he heard, as if a faint, faraway wind, the haunting wail of a flock of newly disembodied souls as they fluttered skyward into eternity, calling to each other in their grief and confusion. He'd seen nature herself turned on her head, the sky above the western, crematoria-end of the camp illuminated at night by a pulsating mantle of red, the sun blotted out by day with the smoke from his own fire pits. That summer in Birkenau, and for miles around, it had rained more gray, puffy flakes of ash than it had water. Turnips from the camp fields often reached the size of small children, tomatoes from its gardens that of cantaloupes.

Queerest of all perhaps, yet fascinating to behold, was the stubborn Jewish devotion to their lunatic God. Despite making it clear that He'd washed His hands of them, they hadn't abandoned Him, even as they lined up to file into the gas chamber. Again, on they'd come all summer, naked as newborns, skinny, knob-kneed old men nervously stroking their long beards, menopausal women whose breasts rivaled their stout haunches in size, budding adolescents with eyes huge and skittish as a deer's. It never failed that more than a few of them were talking as they walked, not to each other but in a barely audible mumble to that unhearing God in Whom, even here in the crematorium, they continued to profess allegiance. Given the shabby way He'd treated them over the centuries, Möll found this intriguing. The Jew was positively gifted at making excuses for his divinity's disgraceful behavior; seldom was he taken aback by His wrath, nor discouraged by His thirst for the blood of His own children. Instead, he preferred to blame himself for his misfortunes, an arrangement, in view of his infatuation with self-guilt and his God's tyrannical self-righteousness, convenient for both parties.

All the *Hauptscharführer* could do was shake his head at such idiocy. Had their tradition of groveling before their sanctimonious Jehovah blinded the Jews to His brutishness? With the merest flick of a finger, He could have made a rubbish heap of Birkenau. And its five sister Vernichtungslagers with it. Yet for the past year and more the transports had continued to roll, the smokestacks to glow a dull red from overuse.

The Norse gods of his own culture's early days were as useless, a bunch of brawling, mead-swilling, overbearing clowns. Nor had the insipid, mooning double-talk of the Christianity that replaced them been much of an improvement. Except, and he had to give it this, in its distinctly un-Christlike vilification of Jewry. He had yet to encounter a religion, in fact, that in the face of even the flimsiest scrutiny it made sense to follow. To put one's faith in a god was tantamount to trusting in the rational benevolence of a four-year-old. A four-year-old intoxicated by his own power.

But for one, that is, though as the masses in their adulation had been wont to do these past years, to regard Adolf Hitler as divine was to do him a disservice. A messiah who'd led his people to unheard-of heights, yes. A giant, a titan, a superman among men, certainly. But a man all the same, born of woman like the rest, which made his attainments that much more impressive.

Now, *Hitler* made sense. One could count on him. He said what he meant and meant what he said, had laid out his intentions for all to see and carried through on them as no other figure, real or imagined, Möll was aware of. It was all there in his *Mein Kampf*, written twenty years ago, and which he'd had to study in SS school. Since its publication, Hitler had made good on every promise he'd penned, none more unabashed and ambitious than two: the acquisition of *Lebensraum*, or living space, for the German people in the east, and the settlement of the Jewish question once and for all.

Nor in pursuit of the second had the *Führer*, in his ineffable wisdom and foresight, hesitated when deciding to make the war holy. It was one thing to be an optimist and hope for the best, another to look at the map and try to be realistic. After Stalingrad and then Kursk, the Wehrmacht would be lucky to keep that part of Russia it still held. North Africa was gone, and the Allies had wasted no time invading Sicily, with presumably Italy next and Greece not far behind. Should the British and Americans cross the English Channel and establish a beachhead in France, this would leave the Axis to fight a three-front war, as opposed to the single one against the Soviets in which they weren't even holding their own.

Möll had no doubt that Germany would somehow prevail. It was still fairly early in the game, and anything could happen. In the meantime, half the railroads in Europe were funneling Jews into Poland, railroads that could be better used by the military both to hamper the advance of the avenging Slavic legions and prepare for the coming of their western allies. It was plain that a priority had been handed down. The needs of the army, the deployment by rail of troops and supplies, were to play second fiddle to the annihilation of the Jews.

As commander-in-chief of the armed forces, this could only have come from Hitler, and though Möll failed initially to grasp the thinking behind it, in time he'd come to bow to its genius. Cleansed forever of its deadliest enemy the Jew, Germany could weather defeat itself and in some future era, under improved circumstances—a favorable political landscape, a strong, new leader—gain the victory twice denied it before. With a Jewish presence still part of the equation, however, there could be no victory, not now or in the future, especially when the vindictiveness of any who might survive the racial cleansings was factored in. It was imperative, therefore, while Germany still ruled from the Atlantic Ocean to the Black Sea, that it dispose of those Jews still under its heel, even at the expense of military necessity.

This was what was meant by the war having become holy, its thrust more ecumenical now than imperialist. One could add magnanimity to the list of Hitler's virtues: by putting the devastation of the Jews before success on the battlefield, he may have been courting defeat for himself, but facilitating triumph for coming generations of Germans. Not to mention doing the rest of mankind a favor in the process.

If one did allow that the war had been sanctified, then it must follow that Auschwitz-Birkenau be recognized as its spiritual center, its Mecca, its Rome, its Jerusalem if you will—a site consecrated by an occurrence unprecedented in history, a system of killing so new and audacious in form and scale, so beyond anything that had come before or was likely to come after, as to approach the supernatural, the mystical, the sublime. That so many had met their end in so short a time and on so small a plot of ground had made that ground sacred. Because of this, the slaughter could be seen as something akin to a religious rite, and he, Otto Möll, an attendant priest at that rite.

And they weren't finished, the SS. There was more work to do. His superiors might not be aware of it yet, but he knew Birkenau was a long way from having outlived its value. What he didn't know was when it would be needed again, when *he* would be needed, but had a hunch it wasn't far off. And when finally, as they must, they did call him back, he would be ready. He was ready now. It wasn't as if he'd been sitting on his duff all this time doing nothing.

Unpropping his feet, he opened the bottom-right drawer of his desk and drew out a scroll of thick paper bound in black ribbon. Tenderly, he untied it and unrolled it atop the papers on his desk. It was a blueprint, painstakingly precise, of that idea he'd stumbled upon a year ago during the cremation of the exhumed hundred thousand: the self-fueling fire pit, in which the liquid fat from the burning corpses was to be collected and used in place of kerosene to keep the blaze going.

After his transfer to Fürstengrube—at first just to fill the time, later as if there wasn't time enough—he'd kept at the project until it was done. He couldn't have been prouder of what he'd ended up with, either, often dragging it out as now for the sheer enjoyment of poring over it. Not only was it as professional a study as one could want, it seemed eminently workable. Simply put, two sloping cement troughs channeled the fat into a pair of collecting basins, from which it could be ladled back onto the fire. He was hoping by now to have constructed a prototype to test it, but had yet to find a prisoner skilled enough in cement to advise him in this. Nor was he going to, not here. The misfits and rejects sent him from the other camps were fit only for burrowing in the earth like the animals they were.

But that was okay. He was willing to be patient. With the Bauhof Kommando awaiting him in Birkenau, he could afford to be. He had other ideas, too, for when he got back, and lots of them. As workmanlike as it was, there remained plenty of room in the system for improvement. How many of these he'd be allowed to put into practice, of course, remained to be seen, but if things were again jumping enough for him to be in demand, so should any suggestions he had to offer. Most were dedicated, after all, to the refinement of that specialty which hadn't only made him renowned but at times indispensable: the disposal by fire, outdoors, without machinery, of ton upon ton of asphyxiated flesh.

Through no fault of his own, Möll never had the benefit of a higher education. The hyperinflation of German currency brought about by Jewish speculators in the 1920's had bankrupted his parents and made any talk of college meaningless. He'd done well in his studies at the secondary level, however, and had been blessed his whole life with an inquiring mind, a hunger for knowledge that led him to explore paths others in his place might not have. Thus his interest in events, current and historical, that shone a complimentary light on National Socialism and its philosophy.

He was also good at figuring things out, for probing to the root of a problem and solving it. He'd always felt he would have made a good engineer if he'd had the chance. If so, he would more than likely be a major by now, building bridges somewhere or air fields, or in armaments production. As it was, even with this latest promotion, he was nothing more than a sergeant still, had to end his sentences with a "sir" when talking to a lousy wet-behind-the-ears *Untersturmführer* fresh out of officer's school. Which was one reason he never considered himself in full uniform until he'd hung the Kriegsverdienstkreuz around his neck. It helped in curbing the haughtiness of his putative superiors, some of who could hardly keep their eyes off the thing.

With the possibilities the fortunes of war had laid at his feet, though, he'd be damned if he was going to let the absence of a diploma hold him back. He'd decided months ago that what he lacked in scholastics, he would make up for with sweat and as much on-the-job training as his schedule would permit. He was everywhere that spring and summer, observing, joining in—the unloading ramp, the undressing rooms, the anterooms to the gas chambers, the ovens, with the Disinfektoren emptying their Zyklon-B into the induction vents. Not content with just the fire pits, he wanted to learn the ins and outs of every phase of operations, from how to handle the poison to handling the people. There wasn't a procedure at which he wasn't present at least once from prep to cleanup; he'd even driven one of the trucks that took the ashes to the Vistula and dumped them. He was working eighteen-hour days and loving every minute of it, absorbing Birkenau like a sponge, getting to know it like a book.

He'd made up his mind, he would be an engineer yet. Maybe not a civil or a mechanical or an electrical one, but if not something qualitatively as great, then certainly of greater service to the Fatherland. The title he'd chosen for himself was *extermination* engineer, the first and quite possibly the last of his kind, a devotee of the art and science not of construction but destruction.

The *Vernichtungs Techniker* by definition created nothing. His output was entirely negative, success measured by how much he subtracted from the world, not what he added. The field was not for the faint of heart, even less the unimaginative. It required man the builder to become man the destroyer, the antipode of what the traditional engineer aspired to.

A tall order, but Möll was enthusiastic about filling it. Indeed, once back where he belonged, in the happy confines of Birkenau, he'd have to insist the suggestions for improvement he brought with him be implemented. Precision was the name of the engineering game, anything less than perfection not to be tolerated. Nor was this the self-important puffery it sounded, a case of ego dragging both perspective and modesty through the dirt. Germany's very existence depended on winning the war; again, not that against Russia and the West, but the war it was waging on that abomination the Jew. With all that was riding on it, with generations to come affected by it, for anyone—especially he who wore the uniform of the SS—to give less than a hundred percent toward that effort wasn't only treason against his country but his race, his tribe, his Volk.

With a last loving look at the blueprint on his desk, he rose from his chair, rolled it up, and put it back in its drawer. The commandant's office came with a small bathroom, a nod to its occupant's status and demanding itinerary. It was to this and its sink that he now took himself, splashing cold water on his face, running wet hands through his hair. Not bothering to dry off, he returned to the window he'd left earlier, and after critiquing his reflection in the glass, looked past it into the black of the Polish night. The distant lights of the unfinished mine still gleamed whitely, and would until the sun made them superfluous. That it was the wee hours of the morning didn't matter to I.G. Farben, its people would have their coal or know the reason why.

Möll was determined to be as single-minded in committing his energies to the task for which destiny had singled him out. The Jew was almost done for; all that remained was to finish the job. Unfortunately, this wasn't going to be easy. Most of the descendants of Abraham left in Europe were in hiding, if not in the homes or on the farms of those outlaw Gentiles protecting them, then with the partisans in the forests. The exception was Hungary, and a major one it was. With its Jewish million continuing to elude justice inside its borders, whatever gains had been made against their kind elsewhere were endangered. It was neither compulsory nor even feasible that every Jew end up a statistic. Not even the SS were that thorough, or needed to be. What mattered was that enough were returned to the hell whence they'd come to keep them from breeding themselves back into relevance. Once this was accomplished, time and a negative birth rate would take care of the rest and eventually render them extinct—unless a bloc of a million of them were left intact to spark their race's resurgence later on.

Möll saw Hungary as critical to both his own and his country's prospects. He couldn't envision Hitler leaving it untouched to fester like a canker in Europe's side, therefore had high hopes it would one day prove the conveyance to rescue him from his exile and return him to his beloved Birkenau. He narrowed his eyes as if to penetrate the blackness outside the window, and the even more formidable distance separating him from the instrument of his redemption. Beyond the lights of the new mine, in a more or less straight line three hundred miles to the south, lay the living bounty of the Hungarian plain, a million lives, if all went as it should, that would soon be intersecting with his.

He was dying to meet them. He planned on giving them a warm welcome, a very warm one indeed. His little joke brought the fourth smile of the night to his face, if but for an instant; he doubted he'd cracked many more than that since his transfer. Was he not himself because it had been a long day and he was tired, or was Fürstengrube, he wondered, starting to make him soft? He wanted to think it the former, and decided the paperwork staring him down from his desk, curse it, could wait until morning. If he felt up to it even then.

*   *   *

As soon as she saw him standing there, she knew something was wrong. There was no reason for an officer to be anywhere near, especially one of his rank. Normally, all she and the Sonderkommando had to deal with during the exchange of the gunpowder were two or three *Schützen* bored out of their skulls, the occasional just as disinterested *Rottenführer*. That an SS captain no less should appear at this diciest part of the operation had Roza Robota in a sweat, the cold sweat of fear.

The Sonder saw him also and didn't know what to do. The boy Wrubel, Yankel Handelsman, Zalman Leventhal, all stood uncertainly to the side of the huge wooden cart they'd just wheeled into the yard from the crematorium, piled high as usual with its small mountain of dead people's clothes. They, too, were aware of the peril they were in, and to a man had gone as pale as the corpses they were used to handling.

The source of their and Roza's discomfiture, SS-*Hauptsturmführer* Franz Hössler, stood inside an open door of the Bekleidungskammer not twenty meters away, arms folded across his chest, watching. If ever a man gave the impression he was onto something, it was he. By not making his presence known until the cart came into view, as if waiting for it to show, he was in effect giving notice that was why he was there—that it was by no means a coincidence that so august a personage should be in so seemingly innocuous a place at so critical a moment.

Leave it to Hössler, she thought, to be the one to find them out. Of all the demons in gray uniforms presiding over the man-made hell that was

Birkenau, the prisoners regarded him as the most cunning. Gifted with a glib tongue, he had no compunction against using it to deceive people to their deaths. Indeed, it was this that had made him his reputation. On the few occasions when those selected from a transport balked at taking the next step in their destruction, be it from the crematorium yard into the crematorium proper or from the undressing room to the gas chamber, Hössler was called in, and with his placating manner and powers of persuasion, invariably convinced them to do as they were told. So adept was he at allaying the suspicions of the doomed that among the inmates he'd come to be known as Moshe Liar.

He was also as pompous and preening as a peacock, a dandy in both demeanor and dress. Six feet tall and darkly handsome, a full head of black hair combed straight back from a high, intelligent forehead, he always looked as if he'd come fresh from a tailor's, his uniform resplendent and creased to a knife-edge. He didn't walk, he paraded, like a ship's captain on his quarterdeck, or someone posturing for a camera only he could see. He'd even been known to wear a monocle, letting it fall dramatically from his eye to dangle from its chain when he felt the situation called for it. His vanity, moreover, was matched only by his cruelty; one had to be a fool to expect more mercy from the ostensibly amiable Hössler than from any other SS killer. Beneath the outgoing, almost likable exterior, beat a heart as hard and black as a lump of seasoned coal.

Such was the dangerous creature come to spy on them, who having left the doorway now circled the clothing cart like a shark checking out its prey. It was a typically raw morning for late-October, all silvery gray, the sun screened behind a field of thin, frozen clouds. It was a broken field, furrowed, as if some cosmic plow had prepped the sky for planting. Not cold, neither was it warm, a steady northerly breeze making it feel cooler than the thermometer proclaimed. As a harbinger of the frigid days to come, it was less a morning to be treasured for its alabaster beauty than feared for the ice storms and arctic winds it presaged. Only the more resourceful of prisoners had coats; the rest had to make do with a single layer of cloth as protection against the glacial claw of winter.

Still, it was of yet not unpleasant. The sun behind the clouds was more like the moon, a ghostly white ball one could look at directly without harm. The pebbles and other detritus dotting the ground gleamed in its luminescent light like gemstones, as did the metal buttons and bars on Hössler's uniform.

How had the son of a bitch zeroed in on them, Roza wondered, or had he? Maybe he just smelled a rat, had a feeling; it was possible he didn't know who or even what he was looking for. Was it his instincts that had brought him here, his policeman's nose? In any case, this was no time to ask either how or why. The only question was *what*, as in what in the world was she going to do now?

Discreetly, she waved the Sonder off, and pulse racing, proceeded to help her co-workers unload the clothing. That she had to get rid of the gunpowder she was holding was obvious, but with it tucked away in a packet in the crotch of her underwear, and Hössler watching their every move, this was easier said than done. As it was forbidden for an inmate to look directly at an SS man, she wasn't able to keep that close an eye on him, but the two times she did dare to glance in his direction it was to discover the *Hauptsturmführer* staring straight at her.

So much for him simply smelling a rat. He hadn't come on a hunch, but to catch them in the act—no telling how long he'd been planning this, looking forward to it. She expected him at any second to order the guards to seize her, and her three accomplices with her.

She couldn't let that happen, not while she was holding. If there was no gunpowder, there was no proof; somehow she had to find a way to lose the stuff, and fast. Not to save her own skin, or even that of her confederates, but to prevent the dissolution of everything she and they had worked for, the end of their all-important, inviolable mission. The mission took precedence. The mission was everything. The flow of explosives to the crematoria mustn't be stopped, should it cost a hundred lives. She had to do something, but what? Her legs all of a sudden felt as wobbly as a marionette's, the palms of her hands damp. It was all she could do not to freeze in panic where she stood.

Instead, it was Hössler who froze, ceasing his circumambulations of the wagon and planting himself opposite its open back end. Wasting no time, Roza sped round to the front. There she scooped up a double armful of clothes, then "accidentally" dropped them, allowing her to squat down in order to retrieve them. Removed for the moment from the captain's view, she was able to reach in her pants, pluck the packet from between her legs, rip the thing open, and strew its contents about.

What happened next stopped her heart in mid-beat. After stashing the empty sack into a pocket of some trousers, and before she had a chance to scuff the gunpowder into the dirt, she looked up to see Hössler bearing down on her almost at a run, his face lit with triumph.

"You there, stop!" he cried. "I said you! Stop right there!"

The crunch of his boots on the gravelly ground sounded like death approaching, the Angel of Death come to wrap her in its wings. In that instant, Roza's future flashed before her eyes: the arrest, the torture chamber, the gallows—the end of all her dreams, of life with Godel, the end of everything. She almost fell to her knees and raised her hands in surrender, though to run and let herself be shot would have been to suffer a fate kinder than the one awaiting her in Block 11.

Yet to her astonishment, he went barreling past her without a glance, as if she wasn't there. Turning slowly, reluctantly, fully expecting to find him kneeling in the dirt behind her examining a handful of gunpowder, she saw him stop only upon reaching the side of the cart across from her. There, her terrified eyes peeping above the heap of clothes she was carrying, stood the real target of his outburst, a Czech girl new to the commando.

Though the youngster looked as if she might faint, Hössler was all smiles. "Don't be afraid, little Jew," Roza heard him say. "It's not you I'm after, but this." Peeling a man's coat from atop the girl's bundle, he held it in front of him, admiring it, before slipping it on. "Just as I thought," he exclaimed, "a perfect fit!"

Then to the girl trembling still before him, "That's all, you can go. Back to your work, get along with you. Oh, and thanks," he scoffed, "for your generosity."

Roza had to admit it was a magnificent coat, worthy of an officer of the exalted SS. Black, supple leather from neck to ankle, buttons of polished ebony, a collar of gray fur—it was the coat of a rich man, a rich Jew Hössler had likely spotted wearing it, probably in the vicinity of one of the crematoria. How long he'd bird-dogged it after that, there was no telling, but was doubtless hoping to find it on this morning's cart. He'd made his way to the Bekleidungs yard not because he smelled a rat but was one, a beady-eyed, greedy, contemptible rodent of a man.

Having got what he came for, Hössler wandered happily out of sight, giving Roza the chance to huddle with her Sonder pals. "Jumping Jerusalem!" she exclaimed on joining the three. "Was I the only one who thought we were done for?"

There was laughter, but it was labored. "I know I was wishing I was somewhere else, that's for sure," Wrubel said. "What I'm *not* so sure of is what in God's name just happened."

"It would seem," Handelsman offered, "that our friend Hössler wasn't here in an official capacity, but to add to what I suspect is an already sizable wardrobe. That black leather trenchcoat—you all saw the thing. We had the devil scared out of us because of a dead man's jacket."

Wrubel glanced at the guards loafing about the yard, none of who was paying them any mind. "That's sort of what I figured," he said, "but I didn't think even the SS could stoop that low. Is there nothing they won't do to bring shame on themselves?"

"And they call us Jews profiteers," Leventhal snorted. "It's they who seem determined to out-shylock Shylock."

Roza smiled at the reference. It was something her bookish Godel might have come up with. "Just be glad," she said, "they're more interested in plunder than in keeping track of that gunpowder of theirs. Not to mention those of us relieving them of it."

"The gunpowder!" blurted Leventhal, touching the heel of his hand to his forehead. "I almost forgot. Shouldn't we, you know, be taking care of business?"

"Nothing to take care of," Roza sighed, "not anymore. I thought for sure Hössler was about to bust us, so I dumped it in the dirt, every last gram of it. And was more than happy for the chance. Every time I looked up, he was staring right at me, or so I thought. Sorry, but who knew? It would have been crazy to try and save it."

"No, you did the right thing," Handelsman assured her, "the only permissible thing. To do otherwise would have been crazy indeed, especially given the lack of urgency these days, after what that fellow Zabludowicz told us, in procuring the gunpowder to begin with. Better luck next time, huh, boys? Although I have to think I'm not the only one feeling pretty damned lucky now."

In spite of the knowledge she'd acted out of necessity, the loss of the gunpowder ate at Roza for the rest of the day. What a waste of something so riskily acquired! She would really have been upset if she, too, hadn't learned from Noah about the sorry state of the revolt, but even then it was discouraging to forfeit so large a shipment. To her practiced eye, it had been a good quarter-kilo if it was an ounce. Most of it had come courtesy of Esther, directly from the safe in Meister von Ende's office. Lately, Roza had voiced some concern at the incautiousness of this, but Esther insisted there was nothing to worry about, and that was good enough for her.

She'd become a big admirer of this Esther Wajcblum, nor was it because of the girl's boldness with the safe. Even though it was indoors, work at the Union Metallwerke was by no means a picnic. In response to Roza's inquiries, no one had anything but bad to say about conditions at the Union factory. Ala Gertner, as a forewoman, had been her main source of information, but she'd canvassed numerous others, and the picture all had drawn of it was bleak.

To start with, a person had to walk a ways just to reach it. The plant was almost three miles from Birkenau, and this a twice-a-day hike, in all kinds of weather, in shoes that didn't fit, on blistered, swollen feet. And when it rained, it was more of a run than a walk; the guards didn't like to be out in the wet, and they had leather whips.

The building itself hugged the ground like an enormous inverted cake pan, sprawling, metallic. Lacking a single window, wrapped tight in barbed wire, it exuded a forbidding air, a perception confirmed upon passing through its doors. Another set of doors and you were in the *Montage*, the main body of the factory, where all five senses were assaulted at once—your flesh by an embracing damp blanket of heat, your ears by the roar and clank of machinery, your nose, eyes, and mouth by a thick yellow dust in the air, as soon as you stepped inside you started choking on the dust.

Most of the interior walls were made of glass, giving the impression you could see everywhere at once, into every room, every corner. The first thing you did see were dozens of female workers seated at both sides of long tables, down the middle of which ran heaping piles of small yellow widgets. These *Einsatzstücken*, or insert pieces, were the casings for the detonators of various bombs, mortar and artillery shells, and had to be measured by hand-held gauges to make sure they met spec. They came from the *Pressen*, or stamping machines, hulking nearby. A ten-chambered mold was filled with yellow powder, the heavy mold lifted and slid into the machine, and after three minutes of heat and pressure out came ten solid pieces. The machines had to be air-hosed after each application to rid them of leftover powder. This was where the dust originated, but where it ended up was in you, breathed into your lungs, swallowed down your gullet, absorbed by your body through the pores of your skin. After several days, you were coughing, feeling dizzy, sick to your stomach. It was commonly assumed that if the Germans didn't kill you first, their toxic powder one day would.

It wasn't easy operating one of the waist-high Pressen, not unlike standing next to a hot oven all day. And those molds weren't just heavy, it was all a girl could do to lift one. It was the kind of machine to sweat the life right out of you, squeeze you as dry as someone wringing out a dishrag. The body could take only so much of this before it gave out, before it sat down one day then couldn't get back up. Sabotage this was called; not surrendering to hunger or exhaustion, sickness or the heat, but daring to slow or stop production on purpose. And there were a hundred other ways to commit this great crime. Going to the bathroom without permission, sabotage! Eating on the job, sabotage! Talking to one of the male workers, sabotage! Stopping for a moment to catch your breath, stretch your limbs, your aching back—sabotage report! Which if you were lucky and not too worn out and weak-looking would land you in Block 11 for a while. If not so lucky then it was off to the crematorium with you, goodbye and nice to have known you, *mein Lieber.*

Making things even worse was you never knew who was watching you, or when. That was why the glass walls. The German Meisters, the kapos, the foremen and women, the SS *Blockführer* and his guard—there were hostile eyes everywhere, eyes able to spot sabotage from halfway across the floor. For twelve long hours, you were under the microscope of those eyes, like a germ on a slide, afraid to so much as start sneezing should it interrupt your work. This was hard on the nerves this living in fear, in a way more of a torture than the heat and the dust, the round-the-clock grind.

The more Roza learned about the ordeal that was the Union, the greater her respect for Esther. That she'd not only survived but excelled in such an environment was a testament to both her stamina and pluck; a spot in the gunpowder room wasn't a position meted out lightly. Her sister Hanka, especially in light of her youth, deserved kudos as well. Compared to the Metallwerke, the Bekleidungskammer in which she'd been fortunate to land was a walk in the park.

What sold her more than anything on the two girls, however, was where they'd been living prior to their deportation. Both came from the Warsaw ghetto, and hadn't only witnessed the history-making uprising there, but participated in it. Actually done battle with the SS! Noah had shared with her what he knew of that glorious fight to the death, which because of his contacts in the underground was substantial. But it was Esther who'd put a human face on the affair. Though she could tell her new friend didn't like to talk about it, after the conversation turned one night to their lives before the camp, she started in on the ghetto and couldn't stop.

"Oh, Roza, we were so scared, Hanka and I, more scared than here, if you can imagine. Before the war, our father owned a factory that manufactured wooden handicrafts. Because of this, after the occupation, he was classified an essential worker; it was his job to make and engrave the crosses for those Wehrmacht soldiers from the Russian front who'd died of their wounds after being shipped to the military hospitals in Warsaw. As a result, he and our mother were relocated to the Aryan side of the wall, a mixed blessing for my sister and me. Though we knew life would be better for them from then on, there we were, two teenagers all alone in the world, a world gone mad and about to come crashing down on us.

"Once the shooting and all the rest of it started, I don't know how many Germans I killed, if any. I think it must have been some, for I was one of those dropping Molotov cocktails from the roofs of the buildings. I can't tell you how amazing it was to be finally fighting back, shoulder to shoulder with other Jews, with men and women who'd had enough of being treated like animals and weren't going to take it anymore. Later, of course, after the Nazis began bombing and setting fire to the ghetto, it was every person for himself. Hanka and I and some others ended up hiding in a deserted apartment building on Mila Street. One day the SS torched it, and we had to jump. It was three stories to a grass courtyard below, and there were soldiers on the other side of it shooting at us.

"Somehow, Hanka and I escaped with no broken bones or bullet holes, and later decided to try our luck in the sewers. Which was about all that was left of the ghetto by then anyway. It took us two days up to our waists in the slime and sewage to reach our parents and safety, but once the ghetto did finally fall, no Jew was really safe in Warsaw, not even essential workers. It was then that all four of us were put on the train to Maidanek. Where, we learned later, our mama and papa were gassed."

Esther fell silent, ran her fingers slowly through the nap of her hair. When again she spoke, her jaw was clenched, her eyes cold.

"I may or may not have killed some Germans," she said, "but if I did, it was too few. Which is why I can't get my hands on enough gunpowder, in the hope that every ounce of it will go toward killing more. The way I see it, the fight in the ghetto isn't over. As long as there are Jews who continue to resist, the battle goes on. And will until there are either none of them or none of us left."

Roza had never seen her so beautiful. Striking to begin with, sheared scalp or no, she belonged to that breed of women whom anger made only prettier. Her big, brown eyes seemed to get bigger, her nostrils to flare provocatively, the signature dimples at the corners of her mouth to deepen even more. Esther's face hateful was Esther's face idealized, as an artist might have painted it.

But it wasn't her beauty that impressed Roza any more than did her familiarity with the Meister's safe. She felt small in Esther's presence. Her escapades in Warsaw made those midnight raids the Shomeir had conducted outside the Ciechanow ghetto look like what they were, glorified games of hide and seek. The girl had fought the SS in armed combat *and* lived to tell the tale, with likely a fair number of German notches on her belt. That had been Roza's dream for going on four years now, ever since the invaders of her homeland had shown their true colors. It was only natural she should be in thrall to someone who'd actually lived that dream, and just as natural, given their similarities of age and disposition, her adulation for this killer of Nazis should have blossomed into friendship. To Roza's delight, the feeling turned out to be mutual. Esther had taken to her as effortlessly as she had to Esther.

She'd never lacked for friends growing up, even if most had been boys. A tomboy herself, she'd preferred the rough-and-tumble company of the male of the species. Her sister Shoshonna was the closest she'd come to a serious girlfriend, a relationship compromised by the very fact of their sisterhood. Neither had chosen, but rather inherited the other, and no matter what, were bound together for life. Would they have found each other if they hadn't been sisters? Roza liked to think so, but in all honesty couldn't say. She'd loved Shoshonna with all the fierceness typical of her, but had to admit they were two different people.

Esther, however, was in many ways her mirror image, and she was able to cut loose, be herself around her as she never had any female. Like the little more than adolescents they still were, in spite of the grimness of their surroundings they spent a lot of time being silly together. They gossiped, exchanged secrets, succumbed to prolonged bouts of giggling, especially when the subject of boyfriends came up. Esther had fallen for a young Pole named Tadek, a handsome fellow who through an uncle had secured a job in the Birkenau laundry. He also held the post of *Schreiber* of a block in D Camp. The position of scribe was a valued one. He or she was responsible for all the paperwork that came into or went out of a hut, such as directives from the camp administration, occupancy and roll-call reports, sick lists, work assignments, special passes, and so on.

Esther was smitten. Not even Hanka could remember seeing her so happy. One day Roza good-naturedly accused her of suffering from camp love with a capital L. She had to agree. "Funny," she said, "that here of all places, in this stinking sewer, this boneyard, I should have come across the man I want to have children with, a man whose heart is no less beautiful than his adorable face."

More than almost anything, as a lot of girls their age did, the two loved to dance, which in gender-segregated Birkenau meant with each other. A dancer since childhood, Esther had once aspired to turning professional and knew all the steps. Soon she and Roza, upon the latter's bribe-fueled visits to her friend's barracks, and more often than not to the delight of an audience, were doing the rhumba, the samba, the waltz and the tango, the American jitterbug even, this last invariably closing with them falling into a laughing heap on the floor. The lack of music was no more an impediment than the absence of male partners; they either dah-dah-dah-ed their own accompaniment or were helped out by those watching. Sometimes in that interval between the night's bread and lights-out, the merriment wafting from Block 2 was more characteristic of a summer camp than one built for mass murder.

Esther may have been the best friend Roza made at Birkenau, but was far from the only one. Marta Bindiger, Ala Gertner, Rose Greuenapfel, Mala Weinstein, Regina Safirsztajn—if she had kept a list, those names would have been at the top of it. All of them, needless to say, met the first requirement her friendship demanded, namely the desire to do whatever it took to see the German beast vanquished, its innocent victims appeased. To this end, each woman was either pilfering or helping to smuggle Union gunpowder.

Other than that, she was attracted to them for different reasons. Because of the coolness she brought to the tensest moments and a talent for letting nothing faze her, Marta played as big a role as she in holding this inner circle of conspirators together. She'd joined the underground not long after Roza and risen as high in its ranks, if in the performance of duties unrelated, especially at first, to the plot. As the importance of her assignments grew, so did her freedom of movement, until it wasn't long before she was showing up everywhere, and with impunity. A Camp, C Camp, the infirmaries, even the men's lagers—there was no limit to her range, nor as a result, the good she was able to leave in her wake. Her official status was as liaison between the Union women and the underground, but though not even those close to her knew how many pies she had her fingers in, she was never too busy for others, had a knack for being there when needed. People were always looking to Roza for strength, to reassure them of their mission, but when she was in want of reassurance and a shoulder to lean on, it was to the imperturbable Marta she would turn.

Ala, by contrast, was a tinderbox of emotions, and never far from combusting. She could be the life of the party or the wettest of mops, depending on which side of the koje she crawled out of in the morning. As with her every sentiment, she didn't try to hide her hatred for the Nazis, and what a hatred it was. She'd have hurled herself off a mountain if she thought it would help avenge her murdered baby Rochele. Whenever the danger of what she was doing caught up with Roza and she felt her own store of courage in need of replenishing, she found Ala's bottomless well of it, reckless as it was, the perfect tonic.

When it came to Mala and Rose, it was their indestructible *joie de vivre* that first drew her to them, and continued to. Both worked in the pressure cooker that was the Pulverraum, Mala on the night shift, Rose during the day. Both had also lost a significant number of family at Birkenau; in one afternoon alone, prior to her recruitment into the conspiracy, Mala had to watch as all three of her sisters were forced onto a Himmelblock truck. Yet both she and Rose refused to give up, to lose their lust for living, but rather made use of it to stave off despair. The method they chose was laughter, often at risk to themselves. Roza would never forget the time, it was a Sunday, Mala gave herself a Hitler moustache with a dab of bootblacking and strutted around half the day without getting into trouble somehow. Nor could she keep from cracking up at Rose's gift for mimicry, particularly—she being half-German herself—when at the expense of von Ende and the other Meisters. But more than just a means of holding grief at arm's length, humor to both women was a form of resistance, an attempt to inject a little normality into not only their own lives but those of others, lives that had become as grotesque as they were ephemeral. In that respect everyone profited from their daffiiness, Roza among them, who when her spirits were needful of a dose of comic relief, knew where to find it.

As for those times her faith in humanity cried out for restoring, all she had to do was spend a few minutes with Regina. The Safirsztajn woman was a walking monument to kindness and understanding. Excluding the SS and those prisoners who'd sold out to them, she didn't have a bad word to say about anyone, insisted instead on always giving people the benefit of the doubt. Regina was a short, moon-faced twenty-three, with in spite of her youth a decidedly matronly mien, who gave the impression that in more conventional times and on a better diet, she would probably have been on the plump side as well.

Just because she was kind, though, didn't make her an easy mark. She hadn't been appointed forewoman of the gunpowder section because she was a pushover. She could be hard if the situation called for it; at any other time, she was everyone's big sister. When Roza sought Regina out it was to feed off her sweetness, her generosity of spirit. In the bloody meat grinder that was Birkenau, which brought out the worst in people, it was good to be reminded that men and women were more than base animals, that they also had something of the angels in them.

She counted others among her friends, too. As with most who'd crossed paths with her, she'd taken a shine to Hanka Wajcblum, the teenager having exhibited the same disregard for danger as her older sister.

Hanka was running as much gunpowder as anyone, and raring to do more. Beneath the pimples, the gawkiness, and the child's stick of a body beat a heart the boldest man would have envied.

Then there were those Sonder to whom Roza was passing the dynamite, a couple of them hailing from her hometown. She'd learned by then that the SS had conscripted an unusually large number of men from the Ciechanow transport for duty in the Sonderkommando, many of them friends she'd made in the Shomeir and elsewhere. The only face she knew from the old days to make the trip to the Bekleidungskammer, however, was a boy named Wrubel, whose father had owned the neighborhood bakery.

Though barely eighteen, Ariel Wrubel had managed to gain the confidence of the Sonder leadership; few were those trusted with the job of picking up the gunpowder from Roza and carting it back to the crematoria. Well on his way to standing out from the crowd physically, already a strapping six-footer broad in chest and shoulder, it was his attitude more than his muscles that had made an impression on Kaminski. His entire family had been extinguished at Birkenau, a loss that instead of crushing him ended up giving him reason to live. From the moment he heard of the revolt, he'd not only been on board but existed for nothing else, less for the chance to save himself than avenge his slaughtered kin. To see German blood spilled was all that mattered to him. Not just another recruit, he was the kind of modern-day Zealot the Battle Group needed, more than ready to lay down his life if it meant depriving some Nazis of theirs.

Roza remembered him as cheerful, outgoing, nor to her eyes had the gruesome realities of his new life changed him. He seemed the same happy kid who used to deliver her family's coffee cake. What she couldn't know was how hard he worked to make it appear so. Or how often he could be heard quietly crying himself to sleep at night.

The only other Sonder from Ciechanow to man the clothing cart was Zalman Leventhal, just recently assigned the duty. Though unacquainted with him until now, she always looked forward to seeing him. She suspected it was because he reminded her of Godel. Not only the same age, they shared the same boyish build, both skinny as flagpoles. They were alike, too, in their love of books. Long aware of her man's infatuation with the printed word, she could tell from his occasional casual reference to Shakespeare among others that Leventhal was also well read. There the resemblance ended, the dour redhead being not half so personable. The similarity was enough, though, for her to regard him with affection, which as far as he had it in him, he returned. Other than Gradowski and maybe Kaminski, no one did he feel more at ease with than Roza. Exactly why he couldn't say, unless it was her smile. He'd grown up clumsy around women, wasn't used to smiles from them, yet here was one, and a pretty one, who gave them freely.

She also had friends she wasn't aware of, men the likes of Leventhal's same Kaminski, and the Steering Committee's Bruno Baum, both of who applauded her from afar yet refrained from making contact. Aside from their having no business in SS eyes to be around her in the first place, what anxieties, they figured, might it have bred in her that two people she didn't know from Adam were in on her secret?

Head and shoulders above each of them, however, the new and the old, the known as well as unknown, stood her staunchest friend of all, her and Godel's best buddy, the famous, the formidable, the one-of-a-kind Noah Zabludowicz. For going on four years, the three had been thick as thieves; not even Birkenau had succeeded in keeping them entirely apart. In the ghetto, meanwhile, they'd been inseparable, and had never failed to project a bond that bordered on the familial—walking arm in arm down the street, seen at all hours hunched together in conversation, sharing clothes, sharing food…. sharing, some said, who knew what else. There were those who whispered of impropriety, even a *ménage a trois*, but they were in the minority, outsiders for the most part. Everyone who'd known or known of them for any length of time was aware also that Roza and Godel were a number, with Noah no more than a platonic third wheel. That this seemed to work for them without giving rise to complications was deemed deserving of praise for all involved.

She on the other hand knew better, having come to realize long ago, to her consternation, that a good part of Noah's affections were far from platonic. A girl would have had to be blind not to notice. Seeing as how she was already spoken for, that he'd never bared his soul and come out with it was to his credit. But love had a way of revealing itself beyond the verbal. There were too many times, too many moments when his guard was down for her not to have picked up on that look in his eyes, that plaintive, puppy-dog stare that could mean only one thing. Nor was there any mistaking the dead giveaway of his smile, which when directed her way was always a shade brighter than it had a right to be. His persona seemed perceptibly to soften when he was around her, from uncowable to something approaching the submissive. He wasn't as exacting with her as he could be with other people. She knew she could do or say just about anything and it would be all right by him.

Not once, however, had Roza held any of this against him. Nor viewed his divergent passion as a betrayal of their friendship. Or for that matter, his and Godel's. Again, that Noah hadn't come even close to acting on his feelings, that he'd had the discretion, the decency to keep them to himself, was in her eyes enough not to blame him for having them. Young as she was, she understood that like an untrained animal or undisciplined child, the heart didn't always behave as it should. Love tended to play by its own rules, and where these led, people were all too often powerless not to follow.

She had once toyed with the idea of confronting him about it, if for no other reason than to clear the air between them. That was the way, after all, she dealt with most problems, not by running and hiding from them, but facing them head-on. Something told her at the time, though, to let this one be, nor in the months, and what became the years to come, had she regretted her decision. Not only had it remained harmlessly unspoken but time was beginning to look as if it might have solved her dilemma for her; without growing any less friendlike or at all distant, lately Noah had been acting decidedly less spellbound. Indeed, she'd started to question how much of it had been her imagination all along—until Marta having stopped by her barracks one November night, the subject of Godel came up.

They sat facing each other on the wooden edge of Roza's koje. "I hear your fiancé's starting to make a name for himself in the underground," Marta told her. "The word is he's been spending a lot of time at Birkenau. The Union plant, too."

Roza frowned. "Yes, I worry about him. That he's—hell, you got wind of it—cutting too high a profile. Pulling too much exposure."

"I wouldn't, if I were you. Worry, that is. I'm sure he knows what he's doing. Besides, his partner is as experienced as they come." Here Marta paused. "How's he by the way? That friend of yours, Noah Zabludowicz."

"Okay, I guess." There was a casualness to Marta's tone that sounded forced, artificial. "What makes you ask?"

"Oh, nothing. Nothing much anyway. I, you know, was just…. you know."

Roza cocked her head quizzically. "Are you all right, Marta?"

"The question is, are you?" She put a hand on Roza's knee. "I'm not the only one to notice you haven't been yourself lately, honey. That spark of yours, that fire we're used to feeding off of is gone. Is there anything you've been feeling a need these days to—to talk about maybe?"

"Talk about?"

"Yes. Involving Noah perhaps?"

Roza was really confused now. "Noah again. What's all this about Noah?"

Marta took a deep breath, exhaled. "I don't know how to say this other than just to say it. It's no secret how the man looks at you, acts when he's around you. Is it something to do with you and him that's had you so preoccupied?"

Realizing her mouth had come open, Roza clapped it shut. "I—I don't believe this," she mumbled, as if to herself.

"I don't claim to, either," Marta said, her expression pained, "but I had to ask. *Something's* been eating at you, that much is plain. I was just thinking if you needed someone to talk to, about anything…."

Slowly, a smile spread across Roza's face, turning it from indignant to affectionate. She took Marta's hand in both of hers.

"I get what you're trying to do," she said, "and appreciate the effort, Marta. That's what friends are for. But believe me when I tell you that Noah, too, is my friend, and nothing more. Godel is the one I love. Always has been and always will be. We mean, God and the Nazi devil willing, to get married one day, have babies, the whole *shmear.*

"Which isn't to say you aren't right about Noah," she admitted. "But what feelings he unfortunately does have for me, he's been man enough to keep to himself. When we do see each other it's as friends, best friends, but again, nothing more. Do you really think I'd be involved in something that might risk my losing Godel? I've lost enough people that I love as it is."

"That isn't what I meant!" Marta cried. Then, "Heck, I'm not sure what I meant. But if it's not what in my own clumsy way I was trying to get at, what *has* been bothering you, pet? As I said, I'm not the only one who's noticed."

"I'm fine, Marta, really. Been under the weather a bit is all, no big deal."

"Under the weather? You've been moping around like a sick turtle for a month now."

"Trust me, I'm good." Roza's voice was convincing—not so her lack of eye contact. "Everything's good."

"Uh-huh." Marta leaned forward until their faces were almost touching. "The truth, Rozhka," she said. "Tell me what's wrong."

But she never did. All it would have done would be to bring Marta down, too. Ironically, it *was* Noah who was to blame for her funk, though it had nothing to do with his misguided amour. After informing the Sonderkommando of Auschwitz's decision to delay the revolt, the next day he'd gone to her with it. He said it only proper that as the brains, heart, and soul behind the gunpowder operation, she be kept abreast of any such changes. He would have hated for something unfortunate to happen with hurry for the present no longer a factor.

Roza was stunned at the news, then disgusted, then despondent. She'd been expecting the signal for the revolt any day, at the very least sometime this year. Now even that was in jeopardy. Unconscionable as it was, 1944 could find the crematoria still standing, still gobbling up the trainloads of humanity filing into them. When was it going to stop, talk turn into action? What in the name of mercy was everyone waiting for? Was this what she and her people were putting their lives on the line for, so that this precious powder, this gray gold they'd been ordered to gather could lie hidden away somewhere collecting cobwebs?

All Roza had were questions. She'd have given a lot for some answers. If she were to persevere on her friends to continue risking their necks, she was going to have to find somebody who could give her some answers.

1944

Winter

The liquidation of the 11th Sonderkommando followed the same pattern as the last few preceding it. One cold, clear February afternoon, the sun a distant circle of ineffectual fire, two SS officers and a platoon of *Schützen* appeared in the yard of Block 13 and the commando was assembled. As there were no transports expected that day, all but a token crew assigned to Crematorium V were present. The presiding officer, SS-*Obersturmführer* Schwarzhuber, a squat, sallow-faced man of about thirty-five, approached them, a clutch of papers in one hand.

Bursts of frost like puffs of smoke accompanied his words. "Men of the 11th Detachment!" he boomed, his voice piercing in the cold. "Two hundred of you have been selected for heavy labor in the Lublin area, mainly the clearing of rubble in the aftermath of Soviet air raids. It is hard work, but you will be well treated. You are to remain at the Maidanek lager in the likelihood of future raids. A train is waiting now to take you to your new home. You may bring what possessions you can fit in one bag."

It was a trick, of course, there wasn't a Sonder who spoke German that didn't see instantly through it, the rest once these had translated for them. But what could they do? Unarmed, defenseless, they were looking down the barrels of automatic weapons. Their only choice, if one could call it such, was to hope against hope the Nazis were telling the truth this time. As slim a chance as this was, it did hold at least some water in that they'd been instructed to pack a bag for the trip. When Lieutenant Schwarzhuber began reading the tattoo numbers on his list, those they belonged to stepped forward as commanded. Inside of an hour, belongings in tow, they were formed into a column and led out of the compound.

Two days later, those left behind, all too aware their turn was coming, learned to their relief that the two hundred had been seen boarding a transport bound for Maidanek. It appeared there was work in Lublin after all, or so they kept telling each other. If it was a hoax it was an elaborate one, and why should the SS go to all that trouble when there were plenty of places right here to carry out a massacre on the sly?

Kapo Kaminski of Crematorium III harbored no such illusions. Those who were on the list and had gone with the soldiers were dead—not only were their four months up, there was no longer any need for them. The transports had slowed almost to a standstill. There might be three or four a week now, and none as big as before; the days of the forty-, fifty-car trains were over. And with them those of the four-hundred-man Sonder. Its kapo expected the 12th Squad, as soon as the Nazis were finished with what was left of the 11th, to end up numbering little more than a hundred.

Irrespective of the danger it posed them all, even the veterans among them now, the increasing dearth of deportees made itself felt in other ways. So scarce was food becoming that the men of Block 13 had been forced to supplement their diet with lagersuppe. Same with the liquor that numbed them to their work; when available at all, it had quadrupled in price. And this with the twin rivers of wealth that had flowed into the crematoria's undressing rooms and out of the Goldarb having been reduced to a trickle.

No one found this more distressing than Kaminski. For one, it spelled the end of Sonder aid to the women of C Camp; his men could barely supply themselves anymore. Even more worrisome was how he was supposed to purchase the weapons those same men would be needing to fight their way out of this hell. So far they had the three hand grenades lifted from the dead Ukranians, two large-caliber pistols, and double that amount of the small-bore pieces the SS used for executions, these being little more than popguns and only effective at close range. From the gunpowder smuggled them, they'd been able to fashion a growing store of crude dynamite sticks, but had yet to devise a reliable grenade. Their reserve of bullets remained woeful as well; it was this more than anything that had him concerned. Say that on the day of the attack they did manage to subdue their guards and take their guns. Would they have enough ammunition, first, to shoot their way out, then once in the forest to hold off their pursuers as they fled?

They needed more cartridges, especially the 19 and 57mm sizes compatible with the German submachine guns and Mausers. These were difficult to come by even with gold and diamonds. What was he supposed to use now, Kaminski wondered, his good looks?

Or to ask himself, as he'd been doing lately, a more realistic question: What the crap did it matter? For to entertain the hope still of manufacturing even a semblance of the revolt as planned could no longer be called optimism, but wishful thinking. It was obvious that the underground had reversed its position. All he'd heard from it, and for close to six months now, was the word *wait*—for the partisans to be ready, for the weather to improve, for the Soviets to launch their spring offensive so the front would draw near enough to allow the escapees the protection of the Red Army.

What wasn't obvious was what had caused this reversal, though in the end that, too, didn't really matter. No Auschwitz meant no partisans, no Home Army, and without it, the uprising didn't stand a chance. Even if the Sonder were to reach the trees, there'd be two thousand soldiers from the camp right behind them, with a like amount from the nearest subcamps, in addition to units of the local Gestapo and police, homing in on them from the front and the flanks. Nor, unable to protect them without the Armia's help, could they in good conscience still attempt to free the thousands from the general population that by accompanying them would serve to spread the Germans thin. The Sonder, thus hung out to dry, might as well have painted targets on each others' backs. Their only hope would be to disband into groups of ten or less and spread their own selves thin, enabling a lucky few maybe to elude the Nazi net. If they succeeded, without the partisans attacking it from behind, in even making it past the inner cordon.

Dashed dreams and dead friends and the SS victorious again, Kaminski mused, the same old song and dance it had been since the ghetto.

But as every man in the commando of the living dead knew, from the oldest to the newest among them, it was have a go at escape, or with the knowledge they had of Sonderbehandlung, wind up dying in any case. Which was why Kaminski, refusing to banish a positive attitude entirely, not only continued to stew over their paucity of guns and ammo but hadn't stopped trying to scratch up more. If his men were left with no alternative but to attempt a breakout alone, then attempt it they would, Auschwitz could rot. Should it accomplish nothing else, he would at least have kept his oath to that long-ago revenant of a moon and blown up the crematoria. And that *did* matter, though to his everlasting sorrow and shame, it might have come too late—with the transports having dwindled to next to nothing—to do a lot of good.

It was motivation enough, however, along with everything else, to keep him plugging away. Just yesterday he'd informed his Battle Group's lieutenants, outgunned and now undermanned as the squad was, to start pumping it up mentally as well as preparing it physically for the fight and flight to follow. As doomed an effort as it likely was, if it was the only option they had, it was the only option they had. Nor did he expect much resistance from the ranks. It beat sitting on their backsides waiting for the SS sickle to sweep through them again, a reckoning that couldn't be far in their future. And when it did happen, pretending it hadn't, that there really was work in Lublin, or whatever fable their duplicitous masters chose to foist on them then.

Kaminski knew they'd have to hurry, though, and hoped to have them ready to go as early into March as he could. The significance of this date, when later it occurred to him, was as hard to believe as it was to choke down: March would make it a full year of the "rebels" not having lived up to the name.

But with news that would first sink his spirits even further then make them soar, opportunity came knocking on the Special Squad's door with it still February. It was typical for the soldiers on crematoria duty to pick one Sonder from each shift to do odd jobs around the building, cleaning up the *Kommandoführer's* office, polishing the Germans' boots, washing the dishes, and the like. The officer in charge of Crematorium V was *Oberscharführer* Voss, and his Sonder orderly-for-the-day happened to be in his office the afternoon an envelope from the Political Department arrived by motorcycle. After reading its contents, a ruffled Voss tossed the note aside and with an expletive hurried out of the room. The Sonder man, left alone, darted to the sergeant's desk and scanned the letter lying there, then once more, slower, to make sure he hadn't read it wrong. It was addressed to Voss, and ordered him to prepare Crematorium V for a major Aktion that was to commence in two days: the destruction by gas of the Czech Family Camp.

The *Familienlager*, designated *B2b*, Birkenau, had been established six months prior with the deportation of five thousand Czechoslovakian

Jews from the model ghetto of Theresienstadt. Two transports totaling five thousand more would follow. Unlike the other ghettos that dotted the map of Europe, Theresienstadt was a showpiece concocted by the Nazis to show the world that the Third Reich's treatment of its Jews was humane. The International Red Cross had been allowed full access to its streets from the outset, was even invited once to inspect the facilities at B Camp.

There were no selections awaiting the Theresienstadt Jews at the unloading ramp. Families were trucked intact to their new residence, nor were their possessions confiscated, their hair shorn, their forearms tattooed. None was subjected to forced labor. There was a school for the children, a small clinic, a smaller library. Pregnant women and babies received extra food, while everyone was permitted one parcel per month in the mail. It was hard to conceive of a Jew enjoying such privileges, though few were those of their people outside of *B2b* to begrudge the Czechs their good fortune. These had an emotional stake in the continued well-being of those lucky ten thousand, taking a vicarious satisfaction from the knowledge that some Jews, somewhere, were being treated as more human than animal.

Which was why it came as such a blow to learn that even these apples of the SS eye weren't immune from the exigencies of SS *realpolitik*. Having by this time lost their propaganda value, and with the Soviets getting ready to continue their advance west, to the Nazis their pampered Czechs had become all liability and no asset.

After Voss returned to his office still in an agitated state and with two equally flustered kapos in tow, the Sonder who'd stumbled upon the Gestapo order quietly left and hurried to inform the Battle Group of what he'd discovered. His story would seem to have been confirmed the next morning when normal operations were suspended in Crematoria II as well as V, and their shifts ordered to begin what amounted to a complete overhaul of both facilities. The Germans wanted everything not only put in good working order but cleaned, painted, and polished by no later than tomorrow evening. Clearly, something over and above the normal was in the offing.

The night before, recognizing both the gravity of events and the opening they presented, Kaminski had called a meeting of his lieutenants. He explained the situation and told them that though a massacre appeared imminent, it was possible it could work to both the Sonders' and everyone's advantage.

"Lady Luck, lads," he began, "looks to be on our side for a change. There isn't a man here, I'm sure, who doesn't realize that for our little group alone to try and break out of this place would be nothing short of suicide. We are two hundred, the enemy thousands. Our only hope is to be a part of thousands as well, which in the original plan meant those prisoners from the camp proper supposed to lam out of here with us. The more of these the Nazis had their hands full with, the likelier it would be for some to slip through those hands."

His audience, aware of this, waited expectantly.

"Without the partisan arm of Battle Group-Auschwitz to help us, however, help I'm afraid we can no longer count on, this isn't going to happen. Even if the time we'd not have anymore would permit our rounding them up and taking them with us, deprived of the Home Army's firepower and command of the forest, any escapees that might make it to that forest would end up sitting ducks."

He didn't smile, but came close. "The Czechs of the Family Camp, though, are a whole other ball of wax. As good as dead already, they have nothing to lose. By refusing to lie down and be killed, and joining forces with us instead, they'd at least have a shot at surviving. A few of them anyway. Perhaps more than a few. Having lived in the shadow of the cremo chimneys for six months, they know all too well what that smoke coming from them is. If convinced they were next to burn, I for one can't see them turning us down. Who could be more up to making a run for it than people who know for a fact that in a matter of hours, they and their loved ones are to be no more than smoke and ash themselves?"

Kaminski was positive that the time to strike was now, that they weren't going to be favored with a chance like this again. He told the men present that in anticipation of their agreement on this, he'd taken the liberty of formulating a plan.

"Before anything, of course, we'll need to get the bad news to B Camp. Not that we can simply sashay past the sentries and announce it. Assuming the extermination order is true, not even bribery is going to get us through the Czech gate. The maintenance commandos, though, have the chops to go anywhere, and I've a friend on a plumbing crew who owes me big time. I should send the Czech Müller from Number Two along with them; he's got a head on his shoulders and speaks their lingo. He'll set the Slovaks straight.

"The *Familien* elders must be made to understand that the only out left them is escape. First, they've got to set their barracks on fire, then with some insulated pliers I trust we can spare them, cut through the barbed wire at the southern end of their lager. The Sonder on shift at the crematoria open that day, meanwhile—and I'll be the first to volunteer to sneak into any that might not be—after overcoming their guards and taking their weapons, will dynamite the death houses and force the inner cordon at the western perimeter. With all of the pistols, our three grenades, and the rest of the explosive, those remaining in Block 13 are to rendezvous with the Czechs, penetrate the eastern perimeter at the auxiliary gate nearest the main one, then head south to the Sola River and the marshes there. If they can make it to these, as you know, the Krauts might not be so eager to follow; that swamp is said to be crawling with as many partisans as snakes."

It was a desperate plan, a crazy plan, but as full of holes as it was, there were some points in its favor. With *B2b* and the crematoria on fire, and the inner guard cordon breached in two places, in the chaos it was going to take the SS time to get organized. This should buy the rebels valuable minutes. And with thousands of people running everywhere at once, the Germans would have to extend their forces yet.

More than this, though, or anything he might have proposed, it was Kaminski's air of calm confidence that carried the meeting and won his listeners over. Eschewing histrionics, without even raising his voice, he managed to inspire them with the same enthusiasm and urgency of purpose that filled him. Which they in turn would that night pass along to the rest of the squad, who ended up reacting much as they had. Seeing as how most probably didn't have many more days left them than the Czechs, they grasped that a rare bit of luck had been dropped in their laps. Come morning, Block 13 bustled with activity as the commando, spurred on by an adrenaline-driven mix of nervous fear and wild hope, began readying itself for both battle and the journey.

Their excitement was short-lived. When Müller returned from B Camp, he brought evil tidings. The Theresienstadt Jews refused to believe they were in danger. They couldn't understand why the SS would have handled them with kid gloves all this time only to turn on them now, and without provocation. It was a most illogical thing to do, so very un-Germanlike. If the Nazis were indeed intent on killing them, why hadn't they done so on their arrival? Why bother assigning them their own camp, a model camp at that, if a mere half a year later it was to be the gas for them?

The Sonder must be mistaken. Where had they heard this awful rumor? Or maybe it wasn't a rumor, but a deliberate lie to try and panic the residents of B Camp so as to enlist them in some hare-brained escape attempt. Sorry, their elders said, but that was what it looked like to them. Show us some proof, they told Müller, and then we'll talk.

There was no proof, of course, so Kaminski had Müller return with the Sonder man who'd been there when Sergeant Voss had received his orders. "This didn't make a dent in them," Müller would grumble later, "this one old man in particular. 'So where is this paper you're talking about?' he said. 'The one, or so you'd have it, authorizing our destruction? Show it to me, and then I will believe.'

"He said something then that I'll carry with me forever." Müller's tone went from exasperated to sad. " 'You tell us to fight back, and then what?' this poor old man pleaded. 'Watch our wives and children, our elderly and ailing, cut to pieces in front of us, mowed down with machine guns? It would be better, I think, to die in each other's arms, locked in a last embrace—in the gas chamber, yes, but clinging tight to one another, allowed the solace of touch, of saying goodbye. And in the dark, we wouldn't have to watch each other die.' "

Not, Müller would add, that either he or any of the Czechs believed it would come to that. They still insisted it was, if not a mistake, then a Sonder lie, the most shameful of lies, and weren't about to concede otherwise unless confronted by hard evidence.

Their position was reinforced when the two-day deadline came and went, and nothing happened. Then another few days with life continuing as before, by which time not a one thought the Sonders' warning anything but a fabrication. Even Kaminski was beginning to wonder if there hadn't been some kind of misunderstanding. Or maybe the undependable Germans had simply changed their minds.

Then on March 6th, the SS informed the leaders of the Familienlager that half the camp was to be sent to the city of Heydebreck in Germany to work in war production. The next day, five thousand of them made the short march to quarantine camp, where they were given rations and extra blankets for the train ride. A stop in Q-Camp was standard for all prisoners transferring out of Birkenau; before leaving, a delousing and change of clothing was mandatory.

It wasn't until the night of the 8th that the Nazi fog of deceit lifted, and the first truckfuls of wide-eyed Czechs rumbled into the yard of Crematorium II. (A second allotment was dispatched to Number Five). The SS were there waiting for them, nor were they taking any chances; floodlights reflected off a hundred steel helmets. The angry barking of dogs added its malefic note, their breath jets of steam in the chill air. Two machine guns on tripods covered every foot of ground. The Germans knew that for the Czechs, steeped as they were in the ways of Birkenau, there could be no misconstruing why they'd been brought here. Abandoning the pretense of the necessity of a shower, therefore, those soldiers equipped with nightsticks lost no time using them. As each truck was waved to a stop and its tailgate lowered, the people tumbling out were beaten toward the steps leading down to the undressing room. The noise was as deafening as it was unnerving, the curses and shouts of the SS, the screams of their victims, the maniacal clamor of the Alsatians and other dogs excited by the smell of blood.

When the dust had cleared, three thousand people huddled in the fluorescent glare of the changing room. Many were bleeding, most weeping, some mute and staring straight ahead at nothing as if in shock. The air in the packed basement was thick with fear and betrayal. Even the children, even the smallest ones, could sense what was about to happen. They held tightly to their parents' legs, eyes big, bodies trembling.

From the double line of soldiers blocking the stairwell came the order to undress. This galvanized the crowd. Cries of "What about Heydebreck?" and "We only want to work!" were soon cracking like pistol shots from out of the welter of moans and sobs. A trio of officers appeared, not to investigate those shouts, but to celebrate the operation's success so far. This was clear from their satisfied smiles, their nodding faces....

And too much for their victims. A handful of these rushed the steps, whether to confront the Germans physically or verbally would never be known, but in an ear-splitting explosion of yellow muzzle blasts were cut down before reaching them. Hardly had the echo of the shots ceased ringing off the walls than the SS stormed forward, and with truncheons and dogs tore into the helpless crowd. So furious was this onslaught that several more were killed before their attackers withdrew.

There was blood everywhere now, the floor slippery with it. In their terror, the people clung to each other, the wild weeping of even the hysterical among them having subsided to a whimper. Again the order to get undressed. But though most made an effort to comply, they weren't quick enough for the Germans. Ignoring the fact they weren't entirely naked, the soldiers advanced again, pummeling the dazed mob into the narrow corridor leading to the gas chamber. In the claustrophobic semi-darkness of this hallway, bedlam once more reigned, people running over each other to escape the Nazi clubs, the demon frenzy of the dogs and the shrieking of their victims even louder in this confined space.

Then suddenly, impossibly, from out of this babel of tears, pain, and SS anger, climbed the sound of a woman singing, a diva's voice, professional, powerful, as out of place yet as beautiful as a rose sprung from a patch of thistles. In the space of a few notes, this rose announced itself the Czech national anthem, and as others took it up, it swelled into a ringing chorus. Upon reaching their destination and starting to file into the death room, their song dissolved into that less official anthem of European Jewry, the mournful, majestic *Ha Tikvah*, Hebrew for "The Hope." It was as if they were making a last statement, a farewell homage to their heritage. Loyal Czechoslovakians they were, and proud to be, but in the end bound less to their country than their religion, their Jewishness being the part of them they held the most dear.

By sunrise of the third day, the Family Camp was no more, the remaining five thousand having followed the first into oblivion. Its dirt streets were as bereft of life as the surface of the moon, the doors of its empty huts banging forlornly in the wind. Not that it would remain that way. Though the Sonder couldn't know, there were twenty thousand Jews left in the Theresienstadt ghetto, most of them earmarked for B Camp. As of now, however, it was a desolate place, inhabited by ghosts, the occasional child's toy in the mud a reminder of what had been.

Kaminski took the whole disheartening episode hard. Always quick with a grin and a slap on the back, or conversely a withering scowl and a rebuke, overnight he became withdrawn and apathetic. Though he made every effort to hide this from his men, so at odds was it with the hardy exuberance they'd come to expect from him that few failed to see the change. When asked what was wrong (as if they didn't know), he denied anything was, but in truth felt as hollow inside as he had since arriving at the Vernichtungslager.

Noah Zabludowicz had no trouble noticing the difference in him, either. The underground had sent him to Block 13 to size up the situation. Having found out about Birkenau's decision to move without them, Auschwitz wanted to make sure, with the Family Camp no more, that Sonder obstreperousness had cooled. They could have saved themselves the effort: the deflating Czech imbroglio had cured both the commando and its kapo of any desire at this point to take on the Germans.

From their first meeting months ago, he and Kaminski had hit it off. They recognized a lot of themselves in each other, not least the soft spot beneath the stolid, he-man exterior for those who were suffering or in need. It saddened Noah to find his normally vivacious friend a defeated shadow of his old self, a sadness compounded by his having someone even dearer to him in similar straits. Roza Robota, too, wasn't herself these days, hadn't been for a while, her usual bravado supplanted by a stubborn moodiness.

Though Noah knew what was troubling both—in Kaminski's case, of course, the Familienlager debacle, with Roza distraught over Auschwitz looking to have lost its appetite for revolt—in neither instance did he have a clue what he could do to help. Until, that is, he arrived at what he subsequently had to admit was the brilliant idea of getting the pair of them together. By arranging for them to meet, putting them in the same room, not only might Kaminski, as head of the Sonder, be able to answer some of those questions causing Roza grief, but if there was anyone whose words could restore the starch to a man, that person was her.

It was a sunny yet biting-cold March morning when Noah passed through the sentry gate into *BIa*, the icy mud crackling like dry twigs beneath his boots. Kaminski had balked at going anywhere at first, but once he found out they'd be joining the operative who'd been feeding his men their gunpowder, he protested no more. Roza was game from the start. She knew all about Kapo Kaminski from her Sonder contacts, and here was her chance to sit down with this founder and commanding general of Battle Group-Sonderkommando—and clarify a few things, was the way she'd put it to Noah. She swore she'd have no problem being there at the appointed place and time, as the blockova of her barracks owed her more favors than she had fingers. Sure enough, but for a couple of Stubendiensten busy with their chores, he found her sitting alone in her block.

On catching sight of her, his heart skipped a beat as it always did; stringent as he was about keeping his love for her under wraps, his body as usual was refusing to cooperate. She rose to greet him, and they exchanged hugs and how-are-you's, their breath like smoke. It was almost as cold inside the barracks as out, and like most of Birkenau's huts, short on windows, shrouded even on the brightest day in a permanent dusk.

"So where is this—Oh," she said, looking past him, "here he is now." Noah turned to see Kaminski's barrel of a body silhouetted in the blazing-white of the open door. Soon the three of them were sitting in a corner well away from the Stubendiensten, Roza having managed to get hold of three folding metal chairs. It was she who spoke first.

"So I finally get to meet the legendary kapo of Crematorium III," she said. "You are aware, sir, I'm sure, that your reputation precedes you."

"What I'm aware of," Kaminski said, subdued, minus his usual bluster, "is that I have the honor at last of coming face to face with a person I've been admiring from afar for a while now."

"You know of me? Ah, yes… Wrubel, Leventhal, and the rest. I hope they haven't been too free with my name."

He shook his head. "Your name, dear lady, is known to a very few only. I've made sure of that. Your bravery, however, has captured the imagination of many. Whenever the courage of my men needs reviving, or when I can see their faith in our cause slipping, I like to remind them that the gunpowder on which much of our hopes are founded comes to them courtesy of a woman—a *woman*, I always take pains to repeat—who would rather die than have the revolt do the same."

Roza fidgeted in her chair. She wasn't good at taking compliments. With a look almost of helplessness, she turned to Noah. "So when do we get on with this pow-wow of yours?" she demanded, but only, he knew, to hide her embarrassment. "I have to think we're not here, no disrespect to you, Mr. Kaminski, to be part of some half-assed mutual-admiration society."

The two men looked at each other before breaking out in laughter.

"No, you're not," Noah said, quickly serious again. "For months now," he continued, indicating Roza, "this one has been after me about the people I work for having put the uprising on hold. Whenever I see her, the first thing she asks is if they've changed their minds yet, usually followed by when in the hell are they going to."

"Can you blame me?" she said. "I'd hate for it to turn out that me and the others had been schlepping that damned dynamite all this time for nothing. That the revolt should be over before it even started."

"Until just a few weeks ago, I kept telling her not to worry, that there was the Sonderkommando still. Which meant there was hope. The Sonder have no choice, I said; for them it's take up arms or die. And no squad knew this better than the 11th. Speaking for ourselves, she and I, we didn't think there was a chance, aware as it had to be of the fate of the ten detachments before it, that this one would let itself be caught flat-footed and marched to its death without a fight."

Noah shook his head, as if he still couldn't believe it. "Boy, were we wrong. Couldn't have been wronger. Please don't think we're judging you, kapo, or for that matter anybody, but as someone I've always admired for his straight shooting, for telling it like it is, perhaps you can shed some light on what the odds are of the next Sonder, the 12th, being the first to wake up and throw off its chains."

For a long moment, there was silence, the only sound the swishing of the Stubendienst brooms on the dirt floor. Kaminski sat with his elbows on his knees, head lowered. A thin smile played at his lips, but that was about it; for all the emotion he showed at what amounted to an insistence he explain Sonder complacency, this normally emotional man might as well not have been listening.

Finally, he raised his eyes until they met Noah's and held them there. The smile was gone, the voice tired.

"I like you, Noah Zabludowicz. Have from the start. No one has been more of a friend to the Sonder than you. But when it comes down to it, you're not one of us, do not suffer what we suffer, and until you've seen through another's eyes, walked in his shoes, you can't truly know who he is, appreciate his situation. Every stripe of prisoner living here is different, with different problems, different needs, and there are forces at work on the Special Squad you'll find nowhere else. Bear with me a few minutes while I lay some on you. Maybe it'll help you better understand where the Sonder are coming from—and where we're going."

As one person, his audience of two inched forward in their chairs.

"As you said, Noah," he began, "you'd think no group of inmates would be more open to revolt than the Sonder. Human nature being what it is, though, they could also be seen as the least likely to risk it. There's no getting around it: in an uprising the Sonder have something to lose. And by this I don't mean all those privileges we're allowed, that long table in Block 13 piled high with food and cigarettes, the civvy clothes and hot showers, the prescription and other medicines, among which I'd have to include the alcohol. These are spectacular to be sure, things a lot of us haven't known since before the ghetto. Some not even then. There are those, too, tied to the camp for other reasons, a wife or girlfriend in C Camp, say, a brother in Auschwitz.

"But this, none of it, is what I'm talking about. When I say the Sonder have something to lose, it has nothing to do with a full belly or some tug on the heart. We of the crematoria live under the axe, and no one knows when that axe is going to fall. They say it's four months, but the 9th Squad lasted almost twice that. Even so, four months of life—four weeks, four days, four *hours*—is not something to be thrown away lightly. And in the eyes of a lot of Sonder, that's what they'd be doing, throwing it away, for the day revolt does come will almost certainly be their last. Especially if forced to go it alone. So they wait and tell themselves they have plenty of time, that they'll start thinking about it next month, get serious about it then. But they always wait too long, and time sneaks up on them like a thief in the night, and before they know it they're standing in formation in the crematorium yard and some *Unterführer* is calling out numbers from a list."

A hint of a smile returned to his face. "Besides, I'd be willing to bet there's not a cremo man out there who doesn't believe that when that axe does fall, it's not going to land on him. Another man, yes, and more's the pity for that, but another's death isn't your own. Somehow, you tell yourself, that if there's any justice in the world, you'll be one of the few to escape the SS head-chopper. People, none more than the young, have trouble coming to grips with the grave, and like a man falling from a tree will grab at any branch, no matter how flimsy. I've heard it a thousand times, and might a thousand more: I've done everything they asked of me, followed every order. Why would the Germans want to get rid of me?"

His voice had grown stronger, surer of itself. He rose from his chair and began slowly pacing, studying the floor in front of him.

"What can prepare a new Sonder, a young man, a boy, for his first shift at the ovens, the sights, the smells, the hair-raising sounds of the gas chamber? Many have never been around a dead person before, and here they are all of a sudden tripping over corpses. There are those who can't do it, those unwilling or unable to face the shock of the crematorium.

These are quickly taken somewhere and shot, or soon get hold of enough sleeping pills to keep from ever waking. Most, however, as disturbing as it sounds, grow accustomed to the job. Or as accustomed as men can get to mass murder on a daily basis. As horrible as it is they adjust to it, learn to live with it, settle into routines.

"To do this, though, they must learn also how to look at human beings as not people but things, piles of dead bodies as nothing more than raw material to be sorted and processed. But that carries a price, for to master this trick of the eye and the mind is to become in the end less human themselves. 'Sonder sickness' I call it, and it can make men not men. Apathy sets in, indifference to not only where they are and what they're doing but what they *should* be doing to put a stop to both their own anguish and the killing. You can see it in the way they move, stiff, mechanical, like machines. As if there in body only."

He continued walking, head down, immersed in what he was saying. Noah was reminded of a teacher in his classroom. Or better yet, a lawyer before a jury.

"It doesn't help that by then time has ceased to have meaning for them as well. Denied any realistic hope for a future, the past is also lost to them, as dead and gone as those loved ones of theirs who inhabit it. Finding it too painful to contemplate either, all they're left with is the present, the next hour, the next day, to think much further ahead is as depressing as dwelling on what was. All that matters then, all they come to care about, is making it from one shift to the next, counting out survival one day at a time. It's easier that way. Easier not to have to think, to give events their head as you might a horse, let them carry you where they will. This isn't exactly an attitude, however, conducive to…. conducive to…."

Kaminski stumbled to a halt, a lost look on his face. In an instant he'd flipped from lawyer to defendant. "Tell me," he begged Noah, "if I'm making any sense." Then to Roza, "Or just making excuses."

"If you have to ask that," she answered, "maybe you ought to reconsider what you're saying. But then you've come up with some good points, excellent points. Noah was speaking for both of us when he said we don't mean to pass judgment—no one has the right to judge you poor souls of the Special Squad. Yours is an unhappiness not seen this side of death. But have you ever wondered if perhaps there's something else at work here, something you're missing, and Sonder misery isn't the only thing to blame for their do-nothingness?"

Kaminski did a double take, looking at Roza as if seeing her for the first time. Then with a smile and a shake of his head, returned to his chair. It was to Noah that he spoke.

"I don't fault you for never telling me how brave this young lady is; that I figured out for myself a long time ago. And I already knew from those of my men in touch with her not only how easy on the eyes she is but how inspirational she can be to the ear."

"Good God almighty" Roza groaned, her cheeks turning crimson.

"You might have informed me, though, friend Noah, that she's also as sharp as a brand-new pair of scissors. My compliments, missy, there *is* something else that's been holding the Sonder back, and I was just getting to it. As your pal here can tell you, I haven't been what you'd call myself lately. Others have noticed it as well. Most hold what happened with the Family Camp to blame, and they're partly right. Has Noah told you the 11th Sonder, what's left of us anyway, tried to persuade the Czechoslovakians to join us in fighting our way out of here?"

"No," she said, "but Zalman, Zalman Leventhal, and some others did. They were still sick about the whole thing, as was I when I heard."

"The way it turned out, yes. It was an opportunity missed. Those poor, clueless Czechs…. I honestly believe, if they'd only let us, we could have saved some of them, along with some of ourselves maybe. But it isn't only this that's had me down. What's really been gnawing at me is that I've been such a fool. That and knowing how many have paid so dearly for my foolishness."

Roza's eyes found Noah's, which were as puzzled as hers. "I'm afraid we're not following you," she said. "What foolishness?"

Kaminski didn't hesitate, but waded into himself like a boxer on the attack. Nor in his self-loathing did he pull any punches. Of all the negative influences working on the Sonder, he said, none were more instrumental in curbing their aggression than the one he'd been saving for last, namely himself. It was he who'd been keeping the more radical of his men on a leash, insisting they be patient until the underground was ready. But later even he could see that the underground was never going to be ready, had no intention of it. How could he have been so stupid and stubborn at the same time? For a year, he'd let Battle Group-Auschwitz lead him around by the nose, ignoring the calls to action from his own Battle Group. Meanwhile, two squads had gone to the gas, and part of a third, men he'd worked with, grown close to, boys who'd looked up to him as to a father. He'd failed them all with his ridiculous bull-headedness, his blindness, might as well have walked them into the death room himself.

"I meant well, I did. Nor am I saying this to try and squirm my way out of anything. Guns were proving tougher to find than expected. Ammunition, too. The lack of this last was especially troubling. We weren't looking to free just ourselves, either; I wasn't the only Sonder back then thinking in terms of busting the whole camp out. But to do this and avoid a bloodbath in the forest, we were going to need the partisans, which according to the underground meant waiting until those partisans were available. So wait for them we did, as the weeks dragged into months, until one day I woke up and blast my bones if it wasn't January. It was only then that it started sinking into this thick skull of mine, Noah, that maybe your bosses were playing us Sonder for suckers."

Noah looked as if he could have crawled under his chair. "I know, and I'm so sorry, so ashamed that I—"

"Stop that. Right now. You were only following orders. Besides, who's to say you would have made any difference? As I said, more than a few of my people had been after me since summer to open my eyes and see how full of manure our so-called allies in Auschwitz were. But I didn't listen.

Not to those I should have. By that time, I'd since stopped listening to myself even."

"What do you mean," Roza said, "you stopped listening to yourself?"

Kaminski appeared to have shrunk in his seat. "You may be thinking, I don't know, that I'm being overly hard on myself, that I was too trusting and let the months creep up on me, but believed nonetheless, as I still do, that the success of any revolt depended on having the underground behind it. That hundreds of Sonder were tricked to their deaths because of this was a tragedy, but who's to say these wouldn't have died anyway if trying to pull off a breakout on their own? Not that this excuses me for failing to have the 11th Squad ready to go, success be damned. How I could at that late date still be playing the patsy to the double-dealers in Auschwitz is beyond me. Sonder sickness? Perhaps. I'm as susceptible to it as anybody, and it'll suck the gumption from a man as sure as Zyklon-B will his oxygen."

He wrapped himself in his arms, shuddered, but not from the cold. "Sad as it may have been, though, it wasn't the loss of those hundreds, nor again, the Czech disappointment, that's had my butt dragging in the mud. At least not by their lonesome. There's something you don't know, something that makes the betrayal of my brother Sonder pale in comparison. It's been a year almost to the day since Crematorium II opened. I was there that first gassing, I and 1,493 Jews from Krakow; never will I forget either that night or that number. The following night, after it was all over but the memory of it, and alone with that obscene memory in the yard of Block 13, I swore to the moon above, a moon as red as the blood I'd washed from my hands the day before, that if it was the last thing I did, if I did nothing else with the life left me, I'd see that bitch of a crematorium and her three people-eating sisters destroyed. Don't ask me how I knocked to it, it's too long and ugly a story, but it was plain that the moon was demanding it of me, demanding that I serve as its instrument in maybe not stopping the killing, but putting the brakes on it before it was too late.

"*Escape?*" Kaminski spat the word. "The revolt was never about escape. Not at bottom it wasn't, not ours in the crematoria or that of any prisoner. Its real aim, its higher one, was to put the death factories out of commission. And I *knew* this, right from the beginning I knew it. But caught up as I became in the dream and drama of escape, in pandering to the underground, I thought we had time. Not all the time in the world, but enough to spring both us and the tens of thousands of Jews here before too big a dent could be made in the hundreds of thousands still out there.

"So I put it on hold, the oath I'd pledged to that bloody moon, shunted it away like a train onto a siding—which was what I meant by saying I stopped listening to myself. We should have blown the cremos as soon as we had enough dynamite, even if it would have meant blowing ourselves up along with them. But who could have predicted they'd be so effective, drain half the continent of its Jews in a matter of months?"

He fixed his eyes on a point on the wall, a faraway look in them. "Now it *is* too late. The hundreds of thousands are no more. The job I did on the Sonder, it was nothing to this. The day my time comes, when it's my turn to die, there'll be a special place waiting for me in hell, a place for those who've not only forsaken their fellow man, but nearly as wicked, their own good intentions."

Neither Noah nor Roza knew what to say. Kaminski's pain had shackled their tongues to the same degree it had loosened his. It was Roza finally who broke the silence, her voice gentle.

"There are two things, it seems to me, Mr. Kaminski, worth pointing out here. One, you *are* being much too hard on yourself. You did what you felt you had to, what you thought best, which in a place such as Birkenau can be difficult to get right. It doesn't do us any good, though, to crucify ourselves when we're wrong. Blame the asshole SS, I say, for putting us in those positions to begin with.

"Second, you pronounce it too late to do something about the crematoria, that they've done their damage already and there's no turning back the clock. I get what you're saying, but couldn't disagree more. To send those monstrosities back to the bottomless pit from which they came is a duty we owe to not only our own people, alive and dead, but to all peoples everywhere, even those not yet born. It's been less than a year since history was made in the Warsaw ghetto, since our brothers and sisters imprisoned there refused any longer to be led meekly to the cattle cars. What has Warsaw taught us, and will one day teach the world when the world learns the story? That the Jew can be as fearsome a warrior as the next person, yes, but anyone with any sense should have known that already. The real lesson, the more valuable one, is that you can either submit to tyranny, roll over on your back and show your belly like a dog, or stand on your two feet like a human being and fight back. No matter that you're no more than an un-battle-tested civilian, weak with hunger, disease, many of your weapons homemade, fighting with all but bare hands against tanks, artillery, and veteran troops—if you've got what it takes inside, if you're determined enough, fed up enough, that can be half the battle. Look at the heroes of Warsaw. For two months, the men, women, and even children of this ragtag 'army' took everything the Nazis could throw at them and didn't back down until there were too few of them left alive, with too little ammunition, to wage war against the students of a rabbinical school.

"It was from Noah that I learned of these martyrs and their glorious fight to the death. He told me all he knew of it, down to the last detail, though I wasn't going to let you go, was I, you poor man, till you did?"

"She can be most persuasive," he agreed, "when she sets her mind to it."

"Of all the pictures he painted of that struggle, however, none moved me more than one. On the third day of the rebellion, the freedom fighters raised a flag high above their stronghold, a blue Star of David on a white field. That flag said it all, its message to the SS clear: 'We will be your slaves no longer. No more will we bow our heads to you. You may kill us, if you can, but never again will you own us.'"

Roza's gaze grabbed the kapo's and held it. "The rebels of Birkenau can send the same message, leave the same legacy for future generations to draw from. If so, it will be said of the 12th Sonderkommando that here were men condemned to the ugliest job in the worst place on earth, men so degraded by guilt, so saturated with death that in many ways they didn't resemble men anymore, who broke free of their bonds to do what none before them had dared. And will have done it with flair, their first act the tumbling of those six gluttonous chimneys that are the evil face of the camp, its center, its heart, the very symbols of what Birkenau is and was meant to be."

Noah had been studying Kaminski as she spoke, trying to size up his reaction to her words. The man's features, however, remained inscrutable. Roza, on the other hand, was starting to heat up. She'd moved to the edge of her chair, her eyes as boiling-black as hot tar.

"But why speak of it as being our *duty*?" she sniffed. "Duty implies obligation. I'd think the Sonder couldn't wait to blast the cremos to rubble, that it'd be a real pleasure, a labor of love for them. Not only have they seen things, done things inside those walls that left a permanent mark on them, a wound that will never heal, but those foul contraptions are the pride and joy of the sadists in charge of us. What more visible a demonstration of German ingenuity and power than those factories for turning living, breathing people into powder?

"There are few better ways than blowing up their death houses to hit the Nazis where it hurts. And we must not forget, after all they've done to us, taken from us, that we can neither hurt nor hate the SS too much. Not many people know this—Noah, a few others—but you could say I owe my life to a young *Oberschütze*. Having thought much about it since, I'd hesitate to call it an act of kindness on his part, but something born more of a grudging respect for my having stood up to him. Stood eyeball to eyeball with him, in fact, a carelessness that should have got me shot, but somehow didn't. I remember what he said, and the look on his face when he said it. 'A Jew with a backbone,' he called me, as if this surprised him, and instead of executing me on the spot or turning me in as insubordinate, went out of his way to give me a favorable report. It was this report that touched off a chain of events that in the end resulted in my transferring out of an Aussenkommando and certain death.

"Though he could hardly have foreseen this, and would probably have desired it even less, that boy of a private did save my life. Should I be grateful and forgive him past crimes he's committed, crimes that as a Death's-head SS he had to have committed, simply because he chose not to commit one against me? Does one small show of human feeling, and a borderline one at that, make up for that skull he wears on his collar?"

Roza made a face that matched the venom in her voice. "I'd waste him in a heartbeat if I had the chance, shoot him down like the dog he is. They deserve no mercy from us, these murderers of children. All they rate is our ill will and the justice coming to them, and until that day does arrive, whatever resistance we can mount against them. Would my *Oberschütze's* death bring back those he's killed or helped kill? Of course not, just as the destruction of the crematoria won't restore a single one of the innocent thousands who passed through their doors. For that, as you said, kapo, it is too late; our beloved dead are past saving.

"There is still time, though, for the Sonder to save themselves, if not their bodies then their souls. A few bundles of dynamite, and pardon my

French, the balls to use them, and they'd be able to call themselves men again."

Kaminski waited a moment to make sure she was finished. When he did speak, it was with an apologetic smile. "Forgive me if I've given you the wrong impression," he told her, "but so taken was I with what you were saying, I didn't want to interrupt. Make no mistake, I do agree it's not too late to deal the Krauts what they have coming. In fact, in answer to your question earlier, Noah, the 12th Sonder will be ready to fight, and that's a promise. Even before this Czech thing came up, my lieutenants and I were working on it, or at least working to steer the commando in that direction. And, if only just, we're back at it now."

Noah and Roza exchanged a quick look. "Outstanding," she said. "And how is that going?"

"Well, as I said, we've just begun, but it is going. This most recent kick to the midsection, as you can imagine, isn't making it any easier, but those still left from the 11th Squad are starting to come around again. We're even making some headway among the new recruits."

"So when might...." Noah stopped, not wanting to sound pushy. "I mean, if I could convince my superiors that the Sonder had made up their minds to go it alone, without help, who knows but that they wouldn't feel guilty enough to offer some."

"When might it happen, is that what you're asking? I couldn't tell you just yet," Kaminski said. "We'll see how things progress. If I had this one at my side to scorch a few ears," he said, motioning to Roza, "it might be a lot sooner. You've got quite a way with words, girl. No wonder you have so many willing to put their heads on the block for you."

"Begging your pardon, sir, but none of those relieving the Germans of their gunpowder could volunteer fast enough, no pep talk needed. Their bravery humbles me. I don't know about you, but I'm sick and tired of hearing about the all-powerful SS. Maybe it's they who should be worrying about us."

Kaminski didn't feel confident in setting a date for the revolt because he didn't know yet what to make of certain recent developments, all of which defied understanding. In a repeat of yesterday, no transports were due. After the meeting was over and he'd returned to Block 13, he secluded himself in his bunk to puzzle once more over what the SS might be up to. If the reductions made in the past few Special Squads were any indication, the Sonder could have expected more men to be winnowed from the 11ᵗʰ by now. But after the two hundred were packed off to Maidanek, there'd been no second list. Instead, the Germans had begun to build the detachment *back up.* Newcomers from both the unloading ramp and the camp started flooding into Block 13, to the point where any further were going to necessitate a second barracks. Already the 12ᵗʰ Sonder was closing on its predecessor in size, and fast. The Nazis were even bringing experienced hands in from other camps, nineteen of them last week from the double crematoria at Maidanek. And with less a need for such numbers than ever.

None of the squad knew what to think, though two of the rumors floating around did have possibilities. The first and most credible, not to mention the scariest, was that the SS were readying Auschwitz-Birkenau itself for annihilation. Those touting this explanation cited the massacre of the Family Camp as but its opening phase, with more lagers to follow. This theory meshed nicely with what had become common knowledge: the German army's mounting reversals on the eastern front. With hostilities to resume in earnest come spring—in other words, any day now—it wasn't a stretch to imagine the SS engaging in wholesale slaughter in order to preempt the liberation of its prisoners by the Red Army.

A second rumor was less plausible, but did have its adherents. These believed a new wave of Jews was poised to inundate the camp, a last-minute multitude the Nazis had managed to drum up from somewhere. The question was where, and there were several answers to choose from. Some posited the Germans who were retreating from Russia driving the Jews still under their control ahead of them. Others saw the SS and Gestapo making one final sweep of Europe, rooting out those who'd eluded them up to now. A few even suggested this might include the heretofore protected Jews of the neutral countries, Spain, Switzerland, and the rest, though the Third Reich would have been hard-pressed to accomplish this at its strongest.

Then there were the Jews of Hungary, enough of them to keep two Birkenaus busy. Kaminski had learned from Noah that as an ally of the Reich, Hungary had been able to keep the SS at bay and its Jewish population intact. For the most part their countrymen regarded the Hebrews within their borders as Hungarian first and Jewish second. Why now all of a sudden, at this late stage of the war, would Budapest give in to German demands and send so many of its citizens off to be butchered?

Kaminski didn't know what to believe, if any of it. All he did know was what his gut was telling him, and it wasn't good. Though he'd seen no reason to bother Noah and the girl with it, an indefinable uneasiness had been growing in him lately, distinct from those other worms nibbling at his brain. What was causing it he didn't know, but there was no brushing it aside; something out of the ordinary was imminent, something as devilish as it was big, he could feel it. It wasn't just jitters, either, at the battle ahead. As suicidal a prospect as the uprising had become, he was looking forward to having a rifle in his hands and a German, as Bruno Baum had once sought to tempt him with, in its crosshairs. Death, his own, no longer meant much to him. He and death had grown to be old friends, and with him a Sonder for going on two long years now, the thought of becoming even better ones wasn't displeasing.

No, the malaise which had taken hold of him wasn't from nerves. It came from a darker place, was continuous, relentless, like the coils of some huge snake squeezing the breath out of him inch by slow inch. There was as little likelihood of him escaping it for more than a few minutes as of preventing what it was trying to warn him of.

But even outside those few minutes, it wasn't all python and dire premonition. He could congratulate himself, for example, in knowing that despite everything he hadn't thrown in the towel. Somehow, from somewhere, he'd found the will to keep traveling the road of revolt, if not with as confident a step as he'd trod it a year ago, at least he was still walking. And the dream still alive. The disapproving moon of last spring might yet be appeased in the present one, a different kind of trumpet topple the walls of a different Jericho after all.

Ironically, the SS had played a part in hastening this, having done themselves no favor by importing the nineteen Sonder from Maidanek. These weren't Jewish civilians but Soviet POWs, hard men hardened further by their violent captivity. They had immediately fallen in with the conspirators. Their leader, a Major Borodin, was an unprepossessing fellow at first glance, his wire-rimmed glasses and rounded shoulders making him resemble more a schoolteacher than an infantry officer. He had a talent, though, his new kapo soon observed, for eliciting not only respect but affection from his men. If they weren't there already, one got the impression they'd have followed him into hell if he asked them to.

But Borodin's value to the cause extended well beyond his aptitude for leadership. He'd been trained in explosives, this was his specialty; indeed, he was more than a demolitions expert, he was an artist. This became apparent when Kaminski approached him with the problem of constructing a serviceable hand grenade using the gunpowder they'd accumulated and what materials were at hand. That same day he succeeded in building a device out of an old tin can that he guaranteed would cause casualties, with luck even kill. Inside of a week, he'd assembled half a dozen of the things, and suddenly the Sonder didn't feel so at a disadvantage, nor escape quite as remote a possibility anymore.

The nineteen had greased the wheels of revolt further with yet another contribution, if inadvertently. Upon their arrival at Block 13, several sported the same blue serge jackets and tan calfskin boots in which some of the two hundred singled out from the 11th Squad in February had departed for Maidanek. Questioned, the Russians told how after detraining, the entire two hundred had been gassed, though not before revealing who they were and where they were from.

Any faith the detachment might still have had in SS integrity was shattered forever. For the Germans to go to the length of masking their real purpose by shuttling the condemned all the way to another camp meant they couldn't be trusted no matter how tricked-out a story they put forth in the future. If they were to have any chance of surviving, the Sonder would have to stop sitting and start doing, grab hold of their destiny with both hands.

Kaminski would lie in his bunk for the rest of the morning. There was much to be done, many new faces to try and win over to the Battle Group. But that could wait. Before occupying himself with anything, he wanted to etch into memory some of the things that astonishing friend of Noah's had said. Her last name might have sounded a funny note, but she was deadly serious. And feisty as a tomcat. One felt braver around her, empowered somehow. He'd fully expected this Roza Robota to be a firebreather, just hadn't anticipated her being so quotable a one. He saw her words having an effect on his men similar to Borodin's grenades, and like those grenades, the benefit in storing them away for use later.

The barracks that morning was awash in pale sunlight, and toasty warm from a pair of furnaces. Though not uncrowded, neither was it noisy. His wasn't the only bunk occupied, most of his fellow recumbents napping, a reader here and there. The conversation that did reach him was hushed. Eventually, he, too, dropped off to sleep, lulled there by the caress of muffled voices. He dreamt he was on a train bound for where he couldn't remember. He was in a coach, not a cattle car, with cushioned seats, curtained windows, a uniformed conductor. He could tell it was spring; the grassy countryside slipping by was a rainbow of flowers.

That he'd forgotten where he was headed both frustrated and dimly frightened him. He wracked his brain, but to no avail—how simple-minded could a person be? Finally, he could stand it no longer and turned to the woman sitting next to him. She was young and dressed to the nines; from beneath a small, coquettish hat and a fishnet black veil peeked eyes no less black, set in a strong but inviting face.

"Excuse me, miss," Kaminski said in a low voice, not wishing to broadcast his ignorance, "but perhaps you could help me."

"I'll try," she smiled. "What is it you need?"

"This may sound peculiar, but I'm drawing a blank where I shouldn't. Would you be so kind as to inform me of our…. destination?"

Her expression clouded on the instant, flashing from solicitous to vaguely suspicious. "Why, Budapest, of course," she said, turning away. "What else would it be?"

*   *   *

The short, slender man in the dashing black uniform, having separated himself from the party, stood alone at the railing taking in the city spread out below. There were other guests milling about on the long, narrow balcony, but none had yet to approach. It was a typical day for mid-March in this part of the world, cold but not uncomfortably so. The sky was more white than blue in the early afternoon sun, an intense, shrunken sun that blazed with little heat.

A young SS subaltern in white serving jacket appeared at his side. "Champagne, sir?" he said, presenting a tray.

The tall, bubbly flutes glistened yellowly in the sunlight. "No, thank you," the man said. If he was to start drinking now, he might as well forget about working later.

He would rather there weren't a party, but it would have been bad form not to show. Even without drinking, it was a waste of half a day, and there was so much to do yet, their work barely begun. He might have declined to appear anyway, formalities aside, but that this gathering of SS and army brass was at least partly in his honor.

"Congratulations, Herr *Obersturmbannführer*," said a voice behind him. He turned to see an SS officer, a lieutenant, whose name he couldn't recall.

"Thank you," said Adolf Eichmann with a slight bow. "The glory, however—or should I say the gratitude?—isn't mine alone. There are others who have worked as hard for this moment."

"You are too modest," said the officer. "Allow me to commend you for that as well."

Eichmann bowed again, then turned back to the railing. He wasn't trying to be rude, he just didn't feel like company, not now. It was why he'd slipped out here, to get away from the press of bodies and the innocuous patter inside. He had a need to be alone for a while with his thoughts, and with this view that never failed to thrill him.

He'd fallen in love with Budapest upon first setting eyes on it two years ago. With its medieval architecture, narrow streets, countless statues and parks, it possessed an Old World charm Berlin couldn't touch. The vista from the penthouse suite of the Majestic Hotel was a good one. Visible, of course, was the winding, silver serpentine of the Danube as it snaked through the city, and four of the ornate Renaissance bridges that spanned it. Nestled against the river was the ancient Jewish Quarter, exotic in its timelessness. Oddly, it was one of his favorite neighborhoods; to walk its streets and bazaars was to enter a portal into the past.

Or maybe it wasn't so odd. Despite the route his life had taken, and though he would never have admitted it, he'd developed, if not an admiration for the Jews, then respect for those isolated nuggets of worth and wisdom to be found in even the most degraded of peoples. This, and much more, would not have happened but for a career decision he'd made years ago. As a new enlistee in the *Sicherheitsdienst*, the Security Police or SD, he'd been put to work keeping files on the Freemasons, as dead-end an assignment as might be imagined. Perceiving in the Jews an infinitely greater opportunity for advancement, he set himself to becoming an expert on that peculiar race. Nor was it long before he was able to pass as such, having submerged himself in a study of its history, culture, religion— indeed, in all things Judaic, down to mastering the basics of Yiddish even.

At which point, it became merely a question of catching the right men's attentions, which he did in the persons of *Reichsführer*-SS Heinrich Himmler and Himmler's deputy, SS-*Obergruppenführer* Reinhard Heydrich, commander of the SD. After several years as Heydrich's assistant, in 1939 Eichmann was appointed director of Gestapo Department IV-B4 of the RSHA, the Reich Main Security Office. As head of the Chancellery's Jewish Desk, he was responsible for implementation of Nazi policy toward the Jews in all occupied territories, making him one of the most powerful men in Europe. Not bad, he reflected as he let his eyes meander this scenic stretch of the Danube, for a man who not all that long ago was working in the warehouse of an oil-field equipment company.

Aside from his humble origins, his encounter with the lieutenant a moment ago had brought home what he'd always considered another drawback to his ambitions. Even today, despite the pinnacles he'd reached, he'd felt a twinge of self-consciousness in this subordinate's presence. A full head taller than Eichmann, broad-shouldered, *blond*.... this was one reason he'd turned his back on the man. No one was more sensitive about his appearance than the colonel, to the fact he resembled more the archetypal Jew than the Aryan ideal. Spindly of build, balding, with a protruding, bony nose and neck as scrawny as a chicken's, he suspected that not even the fearsome SS uniform entirely made up for his Semitic moneylender's image.

Not that there was a whole lot he could do about it, beyond continuing to make sure his achievements superceded his looks. As much as he relished his official title, chief of IV-B4, he took equal pride in those less formal appellations his reputation had earned him. Foremost among these was a name the Jews themselves had given him, the Bloodhound, for his success in tracking them down and handing them over to their fate. To his peers, meanwhile, he was known as the wizard of transportation, the magician of trains, able to conjure rolling stock seemingly out of thin air, fill it with Jews he'd collected from the Norwegian Sea to the Mediterranean, then deliver those Jews relatively intact all the way to the gas chambers in Poland. And this with an increasingly hard-pressed military competing tooth and nail with him for access to both that stock and those rails.

The Wehrmacht had been particularly busy in the Balkans this month, and the direction the war was headed, would soon be even busier. The Red Army had targeted Hungary as the gateway to Austria, and once it finished reclaiming the Ukraine then sweeping south into Romania, the land of the Magyars would lay ripe for the taking. Admiral Horthy, the Hungarian regent and head of state, had seen the writing on the wall and informed Hitler he was withdrawing his divisions from the Russian front the better to defend his country. In truth, he was secretly negotiating an armistice with the Soviets. Informed of this, the *Führer* flew into one of his patented rages and ordered his ally invaded. In little more than a week, Hungary's army was routed, its government toppled, Horthy under arrest—and up to a million previously untouchable Jews suddenly there for the plucking.

Enter Eichmann and the well-oiled German engine of extinction. Actually, the *Obersturmbannführer* and his staff had made the Majestic their headquarters even before the invasion began. With its outcome in no doubt, he'd wanted to get a head start on mining the amazing bonanza of Jews fortune had seen fit to lay at his feet. At the rate the Russians were expected to advance, he wasn't counting on having a lot of time in which to work.

Hungary had long been a boil on Eichmann's backside. Charged with making Europe permanently Judenrein, freed forever from the Hebrew death grip, for two years he'd badgered, cajoled, threatened the authorities in Budapest into relinquishing their Chosen People, and hadn't so much as a single transport to show for it. Now, thanks to the bumbling cowardice of their government, the Hungarian Jews were his at last. This was one reason for the party today, but not the only one. The SS had come, of course, to honor their and their colonel's victory, but the army was there to celebrate one as well. The Wehrmacht had taken Budapest without resistance the day before, and scheduled a ceremonial march of the troops down Nicola Boulevard for this afternoon.

He wondered if maybe he shouldn't be getting back to the party—the babble of voices was insistent, the clinking of glasses, the laughter— but decided he wouldn't be missed a few minutes more. Going over the situation, even briefly, had put his mind on his mission, a subject admittedly never far from his thoughts. Much had been accomplished already, but a whole mountain of work remained.

On the map, the country had been divided into six zones, which at a future date were to be emptied of their Jews one zone at a time. Arrests were still ongoing, thousands of them so far, all the way from leading anti-Nazi political, industrial, and religious figures down to a wide range of common Jews, such as those, to use but one example, found loitering near the bus and train stations, the airports and boat docks. A coalition called the Central Jewish Council was formed; consisting of that doomed people's leaders nationwide, its task was to compile detailed lists of all Jews and their exact addresses. All county and municipal administrations, along with state and local police, were well on their way to being Nazified. Without the help of those Hungarians who sympathized with them, it was unlikely even the Germans could have completed so monumental an undertaking in the time left them.

Still, it would take the Council weeks to draw up its lists, and weeks more for the SS and its minions to round up and herd the people on them into ghettos. By sometime in May, Eichmann hoped, the transports from Zone I should begin arriving at Birkenau. He estimated a travel time of up to four days, depending on which zone the train originated in. Postulating a forty-car train on average, with a hundred deportees to a wagon (the standard Hungarian boxcar was somewhat smaller than the Polish), each transport would consist of four thousand units. How many transports a day could Birkenau absorb? He reckoned three, maybe four; anything above that would be a bonus.

That it would have to be Birkenau by itself couldn't be helped, with Maidanek, although its two crematoria were little more than glorified sheds, perhaps taking on some of the load. The other four annihilation centers were long since shut down. They'd always been considered provisional anyway, the exigencies of last summer, nor with the possible exception of Treblinka, had they been equipped to handle such a deluge of flesh as was coming. Prisoner disturbances had proved the deciding factor in closing two of them, Treblinka and Sobibor, but both, like their counterparts Chelmno and Belzec, had already outlived their usefulness.

It was Birkenau or nothing, though Eichmann was far from worried. Built from its inception to last, it was a remarkable facility, and what was more, not the same camp it had been even a month ago. He'd been keeping tabs on the measures its hierarchy was taking to prepare for the

Hungarians, and was impressed. The most dramatic of these was the building of a new rail spur. Hundreds of prisoners labored day and night laying lines right up to the steps of Crematoria II and III. It was to be a three-track system, complete with a concrete unloading platform even larger than the old one. This "Jewish ramp" would more than halve the time it took to get the payload from the trains into the gas chambers. All roads running to and between the death houses were being resurfaced as well, and construction accelerated in the unfinished *B3* lager. The work, again, knew no clock, the camp lit up at night by the phosphorus beams of anti-aircraft searchlights. The effects warehouses were being cleared out and their contents shipped off to make room. The number of inmates assigned to Canada was at an all-time high, and never had there been as large a Sonderkommando.

Four transports a day was the better part of twenty thousand subhumans. If four-fifths of these were selected for the crematoria straight off the ramp as was projected, not even their forty-plus ovens would be able to cope. Birkenau, however, boasted an excellent fire-pit program. Open-air incineration had the potential to transform the very face of industrial-scale killing and disposal, its capacity dependent only on the availability of fuel. It was this more than anything that had put Eichmann's mind to rest about entrusting the job to this one camp. Say twelve to fifteen thousand bodies on average run through the machinery per diem, and that was lowballing it—at that volume, Hungary could well be rid of its Jews before summer's end.

The mere contemplation of this suffused him now, as it usually did, with a warm, golden glow, set his heart to beating faster.... when the moment was cut short by some commotion from behind. He turned to see a rush of uniforms spilling from the penthouse onto the balcony. Though this stretched the considerable length of the suite, its railing was soon two-deep in expectant faces. It was what everyone had been waiting for, the parade of soldiers down Nicola, the dark mass of them plainly visible to the west and growing larger.

In five minutes, the first of them were passing below. The crowd that lined both sides of the street, mostly local Nazis, was making its crowd noises, behind it a sprinkling of silent, sullen citizens who for whatever reason had chosen to subject themselves to this indignity. The soldiers marched without music, but music wasn't necessary. The boulevard resounded with the metronomic stomp of the goosestep—this was their music. At their head rode a lone horseman, a color sergeant in full battle dress, tall, stately, sword unsheathed. His ebony mount stepping as proudly as the formations behind it, upon drawing abreast of the Majestic, the sergeant raised his sword in salute.

They were magnificent, these troops. The gray column tramped past in stiff, flawless precision, the sun glinting off a solid river of helmets. Fichmann shaded his eyes and strained into the distance, but could see no end to the procession. He was both awed and perplexed at the same time. He couldn't imagine such disciplined, noble legions as these giving up a foot of ground to the Mongoloid rabble of the Russian hordes. How this had happened, and was almost certain to happen again, could only be explained by the sheer force of numbers those hordes were able to muster. Such, he mused ruefully, was the power of vermin, its propensity for gaining the upper hand simply by breeding itself there.

All in all, though, it gladdened the heart to look upon such an army, and after it did finally pass from sight, the mood of the party became even sprightlier. Eichmann was drawn back into it, and not against his objections; animated by so rousing a display of German might, he was ready to be sociable again. At one point, he found himself in the company of a general, three in fact, all from the army, one of them the crusty, curmudgeonly Steiner, a soldier's soldier of the old school, who by this stage of the proceedings was well on his way to getting drunk.

"So they tell me, colonel," he said, the condescension in the word "colonel" unmistakable, "that this is a glorious day for you, too."

"It is a day of which any German can be proud," Eichmann said, ignoring the slight.

"Yes, but you've finally got your hands on those Jews you've been after. Is this not true?"

Eichmann nodded once, curtly.

Steiner turned to General Ehler on his right, and not entirely under his breath muttered, "Which makes it a bad day indeed to be a Jew, those poor people."

While Ehler blanched, Eichmann stiffened. "Those poor people, as you put it, general, are the ones who started this war, a miscalculation they are rightly paying for now. Or are you not aware of the *Führer's* thoughts on the matter?"

"As the simplest of soldiers," the other replied with a smile, "I can only concern myself with those thoughts of the *Führer* that come in the form of his orders issued me in the field. But on the subject of orders," he said, the smile falling from his face, "I've a question, if you don't mind, that's been troubling me for some time now."

"Shoot," Eichmann said, "as long, if you please, as you don't interpret the word literally."

Those listening laughed nervously, relieved at this attempt to break the tension. Only Steiner remained grim. "It has been my experience, in both Greece and the Balkans of late, that without exception, Herr Eichmann, precedence has been given those RSHA transports of yours. And by that, I mean over supply and even armament and troop trains. Time and again, I've watched the military left hanging so that the SS can use the rails to shuttle its cargoes of women and children around. My question is that in these desperate times, this crucial stage of the war, can we expect the same insanity to prevail?"

Eichmann never ceased to marvel at the power of alcohol to loosen men's tongues. Could the fool not see he was flirting with treason? "You mention orders," he told this Steiner. "Well, I'm only following mine. And in answer to your question, yes; the Hungarian transports will have priority over all other traffic."

"At the expense of success in battle? The lives of the brave men fighting the battle?"

"At the expense of Germany itself if necessary," Eichmann said. "There is more at stake here than you apparently realize, general."

"Then you and your whole bunch of—"

"What the general means, colonel," Ehler hastily interrupted, "is that he wishes you and your people all the best in your mission." He then leaned toward Steiner and whispered at some length in his ear.

This had its effect. The man wasn't quite drunk enough to sign his own death warrant. With obvious effort, he composed himself, not that he was done handing out the insults.

"You're right, Karl," he told Ehler. "I should probably shut up now. But first...." Addressing Eichmann, he squared his shoulders. "May your

SS, sir, enjoy the same triumph over the noncombatants of this damned country that the Wehrmacht did against its armed forces. And I mean that most sincerely," he added with a grin.

Though the taunt hardly escaped him, Eichmann took it in stride. He had more and bigger fish to fry than this pathetic relic of the past. In fact, with a grin himself, he sought to be gracious, sort of.

"Allow me, gentlemen, to propose a toast," he announced. A waiter was summoned, glasses of champagne passed around. "To our valiant troops!" Eichmann exclaimed, lifting his glass. "And the many victories over the Jew their conquests have brought us!"

He made sure to stare straight at Steiner as he spoke. Just so there wouldn't be any misunderstanding.

Spring

S-Master Sergeant Möll wasn't having the best of days. Here it was a long way from noon and already there were problems, beginning with the fifth straight morning of a drizzling rain that showed no sign of stopping. An unbroken ceiling of gray overcast so low it felt as if one could reach up and touch it had parked itself above Birkenau and wasn't leaving.

It was a living, malevolent thing, this rain, come to torture him for the sheer pleasure of watching him squirm. Its timing couldn't have been worse. Intermittent, not steady, it was playing havoc all the same with his efforts to get the camp ready for the Hungarians—not undividedly, thank God, but in several critical areas, one of which, the fire pits, could prove calamitous if any more were to remain undug.

As frustrating as this was, however, he couldn't complain too much. Or so he kept telling himself. That he was back at Birkenau where he belonged was more than ample cause for him to count his blessings. Just ten days ago (ten days!) he'd been marooned at Fürstengrube still, when from out of the blue a phone call had given him not only a second chance but the chance of a lifetime. Six months prior, the original commandant of Auschwitz, *Obersturmbannführer* Rudolf Höss, was transferred to the commission at Oranienburg that oversaw the entire concentration camp system. There were rumors of personal gain and other improprieties Höss had committed on his watch, but Möll knew nothing of these, nor cared. What mattered to him was that following the recent fortuitous events in Hungary, the *Obersturmbannführer* had been recalled to Auschwitz on May 1ˢᵗ to supervise the annihilation of that country's nest of Jews. One of his first acts had been to telephone Möll and order him back to Birkenau, not merely to assist in said annihilation but to assume management of the crematoria. Not one, not two, but all four of them.

He, Otto Möll, in charge of the whole show! He'd fantasized such a thing many times, during many a long, empty night in Fürstengrube, but though he'd had a hunch he hadn't seen the last of Birkenau, any thought of the crematoria being his to do with as he saw fit had remained just that, a fantasy and no more. But hardly an idle one. He'd filled it with as many details as he could think of, imagining how he might improve operations were the power his. This served to give him a head start when the call to glory did come. Upon his arrival at his new/old posting, he'd hit the ground running.

His first order of business had been the shuffling of SS crematoria personnel. Having deemed him in his opinion too soft for the job, he'd replaced the *Kommandoführer* of Number Two with First Sergeant Muhsfeld, already top dog at Number Three. The no-nonsense Muhsfeld was not only intelligent and an excellent organizer, but a dedicated killer. Möll had seen him in action, and no one, himself included, was more devoted than the *Oberscharführer* to the holy task of rendering the Jewish bacterium extinct.

Two crematoria, though, he realized, were a lot to ask of one man, so he appointed a brace of corporals to back Muhsfeld up. Number Four, which had for some reason been under the command of a lowly, grossly incompetent *Oberschütze*, he contemplated handing to the debonair Captain Hössler. But the man, as his superior in rank, would have been difficult to control, and was too much the dandy besides to dirty his hands with Krema work. Instead, he appointed *Unterscharführer* Gorges to the post. The fortyish sergeant was a shameless windbag and overly fond of his schnapps (his perpetually florid countenance had earned him the nickname Moshe Beetface among the Sonder), but could be counted on to obey orders, regardless what they were. Which was also why he chose to retain *Oberscharführer* Voss as chief of Number Five; though he, too, drank to excess, and was far too lenient with his SS subordinates, he was a punctilious follower of orders, and as unshrinking a killer as Muhsfeld. Just to be safe, Möll assigned a trustworthy *Sturmmänn* to each, to aid them in their duties, of course, but also to keep an eye on them.

Finally, and in what he had little doubt would end up his best people move, he'd acquired the services of a young sergeant who gave every indication of having what it took to make his own job easier. Actually,

Unterscharführer Karl Eckardt was a year older than he, but so youthful were his features, he might have passed for twenty. Tall, athletic, and with hair so blond it was almost white, he looked every inch the Nordic nonpareil, which should have made the paunchy, freckled Möll dislike him at first sight. But so great was the respect Eckardt had shown him from the beginning, deferring to him with the same humility he would have a senior officer, his new boss took an instant shine to him, a view amplified when the man proved to be capable. He'd been seconded to the crematoria because of his fluency in Hungarian; born and raised in Budapest, it might as well have been his first language. That he also spoke some Polish was almost too good to be true. For now he was keeping this Eckardt close to him as his adjutant, and so in demand was he day and night, so laden with responsibility, that he truly did need a full-time assistant. Down the road, though, he had other plans for him, namely as *Kommandoführer* of what had been redesignated the Bunker 5 complex.

This was the larger of the two provisional gas bunkers decommissioned last spring with the opening of the crematoria, the smaller, unfortunately, having been dismantled for its brick and timber. The old farmhouse-turned-death-house was being remodeled and would once again be used for special handling, this time in conjunction with three new undressing barracks and four fire pits to be dug nearby. Eckardt's linguistic acumen would be invaluable at this new site, and with Bunker 5 located off the beaten path, well away from its four cousins, Möll wanted someone over there he wouldn't have to babysit.

Already he'd had to make a special trip to the complex this morning to assess the harm done one of the new changing barracks last night by the rain. A large tree had dislodged itself and crashed onto the roof. The damage had been considerable and would call for major repairs. Apart from waking up to more rain, this had been the first thing to go wrong with his day, though as he would learn come afternoon, far from the worst.

Following the solidification of his chain of command, he'd turned his attention to the excavation of the fire pits. No one was exactly sure when the Hungarians were due, but once they did start showing up, the bodies would be spilling out of the gas chambers like grain from ruptured sacks. Eventually, the ovens wouldn't be able to keep up, creating a mess repulsive beyond all comprehension, especially with the weather already warm.

It was imperative that most if not all of the pits be functioning when the time came. Why his superiors had filled in the originals and grassed them over was beyond him, but they were irretrievable now; not even he could begin to pinpoint where they'd been, nor could a map be found to aid him in this. The only thing to do was start from scratch, and it was here that the rain proved its most crippling. The dense, sticky clay soil only grew denser and stickier when wet; to the Sonder digging in the stuff, it was as if they were shoveling into half-melted rubber, nor were they able to get any traction in the ankle-deep mud. Möll had ordered five pits finished within the week, but despite a dozen major tantrums, and as many dead Sonder to show for them, had to settle for two. At least he had these, though, and to specification, each a perfectly rectangular fifty meters by eight by two. He could take some satisfaction knowing that these two pits alone would double the incineration capacity of Crematoria IV and V combined.

But there was something other than the Hungarians that had him in a rush, something he'd been dreaming about since Fürstengrube. No, before then—since he'd stumbled onto the idea a year and a half ago while disinterring and burning the corpses of the 110,000. If successful, the self-fueling fire pit could revolutionize the field. By recycling the human fat that would otherwise be lost, one could dig as many pits as required without fretting about the amount of kerosene on hand. At twelve hundred corpses per pyre reduced to ashes every six hours, the only limit to the destruction became not how many Jews a day could be incinerated, but exterminated. The gas chamber was suddenly the weak link in the chain, if one could call, with the addition of Bunker 5's, an easy seventeen, eighteen thousand deaths a day weak.

Möll had experimented with a few table-top models he'd put together at Fürstengrube, but without a full-sized pit to try it out on, his invention remained theoretical. Now he had that pit, and another if required. All he needed to test theory against practice was for this insane rain to quit, and as the morning wore on, it appeared he might finally get his wish. Around nine o'clock, the one big cloud, as if afraid to try the Cyclops' patience any longer, commenced to break up into little ones, these soon tumbling out of sight off to the east.

An excited Möll, blueprint in hand, found Eckardt and made on his motorcycle for the meadow abutting Crematorium V. After assembling a work gang, he picked the driest-looking of the two pits, had it suctioned out, then he and his second, with a ball of string, staked out a strip thirty inches wide extending almost the length of it down the center. Helping them was the prisoner he'd chosen beforehand to be kapo of the crew. When satisfied with the placement of the string, his new boss took him aside.

"I selected you for this job," he told him, "one, because of your experience in cement at the Bauhof Kommando, and two, because you are German. It is not a particularly difficult task, but does demand a respect for detail. Are you with me so far?"

"Yes, Herr *Hauptscharführer.*" He stood rigidly at attention, staring straight ahead.

Möll paced up and down in front of him as he talked. "That blueprint you're holding lays it all out for you. I want two six-inch-deep channels dug the width of the strings each starting at the centerpoint of the pit, then continuing away from each other at a downward angle of seven degrees. That's seven degrees precisely, no more, no less. How many degrees, kapo?"

"Seven, sir. Precisely."

"Each trench is to empty after twenty meters into a reservoir four meters long, two wide, and one deep. You said rebar would be required for these last, but I want the grids laid quick; no reason to make them works of art. And you're sure the trenches won't need reinforcing as well?"

"Not, sir, if we mix their cement with enough rock and scrap metal. That should allow them to hold their shape."

Möll shot him a look that said, You'd better be sure. "Once all is done, if done properly, the completed channels should catch a fair amount of the liquid fat given up by the bodies and funnel it into the two reservoirs. From there, it can be ladled as necessary onto the fire. That much should be clear, but do you remember what I said about the importance of all this?"

"Yes, sir." Upon summoning him last week, Möll had explained his plan. The man had been startled, then sickened by the ghoulishness of it. Not, from a practical standpoint, that it didn't make sense. This was what was so dreadful about it—it made perfect sense. "I remember it…. well. Yes."

"Excellent," Möll said, "for that allows me to add this. Not only is this job of yours, small as it may seem, significant to the future of Germany and its people, our people"—here he came abruptly to a stop and stood facing him—"but to me personally. Do I make myself understood?"

The prisoner could only nod. A large bead of sweat had begun to trickle down his forehead.

"Let me spell it out for you anyway," said the sergeant. "I've been waiting a long time for this day. It means a lot to me. Do you envision anything, *anything*, cropping up that might ruin it for me?"

"Nothing, *mein Hauptscharführer*. All will be done as you say, down to the last detail."

"I do hope so," Möll said, walking away, "as should you, my dear kapo. Trust me, as should you." Halfway up the small ladder to ground level, he paused and turned. "Follow the blueprint, it's as simple as that. I'll be back in three hours. The cement should have set enough by then to do a trial run with water. See that you're here."

He sped off on his motorcycle, Eckardt in the sidecar. It would take at least three hours to dig the thing and for the cement to harden some, and there was much to be done meanwhile back at Bunker 5. He needed, among other jobs, to site and stake the four fire pits he intended to situate there. These would bring the final total to nine, a number he was content with. He found it hard to imagine needing more than nine.

When he did return shortly after twelve-thirty, it was with his German Shepherd Hannibal riding next to him. Unable in his excitement to wait any longer, he'd left Eckardt to finish up at the bunker. He made for the pit almost at a trot, hopping nimbly down without waiting for the ladder. Standing at the center of the apparatus, he studied first one side of the channel then the other. After a long moment at each basin, again he seemed satisfied. Returning to the center, at his order two buckets of water were lowered from above. He poured the contents of one into the left-hand gutter and watched it closely. The water flowed the length of it, then out of sight into the basin. Without pausing, his face expectant, he emptied the second bucket into the opposite side—only to see the liquid slowly form into a pool a good twelve meters from the reservoir at that end.

Those watching looked on in terrified silence. They knew what was coming, nor did it take long. Möll snatched up the first bucket, and wildly swinging both, launched himself at the prisoners nearest. Bashing a few heads wasn't enough for him, however. With a strangled cry, he threw down the buckets and scrambled up the ladder, searching out the kapo he'd left in charge.

"You stupid shit!" he screamed, droplets of spittle spewing from his mouth like tiny, hopping insects. "I give you a simple enough job, and what do you do?" He whistled his dog over. The creature flew to his side, ears up in anticipation. "Hannibal here could have done better! My dog! I ought to—" He looked down at the ground, breathing heavily, as if trying to calm himself. But it was no use. "The hell with it, goddammit, I think I will!"

He whipped out his Luger and aimed it at the man, who closing his eyes, began mouthing a silent prayer. But two seconds turned into five, then ten, and to everyone's disbelief, none more than the kapo's, the gun went unfired. Möll stood frozen, arm outstretched, before giving in and letting it fall. Despite his bungling foreman's sorry performance, he realized that to replace him would take more time than he could spare. Besides, in a way it was his own fault as much as anyone's; he, after all, was the engineer here, and should have led by example, this first go-around at any rate. He'd debated this with himself earlier, but Bunker 5 had beckoned, and he'd thought to save a few hours. Now he'd have to scramble to get back those he'd lost.

Angrily holstering his pistol, he called a guard over and sent him for a pair of overalls. And another for more picks and shovels. Within minutes he was back on the mud floor of the pit with a surveyor's rod, a spirit-level, the rest of the work crew, and a look on his face that promised a bullet to any man who didn't snap to his orders. As for the derelict kapo, he kept him glued to his side. He wasn't going to have the time to install the remaining eight of his contraptions himself, but he'd be damned if his protégé wouldn't be able to in his sleep.

Thanks to his foresight, in case of just this, the concrete was still wet enough to break apart without using jackhammers. In under an hour, the defective half of the channel was gone and a new one in its place. All that remained now was for the cement to harden. He sent the crew off to help their comrades working on Pits 3 and 4, and since his presence no doubt was urgently needed elsewhere, somewhere, everywhere, decided to make a sweep of the entire area while he waited.

After this latest and most demoralizing one, Möll had to wonder what other problems this day had in store for him. At least the rain had ended, and appeared gone for good. Released from its prison of clouds, the sun beat down as if to atone for lost time. He shed his overalls and slipped his tunic back on, though with the heat and humidity having climbed with the sun, he left it unbuttoned. With Hannibal, he set off at a crawl on his motorcycle. He wanted to take it slow, make certain everything was as it should be.

Not that he wouldn't have been tempted to dawdle anyway, the spectacle that swirled around him difficult to resist. The meadow to him was an intriguing study in contrasts. Dotting the lime-green spring grass and gaily colored sprays of wildflowers were ugly, greasy-looking heaps of tools and machinery, everything from hand wrenches to pneumatic drills, spools of wire to electric generators. The 12th Sonderkommando was at six hundred men and growing. Scores of them pushing wheelbarrows and hauling carts crisscrossed the meadow at a run, dodging the big trucks lumbering in and out. The majority of these were busy provisioning the fuel dumps that rose up here and there—more like garbage dumps, actually, nor was this being metaphoric. Protected from the weather by tarps or ramshackle roofs on stilts, they consisted largely of freshly dismembered trees, but also old railroad ties, broken timbers, irregularly cut planks and boards, barrels of methanol, kerosene, and waste oil, and bundles of rags to be drenched in the latter for studding the pyres with. It may have passed for so much trash, but stockpiled and covered it was going to come in handy, especially on rainy days. The fire pits would be as in demand in damp weather as dry.

Möll was in his element. What another might have viewed as nature despoiled, the land scarred, he saw as a thing of beauty, the sum of much planning and hard work. As he wound his bike through the clutter, he marveled at its grimy pageantry, soaked up the discordant music it generated as accompaniment. The noise was without pause, men shouting, motors roaring, the woodpecker staccato of hammers, the distant shriek of chainsaws slicing up the surrounding forest. Though still in a huff over the delay at Pit 1, it was softened some by the sights and sounds of this mad, multidimensional hornet's nest he'd created. Whatever setbacks might arise, and these were to be expected in so vast an undertaking, it never ceased brightening the mood of its newest officiary to know that without him Birkenau wouldn't be close to reaching the level of destructive power it was fast approaching.

Take, for instance, what greeted him when finally he did exit the meadow en route to Crematorium V. Here lay another of those ideas he'd hatched at Fürstengrube. Though no more now than naked rebar, a grid of interwoven steel rods hugging the ground, it would soon be an enormous concrete slab for the crushing of whatever material the fire pits had left whole. Despite the rain having precluded the pouring of a single yard of cement, this would change starting tomorrow, eventually producing a platform stretching sixty meters by fifteen. And another, smaller one at Bunker 5. One advantage the ovens had over their parallels outdoors was the thoroughness with which they consumed their human fodder. During express work, some of the larger bones might survive the flames in varying degrees of wholeness, but as a rule all that remained were crumbly fragments, if that. The fire pits, however, regularly left sizable chunks behind, whole femurs and skulls, burnt to brittleness but intact. To the SS powers-that-were, this was unacceptable; they wanted as little evidence of the dead lying around as possible. Möll had never understood this. He saw no reason to hide, as if ashamed of it, the selfless work they were doing, work he would have thought his superiors eager to take credit for. The world in its hypocrisy might holler some when finally informed of the elimination of Europe's Jews, but in the end, having as much to gain from such a housecleaning as the Germans, could only be grateful.

Were grateful now, it was obvious to anyone with eyes. Or in his case, the one eye. Twice a month, sometimes more, both Russian and American bombers droned above Birkenau, their targets on occasion the factories of Monowitz, but usually headed elsewhere. There could be no question the entire complex had been photographed from the air many times over, nor was it possible to mistake the camp for what it was. The crematoria, the train tracks, the unloading platform, the lines of people filing into buildings with chimneys that vomited black smoke—even without their spies on the ground, the Allies knew all too well what was going on, yet continued to do nothing. It wouldn't have taken a handful of bombers five minutes to disrupt the killings permanently, so why in the name of all that was irrefutable hadn't they?

The answer was plain. The adversaries in this great conflict that had come to be known as the Second World War may have disagreed on a lot of things, but on one clearly didn't: the Jew, their mutual enemy, had to go. If it were up to Möll, he'd have kept the foe informed of the Birkenau body count as it progressed. Maybe then they wouldn't have been in such a hurry to beat a path to Berlin.

But it wasn't up to him. To paraphrase the famous English poet, His was not to reason why, his but to do and die. Good soldier that he was, therefore, and perfectionist to boot, he'd not only conceived of this site for the pulverizing of charred bone but planned to equip it with an array of sieves with which to sift the powder. Misguided as they were, if his commanding officers insisted there be nothing of their victims left behind, then nothing there would be. He had no intention of letting anything bigger than a fingernail clipping get past him.

Not far from where the ash and bone slab was to be loomed Crematorium V. Möll noted with satisfaction that both its chimneys were smoking; a smallish transport, from Belgrade he believed, had arrived earlier. It was always a plus to see smoke coming from either IV or V, given what junk the Mogilevs had turned out to be. He parked his motorcycle, and with his dog behind him, went in search of Sergeant Voss. He found the *Kommandoführer* in the undressing area supervising the transfer of the corpses there to cremation. It was a good thing for him he wasn't only working but seemed sober.

Voss, sweating through his uniform in the closed room, looked startled when he saw him. Möll, as he generally did, got a kick out of the reaction. "Sergeant," he said coolly, parading toward him.

"Good afternoon, *Hauptscharführer*. What can I—You there!" he bellowed at a group of Sonder. "Two at a time, you idiots! If you drag them by the wrists, you can take two at a time, Christ!" Then to his visitor, with a conspiratorial roll of the eyes, "What can I do for you, sir?"

Was this little outburst meant to impress him? Möll was used to that, too. "I was passing by and thought I'd check to see if that new paste was helping any." He'd come up with a different formula for filling the cracks in the furnaces, something hopefully more binding. "Have you noticed any improvement?"

"Some maybe, it's hard to tell yet. So far so good, I guess. I—By the *wrists*, I said, goddammit!"

Möll observed to his chagrin no less than six hundred bodies cluttering the floor of the undressing room. How inefficient these smaller Kremas were! How poorly planned, from entrance to exit. As aggravating a sight as this was, it was mitigated some, to his amusement, when he noticed Hannibal sniffing at the private parts of a stack of females. One advantage of having a dog, he mused affectionately, was its ability to distract its owner from his troubles.

He turned his attention back to Voss. "You do realize, I trust, what is on its way," he said.

"Sir?" the sergeant replied uncertainly.

"Three, four transports a day. Some days more maybe, if you can imagine. In all honesty, do you think your Number Five is up to it? To dealing with such numbers?"

Voss wiped a sleeve across his forehead. "In all honesty, sir, what would you have me say? We will do our very best, that is all I can promise."

Möll had hoped for more, but would settle for this. In fact, in appreciation of the other's candor, and what for him was no small concession, he dropped his normally distant tone for an almost comradely one.

"That is all that can be asked of any of us, I suppose. You are doing a fine job, *Oberscharführer*. Keep up the good work."

Upon his return to Birkenau, he'd found all four of the crematoria, in if not inoperable condition, then well on their way to it, and from little more than a lack of basic care. Among the many shortcomings of Höss's successor as commandant, the weak and ineffectual SS-*Obersturmbannführer* Artur Liebehenschel, was his failure to adequately provide for the death factories. Möll found himself the recipient of a long list of neglect. First and most urgent, all six smokestacks were struggling, half of them close to collapse. Most of the firebricks lining their interiors, those that hadn't already fallen and were clogging the flues underground, had to be replaced, the flues cleaned out, and for good measure the chimneys' exteriors strengthened with heavy iron bands.

Even more damning was the filth that had been allowed to accumulate in all four buildings. There wasn't an oven that looked as if it had been clinkered in weeks. He ordered them cleaned from the inside out, their cast-iron doors repainted, the hinges and rollers oiled, even the brick furnaces enclosing them given a bath. He also had their electric generators overhauled, along with the motorized Exhators that fanned the coke. Each cremation room received so thorough a scrubbing, down to removing the soot many had thought ineradicable, that it shone as if it had yet to be used.

As for the undressing rooms and gas chambers, they were slathered with fresh layers of paint and plaster, all light bulbs changed, windows washed and fixtures polished, drains flushed out, the floors refinished and disinfected. Nothing escaped his notice. Harking back to his original posting at the main camp as groundkeeper, he even had the crematoria compounds spruced up, the lawns resodded where needed, the flowerbeds replenished.

There was more to it, though, than merely giving the place a face-lift. It went beyond the cosmetic, the repairable even. Both Crematoria II and III were in sore need of new elevators, the old ones having turned out to be too light for the job. They'd been running, he was told, in fits and starts for a while, and soon they wouldn't be running at all. At first, Commandant Höss had balked at the cost, but quickly acceded to his sergeant's logic: II and III without elevators were like horses without legs, an engine without oil. Höss put in a rush order for replacements. Möll was also awaiting the arrival of two forced-draft ventilation systems for the gas chambers of Crematoria IV and V, each identical to those existing in their bigger, better-appointed sisters. Mechanical de-aeration wasn't only safer than the natural, but a faster method of emptying the death room of its gas once it had served its purpose.

Though much of the work was done, much remained. He was on the move all day and half the night, had hardly slept since he got here. Not that he regretted losing one minute of that sleep, picturing himself sitting on his butt back in Fürstengrube still. The way he looked at it, those minutes that would have been rendered empty by the semi-coma of slumber were packed full instead of the fascinating business of mass extinction, or rather mobilizing for same, which had its own attractions. The SS were breaking new ground, expanding old frontiers, entering territory unexplored in all of history until now. The world had never witnessed such a blood sacrifice as was coming, nor the holocaust to follow, and there he stood stage center, the high priest, the anti-rabbi presiding at the pyre. It was as if his life, its indecipherable twists and turns, had been leading over the years to this exact point. Never had he believed more vehemently in the greatness the future held for him.

There was no ignoring, too, the fun of being boss, of strutting about like the cock of the roost, master of the regal pose, the theatrical entrance. Especially when that entrance came without warning. He liked the look of fear, even panic, this brought to the faces of both the prisoners and their guards. Möll got a charge out of affecting people this way. It was the ultimate compliment, an acknowledgment from the gut of his utter dominance. Equally bracing, though he hadn't foreseen it, were the many obstacles facing him, which instead of wearing him down served on the whole to energize him. Despite the volcanic eruptions of temper they were apt to unleash, secretly he welcomed these roadblocks, the challenge they presented. Some of them, that is. There'd been nothing redeeming about the week's interminable rain, nor what had happened earlier at Pit 1.

But not everything he'd inherited upon his return to Birkenau was a headache. And by this, what came foremost to mind was the Jewish ramp. It was there, gathering up Hannibal on his way out of Crematorium V, that he decided to make for now, bypassing Number Four (talk about a headache, nor was there a thing he could do about it) and Three as well, which but for its elevator and after its refurbishing, was running so smoothly there was no need to stop in.

The Jewish ramp had been an unexpected treat. Where the initiative for it had come from he couldn't say, except to feel sure it hadn't sprung from the hapless Liebehenschel. More likely from the headquarters at Oranienburg, maybe even Höss himself. Whatever its provenance, it was a stroke of genius. Indeed, such was its potential to hasten the Jews to the fate they'd earned themselves, he relegated much of his time to helping superintend its completion.

Belying, to his surprise, what he'd anticipated upon beginning his tour of the area, his presence hadn't been needed anywhere after all. Until he announced it at the ramp. Some snags had arisen involving supply and distribution, mainly the flow of tools, materials, and such to the work site. Nothing too serious, these were resolved soon enough, but were neither the only nor the biggest problem. One of the tracks had veered off course due to a surveying error, but though the mistake had been caught before too much of the crooked rail was laid, it did take Möll and the other officers no little effort to make the mess right.

By the time they had, another hour had passed. He looked at his watch and almost yelped with excitement. Busy as he'd been, he'd forgotten all about Pit 1. The concrete had to have set by now, enough for him at any rate. He jumped on his motorcycle, dropped Hannibal at his kennel, then raced to Bunker 5 to pick up Eckardt. After arriving at the meadow, he tracked down his kapo and crew at Pit 3 and marched them back to where they'd botched it the first time.

The shadows were starting to lengthen, the sun to lose its teeth. The promise of evening and its cool hung in the air. The two soldiers he'd left on guard had summoned several more while he was away, and these stood leaning on their rifles in anticipation. First into the pit was Möll, followed by Eckardt then the kapo, the latter looking as if he was bound for a funeral, his own. Buckets of water were lowered. Möll grabbed one impatiently, a malicious twinkle in his eye.

"You do realize that if this doesn't work, I'm going to blame you, kapo. For screwing it up in the first place. Fair enough?"

"But—but this last time, sir, you...." There was, of course, no arguing. "Yes, sir. Fair enough."

"I have a good feeling about it, though. Let's keep our fingers crossed. In your case, I would suggest the fingers of both hands."

Möll walked to the center of the pit, and as if warming up, eased into the test by emptying the pail into the good channel on the left. As it had before, the descending ripple of water vanished rapidly from sight. Carefully, almost reluctantly, he repeated the process on the right.

This water, too, disappeared. With a quick glance at Eckardt, he held out his hand for a third bucket and tried it again, with the same result. Without a word, he dashed to the collecting trough on that side, then to the one at the other end. A film of liquid puddled the floor of each. For a brief moment, he lifted his face to the heavens, long enough for those looking down from the edge of the pit to see that rarest of phenomena, a smile untarnished by sadism's leer lighting up the features of the Cyclops.

But it, too, was brief, though he didn't so much walk as saunter back to the centerpoint. "Get your men down here, all of them," he told the kapo, his voice, as with Voss, uncharacteristically civil, "and let's wrap this up. I want that old concrete out of here, the reservoirs siphoned and covered, and the dirt packed down so it won't blow in the wind. And keep your head clear for tomorrow; I'll be expecting you to impress me at Pits 2 and 3."

Once back above ground, he stared pensively into #1. Calm as he appeared on the outside, however, within he was dancing. Gratitude, fulfillment, relief, they were all there, but of that whirl of emotions gamboling inside him, triumph leapt the highest. After years of working his way up from the bottom—from less than the bottom, from digging ditches, for God's sake!—not just recognition but a measure of fame was within reach. Should he guide the Hungarian Aktion to a favorable conclusion, an end this brainchild of his could only further, his career was secured, his prospects limitless. It was far from fanciful to envision a lieutenantship in his future, and from there, who knew? SS-*Untersturmführer* Otto Möll…. the sound of it in his head was enough to tick that head a little higher.

On the other hand, any personal acclaim he might reap was as nothing to the big picture, to the discharging of that sacred oath he as a biological soldier had sworn. For Germany to live, even should it lose the war, particularly then, the Jew must die when and wherever he was found. Who could quantify the revenge of the survivors, should there be any? It wasn't hard to imagine all of Germany turned into one gigantic concentration camp, with its people, the Volk, the master race, on the wrong side of the barbed wire. That was an insanity one must do everything in one's power to prevent, and to the extent that this device sprawling at his feet like the unearthed spine of some dinosaur contributed, however slightly, to the achieving of that goal, therein lay its value and the only true justification for celebrating it.

But in the midst of celebration, even then there was room for doubt. As Möll reveled in the success of this afternoon's demonstration of his simple, yet precisely because of that, conspicuous feat of design, one question persisted, a final nagging uncertainty. He wasn't sure it even merited comment, but called Eckardt to his side anyway. Below them in the pit and the full flush of his reprieve, the kapo was dutifully shouting at his men to work faster.

"What is it, sir?" his adjutant said. "Something is bothering you?"

Möll didn't look at him, squinted instead into the distance. "I don't know," he said. "I'm sure it's nothing, but…. Fat is viscous, isn't it, sergeant? Thicker than water, I mean."

"I believe that is correct, sir. It does make sense."

Möll turned and faced him, his expression almost pleading. "So what do you think?" he said, nodding toward his creation and the mob of prisoners bustling around it. "Is it likely to perform as well with hot fat as water? Can that make a difference, or am I being paranoid?"

Eckardt had to suppress a smile. So his boss had a jigger of humanity in him after all. "I should think it will be fine, *Hauptscharführer*," he replied. "Water, melted fat…. the two aren't *that* dissimilar. I wouldn't trouble myself with it if I were you."

Möll felt better after this, but only some. Walking a little way off by himself, he stared unseeing at the scrum of prisoners below. There was only one way to answer his question for certain, and it wasn't with buckets of water, but with corpses stacked atop each other in neat, sizzling rows, giving up their fat for the Fatherland. He was proud of what he'd done to whip Birkenau into shape, to prepare it for those corpses, but rewarding as it had been, it was as nothing to the adventure to come. To tell the truth, he was starting to grow tired of them, these preparations, as one might of hors d'oeuvres while awaiting the main course. Enough of cheese or salami or whatever on crackers—he was starving, it now occurred to him together with a soundless chuckle, for a man-sized serving of Hungarian goulash.

*   *   *

The sirens started up during roll call, filling the rapidly darkening expanse of Birkenau with their mournful wail. Most of the inmates, the Sonder included, assumed it an air raid, if a little earlier in the night than normal. But Kapo Kaminski and a few others recognized it for what it was.

"It's not a raid," he sought to assure those newer men among them glancing nervously skyward. "It's an escape is all; nothing to wet your breeches over, trust me."

"And how do you know that?" came the translation from Hungarian.

"Because you've been here two weeks and I for two years, that's how. Any more stupid questions?"

Actually, Kaminski knew because he happened to be in on the thing, nor was this the first time Battle Group-Sonderkommando had assisted the Stammlager in fomenting an escape. The Polish underground may have been reluctant to sponsor a mass breakout, but was all for smuggling increments of two or three men out of camp in the hope they might reach the Allies with proof of Nazi atrocity.

Not two months ago, for example, Auschwitz had requested Sonder help in the springing of two of its operatives with instructions to warn the West of the impending Hungarian slaughter. What was needed from Birkenau was an estimate of the number of crematoria dead to date; a description of the extermination process, complete with detailed sketches of the facilities and their equipment; and, if it could be managed, a label from one of the Germans' canisters of poison gas.

"Uh, excuse me?" Kaminski had said to the agent bearing these requests, a Polish electrician by the name of Porebski. "Could you repeat that last one, please?"

"A label from one of the tins of Zyklon-B." The young Pole had been transparent in his effort to sound matter-of-fact.

Porebski, like Noah Zabludowicz, was a familiar face at Block 13. This was all that had kept Kaminski from losing his temper. "I don't know, my man, if your bosses realize it or not, but the Krauts are rather jealous of their Zyklon-B. It's not something they like to share or leave lying around, not even those empty containers of it."

"Of course, but there must be a way to—"

"No, there mustn't, not necessarily. And to get caught trying wouldn't only be fatal but something of a giveaway to what you're planning, don't you think?"

Porebski was apologetic. "I understand, kapo, I'm just repeating what I was told. All we're asking is that you do what you can."

"Easy to ask, hard to do," Kaminski had groused. "But what the hell isn't around here?"

Not that he'd failed to see the value in such a prize. Come the next gassing, a shipment of Greeks, he informed his *Kommandoführer*, First Sergeant Muhsfeld, that two new receptacles for the collecting of gold teeth were needed, as the old ones were rusting through. Muhsfeld, annoyed, wanted to know why his kapo was bothering him with such a triviality and told him to scrounge something up. Immediately, he made his way to the bogus Red Cross ambulance parked in the yard, telling its pair of Disinfektoren that the *Oberscharführer* had sent him for two empty cans of the poison. Despite having participated in countless executions, he'd never seen a tin of the stuff up close. It didn't feel quite real holding in his hands two admittedly ordinary-looking objects that had nevertheless been instrumental in the murder of two thousand human beings. Later, as he struggled to peel the labels off without tearing them, the words on them, stark, straightforward, chilling, imparted the same eerie feeling.

Zyklon-B. Poison gas for pest control. Cyanogen compound.
DANGER! POISON! To be opened by trained personnel only.
Tesch and Stabenow International, GMBH

Within three days, Porebski got everything he'd asked for, and soon after, on the night of April 7th, it was discovered at the Appell that the Jews Alfred Wetzler and Rudolf Vrba were missing from formation. The sirens blared, a Blocksperre was ordered, and within minutes hundreds of soldiers thrown into the search. All night the shouts of men and the barking of dogs could be heard as patrols scoured the vast forbidden zone between the inner and outer guard cordons. The next day the Germans started in on the camp itself, going through every hut, warehouse, workshop, and latrine. They even combed the unfinished areas of *B3*, the Mexico lager, where construction had resumed in anticipation of the Hungarians. Not a pile of lumber or mound of trash was left unexamined, but nothing turned up here, either. It was as if the earth had opened and swallowed the two men.

And so it had. They'd been hiding in Mexico all along, having dug a hole not much bigger than a grave while members of a work crew excavating for a future barracks. They'd situated it outside the barbed-wire perimeter of the lager, a provisional fence in constant flux depending on where the prisoners were working. Upon their dodging into this hole, those in league with them hastily covered it with a roof of boards and a layer of soil, then sprinkled the area with turpentine and a dusting of tobacco in order to throw off any dogs.

For four days and three nights, Wetzler and Vrba crouched in this hot, suffocating den, waiting for the SS to break off the search locally and withdraw the outer cordon. This farthest ring of watchtowers, manned as a rule only during the day, was kept occupied at night if an escape was ongoing. After three days, the schedule would return to normal and the focus of the search be expanded.

On the fourth night, the two fled their hiding place and slipped into the woods. The search in and around the camp having been abandoned, and the area police and Gestapo alerted, the entire countryside was swept, every village and farm watched, all bus and rail terminals, even the gendarmes at the border crossings warned to be on the lookout.

Equipped as they were, though, with forged identity papers and work cards, the Wetzler-Vrba team made it—all the way to London eventually, as Battle Group-Auschwitz was to find out three weeks later. Optimism ran high that the sixty pages they'd brought with them documenting SS crimes past and to come couldn't help but persuade the Allies to rush to the rescue of the Hungarians. For three more weeks, hundreds of eyes scanned the skies above Birkenau, watching for those planes come to rain ruin on the crematoria.

But they never showed. Something had gone wrong. Maybe, it was thought, Churchill and friends had had a hard time believing what was put in front of them, needed to see the pair's bizarre accusations corroborated. So Auschwitz organized a second escape. On this, the evening of May 27th, the prisoners Mordowicz and Rosin failed to present themselves at the Birkenau Appell, and again the sirens sounded. Three days later, the gallows set aside for them remained unused, and Kaminski could only hope that his second Zyklon-B label would help move the Allies to action.

Something had to happen, and fast. Even the Poles were shaking their heads at the rate the Hungarians were dying. Two transports a day now disappeared into the flames, and as everyone knew, this was only the beginning. Soon the count would be upped to three and four, numbers difficult to conceive of.

As for those Sonder whose job it was to dispose of those transports, the recently recruited among them were no more receptive to the idea of revolt than any commando preceding them. Kaminski hadn't expected this; he'd hoped the 12th Squad might be different. Two-thirds of what was now almost a thousand men were Hungarian, meaning they were herding their own people to the gas, feeding their own to the ovens. Their kapo would have thought this incentive enough to make them trip over each other exchanging their gas masks and other gear for dynamite. But the same forces that had blunted the volition and stayed the hands of previous detachments cast their pall over this one, too. Possibly, because they *were* having to collaborate in the murder of their countrymen, to an even greater degree.

It didn't help that they were being worked to the bone in the bargain. Most had neither the time nor the energy even to ponder revolt, much less embark on one. So torrential was the flow of deportees from the unloading ramp becoming, that though all but a few were consigned directly to the chimneys, enough were surviving this first selection to strain the ability of the SS to house them all. Hence the rush to build Mexico out.

It was more than mere exhaustion, however, that was holding the 12th back. Such numbers, such a slaughter perpetrated so brutish an assault on the psyche as to numb not only the senses but the mind, leading one to obey without thinking, to react passively to the lunacy instead of acting against it. A month ago they'd been boys, young husbands, fathers some of them, shut up in transit camps and temporary ghettos to be sure, but still in the bosom of friends and family, their surroundings both reasonably unthreatening and familiar. Now those families were gone forever and they themselves living a nightmare, their waking hours so overflowing with corpses it must have seemed half the world was dying.

Nor could Kaminski in all fairness find it in his heart to hold their uncooperativeness against them. He tried to put himself in their place, to remember his own first days in the commando of the living dead. The honeycomb of mass graves in the meadow behind the old gas bunkers, back in the summer of '42.... the work he'd done there still fueled memories only forgotten in the obliterating arms of sleep. He, too, had once felt as if he was drowning in a sea of dead bodies. He, too, had shut his mind down and let his instincts take over. What was more, he recalled being willing to do whatever it took to stay alive, to do even more than the Germans required of him for another day of existence, one lousy day. How could he fault then these men and boys, as dazed and terrified as he'd been, for feeling the same way? For shrugging their shoulders when he got on his soapbox and began preaching revolt?

He and others in the Battle Group had won some individuals over, Major Borodin and the Russian POWs being notable examples. The bulk of the Hungarians, though, were proving obstinate, which left the conspirators well shy of the quorum they felt necessary for a breakout. The more men they had, the better their prospects of not only blasting their way past the inner cordon but fighting off their pursuers later in the woods. Or at least fleeing in so many directions as to make them difficult to chase down. To Kaminski's advantage, the 12th was by far the largest squad ever; to shake but half the new Sonder out of their lassitude would have sufficed.

But even that was looking less attainable by the day, leaving him with a decision to make. The only recourse he saw remaining to him, painful though it be, was to forget about escape, and as they should have done a year ago, have his men bring the walls of the crematoria down around them. Blow the accursed things up in an act of Sonder suicide. Besides himself, only nine men at minimum would be needed for the job, and should he come up with no more takers than that, he knew just which nine to ask. The problem was the other nine hundred and fifty of his brother Sonder, who if they didn't die in the blasts would fall victim every one to SS revenge. That there was no comparing the loss of these lives with the thousands upon thousands that might be saved hadn't spared Kaminski some long, fitful nights grappling with the problem.

As extraordinary good fortune, and antithetically, the Nazi compulsion to kill would have it, he needn't have agitated over it. Something happened that changed everything, something sudden, jaw-dropping, as powerful and unforeseen as a bolt of lightning. One could have pushed him over backward with a finger when he heard about it.

It was the last hour of the last day of May, nearly as hot and humid a night as it had been a day. A breeze had blown from the south for most of that day, but instead of providing some relief was no more than heat in motion. The sun was already acting the bully, cruelly indifferent even at this early date to the comfort of those below. A pitiless sun, a scorching wind, the sweat snaking down one's spine and it not yet nine in the morning—if this was May, one had to wonder what kind of summer lay ahead.

Kaminski stood in the open doorway of Block 13 taking in the night, a wedge of moon overhead. The barracks at his back was black save for a smattering of candles. Around these, men had gathered to talk in low voices, the only other sounds from inside the odd cough, the buzz of snoring. But for the chirping of insects, the distant barking of a dog, it was quiet outside, too. Victorious sleep held the field, having felled all but a stubborn few.

That he was still standing wasn't by choice. Tired as he was—three transports today, and the day before—his eyes wouldn't stay closed. Every time he lay down, he would pop right back up. Something was keeping him awake, but what?

He was just turning to go back inside and give it another try when to his surprise he heard the gate open, the crunch of shoes on gravel. A figure approached, its stride full of purpose.

Another dozen steps, and his face brightened. "Noah!" he cried. "Noah Zabludowicz! *You* here at *this* hour…. what brings you, my friend?"

"Kapo? Is that you?" Then a curse, as Noah tripped and almost fell. "What luck! I can't believe it. I was afraid I was going to have to wake up most of the block looking for you."

The two men embraced. Even in the dark, he could tell that Noah wasn't Noah. A silly grin plastered his face; he looked giddy, as if he'd been drinking. "So what's the occasion?" Kaminski said. "I don't recollect, sir, having the pleasure, not at this time of night."

"No, you haven't, but then I've never had the pleasure of an assignment such as tonight's. I bring a message, from Auschwitz. From the Steering Committee. Bruno Baum."

He waited, but Noah just stood there, grinning. Kaminski looked at him as he might a crazy person. "Well, you going to tell me or what?"

"Oh yeah, the message!" Noah shook his head as if to clear it, raised himself to attention. What followed, in its stiffness, was plainly rehearsed. "It is my honor to instruct you to prepare your men for battle. The underground has decided an uprising advisable, with you, the Sonder, to lead the attack as planned."

Now it was the other's turn to fumble. "The—the revolt?" was all he could get out.

"The revolt," Noah affirmed. "That's what has me all stupid; I just found out myself, from Commander Baum. He wanted you to know personally and as soon as possible, so here I am."

Kaminski had been about to ask him how in the world he was able to travel between the two camps at night, but the thought had fled him along with the power of speech. "Unfortunately, there is a downside," Noah said, filling in the silence. "It looks as if it's to be a Birkenau operation only. The

as ours to giving a single Jew up to liberation. The first stirrings of the Red Army this spring, limited as they are, have already gobbled up large chunks of acreage. And though it is a good distance still from Poland, the Krauts from the look of it aren't taking any chances of either a Wehrmacht collapse or Soviet thrust catching them with their pants down.

"Not that it was any great trick," he'd said, "for Auschwitz to sniff out what's happening at Maidanek. The installations there, unlike those of every other Vernichtungslager, aren't located in a remote area, safe from prying eyes. One of Lublin's busiest highways passes right by the camp; anyone with a pair of binoculars can tell exactly what's going on inside. The Stammlager's reach does deserve applause, however, in what it has succeeded in unmasking elsewhere. Maidanek isn't the only river of murder spilling out of eastern Poland; entire camps are being liquidated. At Poniatowa, thousands were shot. Machine guns were put in place in each corner of Trawniki, then the barracks, which were clustered in the center, set on fire. The Lublin area has been especially hard hit: Maidanek remains, for now, but the lagers Budzyn, Dorohucza, Osawa, Krychnow are no more."

Kaminski, though properly shaken, had fallen short at first of grasping the implication. Poniatowa, Trawniki, Budzyn…. tragedies all, without question, but also all labor camps, and as such comparatively small. One could see how the Germans might be tempted to make quick work of these. Out of what had to be the dizzying profusion of camps in Poland, however, Maidanek was second in size only to Auschwitz-Birkenau. Noah, who'd been watching for it, finally saw it in his friend's eyes, in the way they'd lit up with something the mind had belatedly wakened to.

"And if at Maidanek," he'd said, "why not here? I get it now."

"Especially," said Noah, "with that werewolf Möll skulking in the wings. Just itching, after he's done with the Hungarians, to wet his muzzle with more blood."

One point had still eluded Kaminski. "Why then, after everything you've told me, is it to be a Birkenau operation only?"

"You mean with the threat of the Möll Plan, on top of Maidanek, why isn't Auschwitz attempting a breakout of its own?" It was obvious from Noah's frown that he'd struggled with this very thing. "The Committee's line is that an escape from both camps would spread the Home Army too thin, endangering the whole business. And since the number of prisoners at Birkenau is many times that of the main camp, to choose between them—well, there can be no choice. Perhaps they're right. I'm not a hundred percent sold, but what do I know? What does anybody know? This, though, I do: I'm in too good a mood to think about that now. Another time, if you please, kapo."

According to Baum, there was a third and final reason behind the underground's change of heart, though hardly had Noah brought it up than Kaminski was questioning it. Aware of the man's basic decency, he suspected him of projecting that decency onto others. He'd asserted, as Noah had it, that Battle Group-Auschwitz—which was to say, those Poles that made up its majority, and who'd been taught at their mothers' knees to hate and fear the Jews—were as repelled as everyone by this new and bottomless slaughter. Though only just begun, already it exceeded the killing frenzy of last summer. The Hungarians flooding the camp were as many as the blades of grass in the meadows, the stars in a hundred skies, with Birkenau resembling nothing less than a small city ablaze. All day and into the night, the Nazi cremation pyres roared, gushing great ramparts of smoke that blotted out the sun. From out of these and the belching chimneys rained flakes of ash the size of fifty-zloty pieces, powdering every surface with a gray, moistureless snow. Like a synergy of noxious fumes released from the bowels of the earth, the lipid stench of burning flesh and kerosene drove every other smell away.

The entire western quarter of the camp teemed at all hours with long lines of deportees fresh from the ramp, lines moving, lines stationary, lines forming, disbanding, reforming, most of them filing eventually into the gaping maws of the crematoria. The roads leading to the death houses were at times so clogged with people that cars, trucks, and even bicycles found them unnavigable. The crowds weren't so much walking as dragging themselves along these paths, weary, disoriented, wild-eyed with thirst, the shuffling of their feet raising great clouds of dust. When there was no wind and the heat hung in blankets, this dust would combine with the smoke to make the greenish air even murkier. Adding to this gloom like the song of some choir of the damned was a steady cacophony of subdued weeping, children whining for water, wails of pain and bewilderment, the growls of the SS dogs and their masters.

Out of sight in the rear of the crematoria or hidden by tall wattles, piles of naked corpses glistened in the sun, the overflow from the ovens awaiting their turn at the fire pits. The rats swarming them often had time to strip the smaller children to the bone. If there was a hell, this was what it looked, smelled, sounded like, a spectacle that might well have moved the Auschwitz Poles to compassion. Or if not that, then shock at the enormity of what they were seeing, and with it an urgency to put the death houses behind it out of action.

That, Noah had said, was what Baum contended anyway. Kaminski had his doubts, but then neither did he much care. Whatever had sparked its reversal of opinion—the Hungarians, Maidanek, Otto Möll, the reading of tea leaves—all that mattered was that the underground had seen the light at last.

The next morning, he was up well before the others. He wanted to catch Shlomo Kirschenbaum as soon as he walked in from the night shift. And both Zalmans, the boy Wrubel, Major Borodin in Block 10. And the sooner Leyb Langfus in the Reinkommando attic knew, the better. There was much to do all of a sudden, and not a lot of time to do it in. As the next couple of days would bear out, however, he and his lieutenants weren't forced to spend a lot of it convincing even the newer Sonder that the situation had changed, that overnight they'd been handed a realistic chance of escaping the bad dream their lives had become. With the Home Army and its guns, and the general population its numbers, the odds of surviving a breakout had grown exponentially.

Emboldened by this, virtually the whole commando cast in. Everyone was assigned a role in the hostilities to come, some specific, most generalized, but all vital to the plan; it was essential each man know where he was supposed to be and at what time. The plan itself would need honing and rehoning, tighter synchronizing, memorizing. What weapons and ammunition there were had to be distributed, and those they hoped to get later from their dead guards earmarked for the men who knew how to use them. Supplies, prior to packing them, had to be stockpiled and carefully, so as not to arouse suspicion. Each rebel would be responsible for acquiring and outfitting a personal pack as well.

For the next two weeks, the respective Battle Groups maintained a continuous communication. Noah Zabludowicz appeared to be spending as much time at Block 13 as his own barracks, ferrying messages, being briefed and debriefed, arranging for all manner of covert goings-on. Within a week, the Sonder had received four pistols and a submachine gun from the Stammlager, along with ammunition. Kaminski drooled over this amazing windfall for half a day before turning all but two pistols over to Borodin and his gun-savvy POWs.

It wasn't only Noah, though, that was running back and forth between Auschwitz and Birkenau. Porebski the electrician and Silver the locksmith—a spindly stick of a kid who didn't make much of an impression on Kaminski until finding out he was the Robota girl's boyfriend—had also become fixtures at Block 13, which though remaining the nerve center of Battle Group-Sonderkommando, was but one of three barracks now housing the oversized 12th Squad.

Other faces, too, began appearing at the compound, none of whom Kaminski could recall seeing before. Most of these showed only once never to return, but there was one Kaminski wouldn't be forgetting anytime soon. Nor was it because the man behind it had been in charge of the detail posing as a maintenance crew that had delivered him the submachine gun. Mordecai Hilleli was the Schreiber of the main camp's Block 16, the Ciechanow hut. He knew both Noah and Roza well, having partnered with them in the midnight raids the Shomeir had conducted outside that town's ghetto. The same age as Noah, he'd joined the camp Resistance the same time as well, and had risen high enough in his superiors' estimation to be entrusted with the job of smuggling weapons. Hilleli was one of those individuals who always seemed in good spirits, unbroken by the brutality around him. Though tall and big-boned, he had the almond eyes and waggish expression of a forest elf, and the sense of humor to match. With Hilleli, if there was a laugh to be had, he was going to find it.

After handing over the machine gun, he marched up to Kaminski. A dozen Sonder looked on. "Apparently, you know the freedom fighter Roza Robota," he said.

"We met, yes," Kaminski nodded, "an encounter I won't soon forget."

"Before setting out on this mission, I arranged to meet her myself at the clothes-sorting warehouse where she works. We had to pass by there anyway on our way here. She asked me to give you a message. Do you have a moment, kapo?"

"For her," Kaminski said, intrigued, "I have two."

"She wanted me to wish you and the commando good luck in battle, and that your every bullet find an SS man. More important, she said, is that your dynamite take care of its intended targets; all of us will be listening for the sweet sound of the explosions. She ended by saying she hoped to run across you later in the woods, where the two of you could proceed to kill Nazis together."

"That's my girl," Kaminski said. "Anything else?"

"As a matter of fact, there is." Hilleli moved a step closer. "She wanted me to give you this." With both hands, he took hold of the other's startled face and planted a kiss on his left cheek. The Sonder watching guffawed their approval, while their kapo blushed a color that would have done Beetface Gorges credit. With a crisp salute and as smartly military an about-face, Hilleli led his men out of the compound.

Yes, he would remember this young Schreiber from Block 16. When he learned later from Noah just what a cut-up the fellow was, he pretty much knew from whom that last bit of encouragement had come. There was no mistaking, however, the author of the first part of the message, nor what she'd meant by the dynamite finding its targets. Roza was reminding him and his men of their obligation to blow the crematoria back to the hell from which they'd come.

Not that their memories needed jogging. The rigging of the death factories for destruction played as important a part in the Sonders' makeready as any. A good amount of the dynamite was taped together into packs of four sticks each, and these secreted under each crematorium's floorboards. Two fifty-five-gallon drums of gasoline per building were kept to fuel the generators that fired the coke and the ventilators that kept it burning. Under the pretext of requiring more to handle the Hungarians, Kaminski was able to have this quantity doubled. A bundle of explosives detonated anywhere near those barrels should result in a fireball sufficient to blow the roof off the place. The demolition teams were to comprise Borodin and his Russians. He'd be sure to have one of these working Bunker 5 that day, a box of the dynamite having already been buried nearby. The kapo wasn't going to leave the SS so much as a broom closet if he could help it.

Though as the shock troops of the revolt, they bore the brunt of gearing up for it and had the transports to deal with besides, the Sonder weren't the only ones to have their hands full. Battle Group-Auschwitz had preparations to make, too, principal of these the mustering and deployment of the partisans. Their chief Cyrankiewicz had to have them in place, undetected, by June 15th, the date chosen for the breakout. The partisans weren't by any measure a unified body, but rather a rubric for a collection of disparate fighting units operating under different leaders. They may have called it the Home Army, but a true army it wasn't. A communications network that left a lot to be desired exacerbated the difficulty of aligning these independent outfits into a cohesive force. With radio transmissions considered too risky and reserved for emergency use only, the principal means Cyrankiewicz had of giving orders and receiving information was by courier. The Resistance had an abundance of agents among those civilians employed inside the camp; it was they who relayed his directives to Krakow and his field generals. And in turn carried all pertinent information back to Auschwitz.

It was neither the fastest nor safest of systems, and as a result called for much caution. To coordinate and then launch the assault, though, was as nothing to the problems facing Auschwitz immediately after the fact, namely what to do with the thousands that will have liberated themselves. As dilatory as it may have appeared to the more radical of the Sonder, the logic behind the underground's former insistence on postponing the rebellion until Soviet troops were in the area wasn't lost on Kaminski. Behind Russian lines lay both freedom and food, behind enemy lines a blood-filled shambles in the making. Among other questions, he wanted to know what steps the Resistance was taking to prevent this shambles. And what the Sonder could do to help.

This had been a thorn in the paw of the Steering Committee since it proposed revolt a year ago. As up in the air as its ability to distance the escapees from the Germans who'd be chasing them was the matter of how and where to hide them afterward. The strategy chosen was to divide this mob at the outset, driving it hard and fast and in smaller groupings for the marshlands straddling the Sola River. Whether this was feasible remained to be seen, but it was the best the Committee could come up with.

As for provisioning such a throng, that, as the sardonic joke making the rounds went, wasn't going to be any picnic, either. The Home Army could manage some food, but it looked to be starvation rations at best until the Russians did arrive. Noah had been instructed to inform Kaminski that any supplies the Sonder might succeed in piling into carts and taking with them would be of benefit.

And so their days passed in a fever of death but also hope, days spent hauling heaps of lifeless flesh from one spot to another, eating meals that tasted of corpses, drinking themselves numb—but in the midst of it all getting ready, actually packing for an adventure so larger-than and affirmative of life as to make the pulse gallop in anticipation of it. The dichotomy was pronounced enough to make a surreal two weeks seem even stranger, so that between it and the lack of sleep and the affright of their work, by the evening of the 14th, Sonder nerves were pulled taut.

Kaminski felt he ought to say something on the eve of their great escape, something over and above a last minute finalizing of details. He called a meeting for midnight, by which hour a representative number of those he wished in attendance should be done with work. (The Germans, as if to accommodate him, had decided to cut the second shift short this night only, for general maintenance and cleaning). Leyb Langfus, living with the Reinkommando in Crematorium III wouldn't be able to make it, of course, nor whomever the SS kept late to clean up. That was unfortunate, but couldn't be helped. He could have scheduled the meeting for later, but the Sonder were going to need all the rest they could get this last night.

Come midnight, six of them sat at one end of the long dining table that ran a quarter of the length of Block 13. Dirty dishes cluttered its top, glasses full to varying levels with a red Hungarian wine. A single oil lamp burned in the center of them, casting a subdued yellow light. Most of the rest of the barracks were asleep. From the rows of bunks receding into the darkness came the deathbed sounds of people snoring, as if gasping their last. Farther down the table, out of the light's range, a few of those still awake had gathered to listen in, gray and faceless in the shadows.

Sitting at the head of it, Kaminski leaned toward Yankel Handelsman on his right. "I was hoping Leventhal could be here," he said, "and that Russian major. And Leventhal's pal, Gradowski. Each fills such big shoes tomorrow, and has to be up on not only his role but those of the men under him. You're as familiar with the battle plan as anyone, professor, and there's so much I've still to do. Perhaps you could take those last two aside in the morning and make sure they know their stuff. I'll catch Leventhal myself at work."

Handelsman nodded. "I can take more than two off your hands if you want."

"That'd probably be a good idea," Kaminski said. "You're in Number Four these days, right? Check on the Greeks Baruch and Errera then, too. And let's not forget Kirschenbaum. If all goes as it should tomorrow, Shlomo will be wearing a *Scharführer's* uniform, in charge of those masquerading as SS."

"Anyone else?"

"No, that should do it. I can handle the rest, starting with Langfus at Number Three first thing in the morning. Which, unless I get on with this meeting, might find us still sitting here."

He rose from his chair and cleared his throat. Conversation stopped as all eyes turned to him. "I called you here tonight," he began, his hoarse rasp of a voice low, "for a couple of reasons. First, it's important that everyone is crystal-clear on what will be expected of him a few hours from now. It's you, after all, who'll be leading the assault, and nothing is more crucial to its success than the order in which it was designed to unfold. Is there anyone the least unsure of that order?"

The weary six eyed each other expectantly, but none spoke.

Kaminski himself looked as if he could have fallen asleep standing up. "I realize you've all about had it for the day, and God knows the sun will be up soon enough. But this won't take long, I promise. Think of it as humoring an old man, who would feel a lot better if we went over the plan of attack one more time."

Kaminski had indeed aged much the last year. Handelsman and his friend Warszawski, who was also present, were almost as old as he, but looked twenty years younger. The stubble covering his scalp and cheeks had gone from grizzled to a uniform white, and the lines in his face had deepened in tandem with the slouch of his shoulders. His eyes, though, were what sealed it, eyes that hadn't necessarily seen more than others, but had perhaps lost more in the process, more of that glow which distinguished those enamored of life from those who'd grown tired of it.

Some of his lieutenants shifted uncomfortably in their chairs, but eager as they were for bed, Handelsman spoke for them all. "You have but to wish it, general, for us to obey."

The rebels' plan, though basically the same as first put forth—still scheduled, for instance, to begin at 5:30 that evening with the ambush of their guards—had been revamped some. This was necessitated more than anything by the squad's size, it having grown so large it occupied three huts now, the original Block 13 as well as Blocks 10 and 11. Two of the wooden clothes carts waited behind each. Upon returning from work, the day-shift Sonder were to load these with the supplies they'd accumulated, break out their stash of weapons, overcome the sentries at the gate, then twenty of them, armed, hurry to the main Appellplatz, where the evening roll call would have started. The freeing of the prisoners there would be the first battle, and the signal for the night-shift Sonder to blow the crematoria. This in turn would alert the partisans waiting in the woods and the men working Bunker 5 to take the respective steps assigned them.

The twenty at that point would return with their liberated prisoners to D Camp, pick up the carts and the majority of their fellow Sonder, and the whole mass make on the double for Crematoria II and III. The hundred left behind, with most of the guns and grenades, were to split up, half proceeding to the *B1* camps, eliminating their sentries, and freeing any inmates they found there, the others seeing to the same at the *B2* and Mexico lagers. All would then head with their charges for Crematoria IV and V. Once the inner cordon was breached and people began reaching the woods, it would become mainly a Home Army show. From there, after the escapees had been divvied up among their partisan custodians, it was on to the Sola and its marshes, with those rebels who were armed and half the Armia men providing a rear guard.

Kaminski queried the half-dozen on not only their assignments but the details of the battle plan as a whole. When satisfied, he leaned forward on the table, resting on his knuckles. If there were any questions, he said, now was the time to ask them.

But for the snoring in the background, all was silent. Finally, "I have one," said a slyly smiling Warszawski. "How much longer, Kapo K, until 5:30 rolls around?"

With nothing more to discuss as far as strategy was concerned, Kaminski could relax some. He looked fondly around the table; never had he felt closer to the faces staring back at him. Instead of being united in the despicable work of the crematoria, they'd become brothers in an enterprise that wouldn't only be saving lives as opposed to taking them but fill every Jewish heart, and possibly the world's one day, with pride that here were slaves who dared stand up to the slave driver, men willing to risk the little life left them for a chance, that was all, just the chance at freedom.

Men like Handelsman, their professor, whose wisdom and constancy had been both a crutch and a comfort to his kapo from the beginning. Or Handelsman's friend Warszawski, who was still grinning at his joke. But maybe he hadn't meant to be funny, not entirely anyway, for there he sat drumming his fingers on the table as if indeed impatient with the clock. That was the way he was, though, some part of him always moving, fingers drumming, foot tapping, that nervous tic he had of running a hand through his hair. One got the impression that if Warszawski ever did go completely still, like a shark that had stopped swimming that would be the end of him.

Or seated next to him, Isaac Kalniak, the same Kapo Kalniak, who by rousing him from his faint and convincing him it was work or die, had saved Leventhal's life his first day on the job at the old Bunker 2. He'd since shaved his beard, but cut as imposing a figure as ever, with the same bull-like build as Kaminski, only taller. Also like Kaminski, he had a genuine affection for his men, and grieved with the same sincerity for those no longer living. He wasn't, however, a grieving man by nature. Had a laugh, in fact, as big and brawny as he was, a laugh not even the crematoria could kill. Kalniak claimed to have been the blacksmith of a small shtetl outside of Lodz, a story born out by his peasant accent, a serious set of shoulders, and the dozens of tiny white burn scars that dotted his huge hands and forearms.

Or across the table from Kalniak, men like Josef Deresinski, a fisherman from up north, the Pomeranian coast. Not much taller than the compact Warszawski, he was as wiry and spry as a baboon; one could imagine him scaling the roof of a crematorium without a ladder. Deresinski walked like a true man of the sea, with an oddly rolling gait, as if still on the deck of his trawler. His hands were as rough and weathered as Kalniak's, but unlike him he was a quiet sort, seldom spoke at all. Then again, the way most saw it, he didn't have to say much; his words, being scant, carried more weight.

But not enough, try as he might, try as all of them had, to open Kaminski's eyes these past months to the stalling tactics of Battle Group-Auschwitz. Even now, a few hours from perhaps exonerating himself some, his blood burned with shame at not having been more aggressive. At allowing a year to go by without raising a finger against the SS. It was a mystery to him that he should have been so damnably cautious yet surrounded himself with such have-at-it officers. It was as if on an unconscious level he'd been trying to compensate for his own inertia.

Not that this was any time to be raking up the missteps of the past, though Ariel Wrubel being there wasn't helping any. When Kaminski looked at him, the teenager smiled, and despite his smiling back, he could feel the tears forming behind his eyes. The precocious Wrubel may have been pushing six-feet in height, with a man's build to match, but it was difficult not to see him as still a kid. His face had yet to lose the artlessness, that child's intrinsic sweetness capable of softening all but the hardest of hearts. The patchy beard he was struggling to grow only underscored his boyishness, a quality, that like Kalniak's robust laugh, not even the crematoria had succeeded in burning out of him. How many such Sonder, Kaminski brooded, men little more than children—men who'd looked up to him and trusted him as they might a father—had he condemned to certain and inglorious death simply because he'd let himself be duped by the underground?

Again, though, this was neither the time nor place for regrets. It was enough that he'd betrayed not only others but himself without crying about it like some little girl. There was no resurrecting the dead. What was done was done. It wasn't a night to look backward but ahead, to set the tone for an escapade as overdue as it was heroic.

He stepped away from the table, and folding his arms across his chest, looked at the floor as if collecting his thoughts. But he wasn't so much attempting to collect as recollect another meeting not that long ago where a pretty, young woman with flashing black eyes had enthralled him with not only her hunger for justice but her rhetoric. Now would be the perfect moment to summon some of that rhetoric, some of the fire that had given her words muscle.

"As I said, lads," he began, raising his voice to include those in the back now, "I called this meeting for two reasons. To answer your question, Yossel, in seventeen hours exactly the clock will have struck 5:30. The day we've been waiting for, living for, is upon us. Having shown, and most impressively I might add, that you know *what* to do on this day of days, perhaps it's right we recall why we're doing it. The easy answer, the one that jumps out, is to try and save our skins. I think it safe to say there isn't a man at this table who doesn't understand that to sit back and do nothing, to trust in God or luck or SS carelessness to spare him, is to be no less than an accomplice in his own execution.

"Some of us, of course, are going to die anyway. Such are the fortunes of war. But there are some who'll be leaving the mud, stench, and murder of Birkenau behind them forever, who will have fought their way out of here, and as the sounds of the German guns grow fainter, are going to stop, look around, and scarcely daring to believe it, realize they might be halfway to freedom.

"Call these the lucky if you want, the confounders of all odds, but they won't be the only ones to triumph today. Every man, live or die, who would brave the coming battle, defy the SS, will come out of it victorious, if not in body then spirit. For no longer the slave, the animal the Nazis would make of him, he will have become a man again, reclaimed that humanity stripped from him. To save our skins? Yes, that's something worth fighting for. But as someone told me once—a slip of a girl no less, but twice the soldier I'll ever be—though Sonder flesh and bone might not survive a revolt, such a feat would go far toward us saving our souls."

Kaminski paused, his gaze sweeping their end of the table. It stopped on a man sitting next to Deresinski. He'd undressed to his undershirt, revealing a trim, hairless body. His features were striking: a prominent nose as sharp and curving as an eagle's beak, high, aristocratic cheekbones, dark, piercing eyes. Though a member of the Sonder for little more than a month, the Hungarian Bela Lazar had worked his way into Kaminski's inner circle. A ready smile and humble manner allowed him to make friends easily, though that wasn't what had led to his acceptance. After the German invasion of his country, he'd refused to submit to the SS edict requiring all Jews to display the yellow star on their clothing, and fled into the woods outside his village. Quickly captured by the Gestapo, he was on one of the first transports to Poland. A member of Squad 59B, the day shift, Lazar alternated between Crematorium IV and the fire pits behind Number Five. He thanked his stars every day that in the performance of these duties, he had yet to come across anyone he knew. This fear of running into familiar faces had made him a tiger for revolt. From his first day in the detachment, he'd been all about turning the tables on the Nazis, and with a fervor that had quickly attracted his kapo's attention.

When the latter's eyes met his and didn't leave right away, Lazar had a hunch what he was going to say next. "For when it comes down to it," Kaminski continued, "it's not about us at all, is it? There's more at stake here than simply saving ourselves, or for that matter the thousands we'll be busting out with us. More important, much more, are the hundreds of thousands to come, and not just the Hungarians, but those doomed to follow them. Who knows how long it'll be before the Russians get here, and you can bet the Krauts won't be pulling up stakes and moving on until they're forced to.

"First, though, the Hungarians. The killing has got to end now. We all knew it was going to be terrible, but this? Hell, the cremos are running eighteen hours a day as it is, twenty! And the transports have only started to roll in. Our friend Noah Zabludowicz tells me there are close to a million Jews in Hungary. Are we supposed to do nothing while a million people go up in smoke, keep shoving them into the fire until it's our turn to bake?"

As he spoke, he'd moved from the head of the table to where Lazar sat, and now stood behind his chair, gripping the back of it. "If it's all right with him," he said, "I'd like to ask Bela here a question. Have you ever wondered, young man, why the word Jericho was chosen as the code name for the revolt?"

Lazar had, in fact, but not enough to inquire about it. Though as familiar with the legend as anybody, he'd never been much of a one for religion, and had relegated it with most other Biblical tales to the realm of the fanciful. "Why Jericho? I no able to tell you, please, sir," he said in the broken Polish he'd learned since he got here, "but that you.... wait for this night for ask me, I think maybe is not.... not accident."

"So it isn't," Kaminski said. Nor was it solely for Lazar's sake that he felt it worthwhile now to chat the story up again. It was for everyone who was listening, whether he'd heard it before or not. "When the first of the crematoria came into being over a year ago, we of what was then the 9th Sonderkommando saw that to leave them standing would amount to a crime almost as great as that of those who'd built them. We likened the obligation to destroy them to that felt by our forebears to take and destroy the Canaanite city of Jericho. Just as the trumpets of Joshua's Israelite army had tumbled those pagan walls, so would we with our dynamite the walls of the death factories.

"As fate and our own shortcomings would have it, however, we failed in the task, with the result that those factories were permitted to succeed at theirs. The heart and soul of our race, the largest concentration of us anywhere—the millions of Jews who over the centuries had set down roots in Europe and Russia—appeared if not already done for, then well on the way to it. The transports slowed almost to a stop for lack of people to fill them."

He raised his face to the ceiling and held it there. When finally he lowered it, his voice had sunk with it. "I blame myself for that failure. Somehow, somewhere along the path of firm purpose, I made a wrong turn, lost my bearings, then compounded the error by refusing to listen to those of my men, to you at this very table, who would steer me right again.

"But now," he said, louder, "I've been given a second chance, the opportunity to redeem my undeserving self. Nor is this, as it was with the Czechs of the Family Camp, a false alarm. This time there's no stopping the wheel of history from turning. The trumpets of this latest Jericho will sound after all, the walls of our enemies dissolve into dust. It mustn't be for ourselves only, therefore, that we do this great thing, but also for the crowds once again spilling from the cattle cars. And lest we forget, the devil take us if we forget, to avenge our friends and families who've perished within those walls."

Without turning around, Lazar reached over his shoulder, and in what was either affirmation, affection, gratitude, or all three, took Kaminski's hand in his and briefly squeezed it. He started to say something, but Handelsman beat him to it. "Well spoken, commander. Thanks for your eloquence, for the power of your words…. words all of us would do well to pass on to our men."

But Kaminski wasn't finished. There was something else, something he could envision Roza Robota closing with. "That isn't the whole of it, however. It's not just for the present that we fight, but the future—not only for ourselves, the Hungarians, the dead, but for the living of the decades, maybe the centuries to come. For as long as the human story is soiled by the memory of Birkenau, so too will it soar with the tale of the 12th Sonderkommando. We rise up today to carve our names in stone, so that men for all time will remember and learn from what we did."

Stove in as he was, Kaminski had trouble sleeping that night. His head spinning with a hundred details, with all that needed to be done still, he would doze off for a while then awake with a start, peer at the window behind him to see if it was turning gray yet. The barracks was silent but for the snoring. It mystified him, with all that lay ahead of them, how his men could have surrendered so readily to sleep. But maybe they hadn't. Maybe some, a good number of them even, were like him, lying in their bunks eyes open, thoughts racing.

Whatever state they occupied now, there could be no maybe about this: it was going to be a long day until 5:30 rolled around. He could picture the Sonder later, those with wristwatches, checking them over and over, thumping them, shaking them, putting them to their ears, refusing to believe only five minutes had passed since they'd last looked at them. Everyone this day would be keeping an eagle eye on the time and little else. Three transports or ten, SS or no, not a lot of work was going to get done. How he was supposed to hide this from the Germans he had no idea, but he'd think of something. He always did.

Summer

Birkenau simmered in the July sun like some hideous brew, a witch's potion of blood, sweat, smoke, and excrement worthy of something the weird sisters might have cooked up in *Macbeth*. No one could remember a summer as brutish as this one. It hadn't rained since May, and with no respite from the heat, it accumulated, grew denser, more concentrated each day, like sediment collecting at the bottom of a pond. People perspired the clock round, midnight, dawn, it didn't matter. The barracks were as suffocating as the airless cells of a dungeon. When the wind did blow, it was a burning, desert wind, or like the acetylene gusts generated by a forest fire.

It was also the longest summer anyone could remember, or so it seemed to the men of the Sonderkommando. The veterans among them couldn't recall working this hard, not even the summer before, when three transports a day hadn't been unusual. Now it was four, sometimes five, though this last was pushing it; twenty-four hours simply weren't enough to dispose of that many people. As for the toll taken on the machinery, all eight of Crematorium IV's ovens had ceased to function, nor would they again, the two furnaces that housed them having cracked literally in half. Number Five's were somehow hanging in there, but sorely needed overhauling, as did not only its chimneys but those of Numbers Two and Three. Most Sonder were of the opinion that if the current pace was maintained, the entire crematory system, that part of it indoors anyway, would end up claiming itself as its last victim.

After the last bone-bruising, mind-numbing, who knew how many weeks, Zalman Gradowski had never been so tired in his life. Yet here he was after his shift on this stifling July midnight sitting on the edge of his

317

mattress, unable to sleep. Not that he was the only one awake at this hour. Dotting the labyrinth of tiered bunks half-filling the attic of Crematorium II, a few candles flickered in the dark. Apart from the negligible little halos of light produced by these, four large shafts of pale moonbeam slanted through the windows set in the slope of the roof, windows that weren't built to be opened, that were for show only, part of the flummery intended to make the death house look ordinary.

It was hot in the attic, and the drone of the electric fans situated about the room were no match for the din of the ovens below. It was neither the heat nor the noise, though, keeping Gradowski awake. July it may have been, but he wasn't the only Sonder who had yet to recover from the calamity of June 15th. There wasn't a man in the squad not trying his utmost to refrain from talking or even thinking about that day, for whenever one did, it only ended up breaking the heart all over again.

Gradowski had made the mistake of doing just that, hadn't been able to rid his mind of it from the moment he'd drug himself out of bed this morning. Today, after all, was July the 15th, one month precisely after the disaster. From sun-up to sundown, he'd wrangled with this congruity, struggling to fend off memory each time it strayed in that direction. But he was fighting a losing battle; with every load of corpses he fed into the ovens, the failure of June was driven home. Now here it was midnight and still he was reliving it, sleep as remote a prospect as a cool breeze.

The euphoria with which that Friday had begun only made the recollection of it the more bitter. After months of waiting and doing nothing but talking about revolt, the time for action was finally, unbelievably at hand. As the green ball of the sun behind its screen of smoke had climbed its molasses-slow way to its zenith, so too had both the angst and anticipation of the Sonder. All signals remained go from their contacts in the Stammlager; the moment of either freedom or death was upon them. Gradowski could feel the electricity in the air, like that preceding a thunderstorm. There was no keeping the rebels now from their appointment with destiny.

At three o'clock in the afternoon, however, a three-man maintenance crew, wheelbarrow loaded with tools, appeared at the gate of Crematorium III. They were in reality agents of Battle Group-Auschwitz, sent to find and deliver this message to Kaminski: the revolt had been called off.

Orders were to stand down. No reason was given, other than to proceed now would make a grave situation worse. Stunned, the Sonder haggled over what to do. The issue was decided for them when not half an hour later, trucks squealed to a stop in front of each crematorium and heavily armed SS poured into the compounds. Operation Jericho was done for. The dream had come to naught. The Germans had been tipped off, how and by whom was a mystery.

But not for long. Gradowski learned the whole awful story from Kaminski. On the 17th, Noah Zabludowicz had showed up at Block 13 looking for him. "How are your men taking it?" was the first thing out of his mouth.

"How do you think?" Kaminski answered. "Look at me, at this face…. that's how they're taking it."

The kapo's expression did indeed say it all. Never had Noah seen it so empty, so drained of emotion, not even after the incident of the Czech Family Camp. The eyes were two stagnant pools, the voice just as dead. There wasn't enough life in it for it to register disappointment even.

"So, not that it matters now, but what happened, Noah? Tell me, what went wrong? I have to assume that's why you're here."

"What went wrong?" Noah repeated, his own face still fallen. "What didn't? You're familiar with Battle Group-Auschwitz's preferred method of communication, with its forces in the field, I mean."

"By courier as I recall, right? You told me once that they thought radio too dangerous."

"Well, that very Friday, that afternoon, in fact, a courier from the Home Army command in Krakow was stopped on his way to Auschwitz and arrested by the Gestapo. Not just any courier, either. This one was carrying papers confirming partisan readiness for the assault on Birkenau, including their estimated troop strength, firepower, and escape routes, and the newest provisions made to deal with the thousands of runaways expected. The date of the uprising was listed as well, and requesting it be corroborated, the exact time even."

"Good God," Kaminski muttered.

"As quick as the SS could get their catch there, he was hauled to Gestapo headquarters in the Stammlager and rushed into interrogation. Not only were the Nazis ecstatic at what they'd muddled onto, they realized their good fortune needn't end there. If they could come up with the names of those in Krakow who'd sent the information, and those in Auschwitz it was sent to, they stood a good chance of decapitating both the Home Army outside the camp and the Resistance within.

"But somehow the courier withstood their tortures, at least until we were able to smuggle some poison into his cell. The man died a hero, but though it could have ended up a lot worse, that doesn't make the revolt any less dead than he."

"So where does that leave us?" Kaminski asked dully, as if he didn't know already.

"Back where we started, I'm afraid. No, further back."

"How do you figure further?"

"The Germans know they've dodged a bullet, but do you honestly think that's going to be enough for them? That they'll simply congratulate themselves on their luck and leave it at that? Brace yourself, my friend, changes are coming. How severe these will be remains to be seen, but on this you can count: just because they've been fortunate in preventing a mutiny this time doesn't mean the SS have any intention of letting that be the end of it. Not until they've done everything in their power to head off another in the future."

And so, as Gradowski was shortly to see, did Noah's words become prophecy. A week after stumbling onto the plot, the Nazis uprooted the Sonderkommando from its quarters in Blocks 10, 11, and 13 and moved it in its entirety into the crematoria. Half of the men were billeted in Number Four on removable cots, the rest in the attics of Two and Three. The idea was to cut them off utterly from the general population. There was to be no recurrence of the underground assisting them in escape should either group be tempted to have another go at it.

To further discourage this, the death-house guard was increased fourfold for both the day and night shifts, and the inner cordon to the west similarly reinforced. Each watchtower of the outer cordon was fortified as well with soldiers on the ground. Block 13 and the rest of the squad's erstwhile barracks were searched, along with the crematoria, but nothing incriminating found. Their weapons lay safely hidden inside walls and under floors.

As the officer responsible for the squad, *Hauptscharführer* Möll played a major role in tightening things up. Having suspected for a while that its members were up to something, after the 15ᵗʰ he was to keep them under a microscope. It was his decision to move them into the crematoria, though if he could have, and he did give it some thought, he'd have extinguished the whole commando and started over. The Sonder themselves had feared this very thing, but as the days passed and nothing came of it, realized that for the SS to do so in the middle of their campaign against the Hungarians wouldn't only run the risk of dooming that campaign but precipitate a hygienic catastrophe, submerging the camp in an ocean of dead bodies.

Möll was well aware that the men of the Special Squad weren't the only ones who bore watching. He had his one eye as well on those whose province it was to guard them; from what he'd seen, some of the SS acted more like business partners of the Sonder than their overseers. Once he'd entombed the 12ᵗʰ in its new lodgings, he had every sentry manning the gates of them replaced. He also let it be known he would personally shoot any soldier he caught abetting the detachment in its illicit comings and goings. *No one* was to be allowed in or out of the Krema yards without a pass. The guards' days of looking the other way in exchange for bribes were over.

The most radical change the SS undertook, however, had nothing to do with the Sonder. With the courier having exposed the underground as in on the plot, and cognizant its core consisted mainly of Poles, the Germans took this opportunity to try and eliminate this bastion of opposition once and for all. They began rounding up the Polish inmates of both camps by the thousands and hustling them off in cattle cars to various lagers inside Germany. They hoped by catching enough meaningful fish in their net to leave those remaining behind both directionless and disorganized. Nor were these abductions confined to just the Poles. The Nazis targeted prisoners of every nationality, particularly those classified as political. Thus were Bruno Baum and a host of others carted away, depriving the Resistance of some of its ablest officers. (Baum went on to survive the war and live in what became East Germany. He resumed a career in communist politics, wrote several books, including a memoir of his days at Auschwitz, and in 1971 died in his bed surrounded by family and friends). The upshot of all this was a Battle Group-Auschwitz left in tatters, not only its chain of command but countless cells fragmented, the labor of years erased overnight.

The underground wouldn't be the same again, and Maidanek notwithstanding, abandoned forever the notion of revolt. It did, however, seek to make the Möll Plan public, forwarding the details of it via Krakow to the BBC in London. Attached, courtesy of its clerical operatives in the *Kommandantur*, the executive and communications center of the Auschwitz administration, were the names and SS I.D. numbers of the worst killers, which the BBC dutifully broadcast in German with the warning that any Nazis suspected of crimes against humanity would be held accountable for them after the war. What impact this might end up having was debatable, but for now was nonexistent. Well after the Allies' threat should have given the Germans pause, the Hungarians continued to burn like so many dead leaves, the smoke over Birkenau to enshroud the sun.

As for those restrictions laid on the Sonder, it didn't take them long to get around at least a few. Where before their segregation they'd had no need of the usual camp rations, now food carriers left the crematoria twice a day for the kitchen, and on top of smuggling back goods from the black market also brought news and other information. Then there were the men of the *Aschekommando*, or ash-processing squad, whose job it was to rid the fire pits of their residue. After the whitish-gray surface covering what was left of the blaze had been hosed down with water, and the clouds of steam this produced had dissipated, the prisoners of the ash team lowered themselves into the pit. Perched atop thick squares of wood sheathed in metal, they proceeded to shovel out the still-shimmering coals. Though protected by gloves, insulated boots, and goggles, severe burns to the arms and head were common, the windier the day the more casualties. Möll had no choice but to remit the graver of these to the hospital barracks, sometimes for several days. There a Dr. Pach, a Belgian Jew and member of the underground, allowed them as many visitors as wished to see them, men like Zabludowicz, Porebski, Hilleli, Godel Silver, who in this way succeeded in re-establishing a dialogue with the crematoria. The older, soft-spoken Dr. Pach, whose pointy chin and shrewd little eyes gave him a distinctly rodent-like look, also made regular house calls—to the death houses, that is, his mission not so much medical as to relay messages and keep each Battle Group informed of the other's activities.

Which at this stage of the game didn't amount to much with either. The underground kept insisting that the abort of June 15th was merely a postponement, a delay until the partisans could be reassembled, and in light of the security changes the SS had made, a new battle plan drawn up. This, as not only Gradowski but just about everyone knew, was a load of hooey. To the Resistance, or what was left of it, armed rebellion had become as bankrupt a proposition as saving the Hungarians. Their appeal to the Special Squad for patience was no more than a ploy to try and prevent it from going off half-cocked and acting independently. Its leaders would have said anything, promised anything to keep Birkenau quiet.

They needn't have worried. There was as little probability now of the Sonder erupting in violence as there was of the Third Reich winning its war. Gradowski could see it in their eyes, the slope of their shoulders: this latest and cruelest of misadventures had bled all the fight, the rambunctiousness right out of them. The SS could have torn down the barbed wire themselves and not been at much risk of losing a single prisoner.

He felt as beat down, as exasperated as the next man. To have been so close and come up empty at the last minute was too much, the final straw in a bulging bushel-bagful of them. The general opinion, unspoken but loud and clear all the same, was that maybe it was time to back off, give things a rest for a while.

Tragically, this meant leaving the Hungarians to the wolves. Gradowski fell backward on his bunk with a sigh; the crematoria were no longer in danger and wouldn't be for some time, perhaps from now on. But there was more to his sigh than that. For as he'd learned firsthand and to his horrified amazement last week, it appeared the SS, if it came down to it, would have been able to get along just fine without them. He'd heard crazy stories about what was going on at the fire pits, but believing these no more than the irresponsible products of overheated imaginations, hadn't paid them much mind—until he had the misfortune of seeing the things in action for himself. The foulest crimes weren't necessarily occurring in the hidden rooms of the death mills. Worse, much worse, was happening out in the open, in the undeceiving light of day.

That he'd been given a glimpse of what to that point he'd refused to take seriously wasn't by any choice of his, but as the result of another's spite. Without intending to, he'd managed to get on the wrong side of his boss, Mietek Morawa. Something about him not showing the young kapo the proper respect. This was the same Morawa who'd locked horns with

Kaminski back in '43, and who those days had been notorious for walking around with a permanent and sometimes murderous chip on his shoulder. The man had mellowed some since then, if not enough to avoid mixing it up with Gradowski that particular day. Words were exchanged, and the next morning he found himself assigned to duty at the Jewish ramp. The Sonder were often called away from their regular posts, especially these last months, to assist where help was needed, though seldom were the oven men and other technicians included. Not that he was surprised to find himself an exception. Morawa might not have been the tyrant he used to be, but didn't appear to have lost any of his vindictiveness.

Traffic was typical that morning for this beehive of a July. Even with the sun but inches above the horizon, the road from the railroad tracks was clogged with people trudging their slow path to the crematoria. Headed the opposite way, he and the two dozen of his fellow conscripts and their guards were forced to negotiate the rocks and weeds on the side of the road. Upon reaching the ramp, it was to find a fifty-car transport parked at the siding, and a platform still overrun with deportees.

It wasn't to help with these, though, that they'd been commandeered. Bringing up the rear of the train were five open boxcars piled high with weathered timbers, old railroad ties, and scrap wood in a hodgepodge of shapes and sizes. A team was already hip-deep in the stuff, piling it into trucks, dripping with sweat, and soon Gradowski and his group were sweating alongside them.

It was punishing work. Most of the wood wasn't only heavy but cumbersome, and bristling with splinters. When a truck could hold no more, it would roar off in the direction of one of two massive columns of smoke, one from the fire pits adjoining Bunker 5, the other from those in the meadow nearest the same-numbered crematorium. Three Sonder clung to the outside of each truck as it left, unloaded it at its destination, and returned in the empty bed. After two hours at the boxcars, Gradowski jumped at the chance to be one of those three, if for nothing else than to catch a few minutes breather there and back.

The truck he wound up on followed a rough, bouncing road outside the barbed wire until it reached the meadow behind Crematorium V. It stopped at a large fuel depot covered with a tin roof, where their SS driver grunted them to work. Forty meters away a long trench leapt with flames, the rolling boil of its smoke obscuring the sky. He'd never been this close to a fire pit. Puffs of ash floated everywhere like huge, dirty snowflakes. So strong was the odor of burning fat and kerosene, scorched hair and seared flesh, it stung the eyes, coated the inside of the mouth with a greasy film. Corpses the bluish-white color of raw sausages littered the ground, waiting for the next fire, while those in this one spluttered and sizzled, their limbs contorting in the heat as if the dead they belonged to were trying to raise themselves. Eight Sonder worked the pit, each wielding a long steel pole, some with stoking forks at the end, some dangling buckets from which they poured what he'd learned to his disgust a while back was liquid fat over any trouble areas. Where the fat hit these dead spots, the fire would flare up and crackle noisily anew.

As he and the others toiled with their truckload of wood, Gradowski couldn't keep his eyes off the pyre, fascinated by the sheer size and power of it. Suddenly, he heard shots, pistol shots and close by, but didn't pay them much attention. Sporadic gunfire at Birkenau was nothing to get excited about. But quickly these grew from sporadic to sustained, accompanied then as well by the occasional fearful shriek. Both shrieking and shots sounded as if they were coming from another fire pit about seventy meters away, but because of the smoke that wreathed the meadow, he couldn't make out their cause.

The guard, having returned to the truck, was attempting a quick nap in the cab. After lugging one of the ties inside the depot, Gradowski darted behind a stack of lumber, hurried to the far side of the shed, found another stack piled almost to the roof, and climbed atop it. What he saw from there took some seconds to sink in, but when it did he drew back in shock, grabbing the edge of the roof to keep from falling.

A line of ten SS stood evenly spaced along one side of the distant pit, each armed with a pistol. It was an execution squad. A pair of Sonder holding a deportee tight by the arms would bustle him or her, naked and defenseless, up to one of the soldiers, who proceeded to shoot whomever was stood before him in the back of the neck. The Sonder would then drag the limp victim as close to the pit as the heat permitted and fling that person into the flames. That the murdered were new arrivals from the unloading ramp and not the camp was evidenced by the long hair of the females. That and the fact there were numerous children and aged among them.

Also evident was that most were being thrown into the fire alive. The screams coming nonstop now confirmed this, screams to raise the hackles and freeze the blood. Apparently, from the stingy pop the pistols were making, the Germans were using the same 6-mm caliber employed in similar Aktionen, and these tended not to kill right away.

Such was the abomination which had tormented Gradowski for going on a week now, and in its horror impelled him to a decision. It had been some time since he'd put pen to paper in his capacity as self-imposed chronicler of Nazi crimes. To say he'd neglected this of late would be to understate; though he already had four jarfuls of damning testimony to his credit, months had passed since he'd buried the last one. Nor had he felt any great urge to bequeath posterity another. With the addition in January of the learned Rabbi Katz from Wroclaw, one of the Reinkommando elders, their closeted little circle of diarists had swelled to six. Figuring he wouldn't be missed if he were to lie low for a while, he'd been content to pass the baton of accountability to them. Now, however, accidental witness though he was to this fiendish aspect of the fire pits, to keep silent would have made him feel complicit in it, a sin he had no desire to add to those he'd already accrued as a cremo man.

He would take up his pen again and write about what he'd seen. More than what he'd seen. For having arrived at this decision, he'd sought out those Sonder forced to assist the Nazis in this fresh obscenity of theirs, the same Sonder he'd accused earlier of exaggeration. From them he'd learned more than he had or ever could have in person, the *modus operandi* of this latest crime in its every detail, from ramp to fire pit.

Those consigned to this worst of deaths were the surplus from the former, having arrived at the latter because there was no room for them in the crematoria. Depending on how far they'd fallen behind, the Germans might divert a whole transport to the meadows. These unlucky ones followed a path into a pine forest until reaching a clearing with a wooden barracks at the far side of it. A wall of smoke blacked out the sky to their left, the air foul with a curious stink. Up to four hundred at a time were herded into the hut, made to strip naked, then hurried one by one through a back door into the grasp of a Sonder, who sped them down a trail lined on both sides by armed soldiers. So disoriented were they by thirst, the frantic pace, and fear of the unknown, they let themselves be led without resistance. At the end of the trail, each was turned over to a pair of Sonder, these grabbing their victim by the arms and rushing him to the row of SS assassins fronting one of the blazing trenches. The crack of a shot, a cry of pain and surprise, then into the flames the person went, followed by even more terrible cries. Occasionally, some of the men and older boys would break free and make a run for it, but were quickly gunned down.

Also shot on the spot were any Sonder who hesitated in their duty. Though few made them as nervous as this one, any Sonderaktion tended to put the Nazis on edge. Deviating as these did from the norm, which was to say outside the controlled environment of the crematorium, there was always the chance they wouldn't go as planned and deteriorate into untidiness, or worse. In this case, with thousands of frightened, jittery people waiting back at the clearing—wondering where those preceding them had gone, where that smoke was coming from, what that smell was—the SS couldn't see the affair to its conclusion fast enough. Woe to the Sonder who gummed up the works, who by either action or inaction disrupted the living chain extending from the undressing barracks to the pyre.

In his quest for information, Gradowski turned this up, too: of all the Nazis involved in this new kind of murder, none had a bigger hand in it than the bestial Otto Möll. Indeed, it was he, motivated by the strain the Hungarians weren't only putting on the crematoria but the Germans' dwindling stock of Zyklon-B, who'd come up with the idea of enlisting his infernal bonfires in double duty. This pleased him as much as any benefit he'd derived from them so far, combining in one neat, time-saving package both the killing and disposal processes.

Those Sonder working outdoors had plenty to say about their fearsome sergeant. Always resplendent in a spotless dress-white SS tunic, the Kriegsverdienstkreuz prominently displayed, he conducted himself with the swagger of a general at his headquarters. Not that he commanded from some rear echelon at a comfortable remove from the fray. Möll was right down there in the mud and the blood, at all hours of the day and night, bouncing between the unloading ramp and the death houses, the two ash-crushing slabs, all nine of his treasured cremation pits. A big part of his duties was to determine which of the deportees selected for extermination went where from the ramp, meaning he had to be aware at all times of each killing site's status. It also meant large groups of people waiting in limbo sometimes for hours while a gas chamber or fire pit was cleared of its dead. Much of his day was spent dashing from one of these groups to another trying to smooth their harried nerves, deflect their demands for the water they'd been promised since the ramp. As empty a promise as it was, to have disregarded such desperate people entirely would have been to invite trouble. The last thing he wanted was a riot on his hands and the panic that might spread from its suppression.

But it wasn't all work for the *Hauptscharführer*. Aside from the pride and satisfaction he took in that work, he was also quite plainly having the time of his life. Busy as he was, he always found room for the odd diversion, accomplished as always at mixing business with pleasure. When presiding at one of the meadows, for example, he kept a soldier at his side armed with a Mauser. On seeing something that displeased him, such as a deportee putting up a struggle, or a tentative or otherwise underperforming Sonder, he would call for the rifle and with a single shot solve the problem. He could drop a man at a hundred meters no problem, pick him right out of a crowd.

This was as nothing, however, to what came over him on those days his blood was up. When things weren't going right, or even when they were, Möll was known to work himself into a furor. According to those who'd seen it, he was no longer quite human then, not in the familiar sense, but a raging, profanity-spewing demon careening from one atrocity to the next. If he wasn't setting his devil dog Hannibal loose on whatever wretches he'd chosen for that bit of fun, he was stomping around with a wild look in his eyes preying on people at random, children and the elderly as a rule, the more helpless and pitiful his victim the better. He might ask an old woman if she enjoyed roses. Then smell this one, he would say, putting the muzzle of his Luger to her nostrils and pulling the trigger. Or yanking up a baby by its heels, sling it alive into the fire or one of the reservoirs of boiling fat, laughing that he'd just saved the Third Reich a bullet. After such a demonstration, he often struck a belligerent pose, legs apart, hands on hips, expression defiant, as if daring anyone present to object.

A more subdued moment might find him positioned where he could see the faces of the deportees when they first laid eyes on the fiery trench, soaking up the terror in those eyes as he welcomed them with a flourish to his "little clambake." Like some kind of leech, some psychic parasite, he seemed to feed off their fright, his own face glazing over with a voluptuary's bliss. Manic or subdued, though, even his fellow SS tried to keep their distance when he was around. Not only was there no telling what he might do—and when really off his nut to whom, not even they felt immune— there were things he did do that to no less than their hardened selves weren't always easy to watch.

Despite having no choice but to anymore, Gradowski still had trouble believing such things possible. That *any* of it was possible, even that not directly involving the demented sergeant. If he hadn't been there and seen it, he might have remained skeptical, but he'd seen it all right, and the comparison it conjured begged to be recorded. Scripture divided the Jewish hell into three realms: Abaddon, the bottomless pit; Sheol, the abode of shadows; and Gehenna, the lake of fire. There was no question which one the desecrated meadows of Birkenau resembled, nor was it because of the pyres alone. The sheer, inundating carnage of it was as evocative as the flames. Not just bodies but body parts lay everywhere. Those fire pits waiting to be emptied of their dying coals invariably sported a macabre carpet of skulls. Smaller, subsidiary pits radiated outward from the ash-crushing slabs, their purpose to burn those odd gobbets of flesh not consumed by the bigger blazes. To see feet, heads, fingers all roasting together in a pile was in its way even more unsettling than watching intact corpses burn.

Also from the vicinity of the slabs came the music of this hell on earth, the mournful, monotonous chanting of those Sonder whose job it was to pulverize and sift the endless flow of cinders from the pits. For some reason, these men were exclusively Greek, Gradowski was never able to find out why. All day they trod the hot concrete tamping their tall, heavy mortars in front of them, turning baked bones into powder, boredom into song. More dirge than song actually, these consisted of one heartrending requiem after another, refrains from the old country so glum and oppressive as to crush the spirit into its own semblance of ash.

With a long, overdone groan, as if in imitation of them, Gradowski hauled himself back into a sitting position on his bunk. Sleep looking less likely a visitor than ever, what with not only June 15th now but the excesses of the fire pits stuck in his head, he figured he might as well begin that very night to put down on paper what he'd come to know of these last. He lit his candle, and gathering his materials, spread them out on the mattress. He'd discovered long ago that there'd never been much of a need for secrecy; not once had anyone asked him what he was writing about in the dark.

It would take him a week to finish his testimony and bury it in the yard of Crematorium II. The pathological Möll inhabited a good deal of the pages, but only as an extreme example of his kind. This latest testament, like those preceding it, was intended to document the evils of the SS as an organization, not simply those of its individual members. If anything, Möll's debauches reflected as badly on the group as the man in that they demonstrated how an individual as twisted and sick as the *Hauptscharführer* could not merely find refuge but thrive in the service of it.

Little did anyone know that the murderous sergeant had arguably worse up his sleeve. If he'd waited another week and a half to bury it, Gradowski could have topped off his account with a bombshell of an ending, a turn of events as unforeseeable as it was devastating. The dog days of this hottest and bloodiest of summers would see Möll perpetrate, if not his blackest infamy, then one that would rip the heart and soul right out of the Sonder. If by some miracle he should live to be an old man, never would Gradowski forget that accursed August night. It was one of the saddest he'd ever suffered, and for a Sonder, he had to admit, that was saying something.

*   *   *

By August the Hungarian Jews were finished, or at least those the SS could get their hands on. In less than three months, half a million of them had disappeared into Birkenau's flames alone, and but for the religious leaders and more politically moderate of their countrymen, and the diplomatic pressure brought to bear by Great Britain, the United States, the Vatican and others, it would have been more. Acceding to the groundswell of condemnation from both within and without, Miklós Horthy, who'd been freed from arrest to serve as head of the puppet government in Budapest, finally stood up to the Nazis and halted the deportation of Jewish "workers" westward. Unable to finish the job they'd started without the cooperation of the government, and with the Red

Army getting closer to Budapest by the week, *Obersturmbannführer* Adolf Eichmann and his staff were recalled to Berlin.

Transports from the east would continue to arrive at Birkenau into September, but grew steadily smaller and less frequent. This didn't bode well for the men of the Sonderkommando, and they knew it. The Bunker 5 complex was shut down, its fire pits filled in, and the dismantling of its gas chamber and undressing barracks begun. With the influx of deportees once again at a manageable level, the SS could concentrate on the badly needed repair and refurbishing of the crematoria. This promised to keep the squad busy for a while, but not forever. Though none was so craven as to wish it, the only way the Sonder were going to feel at ease was if the Germans at this point, with the arrival of the Soviets but a matter of time, should set their sights on those prisoners already inmates of the camp. In other words, in order to justify so large a commando, the number of selections carried out inside the wire would have to start rivaling that made at the unloading ramp.

The liquidation of the Gypsy Camp at the beginning of the month looked to foretell this very thing, especially when coupled with that of the Czech Familienlager prior. Like that of the Theresienstadt Jews, the gypsy *B2e* lager was a family camp, four thousand men, women, and children living in isolation and virtually unmolested. They weren't required to work, wear either the prison stripes or the tattoo, nor have their heads shaved. Unlike the Czechs, they were predominately Catholic and German in origin; not a few of their guards wondered why they were there at all. In fact, they were a pet project of none other than *Reichsführer*-SS Heinrich Himmler, who'd had tens of thousands of them rounded up from all over the continent and sent to the camps, not for obliteration but observation. Long fascinated with the myths and imagery, the lore and archaeology of prehistoric Germany, Himmler suspected the mysterious gypsies of being the descendants of the early Nordic tribes of legend, the barbarian inhabitants of the primeval forests of northern Europe. As far as Nazi ideology went, this was admittedly a reach. The more orthodox of the Third Reich's racial apologists asserted just the opposite, portraying the gypsies as not much different than the Jews in that they were both non-Teutonic and parasitic, a culturally unassimilated infestation from abroad who prospered at the expense of their host populations.

As might be expected, however, Himmler's wishes prevailed; unlike the Jew, the typical gypsy internee lived in relative safety. Those who found themselves at Birkenau had been gathered from the German countryside, and were encouraged to continue their folk traditions and way of life as best they could. What support they furnished the idiosyncratic *Reichsführer's* theory was unknown, but many of the lager guards to whose care this living diorama had been entrusted were grateful for their presence in that they provided a unique break from their soldier's routine. They were often audience to the gypsies at play, the high-spirited music and dances for which this colorful people was renowned. Over the course of their confinement in *B2e*, a lot of the SS had come to be on friendly terms with this exotic parallel of their race; the gypsies weren't only an Aryan people themselves, but German citizens, spoke German, some having served in the Kaiser's army during the previous war.

But with the present war going badly and his own future to worry about, Himmler lost interest in the project. Viewing them now as more of an encumbrance than anything, as well as potential witnesses against him after the war, he ordered the *Roma* exterminated. At Birkenau, under the expert direction of *Hauptscharführer* Möll, this was completed in a matter of hours.

On the hot, muggy night of August 2nd, twenty-five hundred of the disbelieving gypsies were trucked to Crematorium III, the rest to Number Five. What they couldn't understand was why their guards, whom they saw more as protectors, would turn on them for no apparent reason. Like the just as uncomprehending Jews of the Czech Family Camp, they argued, pleaded, wept, but to no avail—an hour before midnight, the pounding on Number Three's heavy gas-chamber door and the choking sobs from behind it slowly weakened and then stopped. Thirty Sonder from Squad 58B, second shift, huddled sweating in the steamy anteroom, hoses and meat hooks at the ready, waiting for the SS doctor in charge to order the door opened.

Suddenly, the stomping of boots sounded from the corridor to their rear. All heads turned to see Sergeant Möll enter the room, a half-dozen helmeted soldiers at his heels. These, armed with machine guns, fanned out in front of the Sonder, Möll in the center. He took a step forward, hands balled into fists, staring at them with such a look of triumphant hatred that there wasn't a one whose sweat didn't turn cold. For several long seconds, he glowered silently at them. When finally he spoke, the voice didn't match the face.

"Kapo Kaminski," he all but cooed, "front and center, please, sir. If you would be so kind."

Such affected politeness was somehow more ominous than hostility. Kaminski, however, complied without hesitation. He'd been expecting this for weeks, had sensed Möll was onto him for what could only be his part in the revolt. Many was the time he'd looked up to find the man staring at him, boring a hole in him, as if to let him know he hadn't got away with anything. The only real surprise Kaminski felt, now that it had happened, was that the bastard had taken so long to call him out.

"Upstairs with him," Möll ordered, following the soldiers as they led their man onto the elevator. And to the SS doctor in charge, "Keep the gas chamber sealed until I get back."

As the elevator door slid closed, Kaminski directed a thumbs-up and a wan smile at his men. Neither inspired much confidence. They could tell this wasn't good, was worse than not good, but immediately fell to trying to convince each other it was nothing, that their kapo's expertise was merely needed elsewhere. As the minutes ticked by, though, the emptier their words sounded, as devoid of substance as the flakes of ash soon to be spewing from the chimney.

Upon exiting the elevator, Kaminski was marched to the morgue and left under guard while Möll checked to make sure all was as it should be in the oven room. Both men and equipment had a workout ahead of them, and come dawn, if not as long a one, their replacements on the day shift. This meant, of course, no sleep for Möll, but that was all right by him; the hardest part of the Aktion was over. The gypsies had been sent to gypsy heaven without incident. All that remained now was to clean up the mess.

With a bounce in his step, he returned to the morgue. The happy task awaiting him there had been long in coming. He suspected Kaminski of being the driving force behind the stymied rebellion, and resented him for not only that but his transparently fake loyalty. Now he had proof of the kapo's treachery, or all the proof that he needed. There were few things that rubbed the sergeant the wrong way more than hypocrisy; it was time to wipe the phony affability from this Kaminski's face forever.

A single weak bulb burned in the morgue's ceiling; shadows grew in the corners like mold. As Möll entered the room, Kaminski rose from the floor. He saw little point in feigning innocence. "It was Mietek Morawa, wasn't it?" he said, his German slow but adequate. "The kapo from next door."

"What about Morawa?" Möll said, his expression guileless.

"It was he who tipped you off, ratted me out."

"Ratted you out? Pray tell, about what? I don't—"

"Lay off it, *Hauptscharführer*. You know perfectly well about what. I'd be glad to spell it out for you, if that's what you're waiting for."

"So you blame Morawa, do you?" Möll laughed and shook his head. "I hate to disappoint you, but you've got it all wrong. If you have to blame someone, I suggest you look in the mirror—there's the man who put you in the fix that you're in."

"And what fix is that?" Kaminski's nonchalance wasn't totally an act.

"Why, you're going to die, my dear fellow. And in a very few minutes. As much as I'd like to, we're not here to chat."

"Die, you say?" It was Kaminski's turn to laugh, a long, mirthless one that echoed off the concrete walls. "I've died a thousand times in the two years I've been here. I died every time I led a child into the gas chamber, then carried his little body out later and sent it up here to be burned. I died when I had to look into some terrified old grandmother's eyes and tell her to keep moving, it's only a shower, nothing to worry about, you're going to be fine. I died when I heard the gas pellets hit the floor and start hissing, at the shrieking that followed and never completely left my head, not even in my dreams. And when the tattoo numbers of my men—boys really, most of them, many of them fatherless all of a sudden, who in their grief and need fixed on me to fill that void—when their numbers were read from a list and they were marched away by you people, killed by you people, a part of me went with them and died as sure as they."

Möll clapped his hands in slow, exaggerated applause. "Touching, very touching. I do believe you missed your calling in life, Rabbi Kaminski. But just what is your point?"

"I should think it obvious: you can't kill a dead man. The dead are past harming. If anything, you'd be doing me a favor by shooting me."

"Well, by all means, let's get on with it then. My aim, if you'll pardon the expression, is to please." Möll loosened his holster strap, rested his hand atop the butt of his Luger. "One question, though, before lights-out. Did you really think you and that degenerate trash you command would succeed? In escaping, I mean. Getting the better of us."

"What makes you think we won't yet? That we won't stop until we do?"

"Because the Jew is by nature a coward. And the SS invincible. Or haven't you of all people, kapo, been keeping score?"

Kaminski lit the room with a smile as big as the life he was about to leave. "We'll see how invincible you are, sergeant, when the Russians come knocking. When it's not defenseless women and children you're up against, but grown men with guns. Your days, I hope you realize, are numbered, Otto Möll, yours and that pack of murdering dogs that—"

"So *you* say!" The freckled face flushed a sudden, deep red.

"That pack of hyenas that wear the grinning skull on their collars. You already know, I can tell, the fate that awaits you and those like you."

"Shut your filthy kike mouth!" The German's color was now alternating between red and pale, one to the other then back again, as from some rare tropical fever.

"I can tell from your face that you know," Kaminski said, still smiling. "That you're more than just angry, you're—what is it? Scared? By God, I think that's it! You're scared because you know as well as I do that someone, somewhere in the not too distant future is going to have both the privilege and pleasure of slipping a noose around your neck."

"I said shut your mouth!" Möll jerked his pistol from its holster.

"And there's a good chance this someone, which I'd be willing to bet is what frightens you the most, will turn out to be, yes, nothing less than…. a Jew."

In the anteroom to the gas chamber, waiting for exactly what they didn't know, the Sonder heard the muffled crack of a gunshot overhead, followed by another. Shortly after, Möll returned by way of the elevator. Having shed the calmness with which he'd departed earlier, he strode excitedly back and forth in front of them.

"Kapo Kaminski is dead! He has been found guilty and executed. His crime was to plot against the camp authorities, against us, the SS!"

Though anticipating as much, several of the Sonder almost collapsed where they stood. Möll continued to pace, his voice shrill.

"That is what awaits all who would defy the SS! There is no future in such foolishness, you cannot win. You will only end up dying stupidly like your kapo. Do you understand? Are you following me?"

Most knew enough German to, but remained silent.

"Say something, goddammit!"

"Yes, *Hauptscharführer*," came the ragged reply. "We understand."

Möll glared at them before ordering the door to the gas chamber opened. "See that you remember it then," he growled as he stormed out.

There were no secrets in the crematorium. As if by osmosis, the men in the oven room knew what had happened and were ready. Two soldiers carried Kaminski in just as the first of the gypsies were coming up on the elevators. He'd been shot in the neck and the left eye, this last leaving a gaping hole. Aside from this wound, his face looked at peace, lips set in a serene smile, that of someone half-awake enjoying the final moments of bed. Leventhal and Warszawski quickly claimed the body and hastened it to a corner, where they spread a canvas tarp over it before returning to their stations. When the day shift showed up at dawn, they were told to keep a close watch over it. The plan was to assemble after the gypsies were taken care of and try to give their poor kapo as decent a funeral as possible.

At ten o'clock, word reached the attic that the men in the oven room were waiting. Not everyone who wanted to was allowed to attend, of course, lest this arouse the notice of the Germans. Only those individuals closest to Kaminski were chosen, with the dayan Leyb Langfus to conduct the service.

When they arrived at the crematory, it was still dark with smoke, but the last of the night's corpses lay at the foot of the ovens. Sergeant Möll, luckily, was nowhere to be seen, and the two SS on duty sat at a table against the back wall deep into a game of cards. Muffle 15 at the far end had been cleared and was ready, and while a skeleton crew continued to work, a collection of men gathered in front of it. Kaminski's body was retrieved from its corner and gently laid on the metal stretcher. As it disappeared into the fire, some of the mourners wept openly. Langfus faced the furnace and spread his arms wide. He'd chosen the *El Male Rachamim*, a ritual prayer for the dead he felt was more personal than the formalistic *Kaddish*. He spoke just loud enough to be heard above the flames without attracting the attention of the guards.

"O, God, full of mercy Who dwells in the heights, provide a sure rest upon the Divine Presence's wings, within the range of the holy, pure, and glorious, Whose shining resembles the sky's, to the soul of Stanislaw Kaminski, for a charity was given to the memory of his soul. Therefore the Master of Mercy will protect him forever, from behind the hiding of His wings, and will tie his soul with the rope of life. The Everlasting is his heritage, and he shall rest peacefully upon his dying place."

The dayan turned to his congregation. "And let us now say…"

"Amen," they responded.

His prayer, if brief, couldn't have been better received, tugging as it did at those heartstrings where grief and ceremony intersect. For a long moment, there was silence but for the clank and rumble of the ovens, all heads bowed as one. Then Langfus, raising his, ventured to speak.

"The death of any person is a thing to be mourned, but none could have hurt more than that of this man. Not only has our leader and inspiration been taken from us, but a dear friend. A friend to many. Hundreds of women survive today because of the food and medicines he had ferried to C Camp. How many of us are alive that he succeeded in talking out of suicide? There isn't a man here who hasn't seen him sit down with a child, a frightened, motherless child on its way to the gas chamber, and somehow comfort it into not being afraid anymore. He could be hard to deal with, stubborn, egotistical, but never hard to like, not for long. For all his faults, he was the best of us, nor shall we see his like again."

Scattered murmurs of agreement. The dayan continued.

"What's important now is that we carry on without him, and by this I mean finish the work that he started. It was Kaminski who planted and then nurtured the seed of revolt, and though he later gave ear to the false counsel coming from the Stammlager and allowed that seed's bud to wither on the vine, in the end he made every effort to revive it, costing him his life in the process. Are we to let our kapo, our friend, die in vain and his dream along with him? I would rather die myself than choose so cowardly a path. I can't help but feel he's somewhere watching us still, waiting to see what we'll do now that he's gone. Would you betray him by doing nothing and permitting the crematoria to stand? Would you carry so damning a sin to your graves?"

For a few seconds, his eyes blazed as hot as the ovens at his back. Then just as suddenly, they and the fire in his voice returned to normal. "It is our duty to see that Operation Jericho outlive its creator. If not to ourselves, we owe it both to him and the thousands of people his vision might yet save."

Langfus wasn't sure where these words of his came from. He hadn't prepared them beforehand, or for that matter planned to say anything. They'd welled up spontaneously from somewhere inside him, almost as if they weren't his words at all, but dictated by another.

Whatever their origin, he was thankful they'd found voice. Not only had they eulogized Kaminski to the extent he thought fitting, he was hoping they might help in their small way to keep the spark of rebellion alive as well. This would soon prove of major concern to their dead commander's lieutenants. Well before August, and as he had after the Familienlager letdown, Kaminski had put the disillusion of June 15th behind him and begun psyching the Sonder up for another attempt at a breakout. This time on their own. Combination optimist and pragmatist that he was, he'd sought to turn a minus into a plus by arguing that freed from the obligation of having to protect thousands of escapees from the camp, the rebels could move faster and disperse themselves more effectively once past the wire. That the squad, too, was now quartered in the crematoria, he'd said, should make up for the lack of partisan help in the assault on this inner cordon. Critical also was his decision to reschedule Jericho for night. Though the commando's guards were to be overcome at the changing of the shifts as before, the main attack was to be delayed an hour and a half so as to take advantage of the darkness. Anything that might complicate the German pursuit was a good thing.

A whole new battle plan had been drawn up. The signal to launch would be the demolition of Crematorium III, followed by that of the others. As soon as each blew, its Sonder were to commence their attack on the perimeter. The weaponry left behind in their old barracks would have been retrieved days before and smuggled into the death houses.

Propelled by the simplicity of this plan and the renewed prodding of its author, momentum was starting to inch forward again, the defeatism of June 15th slowly to fade. In the spirit-killing void left by his death, however, the pendulum of rebellion was once again swinging the other way. Where Kaminski had made his mistake was with Mietek Morawa. Curious as to the reason for the rebarracking of the squad, and the other changes that went with it, Morawa learned of the foiled revolt, and playing a hunch his old rival had been in on it, went to him and asked why he hadn't been included. Though wary of the man, but willing at the same time to let bygones be bygones, Kaminski promised him a role in the next attempt. Contributing to his decision was the potential he saw in the powerful young Pole both to attract conspirators and hasten the revival of rebel morale.

Morawa, unfortunately, wasn't the type to forget a slight, regardless of how long ago it had occurred. He'd held a grudge against Kaminski since forced to share the kapoship of Crematorium II with him back in the spring of '43. His resentment had matured over the months like an expensive if evil-smelling cheese, but he'd refrained from taking a bite of it until the time was right.

His patience paid off. Having got the goods on his perceived nemesis, he wasted no time rushing the minutes of their meeting to Otto Möll. Though most suspected him from the outset, only later did the Sonder receive confirmation of the despicable kapo's betrayal. He got drunk one afternoon with one of his Polish buddies and began boasting in a loud voice of his part in Kaminski's undoing. His indiscretion was soon making the rounds in all four crematoria, and though there was nothing they could do about it now, there were many in the Sonder who also had long memories.

Upon hearing of his friend's death, Noah Zabludowicz had headed straight for Roza Robota with the news. She had a difficult time believing, then accepting the fact. Though they only met once, she'd taken a strong liking to the big, blustery kapo. But as much as his passing affected her, as great was her fear of what his absence might mean to the revolt. To many in the Sonder, he *was* the revolt, in both thought and deed. Such was his influence, she worried, that without his direction the one might never translate to the other.

Her fears were realized at her next rendezvous in the Bekleidungskammer yard with her contacts from the Sonder. Once the packet of gunpowder she'd brought had been safely tucked away in the clothing cart, she took Yankel Handelsman aside to ask him how the squad was handling the murder of its leader. His answer was that it had in effect paralyzed the commando, draining it of all ambition. Nor did there appear to be much hope of restoring it anytime soon. Kaminski, he explained, had been more than just their kapo—he was commanding officer, father figure, and friend all rolled into one. The hurt of his passing was too deep, the wound still too fresh. It was going to take a while for it to heal.

As frustrating as this was, Roza could sympathize. If she wanted to be honest about it, what with the kick in the teeth of June 15th and now this, some of the stuffing had been knocked out of her, too. Not enough to dampen her enthusiasm for the revolt, but then she'd have been likelier to lose her enthusiasm for breathing. She was, however, and almost as difficult to process, starting to have doubts about her mission. One day she couldn't imagine living without it, with not sinking a big part of her energies, her time, her *self* into maintaining the flow of gunpowder to the crematoria. The next, she didn't see the sense in it anymore, especially when balanced against the risks. If the Sonder didn't have enough dynamite by now, when would they?

But as the days passed and August began to wind down, the Nazis carried out a move that promised to make up her mind for her. While the male prisoner-workers at the Union plant were housed in nearby Auschwitz, the females came from Birkenau, three kilometers distant. In order to increase the factory-hours of these latter, hence their productivity, the SS decided to do away with this hike by relocating them to an area carved out of the main camp's Frauenlager. This extension of the women's camp became a miniature lager unto itself, comprised of three barracks only: one for those condemned to medical experimentation, one exclusively for the Union workers, and the third to be shared by the remainder of those and the much smaller group of *Shuhkommando* women, whose job it was to dismantle old shoes for their leather.

Hauptsturmführer Franz Hössler was put in charge of this encampment, and approached his new posting with a proprietary zeal. He was particularly proud of his Union girls, and went to some lengths to elevate them above the common prisoner. Their new lodgings, Blocks 22 and 23, came complete with washrooms, wooden floors, real beds, and sufficient Stubendiensten to keep the huts clean. He even set aside an area in Block 23 to serve as a small cinema. Movies! the women joked. What was next, popcorn?

They were issued clean stripes once a week, and to wear over them a white apron complete with pockets. They received permission to grow their hair back. Their bread ration was increased, not by much, but some. Above all, barring disabling injury or disease, they were to be spared the ordeal of daily selections. Hössler, in justifying this, claimed munitions work too important to permit a revolving door of trainees. Wasn't it to make the women more productive, he said, that they'd been transferred in the first place?

So protective of them was he that they took to calling him Papa Hössler, an appellation that never failed to bring a smile to his face. The SS captain couldn't have wished for an assignment better suited to him. What with the care he took in keeping himself impeccably groomed and attired at all times, his vanity was no secret, and found a perfect outlet in this little corner of Auschwitz entrusted him. Small wonder that he jumped at the chance to play the paterfamilias, even if it was to a mongrel collection of scabby Jewesses.

As improved as the situation of the Union women was, though, their move to the Stammlager was like a knife to the heart of Roza's smuggling operation. There were two and a half miles now between her and those she depended on for the gunpowder. Esther and Hanka, Ala, Rose, Regina and the rest…. after stealing the explosive, how were they supposed to get it to Birkenau? Again, maybe they weren't. Maybe their relocation was a sign, a warning from somewhere trying to tell her to quit while the quitting was good. Whatever it was, and from wherever it came, it didn't appear to have left her a whole lot of choice.

Then during their soup break at the Bekleidungskammer one day, her friend Marta Bindiger took her bowl over to where Roza was sitting and plopped down beside her.

"So…. what are you going to do now?" the Czech asked.

"About what?" she answered cautiously, afraid she'd messed something up.

"Your Union girls have been moved to the new Frauenlager in Auschwitz. How do you intend to keep supplying the crematoria?"

"Oh, that." Roza sighed, looking down at her bowl. "I don't," she said. "I mean, I don't know."

"Which is it," Marta said, "you don't or you don't know?"

"I don't know that, either." She had to smile at her own absurdness. "A part of me is wanting to call the mission a success and be done with it.

To stop while we're ahead, before calamity strikes. If the SS were to catch us, even one of us, packing gunpowder, it wouldn't take much for them to trace it back to the Union, and from there to the crematoria. And that would be the end of any hope of revolt. We've been lucky so far, but how long can it last?"

"And that other part of you?"

"That's complicated," Roza said. "It's not easy giving up something that's figured so large in your life. That you've eaten, slept, breathed, and otherwise obsessed on for what feels like forever. I would think it, if in a lesser way, like losing a child. Besides, if another ounce of gunpowder meant another Nazi dead, I wouldn't mind smuggling the stuff till there wasn't any left to steal."

Marta reached over and took her friend by the hand. "I'm with you on that, girl, and glad to hear you say it. For there may be a way yet to keep the operation going, and with next to no added risk."

"What, you have a plan?" Roza could have kissed her. "Don't tell me you've been losing sleep over this, too."

"Ever since I heard the Union was being transferred. And no, it's not a plan exactly, not yet, but I'm hoping."

Roza grinned and shook her head. "I should have known you'd be way ahead of me on this. Hope, you say?"

"Yes. We'll see. Let me work on it a while. I'll get back to you when I do know something, good or bad."

Marta had a friend who worked in the main camp's *Paketstelle*, or parcel room, where the packages from home for the non-Jewish inmates arrived and were distributed. Every Sunday, a truck loaded with these made the trip to Birkenau. Through the underground, she was able to get a pass to visit this friend and try to solicit her help.

The visit was a success. The woman agreed to accept a bundle per week from one of the Union women, enclose it in a box disguised to look as if it had traveled the postal system, and send it along with the others on the truck. It would be addressed to a different name each time, fictitious, of course, in care of Dr. Pach's infirmary. Marta would pick it up there and deliver it to Roza. She swore they could rely on her contact at the Paketstelle, and sure enough the first shipment came through without a hitch.

Roza never ceased to marvel at the quality of the women she'd surrounded herself with. In a way, a very small way, she pitied the SS, who with their parochial attitudes toward the "gentler" sex stood no chance against the enterprising females arrayed against them. Once again the Germans, through Marta this time, had been bested by their own oafishness, one of many such instances they would one day pay for in blood.

Uplifting a victory as this was, though, it couldn't begin to make up for the transplanting of her people. She hadn't just lost co-conspirators, she'd lost friends, one in particular. But for Noah, she'd never had a friend as genuine as Esther Wajcblum, and wouldn't allow herself even the thought she might never see her again. As if touched by her sorrow, fortune had granted her the chance to say goodbye at least. Upon catching word of the impending move, she'd rushed that very evening to Block 2.

It was getting dark, the day shift having just finished its Appell. The barracks was as loud as one might expect with five hundred women trying to make up for the conversation denied them most of the day. Esther, however, lay alone on her bunk. Her sister Hanka was working the night shift that week.

"Roza!" she shouted, jumping to her feet. "What a surprise!"

They hugged each other longer than they normally would have before sitting down on the edge of the koje. Roza got right to the point. "I heard about the outfit's transfer to the Stammlager," she said. "When is the big move?"

Esther's smile wilted. "Day after tomorrow. Or that's what they're saying."

Roza nodded resignedly, not wholly convinced it was true until now. "Which is why I'm here," she said. "I—I've come to say goodbye, Esther."

"I was afraid that's what this was. I'm going to miss you, Roza, you can't imagine how much."

"What I can't imagine is you up and running out on me like this. Who the hell am I supposed to dance the tango with now?"

Esther smiled weakly. "I used to live for those dances, you know, couldn't wait to see your face come through that door. It wasn't just the dancing, either, fun as that was. Hanka and the others singing, clapping us on, even the blockova joining in…. everyone forgetting herself for a moment, her hunger, her heartache. Those were good times, weren't they?"

"The best," Roza said, "and there were plenty of them. Remember the night…."

For a good half an hour, they managed to forget why Roza was there, filling the minutes with memories instead. And when they'd exhausted these, they simply sat a while, silent, basking in the warmth of what they'd just shared. Roza was the first to speak.

"I never told you this before, Estusia, never came out and actually said it, but almost from the day we met, you've been like a sister to me. In some ways even more than my own dear dead sister. When Shoshonna passed away, a part of me went with her. I may have looked the same, even acted the same, but something inside was missing. Then you came along and it wasn't anymore. Missing, that is. It's as if, I don't know, we were meant to find each other."

Esther could feel the tears coming. Another few seconds and she'd be blubbering like a baby. She bit her lip hard. Again, even harder. If she had to bite it off, she wasn't going to cry—the last thing the situation needed was tears. "If that's true," she said, chasing them away, "and we *were* meant to meet, what's all this about goodbye? That does neither of us any good. Doesn't even make sense really. If it was meant to be, it was meant to last. I say we stop torturing ourselves with 'goodbye' and think of it more as 'until we meet again.' "

"Point taken," Roza said, forcing a brave face herself. "Until we meet again."

Not trusting her emotions, Esther hurried the conversation in a different direction. "There is one thing I've been wondering," she said. "Have you given any thought to what's to be done about the gunpowder? With you here in Birkenau and us in Auschwitz, how are we supposed to go about getting it to you?"

"I'm not sure," Roza said. "Not yet anyway. It's not looking good, that much I do know."

"What about the underground? Can't they help us out?"

"The underground?" Roza's voice dripped contempt. "The SS would sooner come to our aid than those bums. The so-called Battle Group at Auschwitz, don't get me started as to why, is doing everything in its power to keep the lid on the crematoria, Sonder aggressiveness from boiling over. We'd be fools to expect any help from them."

Esther fell back on the mattress, lay there eyes open; Roza could see the wheels in her head turning. "Tell me," she said finally, "and be honest, Raizele. What, in your opinion, are the odds of it happening?"

"As I said, Esther, it's not looking so great. But it's still early, and should I do find a way to keep us in business, you Pulverraum girls will be the first to—"

"No, not that." She sat up again. "I wasn't talking about that. Ever since told we'd be leaving here, I suspected our smuggling days might be over. And that's okay. That I can live with; the Special Squad should have more than enough gunpowder by now anyway. What's bothering me is if they're ever going to use it. If a revolt is still in the cards. I'm not asking for myself, either, or my little sister, or Tadek—the chances of any of us escaping at this point are pretty much nil, I know. But could it be that June 15th, that awful day, was the end of everything we've worked for, been risking our lives for?"

How often lately had Roza agonized over that same question? Not that she was going to add to Esther's anxiety by admitting as much. "An awful day, true, it couldn't have been worse. But what about before it turned awful, before everything unraveled? Surely you remember the excitement of that morning, the anticipation."

"My hands were shaking so, I could hardly do my job."

"Maybe we should be asking ourselves this then, and this is my point: doesn't that morning bode well for the future? The Sonder weren't only ready, they were raring to go, and would have made a warm show of it if the underground hadn't got careless and blown it. But just because things didn't come to a head then, doesn't mean they won't ever. I wouldn't call June the end of anything, but a beginning. If the Sonder can rise to the occasion once, they can again, right?"

Esther nodded eagerly, as a child might. Touched by so ingenuous a response, Roza sought to reassure her further.

"This Sonderkommando, the 12th, isn't like any that came before it. These men have no illusions about what the Germans have planned for them, and now, with the Hungarians a done deal from the look of it, they know their own time is near. They'll fight before they submit meekly to Nazi trickery, fight like cornered animals. Or that's what my friend Noah tells me, and no one knows the Sonder better than he."

This wasn't completely true. According to Noah, following the twin heartbreaks of first June then August, how receptive the Sonder would be to taking up the banner of revolt again was anyone's guess. Even more discouraging was the negative report Handelsman had given her, who being a Sonder himself ought to know. Roza, however, as a charity to Esther, had chosen to overstate the squad's toughness. And with the desired result: her friend's face glowed as if with a light of its own.

"Thank you, Rozhka," she said, "for laying my silly fears to rest. You have a knack for that, you know, a positive talent for making me feel better. What in God's name am I going to do without you?"

"You're going to survive," Roza said, "you and your sister, until the Russians get here and this evil is over. A few more months and it'll all be over. What's a few months? I'm going to come looking for you then, and I'd better find you, and by that I mean alive. Promise me, Estusia, you'll still be alive."

The light left Esther's face as quickly as it had come, and all she could manage was a nod—when suddenly the noisy barracks got noisier, a commotion breaking out in front of the quartermaster's office. It was the evening's bread distribution, chaos as usual, everyone beating a path to that end of the hut.

Roza figured this was as good a time as any to make her exit. She had to leave eventually, and though beautiful as always, Esther seemed so much thinner than she'd ever seen her. Damned if she was going to be the cause of the poor thing missing a meal.

That was what in her consternation she told herself anyway. In truth, Esther had ended up crying in spite of herself, if quietly, a single tear wending its way down each cheek. It was enough, however, that Roza could feel her own eyes starting to mist, and that wouldn't do. That was out of the question. The vow she'd sworn herself that long-ago November on the unloading ramp was binding still: any tears she might in a weak moment be tempted to shed would have to wait for the end of the war. Weak moments were luxuries she couldn't afford, not as long as she and hers remained in SS hands. One last lingering hug, therefore, a whispered "Until we meet again", and she was gone before grief could get the better of her, pushing a path to the door without looking back.

She had a rotten few days after that. She'd wanted to see Ala Gertner off, too, and Rose Greuenapfel, Regina Safirsztajn, Mala Weinstein for sure. Given how it had gone with Esther, though, she knew this impossible now, counted herself fortunate she hadn't run into them that night. One wrenching farewell had been quite enough—call it selfish, call it cowardly, call it what one would, she didn't trust herself not to collapse into a wet, weepy heap if forced to go through another.

But as big a heel as it made her feel to duck out on her friends, that wasn't the only thing that had her in the dumps. From what Noah had implied and Handelsman made clear, the Sonder were no more disposed to rebellion anytime soon than to cutting their own throats. The revolt was as dead in the water as the harpooned carcass of some whale, with what might well have been as little guarantee of resuscitation. Roza's spirits for those few days were at as low an ebb as they'd been since her poor Shoshonna had embraced the lethal fence.

But to her bafflement as much as relief, they didn't stay so for long. Faint at first, stealthy, a feeling began creeping up on her that she was then and still at a loss to explain. There was no accounting for it, yet there it was, as impossible to ignore as the obstinate August heat. It ran like a shiny gold thread through the hanging black crepe of her despair: the utterly improbable yet rock-ribbed certainty that everything was going to turn out all right. Somehow she knew, without knowing why, and regardless of how unportentous it looked at present, that the uprising was far from history, its arrival only a matter of time, as unstoppable as the rise and fall of the sun, moon, and stars.

She didn't know whether to be thrilled or disturbed by this feeling. Was she the victim of her own fantasies, of self-delusion born of desperation, or was she tapping into something outside the pale of human understanding, being given a glimpse through a window not ordinarily open? Whatever it was, sixth sense or nonsense, there was no dismissing what it was trying to tell her. Which left her a choice: she could listen to either her head or her gut, one the voice of rationality but fraught with misgiving, the other of irrationality and hope.

In the end, of course, it was a choice so obvious as to be none at all.

Autumn

T he news broke the first week of September and swept through the crematoria like a fire: Otto Möll was gone, and from the look of it for good, transferred to the subcamp of Gleiwitz as its new commandant. Gleiwitz was one of the larger moons in the Auschwitz orbit, the *Hauptscharführer's* reward apparently for a job well done at Birkenau. Where he was posted to or why, though, mattered little to the Sonderkommando, as long as it was far away. Death and the master sergeant were two sides of the same coin—where he went the other followed, as sure as tails followed heads. Given the impunity with which he'd had a hand in wiping out whole squads in the past, and his undisguised enmity toward the 12th as an incubator of revolt, his departure left its members feeling they'd acquired a new lease on life, able to breathe freer than they had since the spring.

With Möll out of the picture, however, complacency entered it, only adding to Sonder inaction. Aggravating this was a rumor that had begun to make the rounds asserting the SS had decided to put an end to the liquidations that had eviscerated all previous squads. It was well known that these periodic vettings made the Nazis nervous, should the day come that those prisoners selected for "relocation" choose not to go to their deaths without resistance. The rumor was made the more credible by the Germans having yet even to hint at reducing the 12th, and that with it going on seven months since its establishment, a year and beyond for the two hundred of them carried over from the 11th Kommando. What was more, for lack of transports, the night shift had been canceled, leaving one less reason to retain a squad twice as large as any previous. And still the SS continued to do nothing. With their captors looking more content by the week to let sleeping dogs lie, many of the Sonder were starting to act as if they were leading charmed lives.

"Are they blind or just stupid?" Zalman Leventhal asked. "I don't get it."

"Neither," replied his friend Zalman Gradowski. "They're Hungarian, most of them, and I don't mean that to sound prejudiced."

"What *are* you saying then?" The two shared a bench in the yard of Crematorium III, taking in the last of the sunset. The sun itself was gone, sunk out of sight behind the trees, but above these floated a slurry of thin, horizontal clouds aflame in orange and pink. Gradowski had been sent from Number Two to deliver tomorrow's itinerary, an errand that should have taken him five minutes instead of the thirty it was approaching. He could only imagine what kind of hell he was going to catch from his kapo, that prick Morawa, when he returned.

"What am I saying?" Though he resented the innuendo, Gradowski let it pass. "With all the suicides among them this summer from working the fire pits, a lot of the Hungarians aren't long from the transports themselves. New and without a clue, these lack the slightest concept of how things work around here. We can tell them what's getting ready to happen, what happened to all past commandos, but we might as well be speaking Chinese for all the good it does."

"But it's no more than a question of simple arithmetic," Leventhal persisted. "Nine hundred men in the squad and not enough work for a third that many. The number of transports so down, the night shift has been scrapped. How can they not see the danger they're in?"

"By choosing not to look too hard, I guess," said Gradowski. "By hoping against hope things will be different this time. What I don't get is why you should find this surprising. It isn't as if we haven't seen it before."

"Yes, but that was before, *eleven times* before, total. Now there can be no doubt the Germans are liars, that there is no such thing as transfer or reassignment or work somewhere else. Then along comes this latest and most ridiculous rumor ever, and….and…."

In his frustration, he couldn't get the words out.

Gradowski let his gaze float upward. He couldn't recall as colorful a sunset. He'd always felt that the more spectacular displays of nature, be they beautiful or destructive, were God's way of showing that He did in fact exist.

"And the prospects for revolt," Leventhal managed at last, "are even dimmer than they were a week ago. Hell, there *is* no revolt anymore! Those Hungarians of yours no more want to hear about shooting their way out of here than they do the Krauts cutting their numbers down to size."

"They will, you watch. They'll see the light, give them time."

"Time? While the gas chambers continue to fill, the chimneys to smoke? Despite this summer's slaughter, there are thousands yet that could be saved. Or are you forgetting what Kaminski was forever preaching, that the uprising was as much about taking out the crematoria as it was escape?"

"Ah, *Kaminski*!" Gradowski said, pouncing on the name. "Thanks for bringing him up. Know what he told me once, not long before he died? Not that he need have, as I'd already had the ill luck of witnessing for myself what he was talking about. But that's another story. Sitting me down, he confided that what urgency he'd attached to the revolt began to wane after he saw what the fire pits were capable of. It was then, he said, that he realized the Nazis would have been just as murderous even without their ovens and Zyklon-B. And in that respect anyway, though he would carry his guilt for it to the grave, felt a little less of it at having listened to the underground and held the squad back."

"Okay, I'll give you that," Leventhal said. "That I can see. Forget the crematoria then—let's get back to the Hungarians. And don't go telling me, I know you, that the one has anything to do with the other."

"That's exactly what I was going to tell you," Gradowski said. "Am telling you now. Think, Zalman: while we old hands were inside working the furnaces and such, the Hungarians fresh off the cattle cars, being untrained and without skills, were outdoors getting up close and intimate with the fire pits. And reaching because of it, one has to assume, the same conclusion Kaminski and I did. Meaning?"

Leventhal didn't have to think; he may have lacked sympathy, but not a brain. "Meaning," he sighed grudgingly, "while we've been telling them the surest way to save their people was to put the death houses out of action, their own experience was informing them to the contrary. That even without the crematoria, the killing wasn't going to stop. Making them less inclined to court a premature death by rushing into a revolt. Satisfied?"

Far from it actually, Gradowski told himself. He was as upset as his namesake at the miserable turn affairs had taken, as worried as anyone about the future of the rebellion. So much so, in fact, that unlike his partner, he refused to make it worse by surrendering to pessimism. Was, if not fully then at least to a degree, convinced that something somehow, in some as yet undefined way, would end up jolting the Sonder to their senses.

That it should take so divinable and familiar a shape failed for some reason to cross his mind.

The 23rd of September fell on a Saturday, continuing a stretch of remarkable weather. Every day for a week had been a cloudless gem, this particular one having ripened into a dazzling autumn late-afternoon. The lowering sun drenched the yard of Crematorium IV in a golden-red fire, recalling the biblical bush that burned yet was not consumed. The changing of the seasons had come mercifully soon this year, siphoning the meanness right out of the summer. The air had turned cool weeks ago, the shadows seeming to lengthen earlier each day. This probably meant a mad dog of a winter, but at the moment no one cared; the sun, for so long an enemy, had grown friendly.

Number Four was shut down that day, hadn't been used much at all lately. Apart from the dysfunctional state of its furnaces, with the crowds of deportees growing sparser there'd been no call for its services. Making it good for something at least, it served as a barracks now for the main body of Sonder.

At a little after 4:00 p.m., however, it unexpectedly erupted in activity. Five trucks and a staff car rumbled up to its gate and disgorged a platoon of soldiers and two officers. Most of its residents were outside taking advantage of the weather, some kicking a soccer ball around, others simply lazing in the newly benevolent sun. At sight of the trucks, everybody stopped what he was doing to watch. The soldiers ran into the compound and quickly spread out, three of them beating a path for the building itself. Within minutes, every Sonder both inside and out was standing at formation in the yard, most trying without success to appear unconcerned.

Scharführer Gert Busch looked to be the officer in charge. The sergeant, if not liked, was one of the less despised of the SS. As swept up in the practice and philosophy of murder as his peers, he lacked their brutality. Seldom had he been heard to raise his voice, and was generally easy on the Sonder, at times almost sociable. He gave the impression he believed that the bloody business they were assisting in entitled them to a measure of equal footing.

The young *Scharführer* strode forward, his chubby face made the rounder by a broad smile. "Men of the 12th Sonderkommando," he announced, "I bring you good news! A brand-new, modern camp is being built to the west, inside Germany. The security of the Reich requires it. What we require is two hundred of you to help man it, where it's been determined your experience will prove invaluable. I've been told living conditions will be better than here; for one, there'll be no sleeping on uncomfortable cots, and I have it on good authority that you and the SS will be sharing the same kitchen. All who wish to take advantage of this opportunity, please step forward now!"

A buzz arose from the Sonder, but it was only the sound of translation, most speaking little or no German. Once it died down, their only reaction was to look at each other in utter incredulity that after so long, and with so much lately having pointed to its unlikelihood, their final hour appeared to have struck. Nor were any so naïve as to think otherwise. Not a man budged. Not a cough disturbed the stillness. Silence enveloped the yard like a fog.

Busch retreated to confer with his brother officer, the crematorium's *Kommandoführer*, Sergeant Gorges. That they had anticipated such a response was evident from the conference's briefness. Together the two returned to face the assembled prisoners and were soon picking through the ranks checking tattoo numbers. Those Sonder selected had theirs written down, then were directed toward the soldiers, who stood with weapons leveled. Only the men with high numbers were chosen.

These had no choice but to do what the guns told them to, and soon two hundred of them were filing out the gate toward the trucks. They walked like what they were, men sentenced to death, slump-shouldered, heads down, but also like the dupes they knew themselves to be, victims of that false sense of security which had kept their rebelliousness idle. Mortified that in their delusion they'd ignored every warning sign, they marched to their fate without so much as a backward glance. Once they were on the trucks, there were a few halfhearted waves goodbye, but most in their humiliation averted their faces.

Those left behind weren't any less ashamed. Nor the rest of the commando when it heard the news. Each man blamed himself for letting it come to this, for lacking both the foresight and fortitude to prepare for and maybe prevent it. So visceral was their guilt, it made the loss that much more personal, as if a part of their own bodies had been cut away.

To that scattering of them desperate enough to hope the Germans were telling the truth this time, what faith they had began to wobble that very evening, and come the next morning would collapse like a house of cards. Shortly after sunset, those quartered in Crematorium II were shut in its attic for the night, hours earlier than their usual lockdown. As if this weren't fishy enough, they were told a group of specialists would be checking the crematorium's furnaces for efficiency and making whatever adjustments and repairs might be needed. That, as every man who worked them knew, was twaddle; Number Two's ovens were in as good a condition as they'd ever been. All the SS and their ridiculous pretext had done was make the Sonder wonder what was really going on.

They would find out the next morning upon discovering the ovens were far from as they'd left them. In five of the muffles lay the remains of corpses only partly incinerated, several identifiable as belonging to those abducted yesterday from Crematorium IV. Later, they would learn the sequence of events that led to this grisly find. The two hundred had been trucked to the main camp and immediately gassed in an airtight room used to disinfect clothing. After dark, the bodies were returned to Birkenau and Crematorium II, where a team of SS, for the first and only time in the history of the camp, was waiting to burn them.

Whether from incompetence or just plain laziness, it was to prove a poor effort. And as such a mystery. After all the care the Nazis had exercised to be devious to that point, how, the Sonder asked themselves, could they have been so irresponsible as to leave such a revealing mess behind?

At any rate, there could be no doubt now as to their intentions. Nor that they were only getting started. Less than a week after the 23rd, the Germans issued another ultimatum, though in this instance they sought to be clever about it and deflect some of the blame from themselves. *Scharführer* Busch returned to Crematorium IV early that morning and met with its kapo, Shlomo Kirschenbaum, the once-suicidal and withdrawn—but having

353

since found a reason to live—now enthusiastically insurrectionary cousin of Noah Zabludowicz. The city of Krakow, Busch claimed, like Lublin some months ago, had been hit hard by Allied bombers, and three hundred strong men were needed to assist in removing rubble. Seeing as how no group of prisoners was in better health than the Sonder, what he wanted was a list bearing the tattoo numbers of those who weren't afraid of hard work, and he'd be back in two days to pick it up.

As soon as Busch left, Kirschenbaum hurried to spread the word, sending emissaries from Number Four to inform the leaders of Battle Group-Sonderkommando that the SS were at it again. An emergency meeting was scheduled for 7:00 p.m. in Number Two. Handelsman, Leventhal, Warszawski, Kirschenbaum, Langfus, Gradowski—all were present, the Sonder having regained, among other privileges, the freedom of movement they'd lost under the watchful eye of Otto Möll. With the *Hauptscharführer* gone, the guards at the gates had reverted to their old ways and become as venal as ever.

The meeting took place in the *Kommandoführer's* office, a cramped, fluorescent-lit room dominated by a large wooden table that served as the *Ober's* desk. Handelsman opened the discussion. "We all know why we're here," he said, adjusting his glasses, "so let's get down to business. First, is everyone agreed the smart thing to do is comply with this latest demand from our keepers?"

Warszawski let loose a long, disbelieving whistle. "Hold on just a sec!" he said. "Are you nuts? Allow me, professor, to rephrase that for you: does *anyone* agree that's what we ought to do?"

"Definitely not!" Leventhal almost jumped from his seat. "I'd say it was pretty obvious what the Krauts are up to."

"And that is?" Handelsman asked.

"Why, to shift the onus for their next massacre onto us, of course!" Leventhal's face was threatening to turn redder than his hair. "To make it look it's we sending those on the list to their deaths. If you ask me, it's the old story of divide and conquer. The Germans have to be thinking if they can pit one half of the squad against the other, there goes any chance of us uniting to resist this latest purge of theirs."

"Is that what you want?" Warszawski said, gazing at each man in turn. "The Sonder, those left of us, at one another's throats?"

Handelsman answered quickly, before the others could. "That's one way of looking at it," he said, his tone equable, "but try this on for size. Say we did go ahead and give the Nazis their list. Those on it, rather than being surprised—standing with their thumbs up their asses in the crematorium yard waiting for their numbers to be called, surrounded by machine guns—would at least have time to ponder their predicament. And if you were one of them, if you knew beforehand you'd been marked for death, wouldn't you jump at just about anything that offered you a way out of it? Grab at any straw that might save you? Well, just such a straw, gentlemen, is there for the grabbing already. It's called Operation Jericho, and who unfortunate to find himself one of the three hundred wouldn't latch onto it with both hands if it was dangled in front of him?"

"And after that sad show the other day at Number Four," Gradowski hastened to add, "it's not as if Jericho isn't on everyone's lips again. Especially the Hungarians', which most of those taken and put on the trucks that day were."

"Meaning that on top of the three hundred volunteers the list is likely to produce," Handelsman said, "we should have those remaining of their compatriots on our side, who have to figure they're next. Only a damn fool would expect the SS to retain a detachment of five hundred with the transports as few as they are, and growing fewer."

Here he paused until he found the face he was looking for. "Bela, perhaps now would be a good time to share what you told me before."

The Hungarian Bela Lazar, though still learning Polish, knew enough to have followed the conversation so far. His words may have been clumsy, but the voice breathed defiance. "I talk with my people…. more early," he said. "In afternoon. They say they not go with the SS this time. This time they fight if they on the list."

Handelsman folded his hands together on the table. "There you have it: this time they fight. The Nazis' latest bit of shadiness may turn out a blessing in disguise. Providence has intervened, with a little help from German high-handedness, to deliver us three hundred men, and that just for starters, whose only chance at survival lies in blasting their way out of here. What more could we ask? I say we give the swine their list with a big fat thank-you scrawled at the bottom of it."

To something of the amazement of all, the fisherman Deresinski rose from his seat, noisily clearing his throat. Rarely did he volunteer an opinion at such meetings, but the granite in his voice now left no doubt where he stood. "The professor is right as usual, and that should be the end of it. We give the SS what they want and get what we want; we don't and we might not. It's as simple as that."

That Deresinski should have felt the need to speak up was a cue for the others. Gradowski made it clear he was with Handelsman, as did Kirschenbaum. It was Langfus, however, who summed it up best.

"Faced as we are with this latest threat from our masters, I can't help asking how our much-missed dead kapo might have handled it. What would Kaminski do in this situation? And there isn't a question in my mind he wouldn't have passed up this chance to beat the Nazis at their own game, grinning like a fox even as he handed them their list."

With that it was settled. Even Warszawski could see their old kapo doing as the dayan had said, and there was no minimizing the magic Kaminski's name wielded. "Far be it from me to go against the majority," he conceded, running a hand through his hair. "But though I'd love to end up admitting you right and myself wrong, it still smells to me, for all your fancy arguments, you might be opting for the easier route of playing ball with the Germans. Zalman?"

Leventhal shook his head in disgust, but said nothing.

"That's it then," Handelsman said. "Now comes the hard part. Whose numbers are we going to put on the list?"

They would make a start on it that night, culling those individuals who weren't to be on it. *Scharführer* Busch had been adamant that the more experienced Sonder were to be excluded. With the transports still coming in, he'd explained, and the Theresienstadt ghetto among others yet to be liquidated, the SS were against doing without their skilled workers, not even (or so he'd lied) for the six weeks the three hundred would be needed at Krakow.

This was what Handelsman and those in agreement with him were referring to: most of the men left to choose from would be Hungarian. The trick was to pick those who could be relied on to resist, who weren't merely talk; no one wanted it to end up an actual death list. Having set October 7th, a week away, as the tentative date of the attack, they needed to know the people on it weren't going to cave in without a fight should the Nazis decide to lower the boom sooner. That such a preemption would force the rebels to strike before they were ready, with neither coordination nor surprise on their side and in the white light of day, would just have to be. The days of watching their Sonder brothers marched disconsolately to their deaths were over.

As Lazar had informed them at the meeting and would confirm the next day, his fellow lieutenants could rest easy about his people's fighting spirit. They'd sought his help, naturally, in identifying the most militant of the over five hundred Hungarians remaining on the squad. After further sounding a representative number of these out, he failed again to find any who didn't impress him as sincere in swearing to take on the SS with their bare hands if they had to rather than be herded like cattle onto trucks.

For the first time since arriving at Birkenau, apart from those heady days leading up to June 15th, he was proud to call himself Hungarian. Like all in the Battle Group who'd never stopped agitating for revolt, he'd begun to despair at his countrymen ever recovering from that fateful day and the dejection it had sown. Not to mention what those wretches forced to man the fire pits had had to endure. What they'd undergone was enough to suck the life out of anyone. Here it was October, though, and those who hadn't committed suicide or been shot for refusing to work, who'd succeeded somehow in surviving, bruised but not broken, were showing themselves the men they had been in June.

This wasn't the only thing, however, filling him with pride. A great honor had come his way, bestowed on him by no less than his comrades-in-arms. He'd requested it to be sure, would have begged for it if he'd had to, but it was granted him gladly and without reservation: leadership of the team whose job it was to blow up Crematorium IV. As with the other death houses, this was to be done by dynamiting the reserve barrels of gasoline used to power the ovens' auxiliary machinery. Though all eight of Number Four's weren't functioning anymore, luckily this fuel had yet to be removed.

In view of its limitations, of course, the demolition of this particular crematorium would serve little purpose beyond the symbolic. Which didn't make it any the less imperative, not least in the eyes of Lazar. Tens of thousands of Hungarian Jews and untold multitudes of others having suffered a vile death inside its walls, to leave those walls standing would have been an offense in its own right, one only the timid or defeated would acquiesce to. The fire pits had shown the work of both extermination and disposal to be in no way dependent on the crematoria. But that was beside the point. If the Sonder did nothing else, Lazar liked to think, if they were gunned down before even reaching the wire, by destroying those four demonic buildings so close to the SS heart they'd be delivering this message: you Germans may have enslaved, corrupted, disgraced, and even killed us, but despite your best efforts, you've failed to break us. Men we came to Birkenau, and alive or dead, men we leave. Either way we will have won, and as proof of our victory taken your filthy death factories with us.

He was among those, who other than the chance at escape it afforded, saw the revolt as a vehicle for sticking it to their tormentors. The two weeks he himself had spent at the fire pits, brief as this was, had left their mark on him. Never had he been given to anger, even less to revenge, but the SS had taught him how to hate and taught him well, and he'd been aching ever since to pay them back for the education.

Fearing the Nazis would act on their list before the Sonder were ready, the 7th of the month couldn't come soon enough for him. Lazar's was one of the more strident of those voices urging the men in charge of its planning to move the date of the revolt forward. Upon the completion of the list and its delivery to the Germans, the Sonder had worked feverishly to speed preparations. The order of battle remained the same Kaminski had formulated, with one exception. Since there was no night shift anymore, the assault would have to begin no later than 6:00, the crematoria's new closing time. This meant that for at least the first hour it would lose the advantage the cover of darkness would have provided. And more damaging yet, what weapons the rebels would have gained from the changing of their guard.

As for advancing the date, it soon became apparent just the opposite would be necessary. Having everything and everybody in place to go by the 7th wasn't being realistic, not if the revolt was to have any shot at success. A couple of days more could make all the difference. The conspirators agreed, therefore, to aim for October 9th, a decision not as risky as it might have been just a few days before. Courtesy of their friend Dr. Pach, they'd learned of a shake-up in the Kommandantur, namely the transfer and sudden departure of His Excellency *Obersturmbannführer* Höss. With their commandant gone, it would doubtless take the SS a while to adapt to the change in echelon, a period in which they weren't likely to be making any moves. And might also explain, though they'd had it in their possession for some days now, why they hadn't appeared in any hurry to put their list to work. To everyone's relief and no small surprise, life had gone on as normal, its routine uninterrupted, one day piling on another as if nothing had or was going to happen.

Not that the tension emanating from the crematoria wasn't as thick as the smoke on a three-transport day. Sensing something was brewing, Battle Group-Auschwitz began sending people to investigate. Nor did it take long for these to return with evidence suggesting the Sonder were poised for a breakout, prompting the Stammlager to issue Birkenau this warning: due to the danger it posed the inmates of both camps, an uprising was to be avoided at all cost. To what extent the Nazis might retaliate wasn't known, but would surely be severe, especially if any of the Sonder did manage to escape.

Though hardly unexpected, there was some discussion among the rebels as to how best to respond to this. It was decided it would be prudent to pretend to share the underground's concern and agree to discourage any talk of a revolt "should it arise." Having lost all trust in their alleged ally, the Sonder wouldn't have put it past them to tip off the Germans if convinced a rebellion was in the offing. As painful as this was to admit, there was too much at stake to ignore the possibility.

On the morning of the 6th, Noah Zabludowicz hurried from Crematorium II with urgent news for his superiors. If he'd suspected as the Sonder did that his Battle Group's leadership couldn't be trusted, he'd have kept what he discovered to himself, orders be damned. In fact, he would have severed ties with them already. It wasn't as if the thought hadn't crossed his mind; with the unfortunate exit of Bruno Baum from the scene, the Resistance had lost one of its more audacious and principled voices. As Noah saw it, perhaps its only one.

His only aim in gathering what intelligence he could from the crematoria was built on the hope that if revolt was inevitable, the Sonder intractable, his bosses might yet be persuaded to offer at least some assistance. And with what he'd uncovered this morning, there was no time to lose. His new contact in the Battle Group was the Polish activist Ludwig Soswinski, like Baum a member of the Steering Committee. He showed up unannounced at Soswinski's workplace, Block 24, the main camp's registrar and primary records office.

The older Pole ushered him to a cubicle and had him sit, but wasn't pleased. "I told you never to contact me at the job," he said, keeping his voice low. A fortyish, dapper non-Jew with his carefully trimmed mustache and odor of hair cream, unlike the mournful Baum he was normally the gregarious type, but in the studied, vaguely patronizing way of the politician. "Suppose an SS walked in and asked you your business here?"

"I came to check out the lock on the front door," Noah replied. "You people have been complaining about it sticking, am I right?"

Believable a cover as this was, it did nothing to lessen Soswinski's annoyance. "Since you're here, make it quick then. I assume it's something to do with those pals of yours in the Sonderkommando."

"I just talked with one of them, yes, and thought you ought to hear what he had to say. He's one of their top men, and knows whereof he speaks."

"So what is it that's so important it can't wait until later?"

"The revolt," Noah answered. "It's on, and for certain. The Sonder are wise to the Germans' latest attempt to thin their ranks and determined either to escape or die trying. They have weapons and intend to use them. It's for real this time, general. I was told we could expect it three days from now, on the 9th. Sooner, if the Nazis should force the rebels' hand."

"And you were told that by…. this person you met with earlier. One of their 'top men', as you put it."

"Yes," Noah said wearily, prepared for what was coming.

Soswinski rose from his seat, brushed imaginary dirt from the cuffs of his jacket. "We appreciate your efforts, Zabludowicz, ill-considered as they are. And the seriousness you clearly attach to your orders. But just yesterday, Battle Group- Sonderkommando informed us, officially I might add, that no action against the SS was pending. And on the improbable chance that should change, we'd be the first to know. So, as you can see, there is no cause for alarm. Not having been there, I hate to presume, but I'd say the person you were talking to this morning was telling you something he thought you wanted to hear."

"And if he wasn't? Which, I know him, he wasn't—what then?"

"Then the Sonder, in addition to killing themselves, could well end up taking, depending on the extent of Nazi anger, thousands of their fellow inmates with them."

"I would think that'd be enough right there for you to pass my report on."

"It would, my dear fellow, if I had any faith in it whatsoever."

"But—"

"That will be all, Zabludowicz. I don't know about you, but I've got work to do. And if you wouldn't mind, at least make a show of having a look at that lock on your way out."

There was no point in arguing, this Noah *could* see. It was the Poles on the Steering Committee obviously, the blind idiots, who were the ones being told what they wanted to hear. Besides, whom did he, Noah, think he was kidding? To expect the underground to come to the aid of the Birkenau rebels now, with the Red Army little more than a hundred miles away the last he'd heard, was akin to looking for the hand of God to descend from the heavens, and if a little belatedly, smite the oppressor.

His energies, Noah decided, were better spent carrying through on his promise to Yankel Handelsman. In return for the information he'd just wasted on Soswinski, he'd given his word he'd do what he could to smuggle the insurgents some ammunition. It wouldn't be the first time he'd helped them out in this way, but on all previous occasions the Sonder had been quartered in their original barracks. Getting the stuff into the death houses wasn't going to be easy. The first step was tracking down one or two of the civilian workers he'd done business with before; the SS employed dozens of them at Birkenau alone, and in exchange for the gold the Sonder had provided him in the past (and again today), they'd been more than happy to bring Noah whatever he wanted. Except for guns. They wouldn't do guns for some reason, but ammunition wasn't a problem, go figure.

Did he have time? He wasn't sure. He'd need to start the ball rolling this morning, and even then it would be tight. And that was if he actually did have until the 9th. Handelsman had vouched that nothing would happen until then, and Handelsman should know. But for all he or anyone really did know, things could come hurtling to a climax tomorrow.

*   *   *

October 7th dawned still cold from the night before. The morning dew had frozen, coating every surface in white; the barbed wire that circled the crematoria resembled the symmetrical strands of some giant spider's web. By mid-morning, though, the sun had asserted itself, and instead of cold, the day was shaping up to be unseasonably warm. Jackets were shed, windows opened. What wind there was blew from the south, so that well before the sun was high, people were wiping the sweat from their faces.

Though stuffy, the attic of Crematorium III wasn't as warm as it could have been. The facility was closed for the day, which meant no heat rising from the ovens. As the revolt was scheduled for the day after tomorrow, its hundred and sixty residents, not counting the personnel of the separate hair-processing room, were busy preparing for their departure. Some were sorting and packing, some sewing and repairing, some parceling food and supplies; others huddled in small groups going over assignments and strategy.

The prisoners of the Reinkommando were busy, too, though they'd made up their minds months ago that should by some blessedness things reach this point, as much as they were in favor of the plot, they weren't going anywhere. The business of armed revolt was a job for the young, and they in their declining years, with their brittle bones and slow step, would only have been a hindrance. Besides, as men of God, rabbis and scribes, it simply wasn't in them to be a party to violence, be it for the purpose of escape or any reason. They were content to sit by and let the will of God be done, justice be served at such a time and in a manner He saw fit.

It wasn't because of their hated work, however, that they also weren't idle this Saturday. A transport had shown up earlier, a small one, but Crematorium II was still occupied with it. (Number Five was ready to go if another should arrive, but as of now was manned by no more than a token crew). The hair that would be coming from it, with what little that remained unbagged from yesterday, could wait until tomorrow. For in addition to it being the Sabbath, October 7th was the climactic and final day of Sukkoth, the major Jewish holiday of the Tabernacles, or Booths.

Sukkoth was both a harvest festival and a commemoration of the end of the ancient Israelites' forty-year sojourn in the Sinai Desert. A *sukkah* was a small wood-and-canvas structure roofed with pine branches that the people of Moses had used as shelter upon first entering the land of Canaan, and later as temporary housing adjacent to their fields during harvest time. Dancing, singing, and other merriments, evolving on the seventh day into a more solemn ceremony, marked the weeklong celebration, also called the Time of Our Joy. It was a busy day for rabbis everywhere, including, though they lacked a congregation, those presiding in the attic of Birkenau's Crematorium III. Indeed, it was here it might be said to have assumed the most importance, an oasis of Jewish affirmation in a desert of Jewish death and negation.

Though Leyb Langfus in his role as dayan was doing his part to keep the day holy by assisting his rabbi elders with their prayers and other duties, he was also, during the frequent lulls in those proceedings, lending the rebels a hand in the other and larger room. Nor did he see any contradiction in flitting between the two. As respectful of the Divine Will as anybody, he also viewed it as open to interpretation. Who was to say where God's intentions ended and the part men played in helping to advance them began? Langfus was a firm believer that people, when necessary and in a just cause, should use every means at their disposal to further both their personal and the general welfare, which was why, unlike his passive brethren in the Reinkommando, he'd committed to following his Sonder brothers down the path of revolt. And why he was aiding them now in prepping for that journey.

His contribution was largely motivational, but not limited to that. His long, lanky frame moved from group to group bearing words of encouragement, the random embrace or pat on the back, but where an extra pair of hands was needed, the dayan was there with that, too. It was while making the rounds that he glanced out one of the windows and saw a line of trucks approaching from the south. He thought little of it until looking again a moment later, and pushing his glasses up on his nose, watched as all seven of them pulled to a halt in front of Crematorium IV. Even then he failed at first to understand what it meant, until, as if someone had switched on a light, it hit him.

"Oh my God, no!" he said under his breath, but loud enough to attract the attention of those standing near.

"What is it, Leyb?" said Zalman Leventhal, arriving at his side. He followed the dayan's gaze. "What's going on?"

Langfus didn't answer, didn't have to. Though Crematorium IV was half a mile away, it was clear what was up. One of the trucks was already expelling its platoon of SS; the other six, for now anyway, were empty.

"It isn't," Leventhal said in disbelief.

"I'm afraid so," Langfus replied, if finding it hard to believe himself. "The question," he added with a calmness he didn't feel, "is what happens now?"

Yossel Warszawski was meeting with Shlomo Kirschenbaum in a corner of the undressing room of Number Four when he stopped in mid-sentence and cocked an ear upward. He'd been sent to see that the mobilization here was progressing according to schedule, and to deal with any problems the conspirators might be having. When his eyes returned to Kirschenbaum's, they were two question marks. "You hear that?" he asked.

"Hear what?" the kapo said. "Wait.... are those trucks?"

At that instant, one of the Sonder burst through the door from outside. "It's the Germans!" he cried, a wild look on his face. "They've come to—they've come for us!"

A squad of *Schützen* yelling like crazy men was soon bustling everyone out of the building and into formation in the yard. The guns and helmets of the soldiers glinted in the noon sun. As he'd been two weeks ago, *Scharführer* Busch was in charge, only he wasn't smiling this time as he stood before the assembled Sonder.

"The following prisoners," he shouted, "three hundred total, are to be transferred for reassignment. When I call your number, present yourself and proceed to the waiting area." He turned and pointed toward the gate behind him. "I will be starting with the higher numbers and working my way down. If passed over, return at once to your quarters."

After allowing time for translation, Busch bent to his clipboard and began reading aloud. As if not staggered enough, the Sonder were caught short by this curt new tack of the Nazis. There'd been no mention of clearing rubble in Krakow or any kind of work, or of easier living conditions elsewhere, a better camp.... nothing propitiatory at all. It became quickly evident as well that the list Busch had brought wasn't the same one turned over to him last week. As some of their own had warned, that had been a ruse to weaken their solidarity by turning Sonder against Sonder. The SS had made their own list, confining it to those prisoners bunking in Crematorium IV; to have to scour all four death houses hunting down those tattoo numbers the Sonder had compiled would have been both confusing and impractical. As well as multiplying by four the hazard of provoking a confrontation.

It wound up in the end, though, not making a lot of difference. One list was as good, or rather as meaningless as the other. For while some of the Sonder were stepping forward, if reluctantly, when their numbers came up, others were ignoring the sergeant's summons and sneaking back to the crematorium. Soon the quantity of men not responding to Busch's calls grew noticeable; from the sparseness of the ranks still standing before him, it was plain he wasn't going to reach his goal of three hundred. With his clipboard at his side and a squad of soldiers behind him, he started out for the nearby building to find the shirkers and bring them back.

They hadn't gone but a few steps before an angry shout arose in back of them. When the soldiers wheeled, it was to meet a hail of stones hurled by the group of men already selected, who then rushed the guards nearest them. Those still waiting to be called were right behind them. Brandishing crowbars and other tools they'd pulled from their clothing, they actually made a fight of it for a few seconds, felling a handful of Germans. Their crude clubs, however, were no match for submachine guns, and the compound quickly turned into a killing ground.

The air sang with bullets, the dirt jumped with them. The Sonder scattered in panic, screaming, collapsing in bloody heaps, but somehow most managed to reach the safety of the crematorium. The first thing they saw upon flinging themselves through the open double-doors of the undressing room was the figure of Warszawski standing straight and tall with a machine gun in his hands. Though in fact the opposite of tall, he seemed a colossus with that gun at his hip. Soon Kirschenbaum appeared bearing the identical weapon, both having come at the expense of their guards. Two of these, overpowered at the first sound of shots, were beaten to death and their arms and ammo seized; the other two wisely abandoned their posts and fled.

Despite having barely made it out of the yard alive, the sight of such firepower in the hands of their own people instantly revived Sonder spirits. Led by Kirschenbaum, they hurried to break out the dynamite and the Russian Borodin's grenades from their hiding places. They were also in possession of two .45 caliber pistols, four of the 6-mm's, and the ammunition to go with both, a good amount of it. These walls that since their raising had seen nothing but degradation and death now crackled with the electricity of high purpose and hope. Men hustled here and there not at the commands of brute overseers, in the service of mass murder, but to put an end to both it and their complicity in it forever. The Hungarian Bela Lazar had already sped off with his demolition team to move the drums of reserve fuel into the oven room and rig them with dynamite. Operation Jericho wasn't only talk anymore. It was about to elevate more than just Sonder morale.

Warszawski for his part had taken up a position at the doorway, where he was waiting for Busch's men to get a little closer. These, having broken ranks while chasing down the Sonder, were now descending in a ragged line on the crematorium. Unaware the squad was armed, their step was unhurried, their manner relaxed, some even holding their rifles slung carelessly across their shoulders. When finally he started firing, the Germans were near enough that Warszawski could make out the astonishment on their faces. They dropped as if their feet had been yanked out from under them, one never to rise again, one hollering he'd been hit.

An even bigger surprise to the soldiers were the two grenades that followed, forcing them to fall back. There they dove behind what cover they could find, content to wait for reinforcements.

Nor would they have to wait long. Even as the Sonder, flush with victory, were yelling themselves hoarse, two convoys of trucks appeared at separate points on the horizon, one barreling in the direction of Crematoria II and III, the other straight for them. Both were coming from the area of the SS barracks, each leaving a cloud of white dust behind it. As if announcing their approach, the camp siren commenced to wail, its apocalyptic howl ascending like a herald of doom.

"Soldiers!" Kirschenbaum exclaimed. "Already! Not fifteen minutes since we—"

"It was the two guards we let get away," Warszawski said. "They must have reached a telephone and given the alarm."

"So what do we do now?" Panic played at the edges of Kirchenbaum's voice. "Another minute and those trucks will be here. No way we can crack the inner cordon before then."

Warszawski said nothing. He had to think, and fast. *So what do we do now?* Good question, he told himself, repeatedly attacking his hair with a hand—if only he had a good answer. So this was what the long awaited, much ballyhooed revolt had come to: an accidental, disorganized, desperation-driven mess, with as little chance of succeeding, he smiled ruefully, as the damned Wehrmacht had of stopping the damned Russians. Here the rebels were, finally acting the part, true, but with the element of surprise gone, the siren blaring away, the SS closing on them and in force before they'd fairly begun.

And on top of it all, staring them in the face the very real possibility of having to take on the Nazi garrison alone. The conspirators in Crematoria II and III had to be wondering what was going on. Though a screen of trees shielded Number Four's compound from prying eyes, anybody with ears would have had to hear the gunshots and know where they were from. But Jericho wasn't scheduled for two days yet. And not, in any case, at so early an hour. Those Sonder sitting blind in II and III would have to figure out, first, just what those shots were, then how, and in light of the adversely altered situation, perhaps even whether they should respond to them. This was going to take time, something Warszawski and his impromptu companions-in-arms didn't have.

"Listen up, Shlomo," he said, "I have an idea. You go on ahead with the men and start in on the guard towers, while I stay behind with maybe a dozen of them—we haven't the guns for more—and try to hold off the Krauts here, keep them pinned down. Once we see you've broken through the wire, we'll disengage and follow. Leave us the pistols and some of the dynamite and grenades. Between those and this," he said, slapping his machine gun, "we should do all right. What do you think?"

"Good! Or good enough anyway. It might, if we're lucky, get us into the woods at least."

"As for the assault on the cordon, though we are short of guns, there's no need as I see it to stray from the original plan. You'll want to take out the tower nearest you first, blow that section of the fence, then keep the farther one occupied while the men make a run for it. You think the one machine gun will be enough for all that?"

"I don't know, Yossel, but this I do: unless we get moving now, we won't be going anywhere."

As the squad made for its jumping-off points, the doors at the gas-chamber end of the building, Warszawski positioned his men along the wall facing the yard. To the right of his station, he put one of the 6-mm's in the nearer death-room door; this person was to alert him when the inner cordon had fallen. He would then pass the order to withdraw to the three gunmen at the windows helping him defend the long undressing gallery, as would the farther one to the two deployed in the oven room. Each of these shooters had a backup in case he was disabled.

It was in this role and that room that Bela Lazar had set up his bomb, which at the call to fall back he was supposed to ignite. A single fuse connected two four-stick bundles of the dynamite, each taped to a different one of the six barrels of gasoline. These he'd clustered where they might do the most damage, against that side of the inner furnace facing the interior wall.

Hardly had the men taken their posts than one truck after another came grinding to a halt in front of the crematorium gate. Soon soldiers were flooding the yard, and after conferring with those already there, began cautiously to move forward. When the Sonder waiting for them opened up, the SS were once again stopped cold.

But Warszawski knew they wouldn't stay stopped for long. There were too many of them this time. The small-arms fire raking the building grew so intense that he soon found himself forced to shoot blind, only his weapon protruding from behind the wall. When a heavy machine gun started tearing chunks out of that wall, even this became chancy. Not that it slowed him down. He continued fighting like a man possessed, someone out of his mind, and in a sense he was, screaming unintelligibly each time he pulled the trigger but so immersed in the fury of the moment, he didn't realize he was screaming. To the Germans hugging the dirt for dear life, there might have been two men at that door.

Yet even as the blood boiled inside him and the battle churned around him, he was able to keep an ear tuned to the one raging on his right. The fight for the inner cordon had been fierce from the first, with what he'd determined to be Kirschenbaum's gun holding its own. More encouraging still when finally it came was the thunderous crash of dynamite, one explosion, then another, and yet another, the last followed by several short bursts from Kirschenbaum.

Then a sound that took his breath away, made his heart leap in his chest. It was a roar of exultation from hundreds of throats, from men who were prisoners no more but spilling into the yard, past the wire, out the camp, he could tell they were out and running for the woods from the rapidly decreasing loudness of their hurrahs. For two years, he'd been waiting for this sound, dreaming of it both in his sleep and awake. After that long, it felt like a dream still. Who'd have thought the putrid air of Birkenau would ever ring with such a cry, its blood-soaked soil pound with the steps of men racing to freedom?

The gunman he'd posted in the gas chamber came hurtling into the room, his message redundant but thrilling all the same. "They've done it!" he shouted, eyes popping from their sockets. "They're through the wire!"

"You wait here!" Warszawski yelled above the racket of the guns. "I'll get the others and—"

The next second he was sitting inexplicably on the floor, as dazed as if just punched in the jaw. But for a high-pitched electronic whine, he was suddenly deaf in both ears. His first thought was that an enemy grenade had landed near, but a check of his person turned up no wounds. It wasn't until he noticed the far wall of the undressing room in flames, then through the door bits of debris raining from the sky, that he realized he'd been knocked off his feet by something much bigger than a grenade.

It had to have been Lazar. He must have touched off the drums of gasoline early. He picked himself up and sang out for survivors, but only four singed and shaken Sonder stumbled forward. With the just as shell-shocked SS having forgotten their guns for the moment, the six took advantage of the lull in the fighting to slip out of the burning building.

What Warszawski didn't know was that prior to the explosion, the German attack had made some headway. Where the coke storeroom jutted from the building it formed an ell, creating a blind spot, which allowed a squad of soldiers to work its way around to the rear of the oven area. With the rest providing cover, two of them sprinted for the back windows, shot them out, and tossed a grenade apiece inside. The double concussion rocked the room, but protected by the massive bulk of the furnace they nestled against, the barrels of fuel went untouched.

When Lazar came to, the room was crawling with soldiers, the air suffocating with the acrid stink of burnt gunpowder. This told him he hadn't been out for long, though he might have remained unconscious indefinitely but for the sharp, pinching pain that gripped his left side. His first impulse was to see where and how badly he was hit, but he didn't dare move. His partner lay motionless and bloodied beside him, as did the pair of rebels beneath the far window.

The Nazis had obviously mistaken him for dead as well. From what he could see through half-closed eyes, they weren't paying him any mind. One had opened the door to the yard and was signaling his *Kameraden* that all was clear. The other five were starting to gather outside the morgue, from where they planned from the look of it to continue their assault. The most troubling if at the same time enticing sight of all, however, loomed eight meters away. Somehow the soldiers had overlooked the bomb in their midst, and there it sat, beckoning, though setting it off was no longer the simple task it had been. Apart from the SS tramping about, and the others soon to join them, he had yet to determine how serious his injuries were, how far or even if he could drag himself across the floor.

He moved one leg an imperceptible couple of inches, but in doing so had to stifle a cry of pain. So much for that…. his hip must be broken, or his pelvis. He'd be lucky to crawl three feet without passing out. There was no way for him to get to the dynamite, even should he by some chance end up alone in the room. As the hopelessness of the situation began to sink in, what physical discomfort he was suffering became as nothing to the mental. Barring anything short of a miracle, the hated crematorium would continue to stand.

This was too much for him. He'd dedicated himself body and soul to wiping this heathen temple, this altar stained with his people's blood—both its brick and the shameful memory of it—out of existence. Nothing else mattered, not escape, not freedom, not life itself, his or any other. Indeed, he preferred death to failing at his mission, and was within a hair of giving himself up to the soldiers then and there. Better to end it right now, a voice in him urged, than live a minute more with so unlivable an outcome.

And then he saw it. Right in front of him, his miracle, as if materialized out of thin air. It lay under the body of the dead man splayed next to him, plainly, implausibly, breathtakingly—a pistol. It was one of the 6-mm's, the tip of the barrel just poking from beneath the man's rib cage. Small a gun as it was, it would suit his purpose just fine. The question was how many bullets were left in it. All he needed was one. Surely there was, had to be, one.

He gave the room a quick once-over. The soldier who'd stayed behind to wave in the others had gone outside, shouting at them angrily to get a move on. Lazar could hear the thud of their boots as they came running. Now was the moment. There wouldn't be another. He took a deep breath to steel himself against the pain, then lunged for the pistol and yanked it free. Hurriedly, he aimed at one of the bundles of dynamite, fired.... and missed. Too hurriedly! That was stupid! Willing a second bullet into the chamber, he would not be denied, he carefully lined up the sights. He felt someone dash into the room but ignored it, his every nerve, his whole being focused on the piece of metal in his hands. Slowly, infinitesimally slow, he squeezed the trigger, not sure he was even moving it, until with a bang the gun jumped, and even as the bullet left the barrel he knew it was a bull's-eye.

The last thought the young Hungarian had, a millisecond of a thought, was how right and proper it was that a gun meant to be used in executions, that had participated in the murder of who knew how many Jews, should end up an instrument of Jewish revenge.

From the attic of Crematorium III, the explosion wasn't only visible but spectacular. Though the intervening trees hid all but Number Four's two chimneys from sight, there was no obscuring the enormous fireball that mushroomed skyward between them, toppling the inner one on the spot while leaving the other teetering at an impossible angle. What had been the roof rose in a volcanic eruption of supporting beams, boards, and shingles, the heavier pieces hovering briefly in the air before crashing back down, the smaller ones drifting slowly to earth like confetti. The blast shook the ground half a mile away, the windows of Number Three trembling in their frames.

The men watching from those windows, though there could be no mistaking what it meant, greeted the explosion with mixed emotions. There was awe in their faces all right, and pride that this wellspring of so much suffering and death should at long last have been dealt its own death blow, and by no less than their brother Sonder, the very slaves forced to work it. But where one might have thought cheers or some sort of celebration in order, the mood in the room was subdued.

This was because, through little fault of their own, for the men of Crematorium III the fight was over before it started. It might have helped if they'd acted immediately, at the pop of the first gunshots at Number Four, but their reticence was understandable. These hadn't lasted long and were followed by an ominous stillness. That their comrades had resisted those come for them was clear, but from the sound of it, or lack of same, the battle had been brief. And with little doubt as to the victors. The camp siren had gone off, but any prisoner riot, suppressed already or not, would have precipitated that. For precious minutes, therefore, unsure what to do, the men of Number Three did nothing, until to their shock the gunfire resumed, heavier this time and punctuated by the dull whomp of grenades. But as they were to their even greater shock to discover, by then the window of opportunity had already begun to slam shut on them.

In all fairness, it wasn't much of a window. Even if they had reacted faster, it would, like as not, still have been too late. They did scramble to break out the few weapons they had—three handguns, a sack of grenades, another of dynamite—distribute them, and otherwise prepare to head downstairs. But no sooner had they set out than they were to encounter the obstacle that was in short order to prove their undoing.

The only exit from the attic consisted of a narrow outside staircase, a construct their four guards and *Kommandoführer* Muhsfeld, at the wail of the siren, had rushed to secure. Upon the first of the would-be rebels venturing onto the landing, a flurry of machine-gun fire felled them and drove the rest back inside. They tried again with the same result. Whether they should attempt it a third time became quickly academic, for within minutes of their first, SS reinforcements arrived by truck and a hundred guns were trained on the stairs. A mouse couldn't have made it down them alive, or at the other extreme, an elephant.

The conspirators had no choice but to return their weapons to their hiding places, their adrenaline to the place it had come from. Where the electric energy of hope had permeated the room, now the bitterness of a dream shattered hung in the air, as heavy as the heat. Accompanying it was guilt at what they felt was their having flubbed it, at letting themselves be trapped in this prison of their own indecisiveness. Few were those able to meet another's gaze. Meanwhile, from Number Four, the accusatory crack of the guns continued to taunt.

"We should have hit those stairs sooner"—this from one of the Maidanek POWs—"while we had the chance."

Langfus, no less devastated than anyone, saw no reason to beat themselves up over something he didn't feel they were to blame for. "What, in the first five minutes? If we had even that."

"He does have a point, Leyb," Leventhal said. "If we hadn't hesitated, we might—"

The dayan cut him off. "Hesitated? Who wouldn't have? Especially after that first round of firing died down. Don't tell me you, both of you, didn't believe the jig at Four was up then."

No response. He looked past them, his eyes sweeping the room. Not a face did he see that wasn't sagging in defeat or laboring hard to hold back tears. "All I'm getting at," he said louder, addressing more than Leventhal and the Russian now, "is that we shouldn't be down on ourselves for not acting before we did. How long was it after we realized the battle was still on before we were packed and ready to head down and join it? A lousy few minutes? Caught by surprise as we were, I'd say that was pretty good. And then I'd say this."

He pointed in the direction of Crematorium II. "What do you hear coming from our friends across the way? Nothing. Not a sound. It would appear we're not the only ones the Germans were too quick for. If there's any comfort to be had in how things are turning out, I guess we can take some in that."

"So what do you suggest we do, rabbi?" came a boy's voice from the crowd. "There must be something…. something that…." It trailed forlornly off.

Langfus didn't answer. He didn't have an answer, not a very helpful one. "My only advice," he said at last, "take it how you will, is to stop feeling all guilty and sorry for yourselves and direct your thoughts instead to—"

He was about to tell them to pray for the brave men of Crematorium IV, when it blew up, rattling not only the windows but the dumbstruck men who proceeded to crowd them. These stood there as one transfixed by the fireball, the dayan and what he was saying forgotten.

To their further dismay, they would shortly be reminded. Hardly had the roar of the explosion ceased to reverberate than behind them burst the distinctive jackhammer thump of automatic weapons. This was soon accentuated by the deeper thud of grenades. Though it took them some seconds to admit so damning a thing, these could only be coming from Crematorium II. Which meant not only had Langfus been wrong about their "friends across the way" but in answer to the question the boy had posed him, there was something they could do now after all. Sadly, sickeningly, it was to look on in impotent disgrace while the crematoria on either side of them carried the torch of revolt.

And most were too ashamed to do even that. While at this newest outbreak of gunfire, some raced to the windows on the other side of the attic, the rest stayed where they were, unwilling to subject their eyes to something mortifying enough on the ears.

What would have eased that mortification some if it had occurred to them, the conditions existing at Number Two differed markedly from theirs, in one detail especially: it being the only death works in operation that afternoon, half the men quartered within it were already downstairs when the shooting broke out at Number Four. This was to prove crucial in determining those men's response to what at first to them, too, were the mysterious goings-on to the north.

57B was the squad on duty that day, and was hard at it. A small transport from the Theresienstadt ghetto had shown up in the morning, all twelve hundred Czechs having gone to the gas. Bombarded as they were by the din thundering from the furnaces and flues, the men sweating at the ovens would have had trouble hearing a gun if fired directly outside. It didn't take long, though, for word to reach them from upstairs of the commotion at Crematorium IV. What could it mean? The question would assume a new and immediate urgency with the ululating shriek of the camp siren.

To a man they dropped what they were doing and left their stations, gathering in two groups at opposite ends of the room. Their faces were pinched, their talk excited. Rifle fire at Number Four, in its wake the wail of the siren.... could it be the revolt had started without them? How and why, if at all, was anybody's guess, nor were they given much time to parse it out. Soon the chief of the guard bustled in and demanded in broken Polish to know why they'd stopped working.

Kapo Kalniak was in charge of cremation that day, and among those who sensed something big was up. Where before he would have addressed the SS man in front of him with if not subservience then certainly deference, his tone now edged perilously close on the insolent.

"The stiffs can wait, *Rottenführer*," the burly Kalniak said, towering over the corporal. "It isn't as if they're going anywhere."

This elicited a few snickers from the men at his back; the German even smiled, but coldly. Responding more to their laughter than the only half-understood Polish, he reverted to the familiarity of his native tongue. "So I should give you boys some time off in the middle of your shift to have a little chitchat, is that what you're saying? To plot who knows what kind of mischief. Or maybe"—here the soldier, his smile evaporating, drew a nightstick from his belt—"maybe I should give you a taste of this instead."

Without warning, he cracked Kalniak a violent blow to the skull, sending him crashing to the floor like a tree felled. But the kapo, if a tree then as stout and tough as an oak, didn't stay down for long. After shaking his head a couple of times, splattering bright red drops everywhere, he was back on his feet, and having pulled it from his boot, brandishing a short, thick knife. In two blinks of an eye, he buried it in the astonished German's chest, who was dead before he hit the concrete.

The Sonder looking on were horrified. "Oh, swell!" one of them said. "Now what? We'll pay for this for sure, all of us."

Yankel Handelsman, though, like Kalniak, wasn't at all sure. In fact, with the shooting from the north having started up again, both surmised the mystery solved. Today was to be a day unlike any other, a day where their world would be turned upside down, the past and its ground rules, its proprieties and prohibitions, as dead all of a sudden as the soldier at their feet.

At any rate, it was done. There was no turning back now. Whatever the story at Crematorium IV, here the die had been cast, SS blood shed.

"Hurry!" Handelsman said to those nearest. "Take his gun and ammo, then into the fire with him. If we're to get the drop on his pals and make the crematorium ours, we can't be leaving dead bodies around. Not at first anyway."

It took them a moment to comprehend what he was saying. Make the crematorium ours? What was that about? No sooner had they ceased asking each other, though, than they broke into smiles and sprang to action. Before long there wasn't a man in the room who didn't know what was up, so that even as some were loading the corporal into one of the ovens, others were busy in the coke store retrieving the dynamite and grenades hidden inside. Cries of "It's on!" and "This is it!" hailed from a dozen mouths, more shouting their way upstairs to alert the men in the attic.

"This is *what?*" a voice yelled, and in strode the imperial figure of their head kapo, Mietek Morawa, flaunting the thick mahogany cane he'd taken to carrying lately. Since the death of Kaminski, the young Pole had been acting his old self more and more, arrogant, impatient, and whenever he detected what struck him as the least bit of defiance, murderously cruel. Just the other day, he'd beaten a teenaged Sonder so badly for "insubordination" that the boy died the next morning. With his archrival and only restraint Kaminski out of the way, he felt free once again to bully and brutalize.

"What in Christ do you numbskulls think you're doing?" he shouted above the ovens. "Who told you lazy scum you could leave your posts?"

Intimidating as he was with his booming voice and heavy cane, he didn't get very far. Another three steps and a gang of Sonder swarmed him, disarmed him, and stuffed a cloth in his mouth. A rope was found and his arms trussed to his sides, and he was dragged struggling wildly to where Handelsman stood.

His captors were ecstatic. Though none had foreseen it playing out so perfectly, if ever, they'd dreamed of this moment. Still grieving over the loss of Kaminski—and to the veterans among them, a lengthy but not forgotten list of others—at last they had in their power the culprit responsible for these crimes. Handelsman, busy sorting ammunition, glanced at Morawa briefly and nodded once. Without a word passing between them, as if it had been planned out beforehand, the Sonder holding him roped the squirming kapo's ankles together, heaved him onto the metal stretcher attached to the open maw of Muffle 2, and slid him alive into the blazing oven.

It was an atrocious death, but the months had inured the men of the detachment to atrocity; to them the gag-muted screams emanating from the furnace were less an indictment of their own cruelty than the long overdue sound of justice being served. Some even stopped what they were doing the better to drink them in. If nothing else came of their mutiny, at least this one account would have been squared.

Then from the coke store, a shout. "Soldiers, at the gate! Hundreds of them!"

It was true: what appeared two companies of SS were pouring from a line of trucks and into the yard. As if that weren't unnerving enough, seconds later a furious explosion shook the ground. Some feared at first that it was German artillery, until through the windows they saw a titanic spiral of smoke and flame boiling above the treetops from what looked to be Crematorium IV. This dissolved whatever doubt any may have had. The revolt, though two days early, wasn't only on but proceeding full throttle. As if not airborne already, Sonder spirits soared as high as the fiery cloud climbing to the north.

Another of their guards came running into the room only to be jumped and promptly beaten to death. Counting the one Battle Group-Auschwitz had smuggled them in June, this gave the insurgents three machine guns, along with a few pistols. Zalman Gradowski and the last of the men from upstairs showed up shortly with a fourth, having made quick work of the guard sent to secure the attic.

As unaware as their counterparts at Krema IV that the Sonder possessed a single firearm, the SS sent to lock down II approached confidently to within thirty meters of its walls. Which was when the rebels inside opened up with everything they had. The Germans reeled and fell back, tried again, and again were repulsed. After taking cover, they attempted a flanking movement to the right in hope of gaining the rear and attacking from behind, but a hail of bullets from the *Kommandoführer's* office stopped them short.

Thwarted there, the Nazis let loose the pack of guard dogs they'd brought with them, the idea being for these to infiltrate the building and keep its defenders occupied while they moved in. But the dogs, normally so aggressive, wanted no part of bullets and grenades, and slunk back soon enough to their handlers in the rear.

By then Handelsman and the Russian major Borodin and their men had initiated the assault on the barbed wire. The area targeted previously was the southwest corner of the compound, an escape route that took one of the guard towers completely out of play and reduced their exposure to another. What no one had envisioned, what wouldn't have been a factor if the revolt had gone off on schedule and as planned, was the presence of a German machine-gun emplacement not far from that same corner, the barrel jutting from between two mounds of earth fronting a hastily dug foxhole. Put there to anchor the left side of the Nazi line, it prevented the Sonder from nearing the electrified fence to set their dynamite charges. They'd tried, and four men had died before even reaching the wire. As long as this gun remained, the rebels were bottled in.

It had to go, but how? Someone would have to work his way close enough to lob a grenade. Handelsman felt a tapping on his shoulder and turned. It was Deresinski, the Pomeranian fisherman, one of Borodin's little bombs in each of his big, sea-scarred fists.

"Cover me, professor," was all he said, though Handelsman required neither clarification nor convincing.

"You're a brave man, Josef," he said. Then added with a smile, "Hurry back to us, will you? We're going to need you today."

Deresinski took off at a run, then hit the dirt after a few meters and began worming his way forward. From his position in the outer door to the coke store, Handelsman had a clear field of fire to the German gunners. His own machine gun, being of a lighter caliber, wasn't all that accurate at this range, but should enable him to keep the two helmeted heads down once their attacker got close.

Which somehow he did, surprisingly close before the Nazis noticed. They'd been too busy hammering away at the crematorium, but upon spotting him, swung the barrel to their left. Handelsman responded, but without the result he'd hoped for; his ammunition limited, he had no choice but to confine his fire to small bursts, and seconds after he'd stop, the SS gun would bark again.

Deresinski, despite this, managed to get closer yet, finding shelter behind a small knoll. From there he hurled a first grenade. It was a decent toss, exploding just to the side of the foxhole, but as if to mock its ineffectiveness the machine gun loosed another volley. When the second grenade proved as futile, Handelsman hung his head, not only at the other's failure but his own mishandling of the affair. He should have known the major's makeshift contraption would just about need to hit its target square-on to do any damage. Why hadn't he thought to suggest his man arm himself with dynamite instead?

But as he was trying to figure out what to do now, he was abruptly unburdened of the problem. He watched as the fisherman-turned-sapper, lying on his back, reached into his shirt and drew out a small bundle: two sticks of dynamite bound together with black electrical tape. Handelsman's lips parted in wonder.

"Get ready, professor," Deresinski shouted at him from the knoll, "and pour it on this time!" Then with a salute as of farewell, "God go with you all, and remember me to our people!"

At this he lit the fuse, jumped to his feet, and vaulted at a run toward the German position. Handelsman opened up and kept it up, prepared to spend his last bullet if need be. But while this took the machine gunners out of the equation, the Pole's grenades had attracted the attention of others. As Handelsman looked on aghast, a Nazi fusillade from somewhere slammed into the man's stomach and sent him sprawling.

Deresinski, however, though down, wasn't out. Even before setting out from the coke room, he'd made up his mind it was going to take more than a few bullets to stop him. Like a corpse rising from the grave, he lurched to his knees, scrabbled the last few feet to the foxhole, and clutching the dynamite to his bloody middle, threw himself in just as it went off.

Handelsman wasn't the only Sonder watching to lose it. The same snarl of rage that welled up from him tore also from a score of other throats. So savage was the fire now issuing from that end of the building that the SS commander, his left flank now vulnerable and unsure of the size of the force opposite him, couldn't discount the possibility of a counterattack. He got on his field telephone, and soon two small, wheeled howitzers could be seen approaching from the east, bumping along behind a pair of jeeps.

But by then, the Sonder had flattened a section of the fence. The cry went out to the men in the crematorium, who were soon racing through the gap in the barbed wire, loud in their jubilation. The last of them supposed to quit the place, however, unluckily never did. Borodin had entrusted two of his Russians with the job of detonating the reserve barrels of fuel on their way out, but they'd waited too long making sure the building was clear and lay where they'd fallen, victims at the last minute of a Nazi grenade. The revolt may have become a reality, but Kaminski's heart's desire of tumbling all sixteen walls of his latter-day Jericho wasn't to be: Crematorium V because, undermanned, its usual guard had been sufficient to secure it; III from its occupants ending up trapped in its attic; and now II, out of what could only be put down to a bad break.

The one death house, though, burned defiantly for all the camp to see, and no one did this move more than Roza Robota. From the Bekleidungskammer, she could hear the battle surging on both sides of her, and through a window marveled at the gigantic column of smoke rising from Crematorium IV. The one was music to her ears, the other a feast for the eyes, and both together glorious proof that her mission, with all its dangers, its sacrifices, had been worth every one of them.

She was so excited she could hardly contain herself, much less tend to her work at the folding table. But by this time, their guards had other things to think about. Even the warehouse's *Kommandoführer* had grown oblivious to his slaves, kept bouncing back and forth between the telephone and a window, his voice and face tense.

Roza could picture the camp's entire complement of SS in a similar state, and so intoxicating was the image of Nazis in fear of their lives for a change that it felt as if she was no longer standing on the floor but floating above it. Jews fighting back, and with guns! *German* blood staining the ground! She'd been awaiting just this for going on five years now, well before Birkenau, ever since her push for an insurrection in the Ciechanow ghetto had been overruled. How many of her race, of her own family, had perished in the interim? Her mama and papa, her sister Shoshanna, her poor sickly brother Isaac and even frailer Grandma Gemmy.... their ghosts, and those of others, would haunt her forever. But at least now when they came to her, in both her sleeping and day dreams, she would have this to tell them: their deaths, in so far as it was possible, had been avenged. The sword of justice—justice on *earth*, not some problematic heaven—had sought out the murderers and cut their own lives short. The guilty, some of them anyway, not enough of them but some, had been brought to task in this life for their sins, not the next, made to answer for their iniquities while they still had something tangible, something temporal to lose.

As good as this made her feel, the moment would have been even sweeter if her friend Esther were there to share it with her. And Ala and Rose, Regina and Marta, she would have liked nothing more than to celebrate the victorious conclusion of their mission with those of her fellow *provocateurs* most responsible for it. Indeed, with all of the brave men and women, who each in his or her own way, had risked their lives helping to arm the Sonder. She could only hope that wherever they were, the main camp or here, they were able to see and admire the same pillar of smoke as she, recognizing it for the triumphant thing it was.

What Roza couldn't know, and would have put a damper on her mood if she had, was that Number Four would be the only crematorium to go up in flames that day. Or that the revolt wasn't the robust animal it appeared. It didn't take long for those Sonder who'd fled IV in such elation, for example, to discover that their problems had only begun. They'd made it to the woods all right, but now what? Short on weapons, they huddled in the sun-spangled shade of the trees, an uneasy mob dripping with sweat and an almost as material tension. How much of the former was from the heat or an incipient if growing panic was hard to say, but it was plain they were as low on confidence as guns.

Based on those they did have, and with the Germans soon to be hot on their scent if they weren't already, it was decided they would split into three groups of a hundred and some each: one under the umbrella of Warszawski's machine gun, the second under Kirschenbaum's, and the third allotted what pistols were left. This last bunch set out west, the others to the north and northwest respectively, all with the Vistula River as their objective.

It wasn't an especially dense woods, but the undergrowth was matted, the ground uneven, which made for slow going. As they slogged their way forward, the men in Warszawski's group cast nervous glances behind them. After fifteen minutes, he held up his hand for them to stop and pulled a map and compass from his pocket. Both were from the supplies the partisans had left them inside the wire of Crematorium V a year ago.

He leaned against a tree, absorbed in the ragged piece of paper. Around him a handful of younger Sonder had gathered. One of them, a Hungarian, spoke a reasonable Polish. "Are we lost, please, sir?" he asked.

"No," said Warszawski, not looking up. "Just getting my bearings."

"Your…. bearings?"

"According to this, if we are where I think we are, there's a railroad bridge that crosses the river two miles just to the east of here, the line to Katowice."

"And this where we go?"

"This where we go. There's a forest on the other side supposed to be full of partisans. If we can make it to that bridge...."

The Hungarian passed this information to his friends, who nodded eagerly. Then to Warszawski, "And we get to bridge soon, sir, you think?"

"With any luck," the Pole said over his shoulder, already walking. Then with a smile, "And if we don't stand here jabbering all day."

But after half an hour more of battling their way through the brush, the fugitives began to wonder how much of a need for hurry there was. Oddly, astoundingly, the SS didn't appear to be following them at all. Certainly not close enough for anyone to have caught either sight or sound of them. As opposed to their slowing down, though, this only quickened the Sonders' pace. Each step wasn't merely a step anymore but a tiny liberation unto itself. Could it be that freedom, actual escape was in their grasp? Gradually, their mood turned from frightened to almost frolicsome, as if they were on some kind of romp instead of running for their lives.

Some cried out before much longer that they could see the river, see it shining through the trees. "Come on!" they yelled. "We've done it, we're almost there!" These ran impetuously ahead, as carried away as children—

Only to crumple to the ground amid an ear-splitting roar before they'd gone twenty meters. What they'd seen was the sun reflecting off the helmets of a line of soldiers, who now emerged from their cover, firing as they advanced.

"Back!" Warszawski screamed. "Everyone fall back! It's the bleeding Krauts!"

For five seconds his men stood there, still as statues, mouths agape. As they began toppling, though, the stampede was on. Suddenly, the air was as thick with bullets as from a swarm of angry hornets. People were dropping all around Warszawski; he saw a boy running past him get hit in the head, the top of it lifting off as neatly as that of an egg tapped with a spoon. His machine gun for the moment was keeping the Nazis at a distance, but wouldn't for long and he knew it. The woods were bristling with more Germans it seemed than trees, not only in front of them now but to the right and left. From out of nowhere they came, as if sprouting from the forest floor like a goblin army from some dark fairy tale. There was no holding back or even slowing down that many, not with one gun.

He stood his ground for as long as he could, then with a final burst turned tail and ran with the others.

They didn't stop until back at the forest's edge where they'd begun, an upshot made the more farcical by the fact they weren't alone. There to meet what was left of them were the two groups they'd separated from earlier, themselves having stumbled back in wild-eyed retreat. Evidently, they'd walked into the same trap Warszawski and his men had.

He wasn't the only Sonder to feel like a dunce. With them just minutes ago starting to crow at its success, their great escape had turned out to be a great big flop; here they were, the whole humbled, pathetic gaggle of them gasping for air under the same shade they'd set out from. Only this time, and soon, they'd be having company. Desperate, they took refuge in a small thicket rising out the middle of a nearby clearing, just large enough to hold the two hundred of them remaining. When the SS arrived, they commenced at their leisure to take up positions in the woods fronting the periphery of this clearing. The men in the thicket soon looked out on an unbroken ring of steel.

He searched the place up and down for Kirschenbaum, but he was one of the many apparently who hadn't made it back. That was too bad; aside from his having taken a liking to the man these past months, they could have used him and his gun for what was to come. While traversing the thicket, he'd studied the German tree line, counted two heavy machine guns, six, seven hundred men. He continued to peruse it now from behind a fallen log, stretched out on his stomach just inside the foliage.

The SS stared back, silent, unmoving. "What are they waiting for?" Warszawski asked himself, not realizing he was asking it out loud. "Why don't they attack?"

"What, you in a hurry or something?" the man lying next to him said, a grin in his voice.

Warszawski recognized him as one of the Maidanek Sonder. A Lieutenant Ustinov, Borodin's second in command. "In a way, yes," he shot back, unable to share the Russian's breeziness. "I mean, what good does it do to prolong it?"

"That I'm not sure, but speaking for myself, I'd just as soon prolong it indefinitely."

Warszawski, smiling in spite of himself, felt the iron band compressing his skull relax a bit. Maybe this funnyman of a lieutenant had the right idea. "Your name is Ustinov, right?"

"That depends."

"On what?"

"To you, I am Georgi Ustinov, First Lieutenant, Red Army. To them," he said, nodding toward the Germans, then drawing back his sleeve to bare the tattoo, "I am R-5212."

"So, R-5212, answer me this. How does a Soviet officer such as yourself come to speak Polish? And by that I mean better than some Poles I know."

"I was stationed in Bialystock for two years," he said, "until the summer of '41. We all were, which was where all nineteen of us, more or less, learned the language. And where we were captured when the Nazis decided they were tired of sharing what was left of your country with us dirty Bolsheviks. Then, regrettably for them, made the mistake of marching into ours. We nineteen, we suspect, are all that is left of our regiment."

Warszawski had never got to know the Maidanek POWs. They'd been a clannish bunch, sticking mostly to themselves. This Ustinov was about the same age as he, and like him short and sinewy, not a lot of meat on him. Unlike him, though, the man didn't seem the least perturbed by the fix they were in. The pale blue eyes beneath the blondish hair were calm, the mouth a gentle smirk; he might have been sitting in a sidewalk bistro somewhere, sipping his wine and watching the girls go by, than here in this death trap of a woods about to breathe his last.

"So what do you figure happened back there?" Warszawski said, referring to the rout in the forest. "It's as if the Krauts read our minds."

"And that surprises you?" The smirk deepened, but for a second only. "Actually, if you think about it, it's not as mystifying as it looks. They had to have known we'd make a dash for the Vistula—given our exit point, where else were we supposed to go? So they made sure to get there first, and instead of having to chase after us, sat there and waited for us to come to them. After that, it was like tightening a net around a school of fish. They probably set out for the river before we did. Before we even left the crematorium yard."

"Two steps ahead of us, as usual," Warszawski muttered. "Oh well, nothing to be done about it now. Except prepare the men."

"Prepare them for what?" Ustinov said absently, intent on the Germans again.

"Why, to fight, what else? The bastard SS aren't going to sit there forever."

"Fight?" He turned toward Warszawski, an amused look on his face. "Fight with what, may I ask? How many bullets do you have left for that gun of yours?"

He waited, but no answer.

"And it, unless you happened to find your friend Kirschenbaum, our only machine gun. As for pistols, we have three, I've already counted." Ustinov held up a 6-mm. "And this one as in need of ammo as that worthless thing you're holding. There might be a few grenades, a little dynamite maybe, but…." He didn't finish. Didn't have to.

"What are you saying?" Warszawski asked, annoyed. "That we surrender, give up? You do understand, I hope, that we're dead either way."

"We've already given up, or haven't you noticed? Good God, look around you! Look at your men!" With a sweep of his arm, he indicated the shadowy interior of the thicket.

Some of the Sonder were curled up crying softly to themselves. Others milled about as in a daze. Most, however, just sat there, a vacant look on their faces, that expression people wore when they didn't care anymore. When death seemed as acceptable a solution as any. That they were cornered and virtually defenseless didn't help, but Warszawski couldn't but feel that even if it were more of an equal fight, they would still have lacked the will to break the grip of the defeat strangling them. To have caught a whiff of the heady perfume of freedom only to have it snatched away was asking too much of men, of *boys*, who'd suffered so deeply for so long.

He knew then it was all over. And if any doubt lingered, it was squashed a moment later. "Look at that," said Ustinov, pointing to his left. "I guess that about settles it."

A team of soldiers was rolling two howitzers into place on the Nazi line. Redeployed from Crematorium II, where they hadn't been of use after all, they'd ended up here where they could be. Indeed, they were more than capable of reducing the thicket to a heap of splinters. This was what the SS poised at the edge of the trees had been waiting for; no sense incurring needless casualties when the rebels could be dispatched from a safe distance.

As much as Warszawski would have rather gone out in a blaze of glory, he questioned what glory was to be got from being pounded to pieces from afar. He did consider gathering around him those Sonder of a like mind as he and mounting a suicide charge against the Germans. Maybe even manage to take some of the muckers with them. But this would have condemned the men remaining in the thicket to the mutilating terrors of the cannons, a worse death than the bullet in the head likely awaiting them.

No, the Russian, though technically he hadn't come out and said it, was right. There was only one thing to do, and Warszawski had already decided he had to be the one to do it. He wouldn't have felt comfortable asking somebody else.

Moments later, he stepped tentatively from the thicket into the clearing, waving a stick with a white shirt attached. Expecting any second to be gunned down, instead it wasn't long before a group of soldiers filed from the woods with weapons pointed and ordered the Sonder to come out with their hands up.

After disarming them and forming them into a column, the SS marched their prisoners back toward the camp. As they retraced the open ground they'd crossed with such high hopes earlier, they could hear off to the south, miles away, the faint, fragmented cadence of a battle in progress. If anything could wring the scantest jot of something resembling cheer from the black depths of their despair, it would be this, for it meant the revolt hadn't been confined to them alone. Somewhere out there were Sonder that had thrown off their chains and had yet to be subdued, who from the sound of it were giving the Nazis all they could handle.

In reality, though, the sound was deceptive. The rebels fleeing Crematorium II were having difficulties of their own. Things at first had gone well. With the martyr Deresinski having allowed them to blow a path through the barbed wire, they ran, still within the confines of the camp and as planned, down the road that bordered the women's *B1b* lager. On impulse, Gradowski and the teenaged Wrubel stopped, and to give any who wished to follow them the opportunity, dynamited a segment of this lager's fence as well. It was a chivalrous gesture, but an empty one; most of the women were away at work, those few hunkered in their huts too spooked by all the shooting and shouting to leave them.

After penetrating the camp perimeter at a side gate and reaching the woods, the escapees organized themselves into groups of twenty. These headed south by different routes in the direction of the Sola marshes. In addition to the SS pursuing them from behind, however, they soon found themselves facing units from the subcamps of Budy, Rajsko, and Jawischowitz. The Germans in the area had mobilized faster than foreseen, and before they knew it, the Sonder were surrounded.

Despite repeated attempts, they were unable to break the Nazi encirclement. This slugfest in the forest ground on for an hour and a half, and wouldn't have lasted that long but for the weapons the rebels were able to snag from their fallen enemy. Even with these, and as furiously as they fought, they didn't stand a chance. The battered remnant of them that remained, little more than forty individuals, many of them wounded, came at length upon an abandoned barn half-swallowed by the trees. Though even as they piled into it they knew they would never leave it, this was fine by them. Not only were they exhausted, they couldn't have asked for better cover. Here their pursuers were going to have to come in and get them, and when they did, the Sonder had enough fight in them still to make them wish they hadn't.

But even this was to be denied them. The SS, after tracking them there, and upon appraising the situation, rejected the idea of an assault on the barn in favor of setting it afire and smoking their prey out. A few swipes from a machine gun were enough to ignite the ancient thatch of the roof, and soon the gray straw was smoldering in three places.

Kapo Kalniak sat with his back against the barn wall, his rifle in his lap. There was no need to keep a vigil against attack; at the first sign of smoke curling in through the vaulted ceiling, he knew what the Germans were up to. Nor was he alone. Even in the dimness of the windowless old building's interior, the only light that which filtered in through the cracks in the warped planking, he could see in the expressions of the men around him the struggle already taking place in their heads: whether to surrender and give the hated SS the satisfaction of shooting them, or stay where they were and burn alive.

He glanced to his left and the Russian major sitting next to him. He'd always admired this officer and his compatriots from Maidanek for their unfailing bravado, their ability to laugh in the face of whatever came their way. He sought to emulate that now.

"I've heard of jumping from the frying pan into the fire," he said, "but this is ridiculous. I never thought I'd say such a thing, but I'm starting to wish I was back in dear old Birkenau."

Borodin smiled tiredly. "I must congratulate you on your sense of humor," he said. "Especially coming as it does from someone covered in blood." Kalniak was still clotted top to bottom with the gore from his encounter with the Nazi corporal back in the crematorium. "Where were you shot, the side of the head there?"

"Not there or anywhere. I wasn't shot at all. But that's a whole other kettle of fish, and I've something more important we need to discuss."

"And not," Borodin added, looking at the ceiling, "a lot of time to discuss it in."

"My point exactly." Kalniak followed his gaze, and could see not only smoke now but flame licking at the wood. "I'd say that roof has another twenty minutes in it tops. Which means every man here has a decision to make, and pronto. I for one have no desire to be grilled like a lamb chop, but neither do I wish to be stood like some poor sniveling deportee before a firing squad. Or worse, be captured and later tortured for information.

"On the other hand," and here he paused, "there is a third option. Nor would I think a man smart as yourself need be told what it is."

Borodin had to think on this a moment. Finally, helped by the insinuating rise of the kapo's eyebrows, he got it. "Let me make sure I understand. What you're saying is we ought to…. take matters into our own hands?"

"It's the only way. We're dead meat anyway, major, there's no getting around it. It's not a question of if anymore, but how. And apart from guaranteeing us as clean and quick an end as possible, the 'how' I'm suggesting would also send a message to our friends in gray out there: we Sonder may have lost the battle, that's true, but by dying how and when we choose, not on your terms but ours—as free men and not slaves—we win the war. Not by snatching victory but dignity from defeat. And if you SS supermen, you elite of the Third Reich don't like it, tough shit. You can kiss our dead Jewish asses."

Borodin, too, cradled a machine gun in his lap, which he looked down at now as if waiting for it to tell him what to do. When at last he raised his eyes, there could be no mistaking what shone in them.

"Let me just say this: it's as hard to find fault with your logic, kapo, as it is your profanity."

"You with me on this then?"

"I'm with anybody who would give me the opportunity to tell the Krauts, even if posthumously, to kiss my ass."

"Good." The big bear of a Pole drug himself to his feet. "Maybe you can help me find out who might be leaning the same way, and see if we can't change the minds of those who aren't."

Their success would prove spotty. So obstinate were some of the mostly younger Sonder in holding on to life, that against all reason they convinced themselves there might be a chance the Nazis would feel they couldn't manage without them, that after today and the depletion of their ranks, skilled crematorium workers would be in demand. Upon these deluded souls, all appeals to common sense and self-respect were wasted. Once the fire that by then had engulfed the ceiling began sending fingers of flame down the walls, and before that ceiling could collapse, fifteen of them ran out the barn door with their hands in the air, begging the soldiers not to shoot.

A heavy machine gun cut their entreaties short, and within seconds the lot of them lay dead or dying. But as the Germans waited for the rest to show, it began to sink in there might not be any others. This was given further credence when a series of shots sounded from within the barn, not directed at them, but *inward*. These went on for some minutes, one shot at a time, until there was only silence, a silence that said it all, as loud in its implication as the blasting of artillery.

The SS looked at each other, unclear what to do. Finally, the order came to machine-gun the Sonder redoubt from front to rear and back again. When this drew no response, a half dozen soldiers crept from the woods to investigate. On reaching the barn door, cringing before the heat, they peered inside and found what they and everyone were pretty much expecting. Vivid in the yellow-orange light of the fire, upward of thirty corpses littered the floor, a bullet to the head of each.

To keep the blaze from consuming them, the camp's fire-control detail was called and told to hurry. The Kommandantur, as the men in the field were correct in assuming, would require an accurate body count later to make certain none of its pigeons had flown the coop.

That some in fact had, their keepers weren't to discover until the day was almost done. In the running battle preceding the showdown at the barn, two of the Sonder groups fleeing south found their way blocked by the SS reinforcements from Budy, and had no choice but to make a right turn to the west and the Vistula. This, however, put them on a collision course with an even bigger force that had entered the forest from the subcamp of Harmense to the north.

The firefight that ensued was brief. With Harmense in front of them and Budy on their flank, in addition to a platoon from Birkenau still hot on their trail from behind, these rebels, like their comrades, ended up surrounded. But in the chaos, and by dint of sheer luck, twelve of them happened to stumble upon a momentary gap in the German advance and blundered through it unnoticed without even realizing they had.

The farther they ran, the weaker the gunfire and explosions behind them. But not until the trees thinned, enabling them to see a good distance ahead and still there were no soldiers, did they dare to think they might have slipped the Nazi noose.

Handelsman was one of these fortunate few, and Gradowski, and Wrubel. It was he, forging far in front on his eighteen-year-old legs, who after cresting a small rise was the first to spy the river. He let out an excited whoop.

"The Vistula!" he shouted. "I can see it! Come on!"

It was wide at this point, but still low from the rainless summer; here and there a white sandbar poked above the surface like the back of some monster fish. The Sonder spilled down a steep bank to the water's edge, shucked their backpacks and shoes, and tied the latter to their belts. It looked to be a formidable swim, but they figured if they took it in stages, hopping from one sandbar to the next, they should be all right.

Once in the water, though, they discovered the current was stronger than they'd anticipated. Instead of being able to hold a straight line, they were soon drifting harum-scarum downstream. For the less athletic among them, it was the fight of their lives, but they hadn't come this far only to drown. With the help of the sandbars, if many a backpack was lost, all twelve wound up making it to the other side.

But so spread out were they by then, it took them a while to locate each other and regroup. Nor after their bout with the current could they stop and catch their second wind; they had to act on the premise that German patrols were searching this side of the river, too. Soon they were plowing a path through another woods thicker than the previous, the trees spindly but their branches low to the ground and packed tight. Scratched and bleeding from these, sweating like mules, after an hour they were beginning to wonder how much farther they could go.

Suddenly, as if by magic, for none had seen it coming through the impermeable wall of trees, they were standing in a plowed field stubbled with straw. The land to the horizon was an unbroken quilt of such fields, treeless but for the occasional copse resembling a cluster of broccoli. Less than a mile away, they could see a silo and barn, a farmhouse with a ribbon of smoke coiling from the chimney.

"What do you think?" said Gradowski. "It'll be dark before too much longer."

"I'm about stove in," said the man Tevek. "We could at least hide out in his barn until we regained our strength some." And from a young Greek in crude Polish: "Food maybe he gives us."

"I don't know," Handelsman said. "Who's to say he can be trusted?"

"We can't," said Gradowski, "but I'm with Tevek. I'm not sure how much more I can—"

He stopped in mid-sentence, and all eyes followed his. A man had appeared from out of the farmhouse and stood gazing their way. Nor could there be any question it was them he was looking at.

Handelsman shrugged. "Well, that clinches it," he said, and started walking toward the house. Relieved, the others fell in behind him. "Let's just hope our farmer here doesn't hate Jews more than he does Nazis."

As the day hastened to wind down and the sun to lose strength, so too did the revolt. The unearthly caterwaul of the siren had long ago ceased, along with the sounds of battle to the south. That eerie, suffocating silence peculiar to the death camp descended once again on the kingdom of Auschwitz-Birkenau.

But that wasn't the end of it, not yet. Not as far as the infuriated SS were concerned. Though Crematorium IV's fire had been put out, well over half the building was a charred wreck. In back of this ruin, in that part of the yard devoid of grass, the roughly two hundred Sonder who'd surrendered in the thicket lay face down in the dirt, alive but bloodied.

After being marched back to the scene of their earlier triumph and ordered onto their stomachs, their guards had gone to work on them with the butts of their rifles and other clubs. Unable to contain their anger any longer, they'd waded into the prostrate rows of those who'd dared to rise against them. This went on until there wasn't a rebel who'd escaped their wrath, nor a soldier who didn't feel better at having vented it.

Eventually, they were joined on the ground by a random assortment from Crematorium II. These consisted of those prisoners who hadn't fled the building, some from a last-minute failure of nerve (of which there was a smattering from Number Four as well), some who'd left too late and got themselves captured, and a few because they weren't a part of the revolt in the first place and had been found still at their posts. These last, mainly the squad's chief physician and his assistants, were exonerated after a quick investigation and released. Everyone else was kept prone and at gunpoint, the Germans prowling among them begging them to utter a single word or even raise their heads so as to give them an excuse to blow those heads off.

While there wasn't a Sonder who didn't see what was coming, as the minutes stretched into an hour and nothing happened, an obdurate handful clung to hope. What they couldn't know was that the Nazis were merely waiting to find out if there were to be any more prisoners, namely those that might have surrendered in the fighting to the south.

Once it was confirmed, however, that no further captives had been taken, the SS at Crematorium IV were free to bring things to a close. To those of the doomed still thinking they might somehow make it through this, the thought evaporated at the sound of the first pistol shot. Even on their stomachs, heads flat to the ground, many could make out their executioners as they began moving among them, administering the fatal bullet Sonder by Sonder.

Warszawski lay at the extreme northern end of one of the farther rows. To his right was the perimeter's barbed wire and the woods beyond, on his immediate left a man, more a boy actually, whom he recognized at once as an old enemy, the Hungarian Svoboda of all people. Since an earlier scrap months ago, each had made it a point to stay away from the other, or as far away as space and the Germans would permit. Yet here they were in the last minutes of life left them so close they were practically touching each other.

Far from startling him, the bang of the guns barely registered with Warszawski. Not only had he resigned himself to their inevitability the moment he was ordered to his belly, by the time they did appear, his attention was elsewhere. Focused on things both ordinary and strangely unfamiliar at the same time. Never had the trees looked so green, the sky so boisterous a blue. He could hardly tear his eyes from the creamy, billowing beauty of the late-afternoon clouds. The birdsong emanating from the woods sounded as intricate as a symphony, the buzzing of some bees the violin section. With death footsteps away, his time on this earth running down like the sand in an hourglass, his senses donned wings, and as if to make the most of that time, flew him to heights unvisited until now. The soil against which his cheek pressed wasn't just dirt anymore, but a whole little universe of glittering, microscopic silica and cosmic dust. The breeze on his flesh was as cool, as intimate as a lover's touch. He even fancied he could hear the electricity humming in the barbed wire—or was it something else, the hum and throb perhaps that since the beginning of creation had pulsed through every living cell of every plant and animal, that indefinable energy which hadn't only sparked life but continued each second of every day to sustain it?

As out there, even goofball as this was, he found it comforting. Even more the thought that seemed naturally to grow out of it. His hyperkinetic ways having hidden it from him before—those senses of his shuttered his whole life by him hurrying through it without ever stopping to smell its flowers—he saw now with the suddenness and clarity of, well, a gunshot, that he and the birds and the trees and the dirt, even the clouds and the sky with its stars not yet shining, were all part of the same fabric, the same warp and woof of existence, the essential substance of one indistinguishable from the other. That he was about to return to this oneness from which he'd come, from which everything came, filled him with a peace greater than any he could remember. He heard the pistols all right, but didn't. Knew what they meant, but couldn't have cared less.

It helped, of course, that there was another person close by. This end-of-life epiphany of his was all well and good, but it would have been harder to die without having someone to say goodbye to. That this had turned out to be Svoboda only figured, not that he was complaining. In view of the circumstances, did it really matter who it was?

Svobodá had entered the commando late, shortly after the bollixed June attempt at revolt. He'd kept mostly to himself, shying from conversation, except when the talk turned to taking another stab at it. Then he was all ears, eager to hear every detail, loud in hectoring the others to action, to a resumption of arms. Somehow Warszawski got it in his head the boy was a German plant, put there by *Hauptscharführer* Möll to sniff out any further subversiveness. Nor did he try to hide his suspicions. Upon these reaching Svoboda, there was a confrontation, ending badly in what would later prove an unwarranted display of fisticuffs. For the Hungarian wasn't a spy at all, simply one of the more dedicated Nazi-haters among them. Warszawski tried to make amends, but the other would have none of it. The insult had been too great. This only aroused the former's resentment, and stiff-necked as both were, they'd kept the feud alive.

He looked to his left and stared until Svoboda's eyes found his, large, elliptical brown eyes that winced slightly at each crack of the guns. Other than that, they revealed nothing, the dark, gypsy-like features unreadable. From out the curly mop of black hair, a thread of bright red coursed down his forehead. Warszawski, too, could taste blood in his mouth.

"You're not frightened, son?" he was fortunate to be able to ask in his native tongue. Everybody who knew Svoboda at all knew also that his father, half Polish, had bequeathed him the language.

The young Hungarian studied him silently for a moment, then untensed some. "I'd be lying if I said I wasn't, but not as afraid as I thought I'd be."

Warszawski had a feeling the rest of the men in the yard were of the same mind. It wasn't as if the air was free of weeping, but it was nowhere near what it could have been. There was a manliness to this, a nobility that almost brought a tear to *his* eye, not one of pity for, but pride in the mettle of those around him. The kid beside him. Deeper felt than any tear, a sudden tenderness toward this Svoboda swept over him, and with it the urge to reach out to him, to try and blunt the sharp edges of the fear that he knew, despite appearances, had to be working on the boy.

If that boy would let him. "When I was a few years younger than you," Warszawski hazarded, "maybe fifteen, I found my grandfather, who was living with us, dead in his room. He wasn't that old, but had a bad heart, so bad he ended up confined to his bed. It was morning, and I'd been sent upstairs with his breakfast. He was sitting propped up with a book in his lap, but I could tell he was dead from halfway across the room. His eyes were open but unblinking, his body as wooden and stiff-looking as the headboard against which it leaned. My instinct was to bolt for the stairs and raise the alarm, but as panicked as I was, I didn't. You know why?"

Svoboda shook his head.

"The expression on his face. Stopped me right in my tracks. And not, as you might be thinking, because it was horrible. A regular soup of emotions was bubbling inside me, emotions to be expected of a child in that situation—fear, horror, disgust, and not least of all, grief, for I'd loved my grandfather and here he was, gone. But overriding them all, and what kept me from running downstairs, was the look that had frozen itself on that face.

"I set the breakfast tray down and walked up to the bed. That the end had been quick was clear; pain hadn't had a chance to leave its mark. But instead of the fright or at least surprise you'd have thought distorting his features, the lips were parted in a little smile, the eyes brimming over with…. I don't know, call it wonder. Or more like longing maybe. I can't describe it still, but never will I forget it."

Warszawski spat out some dirt that had got in his mouth. "Not at the time that I knew what to make of it. Not at fifteen. What was it that my grandfather had seen in his last moments, perhaps *the* last moment, to leave him looking so, for want of a better word, happy? How, I asked myself, could dying be anything but a sadness? It was only later that I came to suspect—and just a few minutes ago, made-up as it may sound, finally realized for a fact—what that face of his was trying to tell me, his last if unintended gift to his grandson: that death isn't a thing to be feared or even mourned. That it isn't the end of anything, but rather a beginning. Not a door being shut so much as one opening."

Svoboda continued to betray no emotion, his face as impassive as before. Warszawski started to think maybe he was wasting his breath after all, until he noticed that the boy was no longer flinching at the bark of the guns.

"I never did really grieve for my grandfather. It would have been selfish to be anything but glad for him. Not only was he freed of that illness which had made an invalid of him, he'd gone to that place, that uncharted country he'd glimpsed through death's curtain, to enjoy whatever it was that had shown itself to him. The same country we're about to enter ourselves."

As if to underscore this last, a pistol went off louder than any previous; the German gunmen had arrived at the row of prisoners directly behind them. Svoboda didn't look at Warszawski when he spoke, but beyond him, as at something in the distance.

"So what awaits us," he asked, "in this.... country of yours?"

"I'm not sure. Who still in this world can say he knows for certain? It isn't, however, as if I haven't given it a lot of thought over the years."

"And what have you come up with?"

"The same thing that awaited my grandfather. What awaits everyone who travels there."

"Which is?"

"What you've lost in this life that's dearest to you. Either that or something you never had to begin with, but should have. What, if you could only have or have back again, you wouldn't want for anything more."

When Svoboda's eyes returned to his, they weren't the same. No longer inscrutable stone, they'd become two revealing wells of sorrow, openings into a soul in which pain had taken up permanent residence. Warszawski had but to glance at them to understand. How many pairs of eyes like this had he had the misfortune to look into?

"You didn't come to Birkenau alone, did you, son?" he said. "Your whole family was with you."

Svoboda could only nod, his lower lip beginning to tremble.

Warszawski smiled and held out his hand. The boy took it, and after biting his lip until it trembled no more, responded with a pallid smile of his own. When it came their turn and the SS stood over them, they were still holding hands. One of the soldiers nudged the other in the ribs.

"Look, here's another two," he snorted as he reloaded his gun.

After they finished the last of the rebels off, the Germans didn't burn the bodies right away. It was imperative first that they take a final tally of this vagabond 12th Squad; it wouldn't do to leave a single bearer of their secret unaccounted for. They began by matching their personnel lists against both the dead they had on hand and the living who'd sat out the revolt. While this was going on, having already taken care of their own dead and wounded, they had the forests scoured for Sonder corpses and these trucked to Crematorium IV for identification.

Assigned to this task was the crew from Number Five, along with thirty prisoners hastily conscripted from the general population. Unknown to these thirty, though they would learn their fate soon enough, they and the less than two hundred men left from the 12th Kommando were to fill the ranks of the new, reduced 13th.

Once all the bodies were in, and after checking and rechecking their records, the Nazis discovered to their alarm that nineteen men from the old detachment were still missing. Though what was left of Crematorium IV had been picked through earlier, a closer examination turned up the remains of three more Sonder in the debris. This meant a by no means acceptable discrepancy of sixteen. With the sun sinking rapidly, it was decided nonetheless that a night search of both the immediate and surrounding areas be launched. All SS and Gestapo within a radius of a dozen miles were to join in.

It didn't take them long to meet with success. Darkness had yet to descend on the Polish countryside when a farmer in a horse-drawn cart flagged down a patrol out of Birkenau. The soldiers followed him to a barn, where they found the twelve Sonder who hours before had eluded them and crossed the Vistula. They lay fast asleep in the hay, having opted with the farmer's blessing to rest here a while before pushing on under cover of night.

In the rapidly vanishing gray of late twilight, the Germans prodded them awake with the muzzles of their rifles. When the twelve learned they'd been betrayed, they weren't so much angry as sick at heart. To have come this far, this close to pulling off the impossible only to wind up back in the clutches of the Nazi devil! Even as the SS disarmed and frisked them, they muttered among themselves.

Gradowski leaned toward Handelsman. "You think they'll shoot us now or when we get back?"

"I don't know," Handelsman said. "I'm not sure it's either."

"What do you mean?"

"I have a feeling they've something else in store for us."

"Like what?"

"Like Block 35. The interrogation room. Torture. It's what I'd do if I were them, try to wring us for information."

Gradowski hadn't thought of this. "Torture," he said, and shuddered. "My God, I don't know if I—"

"You won't have to. There's no reason to. Not if we choose not to." Handelsman's smile was dark. "I say we die standing up instead of strapped down, go out like men and not so many bloody pieces of meat. I'm for rushing the sonsabitches, ending it right here. Hell, who knows? There are twelve of us and not all that many more of them. If we can get the jump on them…."

Gradowski smiled grimly now himself. "I'd settle for buying just a lousy few seconds. Long enough to get my hands around one of their Kraut necks."

"Count me in," whispered the older Tevek, who'd been listening.

"And me!" hissed another.

"Good," Handelsman said. "Pass the word. And make sure the four Hungarians understand what's going on. Everyone needs to keep his eyes on me, be ready to move when I do."

As it happened, he was right: the Nazis had no intention of shooting anyone. Their orders were to return unharmed any escapees they might come across. Already regretting their impulsiveness at having executed those Sonder they'd taken prisoner, the SS weren't going to make that mistake again. They refused to accept that Birkenau could have acted alone, without help, and saw as they had in June with the captured courier an opportunity in their incessant war against it to gain some ground on Battle Group-Auschwitz. If they played their cards right in the torture chamber, possibly damage it beyond repair.

By now the day had given way to night but for a smudge of gray to the west. The soldiers led their prisoners out of the barn and toward a bridge two miles distant, an electric torch in front and one bringing up the rear. They hadn't gone far when Handelsman darted for the guard nearest him. With a roar the others followed, and instantly all was madness. Wild shouts and the thunder of guns ripped the night apart. The beams of the torches careened crazily about, illuminating a swirl of men running, falling, wrestling, tearing at each other with their bare hands.

Ariel Wrubel managed to grapple his German's machine gun away and blew half the man's head off. Still on his knees, he stitched another up the gut and yet another in the legs before being blasted himself from both the front and rear. Even then, on his back, coughing his life's blood away, he didn't stop squeezing the trigger until they let him have it twice more. Gradowski, his wish granted, strangled his man nearly unconscious before being knocked out himself from behind. Handelsman, too, was only clobbered, not killed. As determined as the twelve Sonder were to die fighting, the Nazis did their best, mindful of their orders, to show restraint. One of their attackers was stopped by a shot to the knee, with three ending up bashed merely senseless.

These were bound hand and foot and a runner sent ahead to fetch a truck. By nine o'clock, two of them sat shackled to chairs in separate interrogation cells. Despite the care taken to get them to that point, however, their Gestapo inquisitors, whether out of anger or overzealousness, came down too hard on the four and wound up bungling the job. By dawn, all but Gradowski were dead. And he, with a fractured skull, slipping in and out of consciousness.

With him of little more use to it now than his murdered accomplices, the Political Department looked to salvage something from its clumsiness. And in the eyes of the SS, there were few things as diverting and at the same time effective at keeping the inmates in line as a good hanging done right. A physician was assigned Gradowski to see that he made it to tomorrow, and carpenters put to work erecting a five-stepped gallows in the yard of Number Four.

The new 13th Kommando was marched there the next morning after breakfast. The weather had cooperated to fit the occasion, an impenetrable fog obscuring everything on the other side of the wire. Even Crematorium V next door had disappeared. The visible world had been reduced to the gutted carcass of the death house, the expanse of the yard itself, and the bright-yellow pine of the scaffold rising from it.

Parading slowly atop this in full-dress black uniform was the patrician figure of *Hauptsturmführer* Franz Hössler. A mix of triumph and disdain pulsed from his face, seeming to darken the air around it. A deathly stillness enveloped the scene, made the more acute by the fog. No calls for quiet were necessary from the guards ringing the assembled men—no one dared even whisper. The only sound was the hollow thump of the captain's boots on the pine.

The silence was soon broken by a Red Cross ambulance coughing to a stop next to the platform. Two *Schützen* slid a stretcher bearing a body out the back and hurried it up the steps to where Hössler was waiting. When they raised it on one end so that it stood vertical to the floor, there hung Gradowski, eyes shut, head swathed in a bloody bandage and lolling to one side, the rest of him tied down with straps so he wouldn't fall out. Suspended above him from its crossbeam was a single crude noose.

Hössler extended an arm dramatically toward him. "Behold the price of disloyalty!" he shouted. "Here is what awaits every dog who would turn on his master!"

Again there was silence, his icy stare sweeping the mass of men at his feet.

"Can you be so blind," he said finally, "as to think you could best the SS? Are you that foolish? There is no prevailing against us, especially not by such as you. It goes against all that is reasonable and right in this world, the natural order of things. Even if the tables were turned, if we Germans were the prisoners and you the guards, it would not stay that way for long. No longer than it would take a lion to get the better of a pack of jackals."

Hössler resumed his pacing, talking as he went. "And where has this mindless stubbornness, this blockheadedness of yours got you? You are still here, and will remain here at our pleasure, but hundreds of your friends and comrades are among us no more. Their lives have been sacrificed for nothing, thrown away in pursuit of the unattainable, in reaching for something that was never there in the first place. You could have prevented this, too, you who stayed put that awful day. But I doubt you even tried. You were as rebellious as they, I'm sure, in word if not deed. You should be ashamed of yourselves! You are as responsible as anyone for this treacherous crime!"

Most of those present had no idea what he was saying, or if so only a sketchy one. What German they did know they'd picked up in the camp. There was no mistaking his poisonous tone, though, nor the gloating expression twisting his features as he continued to rant. They didn't have to understand the words to catch the drift of them.

An exception was Shlomo Kirschenbaum, born and raised in the city of Heidelberg. That he was there to hear the bombastic Hössler at all was by pure chance. Where in the battle on the 7th, Warszawski had presumed him dead when he couldn't find him among those run to ground in the thicket, here Kirschenbaum stood very much alive, his only wound a large knot on the back of his head.

In the forest to the northwest that day, his group, too, had blundered into the SS on its way to the Vistula, and was forced to fall back. It was during this retreat that he ended up a casualty, victim of a grenade. He'd stopped running and had turned to fire a covering burst from his machine gun when a powerful explosion lifted him from his feet. The last thing he remembered was flying through the air, then a blow to the head. Then blackness.

He awoke on his back to someone dragging him by the legs across the ground. Two men actually, both clad in the civilian garb of the Sonder. He cried out, and letting go his legs, they bent over him. Others gathered, curious, and despite his brain not fully working yet, he realized they weren't part of the group he'd been fleeing with. Though Hungarian, one spoke German and said they belonged to Squad 60B, pulled from Crematorium V to help search the woods for bodies. He wasn't the only one they'd found still breathing, but the soldiers, who were everywhere, were shooting those they did. If he wanted to live, he'd better try to stand up.

With some assistance, he was able to, but it took him a minute before he could walk on his own; his pounding head felt so large and unconnected to the rest of him, it was as if he were balancing a pumpkin on his shoulders. During that minute, his rescuers checked him over for wounds, but aside from an ugly bump on his skull, there were none. No trace of blood, either. Somehow the shrapnel from the grenade hadn't even nicked him.

For almost two days now, Kirschenbaum had been waiting for the denunciatory tap on the back. But it had yet to come. The SS appeared to suspect nothing. Later, he would learn that three others from Crematorium IV had also escaped death, one by hiding in the metal flues beneath the floor of the destroyed oven room, two in the belt of trees separating IV and V. The next day, all snuck their way back into the commando, where they blended right in, no questions asked. Upon a subsequent roll call turning up the four Sonder still missing, the Nazis were more than satisfied. They figured that in the confusion of that riotous Saturday, with bodies coming in from all over, they'd simply miscounted and left it at that.

German may have been Kirschenbaum's first language, but that didn't keep Hössler's rantings from being lost on him. He'd ceased listening to this Moshe Liar soon after he'd started spewing his venom. It wasn't as if he hadn't heard it all before, a thousand times before, could probably have finished the *Hauptsturmführer's* speech for him. Tuning him out, he scanned the rows of men around him. This was the first time since the revolt and the massacres it spawned that the 13th Squad had assembled as a whole. Though the majority still bunked in the attic of Crematorium III, a good amount, himself included, had come to call the undressing room of Number Five home.

What he was searching for in the crowd were old faces, if without much success. He did spot Zalman Leventhal a little off to his right, the redhead to his surprise crying softly. He'd long known that he and Gradowski were friends, but hadn't thought the mumpish Leventhal capable of tears.

To his left stood the tall, beanpole figure of Leyb Langfus, also visibly upset, but in a different way. He glared malignantly at Hössler as he spoke, making no attempt to hide his loathing for both the officer and the barbarity he was conducting. Kirschenbaum could relate: hanging an unconscious man, for God's sake! There was an excessiveness to it that communicated pure malice, as if less to deter the Sonder from repeating the folly of rebellion than to rub their noses in the one they'd already fomented.

There were others he recognized that he'd come to know over the months. Filip Müller, the young Sudeten Czech who'd been a Sonder as long as anybody—now twenty, he was seventeen when sentenced to the crematorium. He could have passed for seventeen still but for the centuries-old eyes that stared back at one. Some of the Greeks had been around forever, too, and the Frenchman Maurice what's-his-name, a handful of Russians. There were, however, far fewer remaining than not; almost five hundred of the detachment were gone that had been there three mornings ago. What Kirschenbaum couldn't decide was whether his having been spared was a plus or a minus. On top of the revolt ending up a train wreck, it being for so long his only reason for living, if having to sit through many more such spectacles as today's lay ahead of him, he'd just as soon the grenade in the woods had finished him off.

He was being facetious, of course, if at the moment not entirely. Among his myriad foibles, some of which, to the uninitiated, were often

mistaken for charm, SS-Captain Franz Hössler was a born ham. He loved
to be center stage, regardless if called upon to play the likable guy, the good
Nazi, or more to his taste, the bad. On this occasion, it being the latter, and
the offense in question so reprehensible, he could have railed against those
guilty of it indefinitely. But what before had been a negligible wind began
suddenly to gust, whisking the fog away to reveal ominous clouds closing
fast. Hössler turned his face into the breeze and smelled rain, figured he'd
better get on with the festivities.

He stood legs apart at the front of the platform, arms crossed. "I would
advise you of the 13th to listen to what I have to say in conclusion, and listen
well. Should you be tempted again to think you can win freedom with a
gun, know that you won't be the only ones to die. Next time there will be
others, thousands of others, we'll take out the whole camp and not give
it a second thought. We have a plan set aside for just that, all we've been
waiting for is the justification to use it.

"Do not give us that justification! I warn you, don't push us! Or the
blood of your people will be on your hands, not ours."

With that, he spun on his heel and made for the insensible Gradowski,
still vertical in his stretcher. Reaching up, he pinched him on the cheek.
Again, then slapped him hard across the face. A groan arose from the
Sonder watching, half protest, half plea.

"Shut your traps!" shouted Sergeant Gorges, Hössler's second in
command. As the ex-*Kommandoführer* of Crematorium IV, he'd been
granted this privilege. "One more sound and you will regret it!"

Another slap, and slowly Gradowski's eyes fluttered open. He didn't
know where he was at first; raising his head, he looked about him in
bewilderment. Once the noose was slipped around his neck and made
snug, though, he appeared to understand, looking more sad than afraid.
Kirschenbaum saw him lean forward, and as with the last of his strength,
say something that only the men in the front rows could hear.

Hössler saw it, too, and wasn't the type to share this or any podium.
Quickly, he gave the order and the rope was pulled taut, lifting Gradowski
into the air, stretcher and all. Half dead as he was, the end didn't take long;
a few feeble twitches, a last gasping for breath, and it was over. At that exact
moment, it began to rain heavy, bullet-sized drops, a timing some would
describe later as the heavens weeping in commiseration.

But the mood in the undressing room of Crematorium V that evening wasn't all bleak. A pall, to be sure, hung over the Sonder grouped around their cots, but their grief was offset some by what Gradowski had said at the end. Inaudible at the time to most, it was now known to all. "I am the last," he'd declared, a statement interpreted by those discussing it that night to mean somehow he knew there were to be no more interrogations. That the Nazis had decided to terminate their investigation. This was of special relief to those conspirators remaining from the 12th Squad, every one of who feared he might be arrested next. They could only thank Gradowski, as they saw it, for making his last utterance the dispelling of that fear.

Consoling them further was the news, broken by Battle Group-Auschwitz just prior to the rebellion, that the Red Army was as close as a hundred miles away. With the Russians a possible matter of weeks distant, one had to think the SS would have more pressing concerns than ferreting out those who might know something about an affair that hadn't only come and gone but resolved itself in their favor.

Or as Kirschenbaum heard one of them sitting in the group opposite him ask, "Why would the Krauts persist in crying over the glass of spilled milk that was the revolt with the Bolsheviks on the verge of overrunning the whole dairy?"

The man could very well have been right, but he wasn't buying it. For one thing, he'd ceased to trust Auschwitz a long time ago, and smelled a rat this time, too. It would have been just like them to try to defuse the Sonder powder keg that first week of October by implying that the Russians and liberation were near. Funny that they'd release so seductive a morsel of information at the same time they were begging Birkenau to be patient.

But even if it was the truth, a hundred miles was a hundred miles. Which unless certain conditions were conducive might as well have been a thousand. What, for example, was the extent of German forces in the area, how imposing the Wehrmacht's defenses? Were the Soviets on the offensive or was the front static? What position did Poland occupy in their strategy at this juncture—were there more pressing objectives in the Baltics to the north, the Balkans to the south? A dozen variables were at play and had to be weighed, each of which might find the Russians still a hundred miles away three months from now.

The thing fretting Kirschenbaum the most, however, was the absence of significant, or for that matter, *any* change in the behavior of the SS. A slim two days after the *Sturm und Drang* of Saturday, it was business as usual at Birkenau, the same old routine, the transports continuing to chug in, the chimneys to smoke, the Aussenkommandos to march to work to the music of the camp orchestra in the morning. The Nazis were their usual arrogant, and unless provoked, indifferent selves, not a trace of anxiety in either their faces or speech. All that appeared to concern them was the only thing he'd seen them really care about since he'd been here: that the machinery of extermination be kept well-oiled and running, the assembly line moving, the requisite *ordnungsgëssemer Ablauf*, that orderly procedure so dear to the German heart, maintained as before. They revealed nothing to show they knew the Red Army even existed, much less stood poised scant miles away to descend upon the camp like a plague of locusts.

I am the last.... A touching, one could even say charitable farewell, but to Kirschenbaum impossibly enigmatic as well. Maybe even chiding. The last of the plotters to be held accountable, or the last to have turned words into action and risen against their persecutors? Or if on the off chance directed at the SS—not likely, but not out of the question—a final attempt to try and deter them from making any more arrests? There was no way to know, and as a result less than solid ground on which to tether one's hopes. Yet here he was in a room filled with men doing just that.

He decided he'd had enough for the night. It had been a long, ugly day, and not just because of the Gradowski shamefulness. After leaving the body in its stretcher swaying in the storm, the Sonder found a transport awaiting them, and he'd been tapped to serve in its incineration. He could have stayed up half the night, if he'd a mind to, playing devil's advocate to his bunking mates, but aside from the fact he was worn-out both physically and emotionally, a lot of good that would have done. They were clearly in no mood to hear anything that might throw doubt on their theory.

Besides, what would it accomplish if he were to burst their bubble? That would have been just mean—kinder to let them live in denial while they could. They'd find out soon enough that as opposed to being over, the Nazi inquiry into the events of the 7th seemed from where he was sitting to be only beginning. Anyone familiar with the SS had to figure as much. As long as Soviet guns remained too distant to hear, the men with the silver skulls on their collars and the black of night in their hearts weren't likely to rest until all who'd had the gall to defy them had been flushed out and extinguished.

He drug his cot a little way from the others, where they couldn't disturb him with their naivete, he them with his skepticism. He didn't fall right to sleep, though, tired as he was. As he'd done the previous two nights, and could envision himself doing for many more to come, he lay awake in delicious contemplation of the two Germans he'd killed in battle. How many others he'd wounded who might have died later, he didn't know. But these two were confirmed fatalities, of that there could be no doubt: the one in the watchtower who'd got it in the head, and the other in the forest he'd shot through the heart.

He was not by disposition a bloodthirsty man. Indeed, until Birkenau and the Sonderkommando, the sight of blood had made him queasy. But with the uprising squelched, if Kirschenbaum could be said to have one pleasure left it was replaying in his mind's eye the taking of those two SS lives. Nor was it because of what he personally had suffered in the crematoria at the hands of their insidious fraternity. Or the by far more inexpiable misery it had inflicted on his people, the torture and murder of what had to be millions by now—

But rather the murder of two. That's all, just two, his wife and little boy, both whom he'd picked out of a pile of corpses what felt like a hundred years ago and carried in his own arms to the fire pits in the meadow. It was because of them that he felt warm all over whenever he recalled the two soldiers, because of them that he lay there tonight killing them all over again. And would until sleep drew its cloak over him.

Two for two, it was only fair. If that wasn't justice, what was? An eye for an eye, it was in the Bible no less, a verse so famous the Gentiles had co-opted it, and with as telling a gesture as any of Gentile respect, given it a Latin name. The *lex talionis*, the law of retaliation…. there it was for all to read, in the damn Bible. To use another Latinism, how much more of an imprimatur did a person need?

In fact, if Shlomo Kirschenbaum had still believed in God, which after two years working first the meadows then the crematoria he most decidedly did not, he'd have thought the elegant symmetry of two for two a sign from above.

*   *   *

Coincidental to the revolt of the Sonderkommando having run its course, the main thrust of the gargantuan Soviet summer offensive was also grinding to a halt, if of its own impetus. The final phase of this offensive, named for the fiery Russian prince who'd died fighting Napolean a century and a quarter earlier, Operation Bagration had torn the eastern front wide open and broken the back of the Wehrmacht there once and for all. Three German armies totaling almost half a million men were destroyed, along with two thousand tanks and heavy artillery pieces, hundreds of aircraft. Not only had Bagration reclaimed the Ukraine and Byelorussia in their entireties, along with much of Poland, but save for a few isolated pockets the Baltic republics as well. Which meant that for the first time since the Nazi invasion of 1941, the war in the east would be fought on foreign and not Russian soil.

But none of this had been easily won. The Red Army's losses were even greater than the Wehrmacht's, the difference being that while the Russians possessed both the men and matériel to replace them, the Germans did not. All the same, come October the Soviet giant was exhausted. Except for continued fighting in the Balkans, it would remain relatively quiet for the rest of the year, regrouping and refitting for the final push to Berlin. So that while its forces had indeed driven to a line not all that far from Auschwitz-Birkenau, there they would stay until on the move again in January.

Though the SS of both camps were hardly oblivious to the menace at their doorstep, what concerns they did have they were careful not to show. When the subject did come up in conversation, as when it did in the rest of Hitler's dwindling Third Reich, it was invariably accompanied by the stated if not always heartfelt conviction that their *Führer* would yet save the day, either by means of his legendary cunning, the introduction of a game-changing secret weapon, or some other miracle of arms. With the result that on the surface Nazi hauteur was little altered from what it had been two years ago, when both the Russians and the possibility of defeat seemed a million miles away.

Where the proximity of the avenging Bolsheviks did discernibly affect them was in the negative attitude most displayed toward an investigation into the revolt of the Sonderkommando. As many of the squad's members had predicted, the Germans had more on their minds than getting to the bottom of a plot it had taken them but hours and a minimum of effort to crush. Not that there was any forgetting the casualties they'd incurred that bloody Saturday, but the resentment this bred had been sated somewhat by those they'd inflicted on the Sonder both in the field and afterward. In spite of their faith in Hitler, therefore, and the seeming confidence it fostered, his SS myrmidons at Birkenau weren't as troubled by the past as about that uncertain future threatening to roll over them.

The powers in Berlin, however, were of a different mind. Appalled that a mutiny on such a scale as to make a shambles of one crematorium and deface another should have occurred at his prize Vernichtungslager no less, and by a rabble of Jews, *Reichsführer*-SS Heinrich Himmler ordered a full and immediate inquiry, woe betide all who didn't give it the highest priority. He wanted to know who was responsible, how they had done it, and just as imperative, why it had been allowed to happen in the first place. Not only to punish the guilty and prevent a recurrence, but to mollify his wounded pride. To Himmler, this latest embarrassment was the exclamation point to the insult that had been the Warsaw Ghetto uprising, that contretemps of a year and a half ago that remained the glaring blemish on an otherwise sterling career. He would have those who'd made the Sonder insurrection possible— on both sides of the wire, if it came to that—or he would know why.

One didn't argue with the *Reichsführer*, one simply obeyed, leaving the camp Kommandantur no choice but to keep after it. As a first step, a dozen survivors from the old 12th Squad were selected at random and taken to Block 35. (Exempted were the stokers and other specialists, as there were too few of these left to spare). This, however, was to prove an exercise in futility. Of primary concern to the Gestapo was where the rebels had got their weapons. But once the torture did begin to loosen their captives' tongues, the most any of them relinquished was having heard it was a *woman* who'd supplied the insurgents with their arms. Who this alleged female was, or how she'd pulled off such a feat, they of course had no idea.

A woman indeed! Who did these Sonder think they were kidding? The Gestapo had neither the patience nor time for such silliness (or was it dissembling?), and wasted no more of it dispatching the worthless twelve to the Black Wall. A decision was made to change strategy, abandoning interrogation for the time being in favor of a hunt for physical evidence that might be of help. Had the dynamite and grenades been smuggled to the Sonder intact, or in the form of raw gunpowder they'd used to assemble the things themselves? Either way, where had the explosives originated, the partisans outside the camp or the underground within? The Political Department undertook a search of its own, starting with Crematorium II. Those conducted by the regular soldiery before them had all been on the cursory side, the goal anything incriminating left lying around. The Gestapo expanded this by looking under floors and behind walls, and barely had they begun before they hit pay dirt.

This came in the form of a wooden box the size and shape of a large suitcase discovered beneath the floorboards in Number Two's no longer inhabited attic. Inside it they found what was essentially a miniature workshop, all the tools and materials someone manufacturing homemade grenades might have needed. Included were two small jars of gunpowder, the contents of one the consistency of ground coffee, the other filled with flat, pear-shaped disks of the stuff. It was quickly determined that these last were unique to one place, the Pulverraum of the Union factory adjacent to the main camp.

More of these disks were subsequently retrieved from the rubble of Crematorium IV. The SS were stunned. Suddenly, those prisoners who worked the plant's gunpowder room, all both Jewish and female, looked to be the prime suspects in providing the Sonder that substance from which, as was apparent now, they'd constructed their crude explosives. Women may have played a part in the revolt after all, and a major one. To the idealogues of the Gestapo, this only constituted further proof of the depths to which the degraded Rassenfiend had descended; even their women were capable of foul play.

Fortunately, in as much as it redeemed their chauvinism, another explanation soon surfaced that the Germans jumped on as not only likelier but more palatable. From the moment the dictum from Berlin had arrived, the Gestapo had been a presence day and night at the Union Metallwerke. Where before, his whole shift might pass without a prisoner coming across a single SS, the civilian Meisters and their assistants for the most part running the show, the factory floor now swarmed with uniformed men in implacable pursuit of clues, poking their noses into every closet, every corner. During a surprise search of the workers one night, they found what they were sure was their smoking gun. It was a key to the powder pavilion in the possession of someone it most definitely should not have been, one of the kapos of the plant by the name of Schulz.

That this person should be the culprit was almost as startling as blaming a woman for the crime, he being among the Nazis' more trustworthy servants. Typical of his office, Schulz was one of those men who in the outside world was destined for prison or the gallows, but at Auschwitz had found a home in which his sociopathic tendencies weren't condemned but extolled. A Croatian Jew, he was deported from Yugoslavia to Birkenau in mid-1942, and despite his Jewishness was soon recognized as prime kapo material. Thus began a career of murder, rape, extortion, and assorted other brutalities, culminating in his coveted posting to the Union. He even looked the part of the brute; arms too long for his shortish barrel of a body, a protruding jaw and sloping forehead, combined to give him a distinctly simian mien. Those at his mercy lived in utter terror and abhorrence of him. How a Jew could so wantonly prey on other Jews was difficult to comprehend. One didn't see the Germans, or for that matter the Czechs or Poles as a rule, turning on their own kind.

As faithful a dog as he'd been to them, however, and as improbable a traitor as he posed, the SS thought they had their man and hurried the bewildered Schulz to Block 35 and an interrogation room. They didn't tell him why he'd been arrested until he was sitting across a table from two officers, blinking in the white glare of the light in his face.

"Gunpowder?" he grunted before slumping into gutter German. "I don't know nothing about no missing gunpowder."

"Oh, but we think you do," said one of the Gestapo. "In fact, we believe you know everything about it."

"And what, I gotta ask, sirs, makes you believe that?"

"This," said the other officer. He reached in a pocket and plunked a large metal key on the table. "Look familiar, kapo?"

"It's—it's a key to the boss's office," he said, his face flushing crimson. "So, what of it?" he shrugged, trying his best to sound unflustered.

"What of it, he says!" Both Gestapo men laughed. "This is what," one of them said: "The company's gunpowder is stored in that room. Just *what*, my good kapo, was the key to it doing on your person?"

"If your honors don't mind, I'd—I'd rather not say."

"I'm sure you wouldn't. But I'm afraid we must insist. Why, pray tell, would you have such a key?"

Schulz squirmed in his chair, eyes darting left and right.

"We can do this the easy or the hard way, kapo, it's up to you." The German nodded once toward the shadows in the back of the room. "For the last time, what were you doing with this key?"

He looked up to see three large men standing over him all of a sudden, their soldier's tunics unbuttoned. "Aw right," he said. "I guess you got the goods on me. But not for what you think. I had the key made because…. I was needin' my privacy."

"Your privacy?" the two Nazis blurted as one. "What are you talking about? Privacy for what?"

Aware of the danger he was in, Schulz held nothing back. Since the termination of the Pulverraum night shift months ago, he'd been using the Meister's office for his own purposes. And these had nothing to do with the stealing of gunpowder. His only theft, he swore, if one could call it such, was that of the virtue of the occasional female prisoner he would coerce there in order to have his way with her without fear of interruption. If he was guilty of anything, and why he hadn't admitted it at the start, it was of neglecting his duties on the plant floor in order to slake his appetites on von Ende's leather sofa.

Though beneath the doubtful looks this elicited from his interrogators there lurked the sinking feeling he was telling the truth, they detained him overnight in Block 11 until they could check out his story. Come morning, they rounded up seven of the women and girls from the names he'd given them, and every one, several in tears, confirmed what he'd said. This Kapo Schulz of theirs, the SS realized, may have been an unscrupulous pig, but a smuggler of gunpowder he wasn't, leaving them no recourse but to release him.

And with that, the Gestapo were back where they'd started. Uncomfortable as it made them, they had no choice but to reject their antediluvian approach to gender, swallow their prejudices, and instead of groping about for suspects that fit their preconceptions, follow what evidence they had to its logical source: those females employed at the Pulverkammer. The question was where, or rather with whom, to start. The Kommandantur was already pressuring the Political Department for results; it wouldn't look good to come up empty yet a third time.

The most obvious candidate for arrest was the forewoman of the crew, Regina Safirsztajn. As Vorarbeiterin, it was hard to believe any plot could have succeeded without her knowing of it. A second choice wasn't so easily come by; the Nazis figured their best shot lay in picking a woman who by having transgressed elsewhere or in the past had already demonstrated a disrespect for the rules. Such a person might by nature be more inclined toward the criminal. The problem was that none of the Pulver girls fit the bill. Each had risen to so trusted a position on the basis of an exemplary record.

But with a timing that couldn't have been more opportune, fortune smiled on the Gestapo. It came in the form of a Russian Jewess who worked at the Union named Klara—"Black Klara" as she was known to the other prisoners. It wasn't her dark good looks, though, that had earned her this nickname. As the long-time paramour of none other than the odious Kapo Schulz, she enjoyed a prestige she elected regularly to abuse. It wasn't uncommon for her to put on the airs of a kapo herself, and she could be as pitiless toward the weak and inexperienced as her boyfriend. To the SS, however, she was just another prisoner, so that when she was caught with an unauthorized loaf of bread in her possession, no light offense, she was sentenced to the penal commando. To escape this, she offered to turn in a sister worker she'd seen consorting with a man, which for a Union female was a far greater infraction than hers.

To the delight of the Germans, it was no less than Esther Wajcblum, one of von Ende's girls. Black Klara had spotted her months ago sneaking into one of the Union washrooms with her boyfriend Tadek, and filed the incident away should it come in handy one day. In verifying her story now, the SS ransacked Esther's bunk and found a pencil sketch of Tadek hidden under the mattress. This, too, being against the rules, she and Regina were promptly arrested and taken to Block 35.

It was a frosty mid-October morning, the first real cold front of the season. A long central hallway ran the length of Gestapo headquarters, with offices and interrogation rooms on either side. The largest of these offices was the *Standesamt*, an adjunct of the main registry, staffed by German-speaking female prisoners only. For several days, they'd been busy with the death certificates of vastly more escapees than usual, this seeming to corroborate the rumors floating around of a sizable breakout that had taken place at Birkenau.

Suddenly, one of them, all excitement, burst in from the hall. "There's a young Jewish girl standing with her face to the wall next to Broch's door," she announced. "And another against the wall opposite the restroom. A soldier is watching over them with a machine gun."

Every typewriter fell silent, the women behind them turning to look at each other. "What can it mean?" several asked. Then to her who'd seen them, "Have they been arrested?"

Their questions were more reactive than serious; the presence of the two outside that door was self-explanatory. SS-*Unterscharführer* Karl Broch was one of the camp Gestapo's top interrogators. A man nearing forty, round-shouldered, pudgy, with the tired, cynical if harmless air of the overworked and under-appreciated bureaucratic drudge, few were those nonetheless who didn't give his office a wide berth.

"Of course they've been arrested," said their discoverer, "what else could it be? But arrested for what? One is no more than twenty, the other not much older. What could they possibly have done to wind up here?"

Though they suspected it might have something to do with whatever it was that had happened at Birkenau, none ventured as much. Except for one. "Wally, what do you think? Do you have any idea what's going on?"

The prisoner they called Wally wasn't just the oldest among them but had been interned the longest. She had a reputation for somehow knowing things well ahead of anybody, a talent she had fun attributing to her most distinguishing feature, a long, curving nose that gave her the look of a Grimm brother's witch. She laid an index finger against it now in emphasis.

"Wally has a tracking nose, children. It was created this way in order to sniff things out, and it's telling me that pair out there are from the Union ammunition factory."

"The Union? What makes you say that?"

"Wally's nose," she grinned slyly, "isn't one to reveal its magic." At which the grin disappeared. "Suffice it to say this is connected to the explosions coming from Birkenau the other day, and that those two brave girls in the hall aren't the last we'll be seeing there."

Though they pressed her to elaborate, she went back to her typewriter without another word. The tension in the room was palpable, but as nothing to that later when screams of pain could be heard coming from the direction of Broch's office. Not that these were something the women hadn't been forced to listen to before, just never in the childlike soprano of a girl barely out of her teens. Woven among them was the booming, brassbound bellow of the sergeant's voice.

Half an hour had passed without any screaming when Broch's secretary, the Polish prisoner Raya Kagan, entered the room and asked for attention. An attractive young woman with a pleasant smile and a quiet way about her, not normally given to dramatics or easily rattled, today her voice sounded as strained as her face was haggard.

"The *Unterscharführer*," she explained, "has sent me to inform you not to enter the hall unless absolutely necessary. If you must, you're to have nothing to do with any prisoners waiting there to be questioned. What contact you might attempt will be dealt with severely. He further commands that you say nothing of what you've seen or heard to anyone. If found to have done so, again you will be sorry."

Conscious she could be seen in the role of messenger as endorsing these orders herself, she hurried to add, "It's not me speaking, you understand, but they who sent me."

Her audience seized on her disclaimer as an opening. "Can you tell us then whether the two there now are from the Union commando?"

Raya said nothing, turned and made for the door.

"Or if any of this has something to do with what we've been hearing about Birkenau?"

Halfway into the hall, she paused. "I'm sorry, believe me, but I'm forbidden to say anything. At the risk of my own neck. But what's the rush? Be patient. You'll know the whole story soon enough, I'm sure."

And so they would. The arrest of the girls wasn't the type of thing that could be kept secret for long. Roza Robota would learn of it when her friend Marta Bindiger, on a parcel run from the Paketstelle, showed up at the *B1a* lager that Sunday night. Through her connections, Marta had arranged to have herself transferred from Birkenau to Auschwitz and a job in its mailroom, where she'd been for a month now. Her friend and fellow smuggler there had fallen victim to a heart attack of all things, and in order to sustain the flow of gunpowder, she'd called in some favors and succeeded in replacing her—though no more, naturally, did her trips include the explosive.

With Marta living in the Stammlager, it had been two weeks since she and Roza had seen each other. After securing a measure of privacy at a vacant koje in a corner of the crowded barracks, Roza was brimming with questions. Was it true what she'd heard about the SS investigation, that it had turned up some loose gunpowder and traced it back to the Union?

"Regrettably, yes," Marta said. "And though it took the fools a while to admit the obvious, eventually the Gestapo took two of the Pulver women into custody."

Roza grabbed her by both arms. "Who?" she said, bracing herself.

"Esther and Regina. Came in and plucked them right off the factory floor. They're back now, however; the Germans only held them two days. They're in pretty bad shape, I won't say they're not, but both are already up and walking again."

Roza flew from the edge of the bunk. "Esther," she groaned, "my beautiful Estusia…. and poor sweet Regina! But—" Her brow puckered in confusion. "They were tortured, I take it?"

"I'm afraid so."

"Why for two days only? What made the Krauts let them go? Not that I give a good damn what happens to me, but did they—did they talk?"

"Oh, no!" Marta was vehement. "Good gracious, no! Not a word out of either. How gutsy is that? We're all in total awe of them."

Roza let out a relieved sigh. "Good. Very good. And gutsy as all hell, yes. But—you swear they're all right? *Everyone's* all right?"

Marta smiled, patted the place next to her on the koje. "Here, dear," she said, "why don't you sit back down? And let me catch you up on what happened, from the beginning this time. You'll want to hear it from the beginning; it will make you proud. If you'd like me to spare you some of the gorier details…."

"No!" Roza said, throwing herself down beside her. "I don't just want to hear it, I need to, and that means all of it. Don't you dare hold back a single thing, please."

Esther and Regina, after their release, if hesitant to relive it at first, ended up recounting their ordeal in full. Marta began with them shivering in fear as they stood in the hallway of Block 35. Esther was the first to be led into Broch's office. He asked her, his secretary interpreting, to sign a deposition stating she was guilty of stealing gunpowder. Proclaiming her innocence, she refused. He then said a verbal confession would do, but again she refused. Finally, if it wasn't her, he demanded the names of those who had stolen it. She told him she didn't know, had no idea what he was even talking about. She was then taken to a room where two soldiers were waiting, each stripped to his undershirt and wearing a pair of thin leather gloves. But for a metal desk and a couple of chairs, the room, too, was stripped down, the only illumination coming from a light bulb hanging by a cord from the ceiling. Esther was bound wrist and ankle to a chair directly beneath it, and Broch took up his questioning anew. When she remained uncooperative, he sent his secretary from the room, and at a sign from him one of the soldiers sauntered up to her and hit her square on the nose with his fist.

Soon both were taking turns at her until they'd battered her unconscious. She was revived with a bucket of cold water to the face. Broch, impatient, began shouting at her to confess, but though she could feel her nose was broken and probably her jaw, either despite or because of this, she wasn't sure which, she was more determined than ever not to give in.

Again the fists started in on her—face, ribs, breasts, stomach—the *Unterscharführer* haranguing her between punches. After a while, she could hear a woman screaming from another room. She assumed it was Regina. Only later did she realize the screams were her own.

That evening, the SS carried both of them, fading in and out of consciousness—Regina, too, had been tortured, and also failed to break— to the basement of Block 11 and separate cells. And in the morning, or so the women estimated, the only light being artificial, resumed the interrogation there. When further beatings produced no results, their assailants upped the ante. They were strung up by their wrists, naked, and flogged with leather whips, with a force that on some blows knocked the wind out of them. Even this, though, but for the screams and the begging for mercy it wrung from them, didn't loosen their lips. Finally, the Nazis, in what bore a whiff of desperation, drug them outdoors to the Black Wall and stood them side by side. The last thing they saw as hoods were pulled over their heads was a six-man firing squad lining up in front of them. The Germans told them it was now or never, that they had thirty seconds to give up either some names or their lives. At the order to fire, the rifles thundered, but the soldiers had sent their volley harmlessly into the air. Esther thought her companion shot dead, but Regina had only fainted. When she came to, she started to laugh and couldn't stop, giggling like a little girl all the way back to their cells. Once more that day they were bullwhipped, but again to no effect.

"Filthy bastards," Roza fumed half under her breath.

"Yes, but guess what happened then," Marta said.

From the grin on her friend's face, she didn't have to. "The sorry mothers let them go," she replied.

"The next morning! We couldn't believe it! There wasn't a one of us who thought we'd ever see them again. They were more dead than alive, true, but they were back. Oh, Roza, you can't imagine! You would have wept to see what the Germans did to them. Not only were their eyes swollen completely shut, their whole faces were puffed out to half again their normal size. They didn't look human anymore. Their clothes had to be scissored off them, and carefully; where the whip cut the skin, the blood had glued itself to the fabric. They couldn't talk, much less walk, and we were worried we might lose them yet.

"As I said, though, they're better now. Another week maybe and they'll be able to work again. In the meantime, we're taking as good care of them as we can. Medicine, bandages, extra rations, whatever our courageous Esterke and Gina need, they're getting. Funny thing is, every bit of it is by order of Commandant Hössler."

"What's so strange about that?" Roza said. "I thought he was partial to his Union girls."

"Oh, he was. He practically doted on them, until the authorities began linking them to the plot. Since then, it's as if he's been trying to out-Gestapo the Gestapo in his brutality. They say his spite knows no bounds anymore. As he sees it, as I see *him*, for the commando to have repaid the many kindnesses he heaped on it with so glaring an act of treason wasn't merely a crime against the camp and its administration but an affront to him personally. And he's reacted as a man with his ego might be expected to. Gone is the Papa Hössler who always had a smile and a wink, a cheery *'Guten Tag!'* for his charges, in his place a snarling demon of a Hössler who walks around with a whip at his side now. And isn't shy about using it, among other maliciousness."

"I don't get it then," Roza said. "If he's so eaten up with hate, why is he allowing the two women he should be maddest at everything they need to recover from their injuries?"

"That's just it," Marta said, "it doesn't make sense. Just as it doesn't that the Nazis would release the two after only a couple of days. With a little help from an unexpected source, however, we've succeeded in piecing together a sort of explanation for this last."

"Oh, really?" Roza's eyebrows lifted in surprise. "And what is that?"

"A couple of things actually. One by way of an incident I haven't mentioned yet. While Esther and Regina were still captive, the SS arrested two more women: Rose Greuenapfel from the Pulverraum and Esther's sister Hanka. Not so much to accuse them of any wrongdoing—they were only held a few hours—but in an attempt, we believe, to dig up evidence against the other two. So tight are Rose and Regina, as you know, they might as well be related."

"Some think they are."

"But," Marta said, "instead of reinforcing the Gestapo's case, it would appear that Rose's and Hanka's testimonies might just have undermined it. Crazed as she was at what had befallen her sister—what is the child, fifteen, sixteen, and Esther all the family she has left?—she had the snap to see through a trick the SS tried to pull on her, and not only see through it but use it to her advantage. When the Nazis informed her that her sister had already admitted to stealing the gunpowder, and all they wanted from her was how she herself had learned about the thievery, Hanka said she looked them each straight in the eye and told them they were lying, because there was no way Esther would have. That she in fact hated lies and lying worse than anything. How then could she have confessed to a crime she hadn't committed? Unless, of course, she was being tortured, in which case a person was liable to say anything."

Roza leaned forward. "The little girl said that? To the Gestapo?"

"She did," Marta tittered with something akin to a mother's pride, "but here's the kicker: Rose, in her interrogation, basically told them the same thing. That Esther wasn't only guiltless but wouldn't lie if her life depended on it. Now, you know that had to get the Germans to thinking. Not totally convinced as the idiots are even to this point, I wager, that women could have played a role in arming the Sonderkommando, here they were with two members of that sex continuing to protest their innocence in the face of torture that would have broken most men, and two more failing to take the bait and betray any evidence to the contrary. If that wouldn't make the SS wonder if maybe they were shinnying up the wrong tree…."

"And that's why you believe Esther and Regina were set free?" Roza thought this rather lame, but decided to let it go until she'd heard more.

"Wait," cried Marta, "I'm not finished. There's something else. That help I said we got? From an unexpected source? Well, Israel Gutman, one of our friends from the underground—you know Gutman, don't you? Or told me once you did."

"He *and* his buddy, Yehuda Laufer. The two used to be inseparable. I haven't run into them, though, in, gosh, I don't know how long."

"So Gutman," Marta continued, "takes Ala, our Ala, aside the other day—he works at the Union, too, as foreman of some kind of machine shop—and tells her he came across something she might find interesting. Seems the underground got wind of an audit the Nazis conducted comparing the amount of gunpowder they should have against that which they actually did, and get this: the figures matched! No powder was found missing at all! We were as thrown for a loop as the Germans must have been, until we approached the Pulver team with the mystery. According to them, it was all about what's called the Abfall, the residue left over after the dynamite is compressed into the detonators. Made worthless by the heat from the injector machines, instead of throwing it away as they were supposed to, the women would save it on the sly and use it as a substitute for the fresh. Clever, huh?"

"Inspired," Roza said, "but ticklish."

"Isn't *that* the truth. It always struck me as incredible what our sisters whose job it was to pilfer the stuff were able to get away with, especially with a pair, if not two pairs of eyes looking over their shoulders. Thank goodness Esther, though, bless her heart, stopped plundering the Meister's safe when she did. I'm guessing you remember what happened last spring to bring that to an end."

Roza still blanched inside when reminded of it. "If that Kraut assistant of von Ende's had returned to the section a minute earlier that day, she'd have caught Esther with her hand in the cookie jar. What a mess that would have been."

"A mess indeed. But close a call as it was, it turned out to be a blessing in disguise."

"Sorry, I'm not following you."

"Think about it," Marta said. "No amount of Abfall could have covered up for what would have been missing from that safe if Esther had kept at it. And it was the morning after Gutman said the SS audit took place that she and Regina were released. A coincidence? Maybe, but I wouldn't bank on it. There are those, in fact, who say the danger is passed, that in view of the findings to come out of their inventory, no way can the Nazis still believe the gunpowder supplied the Sonder came from the Union. And have already turned their sights back on the underground and the partisans. Or even, as some have it, abandoned the investigation altogether. I can see how it might be tempting to think along those lines."

"And what does the one named Marta Bindiger think?"

Marta stared straight ahead, as if engrossed in the usual chaotic ebb and flow of a barracks trying to wrap up the night's business before lights-out. When it did come, her answer was vague.

"I guess I'd have to say my opinion is split. I do believe the SS audit, as well as their interviews with Rose and Hanka, contributed to their letting Esther and Regina go. But I also don't see that as being the end of it. I can't help feeling the Germans are onto some trick, a slicker, faster way to find out what they're after. What this might be, I haven't a clue, except for something both girls have been saying since they got back."

"And that would be?"

"They keep telling us, the poor dears, to stay away from them, that the Gestapo are probably watching them to see who comes calling. Can the Nazis be using them to lure more flies into their web? I don't see the point. You'd think their time would be better spent feeding on the ones they have."

"I'm not sure," Roza frowned, "but of this I am: you can't trust those two-legged spiders of yours, not as far as you can throw them. They're up to something all right, and anyone who imagines different is kidding herself."

Earlier in the week, a new face had appeared among those who made up the male contingent of the Union. His name was Eugen Koch, a full-blooded Czechoslovakian, but as he was quick to make clear, only half-Jewish. He wore the striped uniform of a prisoner, but it was tailored to fit, and always clean and well-pressed; a blue armband declared him a subkapo. But though technically he was second-in-command of the revolver machines section, in which various fittings and such were honed to spec, he was all too frequently nowhere to be found, sometimes for hours at a stretch. To be regularly absent from one's workstation was a serious offense, even for a kapo, a rule that for some reason didn't apply to this Koch. It was whispered he had powerful connections, was perhaps even an agent of Battle Group-Auschwitz.

Two things stood out about the new man. For one, he was good-looking, extraordinarily so. In his late-twenties, trim and fit in his laundered tunic, he was a shade over six feet tall, a lush growth of jet-black hair topping a face a movie star would have envied. His eyes were a startling blue, the nose gently flared, the lips sensual, with just the right amount of pout to them. But the likable, pearly smile he was always flashing hid a second defining characteristic, a mean streak that would reveal itself at the slightest inducement, if at the expense of the weak and defenseless only. While his behavior toward the stronger prisoners bordered on the servile, to those he felt he could push around he showed little restraint.

A perfect example of this involved Israel Gutman, foreman of the revolver machines detail. On his shift one day, he saw Koch knock a worker to the ground and begin kicking him, a boy who'd incorrectly loaded a casing into one of the machines. It was a small error and easily rectified, but the Czech screamed he was going to report him to the Germans and have him removed from the commando.

"Hold on there!" Gutman said, pulling him off the frightened teenager. "Get hold of yourself, man!"

Koch tore free of his grasp and spun to face him, his face red. "Who the hell do you think you are?" he spluttered at Gutman. "How dare you interfere! This shitbag was committing sabotage, right in front of me!"

The Vorarbeiter had learned Czech from his friend Laufer. "Sabotage? I don't think so. More like inexperience, if you ask me. The boy is new to the job, give him a break."

"I'll break his skull, is what I'll do," Koch cried, strutting closer, "and yours if you're not careful."

"That I'd like to see," Gutman laughed.

"Oh yeah? On second thought, maybe I'll report the kid and you both, him for sabotage, you for putting your hands on a kapo. What do you think of that, tough guy?"

"I think you're a slimy little worm with more mouth than brains. And you'd better back away if you know what's good for you."

Instead, Koch took another step forward, fists clenched. Gutman drew back his right and let him have one on the chin. That was enough for his opponent, who after picking himself up from the floor and cradling his jaw in one hand, limped away mumbling.

Appalled at his own rashness, Gutman spent the rest of the day and night waiting to be arrested, but to his surprise woke in the morning still a free man. First to meet him at the factory was Koch, with outstretched hand and an apology. And thereafter carried on as if he wanted to be the other's pal. He took, when he was present, to hanging around his foreman's machine, prating away about nothing in particular. The German contributed little to these sessions, never mind the importuning of some of his comrades in the underground. These, when they noticed Koch bending over backward to establish a rapport with him, suggested he sound the man out about joining up with them. Foremost among them was Laufer, always eager to welcome a countryman of his to the cause.

Gutman, however, was leery. Not only had Koch shown himself to be a bully and a coward, even more disturbing was his attitude toward their overseers. Where the other prisoners would fall silent at the approach of a guard, their faces hardening, the young Czech greeted every soldier with a smile, going out of his way to be civil. More worrying yet, Gutman had spotted him more than once deep in conversation with the odd SS officer, and just as bad, the despicable Kapo Schulz. This, of course, could mean nothing; Koch was, after all, a kapo himself, and as such answerable to his fascist bosses. Still, something didn't smell right to Gutman, and he not only dropped any notion of opening up to the newcomer but warned Laufer and the others to keep a wary eye on him.

It was advice they were well to heed, for as he was ultimately to reveal, Eugen Koch was a man who'd sold his soul to the devil. And at bargain-basement prices. In return for elevation to the rank of subkapo and assorted other perquisites, he'd agreed to be an informer for the Nazis. His instructions were to gain the affections of one of several women the Gestapo had targeted, then sweet-talk her into admitting what she knew of the theft of the Union gunpowder. This accounted for the many hours he'd gone missing from his post; he'd spent them making his pretty face known in those parts of the factory staffed by the female workers.

The women chosen were those spending the most time around Esther and Regina, making it a good chance they weren't only friends but co-conspirators. Excluded were any who worked the Pulverraum or the few not employed at the Union, the former because Koch would have had little access to them without arousing suspicion, and the latter for what the Germans thought were obvious reasons. Their blockova was under orders from Hössler to allow the tortured girls whatever succor they required, but to report back to him who was administering it. Koch was then briefed on whom to look for, and sent out to snare the best prospect he could.

And prized indeed did his catch turn out to be, none other than the pivotal if also vulnerable Ala Gertner.

The handsome Czech couldn't have chosen a more efficacious victim. Or one riper for seduction. Never having recovered completely from the murder of her baby Rochele, she'd seemed more moody of late than was usual for her. Not that she was the only one; with some of their confinements having stretched into two years or more, many of the women were feeling the effects, in addition to their other deprivations, of prolonged lack of contact with the opposite sex. Ala, however, high-strung as she was and with a libido to match, was hurting more than most—until the day she began to have trouble keeping a smile from her face. Vanished overnight was any trace of her recent moodiness. She traipsed around now humming little songs to herself, her step as tripping as a schoolgirl's.

When asked what had got into her, she'd smile a little bigger but say nothing, though it didn't take much to hypothesize a man behind her happiness. This was confirmed soon enough once she and the new kapo were seen keeping company, sparingly at first, but before long it was every day, twice a day and that just on the job, who knew what they were doing on their hours off? How they conducted themselves in public certainly shouted romance. Koch plied her with gifts on a regular basis: food, cigarettes, chocolate, even a gold chain that those who witnessed the giving of it saw him fasten around her neck himself. Ala for her part was hopelessly smitten. One could see it in her eyes when she looked at him, in the way she blushed when he was near. Quick, surreptitious kisses, ill-concealed caresses, it was all they could do to keep their hands off each other. Most of her friends were delighted for her, even envious in an unbegrudging way. The two made such an attractive couple, and were so clearly, sweetly in love.

Then there were those who weren't delighted at all, who'd witnessed a side to this Czech that was anything but sweet. One of these was Mala Weinstein, whose talent for seeing past the surface of things to the reality beneath remained as sharp as her sense of humor and propensity for clowning around. If not Ala's closest friend, she wasn't far from it; though they often made deprecating fun of the fact, the similarity of their names pleased them no end. Until its abolition, Mala had worked the Pulver night shift, during which she and Ilse Michel had snuck out their fair share of gunpowder. Afterward, she'd been transferred to the *Spritzraum*, where certain of the Werke's finished products were hosed off and dried before being packed for shipping. A gullible Meister, though, and a fictitious bladder problem, enabled her to take as many bathroom breaks as she wished, permitting her to remain an active link in the smuggling chain.

The first time she saw Ala cavorting with the unctuous Koch, she couldn't believe her eyes. Her friend fallen for a man of such dubious repute! She thought about how she might alert her without appearing to intrude, but even if she could, knew it wouldn't do any good. Others had tried before her, and not only had Ala refused to listen but accused them of meddling in something none of their business, what kinds of friends were they? She'd been denied the attentions of a man for too long, even before coming to Birkenau, and in the heaven-sent person of her adoring, her beautiful Eugen felt she'd stumbled on the answer to a question she wasn't even aware she'd been asking. She'd found against all odds, in the most loveless place imaginable, the love of her life, and wasn't about to let anyone talk her out of him.

Of course, no one, Mala included, realized at first what the kapo was really about. What worried them was their Ala ending up with a broken heart, victim of a characterless cad, which would have been ugly enough but hardly a danger to life and limb. It was only when the rumors flying around him started to take a more sinister turn that Mala grew from uneasy to downright frightened. Fear became panic when working the late shift one midnight, she rounded a corner on her way to the Spritzraum only to see Koch and the factory's new *Kommandoführer* standing off to the side in the shadows. So animated was their conversation, they didn't notice her, the kapo so excited he was waving his arms in the air. Though she couldn't hear what they were saying above the clatter of machinery, one was as pleased as the other, both grinning like Jack-o'-lanterns. As she walked away, she turned to see the SS man pat his companion on the head with the same approval he would a dog.

Her skin went immediately cold. What she'd happened on might well have been innocuous; for all she knew, the two were celebrating an increase in the revolver machines' output. But something inside her screamed otherwise, and where before she'd kept quiet out of respect for Ala's private life, she couldn't now warn her fast enough of the peril she was in.

Aware the Spritzraum detail was going to be short-handed tomorrow—poor Yoli had had her foot crushed beneath a loaded pallet and had probably gone to the gas already, and another was sick with a fever—Mala volunteered to work straight through the day. Knowing that after what she'd seen she wouldn't be able to sleep anyway, this would allow her to run into Ala first thing. It wasn't until noon, though, that she succeeded in following her into one of the lavatories, and knew as soon as she saw her that it was too late.

She was leaning on both hands over one of the sinks. With a start she looked up, her mouth twitching at the corners.

"*Ich hab so moira*, Mala," she said in Yiddish for some reason, quickly rephrasing it in Polish. "I'm so afraid."

Mala, moving closer, could have cried at the sight of her. She didn't look the same person. A tall woman and still shapely despite their meager diet, her body had shriveled into something three times its age. She stood bent over, shoulders hunched, as if beneath some heavy load. The skin of her face was pulled as tight as a scrap of dried cowhide over bone, a bright rash splotching her forehead and cheeks. Underneath it, the flesh was as gray as a corpse's, the mouth a grimace of unrelieved terror.

"It's that boyfriend of yours, isn't it?" she said. "That Koch."

Ala's eyes were a red-rimmed mire of fear and self-reproach. They told the whole story, those eyes, she didn't have to say a word.

Mala put her hand on the wall to keep from sagging against it. So the thing, the frightful thing she'd begun to suspect last night was true: the man was an informer, a Gestapo plant, and he'd got to their Ala as sure as the cockroach he was. "How—how much does he know?" she asked. "Did you say anything about the gunpowder? Talk to me, Ala. What happened, for heaven's sake?"

At this, the words came pouring out of her, but questioningly, as if she couldn't quite believe them herself. "He said he, too, was a member of the underground, and that he already knew what I'd done. That Israel Gutman had told him. He was proud of me, he said, for being so brave; his little soldier, he called me. All he wanted to know was how I'd pulled it off, how I'd been so smart as to get all that gunpowder past all those Nazis. I didn't have to tell him if I didn't want to, he said, it was no big deal. He was just curious, was all, and didn't think it right we should be keeping secrets from each other. That if I wanted to show how much I loved him, and even more important, trusted him, I'd tell him. So…. I did."

"Oh, Ala. Oh God."

"But not everything! I never mentioned any names. At least, thank goodness, I didn't do that. But mine they do have, and pretty soon they'll be coming for me. I'm surprised they haven't yet. All this happened yesterday, making it almost a full—"

"Wait a minute. Yesterday? Hold it right there. Maybe it's not as bad as you're making it out to be." It was a straw, a half a one, but in her desperation Mala was glad to have even it to grasp. "As you said, here you are still. It's been a day and they haven't arrested you. What makes you sure this Koch is the scoundrel you think he is?"

"Because he's disappeared, that's why! I haven't seen him since I spilled my stupid guts to him! *Nobody* has. Besides, I looked up Gutman just this morning and asked him if he'd told Eugen about my role in the plot, or anything about me at all."

Ala paused, looking as if she might burst into tears. "And?" Mala asked leadenly, knowing the answer already.

"Of course not. He was horrified I would even think such a thing. Oh, Mala, what have I done? How could I have been so blind, such a meshugga?"

Here the tears did come, along with great heaving sobs, prompting Mala to scoop her up in a reassuring hug. She hadn't the slightest idea, though, what to say. On the one hand, she wanted to scold her for, yes, being a fool, for compromising not only her own but dozens of other lives by falling under the spell of so transparent a blackguard. On the other, who was she, Mala Weinstein, to blame Ala or anyone for being no more than human, for succumbing to the allure, the illogic of love? She continued to hold the poor shattered thing tight, until slowly the sobs ceased and Ala stepped from her embrace.

"You don't have a cigarette, do you?" she sniffled.

Mala lit one for each of them. Her hand trembling, Ala took a couple of deep drags, which seemed to calm her some. She glanced up at the ceiling, then back to Mala. "They're going to torture me, you know. And I'm not a strong person."

"Don't talk like that, Ala. You're as strong a person as I know, as I've ever known. You've got yourself in a bad fix, there's no arguing that, but it'll only make things worse if you pull others down with you. You mustn't let that happen. Promise me something."

"Promise you what?"

"Should the worst come to pass, should you be arrested, you've got to take yourself back to that first day on the unloading ramp, the day the SS stole your Rochele from you. You're going to have to live it all over again in the interrogation room, maybe more than once, maybe much more, but reminding yourself each time that the men who'll be—who'll be in that room with you are wearing the same uniform as those who murdered your innocent babe. Killed her then threw her away like so much trash. Remember what they did, and how you felt when they did it. Let that be your strength. Let that bolt your lips when they start asking for names.

"And never forget who you are, Alina, and will always be to your people, a hero and an inspiration to them."

It wasn't much, not in Mala's estimation anyway, but did seem to help; Ala's hand no longer shook as she smoked. She was silent for some seconds, staring into space. Finally, crushing out her cigarette, she took Mala by the shoulders and kissed her once on each cheek. "My good friend," she said, showing a brief smile, then without another word walked out the door. She seemed taller as she left, her back a little straighter, more like the Ala everyone loved and looked up to.

Alone, Mala saw no reason to hold it in. Slumping to the floor, she hid her face in her hands and wept it all out, all the grief that arises from watching someone you care for walk away knowing you're never going to see her again. Unlike most everyone, it didn't surprise her when she heard an hour later that some soldiers had come and marched Ala off.

They took her straightaway to Block 35, where Sergeant Broch began that very afternoon the job of prying what his superiors wanted from her. Which in her case, as opposed to Esther's and Regina's, was simplified for the most part to the names of her partners in treason, her own guilt having been established by the artifices of her counterfeit lover. As with her predecessors, her interrogation was confined at first to a series of beatings. Gestapo torture techniques were as varied as they were savage, but as a rule began with an attack by fists, feet, and assorted blunt instruments. The object of this wasn't so much to inflict pain as to daze and disorient the victim, a gambit designed to knock him or her off balance. The way the Nazis saw it, it became tougher for a prisoner to mount any kind of defense with nose and ears oozing blood, eyes swollen shut, lips likewise smashed, the front teeth floating in their sockets.

In their way as bad if not worse than the physical, however, were the psychological effects of torture, even at this preliminary stage. Arguably the most debilitating of these was the sense of alienation it imposed, a feeling of utter and total ostracism at the hands of one's fellow human beings. It was never easy being brave when facing such antipathy alone, and coupled as it was with the remorseless application of pain, few places were capable of generating an aloneness as corrosive as the torture chamber. Isolated, cut off from all support and goodwill, not a sympathetic ear to turn to, a kind word to be heard, a person could quickly begin to doubt both himself and his resolve. Nor was this doubt trained inward alone. One's faith in humanity tended not to last long under torture—was fractured, in fact, by the first slap to the face, then demolished entirely by whatever indignities followed. With the result that its recipient found himself alienated even further, repudiating the fellowship of his kind even as he felt repudiated by them.

To such did Ala now find herself subjected, not only the brutalization of her flesh but her psyche as well. But she held her own against it even after the torture escalated, which in contrast to the two women before her took no time at all. Unlike them, the SS had her dead to rights; she represented their first real break in the case, and they couldn't exploit it fast enough.

Beginning the next morning, they started in on her fingernails. This required four people: Ala herself, bound securely to a chair clamped to the wall; *Unterscharführer* Broch; and two subalterns. One of these, a specialist at the task, sat facing Ala across a narrow table upon which a forearm and hand of hers were pinioned. The second was a soldier conversant in Polish. (The sergeant always sent his secretary from the room during the actual torture—he'd had too many of them faint on him in the past, or disrupt it in other ways). Broch would ask his question through this interpreter, and when Ala refused to answer, nod to the specialist. The man was good at what he did, having from experience devised a system. He would start with a lesser finger and work his way around to the thumb, not ripping the nail out all at once but extracting it slowly, a fraction of a centimeter at a time. In the process, he might jiggle it from side to side, or bend it up and down with his pliers, either action taking the hurt to another level. Once again, the unfamiliar, high-pitched screams of a woman traveled the halls of Block 35.

Holler as she might, though, Ala didn't crack, not even when they strapped her feet to a bench and performed the same obscenity on her toes. When this somewhat to his surprise didn't work, either, Broch had a large washtub sloshing over with water carried in, and her head held submerged in it until she began to go limp. She was then revived, water spewing from her mouth as from a fountain, and the question put to her again.

Another unsuccessful dunking, and the *Unterscharführer* was ready to make it easier on the both of them. "Ala, listen. *Ala*! Are you with me?"

Slowly, she raised her head, still coughing water. Her eyes struggled to focus first on the interpreter, then Broch. "I'm not guilty," she panted, her voice barely audible. "I was just trying to impress my boyfriend. How many times do I have to—"

"All right," Broch said, "you're not guilty. I believe you. But I also think you know who is, which means I could use your help. And to get it, I'd be willing to make a deal."

"You believe me?"

"I believe you."

"What kind of deal?"

She was sitting in a chair, a soldier on each arm. Broch knelt down beside her, his face close to hers. "It would be more a sign of good faith on your part than anything. All you have to do is verify what we already know, that it was Esther and Regina who stole the gunpowder from the Union. That and the name of one of the people responsible for delivering it to the Sonderkommando. That's not so much, is it? Just one name, and I promise I'll never ask for another."

When the interpreter finished, Ala summoned a sort of smile. "And if I agree?"

"You do those two things, show me you're at least trying to cooperate, then you have my word as an officer I won't trouble you anymore. You'll go free today, back to your friends."

She thought on this a moment, then setting her jaw, came to a decision. "It's a deal," she said, "but on one condition."

Broch's heart was beating so hard, he could feel it in his wrists. "What's that?" he said as offhandedly as he could.

"Before I give you anything, you give me back my baby."

"Your *baby*? What baby?"

"The one you people took from me on the unloading ramp over a year ago. You give me back my little girl and you'll have more names than you can handle."

Frowning, Broch rose to his feet. "But you know that's impossible."

"Yes," Ala said softly, her head sinking back down, "I know."

Two more simulated drownings found her as unforthcoming as before. And worse, at risk of slipping away for good; her tormentors almost weren't able to bring her around the second time. Afraid of pushing her too far too fast, they decided to call it quits. Hauling her back to Block 11, they left her in her cell for the night to recover some.

Probing for a weakness, for the thing she couldn't endure, the following day Broch tried substituting fire for water. He went through half of the morning and two lit cigars applying their glowing heads to various parts of her, only to end up having to admit defeat there as well. With next to no experience interrogating females, he was, if by no means at his wit's end, on the path to it. Here was this prisoner, this woman, this *girl*—young, pretty, and if Eugen Koch was any indication, of a demonstrably susceptible and frivolous nature—managing nonetheless, with the gristle of two men, to withstand every hurt he and his assistants were laying on her. This didn't only frustrate but was starting to infuriate him. Still smarting at the way she'd toyed with him yesterday, Broch decided to turn up the heat, literally.

He had Ala tied fast to a metal chair this time, and an electric generator wheeled into the room. A single thick wire coiled from the machine, a large alligator clip sprouting from the end of it.

"What—what are you going to do?" she said. "What is that thing?"

"This," the sergeant smiled, "is the gift of electricity, the answer to both our problems. By making you talk, it won't only provide me what I want but relieve you of your suffering. Unless, of course, you have something you'd like to tell me first."

Ala groaned and turned away, her expression despairing. Broch shrugged, affixed the clip to a leg of the chair, ordered her doused with a bucket of water, and turned on the juice.

Her body arced outward as if to burst the bonds holding it, muscle and tendon visible in sharp relief beneath the skin. It didn't take Broch but a second to realize he'd forgotten something. So loud were her screams in the enclosed, windowless room, he had to shut off the machine until he could find a rag to stuff in her mouth.

Persisting with his questions, he stopped several times to remove her gag, but beyond blubbering for mercy, the words eerily liquid as if she was speaking underwater, Ala had nothing to say. This so enraged him that though he knew better, knew he was messing up even as he did it, the next time he switched the device on, he left it on. Her reaction after twenty unbroken seconds of current was to drop her chin to her chest as if poleaxed, her body as lifeless as the generator Broch hastened to disengage.

She came to back in Block 11, lying naked on the cold, concrete floor of her cell. She could tell where she was by both the tininess and unsparing emptiness of the room, its only "furnishings" the waste bucket in a corner and the single caged light bulb in the ceiling. What she didn't know was how she'd got there, or presuming she was carried there unconscious, how long she'd been out, what hour or even day it was.

She tried to sit up, but it hurt too much to move. The damage wasn't confined to specific areas this time, either. While it was true that the tips of half her fingers and toes were on fire, pulpy cavities seeping fluids where once were nails, and the burns left by the cigars were no less alive and throbbing, the electricity had made one big wound of her whole body. Every joint, every muscle, every bone felt bruised, as if each had been singled out and mangled in due order. She would have thought, it being as freezing cold in the cell as it was, that this might have helped. But instead of numbing her nerve endings, the cold only made them rawer, more sensitive. Whether she would have followed through with it or not, Ala swore to herself that if it were offered, she'd gladly have exchanged another fingernail for a blanket.

But these thorns the Nazis had planted in her flesh weren't her only sources of suffering. A formless disquiet lurked in the dark back rooms of her mind, not anything she could pin down, but there all the same, like a song with no name she couldn't get out of her head. Only this song wasn't fading prior to disappearing as was normal, but rather growing louder, more insistent. Worse, it didn't consist of an unease at things to come, but of something already come and gone, too late to undo. As the hours piled up and turned into a day, then two—she knew this because she was fed once a day—and the Germans continued unaccountably to leave her alone, from out of the mist of that nameless anxiety eating at her, something monstrous, inadmissible was trying to take shape. Her bout with the electric generator had played havoc with her memory. Her recollection of recent events was spotty, including her interludes with Broch and his goons. She remembered parts of these—how could she not?—but there were gaps, particularly in the last and most traumatic of them, of which she recalled little.

Eventually, a question as disturbing as it was impossible to answer crept into her thoughts. Could the generator have broken her and she'd given the *Unterscharführer* what he wanted without remembering it? That the pain it inflicted was something she'd never forget, there could be no doubt. Each time the electricity had slammed into her, it felt as if gigantic hands were trying to rip her in half, wrench her inside out, pulling her skin, her skeleton, her ligaments and tendons in opposite directions, tearing apart not only her body as a whole but each piece of it individually. The last thing she did recall of that final session was thinking she wouldn't be able to stand much more of this, that if the Gestapo kept it up, she could no longer guarantee the stronger part of her holding the weaker in check.

As she would find out later, small comfort that it was, her forgetfulness wasn't so much a case of memory failing her as it was she not having been in her right mind to begin with. With Broch having lost his cool that day and almost killing her, it had taken a good ten minutes to restore her to consciousness, and even then it was only partial. Groggy, unsure of where she was or what was happening, unable to put two thoughts end to end, she'd entered what in psychiatry was known as a fugue state, a waking dream in which she was responsive all right, but as a layman might put it, not really all there. The sergeant, who'd encountered this phenomenon before, saw an opportunity to turn near-disaster into triumph, and quick to take advantage of it swooped on the defenseless, discombobulated Ala. Another round of questions, coaxing this time, crooning, in the lulling singsong of the hypnotist, and like a sneak thief he soon had what he was after.

As a bonus, a small one but a salve to his conscience, it acquitted him also of having to release her as promised in that she hadn't given him the names he'd wanted voluntarily. Not that he would necessarily have done so, but now he could rest easier telling himself he might have.

Esther and Regina were snatched from Block 22 and returned to custody that night, and any hope the SS inquest had run its course, dampened by Ala's arrest and incarceration, now vanished completely. Fear once again stalked the floor of the Union factory, more pervasive a presence than the ubiquitous yellow dust, the heat and the noise.

This was as nothing, though, to the news that broke the next day. Roza, too, had been arrested, sped via truck that morning from her job at the Bekleidungskammer straight to Block 35. Roza Robota in the hands of the Gestapo! It was difficult to conceive of a greater catastrophe. It wasn't just that she knew every female at the Union who'd been involved in the theft and smuggling of its gunpowder, and the males, too. Not to mention the names of the Sonder leaders still living who'd planned the revolt. What loomed even more calamitous were the close ties she had with various key members of Battle Group-Auschwitz. Four in particular stood out: Marta Bindiger, the underground's liaison with the Weichsel-Union women, and three of Roza's Ciechanow connections, Noah Zabludowicz, Mordecai Hilleli, and, of course, her boyfriend Godel Silver. Though all were highly placed in the Battle Group, they weren't critical so much for who they were as whom they knew. In Noah's case, and probably Marta's, this likely extended to the upper levels of the movement's leadership. If Roza were to crack under torture, the damage done the organization might well transcend the incalculable and enter the realm of the fatal. With a cost in human life equally as grim.

Fear no longer inhabited the Union alone, but spread like a heavy, ground-hugging fog throughout the complex. Men and women in both camps prepared for the worst, cringed at the approach of every soldier, made up stories and alibis to tell under interrogation, contemplated suicide. To the bravest, it wasn't the thought of death that had them unstrung, but torture, and not just the unimaginable pain of it. They worried that not able to endure it, they would betray their friends, the cause, the Jewish people. And all that stood now between them and the horror, the disgrace of the torture chamber were four young and manifestly destructible women, one of whom, or so the talk went, had already knuckled under to the Gestapo and sold out the others.

People could only hold their breath and wait to see how the four were going to fare, Roza especially. None who'd crossed paths with her, however briefly, could have failed to notice the fire inside her. Yet how long could she or anyone be expected to bear up when forced without respite to drink from the cup of agony?

Though it was the new prisoner's first time in Broch's office, Raya Kagan knew who Roza was and why she'd been brought there. What surprised her was the girl's attitude—she didn't seem the least intimidated. If anything, she regarded the sergeant and the other uniforms present with undisguised contempt. The young secretary, who'd watched scores of people ushered trembling into this room, couldn't recall seeing a one who'd swaggered in.

But to her further surprise, and that of everyone else, when the Gestapo confession was shoved in front of her, Roza didn't hesitate to sign it. The deposition stated that not only was she the conduit through whom the stolen gunpowder reached the insurgents in the Special Squad but knew the purpose for which they intended to use it. When Broch appeared startled at the ease with which she'd surrendered her signature, she was quick to tell him why.

"Don't get your hopes up, *Unterscharführer*," she said, infusing his SS title with more ridicule than respect. "That piece of paper I put my name to is the only accommodation you're going to get out of me. And I give it freely for this reason: more than just willing to admit my role in the revolt, I'm goddamned proud of it. It was the most satisfying thing I've ever done in my life, and if I had it to do over again I would in a heartbeat. Even if I knew beforehand I'd end up having to answer"—here she leaned to her right and spat on the floor—"to the likes of you."

Raya couldn't believe what she was hearing, and her translating showed it. The words came haltingly, as if by repeating them she, too, might be found to share in their insubordination. Not that she didn't feel a shiver of pride at their fearlessness.

As for Broch, he erupted in applause. "Bravo! Well said, my little spitfire!" he exclaimed. "Refreshing, too, I might add, in contrast to the whining I'm accustomed to. I can tell we're going to get along splendidly, you and I. We will, need I say, have to work on your—what was the word you used?"

Roza glared at him, silent.

"Accommodation, I believe it was, yes. But then if it's convenient for you, we can start on that right now. Frau Kagan, if you'd be so kind," he said, with a nod toward the door. "We'll call for you, as usual, when we're ready."

Despite a temperature in the mid-forties and windy, Raya waited outside the building, smoking one of her last two cigarettes. She wasn't about to subject herself to the inevitable shrieking this time, not from this girl. Not from someone who dared talk to the SS the way she had. But though Broch's bellicose roar reached her even out here, if faintly, it wasn't accompanied by a single cry of pain. Nor would she hear one upon returning inside; other than the sergeant, the only sound was the muted clacking of the typewriters from the Standesamt. Who was this person, she wondered, to endure torture quietly, without so much as a peep?

Summoned to one of the interrogation rooms an hour later, she wasn't prepared for what awaited her. Roza was as she expected to find her, conscious but only just, her face broken and bloody. It was Broch who caught her off balance, sitting as he was at the desk looking like the cat that ate the canary. Holding a sheet of paper above his head, he waved her over. He wanted this typed up immediately, he said, so the prisoner could sign it. Back in his office, hardly had she started on it than the reason for his poorly concealed glee became clear. It was another, more detailed confession, this one complete with names. Roza had conceded passing gunpowder to the Sonderkommando by way of four men: an Ariel Wrubel, a Yankel Handelsman, one Zalman Gradowski, and a Yossel Warszawski. The transfer had taken place each time in the yard of the Bekleidungs depot, under the cover of accepting the clothing of the dead from the crematoria.

Raya couldn't remember seeing her boss so puffed up. Having anticipated in Roza a tough nut to crack, he'd already and with little effort succeeded in wresting multiple names from her. That they weren't the kind of names he was especially looking for made no difference; it was a start. He knew that once a suspect began yielding information, no matter how incidental, it became that much simpler to milk more meaningful data from him later.

Raya was at a loss to reconcile Roza's rapid capitulation. Every indication this latest arrival had given pointed to her being made of sterner stuff. This, though, she had to remind herself, was easy for her to say. The Nazis had had a whole hour to work the poor thing over; the face she'd end up taking out of the room wouldn't be the one she'd walked in with. Such was Roza's condition that once her statement was put in front of her, she had to have help holding the pen while she signed it.

It wouldn't take long, however, for both the *Scharführer* and his secretary, to the ill humor of one and silent apology of the other, to discover their error in thinking Roza a pushover. Two days weren't to pass before her "confession" would prove of less value than the paper it was typed on. For when Broch went off in search of the four Sonder she'd fingered, he found every one was among those listed to have perished in the revolt. His first inclination was to curse his bad luck—then himself, for having been made a royal fool of. She'd tossed him the names of four dead men on purpose, was probably having a good laugh about it still.

He vowed not to underestimate this prisoner of his again. Indeed, in acknowledgment of the exceptional individual she looked to be, he'd already singled Roza out for special attention. Aside from her appearing to be the one portal through which every ounce of the illicit gunpowder had flowed to the crematoria, there was something about her that set her apart, marked her as more of a leader than a follower. That she'd been entrusted to play so vital a part in the rebellion, perhaps even organizing the Union smuggling ring herself, was revealing of the status she enjoyed in the underground. Which made it a better than good bet that she had a working relationship with not only the actual perpetrators of the uprising but those in Battle Group-Auschwitz who'd aided them. It was these, even more than the criminals in the Union and the Sonderkommando, that the Gestapo were after, and Roza just the kind of acquisition who could deliver them. Of course, now that he finally had them in his clutches, Broch had no intention of going easy on any of the women; he looked forward to each contributing in her own way to the investigation. There was no question, however, on whom he planned to concentrate his energies.

Thus did the torture of the four begin in earnest, nor despite her headstart was the half-crippled Ala cut any slack. Every day at dawn, they were escorted from Block 11 in the northeast corner of the Stammlager all the way across camp to Block 35, kept well apart so there could be no contact between them. Once at Gestapo headquarters, they remained separated, each alone with her thoughts and another's screams in her ears until the soldiers came and it was her turn. Shaken by what they were forced to hear for the better part of the day now, many of the Standesamt women took to stuffing their own ears with cotton.

Sometimes Broch would extend these sessions into the night, but normally his charges made the long trek back to their cells by the middle to late afternoon. Rarely were they in any shape to walk it unassisted. Each was held upright by a pair of guards, one on either side, her bare, bloody feet often dragging the ground. Or when even this wasn't enough, on stretchers, unconscious, like the victims of some fatal accident. This was the worst for those witness to these grisly processions, for covered as the girls were every inch it seemed with wounds, they looked, and indeed, might very well have been dead.

There were always prisoners along the route of this Via Dolorosa who would gather to watch. Most were friends of the women, who through the freedom of movement their jobs or connections had gained them were able to travel the camp unhindered. These, aside from confirming the four were still alive, were there to provide what moral support they could. Understanding that to give voice to this support might result in their own arrests, their hope was to try and make eye contact with the sufferers in order to flash them a thumbs-up, a coalescent smile, anything that might let them know they weren't alone, that they hadn't been forgotten, that people were thinking about them, praying for them, suffering along with them.

Well-intentioned as this was, it was also futile. The mauled and mutilated women were in no condition to recognize anyone. If sensible of their surroundings at all, it was of the path directly in front of them, the view straight ahead. Glassy-eyed, heads hanging, they either shambled forward or were dragged, immersed to the exclusion of all else in their pain.

"Here they come," Noah said in the burnished light of the setting sun. "Brace yourself, Godel."

The two stood alone just off the edge of the limestone path. As dreadful a vigil as it was, they'd maintained it every day since Roza's arrest.

Godel Silver began tearing up as soon as he saw her. "Look at her," he said. "My God, her *face*...."

"You can't let it get to you," Noah said. "That's not what we're here for."

Godel turned away, his shoulders gently heaving. "I'm not sure anymore why we *are* here, are you? If I could only get her attention, just once...."

"All we can do is keep trying. I don't know what else we—"

"Well, I do!" Godel wheeled to face him, his tears suddenly angry. "I know what we can do! Me anyway. But then that's why when we're out here—I'm onto you, don't think I'm not—you never stray more than a foot away from me. To keep me from running up to her and throwing my arms around her."

"You mean like you tried to do four days ago? It's a good thing I *was* there. They'd have shot you down, Godel, before you got even close to her. Or hotfooted you off to Block 11 yourself."

"I don't care, let them. It would be worth it. All I want is to hold her one more time, tell her I love her."

Godel, actually, wasn't as "onto" him as he thought. Noah had appointed himself to watch over his old friend, but not only at this excruciating part of the day. Alarmed that he looked to be deteriorating emotionally the more Roza did physically, he'd become Godel's shadow when that was possible, and when it wasn't, had others keeping an eye on him. Roza he couldn't do anything about; her boyfriend, and a double tragedy, he could.

They didn't have any luck that evening, either. She was hauled by them without lifting her head. Afterward, Godel tried to explain himself.

"I appreciate you watching out for me, Noah, I really do, and how terribly you must be hurting, too. But you can't understand what it's like. Roza may be a good friend, your best friend, but to me she's no less than my other half, the light of my world, my lady and wife in all but name only. Not to downplay what you're going through, but as awful as it is, it's just not the same. Just not the same."

But, in fact, it was. Exactly the same—there was nothing Godel was feeling that he wasn't. Never had Noah hated the Germans more than when he saw what they were doing to his Roza, not even when he'd learned of the death of his parents, his sister, and kid brother. His instinct to combat injustice with blows, suppressed out of necessity since his entering the Vernichtungslager, was undergoing its most rigorous test yet. To have to stand impotently by while the love of his life was run through the Gestapo wringer, forced to watch as her body and beauty were reduced to ruin, bordered on the unendurable. If there was a chance, though, the slightest chance she might look up one day and see him there, neither God nor the devil was going to keep him away.

But punishing as it all was, there was one positive to come out of it, if nothing remotely capable of compensating Noah for his grief, then something a man drowning in it could hang onto. As time wore on and the days turned into weeks, he and those keeping track of them realized that something truly incredible was happening. Or to be accurate, not happening. Since the arrest of the four martyrs, not a soul had followed after them. Somehow, in spite of the violence piled on them, their torturers hadn't succeeded in gouging a single name from them. How this was possible no one could fathom; grown men, rugged, raised to be tough, couldn't imagine withstanding what these mere girls were. That they were weakening rapidly was evident. The trip to Block 35 had for a while now been less than daily, presumably because they were requiring more time to recover between sessions. And even then the journey, both there and back, was more often than not by way of the stretchers.

Yet to the reverential astonishment of all, they continued to hold out, their lips to remain sealed, nor did anyone find this more boggling than the SS. An increasingly confounded Broch didn't know where to turn next. Not even his workhorse, his faithful stand-by the electric generator, was getting results, not even when he had the alligator clip applied directly to toes, nipples, genitalia. Despite realizing he'd be lucky to repeat the success he'd blundered into with Ala, in his frustration he went ahead and tried the same approach on Roza, but it not only didn't work, he almost lost her, too.

Since being assigned to the Political Department a year ago, the sergeant had participated in innumerable interrogations, if not all conclusive, then certainly unexceptional. Meaning that as admittedly limited as his experience with female subjects had been, he'd found them, as one might have expected, less troublesome than the average male. Granted, the Gertner Jewess hadn't broken easily. But Broch had considered this more a fluke than a portent, and anticipated little of the same from the three women she'd given up. But now even she had closed tighter than a clam again, and contrary to what both practice and his upbringing had taught him, her accomplices from what was commonly accepted as the weaker sex were following suit.

How to explain this he didn't know, though in Ala's case, if he'd sat down and thought about it, he might have guessed. In her chagrin at learning from Broch later that in the semi-delirium brought on by her overexposure to electricity she'd betrayed the three, she'd have killed herself out of shame then and there if she'd had the means. But lacking these, she instead made a solemn promise to herself that it was going to take more than the Nazis had in their depraved repertoire to extract another name from her. Nor did she foresee this as being insurmountable, if for no reason than she'd also made up her mind to accept what pain lay ahead of her as penance for having got both herself and the others in this spot in the first place. What began with Eugen Koch and ended up in the torture chamber was her fault and hers alone. To compound it now by implicating any more of her erstwhile comrades was a sin she was prepared to suffer all the pangs of hell before committing.

As for Regina Safirsztajn, despite the heroism she'd shown in the course of her first detention, few thought she'd be able to hold her own against the Gestapo's more diabolic torments. Opinion had it she was too kind-hearted and sunny of disposition, too soft psychologically to overcome the concerted animus of prolonged interrogation. But it was just this, paradoxically, that helped stiffen her to it. Such was her sympathy for all those under the Nazi boot that it had fostered in her a loyalty not even torture could erode. As a forewoman, the matronly persona she'd adopted wasn't without basis; though younger than many, she looked upon the women of the gunpowder room and the Union in general as a mother might her children. She'd sooner have signed her soul over to Satan than the death warrants the SS were in effect demanding of her.

Esther was even harder to read, though it didn't take Broch long to figure out that the Wajcblum prisoner wasn't going to be the straightforward proposition he'd hoped. Beneath her deceptively melt-your-heart good looks, something inimical lurked, malignant, he could see it in her eyes, a mortal hatred of him and his uniform that burned below the surface like a fire raging in a coal mine. He'd got a taste of this when he had her the first time around, but unless it was his imagination, this enmity and the contrariness it fueled had grown more pronounced. It wasn't as if she was impervious to pain. While lashed to the chair or the bench, she screamed louder, wheedled more shamelessly for mercy than anyone. But whenever on the verge of falling apart and giving in, she would draw upon some inner reserve and pull herself together.

What Broch couldn't know was that this had less to do with her spite for his kind, or even a fealty to her own, than it did with the love she had for her baby sister. It was a tactic she'd evolved to make sure she stayed her tongue, and it was working. Through pounding it without end into her head, Esther had persuaded herself that should she be driven to the point of spilling names, the first to leave her lips would be that of Hanka. If she was going to betray anyone, or so she made herself believe, it would have to start with Hanka. And that wasn't possible. That wasn't going to happen. All the demons under heaven couldn't have torn that name from her. With this or silence the only choices open to her, nothing the Germans could do would make her talk.

Of the sergeant's four catches, however, none depressed, and at the same time, *im*pressed him more than the one named Robota. He couldn't recall encountering a prisoner quite like her, male or female. Not only did she plead guilty to everything she was accused of but boasted about it. She took a scornful delight, for example, in informing her captors that for nearly two years she'd passed stolen gunpowder to the Sonder right under SS noses, gunpowder she knew would end up taking SS lives.

"And my only regret," she would taunt, "is not having smuggled more. How does that grab you, a twenty-three-year-old girl, a *Jewish* girl no less, getting the best for so long of so many invincible Nazi *Übermenschen*? Doesn't that make you wonder, the thought cross your mind, that maybe you're not so damned *über* after all?"

As expected, Roza paid handsomely for her words. To the Gestapo strongmen, Broch included, taken as he was with her pluck, what would have been just another day on the job became something more when it was she brought into the room. Then it was game on as each strove to outdo the others in being the one to wipe the smirk from her mouth. Not that they'd had much success. For after they'd done their worst, or sometimes even while they were doing it, she was as liable as not to say something to the effect that if it allowed her the privilege of telling them to their faces what she really thought of them, then however hard they might lean on her was welcome.

But again, she would have rated the extra attention even if she hadn't been so smart-mouthed. Her three companions, though far from having no value, meant less to Broch together than Roza did alone. With everything, everybody, every secret she harbored, she was too enticing a plum to be left unpeeled. But in spite of all his efforts to bare the flesh beneath, this plum's skin remained intact. In her unbendingness, the *Unterscharführer* could scarcely elicit a cry of pain from her, much less a viable name. Those she had accorded him belonged predominately to the dead, a couple to men who'd been transferred out of camp. Running out of both options and time, his mood was glum; the outcome of the investigation and doubtless his reputation, maybe even his career, were at stake. The Kommandantur had been breathing down his neck for a month now, demanding to know why he had only the four women still to show for his troubles.

There was a solution maybe, if not a pleasant one. It came in the person of SS-*Sturmbannführer* Wilhelm Boger, also of the Gestapo, and his eponymous invention, the notorious "Boger swing." Not that Broch had any objection to using the major's device, which could be most effective. It was the man himself who gave him pause. Boger was an odd-looking troll of a person, one of those individuals whose appearance perfectly matched his occupation. He might have been born to play the part of the professional torturer. There was something about him that wasn't quite human; he could have passed for one of hell's minor fiends made flesh. No taller than a fifteen-year-old and built close to the bone, not an ounce of fat on him, his ears stuck out at right angles to his head, his nostrils two round holes in his face, like a pig's snout. His lips when they smiled revealed a pair of overlarge front teeth, making it hard to tell which he resembled more, swine or rodent.

It wasn't his off-putting looks, however, keeping Broch at a distance, reluctant even in this emergency to seek his assistance. A rivalry existed between the two and had for some time, precipitated by the major's jealousy at the success of his junior officer. The latter's adroitness in the interrogation room, though he remained unpromoted, propelled him swiftly upward in the operational hierarchy of the Political Department. A ranking member of same, this didn't sit well with Boger, especially with his subordinate being appointed to head more and more cases. He let it be known he considered the sergeant not only an upstart but soft, jumping at every opportunity to cite him publicly for lacking the harshness, the heavy hand the job demanded.

In point of fact, it was this very heavy-handedness that had held the *Sturmbannführer* back: too many of those prisoners assigned him had died under questioning before they could be fully exploited. It was a rare talent who could fill the role either man did, to spend one's days occupied in the methodical demolition of people who'd done nothing to one personally. Even rarer was balancing the ruthlessness this required with knowing when to loosen the screws, as it were. Broch, who had his issues, a short temper being one of the biggest of them, at least made an effort to keep it under control. Boger, on the other hand, was an undisguised sadist, whose relish for doling out pain often lapsed into frenzy. That he relied largely on his namesake swing for results did him no favors, for such were its mechanics that it lent itself to producing fatalities.

It was the simplest of concepts. From a stout metal bar a meter long, a thick braid of steel wire rose from each end to loop over a hook in the ceiling. The resulting contraption hung five feet above the floor, somewhat resembling a trapeze. The victim was handcuffed wrist to ankle and suspended naked from the bar, either facing outward, his spine bent back on itself, or inward, in profile like a giant teardrop. Both positions, especially the former, were painful enough, but as nothing to what was to follow. With his prisoner dangling defenseless in front of him, every body part exposed—face, genitals, buttocks, spine, depending on how he was displayed—Boger, brandishing a large club in both fists, would rear back and let him have it. The clubs that functioned best presented a flat surface, maximizing the damage without delivering a knockout blow. So vicious was the attack, so violent each impact, sometimes the swing would be sent flying in a tight, twisting arc. Or even more horrid, the wretch shackled to it do a complete three-sixty around the bar.

His "talking machine," Boger called it, and not without justification. Unless, that is, he got carried away, and the person he was working on wound up never talking again. Those who did survive the thing were unrecognizable afterward. What had been a face was so much strawberry jam, a human voice a frog's croaking. The skin of the thighs, buttocks, and back was frequently split open, that of the ankles and wrists stripped away by the handcuffs.

It took Broch a whole night of little sleep and a lot of back-and-forth with himself to decide that he had no choice but to hand Roza over to his repugnant adversary. He certainly wasn't getting anywhere with her, and starting to lose confidence he ever would. If he had to swallow his pride to advance the inquiry, so be it, even should it mean his stature take a hit. He was too dedicated the Nazi, patriotic the German to put his own interests before those of the Fatherland.

Besides, who was to say how well even Boger and his toy were going to fare against this Jewish she-devil? Broch had seen her spit, actually spit in the faces of his men even as they were torturing her. A part of him was glad to be dumping the bitch on someone else. Let the big-talking major break his teeth on her a while, see how he liked it.

Some days later, Noah Zabludowicz was summoned by the Steering Committee's Soswinski, who informed him of the curious reports coming out of Block 11.

"You've no doubt heard of the infamous kapo of the punishment block," Soswinski said, "the Jew Kozelczik. His position has earned him the ill will of all, particularly your people, who regard him as a traitor."

"I've heard tell of him, yes," Noah said, "but never had the misfortune of running across him."

"He does, though, it would seem, and fortunately for us, have one friend in the camp. None other than Erich Kulka, Bruno Baum's former lieutenant and one of our top agents."

"Him I have met, several times."

"Anyway, this Kozelczik contacts Kulka just this morning with what could end up good news. Apparently, a woman in one of his cells, tortured half to death, in her stupor keeps mumbling the same thing over and over. 'Bring me Noah,' is all she says, 'I have to see Noah.' "

Soswinski watched his visitor's eyes grow as round and white as eggshells. "According to the kapo," he said, "it's the prisoner Roza Robota. And it appears you're the Noah she's referring to. Is that correct?"

Noah could only nod, too flabbergasted to speak.

"Your mission, should you decide to take it, would be to go to this woman and find out what she wants. I won't say there's not an element of danger involved, but neither can I overstate its importance. What do you think? Are you up for it, Zabludowicz?"

He managed this time to choke out a hoarse, "Yes—yes, of course, I am, sir."

"Good. You're to be in front of Block 11 by nine tonight. Kozelczik will be there to let you in."

From Ala's arrest onward, Battle Group-Auschwitz had sought desperately to communicate with the imprisoned women, Roza in particular, eager to offer what sustenance and encouragement it could, but also to get a handle on how each was holding up. Much, perhaps everything, depended on this. It was vital that the underground have time to prepare, both as a group and individually, should further arrests be in the offing. No one, however, had come close to getting anywhere near the four. Not even Kulka, as tight as he was with their jailer.

Now here was one of their agents being issued an all but engraved invitation. As tantalizing as the prospect was, it was also enough to arouse more than a few apprehensions. Were the SS setting some sort of trap? But if they did suspect Noah of affiliation with the underground, and this a way of flushing him out, why so convoluted a ruse? The Germans could have picked him up whenever they wanted, unless their aim was to trace him back to those who'd sent him.

In the end, it was agreed to proceed with the mission. What cemented the decision was the trusted Kulka swearing to the integrity of his unusual friend. Jacob Kozelczik was an Auschwitz institution; he'd been around nearly as long as the camp itself. The only kapo the punishment block had ever known, he also served as the Stammlager's official hangman. Both jobs he'd earned by virtue of his uncanny strength. Though only average in height, he weighed almost three hundred pounds, most of it as solid as the human mountain he resembled. Adding to his menacing exterior, he shaved his scalp to the skin. In the camp's early days, at the request of the SS, he'd sometimes put on a show by bending heavy iron bars with his bare hands, and other such circus feats. In a more practical vein, no prisoner being led to the gallows or the Black Wall, no matter how much he might resist, could hope to wriggle free of his bone-crushing grip. If need be, he could escort two at a time to the execution site, one in each hand. He was as adept at subduing the violent or panicked, and when necessary extricating these from their cells.

The inmates called him *Shimshon Eisern*, the Iron Samson, and their dislike of him was as intense as their fear. In their eyes, he was a disgrace to his race; that a Jew should so unabashedly collaborate with the Nazis made him no better than his vile masters. Of the handful who thought differently, who knew better, most had arrived at this conclusion from time they themselves had spent locked up in Block 11. There they'd seen firsthand that he was no monster, often sticking his own neck out to provide the prisoners in his care some relief from their suffering. He might slip a victim of the starvation cells a draught of poison so he could die a quick rather than a slow death. Or distribute extra water when in the summer the bunker was like an oven. When administering the "25", as he was required sometimes to do, he was skilled at making a convincing show of it while actually delivering a lesser blow. He also refused to preside at the hanging of children, no matter the pressure put on him. This he left for the Germans to work out on their own. Kapo Jacob was one of those prisoners, like Kaminski and Leyb Langfus, whom the SS for various reasons tended to show a certain permissiveness.

He would test this tendency to its fullest toward the end of the year in a situation involving the four most celebrated residents of his block, but for now wanted nothing but to satisfy the wishes of the one.

Before dismissing him, Soswinski had briefed Noah on what the Steering Committee hoped to learn from his meeting with Roza. But he'd only half-listened. Already his heart was racing, the adrenaline pumping, and all he could think about or concentrate on was actually hearing her voice, looking into her eyes, taking hold of a hand he never in a hundred years would have dreamed he'd be given the chance to touch again. It was a prayer answered, but though he wasn't a praying man, he found himself hard-pressed not to wonder if maybe something, some power beyond his understanding, had taken pity on him in his sorrow and favored him with this kindness.

By 9:00 p.m., Noah stood in the shadows in front of Block 11. The building didn't look much different from its neighbors, a two-story structure of pinkish brick with a dark tiled roof. The only discrepancies lay in the windows, which were barred, and a door of unpainted steel instead of wood. An electric lamp above this door was all that kept the night at bay. He had worried there might be a guard, but didn't see one. That an ice-cold wind was blowing may have been why.

Right on time, and in creaking, metallic protest, the door opened to the unmistakable bulk of the kapo framed in yellow light. Noah followed him inside. In the anteroom to the *Kommandoführer's* office, a soldier his age leaned back in one of three folding metal chairs, feet propped on a wooden table. "Herr *Sturmmänn*," Kozelczik said in German, "this is the cousin I was telling you about." Then to Noah in their native tongue, "The corporal doesn't speak a word of Polish. Feel free to say what you please."

The kapo left the room and returned with a liter-bottle and three glasses. "Sit," he told his visitor. "This shouldn't take long. Have you ever had egg liquor? It's like drinking liquid fire."

Soon the glasses were clinking, the *Prosits* and *Heil Hitlers* flying. Their host suggested Noah down his first shot—"you look as if you could use one"—then pour all that followed under the table. He made sure to give the guard the lion's share of the bottle, who well before they reached the end of it passed clean out. After producing a cot and depositing the limp *Sturmmänn* on it, Kozelczik took a large ring of keys from its peg on the wall.

"You ready?" he asked. "Careful on the stairs, there's no railing."

At the end of a short corridor was another steel door. As if waiting behind it for them to unlock it, an evil stench leapt out at them: excrement and soured urine at first blast, which was awful enough, but underneath it something more ominous yet, the moldy odor of prolonged neglect, a subterranean rot of rancid fungus and decomposing soil, of air so long immured below ground it smelled as if even it had begun to decay. A dozen stone steps descended to a second corridor, this one much longer if poorer lit. A row of windowless doors stretched the length of it on either side. As the two men walked between them, from behind some came an urgent imploring in a variety of languages. Noah recognized the ones in Polish as begging Kozelczik for a blanket, for water, or simply to know what day it was.

Finally, the kapo pulled up at door #14, unlocked it, and swung it open. Nodding at Noah to step inside, without a word he locked it behind him, his footsteps rapidly fading.

It was even dimmer in the tiny cell than the hallway, the only light a single weak bulb overhead. In a corner huddled what looked like the broken carcass of some animal. As he drew nearer, Noah could make out human hands and feet, a naked female torso. He knelt down beside her, not believing his eyes; if he hadn't known it was Roza, he wouldn't have been able to tell. From her scalp, streaks of dried blood ran down a face that wasn't hers, that wasn't a face, so swollen and misshapen it could no longer rightly be called a person's. He laid his hand on her shoulder, but got no response. Gently, he shook it, then a bit more forcefully. At last, she let out a long, deep-throated moan.

"Roza, it's Noah. Can you hear me, dearest? I said it's Noah. You sent for me and I've come. Nod if you can hear me."

Her head moved tentatively up and down, though it took a moment for her eyes to blink open. "Noah? What—what's happening? How did you—where am I?"

"You're in your cell, my brave girl. It's all right, you're safe, it's just you and I."

With his help, she was able to rise on one arm, brought her face close to his. "Is it really you, Noah? I don't believe what I'm seeing. How—how'd you get in here? Past the guards, the locked doors?"

He decided it best to start at the beginning, with her calling out his name from her cell. After that, it was all Kapo Jacob, he explained, and told her, in detail, how without him they wouldn't be sitting across from each other now.

Roza wasn't surprised. "This Kozelczik," she said, her eyes clearer, her voice steadier, "isn't the vulture everyone thinks he is. He has a lousy job, but so do a lot of good people in this plague of a place. He's been sneaking me extra food, when I can eat it, and I would imagine, the other girls, too. He even brought me a blanket the other night, but the Germans took it away."

Noah whipped off his jacket and draped it over her. As he did, he took a closer look at her injuries. He'd seen a lot of ugly things in his days at Auschwitz, bodies at every stage of ruination, but never anything like this. A shocking patchwork of devastation covered her from head to foot: bruises the size of small dinner plates; large, inflamed gashes where the skin had either been cut or burst open as from some savage blow; uncounted lesser lesions and abrasions that glistened blackly in the murky light like so many smudges of used motor oil. Worst of all was what had become of her face. He could only hope he was hiding the revulsion in his.

She couldn't help, though, picking up on it. "It's a good thing beauty," she said, smiling crookedly, "is more than skin-deep."

"You're more beautiful to me than you ever were," he protested, disgusted at himself for letting his show. "How could I or anybody be less than in awe of those wounds, those badges of honor you're wearing? Besides, it's not forever. You'll have healed up nicely, I bet, in no time. Soon you'll be your old self again, pretty as ever."

"Healed?" She'd have laughed if it wouldn't have hurt so much. "Come on, Noah, we both know the Krauts aren't about to let me live long enough to heal. Esther, Ala, and Gina neither. We've each of us a foot and a couple of toes in the grave already."

He wanted to insist this wasn't true, but though he'd spent the last weeks swatting it away every time the thought neared, knew in his heart she was right. And would have made the moment even more awkward if he'd persisted in the charade. Instead, he scurried to change the subject, remembering with relief something that had been nagging at him since leaving Soswinski.

"So tell me, please, Roza, and don't take this wrong, but why me? I mean, how come you've been calling for *my* sorry self? If anyone, I'd have thought you'd want to see Godel. It would seem only natural he'd be the one you asked for."

Though a full two feet separated them, he could feel her body suddenly wilt. That brash grittiness so a part of her, which until then despite her condition looked to be trying to assert itself, sped away like smoke in the wind. Noah was afraid she was going to crumple back into a heap.

"Why not Godel?" She hung her head. "Because I didn't want him to see me like this. Because I knew it would be too much for him, that he'd take one look at me and fall apart. As much as I love and miss him, and can only hope I get the chance somehow to tell him that one more time, I can't have him or anyone falling apart on me. Not now. I need someone strong, someone I can lean on instead of the other way around. I need *you*, Noah," she said, and at this raised her head, though her voice remained as plaintive as those behind the cell doors he'd passed earlier. "My—my what? The center of me, the part that makes me *me*, is as broken as my body. Where before it was all so clear, my path pure and uncluttered, now it's as if I'm wading up to my waist in wet mud. If you could look inside me, take an X-ray of who I am, you'd find me as big a wreck as you see on the outside."

He didn't know what to say. He hadn't expected this. In all the years he'd known her, regardless of how bleak things were, never had he heard her give in to despair. "Roza, I'm so sorry," was the best he could come up with, and felt like the world's champion lamebrain for it.

But she was just getting started. "All we've worked for, sacrificed for, risked our lives the past two years for…. in the end, now that all is said and done, was it worth it? Worth the lives not merely risked but lost? I won't say the revolt wasn't noble in the attempt, or that it lacked glory, but it was far from the big deal we were led to believe it was going to be. Between the cowardice of Battle Group-Auschwitz and the bad luck of the Sonderkommando, it was doomed from the beginning to fall short. Of those who did rebel, not a one survived, much less escaped, while three of the four death houses continue to stand, to suck living people into them and spit out bone and ash. Operation Jericho? Operation Fiasco would be more like it. As much as I miss him and wish he was still with us, a part of me is glad friend Kaminski didn't live to see the hash made of his dream."

Noah opened his mouth to disagree, but she shushed him. "Answer me this. Have there been any more arrests?"

"Since you, none. Your courage, all four of yours, is the talk of both camps."

She managed a weak smile. "It's good to know my three sisters in pain are holding up their end, but...." The smile was short-lived. "But when it comes down to it, again, is it really worth it? Those whose lives we would save with our silence are just marking time; they await an early death as unavoidable as ours. The SS aren't about to let a single Jew from the camps live, and not simply to get rid of us as witnesses against them. Being German, they won't rest until they've carried out their orders, until we on the wrong end of those orders are no more. Is this why we've been offering up our bodies in the torture chamber, to spare people who in fact are as good as dead already?

"But never mind that, or our expendable four selves. Or for that matter the thousands here soon to follow us to the grave. What of the millions that have preceded us in the slaughter, those of our people from not only here but all over who've disappeared from among us like—like beads of dew in the sun? Unburied, unmourned, as if they'd never existed. It isn't the thousands who have me down, Noah, but the millions. After five years of ghettos, of deportations, exterminations, how many Jews can be left? How many will there be a year from now? My heart wants to say enough for our race to survive, but my head isn't so hopeful. My brain begs to differ. I remember once in the ghetto, right before we came to Birkenau, overhearing an SS man boasting to another that one day the only Jews to be found this side of the Atlantic would be those made of plaster on display in museums. Back then I wasn't sure what to make of that: did he really believe what he was saying or simply a fool running his mouth? Now, of course, I know, and can't help thinking that day is fast approaching. That the Nazis may have lost to the Russians and Americans, but won their war against us. That all our hardships, and even crueler, our resistance has been in vain and for nothing."

Noah still wasn't sure how to respond. From the tired flatline of her voice, it was obvious that Roza had hit bottom emotionally, a depth neither she experiencing it nor he observing it knew how to deal with. It wasn't until she started filling him in on what she'd been through, on exactly what a grilling by the Gestapo entailed, that he began to understand. He cringed at what he was hearing, had no idea even the Germans could be such animals. To drink from the bitter cup she had was to become embittered oneself.

Yet plumb his brain as he might to come up with something uplifting, the slightest bit revivifying, he could think of nothing that didn't sound either patronizing or trite. Until, that is, with a clash of cymbals only he could hear, and from out of where there was no telling, the memories of a decade ago came tumbling to his rescue. Having remained buried for so long, that they were retrievable at all was cause enough for wonder. Add to this the fact they echoed the words of a God he'd long ceased talking to, and what emerged was even more improbable.

"I sympathize, Roza, with what you're feeling. I do. From where we stand, with what we've seen—with what we haven't seen but know has happened wherever the SS have set foot—to speak of a future for the Jewish people is to risk sounding naïve, if not downright nuts. After five years, as you said, of murder, it's no easy thing to try and stay positive. Hell, if I'd been through five *minutes* of what you have, I imagine I'd be tempted to lose heart also.

"But there's an argument to be made for optimism, too, guarded though it may be. And it begins with something I've got to believe still strikes a chord with you. Tell me, how much of your Ezekiel do you remember?"

Though well aware she was no more religious than he, that wasn't the angle Noah was pitching. There weren't a lot of scouts from the old H'Shomeir H'Tzair, religious or not, who couldn't recite from the biblical book of Ezekiel. An important part of the Shomeir's curriculum was the study of this book, as its message existed in direct complement to that of the Zionists. The prophet Ezekiel had stood tall as his nation's hope during the Babylonian exile. Though he preached that the defeat at the hands of Babylon was God's punishment for the Israelites, among other sins, having turned their backs on Him by resuming the worship of idols, he also foretold God's forgiveness and their eventual deliverance from bondage and return to the Holy Land. If the Shomeir, and by extension Zionism, could be said to have a patron saint, it was Ezekiel.

"How much do I remember?" Roza said. "I don't know." Even at this elliptical reference to the Shomeir, he thought he could detect a glint of her old self in her eyes. She stared at the ceiling a long moment before making the attempt. "Thus—thus sayeth the…. Lord God," she began uncertainly. "Behold, I—I will take the children of Israel from the midst of the nations where they are gone; and I will gather—will gather them on every side, and bring them back to their own land. And I will make them one nation in the…. land on the mountains of Israel. Nor shall they—nor shall they be defiled anymore with their idols, nor with their abominations, nor their iniquities; and I will save them out of all the places in which they have gone. And I will cleanse them, and they shall be My people, and I will be their God."

She was starting to roll now, to gain confidence. "See, I will instill breath into you, and you will live. Yes, I will restore you, put flesh upon you, cover you with skin and—and put breath into you and you will come alive. See, I open your graves and will raise you from them, My people, and bring you to the land of Israel, to the land that is restored from the ravages of the sword, where people are gathered out of many nations."

When she stopped, Noah could see even beneath its disfigurement that her face had brightened some with the warm light of nostalgia, of happier days, of a time before death replaced life as the norm. He was impressed that she'd retained so much after so long, but even more at the change her recitation had worked on her. Gone as if at the touch of a wand was the morbidness that had ahold of her, in its place a glimpse of the Roza he knew and loved.

"Excellent," he said. "You couldn't have picked a better passage. You get where this is headed, don't you?"

"Yes, I do. I mean…. I think so."

"Allow me then, my beauty, to spell it out. To cheer you with a vision of the future as it could be. What planted hope in the Jewish breast twenty-five hundred years ago can do so today; the prophet continues to speak to us from across the centuries. And what he's telling us is the idea of the Jewish people as inextinguishable. Of Israel as eternal. Or to put a modern slant on it, of Zionism as destiny. The SS, despite their Birkenaus and

Treblinkas, their crematoria and mass graves, will never succeed in killing us, not all of us. We are too many, too widespread for even the Germans to stamp out completely. Some of us, even millions of us, are going to survive. And with the Third Reich no more, a casualty of its own wickedness, Eretz Israel will beckon as never before.

"This time, however, it won't be at the whim of some God that we make our way there, but on our own initiative. What, after all, are we liable to find come liberation but the rubble of our homes, of our families, our past? There is no past for us here anymore, even less of a future. Those left alive, I suspect, will be tripping over each other to make aliyah, to be rid forever of this Europe of blood and tears. Funny how it will have taken a Hitler and his insane hordes to open our eyes, to shock us into leaving where we were never wanted for the only place we ever really belonged.

"But what am I telling you that you don't already know? Of aliyah, that is. Haven't you and Godel been planning for years now to—"

Cursing his truly monumental stupidity, Noah caught himself before he finished the sentence. But too late. That it was a fact the couple, as far back as the ghetto, had talked of starting their lives anew in Palestine one day, was no excuse for his being so incomprehensibly clumsy as to bring what was now a shattered dream to her attention.

But if she noticed it at all, Roza brushed it aside. She'd come to terms with dying in the blossom of her youth, with life's potential unrealized, its adventure cut short. She'd reconciled herself to that not fifteen minutes after her arrest. Of infinitely greater concern to her, as she'd made clear, wasn't the thought of her extinction but that of her people. Now, thanks to Noah having reminded her of where she came from and the ideals she'd grown up on, this at worst seemed less likely, at best unfounded altogether. How she with her Shomeir background could have failed to see this on her own escaped her, but she could at least credit her instincts in having turned in her desolation to someone with the strength to help her overcome it.

And in less time than she'd have thought possible. "You do realize, I hope, Noah, that I owe you more than I can say. That you really came through for me. I had a feeling you would, that you'd know just the words I needed to hear. What you've done is no less than save me from myself, from that whiny little milksop in me. That's somewhere in everyone, I suppose."

"Roza, I'm sure you'd have figured it out for—"

"Because of you," she cut in, not at all sure she'd have figured it out for herself, "I can die in peace now, content in the knowledge that it won't be for nothing, that the struggle wasn't wasted. With you and Ezekiel making the convincing argument for it you do that our people might have a tomorrow after all, who am I, one of you two's biggest admirers, to dispute it? Thank you, Noah, for everything. For being, well, Noah."

"*You* thanking *me*?" This was too much for him. "That's like a doctor thanking his patient for getting well. Besides, what did I do that any friend wouldn't have?"

"You've been more than a friend, and for as long as I've known you. But never more than tonight. And you were curious why it was you and no one else I kept calling for."

His eyes grew suddenly large. "More than a friend, you say," he repeated after her. "I don't think you know, Roza, just how true those four words are."

It was the way he said it, almost with regret, more than what he said. "What do you mean, Noah? I—I don't...."

He didn't answer right away, nor look at her when he did. "There's something I have to share with you that I couldn't before. Something I've been keeping inside me forever. I don't see the harm in letting it out now, though, as I'm hoping you won't. Circumstances being what they are," he said, turning his face toward hers, "the real harm would be in leaving it unsaid."

It was then that she saw what he was getting at. She may have been bloodied, but she wasn't blind; it was all there in those pleading eyes of his, a look she'd come to know well over the years. She'd been waiting for this, living in dread of it for five of them, in fact, though if she wanted to be honest about it, had to admit that was then. Things were different now. With both her own and her future with Godel in ruins, perhaps Noah was right. There had been a time when it would have been in poor taste, even destructive to come out with it, but those days were as dead and gone as the promise they'd once held.

"What is it you're wanting to tell me?" she asked, deciding it best to play dumb, let him do the talking.

Having labored for so long to keep it secret, ever on the watch that in a weak moment he not crumble and blurt it out, now that it was about to

455

be a secret no more he hesitated, unsure how to begin. He decided not to tiptoe around it.

"When you say I'm more than a friend, Roza, little do you realize how much more. I—I've loved you heart and soul from the day I first met you. From the first thirty minutes. Hardly had the waitress taken our order than I'd fallen for you. Do you remember that morning at the Yellow Rose Café?"

To his surprise, she appeared to take his pronouncement in stride. "It was spitting rain outside," she said. "We were drinking coffee. You were much handsomer than Godel said you'd be."

"I don't know about that," he said, "but you remember all right, and a lot better than I thought you would. Even stranger, though, is that you didn't even flinch. At what I just told you."

"To tell the truth, Noah, I've known for a while."

"What, that I was in love with you?"

"I'm afraid so. I never let on that I did because what good would it have done? Or better, what bad might it have caused? That was a can of worms shouting not to be opened, begging to remain shut, for there was no telling what would have come slithering out of it. Nothing very pretty, of that I'm certain. I'm only thankful you had the insight to see it that way, too. And the graciousness to say nothing."

He said nothing now as his brain sought to process what his ears had just told it. When he did speak, it was halting. "So, you knew all along. I was that—that obvious."

Struggle as she did, she couldn't suppress a smile. "I don't mean to sound condescending or anything, my poor Noah, but you had a habit of mooning after me like a lost calf. You couldn't have been more obvious if you'd tried."

Now that he thought about it, he, too, had to smile. "That may have been. I won't say it wasn't. I've been known to wear my feelings like a sign around my neck. But it was never intentional, a ploy to trick you into noticing; I hid it the best I could, and for the best of reasons. You do realize, I hope, Roza, I'd rather have cut off an arm than ever do anything to come between you and Godel."

"Didn't I say how grateful for that I was? I thought the more of you for it as both a friend and a man. But that's all water under the bridge.

Still appreciated, yes, don't get me wrong, but irrelevant. My life is over, and that changes everything. Not least whatever secrets existed between you and me. You've told me yours and were in your rights to do so, to bare your heart without fear anymore of it encroaching on what Godel and I have. But I've got a secret, too, one I'm pretty sure you never suspected."

She sensed his body go stiff. Arranging her thoughts, she pondered how best to say this. "The world can come off as a pretty dodgy place," she began, "when thinking in terms of what might have been. It can be difficult then not to view your life, the events that shape it, as founded on no more than—what am I looking for? Happenstance. I was drawn to you, Noah Zabludowicz, even after I'd committed myself to Godel. Not devoutly enough, even in passing, to consider ever leaving him for you—that I couldn't do, not if my soul depended on it—but drawn nonetheless, deny It to myself as I might. To be truthful, as I found myself sometimes *having* to deny it. We're too much alike, you and I, not to feel that pull of one kindred spirit for another. It's like the coin to the magnet, lightning to the rod; the attraction is inevitable, an edict of nature."

She took one of his hands in both of hers, wincing in pain at the effort. "What I'm trying to tell you, while I have the chance, is that but for an accident of timing, a fall of the dice, I can conceive of myself, Noah, having ended up in love with you as opposed to Godel. That if fortune had seen fit to bring you into my life first, who can say…. what might have been?"

Here she stopped to take a long breath. "There, I've out with it. And feel the better for it. Better in that, like you, I was able at last to say what I've often wished to but couldn't. What needed to be said." She squeezed his hand once before letting it go. "I'd hate to think of me leaving this life without having spoken it, without you ever knowing. That would have been not only cowardly but unfair."

She was right, of course. He hadn't suspected this at all, and it left him for the moment at a loss for words. In lieu of those, he reached up and touched her face, began ever so gently stroking the side of it with the backs of his fingers. As he did, it ceased to be the one the Gestapo had given her. The swelling and the cuts, the blackened, bloodshot eyes, the flattened nose, the fractured cheeks—all either melted away or reconstructed themselves, so that what ended up looking back at him was the vibrant, young face he'd known in the ghetto, as pristine as when he'd first laid eyes on it that day it came waltzing into the Yellow Rose. It was the same face that had swept him off his feet then and continued to now, a mix of seriousness and mischief, severity and kindness that even as it warned you not to get in its way invited you along for the ride of your life. It was a face Noah couldn't have resisted if he'd wanted to, nor would any barbarity the SS could possibly inflict on it ever make it the less enchanting to him.

Upon regaining the power of speech, he would thank her for having the generosity to open up to him when she didn't have to. Though he found it hard to persuade himself entirely that she meant everything she'd said, whether she did or not didn't matter. That she cared enough about him to say it at all made up for more than a little of what he'd suffered all these years longing for her from afar.

In their conversation afterward, there was no more talk of love. Apart from the disrespect it would have made them feel they were showing Godel, it was as if having declared it, or in Roza's case the potential for it, elaborating on it further would have been too painful. Neither the present nor the future offered much comfort in that regard, or for that matter any other, so they retreated instead into the safety of the past. Of those days in Ciechanow before their families, their friends, and their own belief in the inherent goodness of humanity disappeared forever in the fires of Birkenau.

They talked until one in the morning of times gone, better times, of life both before the ghetto but mostly during, when things seemed abysmal but in retrospect weren't so bad. When if little else they still had their loved ones and a modicum of freedom—when they and Godel, inseparable, would inhabit the streets by day, and at night dare to sneak out of that prison without walls in dangerous if exhilarating search of army contraband.

And they'd have continued reminiscing but for the sound of steps approaching, the clank of a key in the door, the door opening to reveal, to their relief but also sorrow, the unsurpassed heft of Kapo Jacob filling it.

"It's time," he said. "That idiot *Sturmmänn* is starting to show signs of life. We'll all be in trouble," he told Noah, "if he finds you down here."

Roza looked up at him and smiled. "Allow me to thank you, kapo, from the bottom of my heart for bringing Noah to me. For being the good man you are. If it should happen I be remembered one day for what I've done, you won't be forgotten, either. Would it be too much, my friend, to ask for one more favor?"

"Not if it's quick, child."

"A pencil and a piece of paper. And I promise to be fast. Just a few words, a farewell, for Noah to take back to my friends."

A desk stood at the foot of the stairs in which the bunker's daily logs and other paperwork were kept. It took no more than a minute for the kapo to return with what she'd requested, and another two of her scribbling away before handing Noah a sheet of paper folded in half.

"If you could see that this gets to the right people," she said, "it would make what lies ahead of me that much easier."

"Consider it done," he said. "And?"

"And what? What are you asking?"

"There must be something else I can do for you, Roza. Or if not me, another. There's no shortage, I hope you know, of people more than willing to risk their lives to help you through this."

"No, nothing else. Not, that is, as you'll see when you read it, beyond what I've set down in that paper you're holding. Unless…. wait a minute. Yes, there is something after all."

She motioned him closer. "I don't wish to pester this Jacob any more than I have already," she whispered, "should he start to think me a nuisance, but maybe you could talk to him about trying to smuggle Godel down here, too. Not right away, not in the condition I'm in, but after the Krauts maybe are done with me and I'm looking a little more presentable. Would that be too much to ask of him, you think? I can't imagine not telling my Godel goodbye."

"No, Roza, I don't see as how it'd be too much at all. He's obviously a decent fellow, despite his reputation. I'll ask him before I—"

There was a rumbling from the doorway as their benefactor, his back to them, made a show of clearing his throat. The message was plain.

"I'll ask him tonight and see what he says," Noah promised. "But speaking of goodbyes, it would appear the time has come for us to say ours."

Roza nodded, and despite having braced herself for this, could feel the tears coming.

"Trouble is," he said, "I don't know how. Or if I even can. How do you tell someone dearer to you than life itself goodbye?"

"Simple," she said, wiping at her eyes. "You get up off the floor, kiss her once on the forehead, then march your ass out that door without looking back. No words. No tears. Just go and don't look back. It may not feel like it, Noah, but it's best that way. Please."

He would stay up all that night, what remained of it. The electric explosion of the 4:30 reveille bell would find him wide awake in his bunk. Indeed, many was the night to come when sleep stubbornly refused to, when he would lie there replaying in his head every detail of those hours in the bunker's Cell #14. Some of them were and always would be a pleasure to recall, but others would haunt him for as long as he lived.

Among this last was the manner of his departure. He'd done as Roza had all but begged him to and left without a word, but it hadn't been easy. Once outside her cell, in fact, unable to help it, he'd turned and would have gone back inside—to say exactly what he wasn't sure, he hadn't thought that far—but for Bunker Jacob emerging from it and blocking his way. As if that weren't disgruntling enough, to his disbelief the man was clutching the gray canvas jacket Noah had given Roza as protection against the cold.

Seeing the anger in his face at sight of it, the kapo explained that he hadn't any choice. The Germans had made it clear, after discovering some blankets he'd furnished them, that the women, not him, would pay for any such trespass in the future.

"Besides," Kozelczik added, "if the *Sturmmänn* should identify this coat later as that of my 'cousin'...."

There was, of course, no arguing with this, any of it. Noah could only swallow his anger and apologize. But as he lay later in the comparative comfort of his bunk, the image of Roza curled up naked and alone on the concrete floor of that freezing cell, with only the burning of her wounds to combat the cold, so filled him with guilt that he tossed and turned like a man in the throes of a delirium. How this didn't wake his brother Hanan, or the other two occupants of their koje, he didn't know.

Nor did it take long before the thought of his coat warming himself instead of her got to be too much, and he tore the thing off as if it were on fire. As tattered and thin an affair as it was, heavily frayed at the cuffs and with holes at both elbows, it was better than no protection at all. During the summer, he'd traded some tire rubber he found on the side of the road and three rations of bread for it, and had been sharing it with Hanan since. It had no lining, but a makeshift pocket had been sewn on the inside. It was while freeing himself from the coat that a piece of paper fell from this pocket and glided to the floor.

It wasn't until then that he remembered what Roza had given him. How could he have forgotten that? He lit one of the candles they kept by their bunk, unfolded the paper, and holding it up to the light started to read. As he did, he could hear the words in his head as if she were speaking them.

"Friends and fellow soldiers," it began, "I send you my final regards. It is not an easy thing to exit this life, but I go to my death without regret, convinced that our fight was a just one. As for yourselves, you have nothing to fear. There will be no more arrests. Despite every cruelty the SS have thrown at us, I and the three brave women imprisoned with me have refused to cooperate. And will continue to refuse. In return for our silence, we ask only three things: that you remember our names, not stop resisting until the battle is won, and most important, never forget your obligation to the dead. They call to you from the grave—your parents, brothers and sisters, husbands and wives, your children—call for the righting of an unforgivable wrong. The Nazis are finished. Their end as our masters is near, but it must not stop there. The dead demand vengeance, that justice be done. Those of you who survive must see that they get it."

Roza closed as Noah would have expected her to, with the Shomeir's traditional farewell: *Chazak ve Amatz*, the Hebrew for "Be strong and of good heart." He would read these farewell words of hers several times that night, for though there was no denying the heartbreak they evoked, he also had to smile at their characteristic spleen. And the feeling it gave him that she was right there beside him, if not in the flesh then the spirit.

It was a feeling that would become the more tangible when happening to glance at it, he saw blood on the discarded jacket, a spot here, a smear there, not red but more like chocolate in the dull yellow light of the candle. He hadn't noticed this before, not in the dark, but as soon as he did he slipped it back on and sat there rocking gently, hugging it to himself.

Winter

By the last weeks of November, the long, golden afternoons and invigorating briskness of autumn had given way to the gelid embrace of its harsher sister season at her meanest. Winter arrived with all its teeth showing from the start. The first real snowstorm had been a violent one that had raged for days, the watchtowers on the other side of the wire barely visible, ghostlike, through the swirling white. After it had blown itself out, the whole of Auschwitz-Birkenau lay half-buried under immense, rolling drifts, as if swallowed by an avalanche. In some places at Birkenau, with its single-storied barracks, the wind had piled these drifts to the roofs. The smothering silence of deep snow clung to the landscape like a blanket, muffling all but the most strident of noises.

But it wasn't only quiet because of the snow. For months the usual clamor from the Jewish ramp had been in decline, the screech and whistle of the trains, the barking of the Germans and their dogs, the growls of the trucks carrying the infirm and old to the crematoria. But for the occasional flurry of activity such as had resulted from the emptying of the Lodz and Theresienstadt ghettos, the transports had dwindled to less than one a day now. Sometimes much less, with two or even three days passing between them. The number of cars in each were fewer as well.

While this hadn't gone unnoticed by Birkenau's general population, no demographic was more acutely aware of it than the Sonderkommando. For unlike the other inmates, whose lot it affected little, to the men of the Special Squad it was a matter of life and death. Without transports, the SS had no reason to keep alive those slaves whose function was to dispose of the living cargo the trains delivered. Especially when what those slaves knew of the operations was enough to hang every German even remotely involved in them. There were two hundred Sonder remaining with barely work for fifty these days, each awakening every morning to the very real possibility of it being his last.

This was as nothing, though, to the blow dealt the detachment before the month was out. Incredible as it sounded, a rumor began circulating that Berlin had ordered the exterminations to halt, which would mean, of course, *no* transports sent to the gas. When this was supposed to go into effect, no one knew, but all of Birkenau was on fire with the news. When it reached the dayan Leyb Langfus, he assumed it no more valid than most rumors he'd encountered since he'd been here, all giddy conjecture and no real substance. And would have dismissed it as such but for the fact it was nearing a week since the unloading ramp had yielded any victims.

That and the odd behavior the SS had been exhibiting of late. Overnight, a good many of them had become mere shadows of their old selves. Gone was the arrogance most had worn like a second uniform, in its place a groping, tentative confusion, as if they weren't exactly sure how to act anymore. Though still abusive toward their captives, their belligerence often lacked the cutting edge it once held, was more subdued, at times almost perfunctory, giving the impression their hearts were no longer in it. A few had taken it a step further than that even, making what looked to be an effort at altering their attitudes entirely. Langfus couldn't be positive, so subtle was the change, but every once in a while thought he could detect something resembling actual friendliness from these last: the trace of a smile, the conspiratorial wink of an eye, an order given civilly that in the past would have been snarled.

But something else was flitting at the fringes of the SS face these days, and there was no misconstruing it. The pale pinch of fear had sunk its hooks in them, the same fear they themselves had inspired for so long. And it was declaring its presence by virtue of deed as well as demeanor. Suddenly, Birkenau was a veritable ant hill of Nazi paranoia. The Sonder found themselves burning more paperwork than bodies as whole truckfuls of the stuff began showing up at the crematoria. True to their reputation for thoroughness, the Germans had kept a meticulous record of their nefarious goings-on: tens of thousands of carefully falsified death certificates, as many more police dossiers and files from the Political Department, a complete accounting of those transportees who'd gone straight from the ramp to the gas and fire pits, the hospital records of all who'd entered there never to return. Now box after box of this and related documentation were disappearing into the ovens, and that wasn't the half of it. Two thousand prisoners were put to work emptying the warehouses of Canada, packing what was judged valuable for shipment to Germany, that which was left stacked into bonfires and burned. Others were employed in disinterring what human ashes had been buried and dumping them in the Vistula. All the camouflage screens and baffles were torn down, the remaining fire pits filled in. Any fuel and other temporary supply depots were dismantled, both ash-crushing slabs laid with grassy sod, and the entire area of the razed Bunker 5 complex planted with rows of young trees culled from the woods.

Clearly, the Red Army was either on the move again or expected to be soon, and in anticipation of its arrival, the SS were trying to cover their murderous tracks. If true, however, and the gassings had indeed ceased, why would the Nazis take such pains to obliterate so much other evidence yet leave the most damning of all, the crematoria, untouched? But for Bunker 5 and the useless shell of Crematorium IV, Birkenau's killing machinery remained not only standing but functional, available in its totality if needed. Perhaps this newest rumor was as baseless as it sounded, and the SS thirst for Jewish blood still unsated.

Langfus and some others decided to investigate for themselves. Though they'd heard trains coming and going several times that week, not a single ragged column of people had made an appearance at any of the death houses. Assuming these trains had been requisitioned to carry off the plunder of Canada, the Sonder had thought little of it. Now with the week almost gone and still no deportees, the dayan, Zalman Leventhal, and the ex-kapo Shlomo Kirschenbaum resolved to meet at the next sound of a locomotive to see what they could find out.

It was a sunny if cold morning, not a breath of wind, the snow piled high and white except where it met the camp streets and had turned into a dirty brown slush. It was a short walk from Crematorium III to a small rise from where the three Sonder had an unobstructed view of the unloading ramp. The transport that had lured them consisted of only half a dozen cars from which the last of five hundred people were descending. All were male and adult, wore the yellow Star of David on their clothing. They also all appeared to be either ill or extremely weak; many of them, unable to stand, lay on the icy concrete where they'd been carried. Instead of forming them into a line and commencing the ritual of selection, however, the two officers present sat in a staff car passing a flask between them while their subordinates huddled before the flames leaping from the open mouths of three steel barrels.

"What do you make of it?" Langfus said. "Why no selection?"

"I wouldn't think they'd need one with this bunch," Kirschenbaum replied. "Look at the poor devils, they can barely walk."

"Shlomo is right," Leventhal said. "It's the gas for these, the lot of them. The Krauts are merely waiting for the cremo trucks, I would imagine."

Seconds later, as if on cue, a dozen of these rolled up and stopped. Once loaded with the five hundred, they went rumbling down the road fronting the crematoria in the direction of Number Five, or more likely bound for the *B2f* lager and the men's Himmelblock. But to the unbelieving eyes of the Sonder watching, they never made it to either, taking a right turn instead into *B2d* and its housing barracks. D Camp, not death! Not for the time being anyway. The three could only stare at each other, stupefied.

Just in case it would later prove some sort of aberration, one never knew with the SS, they decided to keep what they'd seen to themselves, at least until the next transport. To jump the gun on something so incendiary in its implications would have been as unwise as it was irresponsible.

They only had to wait another day. The one that pulled up to the ramp the following morning was larger than yesterday's and composed of a different crowd completely. A thousand people stumbled clumsily down from the cattle cars to stand blinking in the white winter sun. Except this time there were almost no men among them, mainly women and children, a few elderly. This transport, too, was Jewish, but again there was no selection. All thousand were bundled off, with their possessions, away from the death factories and down the path leading to B Camp, their guards showing unusual patience with the slower pace of the aged.

The three witnesses to this observed it in silence. It was Kirschenbaum who broke it, his words giving voice to what the others were thinking.

"That's it then," he said. "We're all as good as done for. This 13th Kommando might as well kiss its four months goodbye; we'll be lucky, I get the feeling, to see much of December."

That Thursday ushered in a welcome break in the weather. By afternoon, the temperature had struggled into the forties, which it would continue to reach into the weekend. By the next afternoon, the camp was swampy with melting snow, well on the way to becoming its normal sea of mud.

At a little past one o'clock, the two inhabited crematoria, III and V, erupted without warning in shouts of "*Antreten! Alles antreten!*" as soldiers moved from room to room ordering the Sonder out. Coming as this did in the middle of the day, before evening roll call, it augured no good. The men formed into rows in their respective courtyards, trying their best not to but fearing the worst.

Abating this fear some, the Germans unexpectedly led both groups out their gates and onto the road. Up to then, it had shown every sign of being a selection, but this was something different, and anything different at this point was a plus. Maybe, the men whispered among themselves as they marched, they were merely needed for a special job somewhere. Both whispers and hope died abruptly, however, upon their crossing the empty train tracks and entering the yard of Crematorium II. A hundred SS waited there to greet them, guns at the ready. Five officers were also present, two from the Gestapo and the *Kommandoführers* of the crematoria, Sergeant Gorges having been reassigned to Number Three. A couple of these were conferring over a clipboard at what could only have been a list of tattoo numbers. It was to be a selection all right, except this time the Nazis had taken precautions. There would be no repeat of October 7th.

Not that the Sonder were in any way up for one themselves. They'd spent the last few days girding for this moment, though despite the report their three workmates had brought back from the ramp, it was difficult to believe—after eight months and even more, three times that much some of them, of living on borrowed time—that their final hour was at hand, death come for them at last. Made to line up, they stood dejectedly in formation, meekly awaiting the inevitable. An unshaven and disheveled Gorges, giving every indication he was drunk, stepped forward and ordered those men whose tattoo numbers he read to depart ranks and wait at the gate for escort back to their posts. This was a reverse of that catalyzing selection of fifty days ago, with those on the list the fortunate this time. First to be called were the squad's half dozen medical personnel. Next, the commando's newest additions, the thirty prisoners chosen as replacements in the aftermath of the revolt. Counted among these, courtesy of SS ineptitude, were Shlomo Kirschenbaum, the Czech Filip Müller, and their two Greek confrères in luck, all of who hadn't only survived the 7th but were able subsequently to sneak back into the squad.

Finally, Gorges shouted the numbers of twenty individuals, as a reserve to man the crematoria if needed, but primarily to assist in their eventual disassembly and demolition. Left behind were a hundred and fifty doomed souls already contemplating the manner of the death in store for them. Would it be by gas, bullet, or something new this time? Again, there was never any telling what might come crawling out of the Nazi brain.

Not that they were to find out anytime soon. For no discernible reason and without further ceremony, soldiers herded the lot of them into Number Two's cremation room and locked its doors. A few of the condemned wondered if this was it, but soon realized with the rest that it was hardly the place for an execution. There was conversation but not much, nor for very long. To a man they withdrew gradually into the private world of their own thoughts, the only sounds then the soft sobbing and random whimper of protestation one might expect of people about to meet their end.

Until, that is, the main door flew open and in strode *Kommandoführer* Muhsfeld, a squad of soldiers at his heels. Try as he did to project an air of nonchalance, both his expression and voice were as stiff as his Prussian spine.

"Men of the 13th Sonderkommando! You are about to begin a new life. Today you will embark for the concentration camp at Grossrosen, where work awaits you in an underground armaments factory. It is important work, and you will be well treated. Trucks will soon be arriving to—"

"Herr *Oberscharführer, bitte*! Please!" It was the dayan Leyb Langfus. Separating himself from the crowd, he approached to within a few meters of Muhsfeld. His German was more than adequate. "We are not children," he told the sergeant, "we know what lies ahead for us. There is no need to insult us with talk of Grossrosen. With your permission, I would make your job easier and speak to the men myself. Trust me, it will be to everybody's benefit, including yours."

Taken aback as he was, Muhsfeld kept his composure. It was an outlandish request, even criminal in its impertinence, but after looking the dayan slowly up and down, he nodded his assent.

Langfus turned to face the others. "Brothers!" he cried, spreading his arms. "Fellow Jews! It is God's inscrutable will that we now lay down our lives. It has been our cruel fate to have participated in the extermination of our own people, and now we ourselves are to be reduced to ashes. Many of you ask why, and not alone with self in mind. You ask why the heavens never intervened to stop the slaughter, to send rains strong enough to drown the funeral pyres, bolts of lightning to blast the crematoria. How could God, you ask, have turned His back on His chosen? Permitted the Gentile to lay waste His children? It is not for us, however, to question God's reasons. As His children, as sons of Israel, we can only trust in and accept them, taking comfort that in His omniscience He knows what is best. That in the long term somehow, somewhere, some day, even Birkenau will have worked to our people's advantage.

"Rather than question God, therefore, I say we put one to ourselves. What do we, the accursed of the Sonderkommando, have to fear of death anyway? After what we have seen, what we have been forced to do, we should look at the leaving of this world as a mercy. Even if by some miracle we were to be saved, what happiness would that bring us? Our families are dead; in vain would we search for them. Our homes are gone, too, stolen by our neighbors if they continue to stand at all. We would return to our towns and villages only to find ourselves unwelcome, uprooted, alone, without friends, shadows of the men we once were, as much like ghosts as those of our loved ones destined to haunt us for what did remain of our lives. For us there would be neither rest nor peace. We would walk the earth broken men, wishing we were dead.

"So why not end it here, right now, today? What sense does it make to pile grief upon grief, one mountain of suffering on top of another? Let us stop weeping, and lifting our heads, go forth to meet this Death whom we have come to know so well, this companion who has followed in our footsteps for so long! Let us confront it not as an enemy but a friend, and show the damned Germans how a Jew can die!"

As Langfus had spoken, his voice had grown in volume and emotion, reaching a pitch as to sound almost angry. It filled the room with all the power of a call to arms. His face was paler and even gaunter than normal, his eyes a darker black than the thick glasses from which they peered— wild, staring eyes, incandescent, like two smoldering coals. He could have passed for a fevered prophet torn from the pages of the Bible, returned from the world beyond to lead his people back with him.

As for Sergeant Muhsfeld, who spoke no Polish and had begun to fidget at Langfus's increasingly inflammatory tone, his concern as quickly ebbed at the effect the dayan's words appeared to have on his audience. But for the low patter of translation, the room fell as still as a crypt, not a sob or sniffle or muttered protest to be heard. Instead of men on the brink perhaps of losing it, riddled with fear, dangerous with resentment, there was a calm to them all of a sudden born of acceptance, of having surrendered to a reality that until then they'd resisted. A pleasantly surprised Muhsfeld, thankful to be spared the embarrassment of having to finish his own transparently phony spiel, would rather a second man who stepped forward to speak hadn't, but went ahead and let him, prepared to shut him up if he noticed the mood in the room reverting.

It was Zalman Leventhal, his countenance nearly as ablaze as that of Langfus. "Heed well, you Sonder, what the rabbi would tell you. He is a holy man, and speaks with the wisdom of the Lord. His eloquence has moved me to add my small part, to remind you of that day not two months ago when we should have gone to our deaths with dignity but didn't. We have been living in shame since, but needn't die in it as well. Look at this as not a tragedy but an opportunity to redeem ourselves. The revolt found us timid—let today witness our bravery. Be the soldiers now that you should have been, were meant to be! Don't shrink from this as from a sorrow, embrace it as you would a blessing! It isn't, besides, as if we didn't know it was coming."

Then in a move unanticipated by him more than anyone, he walked up to Langfus and wrapped him in an ungainly hug. He'd once had his doubts about this strange emissary of God, the same God that back then he himself had renounced for what he perceived as abandoning His people. But true to what the poor dead Gradowski had tried to tell him, his misgivings about the man proved to be spurious. He wasn't at all the sniveler of religious platitudes, the insipid proselytizer Leventhal thought he was going to be. If anything, he did his best to avoid the subject of religion. Eccentric, yes, and head-strong as a mule to boot, but a parroter of Scripture and advocate of blind submission to God's will he most definitely was not; no Sonder had been more in favor of rebellion. What was more, he refused to judge or act superior to any but the SS, was as humble and understanding, as plain *decent* a human being as he'd encountered in this dog-eat-dog place. Once he got to know him, he actually came to enjoy the dayan's company, and from there it was but a small step to giving serious shrift to what he had to say on those occasions when the talk did turn to religion.

And to his discomfort at first, reluctant as he'd been to admit it, a lot of it made sense. Who was puny man to try and outguess his God, to presume to penetrate either the mind or the motives of his Creator? It wasn't long before Leventhal started to question his own motives, saw not only the short-sightedness but the petulance behind them, and from this progressed over time to the recovery of that faith that had once played so big a part in his life. In short, if by no means was it a short or painless process, he was able in the end to get his God back, the loving Father he'd relied on for solace and support ever since he was a child. This would never have happened without Langfus to help it along.

But while it may have made these final months the more bearable, it wasn't until this, his final day, that he reaped the full benefit of this spiritual renascence of his. Now, he told himself, that he was about to meet his God at last, it wouldn't have done for it to be on less than amicable terms. He'd have preferred to share these thoughts with Langfus earlier, and should have, but had never been much good at opening up to others. To compensate for not having done so, and moved by the dayan's rhetoric, he not only hugged him but held it for a moment.

"What was that for?" its recipient asked when Leventhal finally let go.

"I guess you could say for opening my eyes. Unstopping my ears. Getting rid of the rubbish that was clouding my brain. But mostly just for ending up a friend, however unexpected."

If not quite sure what he meant, Langfus nodded as if he was. By then Muhsfeld and his escort had returned whence they'd come, locking the door after them. The room would remain quiet as the Sonder retreated back into themselves, not to bemoan their fate this time but to prepare for it like men. Before returning to where he'd been sitting, the dayan seemed to remember something.

"Zalman," he called to the redhead already walking away, who turned to face him. "Tomorrow is a Saturday, you know," he smiled wistfully, no longer prophet but husband and father.

Leventhal looked at him, puzzled. "Yes, Leyb?"

"Are you as excited about celebrating the Sabbath with your family again as I am?"

The next morning, a detail of Sonder from Crematorium V boarded one of four trucks and was driven into the woods to the west. In a clearing were a hundred and fifty corpses strewn about, which their guards ordered them to load onto the trucks. It was their comrades from whom they'd been separated yesterday, still in their clothes and all horribly burned, many beyond recognition. On the ride back to the crematorium, they were at a loss to explain what might have caused this. Only later, after the ovens had finished the job so mysteriously started, did they learn what had happened. The night before, the Germans had trucked this remainder from the 12th Squad into the forest. There, at a sufficient distance from the camp to hide their screams, they turned flamethrowers on them, burning them alive. According to one of the detachment's doctors, who heard it from Muhsfeld, this was SS revenge for those casualties they'd suffered the day of the revolt.

Not that this was going to satisfy them. The Nazis had plans for a certain and very special group of others they deemed responsible for that day. With the passing of November, the Political Department had halted the interrogation of the four female conspirators it was holding. To both the Gestapo's exasperation and embarrassment, their every effort to extract the information they desired from even one of the four had come to nothing, and they saw little point in continuing to try. To do so, in fact, might have resulted in the last thing they wanted; if the women were to die under torture, it would deprive their captors of trotting them out in front of the other prisoners and hanging them. This the Kommandantur had established early as the only suitable finale to the affair, and for two reasons: to appease a still irate Berlin, which was expecting as much; and because with a crime not only so brazen but potentially catastrophic, a spectacle was required when it came time for punishment. To have the guilty perish anonymously and out of sight in some underground room would only diminish the seriousness of their offense.

With this in mind, therefore, not only were the sessions in Block 35 terminated but the women moved from the basement of Block 11 to cells on the ground floor. These were airier, more spacious, even furnished with cots, and though solitary confinement remained in effect, there was a small barred window high up in each that gave access to the sky. They also received adequate food here, clothing and shoes. The aim of all this was to allow the four to mend some from their ordeal, or enough anyway to be able to walk to the gallows. The less sympathy they inspired among the inmates who'd be watching, the better; the whole point of such a demonstration was to showcase the execution of vicious, self-serving criminals, not pitiable invalids.

Unfortunately for the prisoner Robota, this change in their quarters did have its downside. And a crushing one at that. Their new cells came with a 24-hour guard posted at each. These were under instructions to keep a close eye on the four, checking on them periodically through a slot in the door to prevent them from seeking to escape the noose by way of suicide. They were also meant to put a stop to Kapo Kozelczik's surreptitious mothering of this favored quartet of his, which the Germans had begun to suspect extended well beyond the occasional blanket. And so it had: captivated by the fortitude of these little more than girls, he'd taken it upon himself to ease their lot whenever he thought he could get away with it. He was even in the midst of arranging to smuggle her boyfriend Godel Silver into Roza's basement cell when the Germans up and moved them. Gone now was any chance of that, a realization that for a time not only laid her low but might well have proved the undoing of Godel if Noah and others hadn't been there to see that he didn't harm himself.

Nor was he was the only relation to the imprisoned women whose state of mind had people worried. With the second and final arrest of her sister, the sixteen-year-old Hanka was inconsolable. She'd lost interest in eating, become apathetic and distant, was practically sleepwalking through her shifts at the Union factory. She had to be prodded out of bed in the morning and often retired to it early, well before lights-out. When she did talk it was in monosyllables or words bled of all emotion. Those close to her noticed with alarm the attention she began paying the electrified fence, sometimes coming upon her just standing there staring at it.

One of these was Marta Bindiger. She didn't like at all what she was seeing from Hanka these days, feared for the girl's life. Marta was friends with an inmate-physician assigned to the Stammlager's Ka-Be, a Polish Jew named Dora Klein, née Slawka. Having left Poland to study medicine in Prague, where she'd earned her degree, many of the prisoners mistook her for Czech. A short, petite woman in her mid-thirties, with a sweet, childlike grin and the youthful face to match, her looks belied the life of adventure she'd led. In 1936, after joining the Communist Party in Prague, she made her way to Spain during that country's civil war to practice her profession in the International Brigade. With the victory of the fascists there, she fled to Paris. When that city fell to the Nazis, she served in the French Underground for three years until arrested and deported to Auschwitz—where as a member of the main camp's Battle Group, she continued to oppose the enemies of both her race and leftist ideology. It wasn't so much her Czech background that had drawn Marta to her as it was the doctor's refusal to give up the fight.

She had no trouble persuading her to admit Hanka into the hospital barracks, where she could at least be kept under supervision. As it happened, she received more than just that. With Marta having filled her in on the sad story unfolding, Dr. Klein's heart went out to the teenager, and she took her under her wing personally. Not only did she see that the child was watched, she kept her close to her side whenever possible, to the extent of including her in her daily rounds as a sort of helper. This also served to divert the girl's mind from her sister. On the whole, Hanka proved a surprisingly competent assistant, making up in enthusiasm what she lacked in training. She demonstrated a natural curiosity for all things medical. After the day was done, many was the time the doctor would invite her into her tiny cubicle of a room where they would drink tea while she regaled Hanka with tales of her own experiences in medicine and the promise the science of it held for the future. This was but one of the ways she sought to insinuate herself as something of a surrogate older sister, and not without success. Though continuing in her grief to show the world a glum face, Hanka would visibly brighten when Dr. Klein entered the room.

Marta made sure to sustain a presence as well. She became a regular visitor to Ka-Be, partly in an attempt to cheer the youngster with treasures unclaimed in the Paketstelle, but also to evaluate her mental state. Then came the December afternoon she showed up with a very special gift, not anything one could eat or wear or even see, but one that surpassed any previous all the same.

A nurse led her to Hanka, who was not having a good day. She was lying on her side awake in her bed, wrapped in the bathrobe Marta had brought her last week. The girl was staring into space, eyes vacant, unseeing, so detached from the here and now she gave no sign she knew anyone was there.

"Hanka, Haneczka—look at me, beautiful. Are you listening? I've come with good news."

She did look up but said nothing, her face indifferent. *How good could it be?* her expression seemed to say.

Marta, undaunted, didn't beat around the bush. "There's talk of a pardon!" she cried. "Can you believe it? It's far from certain yet, but there is talk!"

Hanka sat bolt upright, as if a spring had uncoiled beneath her. "A pardon? For Estusia? When? Who said so?"

"Remember me telling you that Kapo Jacob was on our side? That he wasn't only doing what he could to bolster the morale of the girls but looking into other ways he might help? Well, just this morning he told me, what with all the other changes the Germans have been up to lately, that they were giving serious consideration to a pardon. How he knows he didn't say, but he sounded pretty confident."

Hanka was beside herself. She vaulted from the bed, crying and laughing at the same time. "I—I'm—I'm not sure what I am," she bubbled, pressing Marta's hands in hers, "except shocked! Beyond shocked! Does anybody know when they might be released?"

"That's hard to tell. It could be a while yet. All we can do is be patient, not give up hope. You have something to look forward to now, Hanka, to live for. I don't want to see you moping around anymore."

Later, Marta would feel guilty for lying. She would have liked to tell her the truth, but couldn't help but think that would only have made matters worse. She wouldn't have said anything at all if the situation didn't appear to be coming to a head, but to keep Hanka completely in the dark might have backfired, especially if she were to learn what was really going on from someone else. This way, if that happened, she would at least have the lie to use as a defense against it.

There was no pardon. She'd made all that up. But there was news, nor was it all bad. As the days passed and winter solidified its grip on the land, Kapo Kozelczik's compassion for his four most prominent charges strengthened as well. In spite of the soldiers stationed at their cell doors, he was able to sneak them better food, real coffee and hot tea, warmer clothing, toilet paper, toothbrushes, even aspirin and assorted other medicines for their wounds. He made it a point to check on each of them regularly, both to see if they needed something it might be in his power to provide, and to reassure them of the as yet indeterminate status of their cases.

Not that it took long for these to turn out as expected. A week into December, the SS alerted him to prepare for a quadruple hanging to be staged on the grounds of the main camp's new Frauenlager adjunct. As downhearted as this left him, Kozelczik was far from surprised. No one, including the women themselves, needed a fortuneteller to show them what lay in their future.

On the upside, however, while awaiting the verdict, the kapo had had time to arrive at a possible way around it. Nothing foolproof by any stretch of the imagination, but possible. His years as the camp hangman had been quite the education, teaching him not only the techniques of his dark trade but its due process, its legalities. And from what he knew of these, he knew also that the Germans weren't adhering to them. For a crime of the magnitude of which the women were accused, the crime of treason against the state, the SS of the lagers weren't authorized to pass sentence. Orders for this had to come from the courts in Berlin, and in writing. Until he had these in his hands, technically those hands were tied by law. In a statement he submitted to the Kommandantur, therefore, he respectfully declined to take part in any execution unless the matter was handled through the proper channels. And further advised all concerned that should they be tempted to proceed anyway, he in his official capacity would be obligated to file a formal protest.

What did end up catching Kozelczik by surprise, aside from his not being taken out and shot for his effrontery, was the readiness with which the Nazis acceded to his ultimatum. He'd thought it at best a throw of the dice, more bluff than real threat actually, never dreaming they'd comply, especially without so much as an argument. But true, as he might have known, to their slavish devotion to the principle of ordnungsgéssemer Ablauf, the SS declared the hangings postponed until the requisite clearance from Berlin arrived. While the kapo entertained no illusions that it wouldn't, this wasn't what his scheme was about. His hope rather, aware of the legal and bureaucratic red tape the acquiring of such a writ would entail, particularly at this late stage of the war, was that the Russian Army would reach Auschwitz before it did. This loomed a distinct possibility, too, given that the Soviets weren't that far away, with some predicting liberation before the year was out.

Marta by this time was in regular contact with Kozelczik. She knew even before the Germans did what he was up to, but though applauding it and him, and dying to share it with Hanka in order to give her a ray of hope, she couldn't without also disclosing the death sentence decreed her sister. It was this that led her to make up the story about a pardon. And though she felt guilty about it, should Esther and the others end up escaping the gallows, what difference would it make how? Or what she had or hadn't told Hanka? With the way the lost little girl's eyes had sparkled when she'd heard it, it had been a lie well worth the telling.

Marta didn't know what to make of the fantastically fat hangman at first, but soon came to realize he wasn't the devil everyone thought. Behind the scary facade, the villainous reputation and stories to chill the blood, was a man, if this woeful affair was any example, with a heart as extravagantly large as the rest of him. Indeed, to her, he was no less than an angel come to their rescue. It was Esther who'd engineered the link between the two. In response to his inquiring one day whether she needed anything, she'd made two requests: pen and paper with which to write a letter to her sister, and his help in seeing that it reached her. To that end, she recommended he deliver the letter to Marta.

It was the first of several such missives from Esther, their intent to assure Hanka that she was well and in good spirits. And so they had, each drawing a rare smile from the girl. Then came the day one arrived that didn't, that left her, in fact, crying loud tears. After Marta succeeded in quieting her some, she read it and saw why.

"Dearest Hanka, I have missed you so much, my darling, as you know, but never more than today. It hasn't been easy at times, but I have tried to keep my letters to you positive, not to burden you with my troubles. On this longest and for some reason loneliest of days, however, I am finding that difficult. The sunny words just won't come. I sit here listening to the footsteps of the prisoners returning from work, the tramp of ten thousand tired feet making their way back to the barracks for the night. Through the bars of my tiny window, the gray light of dusk filters in. Twilight, if you remember, was always the saddest part of the day for me.

"The sounds of the camp at this hour—the tramping of those feet, the yelling of the kapos, the endless counting and recounting of roll call—all the familiar noises once so hated now seem precious to me, and soon to be no more. Those outside the walls of my prison still have hope, but for me there is none. For me there is nothing, not the companionship of the barracks, not your sweet smile, not the joyful cry of 'Liberation!' one day. For me all is lost, and I want so to live. Oh, Hanka, you cannot know how much I want to live!"

The rest of the letter, a little brighter, attempted to offset this first part, but failed. Marta, after finishing it, felt the urge to weep herself. It also got her to worrying about the condemned four's state of mind; if Esther's was any indication, things weren't looking good. What questions she had along those lines, though, would have to wait. Kozelczik was wary of making his excursions to the Paketstelle too frequent, and neither had managed to think of a reason for Marta to be anywhere near the restricted Block 11.

Days passed before he was back with another letter, this one from Roza. She, too, had entrusted it to Marta, in her case for delivery to Godel. As discouraged as she'd become upon learning there was to be no saying goodbye to him in person, Roza had to thank her stars and the goodwill of her jailer for at least having the chance to do so in writing. As usual, two armed SS accompanied Marta's angel in starched stripes, whether as prisoner guards or bodyguards she never asked. These didn't stray far from the coal-burning stove near the door, this giving the pair the privacy they needed.

Tucking the letter away, Marta got right to business. "So tell me, kapo, our girls know full well what's going on, right?"

"Sad to say, yes. The Germans wasted no time reading each the verdict."

"I figured as much," she said. "Which leads me to assume, too, that you've told them of your plan to get around that verdict."

"If you're talking about my insisting on authorization from Berlin, of course I told them. As soon as I found out the hangings were on hold."

In her eagerness, she touched him lightly on the forearm. "And their reaction?"

He hesitated before answering. "Well, they were thankful, I suppose, each in her way. But...."

"But what?"

"None acted as if she completely bought what I was selling. Then again, why should they? This stunt of mine you would flatter by calling a plan is nothing if not desperate. More wishful thinking, I'm afraid, than a plan. It's been over two weeks now. I was hoping we'd have maybe heard the Russian artillery by this time."

Marta saw his point, and was hard put to disagree. Something he'd said, though, and the hitch in his voice when he'd said it, raised a red flag. "What do you mean 'each in her way' thanked you?"

"It's like this," Kozelczik said. "Two of your friends are holding up as well as can be expected, which after what they've been through is no small potatoes. The one named Regina I have yet to hear complain once, or even ask anything of me. When I am able to supply her some small comfort, she won't touch it until I've promised the same to her three comrades. I've met with her kind of selflessness and quiet strength before. Though when I told her of it she showed little faith my trick to save her would do so, I could see it in her face, she pretended to be all excited about it.

"It was the same with the other strong one, this Roza with the funny last name. She, too, said she appreciated my trying, but I could tell she wasn't optimistic. She's a tiger, she is, that one. Though from the looks of her the Gestapo laid way more hurt on her than the others, I get the feeling they could have pounded on her forever and still come up empty. I've been watching her for two months now and can honestly say she's as full of piss and vinegar as when they first brought her in. She did go through kind of a rough patch when a hoped-for visit from her boyfriend fell through, but has since put that behind her. If you ask me, and as much as I've come to admire her, the SS were smart to put her behind bars. You should see the razor blades she stares at them whenever they show their faces around her."

"And the other two?" Marta asked.

The kapo shook his head. "That, it pains me to report, is another story. Ala, the tall one, is a nervous wreck. She spends a good part of every day pacing her cell. Isn't quiet about it, either; when she's not bawling her eyes out, she's talking to herself. About herself. And what she's saying isn't exactly complimentary, more like scolding than talking. I don't remember seeing a person so eat up with guilt. From what I can tell, she takes the blame for not only her own suffering but that of the others. And for something else: did she lose a child when she got here? At the unloading ramp maybe?"

"Yes, a little girl. Rochele was her name."

"That's it, Rochele. She carries on about her, too. Something about her not fighting hard enough to keep her."

Marta bridled, reflexively making two fists. Every time she thought of Ala and her stolen child, she felt the hate rise in her like water filling a glass. How many Rocheles in this godforsaken place had been pried from their mothers' arms? How many children forced to face the horror of the gas chamber alone?

"Anyway," he continued, "that's where Ala is. What she could have done to be punishing herself so, I can't imagine. When I told her the executions had been called off pending word from the courts, she thanked me for my past kindnesses and wanting to help again this time, but said I needn't lie to her. That she wasn't only unafraid of death but looking forward to it. In other words, she didn't believe me, that or chose not to. Either way, I wasn't about to argue with her."

This was what Marta had feared. As long as the Red Army might yet beat Berlin to the punch, for even one of the girls to give in to despair and decide to end life on her own terms, by means of her own hand, wouldn't be only intolerable but criminal. And Ala looked to be the perfect candidate. She didn't even want to hear about Esther. It was true that her latest letter to Hanka, or at least those sentences about her wanting so to live, would appear to rule out her resorting to suicide. But what with where she was both body and mind now, how certain could one be of this? It was one thing to be ambushed by death, blindsided by it suddenly, another to have to sit in a lonely jail cell day after day in anticipation of it, the suspense, the pressure building, the specter of it never far away, until finally waiting to die is more unbearable than the thought of death itself.

But whether she wanted to hear it or not, Kozelczik wasn't done. "Now the last one, the youngest, that Esther," he said, "she's just the opposite. A wreck to be sure, but far from a nervous one. She wasn't that bad off at first, either. Of all of them, in fact, she seemed the most thrilled at having escaped the awfulness of the bunker. But that didn't last. Slowly she began to sink, brick herself off from reality, until one day I turned around and there she was—or rather wasn't. Not all of her anyhow. And has been that way since. When I brought her the news of the postponement, for example, I had to repeat it several times before she responded, and then it was with so fake, cookie-cutter a smile, I'm still not sure she understood. Or was even listening."

He tried but fell short of a smile of his own. "Then again," he said, "in view of her situation, I'm thinking maybe she's better off where she is."

"Better off?" Marta's voice mimed the doubt etching her features. "You're not worried that like Ala she's in danger of hurting herself?"

"Hurting herself?"

"Getting tired of it all, the waiting, the tension. Giving up and, you know, putting an end to it."

"You don't mean suicide, do you?"

"What else would I mean?"

Here he did strike a smile, if an indulgent one. "What makes you believe Ala is in danger of that?"

"From what you've said, how could I not?"

"Let me tell you how," he offered, "and you can take this to the bank. For if there's one thing I've come to know more about than anything, it's death. I've seen it in all its guises reflected in a lot of different faces, and experience shows me Ala is no closer to suicide than you or I. I've looked into her eyes, and it just isn't there. Whatever it is that's chewing up her insides, she's venting it with talk. That's all it is, talk. Few her age, trust me, look forward to dying, no matter what they might say. Or how heavy their guilt. She'll change her tune, you watch. Probably, should it come to that, the nearer the days get to being her last one.

"As for Esther," he said, returning to her question, "I definitely wouldn't fret myself about her. Suicide is the last thing on that one's mind."

Marta wasn't going for it. "Not to sound glib, Jacob, my new friend, but if it walks like a duck, quacks like a duck, then it must be a duck. It seems pretty clear to me, that retreating as you say our Esther has from reality, she's lost any hope she might have had of surviving it. And having lost that—"

"Hope maybe, yes, but not the will, the instinct to survive. I've seen that plenty of times, too: men on the scaffold twisting their heads to avoid the noose, or when lashed to a post at the Black Wall, struggling to break free. There's something in us, a lot of us anyway, which moves us to cling to life when it no longer makes sense to, when the last shred of hope has been snatched away.

"So it is with Esther, and here's how I know. I began to notice that more often than not when I dropped in on her, it was to find her staring at the window up near the ceiling in her cell. And with an expression of total peace on her face. The other day, curious, I knelt down beside her cot. 'What on earth are you looking at, little one?' I asked.

"No reply, so I followed her gaze. Visible through the bars of the window were the upper branches of a tall pine tree, one of a stand growing just outside that corner of the perimeter. 'Is it that tree out there?' I said, not expecting an answer. But to my surprise she nodded, adding, 'It's amazing, isn't it?' 'It's…. a pine tree,' I said. She ignored what I suppose, if questioned, she would have called my cynicism. 'It keeps me company, that tree,' she said, 'in my loneliness, at my lowest.' 'And how does it do that?' I asked. 'It talks to me,' she said. 'Not in actual words, of course, but just by being there.' 'Oh, it talks to you. I see.' Though I didn't, not yet. 'So what does it say, this tree?'

"She'd been looking at me while she spoke, but now turned back to the window. Her face seemed suddenly to shine with—how can I put it? A kind of cloudy light, like that of the sun in water. These were her exact words: '*I am here*, it says, *I am alive—I am life itself, eternal life*. It tells me not to be frightened, that nothing ever really dies.' "

The way Kozclczik interpreted it, and sought to explain it now to Marta, was that with death so near she could feel its bony fingers on her shoulder, smell its carrion breath, so enamored had Esther become of life, any life—the very *notion* of life—that there was little danger of her being profligate with her own. Even a life as remote from ours as a tree's was a miracle, a gift worthy of celebration and respect.

Christmas this year was in the air as never before at Auschwitz. Not from any doing, needless to say, of its Jewish inhabitants, but rather their keepers. Planted conspicuously in a corner of the Appellplatz was a large and impeccably proportioned forest fir, complete with a silver garland cut out of paper foil. At night a searchlight lit it up in defiance of Russian and American bombers. Other decorations surfaced here and there, mostly affixed but not confined to official buildings and soldiers' barracks. Such display was unprecedented, but also understandable: against the godless Bolshevik armies again on the offensive, the comforting accoutrements of this most Christian of holidays offered both a welcome antidote and distraction. And with the approach of the Soviets, the Germans were drinking more, drunkenness contributing as much to their observance of the season as anything.

With a timeliness that some saw as rewarding their embrace of the yuletide, on Christmas morning the top brass of the camp received a present that couldn't have gladdened them more. Battle Group-Auschwitz was the first to hear the bad news, its agents planted in the offices of the Kommandantur acting quickly to relay it. Shortly before noon on the 25th, a courier arrived by motorcycle bearing something prodigious in his pouch, the written orders from the high court in Berlin sanctioning the execution of the Gestapo's four "traitorous" prisoners. The elated SS promptly set a date for the hangings. Estimating the Russians a month away at the earliest, and to allow themselves time to dress them up in a manner befitting the occasion, the Nazis chose January 5th as the big day.

Word of the courier and his delivery spread rapidly. When Marta heard about it, her first thought was to rush to Ka-Be and check on Hanka. Thankfully, the news hadn't reached her yet, though there was no doubt it would. Dora Klein promised to try and keep the girl's contact with the other patients to a minimum, but there wasn't any isolating her entirely. Upon leaving, Marta started working on getting a message to Kapo Jacob, always a delicate process. She needed to know how the victims of it were reacting to this new and horrible development.

His response was to show up in two days at the mailroom with his customary escort. He'd got her summons, he said, but was also there to give her a note from Esther, to which she'd requested a reply.

Kozelczik's demeanor said it all; his voice was as funereal as the look on his face. Sure the four martyrs had been informed of their fate, Marta cut to the chase. "Level with me, kapo," she said. "How are they taking it?"

"The news from Berlin? Better than a lot of people I've seen in the same straits," he said. There was a spark of pride in this last, but it immediately sputtered out, no match for the inextinguishable sadness that shrouded him. "They appear more resigned to it than upset, as if expecting it all along. Which I guess they were."

"Ala, too, and Esther? They look to be…. okay with it?"

"Ala has settled down considerably, as I told you she would. And it seems to have snapped Esther out of her shell, some anyway. Here, read this." He reached inside his coat and retrieved a slip of paper. "She asked if I could get this to you as soon as possible."

The writing was unmistakably the product of a steady hand, the message concise. "Dear Marta," it read, "I know what is in store for me and go readily to the gallows. I only ask that you take care of my baby sister Hanka. Please don't leave her alone, so that I may die the more easily."

Kozelczik handed her a pencil with which to write down a response. Caught off guard by not only the suddenness of the note but its finality, she, too, was brief. "Esther, I promise," she jotted on the piece of paper, "that I will never abandon Hanka."

Even in the midst of her sorrow, Marta's heart went out to the man standing slumped in front of her. The dreariness she felt equaled that he was showing. "Jacob," she said wanting to hug him, but fearing that might be overdoing it, "hard as it may be, try not to let it get to you. We both knew, everyone did, there was a better than good chance of it coming to this. You can at least console yourself knowing you did everything you could to prevent it. In fact, you've done more than a body could reasonably be—"

He raised a hand as a sign for her to stop. "I don't doubt you mean well, dear, but you're mistaken. As disappointed as I am, it's not what I've tried and failed at that has me upset so much as what I'm going to find myself forced to do ten days from now. Already the thought of it sickens my stomach. Come January, my duties will require me to loop ropes around the necks of four heroic young women whom it would be no exaggeration to say I risked my own neck to save. The gallows will have produced five corpses that day, the fifth and last being that fragment of what is left of my poor soul."

After closing the Paketstelle for the night, Marta went to see about Hanka and found her asleep. But it wasn't the healthy sleep of the naturally spent—so upset was she earlier, Dr. Klein said, she'd had to give her a shot to knock her out. Somehow she'd learned of the warrant from Berlin, and there was no calming her after that. The girl went completely out of her head, would later confess to remembering nothing of the days that followed. But during them, and not only the days but the nights, her maniacal wailing and tortured sobs became a fixture of lager life, audible throughout the camp. They weren't continuous, but liable at any hour to pour forth, this having its predictable effect on the inmates. Less a cry of this world than a howl of pure anguish from the darkest depths of Abaddon, it was a sound to lay bare the nerves, raise the hairs on one's arms. It haunted the prisoners by day and woke them at night, but thanks to Dora Klein's diligence and ample stock of tranquilizers its frequency wasn't what it might have been, she couldn't be expected to keep her patient doped up twenty-four hours a day every day.

There was one prisoner, of course, that it affected more than any. Kapo Kozelczik noticed the change in Esther at once: like Ala before her, she grew agitated, restless, the serenity she'd manifested earlier gone. During Hanka's outbursts, she, too, would get vocal, weeping noisily in shared pain, but more worrisome yet, even with her sister quiet she'd taken to walking her cell, mumbling to herself, falling to her knees and clasping her hands together as in prayer. With the days tumbling rapidly on their way to January 5th, whether this was out of concern for Hanka or fear for herself it was difficult to say. All Kozelczik knew was that as hangman he had a potential problem on his hands, Esther giving every sign of becoming unhinged. To have to drag her hysterical to the gallows was a scenario neither he nor the SS would find acceptable.

Marta, meanwhile, at the hospital twice a day now, was having as little luck as Dr. Klein at getting through to Hanka. The child had fled deeper than ever back into the cocoon she'd spun for herself before Marta had rekindled hope in her with her white lie about the pardon. This time there was no rousing her from her lethargy, not even for a moment. She refused to acknowledge anyone, just lay in her bunk staring silently at the ceiling, until the next fit took hold of her and she'd commence to screeching for her sister, for someone to save her sister, which was when at the more violent of them, there being no reasoning with her and two people needed to restrain her, she'd have to be sedated.

She didn't know if it was because it sprang from someone she'd grown to love as a sister, but Marta had never experienced a sound so abrasive and at the same time heartbreaking as the cries ripped from Hanka when in one of her frenzies. Contained in each sob was all the pathos and pain of Auschwitz, the very essence of the place, a distillate of every vileness perpetrated here in the five years of its vile existence. It was as if through this tormented teenaged girl, all of the victims living and dead that had passed through these gates beneath the mocking *Arbeit Macht Frei* had been given an outlet, a single voice, with which to express their agony, their outrage.

But that wasn't the whole of it. Awakened by the crazed Hanka in the middle of the night, Marta would lie in her koje listening with a combination of pity and foreboding, sad on the one hand for the wretched creature behind the screaming, but also tense with premonition. For there was a balefulness to these episodes beyond mere lament, especially coming when they did in the stillness of the night. As the disembodied, ghostly weepiness of them splintered the quiet, rose and fell in the black air, they seemed to be announcing what everyone knew was just a matter of time now, heralds of an offense those within earshot of them were all too aware but didn't want to admit was near. Or as Marta lying sleepless in the crowded solitude of her barracks read it, the selections at the ramp may have stopped, evidence of the slaughter been whitewashed over, the SS lost some of their appetite for murder, but the Vernichtungslager was a long way from done with them yet. It had at least one more gauntlet to run its captives through, one more perfidious crime to enact. It was only fitting it be foretold, if not by one of its upcoming victims, then someone bound to same by ties of family and blood.

1945

Winter

As different as the two processes were, the deconstruction of the crematoria had several points in common with their construction. The difficulty, for one, involved in tearing them down was in direct proportion to the labor and time expended in the building of them. It had taken most of December to finish the job, and this consisting of Crematoria II and III only; Number Five was kept intact to deal with not only the dead continuing to arrive from the barracks but the apparently as inexhaustible flow of incriminating paperwork. And just as it had been Jews forced to assemble these houses of murder, so were Jews given the task of dismantling the things. The Sonder were split into two wrecking crews of twenty men each, one per crematorium.

The final bond connecting the razing of them to their erecting almost two years ago was in itself a study in contrasts, reflective of the sea change the course of the war had taken. Back in 1942, with Nazi military might and ambitions at their highest, the blueprints for the death factories at Birkenau were drawn up with their architects confident that these were but the first of many such installations to come, to be used in turn, once the Jews were disposed of, against the Russians and other subjugated peoples. Now, with those same Russians approaching Birkenau not in cattle cars but tanks, the Germans were frantic to erase all signs there had ever been any crematoria. To the Sonder employed at this, the analogy that emerged was as heady to contemplate as it was obvious: the destruction of those unholy temples to Nazi terror was but a portent of that awaiting the Third Reich as a whole. Once invincible, unstoppable, victory all but assured, the Wehrmacht and the SS were in irreversible retreat on all fronts, their war and extermination machines grinding to a halt. Just as the walls of his and his henchmen's death mills were collapsing before their self-inflicted dynamite charges, so one day soon would the entire rotten edifice of Hitler's evil empire come crashing down.

But in keeping with their fabled thoroughness and attention to detail, the Germans weren't content simply to blow up II and III and be done with them. First, they had to remove everything that even remotely smacked of what they'd been up to; it was this that had stretched the process of demolition into a month. The object was to conceal the buildings' true function by making the ruins left behind as nondescript as possible. The ovens had to be taken apart, their components cleaned and oiled, then packed for shipment. The electric generators that had sparked the fires were detached and also packed away, along with the ventilating Exhators. The hollowed-out brick furnaces that remained would later receive a bundle of dynamite each. Both coke rooms were doused with gasoline the better to burn. The large fans that had powered the forced-draft systems in the gas chambers were ripped out of the walls, and the induction cones by which the pellets of Zyklon-B had entered the chambers disconnected and trashed. The dummy showerheads were unscrewed and discarded, too. The elevators to the oven rooms took almost as long to disassemble as they had to install, and they as well were crated and marked, along with all other packed material, for shipment to the Grossrosen and Mauthausen camps. The crucibles and other equipment in Crematorium III's gold forge were bundled off with them. Even the wooden benches and wall hooks in the undressing rooms were taken out and burned.

Nor was the blackened hulk of Crematorium IV overlooked. It, too, was cannibalized of impugnable parts, and only then were it and the other two rigged for detonation. The explosions that followed not only shook Birkenau but were felt in the Stammlager. The majority of prisoners being unaware at the time of what they signified, many propounded, hoped, prayed it was Russian artillery. When they learned later what in fact they were, this was almost as cheering.

But while the Germans were busy ridding Birkenau of its homicidal past, at Auschwitz they weren't in the business of demolishing but building. A small project to be sure, yet one close to the SS heart: a brand-new gallows on the grounds of the lager that housed the Union women. Upon its completion two days into January, it occupied a prominent place center-rear of the Appellplatz, too prominent by half, in that it was this much larger than it needed to be. Towering above the electrified fence behind it, a flight of a dozen steps rose to a spacious platform from which two tall, heavy hanging trees grew, united at the top by a single long crossbeam.

The handful of prisoners mystified by its appearance was soon set straight by the others; they were to be witness to the execution of the four conspirators entombed in Block 11. By then the death warrant from Berlin had become the talk of the Union, and all too familiar by now with the enraged state of their *Blockführer*, the women suspected Hössler of having had a hand in locating the gallows where they were. How better to punish not just the four, but with the deaths taking place on its home turf, the entire disloyal commando? Nor judging from the dimensions of this pinewood monstrosity planted in their midst was it to be a simple hanging. If they knew their commandant, and provided as was likely that he was to play a major role in the proceedings, they knew also that he wasn't about to shy from making as sensational a show of these as he could.

No one had to tell Esther's sister Hanka what was going on. She could hear it just fine from her hospital bed, the distant, angry whining of electric saws, the pounding of hammers. She hadn't paid it much mind at first, but as the day wore on it began to dawn on her what these sounds meant. It didn't affect her, however, as one might have thought. Instead of launching into her usual wild allegro of woe, she covered her ears, screwed her eyes shut, and as if afraid to open either, retreated deeper into that safe, hermetic part of herself where the world couldn't follow. And there she would remain, more in exile from her surroundings than ever, no matter what both Marta Bindiger and Dora Klein did to try and coax her out of it.

"This is worse," Marta said, "than when she used to wake half the camp at night. Is she responsive at all?"

Dr. Klein didn't try to hide her concern. "Off and on," she frowned, "but mostly the former. If I badger her long and hard enough, I've found I can sometimes get her to look at me, but that's about it. Though not exactly catatonic, she isn't far from it. It's not looking good, that much I do know."

"Does she eat? Is she eating?"

"Only if somebody feeds her, and not always then. She's already starting to lose weight, can you tell?"

Marta felt powerless. Never far from her mind was her promise to Esther to look after her sister, to see she was taken care of. "So what would you suggest, Dora? There must be something we can do."

As if the solution lay there, the doctor glanced at the ceiling. "Nothing I can think of, except not to give up on her. I've a hunch that time is the only cure for what's ailing our Hanka, and after this sad business with her sister is over, with help she'll be able to put it behind her and move on."

Marta could only hope they'd *all* be able to put it behind themselves, and soon. The strain of knowing what was coming, of living with that knowledge, wasn't easy. God only knew what the four tortured souls in Block 11 were going through, what maggots the noises of the hammers and saws had set to squirming in their brains. She would have given much to intercede in their anguish, to offer what solace she could in person, face to face. The thought of them pining their last days away alone in their cells, without a shoulder to cry on, a friendly ear to confide in—women who over the months and in perilous pursuit of a common cause she'd become more than just friends with, had trusted her life to—was enough to drive her to the same despair that until recently Hanka had howled. For all the good it would do to dream of visiting them in jail, though, she might as well have fantasized about busting them out of it.

In the meantime, the calendar crept laboriously forward, the days seeming to pass in slow motion. Marta's weren't the only nerves stretched to the breaking point. Nor those of the other prisoners. At least one German was also in a sweat: SS Captain Hössler, who the suspicions of the Union women proving correct, had been granted the honor of superintending the executions. The problem was the weather. No sooner had the gallows gone up than a storm to rival any this winter blew in, and had as yet to show any signs of abating. The snow was getting so deep that in places it had piled up twice as tall as a person. The only parts of the scaffold exposed were the two hanging posts and their crossbeam. It was clear the affair would have to be pushed back, the only question being how far back.

Having waited almost three months to avenge what he saw as his betrayal by those cosseted Union girls of his, Hössler's patience was long gone. He'd practically begged the Kommandantur for the honor of organizing and then presiding at the hangings, and now was slavering at the mouth to get on with them. As if his temper weren't foul before, he now raged like a captured jungle cat in its cage, at the excessiveness of this latest storm, the Polish winter in general, his ungrateful commando, the gutter race that could birth such trash in the first place.

"If it were up to me," he let it be known loudly and often, "I'd start with these four then hang every bitch in the Union. Then after that, every Jew I could until the Russians showed up."

More than anything, he worried the storm wouldn't permit him time to gild the lily, to make of the executions the grand ceremony he'd envisioned. Should it drag on much longer he might have to settle for something quick, a blah mediocrity of a hanging no more memorable than any other. Then in the early morning hours of the appointed day, January 5th, he stepped outside his quarters to a glorious sight. The heavy clouds had begun to break apart and would soon disappear completely, unleashing a blinding orange dawn upon the world. The *Hauptsturmführer* would pause long enough to thank the gods, then immediately and with a vengeance set to work.

Before the sun had risen the width of a hand above the horizon, dozens of prisoners with shovels were digging the gallows free of its snow, a bulldozer clearing the Appellplatz of its. Two antiaircraft searchlights were wheeled in and situated in the farthest corners of the yard across from the scaffold, their glass faces leveled at same. Though this was all that could be done for the time being at the execution site, Hössler had plenty to attend to elsewhere. Leaving a *Sturmmänn* in charge, he hurried off with a couple of privates in tow.

Gone was his foul mood; his men hadn't seen him this upbeat in months. Realizing, of course, that there was no chance of him reaping his revenge today, he was more than happy only having to postpone it twenty-four hours. Indeed, just about all that could have dampened his spirits was another round of clouds, but though he must have looked aloft a hundred times that day, he didn't spot a one.

The sunrise of the 6th was as gaudy an orange, the sky as unblemished a blue the whole day. Hössler was all over the place, frantic to make sure everything would be ready on time and all the participants in the drama to come, save a certain four, were properly rehearsed and up to snuff on what was expected of them. He motorcycled a constant loop all that morning and early afternoon between the Frauenlager, the SS storehouses and barracks, Blocks 35 and 11, his own rooms. A spinning top of orders and advice, his energy infected not only the soldiers under his command but those prisoners who'd been drummed into the effort. Even they worked as if imbued with his sense of mission, so that by the time the sun was into its descent, Hössler could congratulate himself there was nothing more to be done.

At 2:45 that afternoon, their Blockälteste and her assistants rousted the women of the Union night shift from their bunks, two hours ahead of time. Told to hurry and line up for coffee, they were subsequently run through the latrine with even more urgency than usual. Why both the haste and the irregular hour was a mystery, as was the presence of a squad of soldiers. That their routine had remained more or less intact to this point, however, did help to ease their concern some, though there was no dispelling the feeling that something less than pleasant lay ahead.

What this was revealed itself upon the five hundred of them filing into the Appellplatz for roll call. The soldiers led them toward the gallows that rose at the rear of it, only today it was an alarmingly different gallows than they remembered. When they saw it, a collective moan escaped five hundred mouths, as many pairs of legs stumbling abruptly to a stop. It took every threat and curse their guards could hurl to start them moving again, and even then all but a few could bring themselves to look at the thing.

Hössler had draped the scaffold in a bright scarlet cloth, creating an enormous splash of red against the white of the snow. Broad swatches of it hung from the handrail attached to the stairs, and from the platform to the ground, all either pinned or pegged down to prevent them from flapping in the little wind there was. Even the vertical beams of the hanging posts were swathed in red. As if this weren't enough, two huge bolts of the same cloth covered the section of barbed wire that ran behind the gallows, a good fifteen meters of it. The message delivered by this and the rest of so overdone a display was twofold. First and foremost, it announced to the women cowering before it that the hour they'd been living in anxiety of was here; the reason their handlers had yanked them prematurely from their barracks was so they might witness the killing of their four comrades. The second part of the message was a symbolic one, and there wasn't a prisoner who didn't read it loud and clear. Though it was to be a hanging and technically no blood would be spilled, Hössler's choice of red as a motif was his way of saying that this production of his, make no mistake, was going to be as violent as he could make it.

The Appellplatz was soon surrounded by soldiers, all heavily armed, some holding back dogs whose mad barking added its note of terror. A dozen female SS roamed between the rows of women, demanding those with lowered heads raise them and keep them there. By now the sun was skimming the higher rooftops, the lengthening shadows announcing the approach of twilight. Signaling the start of the *Hauptsturmführer's* passion play, two soldiers ascended the steps of the gallows and marched stiffly to opposite ends of the platform. Resplendent in black tunics adorned with silver braid, their ceremonial chrome helmets polished to a mirror sheen, each brandished a snare drum also trimmed in silver. Once they'd taken their places facing each other, they began beating an unbroken roll, rapid but soft, these combining to make it sinister. It was the ominous metric of the classic military execution.

To this dirgelike cadence, a formation of SS advanced slowly down a central aisle toward the scaffold. At its head was the brutal and much-feared *Scharführer* Anton Taube, and in the midst of the soldiers two of the condemned, Ala and Regina, both coatless in the cold and wearing identical gray smocks. They walked without faltering, staring straight ahead. Flanked by the SS in their helmets and jackboots, they looked shockingly frail, not unlike a couple of children. As they traversed the aisle, all eyes turned to follow them, a subdued sobbing arising from both sides.

Bringing up the rear was the hangman Kozelczik, who followed them and their soldier escort up the steps to the platform. After dropping the two off beneath the nooses suspended from the crossbeam, their guard faded into the background where it remained at attention. Kozelczik tied the girls' wrists behind them, then he, too, backed away, stood arms folded, face impassive, next to a glowering Taube. Many in the crowd even at this early stage couldn't watch, their eyes instead on the ground at their feet. Seeing this, the SS harpies circulating among them went running up and down the lines of prisoners screaming, "Eyes front! Pay attention! Look to the front!" They stuck the butts of their whips under the women's chins and forced them up, loudly slapping the faces of any who resisted.

Ala and Regina, aloof to the commotion, stared past it as at something far away. They appeared more sorrowful than afraid. To those who'd worked with them, bunked with them, shared food, and swapped stories with them—who'd dreamed aloud with them during the hours before lights-out of the day the Russians would come, the day of liberation—what the two were looking at and the reason for their sorrow was plain. Their eyes were fixed on that world beyond the barracks and barbed wire where not only freedom but the future lay, a future they'd once hoped had a place in it for them.

This ended up too much for the women witness to it. What had been a few muffled, isolated sobs rapidly grew into a chorus. Nor was it a cry of grief only, but anger as well. The SS ringing the yard gripped their rifles tighter, their female counterparts looking uncertainly about.

Staff Sergeant Taube strode to the front of the platform, his tall, bony figure bristling with menace. "Enough!" he bellowed. "Stop your crying at once! For every tear I promise twenty-five lashes!" Pausing, he smiled, a repulsive gash of a smile, like a wound that had reopened. "And as you've learned in your time here, Taube is a man of his word."

At this warning his audience, though unable to stifle it entirely, choked back its pain. Just enough of it remained to underscore the ill-boding solemnity of the snare drums. The slanted rays of the dying sun, meanwhile, falling full now upon the scaffold, bathed each person on it in a dramatic gold. It was no accident that the stage-managing Hössler chose then to make his entrance.

He didn't climb the stairs to the platform, he floated up them, as if borne aloft by some mechanical device. The effect derived from his wearing a long, black woolen cape that hid his legs. A silver chain clasped it at the neck. Rounding out his costume was an impeccable black uniform with every button and bar gleaming, knee-high boots polished to a shine, and as a final touch, a pair of fur-lined leather gloves. His peaked, silver-embossed officer's cap might have passed for a crown. Once atop the platform, he motioned to the drummers to sheathe their sticks, and turning to the crowd, swept his cape back with a flourish. The motion exaggerated, he drew an official-looking scroll of paper from inside his tunic and unrolled it.

It was the death writ from the courts in Berlin passing sentence on the four offenders. Without preamble, the SS captain raised it to eye level and began to read, his voice piercing in the frigid air.

"By order of this highest and most honorable tribunal, and by unanimous decision, it is decreed that the following occupants of *Konzentrationslager* Auschwitz-Birkenau, by endangering the security of the Reich with their actions, be put to death for their crimes:

the Jew Ala Gertner
the Jew Regina Safirstajn
the Jew Roza Robota
the Jew Esther Wajcblum

We leave it to the discretion of the camp authorities to determine the appropriate time and place for this order to be carried out. In the name of the German people and their *Führer*, let justice be done. Heil Hitler!

Signed: Judge Ronald Freisler, President, People's Court
Countersigned: Dr. Otto Georg Thierack, Reich Minister of Justice."

Hössler lowered the paper and glared at the women below, his gaze as spiteful as if he'd penned the words himself. In point of fact, he had edited a good many of them out, omitting the legalese and other trappings that for his purposes he felt diminished the document's impact. Now, having read it with what he trusted was sufficient malevolence, and with one last gloating look around, he was ready to get on with the business of the day.

He retreated to one side, relinquishing the stage to his hangman. Kozelczik stepped forward and went rapidly to work. He took hold of one of the nooses above and slipped it over Ala's head, cinching it tight around her neck. Only then did her eyes return from the distance and dart confusedly about, as if aware for the first time where they were and what was happening. When they landed on Hössler, they went no farther. She didn't speak the words, she flung them at him.

"Today you hang me, you Nazi filth, but your hour will come! Remember me, this face, when they put the rope around *your* neck!"

She was about to say more, but Kozelczik, grabbing that end of the rope resting across the overhead beam, started pulling hand over hand. She rose in three quick jerks, legs kicking, after which he secured the line to a hook in the floor.

Regina for her part was groping for some sort of last words herself, but her heart wasn't in it. Whether cowed by the sounds of her friend strangling to death next to her, or even now too sweet-natured to descend into the adversarial, once her neck was in the noose all she could manage was, "I pray that everyone I know ends up getting her freedom."

Whereupon, she, too, was hauled into the air. Death didn't come easily for either. They lacked the weight they needed to die quickly; despite the recent increase in their rations, the bunker had left them more bone than flesh. For an eternity of a minute, they wriggled on high like a pair of freshly caught fish, gasping for oxygen, mouths opening and closing spasmodically in search of the breath that wasn't there. Their clogs having gone flying, it took another full minute for their bare feet to surrender the last convulsive shudder and go limp.

Throughout, the SS demons in skirts were back at it, shrieking at their hapless charges to keep their heads up. Hössler had made it clear beforehand that he wanted this pig commando of his tuned in to this part of the show as to no other. What no one noticed, prisoner and Nazi alike, distracted as each was by the violence of the death struggle, was the hangman's reaction to his handiwork. In violation of what was expected of him as executioner, Kozelczik had turned his back on the scene. He may have had to hang them, but he wasn't going to watch them die, let the Germans try to make him if they were feeling up to it.

As this gruesome last act of the tragedy played itself out, an uncontainable keening went up from the Union ranks, a sound of utter helplessness and heartache wrung involuntarily from hundreds of throats. Many ignored the blows from their guards and refused to look. Some who did were so sickened by it, they vomited. A few even fainted. At the very least, scarce was the woman who wasn't weeping, if not openly, for fear of Taube, then on the inside, her invisible tears no less the scalding for it.

And above it all from his perch on the platform towered the magisterial figure of the *Hauptsturmführer*, his face a study in contentment as he soaked up the misery from below like an insect nectar from a flower.

Eventually, he approached the two corpses and positioned himself between them, laying a hand on each. To the prisoners at his feet, the black gloves he wore resembled a pair of carrion birds. His features were transformed as well, having adopted a look of exaggerated concern; he seemed on the brink of tears now himself. Instead of crying, however, he let out a long, emoting sigh, then commenced to speak loud enough for all to hear.

"My dear children," he said, oozing sympathy, "I both feel sorry for you and don't. Here you have two friends whose loss has clearly devastated you, two wonderful girls, I'm sure, whose untimely deaths have left a hole in all of your lives. It is always a shame when those young enough to have barely begun living are taken from us. Even more so when there is no good reason for it."

With an affectionate pat to the shoulder of each, Hössler slid from between the bodies and stepped to the front of the platform. Though his expression was still caring, none were fooled. He hadn't earned the appellation Moshe Liar for nothing.

"On the other hand," he continued, a slight edge to his voice now, "it is this absence of a reason, the senselessness behind these two deaths, which tells me to pity you not. For here one must ask, Who is responsible for this calamity? It is not we SS, who had no choice in the matter. Laws were broken, and we as instruments of the law were duty-bound to see the transgressors brought to justice. No, it is you who are to blame for the deaths of these two beautiful young people, you who aided and encouraged them in their folly."

Here he affected a look of wounded amazement. "Do you think I and my associates in the Gestapo are stupid? We know there were more of you involved in the theft of the gunpowder than just the four arrested for it. And even more no doubt, who while perhaps not playing an active part, understood what was going on yet did nothing to stop it. Now look what has happened, and all because of your complicity. I can only imagine the guilt you must be feeling. Did you not realize, are *you* so stupid, that any plot directed against us, your rightful masters, was doomed to fail?"

Though most of the women, their German scanty, understood but some of what he was saying, from what words they did recognize they were able to figure out that he was trying to hold them to blame for the two corpses swinging above them. Outrageous as this was, it was also to be expected of the manipulative SS. One of the oldest and most cherished of their tricks consisted of transferring the onus for their crimes onto their victims or those associated with them. This both eased what vestiges of conscience any might yet possess, while in keeping with that rigorously observed sadism of which they were so fond, rubbed salt into whatever injury they'd inflicted. Given the great wrong he saw this commando of his having done him, Hössler was all about this last. His aim in soft-soaping them at the outset was just that, to soften them up a little, sucker them with kindness. That had been the carrot—now came the stick.

"*Doomed, I repeat, to fail!*" he roared without warning. Suddenly, the *Hauptsturmführer's* expression was venomous again, his mouth a lipless scowl. "And any believing different who would be so rash as to test that belief"—without turning, he pointed to the carnage behind him—"will end up like these, that I can promise!"

For a long minute, he strutted stiff-legged back and forth, arms arrogantly akimbo, wordlessly daring any below to meet his stare. When finally he spoke, it was with a malice that matched that in his eyes.

"Do not make the mistake of thinking the war over!" he shouted. "It is not, nor will it be until Germany says it is. The Third Reich is too powerful to be defeated outright; it will still be here long after you and I are no more. You in particular. There is to be no liberation for you, no freedom in your future. Arrangements have already been made to that effect, just as steps have been taken to prevent a recurrence of your crimes. The Reich is quite aware who its enemies are, from the barbarians advancing on its borders to they who would undermine it from within. Every attempt at this last, every plot, every act of sabotage, no matter how small, will be uncovered and those responsible rooted out and eradicated. Now that you have shown what you are capable of, know that we are watching you. I would advise you to remember this should treason beckon again."

Pausing a moment to let this sink in, Hössler once more changed tack, explaining how deeply it hurt him to think that such elements existed in his lager of all places, he who'd bent over backward to be more of a father than a warden. He warned them, however, not to misinterpret his compassion for weakness. "As much as I care for each and every one of you, am willing to start afresh, to forgive and forget, I will show no mercy to any who stray even slightly from the straight and narrow."

To demonstrate how much he did care, and as a token of good faith (but in reality to settle them down some prior to their heading off to work), he announced that a *Zulage*, or extra ration, awaited them outside their barracks. The next instant he was gone, disappeared down the steps.

Even welcomer than the slab of bread and sliver of horsemeat sausage handed each woman before the march to the Union was not having to undergo a second round of hangings. According to their Blockälteste, the execution of the criminals Wajcblum and Robota was a privilege reserved for the day shift upon its return to camp.

To the relief of these, however, who'd learned from one of their kapos what was awaiting them, an air-raid warning was in effect upon that return, and instead of the Appellplatz they were ushered to their barracks. There, per regulations, they were to remain until the all clear, which to their further relief had yet to come by lights-out. They figured it too late by then to go anywhere.

Hardly had they settled into their kojen, though, than suddenly, shatteringly, the overhead fluorescents flickered on and the blockova and her crew were everywhere in full shouting fury. Within minutes, they'd driven the blinking commando outside and into the arms of a squad of SS-*Frauen*, who formed its members into a column. The mercury hadn't registered above freezing all day, and was dropping by the hour. Hands and feet went quickly numb, but unmercifully the heart continued to feel: the women knew all too well where they were headed.

Upon reaching the Platz, they stared at the gallows as if hypnotized, no more able to tear their eyes from it than put a stop to what it was there for. It anchored the gaze as with a steel bolt. Illuminated by the pair of searchlights trained on it from across the yard, the cloth festooning this instrument of death didn't just show red, it glowed red, as if lit not from the outside but emitting a radiance of its own. Severed from its surroundings, it hovered in the air before them, a blazing, crimson islet adrift in a sea of black. Half-prodded toward it from behind by their guards, half-drawn to it, entranced, like the rat before the snake, the five hundred approached the scaffold with uncertain steps.

Unlike that afternoon, the Union wasn't the only group in attendance. But for the human guinea pigs from the medical-experimentation block, the entire Frauenlager stood at attention in the snow. And along with them a collection of prisoners, all female, from various other parts of the camp, among them those secretaries and interpreters assigned to Block 35 and anyone else Hössler could think of who might have had contact with the accused. His revenge only partially slaked, he was bent on jamming as many as he could into the yard to partake of this encore and final performance. For his Union bunch, of course, he'd reserved the space in front; like the night shift preceding them, he wanted them close enough to the gallows to hear their two friends' every dying gurgle, their last desperate gasps. Since he couldn't hang the lot of them as he would have liked, they'd at least get a taste of what it was to perish at the end of a rope.

Other than the numbers he'd amassed and the inspired touch that was the searchlights, he saw no reason to deviate from the day's earlier presentation. What hadn't crossed his mind, nor could have pleased him more, was that nothing he might have added could have topped what the black of night was bringing. The pageantry, the tension, the terror…. all had been elevated by night's witchy feel to a pinnacle unmatched by that in the first hanging. It wasn't just the searchlights, either; the scene wouldn't have been half so mesmerizing if missing those, yes, but without the hands of the clock having spun their spell, poorer as well in other ways. A grateful Hössler made a note to self should the future find him called to execution duty again: when it came to putting on a show, no noon could vie with midnight for sheer theatrical effect.

If happy before at his success, he was walking on air now. The day was exceeding even his expectations. In fact, all was so shipshape, so in accord with plan and more, despite trying his utmost not to, he couldn't stop waiting for something to go wrong.

Which, of course, since no less than perfection was his object, something did. As their SS escort led the two prisoners down the aisle toward the gallows, neither was playing her part as he'd have liked. Esther walked on unsteady legs, arms outstretched slightly at her side as if for balance. One second her expression appeared glassy, perplexed, the next carefree and smiling. Once she stumbled and almost fell, just managing to stay afoot. It was obvious she'd been drugged, but as minor a wrench in the captain's works as this loomed, it was enough to upset him. There was no predicting what she might do under the influence, and if there was anything he desired less at this point, it was unpredictability intruding on his carefully programmed script.

Everybody figured it was the Germans who'd doped her, but in truth it was a favor her hangman had done her. A quick check on her an hour before had been enough to convince Kozelczik that there was no way Esther was going to make it through this without some sort of help. The weeks of torture, then of waiting for this dark day to arrive—along with her sister Hanka's rending cries having done a number on her—had in the end proved too much. With the ticking time bomb that was the death watch winding down, she lay in a tearful heap on the floor of her cell, begging for her life, rubber-legged with fear. Such behavior, of course, wasn't new to the kapo, nor had he ever known it to turn out anything but ugly. Rather than have the Nazis get rough with her when it was time to go, he decided to take action. Somehow he got some hot tea down her in which he'd dissolved a couple of tranquilizers. These soon worked their magic, so that when *Scharführer* Taube came to fetch her she went without resisting.

Accompanying her on this last, short journey of her life was her friend, erstwhile dance partner, and girlish confidante Roza, though so out of it was Esther she didn't appear to notice. Not that it mattered much, for the SS kept them well separated. There would be no show of solidarity, no handholding on the death walk.

Like Esther's and those of the others, Roza's face wasn't quite healed from the beatings it had absorbed. There was no swelling anymore, but not all of the bruises had completely faded, while some of the scars were there to stay. The shapeless gray shift she wore concealed most of the rest of the damage, with the exception of a not inconsiderable limp. The way she carried herself, however, gave no indication of her having known the torture chamber. Her back broomstick-straight, chin in the air, she walked despite the limp with as military a bearing as the soldiers surrounding her. Eschewing that faraway stare Ala and Regina had seized on, she refused to insulate herself from the grim goings-on. If anything, she gave every sign of glorying in them. Her look was as contemptuous and proud as her step—pride in the crimes for which she'd been sentenced to die, contempt for those about to do the killing. This rankled Hössler as much as Esther's sorry condition.

Not that he was to stay irritated for long, courtesy of a sudden, incredible embellishment to his playbook that he couldn't have written into it even if he'd thought to. It declared itself upon the doomed pair reaching the stairs to the gallows. Esther had to be assisted up the steps by one of the soldiers, and no sooner had they started than a long, shrill scream knifed out of the blackness, not from anywhere near the Appellplatz but so loud as to compete with the roll of the Nazi snare drums. Even after ending, it echoed in the night air, followed by an only too familiar cascade of sobs that left each person shivering in the yard to ask herself how the poor girl had known. Was it mere coincidence or something less explainable that led Hanka, confined in Ka-Be, well out of sight of the Frauenlager, to vocalize her despair at the very moment her sister was climbing the scaffold? She couldn't have timed her *cri de coeur* better if she'd been there, and with foreseeable effect on those who were. A chill distinct from the January cold snaked down every spine, the assembled women turning to look at each other with wide, frightened eyes. As if their nerves weren't laid bare already, now they had the supernatural to contend with. Fear slipped into the Platz on swift, padded feet, circling the rows of prisoners like a pack of hungry wolves.

Hössler grinned like a wolf himself at his phenomenal luck. Just because he hadn't scripted it, didn't mean he wasn't going to mine so serendipitous a sound for all it was worth. He waited until the deranged sister's unsettling serenade had dwindled to nothing before gliding up the steps and onto the platform.

It was different this time all right. The air crackled with an electricity that hadn't been there this afternoon. The *Hauptsturmführer* discovered an extra bounce to his swagger, a mordant glee to his voice missing the first time he'd read the warrant from Berlin. Was it the night, the searchlights, the bigger crowd? Did it matter? Surely the input of the leather-lunged banshee Jew hadn't hurt. Once he'd finished with the court's pronouncement and tucked the scroll away, he nodded to Taube, who clicked his heels smartly and advanced to the edge of the platform.

"*Pulverraum, vortreten!*" the sergeant blared. "Powder room, step forward! *Nach vorne!* To the front!"

No one moved. Testily, his voice rising, he repeated the order. A moment more and Rose Greuenapfel, Ilse Michel, Inge Kutzvor, Genia Frischler, and the two replacement members of the crew had collected tentatively in the main aisle, from where, pushed forward by a couple of SS women, they formed a row directly beneath the gallows. Hössler looked on, beaming. What with the night shift at the Union plant no longer carrying a Pulver detail, he'd been denied this particular pleasure earlier in the day.

While this was going on, having arrived at her noose, Esther broke out in song of all things, a soft, almost inaudible ditty from her childhood she used to croon to her sister when Hanka was a toddler. Now, eyes closed, a remembering smile on her face, she was singing it to her again as if back at their home in Warsaw, singing it as if the last dozen years hadn't happened.

Roza, as someone in back of her bound her hands, fought not to listen. Even now she could feel the tears blooming in her eyes because of it, and the last thing she needed in the minutes left her were tears. That wasn't how she was meant to exit this world. After battling for so long, her whole life it seemed, she mustn't let herself melt into a puddle at the end. She had something to say still, that it was her duty to say, that these women brought here to partake of yet another Nazi atrocity needed to hear. She couldn't allow her emotions to interfere with that, not the pity she was feeling for her friend beside her or the devils she herself was wrestling with. For though all rock-hardness and chutzpah on the surface, within she was anything but. Hide it as she might, there was no shaking the loss tearing at her insides, the regret. It was so wasteful a thing to die at twenty-three, to have so many of one's dreams, so much of one's future stolen. She could only use what strength was left her to try not thinking about this, to gut it up and block it out, banish it along with Esther's song from her head. There was one battle yet to fight, one last appeal to the living on behalf of the dead.

"Remember this night!" she shouted, the words clear and crisp in the cold. "And the faces of the SS you see here! The day is coming soon when they will be the prisoners, you the free. You must survive to that day, use this freedom to help bring them and the rest of the murderers to justice. Only you can speak for the dead, only—"

Out of the corner of her eye, she saw movement to her right as a groan went up from the yard. She turned to see Esther rising into the air, but though she looked instantly away, it was too late. The rest of what she'd wanted to say froze in her throat.

The next thing she knew, there was a rope around her neck, its roughness prickling her skin. Then unseen hands tugged it tight and she felt someone back away from her, realized she had only seconds at most.

"*Nakam!*" yelled Roza Robota, lifting her head high. "Revenge!" she thundered with all the fierceness at her command, and like Hanka's blood-congealing scream earlier, the word echoed off the sky, seeming to sound on even after she herself was no more.

Hössler's routine afterward was a repeat of the day's, the same preening imperiousness, the same speech almost verbatim, first the carrot then the stick before signing off somewhere in-between. Unknown to him, though, both the retaliation he sought against the commando and the fear he hoped to instill in it were mitigated—if partially, but mitigated regardless—by the louder-than-life Hebrew valediction *nakam*. It was a word that reverberated in the imaginations of those who'd heard it, a word that wouldn't go away, something they could latch onto not only during the *Hauptsturmführer's* subsequent harangue but after it was over and they were marched back to their huts. Lying in their bunks that night in the dark, it wasn't toward his spite and petty *Schadenfreude* that the women's thoughts gravitated, or the wantonness of the hangings themselves and the sting these still inflicted, but rather the courage of a frail-looking and defenseless young girl, who even as the noose was seconds away from squeezing the life out of her, had the temerity to spit her final breath at her executioners.

A courage, which when they were ousted from their beds later by the reveille bell, was still with them, keeping their spirits as up as could be expected. Then again, strangely, it was to prove a day for raised spirits, and this despite what awaited them at roll call. The Germans had left the bodies hanging and would for the next three days. They dangled there like two broken puppets drooping from their strings, gently twisting in the breeze.

But as the five hundred huddled in the freezing pre-dawn grayness, dully answering "*Hier!*" as their tattoo numbers were called, a rumbling reached their ears from off to the east. Visible through the gaps between the barracks, a bank of angry clouds darkened the horizon. Though too far away yet to say how serious, it had to be a storm and the noise that of thunder. Hopefully, if as was likely it was headed their direction, it wouldn't be showing up anytime soon; there was still the Appell to get through, then the long hike to the factory and work. Marching in rain, or worse, needles of sleet, wasn't the best way to start the day.

But though none could have guessed, it would develop into the finest start to a day they could remember. For not long after setting foot on the limestone road to the plant, a number of them picked up on something that didn't make sense. The clouds hadn't only failed to draw nearer, they were gone, but the thunder continued distantly, inexplicably to growl. *How could there be thunder without clouds?* they asked themselves. By the time it pulled up to the Union Metallwerke gate, there wasn't a prisoner in the column who didn't know the answer. And wasn't struggling to conceal her joy from the guards.

It wasn't thunder at all. It was the rolling cannonade of battle, of artillery, of the Russians. It was the Red Army on the move, slugging its way westward, who knew how many miles away but close enough now that you could hear its big guns. Just, but you could hear them. Upon the women entering the factory, these were drowned out by the sounds of the machinery, and later at shift's end, on the walk back to camp, to their anxiety the evening was peaceful.

But not for good. That night in the barracks, after lights-out, the muted grumbling from the east would start up again. The dark came alive with a ferment of whispers, until the door to the Blockälteste's room flew open and without her having to say a word, the hut fell quiet again. It would be some time, however, before the usual snoring began. To a woman they lay awake warmed by the noise of the guns, then gradually, deliciously, allowed their refrain to soothe them to sleep, like children borne away by a mother's lullaby.

*   *   *

Marta Bindiger was having as much trouble making her mind up as anybody.

In the wake of the hangings, the Russian artillery continued intermittently to pound away. At first this was encouraging, morale high, but after a while the prisoners began asking questions. Almost a week now since proclaiming themselves, the guns were still no more than a distant booming. Why weren't they getting closer? Had the Soviet advance been stymied? Was the Wehrmacht holding its own, or worse, winning whatever battle was raging beyond the horizon? Everyone's fear was that this man-made thunder might return whence it had come, perhaps for good. Despite having fought its way this far, there was no guarantee the Red Army would be able to stay, much less keep pushing forward.

That Saturday, however, the dawn sun would bring with it a surprise to ignite both the sky and the soul. Barely had it poked its burning head above land than what before one sometimes had to strain to hear now packed a startling punch. To the silent hallelujahs of the thousands standing at roll call in not only Auschwitz-Birkenau and Monowitz but their surrounding subcamps, the artillery had grown briskly louder. If the Russians had been bottled up, they weren't anymore.

To everyone's even greater delight, as the day progressed so did that loudness; the front was drawing nearer even as they listened. By mid-morning the guns had stopped, but would resume later that night, accompanied now by short, white bursts of luminescence, like giant flashbulbs popping the length of the eastern sky.

The next day, all three camps were abuzz with a rumor so shocking it diminished even the arrival of the war at their doorsteps. Every conversation opened with it: the entire complex was to be evacuated by forced march to the west. Come the 16th, by virtue of repetition and the increasingly frantic bustling about of the SS, the rumor had solidified into a *fait accompli*. Few were the prisoners who hadn't resigned themselves to it and now had a critical decision to make. Would it be better to follow orders and embark on this exodus into the unknown, or try to avoid it and stay behind? To leave, especially in this weather, with the temperature regularly dipping below zero—sparsely provisioned if at all, and in the weakened condition most were in—would be to risk an ordeal a good many of them weren't going to survive. Not to mention their having to abandon any thought of liberation, and for who knew how long. Maybe forever.

Then again, what awaited those who opted not to go? Who attempted to hide when the call came, or played too sick or weary to answer it? If an evacuation could be said to have a point at all, it would be that no witnesses were left behind to document the Nazis' crimes. Surely the SS had plans to shoot or otherwise dispose of any who were either genuinely too ill to make the trip or simply malingering. If one *were* able to hide, though, if only until the coast was clear....

This was the predicament facing Marta, whether to go or stay put, aggravated by her having Hanka to look out for as well. It turned out it was this, however, that settled the issue, when on the morning of the 17th she went to check on the girl in Ka-Be and see what Dora Klein might have to say about the situation.

The news wasn't good. "Hanka," said the doctor, "has yet to show the least improvement. In fact, if anything she's worse. She's hardly moved from her bed since the death of her sister, sleeps all the time now. I don't know what to do."

Marta tried to keep it positive. "As you said once before, doc, for Hanka to be Hanka again isn't going to happen overnight. I see patience as still the best medicine for her. Unfortunately, as I'm sure you've heard, the Germans may have something to say about that. If there should be an evacuation, if the rumor is true, do you think she's up to it? I've been leaning more and more toward taking off myself, but I'm not about to leave without her."

"Oh, there *will* be an evacuation. That I learned for a fact just yesterday. An SS officer was here and said so, adding he'd been sent to inform me that all the sick in Ka-Be would be staying behind. That and something else," she frowned, looking away. "Something I think you ought to know."

"What, Dora? Go on, spill it."

"He ordered me to draw up a list of all the Jewish patients. The Jewish patients only. He's supposed to be coming by today to pick it up."

Marta knew what that meant and reached a decision then and there. Indeed, there was no longer a decision to be made. When the time came, she and Hanka were quitting Auschwitz if she had to hoist the girl on her back and carry her out. Before returning to her hut, she asked Dr. Klein what she planned to do.

"Why, I'm staying. I've no choice. What kind of physician would I be if I didn't?"

Marta began preparing for the journey that day, gathering what food and extra clothes she could. Nor was she a moment too soon. By the next night, she was ready—and so were the Germans. At nine o'clock, the Stammlager exploded in a tumult of shouts and running feet, the soldiers descending on the barracks, emptying them, and herding the inhabitants toward the main gate. Even if they were hoping to, most of the inmates were given no chance to hide. Marta was lucky in that, bag of provisions in tow, she was able to sneak out before it came the turn of her block, and by avoiding the camp streets reach the hospital undetected. Hurriedly locating Hanka, she dressed her in multiple layers of clothing, and while the teenager went along with this, when it came time to leave she balked. It took Marta several tries before she got her out the door and into the street.

With the girl continuing to resist, she thought about trying to find a hiding place after all, but the machine-gun fire ripping the night apart made her think again. What could it be but SS murder squads at work? At an auxiliary gate, a bottleneck of mainly female prisoners had formed, and she was quick to see why. The Nazis were conducting a selection with flashlights, turning back any deemed too frail for the trek ahead. Those allowed to pass, Marta and Hanka among them, were handed half a loaf of bread and made to wait on the other side of the gate while their numbers accumulated.

It wasn't snowing, but a vicious wind cut through their ranks, the women fearing that if they didn't get moving soon they might freeze where they stood. Most didn't have even a blanket as protection, much less a coat. Some were wearing rags wrapped around their feet instead of shoes.

The Germans waited until the column was four thousand strong before shouting it forward. A full moon had turned the drifts of snow a neon-white, the night as bright almost as day. Still, it was slow going, the wind pushing them back a step for every three they took. As if Marta wasn't having trouble enough; Hanka, having yet to utter a sound, fought her the whole way. More than once, she had to haul the child out of the snow where she'd flopped. It wasn't so much that she was walking as letting herself be alternately pushed and pulled. All she wanted was to curl into a ball and go to sleep, for eternity would have been just fine with her.

The longer they marched, the deeper the drifts. They couldn't tell whether there was a road beneath them anymore. Their guards began cursing at the struggling column to pick up the pace. "Faster, you dogs! You lazy Jew bitches, faster!" Not long afterward, the first shots rang out. Marta wondered what they meant, until she came across a woman sprawled face down on the side of the trail, the blood pooled beneath her black in the moonlight. More corpses followed. The SS weren't only shooting those who could go no farther and had collapsed, but those lagging behind. This last was alarming, for with Hanka still uncooperative, the two were slipping steadily to the rear. Marta was forced to redouble her efforts; death walked with those bringing up the rear.

Their objective was supposed to be the camp at Grossrosen, but not only was it a hundred and fifty miles away, the soldiers had only a vague idea how to get there. In fact, after two days they had to admit they were lost. The plan then became to walk until they hit a railroad track and follow it to a station, which is how they arrived at the town of Wodzislaw and the large switching yard there. The bigger part of the three thousand prisoners left alive, including Marta and Hanka, learned they'd be boarding a train bound for the huge Ravensbrück concentration camp for women, with the rest to continue, also by rail, on to Grossrosen.

By then the bread issued each at Auschwitz was gone, as were all but a few crumbs of what Marta had been able to scrounge beforehand. Nor were there to be any rations doled out at Wodzislaw. Starving as they all were, though, word of a train lifted their spirits. The prospect of giving those blistered, frozen feet of theirs a respite was more than they could have hoped for.

This, however, was only to prove a different kind of torment. It wasn't into sealed boxcars that the women were loaded, but open wagons, at the mercy of the elements, wedged in so tightly there was no room to sit or even fall down. Later, they wouldn't only sleep but die standing up. For two days and a night, they rode the rails deep into Germany, the snow melting when it hit their heads and shoulders then freezing again, coating them in ice. They could no longer feel their feet, but it hardly mattered; people weren't so much standing as being propped up by the bodies pressing in on all sides. With no choice but to answer the call of nature on the spot, what excretions they were still capable of without food and water froze their shoes at night to the floor. The dead remained vertical, eyes open in accusation, as if to demand of the living how they could have let such a thing as this happen.

Marta and Hanka never made it to Ravensbrück. They were part of the six hundred detrained at Neustadt-Glewe, one of its satellite camps. Here they were given a shower and delousing, a fresh set of stripes, and most extraordinary of all, a bowl of hot soup. Neustadt-Glewe was a labor camp devoted to one industry, a large underground factory for the manufacture of airplane parts. It was overcrowded and muddy and infested with lice, but there was no crematorium or other evidence of murder. From the stories told them later of the ghastly inferno that was Ravensbrück, the new arrivals counted themselves beyond fortunate.

Though the pair wasn't assigned work right away, in the older woman's eyes this was a good thing, even with the starvation rations allotted idle prisoners. Hanka in her suicidal apathy wouldn't have been able to function anyway, a situation that if she were to survive would have to change. Marta plunged into the task with her usual gusto, caring for the teen as she might a sick toddler. She fed her, washed her, held and cuddled her, sang her to sleep at night, but also scolded and got tough with her when she felt toughness was called for. Until one day, with as satisfying a sense of accomplishment as Marta could remember, Hanka began to come around. Slowly at first, almost shyly, a word here, a smile there…. but by the time the two were put to work in February, the girl, if not herself yet, was well on the way to it.

Marta manipulated it so that they landed on the same shift. From six in the evening to six in the morning they riveted metal plates onto wings and fuselages. The plates were heavy and the nights long, and it felt as if there were always more lice on their bodies than food in their stomachs. But each day brought them closer to The Day, and this was enough to keep them going. This and the blessedly warmer weather of approaching spring, that as it did every year but never more than this one, filled people's hearts with the warmth of hope as well.

But the nightmare wasn't over, death as always never far. Without warning one April day, the factory was shut down in the middle of a shift and the entire camp put under a Blocksperre, all inmates confined to quarters. It was still in effect the next morning, and looking more permanent with each hour. For the next several days, denied all food and water, the prisoners wandered their huts in a wallow of fear, sweating over what the Germans might be up to. The artillery that had been blasting for a week now was suddenly louder. Were the SS readying a massacre to prevent their Jews from falling into Allied hands? It would have been an easy thing to set the locked barracks on fire, a solution to the Nazi quandary that would have surprised no one.

Then one afternoon, as they watched through the cracks in the wood, a peculiar sight greeted those in the blocks nearest the main gate. Some of their guards had shed their uniforms in favor of civilian mufti, and with suitcases in hand were making for a pair of automobiles. Inconsistent with the barbed wire, the mud and monochrome gray of the place, the two SS females among them sported brightly colored dresses. More guards followed throughout the day, some leaving in cars, others by truck. Come sunset, there wasn't a soldier to be seen, the gate wide open, the watchtowers empty.

A few of the bolder prisoners decided to investigate. Breaking out of their barracks, they came back moments later with the electrifying news that every German was gone. The word spread, and soon the kitchen block and various storage areas were swarming with people. Their jailers hadn't left much, but what they did dazzled: a small roomful of old bread, another of turnips and some potatoes, an enormous cache of dried vegetable shavings that had formed the basis of their soup. After eating their fill, some loaded sacks with food, and in case the SS should return, ventured into the uncertain black night beyond the gate. Too depleted even to consider this, the majority were left to stay and see what tomorrow would bring.

In the morning, Marta and Hanka awoke to a racket of growling motors and hoarse shouts. The younger pulled the other to her, rigid with fear. "It's the Germans!" she groaned. "They—they've come back!"

Marta wasn't so sure. "Let's find out," she said. "Or better yet, you stay here. I'll be back in two shakes."

When she returned all she said was, "It's not the Germans," and smiled. Hanka let out a loud whoop, and together they rushed outside and joined the others running to greet the men in the strange brown uniforms and bowl-like combat helmets. A mud-spattered tank and a pair of half-tracks sat idling at the camp entrance, prominent on each a large, painted red star.

It was May 2nd, 1945, and just like that they and the mob of ragged, malodorous scarecrows gawking at their Russian liberators were no longer human garbage, but human beings again.

After a week, the Soviets relinquished control of the camp to the Americans. With death no longer dogging their every move and having taken the first steps toward recovery, the question for the rescued would soon become, What to do now? Or more specifically, Where to go? For those who knew their families were no more, who had neither anything nor anyone to go home to, the decision was at once made simpler and more complicated. Hanka was one of these, convinced that for her Poland held only sorrow.

But if not Poland, where? She remembered a prisoner who'd worked at the same table as her at the Union factory, a Belgian girl who was always bragging how special her country was. Belgium seemed as good a place as any to try, and she asked Marta what she thought. As Hanka with Poland, Marta knew that only emptiness awaited her in Czechoslovakia. Upon looking into it, she, too, took to the idea; she'd learned of a special rest camp for survivors set in the majestic Ardennes forest sponsored by the Belgian Jewish community. The Americans had procured a fleet of buses to take the ex-prisoners wherever they wanted, and in a matter of days the two found themselves in the beautiful, wooded hills of the Ardennes.

Marta was to remain in Flander's fields for the rest of her life. She quickly met and fell in love with a young man in Brussels and became Mrs. Marta Cigé. Hanka's destiny, too, was to take an unexpected turn in Belgium. While still at the rest camp, Marta had enlisted the Red Cross in tracking down some of her own and Hanka's family who might have survived. As she'd feared, with regard to hers the search yielded nothing, but to Hanka's shock her eldest sister was found to be living in Palestine. In late 1939, Sabina Wajcblum with her boyfriend Mietek had fled Warsaw and the SS for Soviet-occupied eastern Poland, never to be heard from again. Everyone had presumed her dead, but over the phone in the Red Cross office Sabina explained how she and Mietek had escaped across the Baltic Sea to neutral Sweden, and from there eventually to Palestine. And suggested, since they were the only immediate family each other had left, that her baby sister make aliyah herself.

Hanka was hesitant to part company with Marta, who'd become as much a sister to her as she had been and always would be her savior. But strong as the bond between them was, after Marta's marriage it began to dawn on her that maybe it was time to make a life of her own. In the autumn of 1946, she arrived by ship in Tel Aviv and reunited with her long lost "Saba". A couple of years later she was married herself, and after some years more, her husband's business took them to Canada.

Despite the distances that ended up separating her and Marta, however, be it the length of continental Europe then the width of the Atlantic

Ocean, never in all the decades that followed did she let herself lapse into losing contact with her lifesaver and best friend.

Others survived the camps, some against even longer odds. In the week leading up to the evacuation from Birkenau on January 18th, Shlomo Kirschenbaum and the rest of the Sonderkommando were waiting for the SS hammer to drop any day. By then the Russian artillery had crept so near, one couldn't only hear the shells exploding but feel them through the soles of one's shoes. Kirschenbaum watched the Germans like a hawk that last week, trying to intuit their intentions, read what was in their faces, but so wracked were those faces with anxiety, lack of sleep, and alcohol that there was no deciphering them.

What he did see was a total breakdown in discipline among his fellow Sonder. In what would have been inconceivable just a month ago, orders were obeyed sluggishly if at all, maintenance and cleaning of the remaining death house and its environs ignored. Among numerous derelictions, bodies were allowed to stack up for days running at times, and not even the SS acted as if they cared. To the onetime kapo, it was as if not only the camp but the whole world was coming apart in front of his eyes.

At 3:00 in the afternoon of the 18th, the commando's last hour looked to have come. The writing on the wall had appeared days before when the fifty remaining Sonder were put to work dismantling Crematorium V and loading the salvageable pieces onto trucks. Due to its less sophisticated layout and the number of men employed, this didn't take long. Once the job was deemed finished, the fifty were escorted out the crematorium gate for the last time, heads bent, shoulders stooped, steps faltering, the walking dead.

Instead of being led to their extinction, however, they were taken to the *B2d* lager…. and dismissed. Simply dropped off and forgotten. Looking around in disbelief, they quickly dispersed to mix with the other prisoners, and within minutes had disappeared into the faceless masses of D Camp. Apparently, so disorganized were the Nazis by this point, so fixated on distancing not only their captives but especially themselves from the Russians, they allowed the most damning witnesses to their crimes to get lost in the shuffle. Later that night, still puzzling over the gift of anonymity bestowed them, the misplaced Sonder followed the herd out of Birkenau into the subzero semi-darkness of a full moon. Behind them, they could hear the explosions downing the last of the crematoria they'd somehow outlived.

Not that all of them wound up cheating death, not for long. The mortality that marked the death march, its killing pace, the killing cold, the itchy trigger fingers of the guards, felled the same percentage of Sonder as they did the other prisoners. Shlomo Kirschenbaum, however, wasn't one of them. He and those in his group still hanging onto life eventually arrived via open freezer-train at the Mauthausen concentration camp in Austria. One of the larger and older of the camps, Mauthausen acted as a magnet for the mass of prisoners streaming west before the Soviets. Consequently, it had little space and even less food to offer, though no shortage of either order or discipline. Kirschenbaum hadn't been there but a few days when during one of the frequent and interminable roll calls, an officer roared up on a motorcycle, and dismounting, faced the assembly.

"All prisoners of the Birkenau Sonderkommando," he shouted, "step forward!"

Kirschenbaum nearly jumped out of his skin. Heart pounding, he stole a quick glance to either side. Earlier, he'd spotted several familiar faces in the crowd, all crematoria men, but from what he could see none were budging. The officer repeated the command, and still no response. After a third time, he began walking up and down the rows of men peering into faces, trying to intimidate those he was searching for into revealing themselves. Kirschenbaum couldn't tell how much he was trembling from the cold and how much out of fear now, but luckily the SS man gave up and left before reaching him.

None of the Sonder would sleep easy after that. What with the incriminatory numbers inked on their forearms, the fake names they'd been giving were flimsy comfort. Though impossible to know how deep the Germans would dig to make up for their oversight of January 18th, few were those who believed they'd heard the last of it. Again luckily for Kirschenbaum, or so he thought, some days following the incident he was one of two thousand prisoners selected for transfer to the subcamp at Ebensee. The farther removed he was from the inquisitive atmosphere at Mauthausen, the safer he felt he'd be.

Soon he would realize how wrong he was. The sole purpose of Ebensee was to furnish slave labor for the excavation of vast tunnels in the surrounding hillsides in which to house various armaments to protect them from Allied aircraft. In twelve-hour shifts night and day, the inmates, mostly shoeless, hacked away at the frozen earth, their only sustenance a cold "tea" made of leaves and tree bark for breakfast, at noon three-quarters of a liter of hot water infused with a few vegetable peelings, and at night five ounces of a crumbly something supposed to be bread. Each barracks, built to hold a hundred men (there were no women at Ebensee), contained seven hundred or more, the lice so thick they crawled in discernible waves across the floor. By the time Kirschenbaum found himself there, piles of corpses lay everywhere, the camp enveloped in an unspeakable miasma of death and human feces.

Though work on the tunnels was halted not long after his appearance, people continued dying by the hundreds every day. As an ex-Sonder and in better shape than most to begin with, Kirschenbaum held on. When American forces at long last entered the camp on May 6th, he was one of the few able to welcome them standing up.

After six weeks of convalescence, he felt strong enough to strike out on his own. With his parents, wife, and little boy dead, there was nothing in his hometown of Heidelberg for him, and he couldn't see himself returning to live in Germany anyway. He did have an aunt and uncle in America, though, who were willing to help him start a new life there. In July, financed by Jewish charities, he departed London on a ship bound for New York City. For the entirety of the trip, as he had since leaving Austria, he hoarded bits of food and hid them—under his mattress, in drawers and closets, behind the grates of air vents, in his clothing. To the amused sympathy of those in his adopted land, a month later he was still at it. But in time he came to recognize his obsession for what it was, and that would be the end of it. From then on, he led as normal a life as his memories would permit.

Some nine thousand of the evacuees from Auschwitz-Birkenau ended up at Mauthausen. Many would breathe their last before the Allied armies could get to them, but not all died at the hands of the SS and their helpers, or from the cold, hunger, and disease that prevailed there. As in every camp that received them, it was a mixed bag of prisoners that poured in from the east, including the ex-kapos, collaborators, and other predators shorn of the protection they'd enjoyed under the Nazis. Eager in many instances to take advantage of this were their former victims or friends of victims. High on the list of a lot of these was the rapacious Kapo Schulz of Auschwitz infamy. Unlike his almost as revolting girlfriend Black Klara, who died en route to Ravensbrück, he made it through the death march, but was not to last a single day at Mauthausen.

Officially, in fact, he was never admitted. The camp sat on the crest of a hill overlooking the town of the same name. A steep road wound to the top, where a bathhouse stood through which each new inmate had to pass for a shower and delousing prior to entering the main grounds. Schulz's exhausted, half-frozen column reached this hill after dark. Because there were three thousand of them, it was going to take time to run them through, more than enough for those who'd singled the kapo out in order to exact a justice long overdue. During the march, some soldier friends of his had shielded him, but these were now replaced with a new guard. Under cover of night, his executioners quickly cornered him and beat him to death. Already a few people had lain down in the snow, too far gone even to try making it up the hill. How much notice would one more dead body attract?

The prisoner Eugen Koch would also meet his end at Mauthausen. His body was found in one of the latrines with his trousers pulled down and his throat cut. The two instruments he'd used to seduce Ala Gertner were resting atop his chest—his tongue and his penis. Both Schulz and Koch had held the Grim Reaper off during the long and bloody flight from Auschwitz, only to perish for past crimes once they'd reached their destination. They could have saved themselves grief, maybe even their lives, if they'd simply stayed put. But who was to say that the sword of Jewish revenge wouldn't have caught up with them even then?

Those inmates who did decide to risk avoiding the evacuation not only made the better choice but for the most part got away with it. There were reprisals against some who refused the command to fall out, but these were isolated incidents; shootings did occur, but there was no grand SS strategy, nor any order issued, to liquidate the remaining populations of Auschwitz, Birkenau, or Monowitz. The bombast of the old Möll Plan was revealed to be the empty threat it had probably always been.

The morning following the fateful night of the 18th, Dora Klein ventured out of Ka-Be to reconnoiter the situation. With nothing yet, she thanked God, having come of the roster of Jewish patients she'd been forced to hand over to the Gestapo, she wanted to see how many soldiers might be left. To her relief there were few, and the next day she made it all the way to the main gate without spotting one. Nor did a single watchtower appear to be manned. Unless they were hiding somewhere, the Germans had fled.

This was both reason to rejoice and not to. Before leaving, the Nazis had turned off the power permanently, and no electricity meant, among other mischief, no heating for the hospital blocks. They'd shut the water off, too. Klein and her fellow doctors quickly organized foraging parties from among the nurses they still had and the stronger patients. Their goals were first the kitchen, then the Prominenz blocks, the SS barracks and hospital, and any warehouses the Germans hadn't emptied. They set out equipped with carts that until a few days ago had been used to ferry rations. The initial haul was encouraging, among it a pair of large cast-iron stoves, a hefty supply of wood and coal, some medicines, close to three hundred pounds of turnips and potatoes, and several multi-gallon containers of water frozen solid.

Such bounty, however, wasn't to last; with each day the pickings grew slimmer. Hundreds of the hollow-eyed half-dead roamed the camp, shambling skeletons in rags, searching for food or anything that might prove of value. Those who could no longer walk dragged themselves through the snow like so many giant worms, leaving trails of blood and their own waste behind. Corpses soon lay everywhere, both inside the huts and out. Even if the living had had the energy, the icy ground was too hard for the digging of graves.

In Ka-Be, people were dying at a rate Dr. Klein had never experienced before, nor was there much she could do but stand by and watch. After four days and despite the strictest rationing, the little medicine they'd found and the potatoes were gone, the turnips almost. The stoves were a help, but there were only three of them, one per building, not enough even during the day to bring the temperature above freezing. The only water they had now was that which they got from melting the snow, and it swimming with particles of dirt. Diphtheria and pneumonia stalked the halls, invisible killers, but worst of all was the dysentery ward. The filth there was indescribable. Few of the patients had the strength to leave their beds; the excrement was frozen an inch thick on the floor in places.

On each person's mind, when he wasn't asking it outright, was a question that daily grew more urgent: where in the name of all that was merciful were the Russians? For three days following the evacuation of the camp, the crash of artillery was louder than it had ever been, punctuated at times by the burp of small-arms fire. The German Army in retreat packed the roads outside the wire. Wave after wave trundled past day and night, tanks, armored cars, horse-drawn 88's—soldiers in trucks, on motorcycles, but mostly on foot. They trod in silence, tired, dirty, the picture of defeat, until one day the roads were empty again and would stay so. The noise of the guns followed after this parade of the vanquished, was soon as it had been weeks ago, a morose grumbling in the distance.

To those in the camp watching, listening, hoping, the war had come and gone, passing them by, much as the world had for years ignored them in their torment. Though they kept telling each other that the Russians would be there any day now, in their hearts few could bring themselves seriously to believe it. Too often had the lunatic monster that was the Vernichtungslager made a mockery of their expectations, of rationality itself, distorting what should have been into something improbable, if not perverse.

The only visitors to show up so far were increasing numbers of that bird of ill omen, the raven. Nor with the amount of unattended-to bodies piling up was it any mystery why.

For once, however, the prisoners' cynicism was to betray them. In the early morning of January 27th, the sun not yet free of the horizon, a reconnaissance patrol in white parkas from the First Ukrainian Front of the Red Army scaled a small hill to behold a sight they weren't sure what to make of. Three miles away on the snow-covered plain below them stretched row after row of low rectangular buildings enclosed in a perimeter of barbed wire. They studied it through their field glasses but could detect no activity. An hour and a half later, other, larger patrols descended on what they were to learn was the concentration camp Birkenau, named after the preponderance of birch trees in the region.

What had the Russians confused at first was the immensity of the place. Since crossing the Polish border they'd come across their share of such facilities, but never one so gigantic. And just down the road they were to discover yet another, smaller if no less hideous. At both sites the troops were swarmed by crowds of weakly cheering, living cadavers, gray wraithlike figures with hairless scalps and huge eyes, so impossibly thin it was a wonder any were capable of standing. They didn't resemble human beings so much as inhabitants of another world, a planet of insect-men all long, bony appendages and bulging eyes. Hands reached out to touch the soldiers as if to confirm they were real. Others waved scraps of red cloth in the air. The Russians had seen this before, but many wept all the same, partly out of pity, partly from the shared joy of the moment. It was something one could experience a hundred times and never be prepared for, never get used to.

Among the throng to greet them at the Stammlager were Dora Klein and those of her patients still ambulatory. Three months later, once the Allied victory in Europe was formally declared, Dr. Klein would return to practicing medicine in the place she liked most in the world, her beloved city of Prague. But the idyll wouldn't last. In 1951, she was put on trial by the repressive Soviet-backed regime of Czechoslovakia for speaking against the state, and imprisoned for three years. Upon her release, she returned to the country of her birth and set up permanent shop as a physician in Warsaw.

Rose Greuenapfel and Mala Weinstein, who'd also evaded the death march, were to find basically the same destinies as each other though departing Poland in opposite directions. After liberation, upon discovering her entire family had been wiped out, the one would make her way west to America and in lower Manhattan become Mrs. Rose Meth, starting a family of her own. In answer to the genocidal mania of Hitler and his Nazis, she would give each of her three sons the middle name Dafka, Hebrew for "despite".

Mala by contrast headed east, arriving by illegal ship in Palestine in 1946. There she joined a *kibbutz* and like Rose fell in love, but upon marriage and with the support of her husband chose to retain her maiden name. Her family, too, had been destroyed in the camps, and with a defiance similar to her friend's she sought to preserve their memory as Mrs. Weinstein. Mala also had children, and it was the source of her greatest pride that they were born *sabras*, native Israelis.

Jacob Kozelczik had elected to sit pat as well. The SS emptied Block 11's cells, but to his surprise, considering all he knew, left its kapo behind. Afraid that vengeful prisoners might come looking for him, he locked and barricaded both doors to the building and hid out for the ten days it took the Red Army to show. Not that a living soul, even with the Gestapo gone, so much as came near that erstwhile house of punishment and pain.

Allegations did surface later, though, and the Russians arrested him, but amid the cries for his blood enough of the inmates came forward in his defense to move the conflicted officer in charge to place him in protective custody. There he would stay for a month, after which he was sent by train with a shipment of other prisoners, under the auspices of the Red Cross, to a displaced persons camp in Germany. Later, he would wangle passage on a freighter to Palestine, but the ship was intercepted by the British and he and three hundred other illegal immigrants interned for two years on the island of Cyprus.

When finally he did set foot on the ancestral soil, it didn't take long for Kozelczik's notoriety to catch up with him. Once again he was arrested, and this time arraigned on charges of collaborating with the Nazis. But in a repeat of three years ago, so profuse was the exonerating testimony that he was found innocent and released. He would go on to make a living as a professional strongman and later ringmaster in a highly touted and much loved traveling circus. It was a life that amply suited him. Whatever else the SS had taken from him, the feats of strength he'd once performed for their entertainment had given him a taste for the limelight he never relinquished.

As for the man whom he'd served so well if unwillingly as hangman, Franz Hössler ended up stuffing a steamer trunk full and leaving Auschwitz in a covered truck with an assortment of other officers. Their destination was the Dora-Mittelbau camp in Germany. Come March, with the American Army closing in on it, too, Hössler supervised the forced evacuation of prisoners out of Dora to the smaller installation at Bergen-Belsen. Except by that time the Bergen-Belsen camp was no longer small. Built to house six thousand inmates, by war's end its population had soared to in excess of seventy thousand. With neither the food nor the shelter to accommodate them, people were dying faster than they could be buried. When the British liberated the camp on April 15th, they found fourteen thousand naked bodies rotting in the spring sun.

They also found *Hauptsturmführer* Hössler dressed in muddy stripes, if compromisingly well fed, trying to hide among the prisoners. Appointed deputy commander of this den of horrors upon his arrival, he'd since bathed his manicured hands repeatedly in blood. Irrespective of his crimes at Auschwitz, he and forty-four other SS were brought before a British military court in what was dubbed the Bergen-Belsen trial. Convicted in November, he was executed a month later. As opposed to his sneering prolixity at those hangings he'd conducted, when it came his turn at the gallows he didn't have a word to say.

Another who'd figured conspicuously in the martyrdom of the four young Jewish heroines managed to elude the hangman, though it was never determined if he escaped justice as well. *Unterscharführer* Broch of Auschwitz's Block 35 was last seen in mid-April leaving the Sachsenhausen subcamp of Hennigsdorf by motorcycle, headed southeast to Berlin and his family. By then Soviet forces had entered that city's eastern suburbs prior to encircling it and commencing the climactic Battle of Berlin. Whether he was killed on the way there, or died in the battle, or survived to acquire a new identity would forever remain unknown. No body was ever found, nor the name Karl Friedrich Broch appear on paper thereafter.

A fellow Gestapo officer of his at the camp did in a sense get away with murder. Arrested on three different occasions after the war, *Sturmbannführer* Wilhelm Boger escaped the first time and went into hiding for several years, then was released a second time for lack of evidence and on the basis of his "sound and irreproachable character" as the West German court put it. Finally, in 1965, twenty years after the fact, he was named a defendant at the Auschwitz trials held in Frankfurt. Found guilty of multiple counts of murder, accessory to murder, and torture, even then he avoided execution and was sentenced to life in prison. Where he died in his bed, unrepentant, at the age of seventy-two. He maintained to the end that as a military man in wartime he was honor-bound to do as his superiors commanded—that as he was fond of reciting with more of a smirk, it was said, the older he got, "*Eine Befehl ist eine Befehl.* An order is an order...."

This, of course, became the all but universal rationale, whether public or private, for those Germans guilty of war crimes, from the highest ministers of the Nazi state to the humblest *Schützen* on lager duty. To anyone familiar, however, with the violent fanaticism of his anti-Jewish ideology and proven commitment to the extirpation of the hated Rassenfiend root and branch, it would have come as a surprise to see the psychopathic *Hauptscharführer* Otto Möll of all men trying to squirm his way out of responsibility for his past. Yet that was precisely what the arch-exterminator of Birkenau would do, so much for his famous aversion to hypocrisy. With the Russian hammer-and-sickle bearing down on his Gleiwitz domain, and after turning its population out into the snow, Möll would bounce through a succession of camps before assuming command of the Dachau *Unterlager* of Schwabing. When that, too, was menaced by the American Army's push eastward, he led its inhabitants on a frantic forced march to the mother camp, leaving the ground red behind him.

On May 1st, Dachau itself was liberated and Möll taken into custody. Nor did his captors have to probe very deep before realizing they had a true fiend in their possession. It wasn't until November, though, in front of a United States military tribunal, that he took his place in the dock with the other defendants in the Dachau trial, where instead of standing up for the beliefs he'd lived by, twisted and malign as they were, he not only insisted he'd been acting under orders and against his will at Birkenau but denied ever killing anybody. The only involvement he would admit to was preparing the transports for the gas chamber and other Aktionen, then cremating them after. Never had he personally, he said, either by issuing the command or with his own hands, taken a Jewish or any other life.

But the Americans knew all about both his official duties and individual excesses, and had the witnesses to prove them. They even brought in the ex-commandant of Auschwitz, Rudolf Höss, and put him on the stand.

Prosecution: "Do you know the man sitting to your right shackled to the guard?"

Höss: "Yes. His name is Otto Möll."

Prosecution: "Where do you know him from?"

Höss: "First at Sachsenhausen, and later at Birkenau."

Prosecution: "What did this Otto Möll do at Sachsenhausen and later at Birkenau?"

Höss: "In Sachsenhausen he was a gardener, and at Auschwitz a leader of a punishment commando, then at Birkenau after that was used as a supervisor during the various actions."

Prosecution: "You mean the actions whereby people were executed and then cremated?"

Höss: "Yes."

Prosecution: "You've already told us about an assignment of his in 1942, when certain farm buildings were converted into places of execution. Will you restate what you said about that?"

Höss: "After working the farm house designated Bunker #2, an extermination plant, he oversaw the excavation of old burial sites and the burning of their corpses."

Prosecution: "And later?"

Höss: "Much later, in 1944, during the Hungarian Action, he was in charge of all five of the extermination plants."

Prosecution: "Just what operations was he responsible for then?"

Höss: "In the final analysis, everything. The whole operation, as well as that part of it moved outdoors. In the end, of course, as commandant mine was the ultimate responsibility."

Möll contested Höss's as well as every assertion made against him, blaming the witnesses for either failing to remember correctly, confusing him with someone else, or lying outright on behalf of those "who for whatever reason have it in for me." But the court was unreceptive. At the close of the trial some months later, he was among those pronounced guilty and sentenced to death. On the appointed day, he walked to the gallows with a steady step. He stopped only once during the procession, pausing at the foot of the scaffold to look up at the noose. Those present would say that he wore an expression of befuddlement on his face, as if to question how such an apparition could possibly be meant for him.

Noah Zabludowicz, too, had known Dachau, but only briefly. From Auschwitz, he, Godel Silver, and his brother Hanan (their older brother Pinchas was barracked still in Birkenau) endured the march by foot to Wodzislaw, the freezing ride by rail to Grossrosen, from there to Dachau, and somehow still together, ended up at the subcamp of Mühldorf where they were to remain for over a month on next to no food.

Then one sunny day in late April, they were loaded onto another train, and though they couldn't know it, sent nowhere in particular just to keep them ahead of the Americans. At night, stopped at a deserted station, the three slithered through a small hole they'd found in the car and made a break for it. Too weak, however, to get very far, they were quickly caught and prodded back at gunpoint. Why their guards didn't shoot them was a question none could answer, then or later. At dawn, still sitting in the station, the train was overrun by an American patrol, and over the next weeks its hundreds of occupants nursed back to health at a military hospital set up nearby.

Having survived by the skin of his teeth, the sun of inexplicable good fortune continued to shine on Noah. Toward the end of his recuperation, he received a letter from Italy. It was from his two older brothers who'd made aliyah years before, and were now soldiers in the Jewish Brigade stationed in Bologna. The Jewish Brigade was a gesture by the Allies, once bits and pieces of what was unfolding in Poland started surfacing, offering that persecuted people a chance to play a role in the war. It was a force composed of resident Israelis trained by the British to be combatants, and would go on to distinguish itself in the Italian theater of operations. His brothers had tracked him and Hanan down, as they would Pinchas later, first through the International then the American Red Cross. That they had accomplished this long-distance, unable to leave their unit, made it even more of a miracle to him.

What with the knowledge gleaned from their own emigration experience, and again from afar, they added to the miracle by helping the three find a ship. By August, Noah was sitting on the open deck of the *Eva Louise*, an old rust bucket of a freighter out of Marseilles. She was making good time for her age; in less than a week much of the Mediterranean lay in her wake. The August day in question was picture-perfect, clouds as fluffy and white against the cerulean sky as huge, floating balls of cotton. The deeper blue of the ocean was as calm as the surface of a lake, the wind in his face a light, salt-flavored breeze. It was late enough in the morning that the sun was beginning to flex its muscles, if not quite to the point of him having to shed his coat.

He looked up to see Hanan come to join him. After two days of rain and rolling seas, it was far from uncrowded up top, but was a big enough ship that they could have what privacy they wished. "How is poor Pinchas doing?" Noah asked.

"About the same, I'm afraid." Hanan's concern was lightened by a smile. "Tell me, Noah, how is it that out of three brothers, two should be relatively immune to seasickness, the other half-dead from it?"

"You don't know? Why, it's a scientific fact: the handsomer the man, the stronger the stomach."

"I see," Hanan said, laughing. "That explains it then."

They relaxed into silence, content for the moment to bask in the splendor of the morning. It was the same, they'd discovered, with quite a few survivors of the camps: from the moment of liberation, the world had looked different to them, its colors sharper, its smells and sounds noticeably richer, more vivid. Freedom seemed to have removed a barrier from their senses. Until it ceased to define their existence, they hadn't understood how stultifying barbed wire could be.

Each breathed the salt air like a hungry person the aromas from a kitchen. "So how long, do you think?" Hanan said at last. "Before we get there, I mean."

"A week. Ten days maybe." Noah spoke this to the beautiful blue sea gliding by.

"Do you believe it's true what they're saying? About a blockade?"

Noah turned to him. "I've been intending to ask you the same question."

The younger man frowned, his forehead furrowing. "I have given it some thought," he said, "and yes, I do. Sooner or later, the British are bound to give in to the demands of their petroleum-rich friends, the Arabs, and put the clamps on what has already become a flood of Jews into Palestine. And that spells blockade. At this point, however, I'd think it still on the drawing board. I doubt we have anything to worry about."

There it was, that professorial delivery his egghead brother sometimes used, and that he always found as endearing as it was this time reassuring. "In other words," Noah said, "we've as good as made it to the Promised Land. The only thing that can stop us now is if this tub decides to sink."

"Or the Mediterranean," Hanan added, "dry up in the next week to ten days."

Never one for the hyperbolic language that tended to accompany religion, Noah was somewhat startled by his use of the phrase "the Promised Land." But as he'd realized at least once before—that night with Roza in the basement of Block 11, when in the face of the depression that had hold of her he'd called upon Ezekiel in the hope of jolting her out of it—there were times when it was only fair to give things religious their due. And this voyage was one of them. There was a mystique to engaging in aliyah, to turning one's back on the centuries of exile in Europe and one's face toward the land of one's ancestors, one's origins, which lent it an unmistakably biblical aura. He wouldn't be poring over the Torah anytime soon, or counting the days until the Sabbath, but something of what dwelt in the daily lives of the devout had infiltrated his, if only for the time being.

Then again, there'd been more chipping away at his jealously guarded agnosticism lately than just the imminence of Eretz Israel on the horizon. That not only he but his two brothers, and Godel along with them, continued to occupy the land of the living was so implausible an outcome as to suggest a supraworldly intervention. For going on three long years, they'd succeeded somehow in surviving the Vernichtungslager, when as Noah suspected and was later to learn for a fact, the mortality rate for those who'd trod its unloading ramps fell just shy of ninety percent. At those odds not a one of them, much less all four, had any business being above ground.

That his other brothers should have materialized out of thin air as they did, and at the time that they did, helping to unearth both Pinchas and a serviceable ship, was also cause to make one think. None of it, however, astounded him more than discovering those brothers part of an army. Not a British, or an American, or a Russian, or a Free French—but as difficult as it was to believe—a *Jewish* army, thousands of men, three battalions of them, the first organized and officially recognized Hebrew combat unit since the fall of Judea to the Roman legions eighteen hundred years ago. They weren't parade-ground troops, either. No token soldiers these; they'd bloodied the Wehrmacht in numerous encounters.

Noah was as envious of the two as he was proud of them. They'd told him in their letters of the flag they'd followed into battle, the same blue Star of David on a white field that had flown above the rooftops of Warsaw during that ghetto's doomed uprising. And painted on the Brigade's trucks and artillery, stitched onto its uniforms, was the yellow version of that star, until recently a symbol of subjugation and shame, but now, in this new and unapologetic incarnation, a sight, he imagined, to get the heart to thumping. Sitting on the sun-drenched deck of the *Eva Louise*, he closed his eyes the better to picture what the faces of the Nazi soldiers must have looked like as they watched this bizarre flag approach their lines.

They'd surely viewed it with as much incredulousness as it continued to provoke in him, but also, he wanted to believe, with something more: if not uneasiness at this banner of revenge advancing toward them, then at least the realization they'd been wrong all these years. That to their soldier's way of thinking, with a rifle in his hands and a uniform on his back, the Jew was as much a man, a human being, as any of them.

But the emotions that flag roused in him were and always would be bittersweet. Linked as it was in his memory with the Warsaw ghetto, he couldn't visualize it without also summoning the faces of Ezra and Ehud, those twin brothers of his who'd died there. Or so it was assumed they'd died, as neither the Red Cross nor any Jewish survivor's agency had been able to find a trace of them. In the final tally, when one broke it down, Noah hadn't been so blessed after all: four brothers and a sister slain, both parents, who knew how many aunts, uncles, and cousins.... nor was this taking into account the one person who to him was in many ways the cruelest loss of all.

And on top of everything, now Godel was gone, too. With a sudden pang, it hit him how big a void the absence of his friend had left in his life. As if reading his mind, Hanan chose that exact moment to bare the same feeling.

"I don't know about you," he said, "but I can't stop thinking about Godel. And wishing he were here. I miss the skinny runt even more than I thought I would."

"Look who's calling who skinny. But I feel the same way. As exciting as it is to be heading where we are, it would be that much better if, as you said, he were here with us."

"To tell the truth, I'm not sure yet why he isn't. Why he decided to stay behind. He lost as much family as we did, more if you count—" Hanan could have kicked himself. He'd learned months ago not to blacken his brother's mood by bringing her up.

"If you count Roza, you mean?" Funny, Noah thought, how painful it still was to say that name out loud. "But as I've told you before, and this from what he told me, it was because of her, what happened to her, that Godel couldn't bring himself anymore even to think about Palestine. They'd dreamed, the two, of making aliyah together and raising a family there. In fact, there wasn't a whole lot that mattered to them more. You saw how pumped he got whenever he started talking about it."

"It seemed sometimes that's all he did talk about," Hanan agreed. "I always felt that as much as anything, it's what kept him strong."

"It should be obvious then," Noah said, "why the last thing he'd want would be to make the trip without her. For Godel, the land of milk and honey would have ended up instead a land of ghosts and regret, a constant reminder of both the woman and the dream that had been stolen from him. Come on, little brother, you're smart enough to—"

"All right, I get it. Pretend I never opened my mouth." For a long minute both were quiet. "Tell me this then," Hanan asked. "Did he say if Canada was still in his plans? Ottowa, wasn't it?"

"I think so," Noah said, looking back out to sea. "He has family there apparently, some sort of distant relatives. He sounded pretty undecided about it, though. Who the hell knows? Or for that matter, cares anymore?"

Hanan had been waiting for such, which was why he didn't let his brother's sudden brusqueness offend him. It happened every time Roza's name came up. The kindest thing then was to give the poor man his space, allow him to work his way through the grief still hobbling him. As much as he was lapping up the sun and fresh air, Hanan smiled and said he'd better return below and check on Pinchas.

Eventually, Noah made his way to the prow of the ship. He usually did, it was his favorite spot. Standing there gazing at the sea and sky ahead reinforced the sensation of leaving the past and its memories behind. The sun was high enough now to urge him out of his coat, which he wouldn't have been wearing to begin with if it hadn't been *the* coat. There'd been some pilferage on board, nothing major but worrisome, and though it would have taken a petty thief indeed to give so shabby an article of clothing a second glance, he wasn't taking any chances. Later, once settled in his new country, he would lock it away in mothballs for safe keeping, but until then he wasn't about to leave it to the mercy of strangers.

He'd kept the coat on or near his person ever since the night Kapo Kozelczik had handed it back to him outside of Roza's cell. Never much to look at, half-rag at best, it bore the grubbiness now of a year's unlaundered use; able to sponge-wash it some following his captivity, to have it done right and dry-cleaned would have removed the bloodstains as well as the dirt. And these were one of the only two *memento mori* he had of his murdered Roza, the other being the farewell letter to her friends she'd left in his care that same November night. This, too, he'd kept close, secreted away all these months in the inside pocket of the coat.

He drug it out now for what seemed the thousandth time and began to read, not for its content, which he'd come to know by heart, but to let his eyes wander the loops and whorls of a handwriting that couldn't have been more of a treasure if penned in gold. It served the same end as her blood on his jacket: both were so singular, so personal a part of her as to make him feel when connecting with them that she was right there beside him, as real as if resurrected from the grave. Many were the times, in fact, when his guard was down, that he would look up fully expecting to see her standing there, smiling at him with that smart-alecky grin of hers.

He could tell, too, deep within himself, in his heart, his bones, that she would never be far away, no matter what the future brought. Though he had yet to concede it much thought, there was undoubtedly a wife in that future, and hopefully children—if the bogeymen in the gray uniforms hadn't come along when they did, there was little question but that this would have occurred already. Which wasn't to say that when he did meet the woman he wanted to spend the rest of his life with, though that life last a hundred years and produce a dozen little Zabludowiczes, there wouldn't continue to be a place in some corner of his soul for the woman once known as Roza Robota.

With a frown he remembered the day he first heard the word Auschwitz, he and his family part of a frightened mass of people crushed together inside an airless cattle car. He remembered the foreboding born of the mysterious stench in the air that would turn out to be the work of the ogre Otto Möll. And the uncertainty that gripped them as the train slowed and left the main track, a nebulous dread at what was coming that wrung a hundred questions from as many throats, but no answers. He recalled wishing in his anxiety that Roza was there standing next to him, but she and Godel had got lost in the crowd at the Ciechanow station and were in another car. Grown man though he was, and no stranger to courage, he would have welcomed some of hers in those terror-ridden minutes. Instead, he'd tried to pretend the girl squeezed against him was Roza, but that hadn't worked at all—she was shaking with a fear even greater than his. By the time the train glided to a halt, wheels squealing, it was all he could do to keep from trembling himself.

But never again would there be cause for either trembling or pretending. Not should Noah, if such was possible, find himself again facing something as scary one day. Roza would always be there with him, as concrete a presence as she was right this moment. Together, arm in arm, they leaned against the railing at the frontmost edge of the ship, scanning the open ocean stretching limitless ahead…. and would be standing in the same spot a week and a day later, Hanan and Pinchas alongside them, watching the sliver of dusky land wavering on the horizon grow bigger, more solid before their eyes.

About the Author

Fascinated from an early age by the Holocaust, J. Michael Dolan has used his talents as a historian and novelist to bring the heroic if little-known story he sets forth in Trumpets to life.

A traveler in his youth, he has lived in many places, some of them exotic, but recently moved outside of Austin, Texas to be near his family and because it is a magnet of a city for the freethinking young—or in his case, the young at heart.

Taking a break from the horrors of the Holocaust but not the fertile ground of Jewish history, he is currently working on a novel set in the Roman-occupied Palestine of the 1st century A.D.

For more, visit www.jmichaeldolan.net.

A Partial Bibliography

*Lore Shelley (editor), *The Union Kommando in Auschwitz, Vol. XIII* from *Studies in the Shoah* (University Press of America, 1996)

*Filip Mueller, *Eyewitness Auschwitz: Three Years in the Gas Chamber* (Stein and Day, 1984)

*Primo Levi, *Survival in Auschwitz* (Touchstone, 1996)

*Primo Levi, *The Drowned and the Saved* (Vintage Intl., 1989)

*Ysrael Gutman and Michael Berenbaum (editors), *Anatomy of the Auschwitz Death Camp* (Indiana University Press, 1994)

*Victor E. Frankl, *Man's Search for Meaning* (Pocket Books, 1984)

*Dalton Trumbo, *Night of the Aurochs* (Viking, 1979)

*John Toland, *Adolf Hitler* (Doubleday, 1976)

*Robert Jay Lifton, *The Nazi Doctors* (Basic Books, 1986)

*Tadeusz Borowski, *This Way for the Gas, Ladies and Gentlemen* (Viking Penguin, 1967)

*Anna Heilman, *Never Far Away* (University of Calgary Press, 2001)

*Otto Friedrich, *The Kingdom of Auschwitz* (Harper Perennial, 1982)

*Miklos Nyiszli, *Auschwitz: A Doctor's Eyewitness Account* (Arcade Publishing, 1993)

*Rebecca Fromer, Steven Bowman, *The Holocaust Odyssey of Daniel Bennahmias* (University of Alabama Press, 1993)

*Marco Nahon, *Birkenau, the Camp of Death* (University of Alabama Press, 2002)

*Olga Lengyel, *Five Chimneys* (Chicago Review Press, 2005)

*Albert Speer, *Inside the Third Reich* (MacMillan, 1970)

*Howard Blum, *The Brigade* (Perennial, 2002)